# SURRENDER to the WILL of the NIGHT

# SURRENDER to the WILL of the NIGHT

## BOOK THREE
## OF THE INSTRUMENTALITIES OF THE NIGHT

# GLEN COOK

**TOR®**

A Tom Doherty Associates Book
New York

sf

SURRENDER TO THE WILL OF THE NIGHT

A Tor Book
Published by Tom Doherty Associates, LLC
175 Fifth Avenue
New York, NY 10010

www.tor-forge.com

Tor® is a registered trademark of Tom Doherty Associates, LLC.

ISBN 978-0-7653-0686-9

First Edition: November 2010

Printed in the United States of America

0  9  8  7  6  5  4  3  2  1

*For the good folks who put on the wonderful Austin World Fantasy Convention—thank you!*

# SURRENDER to the
# WILL of the NIGHT

The ice is coming. It might mean the end of the world. But mortal men harken only to their hunger of the moment.

# 1. The Grail Empire: Forest of Night

Eighteen remained of the seventy Chosen who had departed chill Sparmargen, holy hunters headed south. Most had been injured or were wounded. Five had to be kept tied into their saddles. Once they stopped outside the gateway they discovered that Drengtin Skyre had been dead so long his corpse was cold. His pony was in a state of supernatural angst.

There was nothing remarkable about the gateway. It was an opening in a rail fence. On this side there was ice and a frosting of hard snowflakes. A manic wind hurled dead leaves about aimlessly. The world beyond the fence might be warmer. The leaves there were sodden. The wind could not pick them up.

The ragged, pale pilgrims with the bones and small skulls in their hair stared at the wintered wood. Something built of gray stone could just be discerned through the skeletal trees. Each sacred assassin hoped their quarry was there, so this harsh quest could be brought to an end.

From among them came Krepnight, the Elect. He wore somewhat human form. He was a divine artifact. His left hand had seven fingers. His right bore six. His toes matched that pattern. He had no hair on him anywhere. His skin seemed impossibly taut and shiny and shone a sickly snot green with irregular patches of deep reddish brown. His cheekbones were exaggerated. His eyes were those of a great cat. His teeth were sharp and numerous and serrated at their back edges.

Krepnight, the Elect, had sprung forth full-grown from the imagination of Kharoulke the Windwalker. He existed for one purpose. Its target lay just a bit more than an arrow's flight ahead.

Krepnight, the Elect, urged his frightened mount forward. He ignored the sign beside the gateway, BEWARE THE WOLVES AND WERE, in faded Brothen capitals. He could not read, anyway.

Nor could many of his companions. None, the language of this land.

Krepnight, the Elect, paused after a four-hundred-yard advance. He faced a small castle from barely a hundred feet. Its drawbridge was down, spanning a wet moat eight feet wide.

Krepnight, the Elect, could not cross running water without help. The water in the moat was in motion.

Water was not relevant.

An arrow slammed into the artifact's chest. It drove through till fourteen inches protruded from his back. The shaft was thick, oak, tipped with armor-piercing iron. Krepnight, the Elect, rocked back after the impact, then just sat petrified in his saddle.

Brittle cold air swirled round him. He felt every breath.

He could do nothing.

Two old men came across the drawbridge. One carried an iron shovel, the other a rusty bill. Shovel man took the reins of the divine artifact's mount and led him away, the horse quaking in terror. A hundred yards on, at the brink of a gully, the bill man used his tool to unseat the rider, who tumbled into the little ravine.

Both old men shoveled and dragged dirt, sticks, stones, and fallen leaves onto the immobile body.

The light went away. A long time passed. Ravens watched quietly from the trees. Wolves came to consider the fallen artifact and be amused by his misfortune.

In time, the pilgrim's companions found the divine artifact. They dug him out. One broke the heavy arrow and drew the shaft. Krepnight, the Elect, shook off the dirt and leaves and got his feet under him. The crows above chattered eloquently about this grand practical joke. The wolves kept their distance but their body language bespoke cruel contempt.

There were shamans among the Chosen. They stayed close as Krepnight, the Elect, resumed his advance on the castle. They suppressed the power of the water. A dozen men were within touching distance as Krepnight, the Elect, crossed that drawbridge and carried his god's will into the rustic citadel.

A blinding flash. A vast roar. A thousand needles of agony. An irrevocable death for Krepnight, the Elect, and all who walked with him.

While the corpses still shook and twitched wolves hit every man who had passed the warning sign.

Three younger riders, left outside by their captain, flew off to report the disaster.

Ravens followed. Mocking.

The Night knows no special love for those who consider themselves its own. Of the three, two fell victim to ruthless minor Instrumentalities. The last was too mad to report anything useful when he did win through.

His return was information enough.

His god rewarded him as gods do. It devoured him.

# 2. Lucidia: In the Eye of Gherig and the Shadow of the Idiam

The wind had an edge like a rusted saw. No man living remembered such cold in the Lucidian desert. For sure not when full winter had not yet arrived. Some had seen snow before—in the distance, on peaks in the highest of the high ranges.

The stone tower atop Tel Moussa offered an outstanding view for leagues around. Built by crusaders to watch for invaders from Qasr al-Zed, the watchtower had been captured by Indala al-Sul Halaladin, Wielder of the Sword of God, after he crushed the crusaders at the Well of Days. Now it was home to desperate fugitives from Dreanger who had taken service with Muqtaba Ashef al-Fartebi ed-Din, the Kaif of Qasr al-Zed.

The cruel wind plucked at the graying hair and beard of Nassim Alizarin. They called him the Mountain. He was a man so large only western destriers could carry him. And he required a string of those when he traveled. He wore them out quickly.

Nassim turned slowly. The Unbelievers had chosen the site well, though they built on foundations set down ages past. A hundred armies had traveled the road below, headed one direction or the other, since men learned to make war. Nassim thought more would come and go before long.

A solitary horseman approached from the south, bent over his saddle, miserable. That would be the old man, Bone, back from a circuit of Sha-lug outposts along the far borders of the Crusader states. Behind Bone, crouched like an evil sphinx on the horizon, loomed the dark silhouette of Gherig, the Crusader stronghold no mere mortal could hope to capture. The Brotherhood of War manned Gherig. Sometimes those hardy warrior-priests approached Tel Moussa, hoping to draw out the fugitive Sha-lug. The Mountain would not play. In the best times he had fewer than four hundred followers scattered across the Realm of Peace. His war with his onetime friend, Gordimer the Lion, Marshal of the Sha-lug, was not going well. Most Sha-lug agreed that the murder of Nassim's son Hagid was an abomination. Yet they did not see that as an excuse adequate to justify bloodshed between brother warriors.

The essence of al-Prama was submission. The essence of being Sha-lug was discipline.

The Master of Ghosts, al-Azer er-Selim, joined Nassim. He cursed the bone-biting wind. Softly. The Mountain tolerated neither blasphemy nor the invocation of demons. Az asked, "Is that Bone?" His eyes were no match for those of the General.

"Yes. And bringing no good news."

"Uhm?" Az looked northward and slightly to the east, toward the Idiam, that harshest of deserts. Az dreaded bad news. If it turned bad enough—so bad that Muqtaba al-Fartebi no longer saw any value in supporting a Sha-lug splinter faction against the Kaif of al-Minphet— then the only safety might lie in Andesqueluz. The haunted city.

The Mountain read his stare. "We'll never be that desperate. The Lucidians need every blade. The Hu'n-tai At threaten in the north and east. Once Tsistimed the Golden finishes devouring the Ghargarlicean Empire he'll turn on Lucidia."

Below, the weary rider began the climb to the tower. Would he make it? Did he have strength enough left?

Bone was old but those who knew him never bet against him.

"How does he stay alive?" Nassim asked.

"Uhm?" The Master of Ghosts now stared a couple of points south of the line that would bisect the Idiam. Toward the Abhar River and the northern end of the freshwater lake the locals called the Sea of Ze-bala. Scarcely a day's walk away. It could be seen glistening on a sunny day. Beside that lake, to the south, lay the village Chaldar, birthplace of the Chaldarean religious error. One of the Wells of Ihrian lay near Chaldar. Az could not recall its name.

He had begun to have memory problems.

"Tsistimed, Ghost Master. How can he still be alive? He's been the King of Kings of the Hu'n-tai At for two hundred years." And was still fathering princes who grew up to rebel against him.

Az shrugged. "Sorcery." The all-purpose answer. "Let's go greet Bone beside a fire."

"In a moment." Nassim stared toward Gherig, now. And slightly north of that fastness, toward the Well of Days, where the crusaders had suffered their worst disaster ever. He pointed quickly, here, there, yon, naming the Wells of Ihrian. "The Well of Remembrance. The Well of Atonement," and so forth. "If you connect them all with lines, those lines almost perfectly define the Plain of Judgment." Where a hundred battles had been fought across the ages. Where the final conflict between God and the Adversary would take place, according to all four religions with roots in the Holy Lands.

"Really?" Az replied. He was learned but no more religious than he had to be to survive amongst the fiercely religious. "Could there be a connection with the weakening of the wells? Would we be better off if Indala had slaughtered the crusaders on the Plain instead of in the wastes overlooking the Well of Days?"

"It's a thought. For someone more connected to the Night than I."
Nassim headed downstairs.

Bone fit his nickname. There was little flesh on him and his
skin was sickly pale. Az feared the old company would shrink again
soon. Only a handful were left. And their captain was far away, being
someone else. Given no choice by Heaven or Earth.

Someone brought broth for Bone, Az, and Nassim. The Mountain's
lieutenants gathered. Bone was nearest the fire but could not stop shaking. The Mountain called for more fuel. Bone squeezed his mug with
blue fingers and sipped. He began to thaw, to peep out into the world,
to be relieved to see Az close by.

"I bring no joy," the old man rasped. "They have forgotten us." But
that was not the message he had come to deliver. "I have that wrong.
They haven't forgotten. They can't bring themselves to care enough to
turn on the Marshal. The Rascal is a different story. They would cut him
down if they could lure him out of hiding. The Lion himself would do
so. But none yet despair enough of Gordimer's leadership to turn against
him. Our secret friends have begun to fade. They say we've offered no
alternative, only an end to what stands."

The Mountain sighed, sank onto a low divan. It was true. He had
gone to war against Gordimer and er-Rashal al-Dhulquarnen. Wicked
though those two had been, they had been the law in the kaifate of al-
Minphet. Gordimer still was. The Sha-lug and the Faith were greater
than the sum of any crimes. Before all else, there must be a Marshal. And
a law. Else, Dreanger would slide into chaos. The Holy Lands would be
lost.

Lucidia—the kaifate of Qasr al-Zed—could not put an end to the
outsiders. Indala al-Sul Halaladin was old. Unlike Gordimer, he was
too honorable to seize all power for himself. He bent his neck to the
whims of his Kaif. And had to concentrate on the ever-waxing threat of
the Hu'n-tai At.

"It's true," said the Mountain. "I am undone by emotion. And have
dragged you all with me. We are become Gisela Frakier for Muqtaba al-
Fartebi." Gisela Frakier were those most loathed of Believers, Pramans
who served the enemies of the Faith for pay. Gisela Frakier patrolled
and enforced the boundaries of Rhûn, backed by the Eastern Emperor's
professional armies.

Ancient tribal rivalries compelled some Faithful to become Gisela
Frakier. In the time before the revelation brought in by the Founding
Family, religion had been a critical part of tribal identities. Throughout

the range now blessed by the Faith the tribes had been divided equally amongst Devedian, Chaldarean, and animistic devotions.

In the mouth of Nassim Alizarin "Gisela Frakier" became uglier than "apostate."

"If we have a kaif," Nomun observed. Nomun had turned rebel when the Lion took his daughter into the Palace of the Kings at al-Qarn. Nomun had been a brilliant captain in the field. Further, he was steeped in book lore and had a reputation as a consummate surgeon. It would be the Nomuns of the Sha-lug, as their numbers increased, who ended the tyranny in al-Qarn.

"If we have a kaif?" Nassim asked.

"Al-Fartebi is sick again. Rumors whisper poison." As always they did when a man of standing became ill. More often with Muqtaba al-Fartebi than others. Muqtaba had poisoned his predecessor. There had been talk of setting him aside because of the threats of the Hu'n-tai At, the resurgent Crusader states, and increased pressure from al-Minphet. And Muqtaba would have gone but for Indala al-Sul Halaladin. All the world feared Indala's displeasure. Some believed the Hu'n-tai At were withholding their fury only because they did not want to waken the genius of the Battle of the Well of Days.

"There's debate about who should replace al-Fartebi. Indala refuses the role. As always. But two of his sons have shown it no disdain."

Civil war? Always a possibility where posts were not passed on according to blood. Nassim said, "Indala trained his sons to be warriors. The Kaif should be a holy man."

Several men snickered. Native Lucidians all. Few recent kaifs had been truly holy. Some claimed Muqtaba's frequent illnesses were the result of his dedication to vice. To his fondness for absinthe in particular.

The Mountain considered Bone. Bone seemed to have shrunk into himself. "All that means nothing to us. Our world is Tel Moussa and the watch on Gherig."

Al-Azer er-Selim observed, "There's always the option of returning to the west."

"Not for Nassim Alizarin. I stay. I abide. If I have to flee into the Idiam, I will. I'll play the trapdoor spider. My hour will come. God delivers the wicked into the hands of the righteous. I'll be as patient as the mountain."

Az and Bone stirred uneasily. They had seen the Idiam. They had visited the haunted city, Andesqueluz. Both knew that "the Mountain" was one translation of the name of the chief god in the pantheon that held sway locally before the rise of the modern religions. And of late madmen had been trying to resurrect fallen gods.

Asher and Ashtoreth, the Bride of the Mountain, were recalled only in ancient bas-reliefs, notably on walls in Andesqueluz. But it would take only one mage, absent a conscience, to conjure evil into the world. Er-Rashal al-Dhulquarnen had tried to resurrect Dreanger's ancient horror, Seska, the Endless.

"Az?" the Mountain inquired. "Something on your mind?"

"Only what's always there. Dread of the machinations of the Instrumentalities of the Night. And of the Night's human pawns."

The Mountain bowed his head slightly. "Thank you for reminding me. My great sin is selfishness. I think of my desires instead of the good of our souls."

## 3. Alten Weinberg: Celebrations

The Captain-General had been assigned a three-story, eighteen-room limestone monstrosity for his visit to the seat of the Grail Empire. The house came with a staff of twelve. It belonged to Bayard va Still-Patter, son and heir of the Grand Duke Ormo va Still-Patter. Empress Katrin herself had ordered Bayard to vacate in favor of the Church's leading soldier.

The Captain-General, Piper Hecht, and his party had come to Alten Weinberg in company with King Jaime of Castauriga. Who had dragged a sizable portion of his subjects hundreds of miles to celebrate his marriage to the most powerful western sovereign. The Captain-General, it appeared, was in favor with the Empress, though they had encountered one another only twice before, never to speak.

Three days after arriving Hecht listened as Kait Rhuk said, "We can't figure it out but this woman definitely has something in mind for you."

Nervous, Hecht paced and wondered if Katrin's game involved her younger sister, the Princess Apparent, Helspeth. He had no one to share thoughts with. His intimates he had left in the Connec to manage the Church's offensive against revenant Night. Those who had accompanied him here were lifeguards, clerks cum spies from Titus Consent's staff, or belonged to Kait Rhuk's weapons gang—the latter along in case the Night offered some unpleasant attention. And there was his adopted son, Pella. Plus Algres Drear, a Braunsknecht, or Imperial guard, who had been rusticated to Viscesment after offending the Empress and members of her Council Advisory.

Captain Drear told Hecht, "I've sneaked around as much as I dare.

He's right. She's up to something. No one knows what. The Council Advisory are concerned."

Empress Katrin was an Ege. Her father's daughter. The Ferocious Little Hans frightened them still, though he was now years dead. Johannes's unpredictable daughters frightened them more.

"I'm surprised they haven't thrown you into the stocks."

"People don't see what they don't expect to see. Algres Drear is off in Viscesment protecting the Anti-Patriarch. The few who do recognize me tell me I got a raw deal."

Hecht had walked the streets himself. He had not learned much. He did not understand the language well enough. Nor did he have the time to fit himself in. More, he could not persuade his chief lifeguard, Madouc, that he would be safe wandering around.

Pella, though, had grown up on city streets and could slip his minders easily. His big problem was the language.

Alten Weinberg was more crowded and excited than any local could recall. The coming marriage had the world agitated. It might be the critical marriage of the century. It could render permanent the Imperial rapprochement with Brothe, ending centuries of warfare between Patriarchy and Empire. If Katrin produced a son to assume the Imperial ermine it would also give the Empire a foothold in Direcia. And would provide Jaime a shield against the ambitions of King Peter of Navaya.

"WE SAVED HIM FROM A GANG OF THIEVES," PRESTEN REGES TOLD Hecht. Hecht considered Pella. The boy was filthy, his clothing torn. "We don't think it was political. The local soldiery wouldn't let me bring the thugs along for questioning."

"Tell me, Pella."

The boy's story supported Presten's estimation. He had become too curious about something, then had betrayed himself as an outsider. An open invitation. "I messed up, Dad. I forgot where I was."

"Lesson learned, I hope."

"I'll be more careful."

"Did you find out anything for your trouble?"

"A lot of people don't like this wedding. But that's not a secret."

Katrin Ege was unpopular because of her accommodation with the Brothen Church.

"It isn't." Hecht worried for Katrin's sister. There were factions eager to move Helspeth into the top spot, hoping she favored her father's policies. That put the Princess Apparent at risk from Katrin's friends.

Helspeth tried to be neutral and to maintain her sister's love. But simply by existing she became a fulcrum and rallying point.

It was early. Hecht had spent his waking time, so far, breaking his fast and studying dispatches from the Connec and Patriarchal garrisons in Firaldia. He had learned little to cheer him.

Carava de Bos approached with a small, black wooden tray on which lay three letters, their seals unbroken. De Bos managed the delegation's clerical functions by day. The night clerk was Rivademar Vircondelet. Each doubled as a spy. Both were protégés of Titus Consent, chief spymaster and record keeper of the Patriarchal forces. And friend of the Captain-General.

De Bos said, "Recently arrived letters, sir. In order of arrival. Also, a gentleman named Renfrow has asked to see you. Shall I make an appointment?"

"You don't know who he is?"

"*He* thinks he's important."

"And that would be true."

"Shall I make an appointment?"

"No. Send him in. The rest of you, clear off. Madouc. I don't want the servants eavesdropping." Bayard va Still-Patter expected his people to spy. They tried hard. And were ferociously inept.

Renfrow was nondescript. He wore seasoned clothing like nine of ten people in the street, was average in height and unremarkable in his features. His hair betrayed specks of gray. Hecht had been close enough to smell the man's breath on several occasions but could not recall the color of his eyes.

Hecht watched Renfrow approach. Renfrow was surprised to see Algres Drear. Pella, Hecht sensed, remembered Renfrow from the Knight of Wands a couple years ago.

That boy had a dangerous memory.

Hecht considered the letters. He recognized none of the hands. One seal was that of the Patriarch. The others belonged to the Empress and her sister, respectively.

These morning reviews happened around a table capable of seating a dozen. Hecht folded a couple maps and turned over two reports that had not gone away. Renfrow took it all in at a glance, lingering an instant on the letters from the Imperial sisters.

Hecht said, "Sit. If you'll be more comfortable. I intend to." He settled.

"I appreciate you seeing me so fast."

"Our talks are always interesting. And I've grown bored. I should have waited and come here a week behind King Jaime."

"I can't imagine being bored in this political climate."

"Not my politics."

"You could be wrong. I think. There are secrets even I can't ferret out. Secrets hidden from Ferris Renfrow in particular."

"I can understand that."

Renfrow flashed a conspiratorial smile. "If I asked, would you explain why Algres Drear is with you? I pulled a lot of strings to get him rehabilitated enough to go be one of Bellicose's Braunsknecht guards."

"Bellicose told him to come."

"I hear you and Bellicose have developed a mutual admiration."

"True. Is that why you're here?"

"No. I wanted to warn you to be careful."

Hecht merely raised an eyebrow.

"Dark things are stirring. Rumors reach me, second- or third-hand, from sources not even marginally reliable. The Night is abidingly disturbed by what you've been doing in the Connec."

"I wouldn't be surprised."

"You have powerful enemies. Over there."

Hecht, never quite convinced, nevertheless nodded.

Renfrow produced a folded paper from inside his shirt. Hecht winced, half expecting a crossbow bolt. Madouc would be watching. Madouc did not like sudden movements near his principal.

Renfrow opened the sheet, smoothed it.

"What is that?"

A talented artist had drawn a face, the side of a head, and an unusual pair of hands.

"Life-size," Renfrow said. "Killed north of here some weeks ago, along with several barbarians who wore animal bones and skulls in their hair."

"What was it?"

"I'd hoped you would know. You're the man from Duarnenia. The veteran pagan fighter."

"Not a pagan fighter. I left before I was old enough to visit the Marshes. But the Sheard had nothing like this helping them."

"You're a mystery wearing a cloak of enigma, Captain-General. The men with this thing had some connection to Kharoulke the Windwalker."

"Then you're looking at the wrong pagan gods. The Sheard have nothing to do with Kharoulke. Or any gods of his generation. Kharoulke hails from the farthest north. From the lands of the Seatts. And beyond. Kharoulke was displaced by the gods that our God overcame when Chaldarean missionaries converted the north. I've heard rumors about the Windwalker returning."

"You surprise me again by being so well informed."

"I have friends in low places."

"No doubt about that."

"Sir?"

"I've found that while almost no one recalls a boy named Piper Hecht making his journey southward, to take service with the Patriarchs, records of his service with several local garrisons exist. He never stayed anywhere long."

"Some captains kept records obsessively. I caught the habit myself. My people can account for every copper that ever touched our hands. Good record keeping lets you show your employer what you've accomplished and why it cost so much."

"And still they complain."

"Of course. This thing." Hecht tapped the drawings. "You should've brought the corpse. That would cause a stir." Maybe get some attention paid to some of the more serious threats to the world.

"Its flesh corrupted and melted within hours, though there was snow on the ground and ice in the trees. Neither ravens nor wolves would touch the flesh."

"Something of the Night."

"Undoubtedly. But what?"

"I'm not the man to ask. But I know who that man might be." The Ninth Unknown. Cloven Februaren. Lord of the Silent Kingdom. Possibly the most powerful sorcerer alive. And the least predictable. "Unfortunately, he's in Brothe. Like most of the Collegium, waiting for Boniface to die."

"What do you hear about that?"

"Hugo Mongoz might outlive half the men who elected him." Hugo Mongoz being the name of the Principaté who had chosen the reign name Boniface VII when he became Patriarch.

"Isn't Bellicose supposed to succeed him?"

"That's the deal. I have orders to enforce it if the Collegium tries to take it back. I'll do what Boniface wants. Bellicose is a good man. Who may not last as long as Boniface has, despite being thirty years younger."

"Drear should be with him, then. Not here."

"Bellicose's health will do him in. Not assassins. He sent Drear to be his representative at the wedding. As I'm standing in for Boniface."

Ferris Renfrow kept his opinion to himself.

Hecht understood. "Bellicose knew what he was doing when he sent Drear. It's because of how he was treated here when he was a bishop."

Renfrow chuckled. "The pro-Brothen party were feeling their oats."

"Is that all? I do have work to do."

"I have ten thousand things. Nine thousand nine hundred you won't help me with. So I'll just leave you with another word of caution. You may have enemies you know nothing about."

"You hear that, Madouc? Now you can nag me with the report of the Imperial spymaster himself." Hecht felt less humor than he pretended. Madouc would, indeed, mention Renfrow's warning every chance he got. It irked him that he would have to pay attention. He was exposed, here. And there were people who did truly believe the world would be a better place without Piper Hecht in it.

Madouc just smiled. More than did Hecht himself, the lifeguard looked forward to putting Alten Weinberg behind and getting back to murdering the Instrumentalities of the Night.

Ferris Renfrow said, "I've done what I had to do here. Which is warn you not to relax."

"I do get lax, sometimes. Madouc never does. Madouc is an Instrumentality in his own right."

"Cherish him, then. Honor him. Most of all, listen to him."

Hecht asked, "Madouc, did you put him up to this?"

HECHT GATHERED CARAVA DE BOS, MADOUC, AND RIVADEMAR Vircondelet as soon as Ferris Renfrow left. Pretty blond Vircondelet could not stop yawning. Hecht stared at the letters on the black tray, longing to dive into them. "What have we found out about Renfrow? Anyone?"

De Bos and Madouc deferred to Vircondelet. The sleepy Connecten, a Castreresonese, had the potential to exceed his mentor, Titus Consent. "A Ferris Renfrow has been involved in Grail Empire politics for more than a hundred years. This Ferris Renfrow claims to be the son of the Renfrow who served the two Freidrichs and the grandson of the Renfrow who served Otto, Lingard, the second Johannes, and the other Otto. Every Ferris Renfrow frightened everyone around him. People won't talk about them much. If a mortal can be considered an Instrumentality, Ferris Renfrow qualifies. He's the living patron tutelary phantom of the Grail Empire."

Hecht asked, "Is there a woman in any of the Renfrow lives?"

Vircondelet said, "I haven't connected any Renfrow with any particular woman. Maybe they do like you and adopt." Pella had just stuck his head in. He saw that he would not be welcome.

Maybe Renfrow's family was like the Delari. Each generation produced out of wedlock, one after another.

Vircondelet kept on. "The princesses, Katrin and Helspeth, are the only women in his life of late. That's because he's the guarantor of Johannes Blackboots's will and Bill of Succession."

"Proceed on the assumption that all Ferris Renfrows are the same Ferris Renfrow. And keep digging. Find out who his enemies are. They're bound to gossip."

Carava de Bos said, "No one here has made much of it, but Renfrow appeared at court, filthy and wounded, with news of the victory, only hours after Los Naves de los Fantas."

That startled Hecht. He hoped it did not show. "How could that be?"

"The critical question, right?"

"Keep an eye on him." Hecht glanced at the letters. He could wait no longer. "All of you. Back to your duties. Vircondelet. Go back to bed."

THE CAPTAIN-GENERAL TORMENTED HIMSELF. HE OPENED THE LETTER from Boniface VII first. He had no interest in it whatsoever. It told him its author had had a premonition that his hour on the stage was about to end. And begged him to make sure the agreements with the Viscesment Patriarchy were honored. By force if necessary,

In Hugo Mongoz's estimation, most of the Principatés of the Collegium were slime weasels interested only in filling their own pockets. They would ignore the agreements if they thought they could.

Hecht burned that letter. It was a waste of paper. Though Boniface could not be sure that his will would be executed. Unless he watched from Heaven as his Captain-General enforced his wishes.

Hecht read the letter from the Empress next. He dreaded what might lie inside that from the Princess Apparent.

Katrin Ege, Empress of the Grail Empire, with a string of subsidiary titles that filled half a page, requested the attendance of the Captain-General of the Patriarch of the Brothen Episcopal Church. . . .

The flattering crap went on and on. Piper Hecht was not one to be turned and shaped by that. But he let it play. And composed an equally florid, disingenuous, and dishonest response. Yes. He would see Her Grace, the Empress, Katrin. . . . Time and place, Katrin's choice.

Katrin's request was echoed by Princess Helspeth in her brief letter. Which he read over and over, looking for the slightest nuance.

IN ONE HOUR HECHT WOULD PRESENT HIMSELF TO THE WOMAN WHO, at the moment, was the most powerful ruler in the western world. He was trapped in speculations about what might be on her mind. Alone.

Pella was away wandering the city with one of his handlers. Madouc had expressed serious reservations.

Alone he might be. In the room where he slept. But one of Madouc's men was right outside.

Some things needed no doors to get inside.

Hecht was rereading Helspeth when the flames of his candles danced briefly. "Cloven Februaren?"

"You've grown more sensitive. We get you more time in the Construct, you'll be able to smell me coming."

Hecht looked toward the voice. He saw nothing till the man materialized by turning to face him. He was old, small, weathered, all clad in brown. His eyes, of uncertain color in that light, sparkled with mischief. His hair needed a trim. And combing.

Cloven Februaren. The Ninth Unknown. Grandfather of Principaté Muniero Delari, the Eleventh Unknown. Who claimed to be Piper Hecht's natural grandfather. Cloven Februaren was more than a hundred years old. Probably more than a hundred fifty. But he lied a lot. And he had the sense of humor of a ten-year-old.

Hecht glanced at the door. Who was on duty? Madouc's men knew their principal sometimes became involved in spirited discussions with himself. Only Madouc dared step in to make sure they did not turn violent.

The old man said, "Well?"

"Uhm."

"So it's going to be one of those intellectual discussions?"

Hecht smiled. Which felt odd. "Philosophical, perhaps. I just realized that I seldom smile."

"Your sense of humor has atrophied. What is it?"

"Sir?"

"You summoned me. You must have a reason."

Hecht managed to hold his tongue. He had done nothing of the sort. But he had wished that he could see the old man.

"I didn't, but I'm glad you're here. You can help with a couple of things." Hecht talked. In particular, about what Ferris Renfrow had said. "I'm interested in all that. And even more interested in finding out about Renfrow." He related what little de Bos and Vircondelet had unearthed.

The longer Hecht talked the more agitated Februaren became.

"You're disturbed. Why is that?"

"An unhappy suspicion. Has anyone accused the man of sorcery?"

"No. But he scares everybody. And has done for as long as you have. And he does things he shouldn't be able to do."

"Which you would accuse me of, too. I'll check his record, then. As he seems to be checking yours."

"More than once he's told me he believes I'm Else Tage, a captain of the Sha-lug pointed out to him in al-Qarn when he was visiting Gordimer the Lion and his wild sorcerer."

"That would be when he acquired the boy. Armand."

"Yes. Osa Stile. Muniero Delari's erstwhile bed pet. Now playing night games with Hugo Mongoz himself."

Flash of the Februaren mischief. "And getting nothing to his friends outside Krois. The Dreangereans think he's dead."

Hecht steeled himself. "Have you seen Anna? And the girls?"

"No. But Muno has them to the house regularly. Anna misses you. She and Heris have become friends. And Heris has become adept with the Construct."

Hecht was surprised at how emotional he was about his makeshift family. Anna Mozilla was not his wife but he ached with longing for her. Vali and Lila were not his flesh but he missed them more than his true daughters. Of whom there were two. Almost forgotten. Along with a real wife. Whose face he could no longer picture. None of them seen in years, and then usually only for a few brief hours before the Lion sped him off on some other deadly mission.

Cloven Februaren told him, "You're not a bad man, Piper Hecht. Neither was Else Tage. We're all slaves of circumstance. And circumstance can be crueler than any devil."

Hecht understood. It was what he needed to hear at that moment. Except: "The Adversary is determined to drag me down."

"And? Are you going to claim some special place on the Rolls of Temptation?"

"Helspeth." He had said nothing to anyone, ever before. "The Princess Apparent. I have an obsession. From the first time I saw her, as a captive in Plemenza. I saved her life at al-Khazen. The insanity is mutual. We've exchanged guarded letters. I'm here, now. In Alten Weinberg. With Helspeth less than half a mile away." Hecht was astonished. He was confessing what he was barely able to admit to himself. "I'm terrified that I'll do something mad. That I'll ruin myself and drag the Princess with me."

The humor and mischievous sparkle fled Cloven Februaren. "Wow. Seeds of an international epic. I'd better shelve my lesser concerns and concentrate on this wedding. It is still on?"

Hecht did not catch the gentle sarcasm.

"Katrin worships the ground Jaime walks on. Though Jaime needs a good solid ass-kicking, to borrow a notion from Pinkus Ghort."

"Who is getting fat commanding the City Regiment. Bronte Doneto and Pinkus Ghort make quite a team. Lords of Brothe, now, those two. What's wrong with Jaime?"

"He's much too impressed with King Jaime. He worships the man. And thinks the rest of the world should join in."

That brightened the old man's evening. He said, "Sounds like an opportunity."

"As may be. . . ."

Madouc invited himself into the Captain-General's bedchamber. He glared around suspiciously. "Who are you talking to?"

"Madouc?"

The chief lifeguard had suffered this before. "Gerzina heard voices."

"Did any of them yell for help?"

"No, sir. But it's a given that the man we're protecting doesn't have the God-gifted sense to call for it."

Hecht was irked. But did not have the strength of conviction to tell Madouc that he was wrong or was getting above himself.

Something had to be done. They were too much at loggerheads, letting personalities get in the way of common sense. Someday he would bring Madouc's worst fears to fruition by thoughtlessly disdaining the man's advice. Meanwhile, Madouc exaggerated every slight in his own mind.

Friction. It had to be overcome. Somehow. Madouc was a good soldier, wasted in his current assignment.

"If you were Master of the Castella Commandery, Madouc, what job would you see yourself best suited to do?"

"Sir?"

"If you could pick your job, what would that be?"

Hecht did not expect an answer. Unless as some formula. The Brotherhood of War had countless rules they did not share with outsiders.

"Given a choice, I'd master one of the commanderies in the Holy Lands."

"And protect pilgrims? Interesting. Have you asked?"

"The Brotherhood has begun to turn its face westward. Maybe because the west has begun to turn away from the Holy Lands. You and I have been involved in two crusades, now. Neither overseas."

Madouc's anger at his principal had transformed itself into anger at his own order.

"Have you asked?"

"No."

"You should. A man ought to do God's work in a way that comforts his soul. He'll do a better job."

Madouc had nothing to say about that.

"I suppose I ought to start getting ready."

"Sir?"

"Letter from the Empress. Commanding me to attend her in privy audience. After the evening meal. That's all I know."

"There's one thing you need to address. We caught that man Bo Biogna trying to sneak in here. I know you go back a way so I'll defer to your judgment. He's been asking a lot of questions about you, here, in Hochwasser, and elsewhere."

"Principaté Delari warned me about this. Principaté Doneto considers me a traitor to his personal cause. He wants to find something bad about me from before we saved him that first time in the Connec. I've given him no ammunition since. Except by faithfully serving each employer instead of being his secret agent."

"Will he find anything?"

"I doubt it. I never stayed anywhere long. As soon as I got up a stake, I headed farther south. Well, wait. I did steal a sack of turnips once, right after I started. Some bullies took my knife and cheese. . . ." He stopped. Madouc was astonished, hearing him open up. "Where is Bo? I know exactly what he was up to."

"HARD TIMES?" HECHT ASKED WHEN BIOGNA CAME IN. BO WAS NEVER a big man. The rags he wore hung loose. Hecht recalled them when Biogna filled them out.

"Yeah, Pipe. How's it going?"

"You've lost weight."

"Been going some cold, harsh places."

"So I hear. You know you got Madouc's guys all flustered."

"I just wanted to see Joe. I heard he was here with you."

"I thought so. I sent for him. You'll understand if we don't give you the run of the place. These others don't know you like I do."

Biogna's gaze turned furtive for a moment.

Hecht asked, "You run into anything interesting up north? Like wild riders with animal skulls braided into their hair?"

"Nothing that outrageous. Just the Night being busier than it used to. You'd better carry some charms if you need to go out after dark. It gets worse the farther north you go."

"Find out anything interesting about me?"

Biogna grimaced. "You didn't stay anywhere long. Hardly anybody remembers you. But there's always good things about you in the records."

"I wanted to get to Brothe. I worked when I needed money. When

I ran into you guys was the first time I let myself get distracted from my goal."

"Paid off, though. For all of us. Especially you and Ghort."

His good humor abandoned Hecht briefly. It had not worked out for most of the men of their little band. They were buried near Antieux.

"Yeah," Biogna said. "For them as survived that nonsense. And Plemenza, afterward. We ain't doing so bad. Hey! I met your brother."

Hecht could not have been more startled if Biogna had pulled a knife. "What?"

"Your brother. Tindeman. You mentioned him a couple times."

"But he's dead."

"Looked pretty healthy to me. Gone gray in the hair, though. And he's got a nasty purple scar across his face that makes it hard for him to talk. But he's alive and kicking. He's an artillery engineer in Grumbrag."

Hecht was too surprised to improvise. How could the Ninth Unknown have placed live people to support his backstory?

"You seem overwhelmed," Biogna observed.

"I am. I've never been so surprised. I always thought I was the only one left. The fighting was really awful that year. Almost everyone on the Grail Order side was killed. Even if the Sheard were broken."

Hecht was saved the need to dissemble further by the arrival of Bo's friend, Just Plain Joe.

Joe was a big, slow, dull man with a genius for managing animals. Though he was a private soldier—Joe wanted no more responsibility—Hecht considered him one of his dozen key men. Joe knew animals. The Patriarchal army could not operate without countless animals if he wanted it to remain an effective, modern force.

Joe had cleaned up. Which explained why it had taken him so long.

Hecht said, "Look who's here."

"Yeah. They told me. Hey, Bo. Hey! You don't want to get too close. I didn't get that clean."

"Look at me, Joe. Do I look like I'm ready for parade?"

Hecht called for food and refreshments. His lifeguards watched, carefully blank, while one of the more powerful men in the Episcopal world relaxed with a stable hand and a would-be trespasser.

Hecht had formed strong bonds with these men, Pinkus Ghort, and others who had not survived. Their variable fortunes since had not broken that bond. Even when they worked at cross-purposes.

Carava de Bos appeared. "I'm loath to interrupt, sir. But you have to see the Empress in just two hours. You need to eat and dress."

"Thanks. Joe, Bo, duty calls. You guys enjoy yourself. Cederig."

Speaking to one of the lifeguards. "Mr. Biogna can stay as long as he likes. But he's to go nowhere except here and the stables."

Biogna would want to say hello to Joe's tutelary mule, Pig Iron. Pig Iron had been with Joe since the beginning.

Hecht considered that mule a sort of philosophical signpost. The beast had an attitude toward the world. It served him well.

Hecht considered himself stubborn and nasty, too. Though he had yet to take a bite out of any of his friends.

CLOVEN FEBRUAREN TWISTED INTO EXISTENCE WHILE HECHT WAS dressing. Without help. He insisted on dressing himself, as much as he could, despite the status he had attained. It was almost as good as having a slave whisper in his ear.

The old man said, "I overheard your friend's report. About finding your brother Tindeman in Grumbrag. I'm not guilty of that. My contributions to your backstory consist of false entries on minor payrolls. Did Begonia say anything he couldn't have gotten from what you've told him about your past?"

"Yes. That someone I made up is alive and kicking in a city halfway between here and the permanent ice."

"You think he told the truth?"

"Bo? I don't know. He's a clever little weasel. He could be running a game suggested by Bronte Doneto. To see my reaction. Only, I'd be more inclined to suspect Ferris Renfrow."

"You've told the same tales so often you believe them yourself—unless you stop to think. You had Muno doubting facts about which there was no question, you lied with such conviction."

Piper Hecht was not one hundred percent convinced that his "true" origins had not been sold to him the same way.

"True, I suppose. And Renfrow has spies everywhere."

"Or he'd like us to think he does."

"Maybe not so many as when Johannes was alive, but plenty. He's thoroughly dedicated to the Grail Empire."

"I'll try to see this Tindeman Hecht."

"I have to call somebody to help me with these last few laces. Some things I just can't manage alone."

"I can take a hint."

FOR THE AFTER-DARK WALK TO WINTERHALL, THE EGE MANSE IN Alten Weinberg, Madouc insisted on a guard that included both Kait Rhuk's falcon teams, their weapons charged with godshot. Every man carried a brace of primed hand falcons and a burning slow match.

Madouc absolutely expected an attack. An enemy would get no better chance.

Madouc thought not only about guarding his principal but about what potential assassins really hoped to accomplish.

Assassinations, in Madouc's estimation, were highly symbolic, meant to make a mighty declaration. If he could guess what that might be, he should be able to guess when and where a killer would strike.

And he was not wrong. Though tonight's would-be killer was but one starving, deranged spearman who charged out of the darkness, shrieking, intent on throwing his weapon.

"What did he say?" Hecht asked after the man had been rendered unconscious, tied, and turned over to local troops drawn by the bark of a hasty hand falcon.

"Something about Castreresone. We did something there that he didn't like."

Winterhall resembled the va Still-Patter house, built larger. Why did the Empress want to meet away from her palace? The grandeur there would overawe a beetle like Piper Hecht.

Madouc opined, "She knows you've seen Krois. You've seen the Chiaro Palace and the Castella dollas Pontellas. Her palace wouldn't intimidate you. And she might want to be away from all the eyes and spies that go with a palace. Here she can talk with only a few noses poking in. Here she can get away from her fiancé."

Rumor had King Jaime making himself thoroughly unpopular by acting like he was in charge. Katrin supposedly would not admit his bad behavior but had taken steps to neutralize it.

"Be interesting to see how much control she lets him have after the wedding," Hecht said. Katrin Ege was used to having things her way. Often even over the objections of her Council Advisory.

"Indeed," Madouc replied.

"What is that?" Hecht indicated construction they were passing. It could not be seen well by torchlight.

"Something being built by bankers from the Imperial states in Firaldia. Their own private fortress. You see more and more of them in northern Firaldia. Just round stone towers with only a few windows up high and just one small entrance maybe fifteen feet above the street. Good enough in family and city politics, where you don't see heavy weaponry or extended sieges."

Hecht recalled capturing a somewhat similar citadel in Clearenza, when Sublime V wanted to punish the local Duke. That place had had a ground-level entrance, though. And a larger footprint.

The Captain-General had to shed most of his party outside the Ege

palace. And all of his weapons. Unarmed, Madouc was allowed to accompany him as far as the doorway of the sizable room where the Empress had chosen to see Hecht. He remained outside with a brace of
humorless Braunsknechts.

The room was drawn from an eastern potentate's fantasy, all silken
pillows in bright colors. The air was heavy with rare incense. Six
women were present. Hecht recognized the Empress and her sister.
Katrin had aged badly. The other women were unfamiliar. They would
be ladies-in-waiting, wives or daughters of important nobles.

It was a torment, avoiding staring at the Princess Apparent.

One of the women seemed aware of his problem. She looked him
straight in the eye, mocking and flirting.

"Captain-General, come forward," the Empress ordered.

Hecht pushed himself. He was able to pursue ceremonials under
fierce pressure. He did those things an empress would expect, but once
he completed his obeisance he dared say, "This is irregular in the extreme, Your Grace." He understood that honorific pleased Katrin, though
it was more suited to a Prince of the Church.

"It is. Yes. Sit. Be comfortable."

The Captain-General did as instructed. The Empress had gained a
regal air along with the haggard look. Helspeth had gained . . . something dangerous. More magnetism than in his frightened fantasies.

Katrin continued, "There are matters I want to raise with you.
I couldn't, elsewhere. As it is, my Council Advisory will fulminate and
bluster when they hear about this. Jaime will be petulant. But not
enough to endanger his chance to become Imperial Consort."

The woman with the challenging eyes approached the Captain-
General. She brought coffee in a little cup so thin the fluid level was
evident from outside. The odor said this was the finest Ambonypsgan,
smuggled through Dreanger and so expensive that only kings and
princes dared enjoy it.

There was a message in the appearance of that cup. The Empress
knew a lot about Piper Hecht. Including his fondness for coffee.

The woman who brought the coffee murmured, "Compliments of
the Princess."

She knew.

A glance at Helspeth. The Princess Apparent was not behind that
message. She had best hope this woman was a true friend.

"Thank you for the coffee, Your Grace. I haven't had the pleasure
in some time. How may I be of service?"

Encounters of this sort often dragged on, no one speaking to the
point, everyone looking for some bit of leverage. Hecht was impatient.

"Two matters, Captain-General. Possibly more, later. Firstly, the Remayne Pass. You came that way?"

"I came with King Jaime. Who went the northern way. He had reservations about the pass."

"Because the thing my sister squashed there has found new life. In a smaller way. It's making trouble but I can't unleash my ferocious little Helspeth again."

So. She had heard the whispers marking Helspeth as the truer child of the Ferocious Little Hans.

Helspeth was not pleased. That was clear. But, as mentioned in more than one careful letter, she meant to be the perfect younger sister and Princess Apparent.

"And?"

"Only the Captain-General of the Patriarchal forces has the power and means to eliminate this pest. The Empire will bear the expenses. Including indemnities to the families of anyone lost in the hunt."

Hecht took a tiny sip of coffee. That could have been arranged by go-betweens. Even if Katrin was flexing her Imperial muscles for the benefit of men who had been pushing her this way and that. Who might be inclined to do more pushing, more vigorously, these final days before the wedding.

Once trivial opposition to her choice of husbands had grown dramatically since King Jaime had become available for direct assessment.

Only Katrin remained infatuated.

Katrin proved capable of cutting through when she wanted. "That's my lesser problem. I have something bigger in mind. First, though, I want your oath never to discuss it outside this room. If we can't come to an accommodation."

Hecht thought the Empress naive if she believed anything discussed here would remain secret. The ladies-in-waiting had husbands who wanted to know. Someone would tell someone, in strictest confidence.

Hecht toyed with blond hair he had let grow long. And was considering pruning back. Strands of gray had begun to appear. "I can make that commitment. But my silence won't keep the secret."

"No doubt. The great symbol of the Empire is the eagle. But I'm surrounded by vultures."

"I'm sorry to hear that."

"But you're not surprised."

"The price of power, Your Grace. The higher you rise the more parasites you accumulate."

Katrin rose from her cushions. Helspeth did the same. The Empress said, "Come with us. There's a quiet room back here."

Every lifeguard and lady-in-waiting began to stir, driven to protest. Katrin snapped, "My ferocious little sister will guard me against the wicked Brothen."

Moments later the Empress herself shut the door of the most austere quiet room Hecht had seen. The walls were bare stone that sorcery could not penetrate. There were no furnishings.

Hecht studied the milky rock sheathing.

"Captain-General? I promise, it's real. The best stone, from the quarry where Aaron and his father worked."

"I was looking for cracks. An acquaintance—he belongs to the Collegium—can spy on a quiet room if there're cracks anywhere."

"Muniero Delari."

"Him. Yes."

"Helspeth. Stop that."

The younger woman was trembling.

"All right." The Princess Apparent feigned an abiding interest in the integrity of the stonework.

Katrin said, "I'll get straight to it. Excusing themselves one way or another, someone will force that door soon. Captain-General. I want to hire you away from the Church. You, your staff, and all your professional people."

Helspeth gasped. "Katrin?"

"Your Grace?"

"I swore an oath when I was crowned. Only my confessor knows. I mean to make the pilgrimage to the Holy Lands. Leading a crusade. I want you to be its commander."

That Katrin might launch a crusade was no secret. But . . . "I don't know what to say."

"I've been surrounded by the great men of the Grail Empire my entire life. The best of them, like the Grand Duke, are petty, self-serving, and would backstab any other lord I might appoint my champion."

Hecht started to protest.

"Bad choice of words, Captain-General. Not champion. Supreme commander. General of generals. For the same reason you were made commander of the Brothen City Regiment. You have no ties to any faction."

"So all your dukes and grafs and ritters would be against me because I'm an interloper."

"My father developed tools for handling that sort. I haven't deployed them yet. Once this marriage is made I intend to put together a new Council Advisory. Jaime and the Patriarch back me."

"Possibly. I suspect Jaime will be a nuisance, determined to control you."

Katrin's temper flared. It was true. She would hear nothing against Jaime.

Hecht stole a glance at Helspeth, who had been stubbornly silent. That startled her. She said, "Surely you'd find service with the Grail Empire an important step forward, Captain-General." Her voice was breathy. It wavered.

Katrin clearly appreciated the support but was puzzled by her sister's shyness.

"It would be, indeed," Hecht said. "I can imagine no greater honor, nor any task more challenging, than being warlord for the Grail Empire in such a holy enterprise. But . . ."

"But?"

"A crusade would be expensive in the extreme. Even if every fighter volunteers, wages still have to be paid. Men have to eat. Their animals have to eat. Weapons have to be purchased. Armor . . ."

"There should be wealth enough, Captain-General. Despite the costs of the Calziran Crusade, my father was frugal. He left a sizable treasury. My brother not only preserved that, he added to it. Despite the jackals surrounding him. Likewise, the current Empress. Who expects to come into substantial additional riches soon." A remark she would not pursue.

"I have a contract with the Patriarch," Hecht said. "At his will. In effect, I'm his till he loses faith in me. Right now I'm engaged in a bitter campaign to exterminate revenant Instrumentalities in the End of Connec. They refuse to go easily."

"As with the thing Helspeth defeated."

"I'll do what I can about that."

"And when Boniface goes?" Helspeth asked, voice stronger now. "Will you be free then?"

"No. Bellicose of Viscesment will be the next Patriarch. To reunite the Church. I've sworn to stand behind him. In case the Collegium try to renege on the Church's promises. It's a pity Boniface became Patriarch so late. He might have earned a place in history, given more time. He's the best Patriarch I've known."

"Bellicose won't last long, will he?"

"Boniface may outlive him. His health is fragile."

The hammering on the door began. Helspeth said, "That took longer than I expected. You're starting to scare them, Katrin."

"They'll have a reason after this. Captain-General. What will it take to bring you here? Will Boniface or Bellicose let me buy you?"

Hecht managed not to eye the Princess Apparent. "Not as things stand. They both have uses for me."

"If you did serve me would you be just as loyal?"

"Yes. My integrity is what I'm selling. Those people out there do seem to be getting impatient."

"They'll regret it." The Ege steel rang out.

For the ghost of an instant the tips of Princess Helspeth's left hand fingers brushed the back of Hecht's right. The effect was electric. He jerked. Helspeth gasped. Katrin paid no mind. The door had begun to open. She was headed that way in a blistering rage.

THE NINTH UNKNOWN WAS IN A SERIOUS MOOD. HE MADE NO NOISE to attract the lifeguard outside Hecht's bedchamber. He whispered, "Wake your dead ass up, boy. We've got problems."

Hecht surfaced from a dream featuring Helspeth and him engaged in activities that could compromise the Grail Throne itself. The old man had a hand over his mouth. That was not necessary. Hecht whispered, "What?"

"Boniface had a stroke. You need to get back to Brothe."

"I'm stuck here till after the wedding."

"There might be a coup. Bellicose hasn't reached Brothe yet. And neither Muno nor I can get close enough to prop up Boniface's health."

"Damn!" Hecht swore softly. The timing was awful. "Can you disguise yourself?"

"What?"

"You can manage not to be seen at all. I know. Can you pass as someone you're not?"

The old man frowned his question in the weak light of a lone candle.

"Can you deliver letters without giving yourself away?"

"I'm listening."

"I can send orders to the garrisons near the city. And my people in the Connec. If you take the long strides in between, my forces can be in place ahead of time."

"Send for pen and ink. I'll find a way." Februaren turned sideways and vanished.

Hecht summoned the duty lifeguard. "I need quills, ink, paper, and sand. Right away." He had wax and a candle.

Armed with the appropriate tools, he began writing orders.

Cloven Februaren reappeared. "Too bad you didn't have more time with the Construct. You could handle this in person."

"Wouldn't be smart to let people think I could be two places at once."

"Good point. Better than good. What were you and the Ege chits doing in that quiet room?"

Hecht forgot his promise first time he was asked. "Katrin wants to hire me to lead a Grail Empire crusade into the Holy Lands."

"My. My, my. The Palace is going mad, wall to wall, wondering what went on in there. No one thought of that."

"It caused some excitement?"

"King Jaime and the Council Advisory are livid. They're blaming Princess Helspeth. Only Jaime has said anything within Katrin's hearing. She's dismissed everyone she saw when she stepped out of that quiet room."

"Good for her. I hope she goes for a clean sweep. Have you learned anything about the Night thing Renfrow reported? Or my purported brother?"

"When would I have had time?"

"Right. One does take an advantage for granted quickly, doesn't one?"

"You may. I don't. Seal the letters you have ready. I'll move them along. Leave the rest here, addressed. And make sure no one can get in here when you're gone."

Hecht grunted and folded, then applied wax. Within the minute the Ninth Unknown was gone again.

HECHT SETTLED BESIDE KAIT RHUK. RHUK ASKED, "WHAT HAVE WE got, boss?" Hecht did not mind the informality. Rhuk did his job. Well.

"You talk much with Prosek about the thing in the Remayne Pass?"

"Yeah. We designed our attack strategy based on what he learned there. Why? Something on the fire?"

"That interview I had with the Empress. She told me the thing is making a comeback. And hopes we'll do something about it."

"We can handle it. Our munitions are way better than when Prosek went after it. One good hit should take it out."

"Good. So. We'll deal with that. After the wedding."

"There isn't much to do, here. For us."

"So?"

"So I've hung around a lot with guys who humped into town with the high and the mighty."

"And?"

"There are incredible career opportunities for men in my line. Especially up north."

"Kharoulke the Windwalker."

"Not yet. Not directly. But his cult is back. That's weird, isn't it? The wells of power start drying up and, suddenly, we've got ten thousand more Instrumentalities plaguing us. You'd think it would go the other way."

"Slow down." Rhuk had a substantial accent. It thickened when he became excited. "Do you know what you'll do if we do come up against an Instrumentality like Kharoulke?"

"More developed than Seska was. Probably bend over and kiss my ass goodbye."

"Because?"

"At some point an Instrumentality should become powerful enough to see ambushes ahead of time. Then it'd stand off and do you wicked. With a platoon of first-string sorcerers I could lure him into a trap that didn't look like a trap until the firing started. If the first salvo was accurate I could finish him before he pulled his shit back together. But if I didn't get him the first time I'd never get another chance."

"Not what I'd hoped to hear. But pretty much what I expected."

"You ask me, boss, if you want to handle a demonic assertion like the Windwalker, you better get the Patriarch on the case with God. Get Him to come out and flex His muscles the way He used to do in the olden days."

An interesting suggestion. But not especially useful.

Hecht suspected that God would not show up.

His faith had suffered serious ablation lately. "Think about the Kharoulke problem. If we ever face something that big it'd be handy to have a strategy set."

"Of course, sir."

Kait Rhuk was dedicated. He would do that. When he was not busy catching whores.

CLOVEN FEBRUAREN CAME AND WENT. IN THE MAIN, HE BROUGHT good news. Buhle Smolens was headed for Brothe with five hundred crack mountain infantry. Patriarchal garrisons throughout Firaldia were on alert. The Master of the Commandery, the new Brotherhood chieftain at the Castella dollas Pontellas, Addam Hauf, would quarter Patriarchal troops there, meaning the Brotherhood would back the Patriarchal forces.

The Brotherhood existed to make war in the Holy Lands. They

could not do that without support from the west. Internecine squabbling anywhere meant reduced resources available to those determined to liberate God's homeland.

The Captain-General was satisfied that everything possible was being done. If Boniface hung on for a week, a smooth succession would be assured. Buhle Smolens would be close to the Mother City. The Captain-General would be headed south.

The Ninth Unknown said he thought the Patriarch would last a month.

He was able to get that close, now he had begun to put thought into the effort.

Cloven Februaren began to show the strain of trying to hold everything together. Hecht told him to ease up. If it looked good, let it ride. Let it work itself out.

Advice he had to take himself. He could not walk away before the wedding.

THE WEDDING DID COME, THOUGH THE WAIT SEEMED ENDLESS. AS AN anticlimax. Being Boniface's representative, the Captain-General watched with the attendant clerics. He played no part himself, not being in orders. Pella was not allowed to join him. The boy remained outside the Holy Kelam and Lalitha Church, shadowed by Presten Reges and Shang "Bags" Berbach. The lifeguards were frantic. If ever someone wanted to get at the Captain-General through his son, this was the time.

Holy Kelam and Lalitha was one of the great churches of the Grail Empire, rich in architecture, furnishings, and decorative detail. It was an object of pilgrimage. Relics of both Founder namesakes were buried beneath its altar. The lame and sick came to light a candle and pray to Lalitha, who had wrought miraculous cures while living.

The Captain-General spared little attention for the wonders of the church. He focused on the wedding party. On Princess Helspeth and King Jaime. There was little mystery about his interest in the Princess Apparent. The Adversary had found a foothold inside his soul. He did wonder why the Direcian monarch interested him, though.

Attitude? The man was sure to be trouble. Everyone watching could tell he was impatient to get this nonsense over. That he was eager to start throwing his weight around.

Jaime was headed for a world of disappointment. Katrin might be besotted, might be fawning over him, but she was Johannes Blackboots's daughter. No pretty Direcian would win control of the Grail Empire simply by wedding her.

And if she did surrender all reason?

The Council Advisory would step in. A dozen grim old men and their grimmer women. They watched from the floor, afraid that they had erred by agreeing to this match.

They could tell that the Castaurigan had ambitions unfettered by reality. He expected to outshine Peter of Navaya, using his new spouse's wealth and power.

Could he be that blind? His bride meeting privately with Boniface's military commander had outraged him. He had no idea what might have been discussed, but was aware that the Church was little interested in glorifying Castauriga or its king. The Church was cozy with Peter of Navaya.

King Jaime would be in a tight place with the Church. The outstanding characteristic of his wife was her devotion to Brothe. That was her external strength and her great political liability inside the Empire.

Hecht leaned nearer the Archbishop beside him, Elmiro Conventi. Conventi represented several Imperial cities in northern Firaldia. "We need to watch this King. He'll intrigue with the anti-Brothens if he can't bully the Empress."

The grossly fat Archbishop first showed annoyance, then grasped the suggestion. "Excellent observation. I'll pass the thought along."

The ceremony was a long one. It did not just join a woman and a man, it formalized an alliance and founded a dynasty.

Piper Hecht thought he had been in the west long enough to be acclimated to its weirdest customs. He was aghast when he discovered that the grande dames of the court were, at this late hour, jockeying to be chosen to witness the Empress's defloration. There would be five. Tradition assigned the respective mothers and the bride's aunts the task. Neither Jaime nor Katrin had a living mother. Jaime had brought no sufficiently exalted Castaurigan women. He tried to refuse the ceremony. The court harpies would have none of that.

They wanted to see the Ege chit humiliated.

Somehow, the Empress, Alten Weinberg, the Grail Empire, and the greater world got through the night. As did the Captain-General of Patriarchal forces.

Madouc assured him, "Only the highborn endure that. Before the conversion to Chaldareanism, girls lost their virginity early. They seldom married before they proved their ability to bear children. It's still that way for the peasantry. But the nobility consider it imperative that there be no doubts about paternity. No man wants to leave his patrimony to a child not his own."

"I understand." Without fully comprehending. "Yet most women here young enough to be interested seem to indulge in liaisons with men who aren't their husbands. Some with more than one man. While the men are involved with women not their wives."

"The underlying consistency is hard for outsiders to grasp." Madouc's tone was caustic. "The romanticism of the jongleurs is to blame."

"Meaning?"

"They say marriage is a business arrangement. Love is something else."

The Praman world had its love stories. Its fables of deceit, betrayal, and cuckoldry, usually illustrating the weakness of the cuckold. In real life even the suspicion of infidelity could lead to a harsh death. Here, everyone winked at it—even when one's own woman was concerned.

And yet, Piper Hecht could not see Helspeth Ege and keep his thoughts channeled into propriety.

THE POST-NUPTIAL CELEBRATIONS WENT ON FOR DAYS. TWO PASSED before the Captain-General could leave without giving offense. He left the borrowed house in better condition than he had found it, with an effusive letter of gratitude to the younger va Still-Patter.

The Braunsknecht captain, Algres Drear, rode with him. "My greatest appreciation for your efforts on my behalf, Captain-General," he said, on the road south of Alten Weinberg. "The Princess Apparent would've had me back if she could. But her sister won't forgive me. Nor will those old men she made look like fools and cowards in the Remayne Pass." Having mentioned the pass, Captain Drear became nervous.

"I'm glad you're along. You were there before. You can help plan."

"You truly intend to deal with the monster?"

"I told the Empress I would. Kait Rhuk says we're a hundred times more ready now than Prosek was then." He glanced over his shoulder. There were four falconeers back there who had survived the last ambush. They had been injured, then taken captive by the Imperials, who had hoped to pry the secrets of the falcons out of them. They had betrayed nothing because they knew nothing.

"I'd apologize," Drear said, following his glance. "But you'd know I wasn't sincere. The Princess Apparent was livid. She has an overly developed sense of honor."

"Something like her father?"

"Johannes Blackboots could put his sense of honor aside if the stakes were high enough."

"I suspect the Princess would, too, given a real need. We're few of us morally and ethically inflexible. Those who win the great reputations are those who are least obvious about it."

"A cynic."

"Perhaps. I count myself a realist. I'd forgotten these mountains are so big."

The Jagos climbed to the sky, each peak clad in a cape of permanent ice.

Drear said, "They've changed a lot, just in my lifetime. There's a lot more ice and snow now."

Princess Helspeth's folly in the pass had earned her no detractors among the people of the region. Their livelihoods depended on having travelers use the pass.

The Captain-General paused to rest his animals and ready his gear before entering the pass. The village was called Aus Gilden. It was unlikely ever to be known for anything but its utility as a jumping-off point.

A courier from the Connec overtook the Captain-General there.

He gathered the band in the evening. "I've had a message from Lieutenant Consent. Our brothers in the Connec had a productive few weeks while we languished in Alten Weinberg."

Laughter. Every man had seized the opportunity to do everything but languish.

"Prosek cornered and dispatched Hilt and Kint on consecutive nights. He's close behind Death, now."

Someone called, "Let's hope that goes well."

"Hagan Brokke twice destroyed large gangs of bandits, with the assistance of Count Raymone. Clej Sedlakova cleared several towns *and* ambushed Rook. Who, unfortunately, managed to slide away again. But badly weakened. That leaves only Shade running free and uninjured." Skilen and several lesser revenants had fallen already.

The men did not cheer. They were not that sort. But they had pride in accomplishment. Kait Rhuk said, "Let's hope it's as easy up ahead."

"You foresee problems? The monster can't offer anything like the threat it did to Prosek."

"I like to be ready for the worst."

An outlook Piper Hecht approved. If you were prepared for the worst you would seldom be caught unready.

THE NINTH UNKNOWN APPEARED OCCASIONALLY BUT THERE WAS little chance to talk.

It was a comfort, knowing the old man was watching.

Drear warned, "We're coming up on where it happened."

Those who had been with Prosek before began pointing out and explaining.

Hecht sent most of the party to make camp at Prosek's old site. A caravan headed north soon filled the pass anyway. Hecht and the veterans of the previous encounter, with Madouc, pushed on against the flow.

They found little evidence of the previous encounter. Even the scars on the rocks had faded.

Hecht said, "Let's get an early start tomorrow."

Returning to camp, Hecht found the north-bounds settled not far off. He sent Kait Rhuk to ask if anyone had seen anything unusual.

No. They were too many for the monster to trouble.

"So are we," Rhuk opined.

Hecht feared so. And did not know how to hunt the thing. "I didn't think this through."

THE PATRIARCHALS MADE SUCH EXTENSIVE PREPARATIONS TO RESIST the Night that the Firaldians nearby mocked them. Every ward got set out. Every man carried at least one handheld firepowder weapon. Both falcons were charged with godshot. Falconeers sat close by them, nursing slow matches. Huge fires illuminated the camp.

And still doom nearly had its way.

A severe itch gnawed at Hecht's left wrist. He knew he was dreaming, yet knew the itch was real. He had to wake up. He could not. The sense of déjà vu tormented him. He had been here before. Not in this place but in this situation. Aware but unable to respond as something terrible closed in.

Reason gained ground. This had happened before, in the Ownvidian Knot. He had awakened enough to shake Bronte Doneto out of the spell controlling him.

A falcon barked. Utter astonishment, like a living force, engulfed existence. Then black pain, followed by an instant of realization that the impossible, extinction, was at hand. Then a swift descent into a vacuum of never-will-be-again.

The impact was so brutal Hecht could barely drag himself out of his tent. He was soaked with sweat, shaking. His left wrist ached like it had been broken.

It was worse for the others. They had no protective amulets. The pale light of drained fires feebly illuminated men writhing, or so smitten they lay as though dead, eyes open and rolled back. Yards from the smoking muzzle of a falcon steam rose from a circle of blackened earth. An egg, still so hot it yielded red light, lay at its center.

"Good work, men," Hecht tried to say. Nothing came out. His mouth was too dry. Nor, he saw, did anyone really deserve the accolade. The duty falconeers were down, in attitudes suggesting that they had fallen asleep.

That thing in the Ownvidian Knot had sent a wave of sleep before it, too.

Cloven Februaren. "Thank you, Grandfather." He should see about Pella, now.

"What?" Algres Drear, stumbling, appeared. He offered Hecht a hand up.

"My ancestors were looking out for me." A suspiciously un-Chaldarean thing to say.

"Maybe. It's the same as that night in the Knot, isn't it?"

"That would be my guess."

"And it wasn't the thing we're here to destroy."

"I doubt it. This would've been what they call a bogon. A sort of prince of the Night. The way it was explained to me before. Why are you in such good shape? Compared to these others."

"I was asleep behind that boulder. I guess it shielded me from the worst."

Hecht eyed the boulder. He saw nothing special. Maybe it was laced with iron or silver ore. Maybe it had been shot up during Prosek's adventure here and had rolled down the mountain since. Maybe rock was a solid enough barrier in itself. No matter. "Let's see what we can do for these people."

"Why are you up so easily?"

"I have friends in the Collegium. They gave me protections against this stuff. Though I'm asking for more, after this. I'm not feeling that grateful to be alive right now."

"A bitching soldier is a happy soldier."

Hecht managed a chuckle.

There were no deaths. No one had anything broken or torn. Nobody needed sewing up. But hearts and souls had been brutalized. Fear had found a home. Faith had suffered a severe strain.

Hecht told them, "Never forget. *We* survived. *We* won. It's the Night that needs to be afraid. The Night that has to get out of the way."

The pep talk helped. A little.

HECHT DECIDED TO INVEST ANOTHER DAY IN RECUPERATION. HE hoped for some sign from Cloven Februaren. None came.

Next morning Hecht got everyone moving as soon as there was light to see.

He squabbled with Madouc. He wanted to be out front. Madouc would not suffer it. The lifeguard carried the day.

Hecht had decided to give in whenever his own desires were not critical to the work at hand. He did not have to be out front, he just wanted to be. Acquiescence now would ease relations and make it easier to overrule Madouc when taking a risk might be useful.

Pella eyed him suspiciously. He asked no questions. Hecht suspected he understood. The boy was quick and smart. Too bad Madouc was just as smart and even quicker.

Progress was slow. The men out front were not eager to find what the travelers from the south had missed. Their Captain-General rotated the point frequently.

The Remayne Pass opened out some. Slopes curved up to either hand, covered with scrub and modest evergreens amongst scattered boulders tumbled from farther up. The peaks caught the rising sun first. Those shifted quickly from orange to a white too brilliant to look at.

A stream rumbled beside the road, carrying frigid meltwater.

The air grew thinner and colder.

Hecht dropped back to the pack train, fell in with Just Plain Joe and Pig Iron. He did not say much. Neither did Joe. Pig Iron kept his own counsel. There was no way Hecht could explain his need for time shared with Joe.

Just Plain Joe was one of his oldest acquaintances this side of the Mother Sea. Pinkus Ghort and Bo Biogna dated from the same time, and Redfearn Bechter from just days later. Only Anna Mozilla went back further than did they.

Joe had no agenda. Joe lived each day as it came. He made life easier for the animals. Hecht could relax with Joe. He didn't have to explain anything, guess about anything, do any planning, be anything but a guy Joe knew.

Joe was in one of his social moods. Fifteen minutes after Hecht joined him, he asked, "You in a big hurry, Pipe?"

"Always. It isn't necessary, though. Probably."

"I keep looking at that river and thinking they ought to be some good trout fishing there. In one of them pools where the water takes a break before it goes charging off again."

"You want to have a fish fry?"

"Been a while since I had a mess of good cold-water fish. Better than anything they got down in the lowlands."

"When's the best time?"

"Afternoon? After the sun warms the water some and there's bugs out. Early evening is maybe even better since there's more bugs then."

"We come to a place that looks good, give a holler. Those men up front need a break."

"They're pretty worried, eh?"

"The monster had a bad reputation, back when. I think we'll have trouble finding it now, though."

"That wasn't it the other night? That was rough on the horses."

"Rough on all of us. No. That was one of those bogon things like the one in the Ownvidian Knot that Principaté Doneto chased off."

"Uhm." Joe went back inside himself and relaxed. Maybe half an hour later he emerged to chat briefly about ways to reduce disease amongst the army's mounts.

A small party northbound had no news about the monster but did report that all Firaldia was holding its breath over Boniface's health. The Patriarch made good progress for a few days, then suffered grave setbacks. On his good days he pursued his work ferociously. He had made great headway with the Eastern Church. He was close to a modus vivendi that would soothe the factions in the Connec. The ancient peace of those provinces was about to be restored.

If Boniface just had the time.

That alone should have the poisoners swarming, Hecht believed. Too many people, inside the Church and inside Arnhand, had become deeply invested in abuse of the End of Connec. Thieves, all, except for a handful of fanatics.

The column halted. Kait Rhuk and the men up front spread out, getting ready for trouble. Hecht hurried forward. His lifeguards closed in but did not stop him. This needed doing.

"Rhuk. What do we have?"

"Injured man up ahead. Maybe dead."

Rhuk had the man covered from several angles, no one closer than twenty feet. One falcon was sited so that it could fire at anything coming out of the only cover nearby.

"He's breathing," Rhuk said. "I see that now."

The man lay sprawled among the rocks like he had fallen out of the sky. He was large and wore nothing but a massive growth of washed-out reddish hair. The dense rat's nest around his head and face contained streaks of gray. He had not been eating well.

"Been in a few scrapes, looks like," Madouc said. "I've never seen so many scars."

"Missing his right hand, too," Rhuk said. "Want me to go wake him up?"

"No. Nobody get in the line of fire."

Everyone eyed the brush up the hillside. Was this man bait?

Hecht said, "I've seen this man before. I'm trying to remember where." The memories came in a rush. He did not want to accept them. "Below the wall of al-Khazen. This was one of the soultaken." Whose death tussle with Ordnan and the Choosers of the Slain had cursed him with ascension to Instrumentality status.

"Target both falcons on him. Have every hand weapon ready."

"Sir?"

"That's our quarry. The man who became the monster."

That caused a buzz. And brisk preparations.

"Say when, sir," Rhuk said, slow match in hand.

"Not yet. Only if he does something threatening." This needed closer examination. He was aware of no instances of this soultaken returning to human form. There must be a reason. "Pella. I have a job for you."

"Dad?"

"Round up some throwing stones. Chunk them over there. Try not to hit him in the head."

"All right."

"Rhuk. The rest of you. No firing without my order."

Pella threw. He did not miss. The body yonder twitched.

Where was the Ninth Unknown?

The hairy man shuddered. He forced his way up off the rocks. His naked skin bore fresh abrasions, several extensive and evidently painful. He got into a sitting position, shuddered again, rested his hands and chin on his knees.

"What now?" Kait Rhuk asked.

"Wait. Pella. That's enough."

The wait was a long one. At last the naked man shuddered, lifted his head, peered round with bleary eyes. He showed his palm weakly, in response to the martial display.

"Don't anybody relax," Hecht said. "Don't take any of this at face value." He told the naked man, "Speak."

Hecht could not decipher the answer. He did not move closer. The soultaken had been created specifically to destroy him. It might not be able to abort its mission.

"Captain-General?" Rhuk wanted instructions. Again.

"Wait."

"Food," the soultaken gasped. That was clear enough.

"Toss him a loaf. And a hard sausage. Somebody. Don't get in the line of fire."

Algres Drear volunteered. He approached the naked man from

uphill, avoiding the sight lines of the falcons. He tossed a loaf and a sausage into the man's lap.

The soultaken ate with glacial haste. A party came up from the south. Threats kept them moving. The news they carried was not encouraging. The Five Families of Brothe were maneuvering heavily, determined to reject the ascension of Bellicose. They might try to lock foreign Principatés out of the Chiaro Palace to keep them from voting in the next Patriarchal election.

The news angered Hecht. He wanted to rush ahead to the Mother City. Those idiots! Was it impossible for them to deal honorably? Impossible to stand by agreements already made?

But this situation had to be explored first.

He could just blast the soultaken. In this form he could be torn apart easily. But. There must be a reason for his having changed shape.

"This may take a while. Anybody know this pass? Is there a good campsite up ahead? I can't remember."

Again, Algres Drear volunteered. "There's a marshy meadow about three miles on. It was a campground before the monster came."

Hecht said, "We need to dress this man. I'll buy from whoever is willing to give something up. Something that will fit, Carolans."

The soultaken was big. The soldier Carolans barely came up to his chest.

Size and the fact that few of the men bothered to carry extra garments around made clothing the naked man a challenge.

The man devoured every crumb given him. His color returned. He got his feet under him. He dressed himself.

He submitted while silver was placed round his neck, while his wrists were bound behind him and his ankles were connected by a leather hobble.

Before resuming movement, Hecht asked, "You have a reason for what you've done? Other than trying to engineer my murder?"

The captive grunted. "Must talk." But that was all he said that day.

THEY HAD NO LEG IRONS OR FETTERS. A NEED HAD NOT BEEN FORE-seen. The prisoner made do with hobbles while he traveled. In camp his captors attached a rope to a stake driven deep into the earth and tied the other end to his left ankle. Another rope ended up tied around his waist. A ready falcon always pointed his way—even after the rain arrived.

The Captain-General had a tent raised to shelter the sentinel falcon.

The prisoner remained in the weather.

Camp set, watch posted, men fed, animals settled, Hecht went to talk to his guest. His lifeguards were close by, armed with firepowder weapons charged for use against the Night.

Hecht brought a camp stool. He settled out of the line of fire. "I'm ready to talk." Drizzle fell.

The prisoner pushed emptied bowls to the limit of his reach. No one blocked any line of fire collecting them. "This will take a while. The change drained me more than I imagined possible. I'd forgotten how to be human."

Hecht was surprised. The man was articulate. But his accent was brutal.

"You knew we were coming."

"Yes. And why. There are few secrets from the Night. But Instrumentalities don't understand human time. If they did, the Godslayer never would have been born. Till he acted the first time, though, the Night could never be certain that he had been."

A theory previously proposed by Muniero Delari and Cloven Februaren.

"If the Night knows the future, why try to direct it?"

"There are countless futures. Some elements are unavoidable. At the same time, countless possibilities have to be eliminated."

Hecht sat silently. The prisoner was content to wait. And indifferent to the weather. He did lean back and open his mouth to catch what liquid fell to him.

He had been given nothing to drink.

Hecht said, "I can't help thinking you're too articulate to be Asgrimmur Grimmsson from Andoray."

"Svavar suffered on behalf of his brother and his gods. Like a sword thrust into the furnace repeatedly, then hammered hard on the anvil. Most of this Asgrimmur came from those gods, garnered unwanted as they died. This Asgrimmur has seen much that that Asgrimmur never suspected."

"If the Night can't tell time how did you manage to get into my way at the right moment?"

"I'm not that far removed from humanity." Talking was a strain. This man never was a talker, nor much of a thinker. But slow waters carve deep canyons, given time.

"Let's get to the heart of it. Why put yourself in my hands?"

"Kharoulke the Windwalker. In too many potential futures the wells of power keep weakening. The earth grows colder. The Windwalker waxes stronger. He could become greater than he was before.

There are no Instrumentalities capable of contesting what he might become."

"How can this be?" That was really a gasp of disbelief. God Himself would crush the devil.

But. The God of the Chaldareans, of the Pramans, of the Devedians, of the Dainshaukin, was a God fragmented into all the thousands of places where He was worshipped. Some believed there was no longer any way that He could pull Himself together again.

"The ice will keep spreading. Someday, no power will be able to challenge Kharoulke within that realm. Already he's found souls willing to work his mischief beyond the ice. The gods of the hot lands will weaken as their believers die and their churches are crushed by the advancing ice."

"And you care, why?"

"The Windwalker's return is largely my fault. The events that created the modern me filled me with insane rage. That drove me to avenge myself on the gods who made soultaken of me and my brother and murdered the rest of our band."

Hecht nodded. "You bottled them up inside a universe inside the realm of the gods they created for themselves. Freeing the Windwalker from bonds that had held him for millennia."

"Yes. Though Kharoulke isn't the only one. He just awakened first. He's forcing the other Instrumentalities of his age to become appendages of his will."

"Why come to me?"

"You are who you are. You are what you are. You are the only means by which I can correct my error. I'm awfully thirsty." That last stated as though by a second, different personality.

Hecht had a bucket of water brought.

Later, the prisoner said, "There is no way I can reassure you. You must, of nature, distrust me. Though I promise you that the lesson of the ambush, where I came within inches of death, hasn't been lost. All that shot, all that terrible silver, burned the madness out of me. Since then I've done only what I must to survive and recuperate. No travelers have died because of me."

Hecht stared thoughtfully. This sounded like an educated man of breeding, not a pirate ripped out of his own time by pathetically scheming lunatic gods.

"What do you want help doing?"

"I have to go back north. I have to rediscover the way into the Realm of the Gods. I have to free them. In some way that leaves me healthy. Once loose they'll have no choice about fighting the Windwalker. He won't give them an option. They imprisoned him ages longer than I've imprisoned them."

"That's a lot to think about. And there's bound to be more."

"True. See to your obligations. There's no rush. The Windwalker is still weak. And will be for years. Though weakness is relative. And he'll get stronger as the ice advances. One day he'll become strong enough to reach beyond the ice. When that happens this world's days will be numbered."

Good Praman or good Chaldarean, Piper Hecht heard little that could be encompassed by the faiths and prejudices of his experience.

"You don't need to trust me. I don't expect you to trust me. But I'll accompany you, causing you no harm, to Brothe. Where I can be examined by those able to determine the truth."

"Can you travel hurt?"

"I heal fast."

But not thoroughly enough to regenerate a missing hand.

"WHAT WAS THAT ABOUT?" MADOUC ASKED ONCE HIS PRINCIPAL WAS safely away.

"He has a message for our masters. From the Night side."

"What?"

"He's deserting. The Night. Because of horrors that are going to come. If we aren't forewarned and prepared."

"What?" Incredulous this time.

"I'm telling you what I heard. He talked me into taking him to the Collegium for examination."

"He is the monster that has been plaguing the Remayne Pass?"

"And other areas across the south slopes of the Jagos. Yes. Though he's been quiet since Prosek mauled him."

THE MONSTER WAS RIGHT. HE DID HEAL FAST. AND MADE HIMSELF useful, too, once he recovered. But no one trusted him. Ever. Not even Just Plain Joe, who was incapable of seeing evil in anyone else. Pig Iron had nothing to do with him. And where Pig Iron led the rest of the animals followed. Asgrimmur walked every inch of the road to Brothe.

He wanted to be called Asgrimmur. He did not want to be Svavar, though he had been called that since childhood.

Asgrimmur Grimmsson had, at last, done something to win the approval of the elders of Snaefells. Two centuries after the last of them crossed over.

The road south passed through numerous counties, duchies, city-states, and pocket kingdoms. Some were Patriarchal States. As many more were Imperial. The most daring claimed to be free republics. Veterans of the Calziran and Connecten Crusades made up the Patriarchal garrisons. Hecht gathered those as he advanced.

Three thousand men went into camp in the hills northeast of Brothe, the troops under strict orders to do no damage to vineyards, olive groves, truck farms, farmers, or farmers' daughters. The Brothen peoples, of all classes, were neither to be offended nor aroused.

The guards at the city gates had orders to prevent Patriarchals from entering. However, they lacked all suicidal inclinations. When Pinkus Ghort raked them over the coals later they would be healthy enough to enjoy his fury.

Hecht went straight to the Castella dollas Pontellas. The Fortress of the Little Bridges was the commandery of the Brotherhood of War in Brothe. The fighting monks had close ties with the Captain-General. For the moment.

Asgrimmur accompanied Hecht. As the great monuments and palaces along the Teragi came into sight, the Instrumentality said, "There is a cruel something hidden beneath this city. An evil something that feeds on fear."

Pella said, "Dad, I thought Principaté Delari said he'd get rid of that."

"He did say, didn't he?"

"And he said he did it."

"Maybe he was wrong."

"When can we see Mom?" Pella hardly pretended not to be manipulating those who had taken him in. Hecht did not mind.

"Soon. I have to see Colonel Smolens first. I have to get our new friend set up where people won't worry about him."

Trouble was likely if anyone connected this man with the northerners who butchered their ways through Brothe during the run-up to the Calziran Crusade. The Brotherhood of War, in particular, nurtured an abiding grudge.

"Presten and Bags can take you if you just can't wait. But you'll have to stay inside once you get there. They can't stay around to look out for you. They have families they want to see, too."

"Can I? I can't wait to see Vali and Lila."

"Go. But remember. You can't leave the house. You *can't*!"

"I got it, Dad. I got it."

# 4. Stranglhorm, at Guretha,
## Shadowed by the Ice

Stranglhorm had been the seat of the Master of the Grail Order for two centuries. A sprawling fortress of small city size, it never faced a serious threat, though it had been besieged a dozen times. The fortifications expanded with the decades. Growth ended only after the Grail Knights pushed the frontiers of the faith so far out that countless subsidiary strongholds had to be built to protect roads and shrines, and to provide local sanctuaries. The pagans called their lost territories the Land of Castles.

Stranglhorm crouched on a moraine, brooding over a bend in the Turuel River, which emptied immediately into the Shallow Sea. Once the waterfront had seethed with activity. A city, Guretha, took life alongside the river, then spread across it, trailing stone bridges behind. But now Guretha was a city swiftly dying.

The Shallow Sea had grown shallower. The Grand Marshes had drained or had frozen. New land had been exposed by the recession of the waters. Navigation had become impossible, except in fits and starts when the tides were favorable. A new breed of ship had come into being. It was wide, had a shallow draught, and was stout enough to survive periodic groundings. When the waters were not frozen.

The northern gulfs of the Shallow Sea no longer thawed. Colonies of sea people no longer existed east of the Ormo Strait. In fact, the mer were almost extinct. Only a few colonies, much diminished, survived in the Andorayan Sea, around underwater wells of power still leaking feebly.

Most all Andoray lay beneath the ice. North Friesland, likewise. During winters the Ormo Strait threatened to become covered with great arching bridges of ice.

The tidal currents were too fierce for the strait itself to freeze. Their power would be tamed only after the level of the seas fell a lot farther.

Where there was any warmth at all hardy men held on, confident that God would turn the seasons. That the wells of power would wax strong again. As in legend they always had.

The Chaldareans of Duarnenia and principalities east of the Shallow Sea had withdrawn to Guretha and other coastal cities established by the Grail Order. Many continued on, desperately, following the Shirstula River south into countries where they would be unwelcome because of their desperation. Clever kings and princes used some to begin clearing lands abandoned since the plague-ridden end days of the Old Empire, when populations had fallen by more than half.

A strange, small army came to Guretha, out of the icy wastes. All thin folk with bones and skulls in their hair, carrying standards made of flayed manskin and totems built of human heads and bones. They seemed half dead themselves. There were no elderly among them. They brought their women and children right up to the edge of the fight. Their eyes were empty and hollow. They reminded their enemies of the *draugs* of yore, the dead who rose against the living. They did not talk. They attacked. They took food where they found it.

Guretha resisted. Of course. The Grail Knights fought. They committed great slaughters. But wherever resistance solidified something irresistible soon appeared. It wore the shape of a man but had seven fingers on its left hand, six on its right. It was a foul, pale green with hints of brown patches. Its skin appeared polished. It had hard cat's eyes and smelled of old death newly freed from the ice. It carried a cursed two-handed sword so ancient it was made of bronze. Though soft metal, that blade did not yield to the finest modern steel. It broke through the stoutest shields and breastplates.

The Grail Knights were veterans of long wars. They did not waste themselves on forlorn hopes. Two encounters convinced them they could not overcome Krepnight, the Elect, hand-to-hand.

They stopped fighting. Gurethens who were quick retreated into Stranglhorm. Laggards fled across the bridges to the south bank of the Turuel. The city militias held the bridges. The invaders tried to flank them by crossing over in captured boats.

Krepnight, the Elect, stalked the Grail Knights to their fortress. Archers and crossbowmen kept the accompanying savages at a distance. They were a mob, not an army. What drove them? They were starving, yet seldom allowed themselves to be distracted by food or loot.

The Grail Knights withdrew, over the great drawbridge spanning the dry moat in front of the fortress gate. Engines atop the wall laid missile fires on the attackers. Krepnight, the Elect, suffered several hits. The savages yanked the offending shafts out of him. He forged ahead, undeterred.

Fierce, panicky shouting broke out inside the gate. The drawbridge had risen but a foot when its chains jammed. Then the outer portcullis fell five feet and refused to descend any farther.

Shrieked, frightened orders rattled around inside Stranglhorm. Get the inner portcullis down! But the backup refused to budge.

Decades had passed since the machinery had been asked to do anything but sit and rust.

The attackers cried praises to the Windwalker. They wanted to swarm across that drawbridge. But they would not move ahead of Krepnight, the Elect.

Krepnight, the Elect, would open the way.

The weird thing stepped up onto the drawbridge and crossed, sharp teeth betrayed in triumph. A Grail Knight in full battle gear, astride a huge charger, appeared behind the partially descended portcullis. He bellowed an order that it be raised so he could couch his lance and dispose of the monster. But the portcullis would not rise, either. The Grail Knight turned away, swearing by the body parts of the Founders that he would slay the monster once it came into the forecourt.

Krepnight, the Elect, advanced like confident doom. Today would see the end of Stranglhorm, Guretha, and these faint champions of a spineless southron god.

Krepnight, the Elect, ducked the portcullis and strode forward, charmed sword tasting the darkness of the passage.

Came a roar like all the thunders of a vast storm unleashed at once. Pale, eye-watering smoke billowed out of the gateway. Savages fell by the score, slashed into chopped meat.

The Grail Knights and their hardy foot swept beneath portcullises miraculously healed, then across a drawbridge suddenly fallen into place. The butchery began. Man and boy, mother and child, no mercy was shown. The heathen had shown none themselves. Few escaped. Only a boy named Boogha lived to carry news of an inexplicable defeat. And he died cruelly for having disappointed the Windwalker.

## 5. Lucidia, Tel Moussa: Sorrowful Truth

Nassim Alizarin faced the visitor across a low table. The meal was the best he could provide. That it was a sad failure would tell this boy too much. Would give him something to carry away with him.

The Mountain remained carefully composed. His age and former status left him unschooled for accepting a boy of sixteen as his superior. Birth meant little among Sha-lug. The slave warriors began as equals and established status by deeds. But this was Azim al-Adil ed-Din, grandnephew of Indala al-Sul Halaladin, upon whose sufferance the Mountain depended. The great Indala's not so secret ambition was the unification of all al-Prama into a single kaifate that could concentrate fully on the liberation of the Holy Lands.

Amenities complete, it was time to approach the point. But the boy demonstrated a decorum beyond his years. "The Arnhanders of Gherig. How do they behave?"

"The current crop are pirates, not holy warriors. They extort bribes from every caravan coming through from Dreanger or the coast. And call it taxation."

The boy laughed. "We do the same. And charge every Chaldarean a head tax simply for being Chaldarean."

Nassim missed the point. That was a "So what?" That was as God Willed it. "Mark me. One day Rogert du Tancret will overstep. He has no respect for God or al-Prama." In this Nassim said nothing that even the Crusader lords did not whisper among themselves.

Rogert du Tancret was a powerful warrior but not a man given to considering the consequences of his actions. He was lord of a crucial border bastion, in continuous contact with the enemies of his religion. Having not one diplomatic bone in his body, he was not the man to occupy so delicate a post. The Crusader lords all agreed.

But they would do nothing to move Rogert out of the crucible. It mattered not if he was a dangerous fool or a drooling idiot. His patrimony could not be denied. Further, Rogert had blood connections with most of the grand families of the Crusader states and many in Arnhand. Not to mention, he stood high in the affection of the Brotherhood of War, for title to Gherig and its dependencies would pass to the fighting priesthood on Rogert's death.

By right, of course, the way those people saw things. The Brotherhood had chosen the site for Gherig, had designed the fortress, and had provided the captive artisans to build it.

Nassim shook off his reflections. Rogert would face his hour in time. It was Written. He needed to attend this pup from the warlord's clan.

The boy said, "It doesn't look like there'll be a significant threat from the Unbeliever anytime soon. My granduncle's agents in Rhûn and the west say the Patriarchy is too fluid and confused to get up to any mischief here. And the Grail Empire is ruled by a woman."

"A good time, then, to push the interloper out of the Holy Lands."

"True. On its bald face. But God, in His Infinite Mercy, may offer us a different test of faith."

"The Hu'n-tai At." The Mountain had heard that the horse peoples were not satisfied with the destruction they had wrought in the Ghargarlicean Empire. Far outposts of the kaifate had suffered their attention of late. Several scouting forces had roamed through the northeastern dependencies. The mountains and deserts up that way had served to protect better than had the local armies. But now the Hu'n-tai At could strike directly west out of conquered Ghargarlicea.

"Tsistimed the Golden. He'll come. And he's never been stopped once he decides to add a city to his empire."

The Hu'n-tai At did not "add cities" to their empire. They looted them, then destroyed them, leaving only ash, ruins, and starvation.

The boy added, "The nomads are suffering from the changing climate. Snow and ice claim more pastureland every year."

Old news. "Which we've heard all my life. A Hu'n-tai At scouting force was caught inside the Holy Lands a few years ago. Near Esther's Wood." And crusaders, Lucidians, and Dreangereans alike had combined to exterminate them.

The boy inclined his head. "Someday it will be a reconnaissance in force. Tsistimed is considering sending one of his grandsons with ten thousand veterans."

Nassim was impressed with the quality of the warlord's intelligence. He said as much.

"There are Faithful among the caravaneers who travel the east road. They talk to Faithful among the Hu'n-tai At. And Tsistimed does little to conceal his ambitions. It matters not if his enemies know his plans. They'll be crushed anyway."

The Mountain knew that kind of arrogance well. His erstwhile friend Gordimer the Lion had it in plenty.

It would be interesting to see the Lion and the Golden butt heads. Though neither was in his prime, now.

The great terror of the east had become an armchair warrior, they said.

He was ancient.

No one living remembered a time when Tsistimed the Golden and the Hu'n-tai At were not a storm beyond the northeastern horizon. No one living recalled a time when captains and kings were not more interested in local squabbles than in preparing for the onslaught to come.

"How does this concern us?" Nassim asked.

"Tel Moussa overlooks the road armies use to march to and fro between Dreanger and the lands between the rivers. The road armies follow north and south crosses that road southwest of Gherig, at the edge of the Plain of Judgment, by the Well of Remembrance."

Nassim nodded. As a youngster he had known veterans of the Battle of the Four Armies, that the Arnhanders called the Battle of the Well of Remembrance. Hard feelings from that still poisoned relations between Lucidia and Dreanger. "An important site. The crusaders were defending it when they stumbled into the trap set by your illustrious relative."

"Any Hu'n-tai At army will follow the traditional route."

"Any army must go where the water is."

"Just so. And for reasons to do with water and grass, my illustrious relative, as you name him, has convinced the Kaif to remove from Mezket and Begshtar to Shamramdi. The plains round Shamramdi are well grassed. The wars of the future will demand many more horses than we have today. Mounts will become a particular problem if we can't buy them from peoples who have fallen under the dominion of Tsistimed."

"I see." Nassim had been in the presence of the Kaif of Qasr al-Zed several times. "What does the Kaif think of the changes?"

The kaifs of Qasr al-Zed had ruled from Mezket for four centuries. And religious leaders everywhere were known for resisting change.

"He was reluctant. But he does as he's told."

As did Karim Kaseem al-Bakr in al-Qarn, Nassim reflected. The Lion lurked behind every fatwa from the Kaif of al-Minphet. More troubling was the Mountain's suspicion that er-Rashal al-Dhulquarnen still dictated Gordimer's decisions, whether or not he had been outlawed.

"As should be in matters of war."

"We trust in God but remember that God helps most those who plan best."

Nassim laughed aloud, definitely beginning to like the boy. There was much of his granduncle in him. He wished Hagid had been such a boy. Though Hagid had been strong in his own way. He had crossed the White Sea alone to warn Else Tage of er-Rashal's evil perfidy. Which burst of courage had gained him nothing but death.

Which burst of courage had driven a mortal wedge between Gordimer the Lion and his friend since boyhood, Nassim Alizarin, the Mountain. The back draft from which burst of courage swept through the Sha-lug like a blistering desert wind. But which, in the end, changed nothing. Few Sha-lug would put aside what they had always known, however repugnant they found what had been done to Hagid.

The boy returned to his primary interest. "The Hu'n-tai At will come soon. Maybe this summer. We are at that stage where we must give God every assistance by preparing to execute His will."

Nassim nodded. "And?"

"This is a critical outpost. Signals from Tel Moussa can carry warnings down the road, or back to Shamramdi."

True. A lookout in the mountains to the northeast could relay signals to Shamramdi in just one transfer. But to the west . . .

The boy smiled. "To the west is Gherig. Only Gherig, of the crusaders. Gherig, of the foulest Arnhander of all, Rogert du Tancret."

"Yes."

"Yet Black Rogert is right there in the path of *anyone* headed into the Holy Lands."

"The adder cares not whose hand it bites."

The boy nodded. "The Hu'n-tai At will ride around Tel Moussa. They'll bypass Gherig. They'll want to seize the Wells of Ihrian first. If they're defeated, which hasn't happened yet, they'll try to destroy the Wells."

"Are they that wicked?" The Holy Lands were the heart of the world. During all the thousands of years that men had fought over the Wells of Ihrian none had been mad enough to try destroying them so they would not benefit anyone else. But the Hu'n-tai At had the reputation. They killed. They plundered. They destroyed. Those who were not of the horde could not comprehend. The horde was determined to destroy settled civilization.

"They're that wicked, General. That wicked, and more. They're enemies of everyone who isn't Hu'n-tai At."

"Taking that at face, what are we to do here?"

"Assuming you'll stand your ground?"

"We've taken this place under obligation. We'll fulfill that."

"That's what I was sent to find out. That being the case, I'm supposed to tap your thoughts about how best to absorb and crush a Hu'n-tai At invasion."

That puzzled Nassim. He said as much.

"Sha-lug think differently. You're one vast brotherhood, strongly disciplined, centrally ruled. My granduncle must, of necessity, gather men from a hundred tribes, captained by proud chieftains who'd rather fight old vendettas than unite against an outsider. He tried to create his own guard, like the Immortals of the Kings of Kings of Ghargarlicea, without notable success. The central problem being the expense of maintaining the force."

The Mountain allowed himself another nod, as much respect as assent. Indala al-Sul Halaladin had done well, teaching this one. Few Sha-lug had as solid a sense of history and their place in it.

"I'll do what I can," Nassim said. "It is written: We must defeat the enemies of God before we can settle enmities within the Realm of Peace." Which name he spoke with a cynical sneer. There was no peace inside the bounds spanned by God's Peace. Because men did not just demand submission to the Will of God, they demanded submission to themselves. Nor could they agree what the Will of God might be.

# 6. Navaya Medien: The Tired Man

The student waited till the Perfect completed his meditation. He carried a letter addressed to the old man. That letter had spent months in transit, tracing Brother Candle from retreat to retreat. In a community less honest and dutiful it would have gotten lost long since. With the Seekers After Light, though, delivery was assured, barring divine, diabolic, or villainous intercession.

It had survived hundreds of miles and dozens of hands crossing the Connec and the Verses Mountains to reach the remote Maysalean monastery at Sant Peyre de Mileage in Navaya Medien.

The old man rose. The youth's presence startled him. "Jean-Pierre?"

"A letter, Master. For you. I didn't want to disturb you."

"Good." The old man responded slowly. Not because of any infirmity but because the boy spoke the Medien dialect, a cousin of that used in the western Connec. It did funny things with consonants. You could confuse words that sounded familiar but then made no sense in context. "It certainly could wait those few minutes."

Brother Candle did not reach out for the letter. He wanted no contact with the world. He had been out there so long, till recently, that he had fallen from Perfection. Far from Perfection. Only now, after months, had he gotten solidly onto the Path again.

The letter was filthy. He did not recognize the hand that had written his name large upon the wrapping. He suspected that had been added in transit because the original had grown so ragged. He saw nothing to indicate a source.

"Aren't you going to open it, Master? It might be important."

It would be. Of course. Extremely. To the person who had written it. He considered the possibilities. Whatever this correspondent had to report, it would not be good.

"My fingers aren't working well today, Jean-Pierre." He pronounced the name in the Connecten manner. Here, it was Jean-Peyre. "Read it to me, if it please you."

The boy was thrilled. He could show off for the monastery's great celebrity. He could demonstrate how well his lessons had taken.

Jean-Peyre took the letter back, removed the wrapper with great care. He made sure nothing had been written on the back of the paper. There had been but it had nothing to do with the letter. Unless a baker somewhere wanted Brother Candle to know details about quantities of flour and eggs and the rising cost of fuel to fire his ovens.

The inner wrapper was, indeed, the worse for wear. But its sender had foreseen its travails. There were additional layers of protection—

one such discarded calculations by a military quartermaster—before Jean-Peyre found the jewel at the heart.

"All right, Master. This wrapper says, 'To the Most Illustrious Perfect Master, Charde ande Clairs, known as Brother Candle, greetings.'"

"That doesn't sound promising." Few people knew the name he had worn before he had set out along the Path.

"That part is signed 'Bernardin Amberchelle.' Is that a name I should know, Master?"

"No, Jean-Pierre. Bernardin Amberchelle is a cousin of Count Raymone Garete of Antieux. A ferocious devil. I never suspected him of being literate. His world is defined by sharpened steel."

"Maybe he had a scribe write for him."

"Most likely." Nobles did that. Those who were dim enough to trust their clerics completely. "That explains it. Go on."

What followed was a rambling history of Count Raymone and his spouse, Socia Rault, since Brother Candle had left them to find the Path again. There was much about the slaughter of foreigners and an alliance with the Church's Captain-General.

Odd. Count Raymone had spent years bloodily resisting the will of Brothe.

The letter eventually got to Amberchelle's point. Which was what the old man feared it would be.

Bernardin Amberchelle begged Brother Candle's return. Socia, for whom the old man had cared through the horrors of the Connecten Crusade, desperately needed his guidance and mellowing influence.

Socia's brothers had all been slain in the past year. None had left a legitimate son. But that was beside Amberchelle's point.

Socia had become a blood drinker. Her thirst for revenge had begun to influence her husband's decisions. The only hope for Count Raymone or his Countess was to spark their respect for the Perfect Master.

Jean-Peyre looked up. "That's all, Master. Except for a signature and a seal."

Brother Candle groaned. The sins of his past were overhauling him. If teaching was a sin.

How bad must it be if someone as vicious as Bernardin Amberchelle was distressed?

Jean-Peyre was frightened. He sensed what the letter failed to state explicitly. He saw a chance to impress the Master. "Would you like to dictate a reply, Master? I have a clear hand."

"Perhaps later, Jean-Pierre. Once I've digested the message. See me this same time tomorrow."

Jean-Peyre could not restrain a slight bow, though that was discouraged amongst Seekers, where there were supposed to be no classes. He gave the letter to the old man and got out.

Brother Candle carried the missive to his cell, where he was profligate in his use of candles as he read and reread.

THE OLD MAN WAS NOT AT HIS MEDITATIONS WHEN JEAN-PEYRE arrived to record his reply. He rushed to the old man's cell. Brother Candle was not there. Before long the monastery was in an uproar. The missing Maysalean hero was so old. The monastics feared the worst.

The mystery ended when a sleepy deacon—the antique who kept the cemetery—reported having seen Brother Candle headed down to the village that shared the monastery's name. He carried a staff, a small pack, a blanket, and a water bottle. He wore rags, so it was likely that he planned a long journey.

The younger students begged the abbot to let them bring the Perfect back. He was too frail for today's wild world. There were brigands everywhere. The Night was astir as it had not been since the early days of the Old Empire. And enemies were tormenting the End of Connec again.

The abbot sent the students back to their studies. The Perfect Master knew what he was doing. He was Perfect.

Already eight miles away, climbing the long slope out of the valley of heretics, Brother Candle increasingly suspected that he had no real idea what he was doing.

Once again he had allowed the world to intrude upon Perfection.

## 7. Mother City: Time of Changes

Rumor said the Five Families were furious. Rumor had their supporters in the Collegium gnashing their teeth. They were irked by Boniface's stubborn refusal to get out of their way.

They were further incensed by the swift arrival of the Captain-General, whose commitment to the vision of Hugo Mongoz was common knowledge. Before his advent gangs roved the streets, bullying the retinues of rustic Principatés, often coming to blows.

The City Regiment did little to control the violence. That said a great deal.

Someone had a firm grasp on Pinkus Ghort's leash. Piper Hecht suspected Principaté Bronte Doneto. Doneto, of the Benedocto family, wanted the disorders to continue.

The arrival of Patriarchal troops stilled the waters swiftly.

The Captain-General answered only to Boniface VII. Boniface had asked for peace in Brothe for months.

Peace there would be, now.

PIPER HECHT MEANT TO STEAL EVERY MOMENT HE COULD WITH ANNA Mozilla and the children. And received an outstanding gift his first visit. The children surrounded him immediately. Pella was proprietary, having just spent all that time in the field with his adoptive father. Lila was shy. He had not been around much since her arrival. She kept looking to Anna to see if she was doing the right thing.

Vali was the amazing one. First, she had grown dramatically. She promised to become an attractive woman. But the greater thrill was having her hug him, then say, "Welcome home, Father." Plain words. Straight out. Speaking in his presence for the first time ever.

Hecht hugged her back and looked over her at Anna. Anna smiled, nodded. Vali had regained her ability to trust. Vali had enlisted fully in their makeshift family.

Pella said, "We thought you'd never get here."

"You and me, both. Every time I started this way they found something else that had to be handled right now. Otherwise, Mother Church and the Episcopal world would go under before sundown."

Anna said, "You're here, now. Leave the world outside. Madouc sent word you were coming. The children made a special meal."

"Wonderful." He could smell the mutton cooking. "I wish I knew how to tell you all what an anchor you are to me when I'm out there." Which he meant absolutely, however hard temptation might nip.

"Tell us about the wedding!" Vali enthused. Lila nodded. The older girl would break no hearts. Nor get a chance to do if her background came out. "Pella wouldn't."

"Because they didn't let him inside." He settled at the table, began describing the Imperial wedding.

The girls rushed back and forth with food. Hecht talked only when both were there to hear. Pella remained seated, Anna judging him to be too old now to run with the girls.

Anna no longer had servants. She did not trust herself or the children not to give something away. And they all had secrets.

Vali wanted to know what King Jaime looked like. Was he as handsome as they said? Lila wanted to know what the Empress and her sister wore. Lila was almost appealing when she was excited.

"Jaime is as pretty as a man can be. And as spoiled. He makes enemies almost as fast as he can talk. He won't stop saying stupid and
offensive things. The Empress and the Princess Apparent were stunning.
Their gowns cost more than any of us can hope to see in our lifetimes.
Katrin wore gold. Helspeth wore silver. They were soaked in gems and
pearls. Katrin favored rubies, Helspeth emeralds. The ladies of the court
were nearly as gaudy. I do wish you could have seen them. But I'm still
thinking it was a miracle that I was invited."

"That is curious," Anna observed.

"They said it was because Boniface can't travel. After the crusade
in the Connec, I was better known than anyone else connected with the
Patriarch."

"You were invited when Pacificus Sublime was Patriarch, too. And
he wasn't handicapped."

"Are you sure? He went way before his time."

Anna shrugged. "It just seems strange."

"I won't argue with that."

"Pella says you had a private interview with the Empress."

"I did. She tried to hire me away from the Church. So maybe that
explains why I was there."

"What? Why?"

Lila asked, "You aren't going to do it, are you?" In a voice so soft
Hecht almost missed it.

"No. She wanted me to lead a crusade to the Holy Lands. I don't
want that. I'd have to deal with all those pompous idiots. . . . Never
mind. I have a job here. At the moment, to ensure an orderly transition.
But let's don't talk about that. You girls tell me what you did while I was
gone."

ANNA WAS MORE THAN USUALLY DEMANDING THAT NIGHT. SHE WAS
troubled. It took a while to get her to open up. "I'm afraid," she said.
"All the time, anymore. Not terrified. Just always anxious."

Hecht held her close. "Any special reason?"

"I worry about the girls. That evil thing is still out there. Principaté
Delari keeps saying they got it, but it keeps coming back. Plus, Principaté Doneto has people trying to find out things about us. If he digs
deep enough . . ."

"He'll get his digging fingers lopped off. The Ninth Unknown has
created entire lives for us based on what we've told people. Pinkus
Ghort's special spy, Bo Biogna, dug up my service records all the way
back to Grumbrag. And in Grumbrag he found a man who says he's my
brother."

Anna stiffened. "Really?"

"He told me so himself. I saw him in Alten Weinberg. He came by to see Joe." He did not have to explain. Anna knew about Bo Biogna, Just Plain Joe, Ghort, Hecht, and their shared adventures.

Hecht added, "You're protected. Never doubt it. Principaté Delari will watch out for you. Cloven Februaren, even more so. I wouldn't be surprised if they don't have a squadron of Night things guarding your house."

"Why would they do that?"

"Because they want things from me. And they're more likely to get them if they look out for you and the kids." Not to mention, they were basically decent men.

Anna started to ask something, decided against it. Probably about something she knew he would not discuss. "You may be right. Heris visits us at least twice a week. She always prowls around outside like she's looking for something."

"There you go." Heris? Muniero Delari's granddaughter. Hecht's sister. Who, like Hecht himself, had no talent for sorcery. But talent might not be necessary with Delari and Cloven Februaren behind her.

Hecht was not sure what his grandfather, and his grandfather's grandfather, were all about. He was no longer the naive Else Tage who had taken a picked band into the Idiam, to plunder the tombs of Andesqueluz. Piper Hecht, Captain-General of the Patriarchal armies, took no one at face value. Neither his enemies, nor the least of his friends and allies. Saving only Just Plain Joe.

Everyone had a secret agenda.

THE CHILDREN SMIRKED AND GIGGLED AT BREAKFAST. HECHT IGNORED them. He was in a good mood. It was a fine day. He had no obligations. He planned to stay right here and do nothing.

Anna was not so cheerful. Looking further ahead, she was anticipating Hecht's inescapable eventual departure.

Lila made breakfast. Hot bread. Honey. Some fiercely tart little green grapes harvested far too soon. And sausages that seemed to be half fennel. She explained, "This sausage is the kind my mother made. The Artecipean way."

"Very good. Spicier than I'm used to, though." And mostly pork. Of course. These westerners seemed determined to cleanse the earth of swine by devouring the beasts faster than they could breed.

"Vali. Now that you've learned to talk, why don't you tell me all about Vali Dumaine? What's the big mystery? What's the big secret?"

The girl's lips twitched and twisted. Habit died hard. But she had known this would come. "I made it up. All of it. I heard some Arnhander crusaders at the Ten Galleons talking to the Witchfinders. We didn't know they were Witchfinders then."

"Continue, please." She seemed to think that she had explained.

"The crusaders had been told to go to the Holy Lands by the Arnhander king. The old one. The one that died. Anne of Menand got him to make them go. They belonged to a count she wanted revenge on. His wife was named Vali Dumaine. I liked its sound. So I made up the story that Lila told you that night in Sonsa."

Hecht looked at Lila, who stared at the floor. "You believed Vali?"

"Not really. But I wanted to. So I pretended. I didn't want her to do what I had to."

Hecht guessed Lila to be fourteen. Even back then, she would have been an experienced prostitute, her virginity auctioned nightly by her mother.

"God will reward you, Lila. I'm sure of that. So. Vali. Who are you, really? The daughter of Bit's relative from Artecipea? She told one story that ran that way. Another made it sound like you had been sold to the house."

Lila said, "Mother never told the whole truth. She couldn't. Not even to herself."

Hecht thought a woman would have to be skilled at lying to herself to survive in such a hard trade.

"I don't remember any more, Father. I was too young when I came to the Ten Galleons."

Hecht did not pursue the matter. It was not crucial. Let the child be what she wanted. Anna would set her on the path of righteousness.

Hecht had another sausage. Vali watched, obviously anxious. He winked. She jumped. "Lila. How are you doing?"

The older girl was surprised to be asked. "Good. Considering. This is an interlude I'll enjoy as much as I can."

Hecht's turn to be surprised. Not because Lila was insecure but because she had assumed a fatalistic outlook so early. Her life must have been harsh indeed. "You have a place here. As long as you like. You're family, now." Which could end with one slight political crosswind.

Hecht said, "Everyone listen. Life is unpredictable. Mine maybe more than most. Other people don't have giant worms come out of the ground after them. If anything happens to me, ever, all of you get to Principaté Delari's house the minute you hear about it."

"Why?"

"Anna?"

"Why would we be safer there than here?"

"Because Muniero Delari is who he is." And because Cloven Februaren made his home there, as well. The Ninth Unknown might be the most powerful sorcerer in the west, if not the world. Though he hid it well.

"I understand that. What eludes me is the Principaté's motives for caring about me or the children."

"Ah, I can't really explain that."

"Can't? Or won't?"

"Fifty-fifty. I know some things. I suspect some things. And I know there's more that I don't know. One thing I do know is, the umbrella of the Principaté's protection casts its shade on this family. Accept it. Enjoy it, the way you will the weather we'll have today."

Pella rose. He had not spoken for some time. Not even minimal table courtesies. "We can't enjoy the weather. We aren't allowed. Some people aren't afraid of Principaté Delari." He left the kitchen. A moment later Hecht heard the front door open. Pella would be staring out into the fine morning and, no doubt, would be incensed because he could not go run the streets.

Hecht murmured, "All life is compromise and trade-off. He can't run the streets but he isn't starving." And he had learned to read. And he had begun to learn a trade.

"Trade-offs," Anna agreed.

Hecht wondered how she meant that.

"DAD," PELLA CALLED. "THERE'S SOLDIERS COMING. PATRIARCHAL Guards."

Anna said, "And there goes the one day we thought we had."

Pella made a startled squeal. Hecht rushed to the front, armed with a kitchen knife.

Heris stood six feet from Pella, who was framed in the doorway. The boy was pale. The woman had her hands spread to indicate that she was not dangerous.

"She came out of nowhere, Dad! I was watching the guards. When I turned around, there she was. And I was in the doorway the whole time."

Heris said, "I'm no good at this yet. I meant to hit that breezeway down the street, across the street. A memory of this room got in the way."

Anna and the girls crowded together behind Hecht, gaping. With Anna eyeing him suspiciously because it was obvious that he understood.

Hecht asked, "There's a reason you did this?"

"Grandfather wants you to know that those men are real Patriarchal Guards."

Hecht had not thought otherwise. Yet. But he would have done if
the soldiers were not men he recognized.

"Has something happened?"

"Boniface has taken a bad turn. He'll want to see you."

News Delari must have gotten from Cloven Februaren. "I see."

"Also, I'm supposed to tell you you're all to come to the town
house tonight." Heris looked him in the eye. "It's important, Piper."

"The old man's wish is my command."

"And the old, old man's."

The Patriarchal Guards arrived. They formed up outside. Their
corporal came up to the door with a letter case. Pella called, "Dad."

The letter case contained only a brief note in a shaky hand. It urged
the Captain-General to pay his final respects to Patriarch Boniface VII.

"It's serious this time, sir," the corporal said. "He doesn't have
long. Everyone says. He's determined to see you before he goes."

"I see." Though he did not, really. "Anna, maybe you should take
the kids to the town house now." That place was no fortress but it
would be safer than this if troubles followed Boniface's passing. He
would get his own men down here right away.

Hecht wanted to ask Heris if it was a problem, the family showing
up now. . . .

Vali said, "She just kind of turned sideways and wasn't there anymore." Her eyes were huge. "How did she do that?"

Anna, however, was suspicious. "What was all that? Never mind.
I understand the need. I just hope nobody decides to loot this place
while we're away."

"Don't worry. There are watchers. And I'll send some of my men.
Corporal, I'll make myself presentable and be right with you."

HUGO MONGOZ LOOKED ALL OF HIS EIGHT DECADES, AND MORE.
"Out!" he rasped at his attendants. "All of you! Begone!"

The Patriarch had made prior arrangement with his guards. They
began removing the physicians and hangers-on. They were not gentle
with any who resisted.

"You arrived in time," Boniface said.

"You're a stubborn man."

"I won't let my Church slide into the grasp of those who want only
to aggrandize and enrich themselves."

Hecht did not ask why Boniface wanted to be different.

"You'll observe my Will and Testament?"

"That's why I hurried down from Alten Weinberg. I know Rocklin Glas. He's a good man. He'll be good for Mother Church. But he has drawbacks."

"Which are?"

"You must know. He's a cripple. Unlikely to outlive you by long. And he enjoys the enmity of every Principaté interested in assuming the ermine in order to aggrandize himself and his family."

"True. Mustn't forget the Five Families. Have they put forward an alternative to Bellicose?"

"No, Your Holiness. They'd have to fight it out amongst themselves, first. None of them have the charm to get the others to elect them."

"Make them fulfill my promises."

"I will."

"Suppress the Society. Don't let that whore in Salpeno seduce anyone else the way she did Sublime."

"These things will be done. Are being done already."

"Excellent. Excellent. I can go on satisfied that good men are in charge. Come here." The old man's voice had been weakening. Hecht knelt beside the sickbed. Mongoz exuded a sour odor that could not be masked by rosewater. "Tell Cloven Februaren I'll haunt him if he doesn't take care of you." He laughed at Hecht's surprise. The laughter turned into a coughing spasm.

"Yes. I know he's out there. I know what he's doing. He was always a busybody. With a juvenile sense of humor. But good at heart."

"So it seems."

"And a useful ally to someone like yourself."

"Yes."

"Pray with me."

Hecht did so.


PRINCIPATÉ DELARI COULD NOT WAIT TO GET HECHT INTO HIS SILENT room to ask about his visit to Krois. "The Patriarch had you in?"

"He wanted assurances that his plans will be carried out after he goes. And he wanted me to relay a message to your grandfather."

"Uh?" Delari's right eyebrow shot up.

"Seemed to know all about him."

Delari scowled. "Makes me wonder who else knows more than he should."

Heris joined them. She brought two permanent members of the household staff, Turking and Felske, who were married. The cook, Mrs.

Creedon, seldom left her kitchen. Heris said, "Anna and the children are changing. Do you have anything that needs bringing in and putting away?"

"I have a couple of lifeguards outside. They could be made more comfortable." Madouc's men had caught up with him coming out of Krois.

Heris gestured. The couple hurried off. Hecht glanced at Delari. "She's grown more sure of herself."

"Blame it on the Ninth Unknown. And the Construct. Will you be able to spend time with us there, this time?"

"If I can. But I doubt it. I'm here to make the Collegium behave. Heris, what the hell were you doing, materializing in Anna's sitting room? I have trouble enough explaining things without that."

"I missed. I told you. The old man isn't the best teacher. He mostly lets you figure things out for yourself. He isn't around ninety percent of the time."

Hecht faced Delari. "You said Heris and I have no talent for sorcery."

"Inborn, less than some stones, certainly."

"There are a million magical stones in folklore and myth."

"My point. But in this case Cloven Februaren is just harnessing the Construct. The magic is in that. You could learn the trick if you spent a few months down there getting in tune."

"Anyone can learn?"

"Given time and the inclination."

"Including the people that work down there?"

"Within severely constrained limits. That's how the women get in and out without falling foul of the Palace guards. Enough, for now." Anna and the children were arriving.

Anna was stunning in something she had found in the apartment set aside for the family. Vali and Lila were not quite so remarkable but were well dressed, too.

Hecht suppressed a chuckle.

Pella had been outfitted like a young lord, complete with silken hose and slippers with bells on their upturned toes.

"Marvelous," a new voice opined. And there was the little old man in brown, Cloven Februaren. The Ninth Unknown. "Yet there's something wrong, here."

Felske stepped into the room to ask, "Your Grace, Cook would like to know when the meal should be served."

"When she has everything ready, I expect."

Almost simultaneously, Februaren said, "These kids don't fight. Brothers and sisters should be like cats and dogs. The girls should be scorching the boy about being dressed like that."

Hecht observed, "Some young people are more civilized than others. I saw Hugo Mongoz today. He had a message for you."

"I heard it. I took it up with him personally after you left. The only man we need to worry about is Bronte Doneto."

Hecht glanced at his family, all eager to eavesdrop. "Doneto? As a concern other than what we have already?" Doneto was digging. Doneto held Pinkus Ghort's leash.

"Friend Bronte has his eye on the Patriarchal throne."

Not unlikely, on reflection. "He seems a little young." Again, Hecht indicated the family with a glance.

Februaren said, "Might as well bring them in a little way, Piper. It's true, what they don't know they can't betray. But what they don't know can let them tell things they wouldn't if they knew what was going on."

That worried Hecht. Family worried Hecht. Family made you vulnerable. His enemies would not withhold their cruelties because he did not share his secrets with Anna and the children.

"I don't like it. But you're the expert. I'll defer to your judgment."

"Why, thank you, Piper." The old man chuckled.

"Teach Heris better aim with the turn sideways trick."

"I heard. She just needs practice. And more concentration. Well. Here they come. And it looks like Muno has laid on a leg of lamb."

Principaté Muniero Delari, within the confines of his home, disdained many Firaldian customs. Among his steps away from the customary was, he let children eat with adults. Though he was not so relaxed that he tolerated their chatter during the meal.

Turking and Felske presented the initial courses. Delari remarked, "I'm as uncomfortable as Piper, Grandfather. For different reasons. If you insist on baring souls, I suggest we save it for the quiet room, over coffee."

"Conceded. One of my failings," Februaren told Anna, flashing a big, boyish grin. "I've never been sufficiently paranoid. Gets me into trouble all the time."

"So has your childish sense of humor," Delari said.

"It's just not possible to resist sticking a pin in, here and there." The old man grinned again.

Hecht changed the subject. "What's the problem with the thing in the catacombs? First, I hear it's been hunted down and destroyed. Then I hear that it's on the move again."

Amazing. Principaté Delari actually reddened. "I don't want to sound defensive. Or whiny. But it keeps getting re-created by the needs of the populace."

Anna asked, "Why would anyone want a monster that creeps around, doing evil?"

"Nobody wants it consciously. But refugees have a powerful need to be scared of the dark. They're from rural areas where the Night was never a friend. The city is different. Night is almost as safe as daytime. Pinkus Ghort makes it so. So the monster fills their need to fear the dark. We destroy one, the belief and need seizes another minor Instrumentality and feeds it. Belief channeling power toward its object."

Hecht asked, "You mean . . . ?" He got no chance to ask.

Cloven Februaren interrupted, "The way to fight that would be to start some rumors that make the believers lose faith."

Then the earth shook violently.

"What in the hell?"

That was Turking, suddenly terrified.

"Earthquake," Anna suggested.

Piper Hecht had heard that sound toward the end of the siege of Arn Bedu. But that explosion, of a ton of firepowder under a tower, had not lasted so long, nor had shaken the mountain so vigorously.

"That's southwest of here," Delari said.

"Maybe the magazines at Krulik and Sneigon." The Krulik and Sneigon Special Manufactory produced the firepowder and firepowder weaponry employed by the Patriarchal armies. Its destruction would be a huge disaster.

"Not a good thing," Cloven Februaren said. "You'd have to start from scratch. Unless somebody had a few eggs hidden in other baskets."

The three men moved out into the weather. Illuminated smoke rose into the overcast. "That's not the Devedian quarter," Hecht said, which was where Krulik and Sneigon were located. "That's closer. And not big enough to be Krulik and Sneigon."

"I'll take a closer look." The Ninth Unknown turned sideways and disappeared.

Anna and the children saw him go.

"Hush!" Hecht snapped. His lifeguards were closing in. Madouc himself appeared. Hecht asked him, "Any idea what just happened?"

"Your guess would be as good as mine, sir. But I suspect that a firepowder magazine wandered too close to a spark."

Interesting. Everyone assumed the explosion was accidental. What if it was not?

A flash shone while Hecht wondered how someone outside the military supply chain might have gotten hold of that much firepowder.

The rumble did not arrive for several seconds. Hecht immediately guessed that to have been one standard twenty-four-pound firepowder keg.

Cloven Februaren said, "You have more resources than you're ready to admit, boy."

Hecht jumped. The old man had returned. Without startling Madouc. Though Madouc was always suspicious of the old man in brown.

"Uh . . ."

"My sentiments, too. The bang. It was at the Bruglioni citadel. They must have had their cellars filled with firepowder. Everything fell straight down, into the cellars, then on down into the catacombs."

The light was not good. But Hecht would have sworn the old man was distressed.

Februaren said, "No one in there could've survived. It's worse than the hippodrome collapse."

Principaté Delari stirred. Having been responsible for that. He had used a keg of firepowder to attack the monster of the catacombs in exactly the worst possible place.

"What shall we do?" Hecht asked.

Madouc suggested, "Staying out of the way would be appreciated by the city authorities."

Delari agreed. "Good point. They're irritated enough, having to put up with Patriarchal troops. Sit still. Let them work. They're competent. If they want help, let them ask."

Hecht nodded. Reluctantly. He had grown accustomed to doing what he thought was right, without consulting anyone.

Anna took hold of his left bicep. "Why don't we go inside? Life could get exciting out here."

The instant he was out of sight of the lifeguards Cloven Februaren turned sideways.

"How does he do that?" Anna asked.

All three children babbled, Vali loudest. "Maybe *what* is he doing would be more interesting."

"Dreaming the Construct," Heris said. "And that's all you need to know now. And you're not to repeat that to anyone."

Hecht glanced at Principaté Delari. He had seen no evidence that Delari could, or did, "dream the Construct." Why not? If it was so easy that Heris could learn?

Delari said, "We still have dinner to finish. Further discussion can wait."

\*    \*    \*

THE GATHERING IN THE QUIET ROOM DIFFERED ONLY IN THAT ANNA was present. Always before she had been asked to stay away. Heris arrived last, bringing coffee. Her great talent. Brewing the rare and incalculably expensive beverage.

Muniero Delari shut the door. Lined with stone, it was immensely heavy. He said, "Anna, you're a remarkable person. As near perfect for our Piper as a woman could be."

"But?"

"Yes. Right. I do have a but. I'd rather you weren't here. What you don't know can't hurt the rest of us. But my grandfather says your ignorance could be a more deadly threat to you and the children. And the four of you have become important to us."

This was new. Hecht sipped his coffee quietly, occasionally glancing at Cloven Februaren. The ancient had been away only minutes. He seemed content to sip coffee and look smug.

Anna looked to Hecht for support. He said, "I don't know where he's going. But you don't need to be scared."

"Let's jump right into the cold water," Delari said. "Heris, in addition to being the top coffee artist in Brothe, is Piper's older sister."

Hecht started. Then realized that almost everything Anna needed to know piggybacked on that one statement. Anna knew pretty much everything else about Heris.

Anna said nothing for more than a minute. Finally, "You're all related. Grade Drocker was Piper's father. Which explains a lot. But . . ." She stared at Hecht, eyes wide. "You fired the shot that caused his death."

"I didn't know who he was. I'm still not sure what difference it would've made. He meant to kill me. He'd tried before. He got two of my friends instead. He didn't know who I was, either. Till around the time I went into the City Regiment, when he did a turnaround and started sculpting my career."

"And his father took over when he went."

Muniero Delari made a slight bow toward Anna. "More coffee, Piper?"

"Always. You know I'm addicted."

Cloven Februaren leaned nearer Anna and, in a stage whisper, said, "Here comes the really grim part."

Delari scowled. "Can't you be serious about anything? Two hundred years old. The most powerful sorcerer in the world. And any one of Anna's children is more serious and responsible."

"Being serious now, Muno. Putting on my stern face and acting my age."

A flicker of smile cracked Delari's scowl. "He had a point, Anna. Obliquely. You've just been included in some extremely dangerous knowledge. The only people who know all that are in this room. Others—er-Rashal al-Dhulquarnen in Dreanger comes to mind—know Piper isn't what he pretends to be. None of them know the whole truth. They can't find it. The records have been destroyed."

Februaren said, "The bush he's beating around is, if anyone finds out it'll be because somebody in this room right now tells somebody. And that wouldn't be healthy."

"Hey!" Hecht said. "Don't you threaten . . ."

"Sun comes up in the east. Tides come in and go out. I'm stating facts. Cold facts."

Delari said, "Anna, you've been whining because you haven't been included in all of Piper's life." As Anna frowned at Heris. "Now that you're included, you can't walk away."

The Ninth Unknown said, "You came to Brothe from Sonsa because your former husband's secret employers insisted. Are you still reporting to al-Qarn?"

Hecht grew more nervous by the second. This could not end well.

"Not for almost two years. I'm sure those people wrote me off for being too close to Piper."

"That's good," Februaren said. "The point's been made. Piper, fill us in on your adventures."

The old man and Principaté Delari hardly interrupted, though Hecht did not have a great deal to report that Februaren had not already picked up during his random visits. Both seemed particularly interested in Asgrimmur Grimmsson.

"What did you do with him?" Delari asked. "I'd certainly like to talk to him."

"Me, too," Februaren said. "A man who became an Instrumentality, then a man again. Interesting stuff."

"He's hidden in a room like this down under the Castella. Hopefully not attracting attention. I didn't know where else to put him. He wants us to help him free the Old Gods he trapped after he turned into a monster. The unintended consequence of that was the liberation of Kharoulke the Windwalker. As the world is becoming a paradise for his sort."

"More coffee, Anna?" Heris asked.

"No. I've had enough. Of everything. I need some time alone." Her world had become far more vast and dark in just a few minutes.

\*       \*       \*

AS HE PREPARED FOR BED, HECHT OVERHEARD VALI ASK ANNA, "SO did they finally tell you what's going on?"

"Yes. And now I wish I'd minded my own business."

"Devedians say, 'Have no congress with sorcerers.' "

"Which makes them smarter than most of us think."

THE CAPTAIN-GENERAL VISITED THE FALLEN BRUGLIONI CITADEL. Four lifeguards and Kait Rhuk's fire team accompanied him.

The Bruglioni stronghold had covered several crowded acres. Surrounded by a curtain wall, it had included gardens and outbuildings as well as the fortress that served the family as home and headquarters.

That was all rubble in a hole, now.

Madouc whispered, "Sir, here comes Colonel Ghort, his own self."

People made mock of Pinkus Ghort's rustic speech—which came and went according to a formula best know to Ghort his own self—and of his dress. But Hecht had heard no one but Ghort himself denigrate Pinkus Ghort's intelligence.

Ghort said, "You musta hauled some major ass, getting down here from Alten Weinberg so fast, Pipe."

"Promises to keep. What happened here?"

"Firepowder accident. Believe it or not, people survived that. Most of the servants. Gervase Saluda and Paludan Bruglioni, both. Though they're both bad hurt. Paludan might not make it. Saluda was just leaving when it happened. Lintel came down and crushed his legs. He'll probably never walk again. The rest of the family are still down there. Along with a fortune in rare wines. I'm told." Ghort sounded more distressed about the wine than the trapped Bruglioni.

"They had a fine cellar when I worked here. You sure it was an accident?"

"It was pure stupidity. We have a witness who heard an idiot Bruglioni nephew brag that he was going to steal some firepowder and make his own fireworks. He was carrying an open lamp instead of a closed lantern."

Hecht stared at the rubble. Dust still swirled in the hole. He tried exercising his cynical side. "Who'd profit if it wasn't an accident?"

"Same folks as will anyway. Anybody in the Five Families who ain't named Bruglioni. This should about do the family in."

Kait Rhuk said, "Permission to interject, Captain-General?"

"Go ahead."

"Colonel. Why would the Bruglioni have had enough firepowder to do this? Not to mention that—I think—legally, firepowder is sup-posed to be made exclusively for us. The Patriarch's men."

"Good point," Hecht said.

Pinkus Ghort did not quite look Hecht in the eye. "The Collegium say they're part of the Patriarchal armed forces, Pipe. Looking at it real-istically, firepowder manufacturers are producing more than you're buying. Your conquest of Artecipea took care of the saltpeter shortage. They're turning a tidy profit on the extra production." And, perhaps, certain individuals charged with enforcing the rules were getting a share.

Hecht glared toward the Devedian quarter, yet was more irked with himself than those people. This he should have foreseen.

There was nothing more likely to facilitate the redistribution of wealth than a new means of killing people. Though handling and em-ploying firepowder effectively required skill.

Skilled firepowder handler Kait Rhuk asked, "How long before we see firepowder weaponry in the hands of our enemies?"

"Let me guess," Hecht said. Loosing his sardonic side. "As long as it takes someone to work out a good formula for the stuff?"

Rhuk snorted. "If that was true we'd be up to our asses in bad guys with firepowder toys. The formula ain't no secret. Every apothecary and chemist in Brothe knows it. What they don't know is how to put them together. If it was me, I'd have somebody I really trusted permanently in-stalled at Krulik and Sneigon. I'd babysit them day and night. I'd use somebody who'd cut a throat anytime the mood hit him. Somebody who ain't weasel enough to get rich on the bribes he was gonna be offered."

The Captain-General did not want to operate that way. But he saw the point. Men who wanted a fast profit, right now, would happily sell the most wonderfully murderous tools to the worst enemies of their own state or people, somehow oblivious to the fact that those weapons might bite back.

The Rhûn had a ferocious secret weapon. They called it nephron. It was a thick, heavy liquid that, once fired, could not be extinguished. It had to burn itself out. Rhûnish merchants would not sell the formula but willingly sold nephron itself, even to Sha-lug who used it against the Eastern Empire's soldiers.

Human minds did not seem large enough to encompass an obliga-tion to eschew profit if making it required providing a means to de-stroy one's neighbor.

Pinkus Ghort said, "Hey, Pipe. You lost in there?"

"What?"

"You went away someplace inside your head. I was afraid you got lost."

"It isn't that vast a landscape, Pinkus. Pinkus, knowing you, you've found a source for the best wine in town. *And* you've found some way to get in touch with what's going on in the underworld."

Ghort gestured with both hands, as though playing with a balance scale—or pair of breasts. "Thus. So. I try. But, really, all I need to do is put on a show that'll keep the senate happy."

"Bronte Doneto is who you need to keep happy. Him and the old men of the Church. Not the old men of the city."

Ghort shrugged. "Pretty much the same crew."

"They're wearing you down. Aren't they?"

Ghort shrugged again. "How can you tell?"

"You don't even bother to talk bad about them."

"A man gets addicted to eating regular."

Hecht faked a laugh. "What are you going to do about this?" He gestured at the hole where the Bruglioni citadel had stood.

"I reckon I could get a shovel and start filling it in. But I don't suppose that's what you mean."

"No." Smiling. Attitude was a big part of what made Pinkus Ghort Pinkus Ghort.

"I'll get some of the old farts from the Collegium to come exercise their talents. Give them a chance to show off. Them antiques have egos like you wouldn't believe. When they figure out it was really an accident, then I'll grab my shovel. It they decide somebody did it, I'll hunt the asshole down and drag him in begging me not to turn him over to the Bruglioni."

"Good for you, Pinkus. You want to come by Principaté Delari's town house some evening, I brought you half a dozen bottles of white wine from Alten Weinberg."

"Hey. That was thoughtful."

"It was, wasn't it? I'm warning you, though. It's different stuff."

"Good. I hear you had an interview with the Empress her own self."

"I did. She offered me a job."

"Shit. That's some shit. I guess you said no."

"I said no. I'm not ready to break in a new set of crazy old men who are out to sabotage me."

"I smell rank cynicism, Pipe. You promised you'd work on that."

"I do. Every day, right after my prayers."

"That don't exactly boost my confidence. Did I ever catch you praying? I don't remember if I did."

"You'd have to be sneaky and fast. I try to keep it between me and God."

Ghort chuckled. "I don't even bother anymore. My god is on a five-century bender and don't have time for mortal trivia."

Hecht understood Ghort's attitude but could not, himself, thumb his nose at the Deity. Whichever One He might be. He asked, "What's your boss up to?"

"What do you mean?"

"Where'll he stand when Boniface goes? I'm hoping he doesn't put you and me in a difficult position."

"You mean to enforce the Viscesment Agreement."

"I swore an oath."

"And the City Regiment, in our myriad, wondrous forms, will be blessed with breaking up the riots."

"They get to be too much for you, Krois or the Castella can whoop and six thousand veteran Patriarchals will be here overnight. Fifteen thousand in a week. There's only going to be one next Patriarch."

"Easy, Pipe. No need to get all intense."

"Just want to make my point."

"Consider it made. But you won't make yourself popular."

"I have to do the right thing."

"I give up. It won't matter a hundred years from now, anyway."

There was room to debate that. Hecht saw no point. It was hard enough to get Ghort to worry about next week.

Ghort said, "Tell me about your god-killing adventures in the Connec. And Alten Weinberg. What was that like?"

"The interview with the Empress was as interesting as it got. The wedding was just long, boring, and hot. And way overdone."

"No shit? Is Katrin still as good-looking as she was when we saw her in Plemenza?"

"Time hasn't been kind. The Grail Throne is a cruel taskmaster."

"She made it hard on herself, changing sides in the Imperial squabble with the Church."

"Definitely part of it. Jaime won't help, either."

"Not the big, handsome hero, eh?"

"Not so big. Definitely handsome, in a southern kind of way. And he did show good at Los Naves de los Fantas. They say. But he doesn't have a much finer character than our onetime friend, Bishop Serifs."

"Not good."

"And Katrin won't see it."

Ghort stared down into the hole. "You see something moving there, Pipe?"

"Where?"

Ghort pointed.

Squinting, Hecht could just make out . . . "Rhuk! Front!"

Kait Rhuk shoved gawkers aside, rolled his falcon to the lip of the sinkhole. Lifeguards closed in. Hecht snarled, "You men! Stand back! Rhuk. Your eyes are better than mine or Colonel Ghort's. Something is moving down there where that furniture is all tangled up. Get a sight on it."

"That looks like somebody trying to wave," Rhuk said.

Ghort said, "I'll send somebody down."

"Have them do it from the sides, please," Rhuk said. "They don't want to get in my line of fire."

Ghort's men were halfway down, descending from both sides. The wreckage began to shift.

Hecht said, "Brilliant, putting your men on safety ropes."

Ghort's response vanished in the roar of the falcon.

As the ringing in his ears receded, Hecht heard Rhuk shout, "Am I good, or what? Took it out first go!"

The Captain-General held his tongue. Rhuk could be given hell later. Then he smelled something, faint but familiar. That odor had been present elsewhere after a falcon had challenged some Instrumentality of the Night.

Then the smell was gone. Rhuk's team, using the City Regiment's ropes, descended into the pit, armed with the jars they used to harvest the leavings of the things they murdered.

After a while, Pinkus Ghort said, "Your guys are really good at what they do, Pipe."

"Yes. Rhuk scares me sometimes." He scratched his left wrist.

Rhuk scared himself, this time. While digging a smoldering hot egg out of the rubble he knocked a hole in a fragile wall, opening the Bruglioni family crypt. Where several desperate human beings had been trapped since the explosion. They climbed all over Rhuk, running to the light.

It was about then that Hecht caught his first glimpse of the old man in brown moving amongst the onlookers. He needed to talk to the Ninth Unknown. His amulet had not warned him that danger was so close.

OVER A LATE MEAL FEBRUAREN REMARKED, "IT WASN'T A FULL-fledged baron of the Night. But near enough. Your problem with the killing thing should ease up, now, Muno. This thing had been spinning off bits of itself to become foci for that monster parade."

Hecht did not understand. Principaté Delari did. That was good enough. Hecht said, "This morning may have exposed a problem. My amulet provided no warning."

Februaren frowned. "None?"

"Nothing but a persistent itch. Which started after Rhuk shot it."

"They're adapting. I'll have to adjust. Maybe the ascendant can help."

Hecht asked, "How're you doing with my pet Instrumentality?"

"The soultaken?"

"Only one I have. I don't even know where you've moved him." The old man had insisted that the soultaken be taken out of the Castella, away from the nosy Brotherhood. Especially the Special Office and its Witchfinders in particular.

"He's bricked up inside a tower. No doors. No windows. And nowhere you need know about. He's teaching me about himself. And working on a plan to . . . But you don't need to know that, either."

"Why not?"

"You've shown a terrible inability to keep your mouth shut lately."

Everyone fell silent. The whole table stared at Hecht.

He awaited an explanation.

"And you don't even know it. Who swore an oath not to reveal what he discussed with the Empress inside her quiet room? Who has, since, told almost everyone who will listen?"

"There was a crack?"

"There are a dozen cracks. In the ceiling. In the floor. The place is old. It's settled. They don't keep it up. Why break your word?"

"I'm sorry. I never thought about it. It wasn't that big a thing."

"For you. For you, it's a feel-good. Look at me! The Grail Empress herself wants me to be her Captain-General. But for her it could be crippling. She has enemies everywhere. Luckily, for both of you, I made the people you told forget. I hope. I don't know what they might have written down."

Hecht felt like a small boy caught red-handed in a shameful act. He *had* promised. And should have had the sense to see the implications for Katrin. In fact, he had. But just had not thought about it.

"Maybe I'm not equipped to operate in so rare a political atmosphere."

"You'll be fine," Februaren said. "If you focus on your work. And don't get distracted by thoughts you shouldn't be thinking."

Time to change the subject. "Have you seen my brother yet?"

That got looks, all round.

"No. I'm working dawn to dusk trying to put enough more hours into the day so I have time to do the things I have to do along with everything everyone wants me to do."

Heris demanded, "What brother are we talking about?"

Hecht said, "A soldier in Grumbrag is masquerading as Piper Hecht's brother Tindeman. Bo Biogna found him. He convinced Bo. My guess is, they didn't have a lot of language in common."

Pella said, "I thought all your family was dead, Dad."

"So did I. I still think so."

"Then who . . . ?"

"An imposter."

"But . . ."

"No point speculating till we talk to him." He could think of several explanations, all of evil intent.

The Ninth Unknown said, "I'll find him. After I deal with more pressing matters here. The transition to Bellicose has to go smoothly. And I want all of us to come out the other side healthy. Piper in particular."

Heris said, "I could go."

Februaren and Delari scowled ferociously. Both shook their heads.

Heris grumbled, "You said I'm ready to manipulate the Construct."

"Not that ready," Februaren said. "Not to go somewhere you've never been. Not somewhere that far away."

Principaté Delari, not unkindly, asked, "What language do they speak in Grumbrag?"

Heris seemed even more deflated. "Probably several. Including Church Brothen."

"Could be. If you were going to interview a bishop, or someone educated, you'd manage."

Februaren said, "There's plenty you can do here, Heris. But you have a long way to go, romancing the Construct, before you can go places you haven't already been. Muno can't do it."

Delari said, "Muno can't do much of anything with the Construct. There's something lacking in the man."

"If you tell the Construct you can't connect with it, Muno, it takes you at your word."

"Yes, Grandfather."

Both old men checked their audience. This ancient dispute probably antedated the births of everyone in the room.

It did not need airing now. It should not have taken place in front of the children. Hecht thumped the table.

Februaren said, "You kids don't repeat anything you hear in this house. Understand?"

He got wide-eyed nods from Pella, Lila, and Vali, none of whom had seen the ancient this intense before.

"Lives could depend on your silence." He told Hecht, "Bragging is how criminals get caught and men with deep secrets deliver themselves to their enemies. It's bonehead human nature. We all want to look special. Knowing something is one of the best ways."

Februaren glared at the children some more. "It would be your own lives, most likely. If somebody wicked decided you knew something he could use against Muno or Piper."

Hecht suggested, "That being the case, why not take steps?" He caressed his left wrist.

"There may be hope for you yet, boy. Only, that means it'll be even longer before I go take a look at your brother."

Anna was subdued in her lovemaking that night. She understood that she had slipped deep into the struggle with the Night. And those she cared for had been drawn in as deeply, or deeper.

"Piper, the children don't deserve this. They've already suffered too much."

"I know." He did not remind her that all three had, already, enjoyed more good fortune than did the run of orphans.

THE CAPTAIN-GENERAL SUMMONED KRULIK AND SNEIGON TO WHAT Kait Rhuk bemusedly called a "Come to the Well of Atonement" meeting. It did not last long. Neither Krulik nor Sneigon had leave to speak. Rhuk, backed by Brothers from the Castella, confiscated their sales records.

The excitement was meant to prod the Deves into talking to one another. A man who turned sideways could eavesdrop and discover what secret sales contracts had been accepted off the books

Hecht would not confiscate firepowder or weaponry sold on the sly. He lacked authority. But it might be useful to know where it had gone.

The vast majority of what Krulik and Sneigon had sold behind the curtain had gone into the Grail Empire, to people who did not hold their Empress in high regard.

Katrin was fortunate that her malcontents disdained one another too much to join forces. Internecine warfare was an ancient sport amongst the Imperial nobility.

Johannes Blackboots had kept the peace. Lothar had not lasted long enough to make mistakes. Katrin's peace was holding because every villain knew Ferris Renfrow was watching from the shadows.

Would adding falcons make much difference?

Unlikely. Even the best weapons were of little use against anything but the Night. Their battlefield value was psychological rather than practical. They made loud noises and a lot of smoke.

\*     \*     \*

WHEN THE END CAME FOR BONIFACE VII, DESPITE THE NINTH AND Eleventh Unknowns, there was no dislocation. Bellicose was in the chamber, praying over Hugo Mongoz. As were physicians and key Principatés. History demanded witnesses.

Also present were Hugo Mongoz's children, fathered before the old man began to prefer boys to women.

Two score more people waited outside the dying room, among them the Captain-General of Patriarchal forces. And Boniface's toy, Armand. Who seemed wary of the Captain-General. And very worried.

Hecht waited with Addam Hauf, one of the Masters of the Brotherhood. Hauf had come over from Runch, on Staklirhod. He was a tall man in his early fifties, all muscle and sun-baked leather. Neither man realized they had crossed swords in the Holy Lands, long ago. Hauf observed, "The Princess fears for his sweets and pretties."

"Don't waste pity on him. He's been underfoot forever. He always finds another keeper."

Hauf grunted an interrogative. So Hecht explained. Without revealing what Armand really was.

Hauf asked, "He seems afraid of you."

"I'm close to Principaté Delari. The lover he abandoned so he could catch himself a Patriarch."

"Hard feelings?"

"Not on my man's part. He was glad to get shot of the boy. It was a strain keeping up." And keeping Armand away from secrets. For Principaté Delari had known that Armand spied for Ferris Renfrow.

"You know this man from Viscesment." A statement that asked a question.

"I was impressed. He's another like Boniface. He talked fire and brimstone early. He went after the Society with amazing ferocity. He reined it in when Boniface showed that he'd be reasonable. His liability is the same as Boniface's. Bad health. He won't last long. And I see no reasonable successor. There'll be the traditional dogfight amongst a lot of bad choices."

The remark about suppressing the Society sparked a nod from Hauf. There was no love between the Society for the Suppression of Sacrilege and Heresy and the Brotherhood of War. The Brotherhood did not like the Society's obsessive focus on heresy in the Connec. That diverted resources from the fight for the Holy Lands. That was the struggle that needed concluding, favorably, before all others.

Principaté Flouroceno Cologni stepped out of Boniface's dying chamber. Four Principatés from the Five Families waited attendance on the dying Patriarch. Gervase Saluda was not recovered enough to take his place on behalf of the Bruglioni. Principaté Cologni said, "His Holiness has passed over."

Servants and lesser priests scurried out. The forms of mourning had to be observed. They would commence immediately.

Among those who hurried out Piper Hecht particularly marked Fellau Humiea, an odd creature recently nominated to become Archbishop of Salpeno by King Regard. Meaning Anne of Menand. As always with the leading men of Arnhand's capital, Humiea stood accused of having lain with the King's mother.

"Trouble?" Hauf asked, noting the Captain-General's stare.

"Possibly. I don't know what they're thinking in Salpeno."

"I wouldn't be disappointed if a boulder fell from the sky and smashed Anne of Menand. The only help we've gotten from Arnhand lately is her son Anselin and six knights."

"She sees no personal advantage from freeing the Holy Lands. Offer to make her Empress of the combined Crusader states."

Hauf chuckled. "That might work. Though she'd probably strip the Holy Lands of treasure and sacred artifacts and abandon them to the Unbeliever."

Hecht nodded. An exaggeration. But where Anne of Menand was concerned, every canard contained an element of truth. "My vigil is complete. I should get back to the Castella, see if there's news from the Connec."

"Difficult, managing a campaign from hundreds of miles."

"Difficult, indeed. I had almost unnatural luck putting together a competent, trustworthy staff and officer corps. They don't miss me much when I'm gone."

"An interesting phenomenon. Unseen outside the warrior orders, at least since the Old Empire."

The Captain-General grew uncomfortable. Master Hauf might be implying something. Might even be accusing. "Sir?"

"Just reflecting on the unique thing you've created these past few years. An army that doesn't disperse during the winter, planting, or harvest. An army not structured around leaders who command by right of birth."

Hecht interrupted, "My little heresy. So long as my employer doesn't object, I'll choose my officers based on talent. Too, no one of exalted birth ever asks to become one of the Patriarch's men."

"Men of noble birth come to us. Or raise forces of their own to take into the Holy Lands. Do you hear much about our comrade order, the Grail Knights?"

"Last news I had from up there was that one of my brothers might still be alive. Which I'm not prepared to believe. I left in the worst season. The pagans had found a war leader acceptable to most of the tribes."

He stopped, shivered as though retreating from painful memories.

Master Hauf nodded. "Some new horror is afoot up there. News came down the amber route, through the Eastern Empire, about an attack on a Grail Order stronghold called Stranglhorm. The Grail Knights were victorious. But the behavior of their attackers, and the sorcery supporting them, is unsettling."

Hecht was moving now, headed for the Castella, slowly. Addam Hauf paced him. The Master was headed the same way. "We faced strangeness and sorcery in Calzir and Artecipea, both. We're still cleaning up a mess in the Connec."

"I'm guessing this is more of the same."

"Kharoulke the Windwalker."

Master Hauf looked startled.

"There's been talk. The Principatés are interested. So were people in Alten Weinberg when I was there. So. Work is being done. Of what value time will tell."

"Include the Brotherhood when you learn something interesting. If you can."

"Of course. Though you seem better informed than I. I hadn't heard about an attack on Guretha. How bad was it?"

"The pagans were particularly destructive."

"I've never visited Guretha. It was supposed to be a great city. By the standards of that part of the world."

"I suppose the ice will have it before long, anyway."

PIPER HECHT CLOSETED HIMSELF WITH HIS CRONIES INSIDE ONE OF the Castella's quiet rooms. Force of habit. He did not expect to share any secrets but you never knew what someone would say to excite an eavesdropper.

"I want to know more about Master Hauf. He doesn't have a reputation that precedes him."

Buhle Smolens said, "Bechter says he was new to the commandery at the Castella Anjela dolla Picolena. He came to Runch out of the Holy Lands with a solid reputation as a battlefield leader. His family has connections with the lords of several Crusader states but he's no politician himself. His claim to fame is that Indala al-Sul Halaladin counts him a friend."

"How could that be?"

"They've had chances to do malicious harm but never dishonored themselves. Bechter thinks Hauf was promoted because he's too honest and honorable. There were men who wanted to get him out of the Holy Lands. Where a lack of scruples, morality, and honor has begun making the Brotherhood look bad. Bechter thinks Hauf is here looking for a few good Brothers to help scour out the corruption."

"Interesting. Strange, but interesting. Slip him what we know about the Witchfinders in Sonsa. Tell me more about Hauf and Indala."

Colonel Smolens launched a convoluted tale of treachery and chivalry centered on one Rogert du Tancret, the violation of a holy truce, the kidnapping of Indala's sister, and the Brotherhood's intercession. In the person of Addam Hauf. Whose effort forestalled a war that might have pulled in Pramans from across all three kaifates. As it was, several mountain counties in the northern Holy Lands passed from Chaldarean to Praman control.

Rogert du Tancret remained unabashed. He continued to provoke the Pramans.

Smolens said, "Rogert fears no one because his fortress, Gherig, is unassailable."

Once, when he was Else Tage, Hecht had seen Gherig. And even from many miles away that fortress had been grimly intimidating.

Some—most—strongholds were just piles of rock, however big they became. Gherig, though, had a personality. It lay crouched on its stony mountaintop like the home of earthly evil. It radiated the sense that something terrible could happen at any moment.

No. Evil was not right. Gherig was more like the Night. Neither good nor evil, except as one chose to behold it. Gherig simply was powerful and predatory. And, evidently, was these days in the hands of a master suited to it.

"Not important to us," Hecht said. "We have troubles of our own. In the Connec."

"Letter from Sedlakova came this morning. They're having real trouble cornering Rook. Who gets a little stronger and smarter each time they take out some other revenant."

"How did they get him the first time? Are there records?"

"You mean the Old Brothens?"

"Yes. Find out how they pinned him long enough to bind him."

"The ancients exploited the nature of the god they meant to confine."

"Research it. I'm going home. Which, this once, I'm not looking forward to. Anna and I are going to have a row about Pella going with us when we go out again."

There was little reason to remain in Brothe. Bellicose's ascension was not being disputed. The loud grumbling was all about his not yet having selected a more clement reign name. Hecht only needed the new Patriarch's confirmation before he returned to the Connec.

"I'll be glad to get out of here. What're you going to do with the Braunsknecht?"

"Drear?"

"Him."

"Take him back to Viscesment and put him in charge of the Imperial pullout."

"And me?"

"Drag you back and make you work. You've had your holiday."

Smolens snorted derisively.

Hecht said, "We don't need to be here. Good guys and bad, they're doing what they're told."

"Only because they've seen the new guy and he looks like death on a kabob skewer. They figure he won't last a year."

Hecht had seen Bellicose, briefly, and agreed. But the Ninth Unknown thought the man might not be beyond help. "He might surprise them."

"I hope he does. I liked working with him in Viscesment." Smolens shifted footing dramatically. "We really do need to maintain a presence here. A lobby with the Collegium and an inspectorate to ride herd on Krulik and Sneigon. Those bastards will sell weapons to anybody with money."

"I'll leave Rhuk. Like Prosek, he keeps coming up with marvelous ideas. Being here, he'll have the chance to try them right away. I'll get him the tools he'll need to handle those people if they don't behave."

Smolens put his feet up. "I think, was I Krulik or Sneigon, I'd have seen this coming. I'd be setting up a manufactory somewhere secret. Maybe several."

"Worth thinking about." Hecht decided to mention it to Cloven Februaren. The old man would find the potential for mischief invigorating.

THE RELAXED STATE OF THE MOTHER CITY WAS EVIDENCED BY THE size of Hecht's escort. Just four lifeguards accompanied him to Anna Mozilla's house. And no one in the streets paid attention.

Which made Madouc especially nervous. Naturally.

It had been some time since someone had tried to get the Captain-General.

*    *    *

HECHT SURPRISED ANNA AND BROKE PELLA'S HEART BY NOT ARGUING
when the subject of the boy going back to the field came up. He told
Pella, "I want you to study with the Gray Friars at Holy Founders. To
learn the things you need know to do what Titus does."

Anna was startled. "Is there something wrong with Titus? Noë
hasn't said anything."

"There's nothing wrong with Titus that a visit home wouldn't
cure. I'm thinking about Pella, not the army." Said with a meaningful
look.

The children did not know the extent of the connection with Muniero Delari and Cloven Februaren. Those were just nice but weird old
men who had them round to visit. Who gave them small but expensive
presents.

"Which reminds me. Heris was here today. The Principaté wants us
to come for a late dinner. A coach will call."

"An invitation with muscle behind it."

"She said the old man wants a last visit before you leave."

"Really?" His plans remained vague. He wanted to see more of
Pinkus Ghort. He wanted to sit down with the man who had been a
monster. He wanted to get a real feel for the political tides in the Collegium and city.

"Have you decided when you'll go?" Anna asked.

"No. I had a message from Sedlakova today. They're having trouble.
The squatters from Grolsach keep getting underfoot. Count Raymone
can't seem to sort them out."

"NOT TO MENTION PROBLEMS WITH ARNHANDER INCURSIONS," PRIN-
cipaté Delari said when Count Raymone Garete came up during dinner. "Small bands, so far. A few straw knights and poorly equipped foot
soldiers following some righteously indignant veteran of the Society
adopted by Anne of Menand when Boniface VII dissolved the order."

"There'll be trouble from that direction?"

"Grandfather thinks so. Maybe as soon as news of the Interregnum reaches Salpeno."

Legally, Bellicose had to wait out twenty-six statutory days of
mourning before he became fully infallible.

Hecht said, "I got messages off as soon as Boniface went. Arnhand
won't catch anyone by surprise. Where is your grandfather?"

"He'll be here later. He finally went to Grumbrag. From there he
was going on to someplace called Guretha."

"A second opinion would be useful."

"Second?"

Turking and Felske came and went with the courses. Mrs. Creedon appeared in the doorway twice, possibly hoping for a compliment. Hecht paid no attention. He barely noted that everyone but the old man was keeping quiet.

Heris finished eating and went to the kitchen.

Cloven Februaren ambled in and settled at Heris's place, pounded the table with the pommel of his knife. Delari said, "Gracious of you to make yourself presentable before you joined us, Grandfather."

Februaren was filthy. And stank. The children, though they enjoyed the old man most of the time, edged away.

"Too hungry. Hungry work I've been doing. Couldn't find your brother, Piper. I think somebody was working you. The rest we'll talk about in the quiet room. Food!"

Everyone exchanged glances.

"What?"

Heris returned with the coffee service. Turking and Felske came armed with sweets. Mrs. Creedon beamed from the kitchen doorway. Heris poured coffee for Hecht first. "Happy fortieth," she told him. Then everyone congratulated him on having reached forty.

He could say nothing. He dared say nothing. He had had no notion of when his birthday was, nor even, for sure, his exact age. He supposed Heris must have worked it out. He could not ask.

"I don't know what to say. I've never had a birthday, or a name day." Which was true despite his dissembling.

Heris said, "I wanted to invite some of your friends, too. Colonel Ghort and that man with the animals. And some others. But Grandfather gets nervous about having strangers in the house."

Principaté Delari said, "The times are trying. Outrageous paranoia is the only rational response."

Piper Hecht watched his children enjoy their first encounter with coffee. Two out of three rolled up their lips. Vali, though, nodded. None of them had a problem attacking the sweets.

Before he took his cup up to the quiet room Hecht had a few quiet words for Mrs. Creedon.

"Visited a city called Guretha," Cloven Februaren said. "Lots of dead people there. Mostly not Gurethan. The city will have to be abandoned, anyway. Unless the climate turns. It can barely support itself. Importing grain. But the Shallow Sea has fallen so far that soon it'll be impossible for the grain ships to get there."

Hecht told what he had heard of Guretha from Addam Hauf.

"Accurate enough. They have better communications through the Eastern Empire."

"Or sorcerers paying closer attention," Delari opined.

"That, too. From Guretha I went to several other places on the edge of the ice. It's the same everywhere. Desperate savages and something not human. The monster is the one from Ferris Renfrow's drawing. At Guretha the Grail Knights lured it into the castle gateway and killed it with a blast of godshot. The falcons were Krulik and Sneigon products. Meaning they got there awfully fast. The charges were from the same generation that killed the worm on the bank of the Dechear. The falconeers were Deves contracted to the Grail Knights.

"I found Devedian falconeers several places once I looked. Those people need to be reined in."

Hecht said, "We should've expected it. I knew they'd arm themselves better. That was my unstated reward for all the good they've done me. But I never meant them to arm the world. I'm going back to Krulik and Sneigon. If I find anything suspicious . . ." What could he do short of filling graves? The firepowder genie was out of the bottle. He would have no more luck stuffing it back in than the Night was having ending the threat of the Godslayer.

Cloven Februaren asked, "Who told you about your brother?"

"Bo Biogna. An old friend. I met him the same day I met Pinkus Ghort and Just Plain Joe. He's one of Ghort's sneak arounds, now."

"I know him."

Muniero Delari sighed.

Hecht asked, "Is there a problem, Grandfather?"

Delari said, "I'm just tired. Helping Hugo Mongoz, and now this new man, stay alive is exhausting. Health sorcery is the most draining kind."

Also the most common, though the majority of people with a healing touch had only a small portion of the gift.

Delari continued, "And Piper's Nightside defector isn't helping. Because of him I'm getting less assistance than I'd hoped." He looked pointedly at his grandfather.

"You'll get more help, Muno. Once Piper goes back to the Connec he won't need guarding so much. And if you really wanted to ease your load, you'd let Heris do the easy stuff down in the Silent Kingdom."

"But . . ."

"But you want to manage everything yourself. Every little facet. So they all get everything *just* right."

"But . . ."

"I know you, Muno. I used to be you. I still can't help poking my nose in. But not so much anymore. Look. Heris is a grown woman. She'll be right there with the Construct. She can yell for help. If the end of the world comes, she can translate out."

Sounded like the old man was trying to convince himself. "I won't need guarding so closely? Is there something going on that I haven't been told?"

"No," Februaren said. "But you're in Brothe. Brothens have strong opinions and act impulsively."

The Ninth Unknown was an accomplished liar. Hecht did not believe him.

Februaren revealed a small, smug smile. "Once you leave the rest of us will have time for the Construct, for investigations, for conspiring with the thing you brought out of the Jagos."

"I've overstayed my welcome."

"And you said the boy isn't bright enough to lace his own boots, Muno."

THAT NIGHT WITH ANNA WAS MORE MELANCHOLY THAN USUAL BEfore Hecht's departures. She seemed sure she would not see him again. She did not want to talk about it and would not be reassured.

Hecht had just swung his legs out of bed, rising to use the chamber pot, when the earth began to shake. A rumbling came from the south. Earthquake and thunderstorm in concert?

No. This was what had happened the night the Bruglioni citadel went up. Only more sustained.

"What is it?" Anna asked.

"Krulik and Sneigon," he said as the children rushed in. "Paying the price of perfidy." He was sure. He knew the collector, too.

That old man was one cold, murderous bastard.

THE HOLE IN THE GROUND WAS TEN TIMES THAT LEFT BY THE Bruglioni explosion. It continued to smolder. Minutes ago there had been a secondary explosion down there somewhere.

Pinkus Ghort observed, "We're gonna need a new law. No more stowing firepowder in the cellar or the catacombs."

"That should help." Hecht watched Kait Rhuk.

Rhuk and two hundred Patriarchals were searching the rubble, recovering the occasional corpse. But that was not their principal task. They were watching the Deve rescuers and confiscating firepowder weapons. And unexploded firepowder, where that turned up. Carefully.

There were a lot of weapons. Many more than contracted for by the Patriarchal forces.

Hecht noted several senior Deves watching. Nervously. None were men he knew. The Devedians he had known in his early days had all died, many by suicide.

That old man was a ruthless bastard.

THE KRULIK AND SNEIGON WHO HAD GIVEN THEIR NAMES TO THE business had died in the explosion. Hecht collected those likely to take over, all from the Krulik and Sneigon families. "I'm not happy," he told them. "My principal isn't happy. We feel betrayed. Our very generous contracts have been violated repeatedly, even after our warnings." He glared at the Deves. "I'm not feeling especially sympathetic today. But I give you one last chance.

"The people who worked here were the best at what they did. They can go on doing it. Somewhere where there'll be less devastation next time there's an accident."

One hundred eighty-one dead had been recovered already. Most had been denizens of the tenements surrounding the works. Scores continued missing. It was a miracle the fires had not spread through the whole crowded Devedian quarter.

Damp weather had proved a blessing.

"I didn't plan this but I'm not unhappy that it happened. Though I do wish I had that firepowder back."

DEPARTURE FOR THE CONNEC HAD TO BE DELAYED. HECHT AND A band of lifeguards took the damp road to Fea, the village where the creature from the Jagos was being kept. Hecht enlightened no one about the reason for the trip. Madouc was in a sour mood. No tempers were improved by the ongoing drizzle.

Feeble rains had fallen irregularly since the explosion at the Krulik and Sneigon works. Old people complained about their joints and proposed unlikely theories to explain the weather. Those in the midst of life were amused because their elders usually claimed everything was bigger, brighter, prettier, deadlier, and just generally more so in every way in decades gone by. Not so, the rain.

Hecht's destination proved to be at the heart of Fea, a tower seventy feet tall. It was a primitive example of architecture beginning to appear in various republics and even a few Patriarchal cities where local politics could overheat. Entry was accomplished through a doorway sixteen feet above ground level, after climbing a ladder. Its few windows were archer's embrasures well above that. Food and water, sufficient to endure a brief siege, were stored inside.

The towers were not fortifications in a traditional sense. City politics being volatile, they needed to protect their owners for hours only. Days at the most. Rioters seldom came equipped with siege trains. Or martial determination.

Hecht thought these family fortresses might be worth consideration in the Collegium. They could make difficulties for Patriarchal troops trying to control local disorders.

This tower was different from similar towers in that the ladder was stored outside. The Captain-General swung that into place. "Wait here, Madouc. I won't be long."

Madouc did not want to risk his principal to a thing that had harvested lives by the score. He argued. But Piper Hecht had no fear. Asgrimmur Grimmsson had reclaimed himself from the Night.

"Madouc, I do most everything you ask. Even when I don't see the point. But not this time. I need to talk to this man alone."

Madouc reddened. Would this be the one time too much?

But Madouc controlled himself. He had his men hold the ladder.

"Thank you, Madouc." Hecht climbed. He felt it in his thighs. Too much comfort lately. And too many years.

The tower door swung inward at a touch. Hecht swung off the ladder, stepped inside. He saw no immediate evidence that the place was occupied. He moved through the gloom to a narrow stairs that had no rail. Stepping carefully, one hand against the wall, he climbed a riser at a time, testing each before he put his weight on it.

His eyes adjusted. And the light did grow stronger as he climbed, sneaking in through the unglazed embrasures above.

How had Cloven Februaren gotten hold of this place? He supposed the villagers would have reports, thirty percent fiction and sixty-five percent speculation.

"Godslayer. Welcome to my mansion in Firaldia."

"Soultaken. I'm glad you're enjoying the Patriarch's hospitality."

"I don't think your old man has much to do with it. Except insofar as he executes the will of the All-Father."

Hecht found himself in a round, featureless room boasting few comforts. Archer's embrasures marked the points of the compass, designed to accommodate crossbowmen. Hecht tried to hide the fact that he was winded.

"The will of the All-Father?"

"Unless my brother Shagot lied, one of our rewards for destroying the Godslayer would be a stone-built mansion in warm Firaldia. Warmth being a huge luxury and giant temptation for wild young Andorayans. Who believed everything could be theirs if they had the will to take it."

"I must confess, you're entirely unlike my preconceptions of an Andorayan pirate."

"I'm not that Svavar anymore. He was ignorant and shallow and an embarrassment to his people. And wasn't bright enough to see it."

"So how . . . ?"

"When you're trapped inside the monster of the Jagos you can't do much but think. And taste the Night. And sample the unfortunate minds and souls that get in your way. You become as aware of the beast you were as you're aware of the horror you've become. All that time thinking could drive you mad. Unless you re-create yourself in a shape more acceptable to yourself. I think most ascendants must go mad. I'm probably barking mad myself—though I keep trying to convince me that I was doing my stint in Purgatory and I'm just fine now. A diet of iron and silver does wonders for clearing the mind."

Hecht moved to an embrasure, looked out on countryside that had changed little in two thousand years. In all likelihood those vineyards and olive groves and wheat fields had been where they were before the rise of the Old Brothen Empire. There were ruins down there the Feaens claimed antedated the Old Empire. Ruins no one disturbed. They were part of a pagan graveyard protected by the insane fury of cairnmaidens, children buried alive so their angry ghosts would guard the burying ground.

Even devout Chaldareans would not test those beliefs.

"Nor should they dare," the soultaken said, as though reading Hecht's thoughts writ upon his face. "Those murdered children are as-cendants themselves, of the most terrible sort. Though very small. The world is fortunate they can't grow and can't sever their connection to the ground they guard. I've tried to talk with them. I can't. Their rage is impenetrable."

"Once upon a time, when the Faith was young, the saints set out to free the cairnmaidens and lay them to rest."

"So they did. Once upon a time. But it was cruel and painful work. And thankless. Changing the official religion didn't change the superstitions of the country people. When those early saints passed over they left no apprentices to carry on. Idealism flees all faiths early."

Hecht moved to another embrasure. From this he could observe Fea itself, and Madouc nervously pacing. He stuck an arm out and waved to demonstrate that he remained among the living. "You wanted to see me."

"In a sense. The old man who comes has a very one-sided mind.

He doesn't want to talk. He wants to ask questions that produce defin-
itive answers. But he doesn't know how to ask the right questions."

"You're hoping I'll sit around chatting, wrestling the world's travails? I'm not the right man. I'm a soldier. I solve problems by killing
people and burning things till the problems go away. I seem to be good
at that."

"Better than most of your contemporaries. Your weakness is your
inability to be ruthless."

Recalling the Connecten Crusade, Hecht considered a protest. He
forbore. The soultaken was right. He had made examples in an effort
to chivvy potential enemies away from the battlefield. But his thinking
had been local and limited, concerned only with the immediate future.
Ten years from now, if the Patriarch sent him against Arnhand, no one
would be intimidated by what he had done then.

The Old Brothens said war was neither a game nor a pastime. If
a man was not willing to pursue it with all his strength, with utter
ruthlessness, he should not go to war in the first place. In the long term,
ruthlessness saved lives.

An enemy had to be stripped of all hope. Before the killing started,
if possible. He had to know that if war came it would not end till someone had suffered absolute destruction. The Old Brothens always had
the numbers. Not to mention superior discipline and skills. And utter
ruthlessness.

"I see what you mean."

"Good, then. In time to come you'll need to be less gentle."

"What?"

"I am become a child of the Night. Though I've resumed my original shape part of me is still entangled in the Night's boundless sea.
I know what the Night knows. Like most Instrumentalities, I have
trouble organizing that so it makes sense inside this world's limitations.
The toughest chore is to anchor information at the appropriate place
on the tree of time."

"The same problem your Old Ones had when they conscripted you
to murder me."

"Exactly. They read the causes and effects incorrectly, then misin-
terpreted the results. By trying to defeat the future they wrote their
own downfall."

"Be careful what you wish for."

"Exactly."

"I'm trapped climbing the tree of time myself. I have places to go
and things to do according to the workings of this world."

"True. A point I wanted to make. The reason I wanted to see you. I am an Instrumentality, now. Almost a new thing. My eyes are open to the Night. But I'm still human enough to see how I could be of use to an enemy of the Night."

"You're volunteering to spy?"

"Sort of. First I have to undo what rage made me do after my suffering at al-Khazen."

"So you said. Yes." Hecht was not ready to take the Night at its word, or at face value. Slippery was a defining characteristic of the Instrumentalities of the Night, be they gods or woodland sprites.

"Trust you need not invest. Judge by results."

"You want to help in the struggle, feel free. A window into the supernatural realm would be priceless. But I can't manage it. The old man will have to do. He can get any really useful information to me quickly."

"He could teach me that traveling trick."

"He could. You never know. He's always got another surprise up his sleeve. But I wouldn't count on it."

"We have an understanding?"

"I'm not sure. I'm not clear on what you want for you."

"At its simplest, absolution. Asgrimmur Grimmsson, as Svavar, was a terrible man. Not as bad as his brother Shagot, but a waste of flesh. What Svavar became might be worse—though that was circumstance, not intent. The ascendant absorbed power from two major Instrumentalities—which left him the slave of the qualities that made Svavar so awful."

"But you're a changed man now." Hecht could not suppress his skepticism.

"The power of the metal to burn out evil and self-delusion can't be explained in any way that would make sense to you. For weeks I've looked for an explanatory metaphor. There must not be one. Just say silver ripping through me constituted a baptism of the soul and spirit."

Soul and spirit? The remark bore a suspicious odor. Some heretics believed men had two souls, consciousness and spirit. Hecht did not know the details. He shied away from deviant thinking.

The ascendant guessed his thoughts. "There's a saying to the effect that there are more things in heaven and earth than we know. That is true beyond mortal imagining. For every Instrumentality you know there are a dozen in the air, the water, and the earth below. You know nothing about them because they never interact with human beings. They've always been insignificant in the history of your world. And always will be if they're left alone."

Hecht was becoming impatient. What the ascendant really wanted was company.

"I'll release you in a moment, Captain-General."

Hecht could not move.

"Those like Kharoulke prey on benign Instrumentalities. That explains how the Windwalker gets stronger when the wells of power are dying."

"Not a secret."

"Of course. But the dark Instrumentalities have never been so efficient. Not even Kharoulke's generation, before they were defeated and constrained. They've changed. They've become devourers."

Hecht noted the use of "they." "There are others? Besides the Windwalker?"

"Yes. They're still blind and only beginning to waken. But mortals are looking for them, wanting to quicken them. Hoping to *become* them."

"Er-Rashal al-Dhulquarnen."

"First try. Go. Enjoy your war. Cleanse the Connec of revenant Night. But your success won't stay that nation's doom."

Hecht could move. He did so instantly, despite having a thousand questions.

The ascendant was amused.

Cloven Februaren should be careful. This thing was no dim pirate.

BROTHE WAS CALM. PINKUS GHORT TOLD THE CAPTAIN-GENERAL, "I almost wish you could stay around, Pipe. It's so quiet."

"Enforce that yourself. You have the power and the men."

"And could be out of a job. I'm not on the payroll to keep the peace. I'm here to make sure Brothe runs the way Bronte Doneto and the Five Families want it to run. In that order. They could hardly care less if the lower classes murder each other. And they're behind the Colors."

Those political parties, once just passionate partisans of various racing teams, had been quiescent since the collapse of the hippodrome. Which had been reconstructed sufficiently that a partial racing season was set for the coming summer. Street politics would come along with. Had begun already and were in abeyance only because the Patriarchal garrison was intolerant of disorder.

Hecht said, "I'll enjoy it from afar. If it gets to be too much, come see me. The militias of the various Patriarchal States desperately need reorganization."

"Thought you already did that."

"I tried. Against a lot of inertia. A couple more tries, I'll get them hammered into a tool that's ready to use when I need it."

Something flickered behind Ghort's eyes. A shadow. A thought he did not care to share. "I'm glad I'm not at the tip of the spear no more. Here I've got some control over my life. I can squirrel away a little wealth."

Hecht filed that for consideration. That would be Pinkus Ghort expressing shadow thoughts as plainly as he dared.

HECHT HAD A ROW WITH PELLA. THE BOY DID NOT WANT TO STAY BE-hind. Hecht ended it. "I promised Anna. I keep my promises. If your studies don't keep you out of trouble, Principaté Delari can find something for you to do."

MADOUC VISITED HECHT IN HIS OFFICE IN THE CASTELLA. "CAPTAIN-General."

"Madouc." Coolly. Displeasure carefully constrained.

"I want to withdraw my resignation. If you will permit."

"What's changed, Madouc? I'll never be any different."

"I understand. I was tired and frustrated. The trip to Fea, with all that bad weather, broke me. I've had time to get over it."

Hecht had not replaced Madouc. It was not a pressing concern. "All right. Get caught up."

"Thank you, Captain-General. I'll try to be less prickly."

CLOVEN FEBRUAREN TOLD HECHT, "ADDAM HAUF TOLD MADOUC TO come back. He got bumped up two stages inside the Brotherhood hier-archy and proclaimed chief observer of Piper Hecht. You'll see some changes among your lifeguards. Several who aren't Brotherhood will go. Others who are will be replaced by men less captivated by you per-sonally."

"Ah. So now I'll be like the old-time emperors. Protected from everything except my protectors."

"Seems to be the idea."

"I shouldn't have let him come back."

"Better the devil you know."

"Possibly."

"Take care. I won't be around much anymore. Other chores need my attention."

Hecht said only, "I'll miss you, then."

"The Connec should present no special challenges. Just be alert. And let Madouc do his job. He's good at it. When you let him be."

"I get the message."

THE CAPTAIN-GENERAL UNDERTOOK ONE LAST UNPLEASANT CHORE before leaving Brothe. In company with his lifeguards he rode out to a small Bruglioni estate southeast of the Mother City.

Gervase Saluda had recovered some. He now occupied a wheeled chair. A blanket covered his lap. "To hide the fact that they took my left leg," he said in response to Hecht's glance. "Gangrene."

"I hadn't heard."

"You're a barrel of surprises, Captain-General. I never expected you to come out here."

"I've moved on but I do owe the Bruglioni. Without you I'd be just another sword looking for work."

"I doubt that. The gods themselves watch over you."

Not a particularly apposite remark from a Prince of the Church. But Hecht was not treating Saluda as a Principaté.

"I have been lucky. And the Bruglioni haven't. What will you do now?"

"Recover. And try not to turn bitter."

"For the family. You understand? You are the Bruglioni, today. I hear Paludan hasn't died, but isn't much alive anymore, either. He can't manage anything. His surviving relatives aren't going to do the Bruglioni any good. Which, I should think, puts you in a fix."

There was pain in Saluda's expression. He had not yet shaken his physical distress sufficiently to explore his future.

"You're the Bruglioni Principaté," Hecht said. "But will that last if there isn't a Bruglioni family behind you? The other families don't love you."

"I know. They think Paludan chose me because I was his lover. That's not true. Or because I have some unnatural influence over him. Never because I was the best available."

"You were the best. You're still the best. But if Gervase Saluda doesn't step back from the Collegium and take charge of the Bruglioni fortunes, the family is going to collapse."

After a moment, Saluda said, "I should just roll this chair onto the Rustige Bridge and right off into the Teragi."

"A simple solution but not the one I hope to see."

"Yes?"

"I'll help if I can. For what good that is, with me away in the Connec."

"Oh. Good on you." Saluda looked skeptical.

THE CAPTAIN-GENERAL REACHED VISCESMENT AT THE HEAD OF troops numbering several hundred more than he had detached to keep order in Brothe and neighboring Firaldia. The new Patriarch had authorized the use of any force necessary to clear the Connec of revenants. And, in a secret directive, of agents of the Society for the Suppression of Sacrilege and Heresy. Too many members of that harsh order had gone underground rather than disband, their defiance fertilized by Anne of Menand's covert support.

Hecht carried letters from Bellicose authorizing Count Raymone Garete to act against any monk or priest who refused to conform to the will of the Patriarch. Though he could only catch the renegades and turn them over to the ecclesiastical courts. Where they were too likely to be judged by sympathizers.

Clej Sedlakova, Hagan Brokke, and other trusted staffers assembled at Viscesment, in the Palace of Kings. With the Anti-Patriarchy ended, the Palace stood empty. The Patriarchals took over, which reduced the strain of their presence in the city.

Nothing critical needed deciding. The staff had managed well in their commander's absence. "Makes me worry," Hecht told no one in particular. "You men are either so good you don't need me, or the job is so easy any fool can do it."

His staff were all shrugs and smiles.

A feast of sorts filled Hecht's first evening back. In attendance were the magnates of Viscesment and nobles of regions nearby. Count Raymone Garete and his bride Socia, and the Count's more noteworthy henchmen, also attended. Senior churchmen were well represented, as well. They divided into clearly identifiable factions.

Bellicose's friends formed the larger party. The other, called Arnhanders by their opponents, recognized the current state of affairs only grudgingly. And openly hoped for the end of Bellicose's reign.

The Arnhander party did, in fact, consist almost entirely of outsiders who had come into the Connec during the crusader era.

Though officially only a lieutenant, Titus Consent had contrived himself a seat at Hecht's left hand. Hecht supposed the rest of the staff had schemed to make that happen. Titus was in charge of intelligence. He would have a lot to report. Especially about those personalities of interest in attendance.

Consent whispered, "I'm still huffing and puffing from the rush to get here." He had been in the field.

"Well, you made it." Hecht noted several churchmen watching the exchange keenly. "Don't take it personal, but you look like hell." Consent did appear to have aged a decade in just a few months.

"Stress. These assholes want me to be you when you're not around. No! Listen! We just got Rook cornered. Finally. In the Sadew Valley."

"Isn't that where he first turned up, back when?"

"Yes. The place must be important to him."

Hecht flashed a sinister smile at one of the more notorious clerical agitators. The man wanted to be defiant, dared not. The Captain-General of Patriarchal forces did not, unlike the temporal powers, *have* to defer to the ecclesiastical courts. Which had led to occasional instances of harsh, summary justice.

"How soon will it be over?" With Rook stricken from the roll of revenants there would be no more demand for a Patriarchal presence in the Connec. Except for Shade. He had heard nothing positive about Shade. Yet.

"A while. It's a loose cordon. They'll tighten it slowly. They don't want to get in a hurry and let him get away again."

Hecht wanted to ask about problems in the force. But practical matters had to wait. He had powerful people to entertain, seduce, overawe.

# 8. Faraway East, the Oldest City: A Slender String

How old was Skutgularut? Only the Instrumentalities themselves might know. Old enough to have been there in the Time Before Time, if its people could be believed. Old enough to have been there before men learned to write. Across the ages Skutgularut, anchor of the northern silk road, had been attacked, besieged, even conquered countless times. Never totally, not even by Tsistimed the Golden. Skutgularut was a place of high honor, sacred, that even Tsistimed could reverence. It was a place where scholars gathered. Where sorcerers met to study and experiment. It was a city at whose heart lay a small but utterly reliable well of power. A well never known, in all history, to have waxed or waned. For which it was called the Faithful.

Once Skutgularut yielded to the seductions of the Hu'n-tai At, Tsistimed made it his western capital. With age he came to favor the city's famous gardens. The city prospered, for it no longer experienced war. Bandits dared not trouble the great caravans traveling the silk road. Those who tried were hunted down, man, woman, and child.

The aged Tsistimed seldom left his beloved gardens. He gave warring over to his sons, grandson, and the sons of his grandson. But he could not resist the call of adventure when the Ghargarlicean Empire collapsed. He had to tour the famous cities that were now his own.

The grand warlord of the steppe did not look like a man over two hundred years old. Those who came to grovel before him saw a man in his prime. A man with many years still ahead.

Age had overtaken Tsistimed only on the inside.

He was just plain tired of it all.

THE SAVAGES CAME OUT OF NOWHERE. THERE WAS NO MORE WARNING than a few rumors of strange things brewing to the north. Then the men and women with the bones and skulls in their hair were everywhere, killing and destroying. Amongst them walked a thing in near-human form, with too many fingers, no hair, and spotted skin. Later, some claimed it had eyes like a tiger. Others said it was ten feet tall. All agreed that it was terrible. Invincible. Immune to the bite of any lone piece of iron but not to the cumulative effect of ten thousand.

The thing eventually fell. Eventually perished. Eventually melted into a pool of puss inside the temple that housed the Faithful.

Survivors agreed that pollution of the well had not been the thing's desire. It had hungered for a direct drink from the Faithful.

The savages turned more ferociously destructive after their tutelary went down. They left Tsistimed's palace a smoldering waste. They wasted most of Skutgularut.

Only a handful lived to flee into the icelands to the north.

THE HU'N-TAI AT COURIER SYSTEM WAS SUCH THAT TSISTIMED learned of the attack while the destruction of Skutgularut was still under way. He ended his progress through Ghargarlicea and turned north.

The eastern world huddled into itself. The Night trembled.

There was no fury like the fury of Tsistimed the Golden.

# 9. Realm of the Gods: The Ninth Unknown

Cloven Februaren now spent most of his time with the soultaken. The soultaken did not enjoy the isolation of Fea, though he understood its necessity. He was not accustomed to being confined.

The old man said, "I sympathize completely. I do. I get ferociously restless when I have to wait. Be patient just a while longer. We'll move as soon as my other obligations are covered. So. Here. More maps. So we can narrow the search."

"You don't listen, old man. I've told you, I know where it is. I've been there. I spent a long time there, trying to shut it down." But that the ascendant would not discuss except in the vaguest possible way. That must have been a time of great stress. Or there were secrets the ascendant did not wish to reveal.

The Ninth Unknown was inclined to suspect the latter.

"You know where it was a few years ago. The world has changed. What did the non-divines do after your vengeance raid? Did they leave? Did they close the way behind you?"

The Svavar of old peeped out occasionally. Notably when the soultaken thought the Ninth Unknown was deliberately inventing obstacles to getting on with what needed doing.

Februaren's concern was genuine. He wanted to invest the least possible time accomplishing this mythic jailbreak.

"THERE'S NOTHING MORE I CAN LEARN FROM HERE," FEBRUAREN told the soultaken. Failing to mention that he had visited the north on his own and had failed to find a trace of the higher realm—though he had found where the entrance had been before. A powerful resonance remained.

The god realm was still there, over on the other side.

"It's finally time to go?"

"It's time."

"Let's do it, then."

Asgrimmur Grimmsson began to change.

Februaren barked, "Wait! There isn't room in here."

The soultaken had swollen, shredding his human apparel. The buds of numerous legs had begun to show.

He reversed the change. "Good thinking." He swarmed downstairs, through the door, down the ladder, to the ground. When the old man caught up he was well on toward resuming his former monster shape. And looking notably healthy—though his hand remained unrestored.

Odd that a demigod would not be able to replace a lost appendage.

Februaren sighed repeatedly. Would the ascendant remain rational and amenable after the change? No way to know. Asgrimmur Grimmsson was unique in modern times.

The people of Fea did not stay around to watch the change.

Soon the only humanity remaining was the monster's head. Which migrated down to its belly. A ghost of a face using a voice barely audible told Februaren, "Climb onto my back."

Februaren gathered his belongings. The climb was difficult. Terribly frightening. Yet compliance left him with arrows in his quiver.

He had the Construct, always.

The soultaken did not yet know much about his ally's capabilities. Said ally meant to keep every secret he could. The enemy of my enemy today could well move to the head of the enemies list tomorrow.

The monster's shoulders were broader than those of a horse, and less soft or warm. Nor were there ready handholds. Just some bristles almost as fierce as porcupine quills.

The monster surged up. It began to move. It gathered speed fast. Countryside streaked by. Februaren gasped for breath, shook in fright— and enjoyed every instant. He was not one of those old men who disdained novelty.

He settled into the rhythm.

The monster stuck to wild country. That meant traveling rougher terrain. The journey took longer than it could have. Yet Februaren was astonished to see the sunset-stained peaks of the Jagos in just a few hours.

Once darkness fell the monster took to the roads to make better speed. Darkness did not hamper it.

Februaren worried about what the darkness might conceal. Worry was wasted. The ascendant created its own bubble of immunity or invisibility.

Dawn found them well into the Empire, racing past amazed peasants. Instrumentalities seldom materialized these days. Though travelers' tales from the north promised excitement to come.

The feel of the world began to change. Each league onward seemed more charged with reality, with a growing electricity. Had it been like this in the dawn times, when magic was everywhere? The old man worried. Why had he not felt this when he came north by way of the Construct? Was it something you had to come to gradually, giving it time to grow around and through you? Was it the hope of this that drove er-Rashal al-Dhulquarnen's cabal?

No. They could not know about this without having experienced it. They wanted immortality. They wanted to become Instrumentalities in their own right.

In a world charged like this everyone would be a demigod.

Reality took a fat bite out of fantasy.

The wells of power were dying. This might be an island of magic in a desert of power, nothing more. One that had not existed long. It was not yet overrun by ravenous things of the Night.

The Ninth Unknown felt those moving all around, headed the same direction. A reservoir of power must have burst, emptying in hours instead of ages. It had happened before, a sort of volcanic burst. The last in the west had taken place almost two thousand years ago, in the eastern reaches of the Mother Sea.

Did the monster understand human speech? Februaren shouted, "We have to hurry! This will draw Instrumentalities from everywhere." Including Kharoulke the Windwalker, who would take most of the power. Unless the source was too far beyond the edge of the ice.

The ascendant sucked it in as he ran. Februaren felt it growing stronger beneath him.

They were crossing the fields of Friesland, where snow was melting in the shade only because of the advent of the power, the epicenter of which lay somewhere to the west. Which meant somewhere out in the Andorayan Sea. In unfrozen water. The Windwalker of antiquity could not cross open water except to step over it, hop from island to island, or walk a bridge. Could that still be true?

No matter, really. Kharoulke could come to the edge of the Andorayan ice and suck up power from there. But without being able to hog the trough.

The monster reached the shore. It stopped, sank down so the old man could dismount. Then it shrank, folded in on itself, flowed, becoming a huge, naked man with an immense complement of red hair. "I can go no farther in that form." He pointed westward. "That's already fading. There'll be nothing left in a week." He shook like a huge dog. "It feels good!"

Februaren thought any Instrumentality would say the same. "I hope Kharoulke is so far off he can't take advantage. What next?"

"The way has to be out there. I'll become something that swims."

"I was afraid you'd say that." Knowing that he had done it before.

"A little water never hurt anyone, old man."

"Good point. Unfortunately, that's not a little. That water goes on for a thousand miles."

"No. The southern tip of Orland is just a few miles out. It's low and swampy. We'll have to swing around it to reach the true open sea."

The man who had been Asgrimmur Grimmsson walked into the surf. "The way is out there. You'll have to take your chances." He began to melt. And expand. He turned into a whale of modest size, twenty-three feet from fluke to snoot. Februaren walked into the water up to his waist. He got soaked by the little breakers rolling in.

Slimy skin. He could not mount up. The Instrumentality took pity and grew handholds. Once he was astride its shoulders a sort of saddle formed beneath him.

"Excellent. Just don't sound."

THE WHALE SWAM CIRCLES WHERE THE GATEWAY OUGHT TO BE. IT could sense the Realm of the Gods. Somewhere.

The Ninth Unknown felt it out there, too. But the way was closed.

The whale grew a grotesque caricature of a blind-eyed face in front of its blowhole. The mouth produced spectral sounds. "This is the place. But the Aelen Kofer have blocked the way."

Who could blame the dwarves? Nothing good came from outside. And the affliction of tyrannical gods had been resolved inside.

"How fine have your descriptions been? Did you exaggerate anything to make the Realm of the Gods sound more glorious, more dangerous, or more exciting?"

The whale did not respond for so long that Februaren began to fear that it might refuse.

But, then, "The bridge. The rainbow bridge. It broke. I did not report that." After an exchange prolonged by the whale's slow replies, Cloven Februaren concluded that Asgrimmur Grimmsson had been at pains to accurately describe the private universe of his boyhood gods. And began to suspect that ascension had changed the man's brain in ways not immediately obvious. Those might be characteristic of many other Instrumentalities.

Dealing with the ascendant reminded Februaren of the difficulties of raising a mildly autistic child. Which he had done, in the long ago. A son, Muno's uncle Auchion. Love, training, and sorcery had allowed Auchion to live a normal, if truncated, adult life.

"Wouldn't that be some shit?" the old man asked the salty air. "If the gods were autistic?"

It would explain a good many puzzles.

"Wait here," Februaren told the whale.

"How long?"

Not where was he going, nor how could he get there from the middle of the water, but the most basic, literal question.

"For as long as it takes to open the way. Eat if you get hungry." He saw seals at play in the distance. There must be land of some sort nearby.

Was the whale the kind that ate seals?

"But stay close."

ASGRIMMUR GRIMMSSON'S REPORTS WERE SO DETAILED THE NINTH Unknown managed to build a fine, if colorless, picture inside his head. Hand in hand with terror he took hold of the hidden strings of the Construct and stepped into what might turn out to be eternity. He could not know if it was possible to slip into the other world until he tried. He could not know—granted success breaking in—if he could get back out if he could find no means of opening the way from within.

Cloven Februaren was two hundred years old. More or less. He had taken risks before. But never quite so blindly, betting against such unpredictable odds.

He took the first step still wondering what secret need compelled him to engage in such blatant folly.

There was the sense of walking through starless, frozen night that accompanied every romance with the Construct. Then he was awash in a silvery light.

The Aelen Kofer must have scrubbed out all the color before they went away.

Cloven Februaren found himself inelegantly sprawled on a stone quayside, facing a mountain. A harbor lay behind him. One lone ship rode alongside the quay. It could have been a ship of legend. But even the legendary suffered from neglect.

That whole world had suffered from neglect.

Where were the Aelen Kofer? He had expected dwarves—though the ascendant thought those might have sailed away in the golden barge of the gods. But what ship, then, moldered at quayside?

"Should have paid more attention to my mythology studies," Februaren grumbled. The dwarves had not been seen in the human world. Ergo, they must have stolen away into another of the realities to which this world was connected.

Were there not several such overlapping realms involved in the northern cycle? The land of the giants, the world underground, a frozen land of the dead, somewhere where elves ran rampant?

What did it matter? He was here. He was alone. He had to go on from there.

He needed to open the way. It did not look like there was a lot of food lying around. The contents of his knapsack would not last.

Sweet irony. To starve to death in heaven.

The old man looked up the mountain. The Great Sky Fortress up top was a ghost almost completely hidden by clouds. The rainbow bridge was partially visible below, showing hints of the only color around.

The bridge was broken.

Sufficient to the hour that problem. The trial of the moment was to open the way for the return of this world's doom, Asgrimmur Grimmsson. A notion that birthed a grim smile.

Awakenings, revenances, most always featured the return of old evils thoroughly dedicated to the pursuit of greater evil. Not the correction of good deeds gone rotten.

## 10. Alten Weinberg: Sisters

As often as she dared without sparking the Imperial wrath, Princess Helspeth begged leave to return to Plemenza. Telling Katrin, honestly, "I want to get away from the politics." Making it sound general. Avoiding specifics because it was the specific that terrified her.

Katrin married was worse than Katrin the virgin. This shrew hated the world because, it seemed, she had chosen her husband so poorly. And could not admit her error.

Jaime had lost interest as soon as it was clear that he would never become Emperor himself. Though for some time he did perform his duty in an effort to create an heir.

More often he lay with some woman of the court. Or with a dusky little mistress he kept in an apartment not far from the Palace.

Alten Weinberg eventually lost its appeal. Jaime returned to Castauriga.

His argument for going was sound. He was king, there. His kingdom was being pressed by its neighbors. Had Peter of Navaya not been distracted by grander ambitions he might have gobbled Castauriga already.

And there were stirrings in Arnhand, aimed at the Connec. That could pull in the Chaldarean Episcopal princes of Direcia. None of them wanted a stronger Anne of Menand behind them.

The politics Helspeth wanted to escape were those of religious factions. Most of the nobility would not accept Katrin's accommodation with the Patriarchy. They wanted to put forward the Princess Apparent as their banner in the struggle to bring back yesterday.

Helspeth would have no part of sedition. And made that plain to anyone who came to her with a scheme.

Katrin adamantly refused to let Helspeth leave the capital. She did not want the Princess Apparent in residence where she could not be closely watched.

There was a huge strain between the sisters. Helspeth was terrified she could end up imprisoned again. Or worse. And had reason to fear. For Katrin's advisers suggested extreme measures regularly.

The gathering storm broke when Katrin announced that she was expecting. Again.

She had become pregnant almost immediately after her wedding. That child spontaneously aborted in the sixth week. The days following had been hard. No one knew what to expect. Katrin flew into rages with no apparent provocation. The rages fled as quickly. She became deeply remorseful, countermanding draconian orders issued while she was angry. The court adapted by pretending to pursue her cruel directives while hoping she would change her mind.

Katrin seldom followed up. She forgot.

But sometimes her people, frightened of a future without Katrin in it, did not ignore her maddest orders.

The Empress's behavior drove more and more nervous nobles into the camp of those who thought life would have to be more congenial with a different sister occupying the Grail Throne. Which thinking terrified the Princess Apparent.

Katrin's announcement, scarcely four weeks after Jaime's departure, brought peace. Her irrationality went away. She buried herself in the work of empire, and in preparations for the baby's arrival. She assured everyone it would be a son, a strapping heir to the mantle of Johannes Blackboots. She would name him for his grandfather. She drove women of the court to distraction with pregnancy talk. She slept much less than before. This manic phase appeared endless.

Which frightened some of the court more than had her earlier psychosis.

Everyone avoided mention of Jaime of Castauriga.

Jaime was a subject Katrin would pursue with more intensity than her pregnancy. Jaime had become a demigod who bore no resemblance to the living man. A man even Katrin's most devoted supporters hoped was gone for good.

HELSPETH HAD BEEN SUMMONED TO DINE WITH HER SISTER. SHE dressed dowdy, determined not to outshine Katrin, whose looks had declined alarmingly. She found Katrin in an expansive mood, inclined to sisterly intimacy. Helspeth played along, afraid a hammer would fall just when she least expected.

Katrin said, "I'm so lonely, Ellie. Jaime is gone. I don't have any-body. These people . . . They're not my friends. They just want to use me."

"Kat, you've always got me. If you'd just accept that. I don't want to be anything but your loving sister. That's all I need to be." In the back of her mind was a hope that she could scuttle efforts to find her a husband. One who would take her far from the Empire.

The search always livened when Katrin was in a good mood. With her expecting, now, there was no perceived need to reserve the Princess Apparent against the unexpected.

A baby would be easier to manipulate if Katrin suddenly went away. Helspeth, many feared, was too much like her father. She would be difficult despite her sex.

An hour of Katrin's insecurities fled. Helspeth suspected her of making some of it up, purely for the pleasure of being reassured.

Then Katrin said, "I hear that Braunsknecht captain, Algres Drear, is back in the city."

"I didn't know that. Why?"

"They ran the Imperials out of Viscesment. After the Captain-General made sure his puppet was settled in Brothe."

"Really? He didn't strike me as that kind. More a loyal soldier."

"He must have turned my offer down because he knew he was in a position to make the next Patriarch."

"I never thought of that. Though I don't see why he'd be chasing revenant Instrumentalities through the End of Connec if he could be the man behind the Patriarch in Brothe."

"He'll have a reason. That man is too slick."

"Just because he turned you down?"

"Doesn't make any sense, otherwise."

"Sure, it does. He gave his word. He'd have jumped at the chance if he hadn't already promised his service to someone else."

Katrin eyed her oddly. Was she too intense? She did not think so. But she ought to back off anyway. This was not the first time she had shown unbecoming emotion when the Captain-General was the subject. People might wonder.

She wondered herself. She was an adult, rational woman. Why the obsession? Why the secret letters? Having witnessed Katrin's obsession with Jaime of Castauriga she feared she might succumb to a similar madness.

A lady of the court interrupted, "Lord Maeterlinck begs your in-dulgence, Empress. Ferris Renfrow has arrived with important news. The Graf believes you should be made aware as soon as possible."

The interruption angered the Empress. People just would not stop butting in with things that could wait. For weeks, for all she could do anything about some of them. With the old men it was always the crisis of the moment. Were they determined to test her to her limits?

Helspeth whispered, "It's not Claudelette's fault. Be gentle. She's doing what she's supposed to do."

Katrin muttered angrily.

"Take it out on fon Maeterlinck. He's the villain."

Easy to say when she was not the girl who had to growl at one of the old warhorses. Simpler to take it out on a woman who could do nothing but bow her head and take it.

"All right, little sister. I'll let you show me how."

Ouch! But Katrin did no such thing.

"Claudelette. Inform the Graf fon Maeterlinck that I require him to assemble the Council Advisory and other appropriate individuals within the hour. No excuses."

The Empress grinned wickedly. "That, little sister, is how *I* deal with the Maeterlincks. Now he has to make himself unpopular with fifteen or twenty cranky old men. Most of whom won't arrive on time. So they'll look bad in front of their Empress. A few will actually blame fon Maeterlinck."

"Are you going to change?"

"No. I'll show up breathless and inappropriately dressed. I'm so devoted to the Empire. Which should make the Council that much more irked at Maeterlinck if this is just another routine report being exaggerated into a millennial threat to the Empire."

A parade of insignificant crises did arise. Helspeth suspected there was less malice behind them than Katrin wanted to believe. Men like the Graf fon Maeterlinck just wanted to be reassured that they were important to the Empire.

HAVING ACKNOWLEDGED THE IMPERIAL DIGNITY OF THE EMPRESS and Princess Apparent—perfunctorily—a tattered and filthy Ferris Renfrow declared, "There wasn't any need to convene the Council in emergency. My news may be dramatic but it doesn't require an immediate response. It may require no response at all."

Katrin's glare very nearly melted the Graf fon Maeterlinck.

Maeterlinck had shaken the hornet's nest before finding out what brought Ferris Renfrow here. And Renfrow had let him think the news would be earth-shaking so he would stick his fingers in the meat grinder.

"Renfrow? We're here. Let's have it."

"Arnhander crusader forces raised by Anne of Menand and

renegades from the banned Society for the Suppression of Sacrilege and
Heresy have invaded the Connec. The largest force, commanded by
King Regard, is headed toward Khaurene, out west. A second army is
working its way through the mountains toward Castreresone. The
Archbishops of Salpeno and Pernoud are its commanders.

"A third force will come down in the east, following the Dechear.
It's supposed to reduce Antieux, then follow the example set by the
Captain-General during Sublime's Connecten Crusade. This army con-
sists of those who have angered Anne of Menand. They've been or-
dered to crusade or face severe disfavor. I expect Anne hopes Count
Raymone Garete will eat most of them up."

Helspeth had begun breathing rapidly. She bit her lower lip.

Katrin said, "It's true. It's not crucial. But now we're here." Scorn
edged her words. "Those who bothered to respond." She glowered. "So
let's discuss it. How is Brothe likely to respond? I'd expect wholesale
excommunications. At the least. No Patriarch tolerates defiance from
the temporal authorities. And what will the Captain-General do?"

News delivered, Ferris Renfrow had eased aside. Helspeth thought
he seemed particularly interested in her reactions. But she had been living close by a sister who turned ugly in an instant. She revealed nothing.

Practically, the news meant little to her.

Not so to the old men. Already there were whispers about this
town or that, on the frontier, which really ought to be part of the Empire. Though the Empire had been nipping off bits of Arnhander territory for decades, whenever Arnhand became preoccupied elsewhere.

Helspeth asked, "What will King Brill do?"

Santerin was always at war with Arnhand. The kings of Santerin
seldom disdained an opportunity to raid and capture towns should the
generally feeble central Arnhander authority turn its back.

Katrin welcomed the interjection. "Renfrow?"

"I can't say for sure. I haven't heard from my sources. But King Brill
should do what Santerin's kings always have. Though Anne of Menand,
being smarter than the last dozen Arnhander kings put together, might
have made arrangements ahead of time." Renfrow gave the Empress a
sharp look. As though to suggest that crusades were not to be undertaken on a pious whim.

"How would she do that?"

"King Brill hungers for more titles and territories. She could relax
Arnhand's claims to some of the more fractious border counties till
she feels strong enough to take them back."

Katrin stepped down from her high seat. She walked among the
Councilors, and around them. Her father shone in her then. That made

the old men uncomfortable. "Have we heard anything from Salpeno? Officially? Or has someone forgotten to inform the Empress?"

Renfrow said, "Your Grace, if I might?"

"Go ahead."

"Strong as she is herself, Anne can't conceive of a strong woman. She'll need her nose bloodied before she considers the Empire worth her worry."

"Is that so? Lord Admiral. Grand Duke. You two are always spoiling for a fight. Arrange for demonstrations along the frontier."

Helspeth asked, "Should we undermine Anne's effort in the Connec? She'll be more of a threat if she gains the strength and wealth available there."

Katrin asked, "Renfrow? Any thoughts?"

"No. Except to note that no good for the Empire will arise from any success Anne might enjoy. Also, we have to consider the fact that there's another unhappy truth out there. The physical world is changing."

"Meaning?"

"The winters are getting longer. Seas are getting shallower. The far north is going under the ice, fast. Permanent snows in the Jagos and other high ranges are several times more vast than just ten years ago. The wells of power, everywhere, keep getting weaker. Meanwhile, old evils, Instrumentalities from the Time Before Time, have begun to ooze back into the world."

"No big revelation there, Renfrow. Why bring it up?"

"Because it's going to get worse. While we stay focused on war and politics as usual. You're looking to try another crusade into the Holy Lands . . ." The spymaster stopped before he said something risky.

Johannes Blackboots had allowed Renfrow the freedom of a court jester. Johannes had found his forthright observations useful.

Katrin Ege was more traditional. She preferred to be told what she wanted to hear. But she had not lost all affection for the truth. She might not like what she heard but she could cope with it. So far.

Helspeth did not expect that to last much longer.

Katrin's connection to bitter reality frayed by the hour.

Ferris Renfrow bowed and began to retreat from the presence, one step at a time.

Helspeth watched. He was not afraid. He just wanted to go away. He had delivered his information. He had tried to make a point. No one cared. Now there was work to be done elsewhere.

Helspeth understood. And could not care herself. She could focus only on the fact that the Captain-General would soon be caught in a political pinch.

# 11. Tel Moussa: A New God Talks Back to Father

One bronze falcon lay hidden in the tower at Tel Moussa, its existence known only to Nassim Alizarin and two cronies. The Mountain had hired it made—the tube only—by a renowned Dainshau founder in Haeti, a city in Rhûnish territory. It was smaller than falcons elsewhere. This Dainshau cast the weapon believing it to be something intended for use in a Devedian temple.

The Mountain had mounted the falcon on a goat cart. Everything Nassim knew about its use he had learned during the campaign against Rudenes Schneidel, by watching his Unbeliever allies. The firepowder—what precious little he possessed—had been purloined from Sha-lug stores in al-Qarn by sympathizers and smuggled north an ounce or two at a time.

Alizarin had powder and shot enough for a dozen discharges. He did not try to accumulate more. He was sure his weapon would not survive that many firing cycles. Bronze was not the best metal for casting falcons. Brass was better, iron best. But only the Deves out west had mastered casting iron tubes that cooled without developing fatal flaws. Gossip out of al-Qarn said the stubbornness of the iron had been a greater irritant to er-Rashal al-Dhulquarnen than all his failures in the west.

Which adventures he had sold to Gordimer the Lion as preemptive machinations meant to cripple the west's ability to launch fresh incursions into the Holy Lands. Or, as the Marshal so feared, against Dreanger itself.

The Rascal was back in al-Qarn, momentarily rehabilitated. The Lion needed the sorcerer more than he abhorred the man.

Each year left Gordimer more frightened of the future. The prophecy concerning his doom came nearer fruition every day.

It might be a blessing to the Sha-lug, Dreanger, and the kaifate of al-Minphet, all, if someone were to slip the Marshal a taste of poison.

Nassim Alizarin set little store by omens or prophecies. Nor had he been inclined to be God's most faithful servant since his son's murder.

The Mountain stared at his half-eaten meal. Was there any point to going on? Looking back, it seemed his very soul had been invested in Hagid.

El-Azer er-Selim interrupted, "Riders on the Shamramdi road. Coming our way."

"Meaning we're about to be blessed with demands from our lords."

Az bowed slightly, said no more. Garrison duty at Tel Moussa was not difficult. Its one great demand was patience. But the Mountain treated every message from the Lucidian capital as an imposition. Though he never failed to do as he was asked, nor did he not do it well.

"YOUNG AZ!" ALIZARIN SAID, PLEASED TO SEE AZIM AL-ADIL AGAIN. "Old Az didn't tell me it was you."

The Master of Ghosts said, "Old Az doesn't see that well anymore."

The boy said, "My pleasure, I assure you." He launched into flowery flattery, a sure sign he had been taught well at his granduncle's court.

The Mountain said, "I'm getting old, boy. I may not last through all this. Have your companions been seen to?"

"They won't want much. We'll head back as soon as you and I finish talking."

"My lord! You mustn't subject yourself . . ."

"I must. We all must. Something dramatic is happening with the Hu'n-tai At. Some unknown force attacked Skutgularut. Left it in ruins. Tsistimed is calling in all his sons and grandsons and their armies. There'll be a huge event of some sort."

"Maybe the old man will beat his brains out against whoever did it. What does it mean to us?"

"To you, very little. To Indala al-Sul Halaladin it means tribes on the periphery of the kaifate will feel more comfortable about defying the central authority. Few of their chieftains can think ahead far enough to understand that they'll need protection again next summer."

"I see." Governance was difficult when communications seldom exceeded the speed of a galloping horse. "Again, what part am I to play?"

"My illustrious relative begs your assistance in an entirely different matter. The beast du Tancret has offended al-Prama again. Deliberately."

"The lepers?"

"You heard?"

"The caravan master came here. He begged me to punish Rogert. I showed him our weakness and told him to make his case at court. I see that he did."

"He did. Indala's anger was boundless. Among the women in the caravan were two of his brother Ibid's granddaughters, Needa and Nia, returning from a visit to the antiquities of Dreanger. No. They weren't defiled. Not even Rogert du Tancret would dare that with any but slaves and pleasure women. But the girls were among those 'guests' he forced to dine in Gherig, then served using lepers."

"I sense a particular interest on your part, young Az."

"One of the girls, Needa, could be my betrothed." In answer to the general's lifted eyebrow, "The relationship is remote. Indala and Ibid had different mothers."

The old man nodded. The children would be sufficiently distant to marry.

"What do you require of me?"

"The beast dared that insult only because my illustrious relative was preoccupied with Tsistimed. But now the Hu'n-tai At have turned their faces. Indala would like to seize the moment to punish du Tancret. Permanently."

"Again, what do you require of me?"

"That you insert a spy into Gherig. Some of your followers have visited the west. They should be able to play Gisela Frakier well enough to fool the Arnhanders."

"Sad hope," the Mountain said. "I've tried. Twice. Both men were caught. And thrown from the wall. A gesture of contempt. As though they were trash, not worth torture or ransom. One man, abd Ador, survived. You can talk to him. He's had nothing but time to think about what went wrong."

"The paralyzed man in the wheeled chair downstairs?"

"Him."

"Why do you keep him?"

"He hasn't asked to die. He isn't ready for Paradise."

The youth's eyes narrowed. A preference for pain and incapacity over Paradise suggested a feeble level of faith.

The boy was brilliant. Well educated. But he needed seasoning in the world outside palace walls.

"It's his choice, youngster. We're Sha-lug, not some rabble turned out of a prison that won't wait for the wounded to die to bury them."

The boy inclined his head slightly, conceding the point.

Alizarin said, "There may be a way to get inside Gherig that hasn't occurred to us. I'll find it. Betimes, your illustrious relative might try to lure Rogert out and destroy him."

"Such plans are being considered, General. But the Arnhanders aren't fools. Gherig sits on the frontier of the Holy Lands, surrounded by princes and principalities, tribes and chieftains, towns and townsmen, any of whom is likely to betray any of the others, or us, for a fistful of copper. And never suffer a pang of conscience."

"The alternative would be to isolate the fortress."

"Harder on the Faithful than the Unbeliever. Gherig can withstand a prolonged, determined siege."

"I understand. I don't mean a siege. Instead, just deploy raiders.

Cut Gherig off. Attack anyone going in or coming out. Lay on the occasional small sorcery to worsen the misery of servants, soldiers, and merchants who are inside and have to watch the rest of the world go on."

"I see. Shield the world from Rogert du Tancret by caging him. With people who will come to realize that the only way to change their fortunes is by stepping over his corpse."

"Exactly."

"Not particularly satisfying. But it might appeal to my uncle's sense of humor."

A soldier, Hawfik, interrupted, "Pardon me, General. Riders are approaching. They're from Dreanger. The Master of Ghosts says it's time to be wary."

"Az? But . . ." But old Az was no longer in the chamber, lurking at the edge of awareness. "This could be trouble, young Az. We've been expecting the Rascal to try to silence us, now he's back in favor."

Alizarin had been awaiting a counterstroke since the fall of Rudenes Schneidel. It had taken time because the Rascal had had to worm his way back into the Lion's good graces.

The boy waited quietly. Alizarin suggested, "Stay here. Make yourself known quickly if we fail to defend ourselves. Er-Rashal won't want to offend Indala."

"Er-Rashal offends my uncle by existing. I won't hide from his lackeys."

Quick, the general thought. The boy recognizing that the Rascal would not waste his own time on an upstart rebel.

Al-Adil asked, "How does your Master of Ghosts recognize trouble from so far off?"

"Az is a very minor sorcerer. But quite good within his abilities." Enough said. Indala's loathing for sorcery was well known, and shared by his associates. "He knows."

Alizarin went to the small balcony overhanging the tower gate. The tower itself was just a few feet wider than the gate itself on that face. It formed a widening wedge behind, climbing Tel Moussa. There was a six-foot dry moat in front of the gate with a bridge that could be taken up and dragged inside. Alizarin had yet to see that done. Behind the gate, the way rose steeply. Any attacker who broke through still had to attack uphill.

The general found that Az had wasted no time waiting for orders. The men had been turned out. They were at posts away from the gate. Which stood open.

He considered the party of four approaching. Two Sha-lug. And two pretending to be Sha-lug. One of those radiated the arrogance Alizarin associated with er-Rashal al-Dhulquarnen.

The senior Sha-lug looked up. The Mountain did not recognize him. The man said something to the sorcerer. Alizarin told al-Adil, "Time to fall back. Just in case."

Soon afterward, a flash and howl spoke eloquently of interesting events outside. Nothing passed the wards denying entrance to things of the Night.

The boy was startled. "I didn't think . . . I can't believe . . ."

"When you return to Shamramdi you can say you saw it yourself."

"If I get back. What can you do against that? Your Master of Ghosts . . ."

What al-Adil might have said, doubting Az's abilities, vanished in a huge roar. The tower shook. Stones groaned. Dust fell.

Almost immediately horses began screaming. As did men. Or a man.

Alizarin returned to the balcony.

All four riders were down. Two lay still. The sorcerer was the human screamer. The other wounded man was focused on reattaching his right hand to his wrist.

Two horses were in flight, one on three legs. Neither appeared to be wounded. The cripple must have hurt itself trying to get away. The two fallen animals would have been in front, bodies shielding the fleeing pair but not their riders.

"Excellent," Alizarin said. Though he mourned the fallen Sha-lug. Their crime had been to be in the wrong place with the wrong man. "Let's see if we can salvage the sorcerer. He could make an interesting witness. Should your uncle be interested in what he has to say."

"No doubt of that."

"You have reservations?"

"He's still a sorcerer. And I have no resources for managing him."

"We'll fix you up."

Arriving down below, Nassim found his precious falcon defunct. "Az?"

"We overcharged it, sir. To make sure we put enough stuff in the air."

"Deal with those horses. And the wounded. If the sorcerer looks like he might live, save him."

Az met the Mountain's eye. He nodded, went back to work. Comrades from his old company joined him. Bone shouted, "We can save the one with the hand gone if I get a tourniquet on him now."

"Do it," Alizarin called back. "We'll kill him later if he needs it."

Mohkam, one of Bone's band, said, "They never saw us coming out of the bright sun, General."

Azim al-Adil observed, "That sorcerer's arrogant certainty astonishes me."

"We'll ask him about it." Alizarin moved, the better to watch Az.

The Master of Ghosts ignored the sorcerer's pleas for help. With assistance from two companions he removed the forefinger and little finger from each of the man's hands. That would end his gesture magic. Then they punched a hole through his tongue. Through that they threaded a strip of silver, bent and twisted its ends together. There would be no verbal magic, either.

Only then did they bring their captive into the tower.

Nassim said, "I trust you'll be able to wait till he's ready to travel, young Az."

"I can. But you'll need to send a message."

"I'll have the signalmen get started. It'll be a long message. I need to catch those horses, too. And we have bodies to bury."

Nassim Alizarin al-Jebal was pleased. This had been a good day. The Rascal's beard had been well and thoroughly yanked, then twisted. Word would spread amongst the Sha-lug. Some might question continued allegiance to a Marshal who let such schemes be woven around him.

"Bone! Tomorrow you go back to Haeti. Tell our Dainshau friend his bronze chalice is so favored by our congregation that they want to add three more just like it."

Bone sighed. He was too old. But he did not argue. Nor had Nassim thought he would.

Bone was Sha-lug.

## 12. The Connec: Confrontations

The circle had closed. At last. Rook had proven slicker than a barrel of greased snakes, according to one veteran of the interminable campaign to eliminate the last of the Old Gods resurrected by Rudenes Schneidel. Hecht told Clej Sedlakova and Titus Consent, "I'm worn out. And I wasn't here for half the work." He glanced eastward. First light limned the Connecten hills. "There's no way he can slide out again?"

Sedlakova waved his one arm in exasperation. "No! Hell, no. Only, he's managed twice already when I promised he couldn't. So, no,

I won't guarantee anything. He could turn into a flock of crows and fly away. One of his appellations is Prince of Ravens."

"Easy, Colonel. You have nothing to be ashamed of. None of you do." That thing about the crows, though . . . Some of the old Instrumentalities had done stuff like that. Another of Rook's appellations was Lord of Flies. If he turned into a million flies, what hope would there be, ever, of eliminating him?

On the other hand, that would be the ultimate act of desperation by the revenant. What hope would even a god have of pulling a million flies together again, far enough away to be safe? How many would survive? How many would become distracted by carrion, offal, fecal matter, or mating imperatives?

Rook would never become that desperate.

The world lightened. Dawn illuminated the hilltops. Rook and the lesser Instrumentalities attached to him would be shrinking down into the deeps of the valleys, looking for places the light never reached. The sprites and bogies did not interest the Captain-General. He needed to get this one last, stubborn revenant. Then he, and all who were part of this campaign, could go home to their families.

Hecht turned, hoping to see an unusual shadow, or movement in the corner of his eye, to assure him that these events were being observed by the Lord of the Silent Kingdom, Cloven Februaren. The Ninth Unknown. Grandfather of his supposed grandfather. Who had been there in the shadows, making sure all went well, throughout the Connecten Crusade and the campaign on Artecipea.

But the old man never showed. Hecht hoped for the best and feared the worst. He did not want to lose the aid and friendship of that too often sophomoric old man.

Muniero Delari had been training his whole life to step into Cloven Februaren's role. But Hecht was not entirely confident of Delari. The Eleventh Unknown did not have the command of sorcery of the Ninth—despite his reputation as the big bull sorcerer of the Collegium.

"One more hour. We'll have him where we want him," Titus Consent promised. "And when the bang-bang stops, I'm heading for Brothe. I'm going to have Noë making some noise."

Hecht cocked his head and eyed his intelligence chief. It was unlike Titus to be that crude.

Only Sedlakova was in earshot. Consent added, "Been a damned long time, Piper. You got to visit Anna. . . . Noë will probably be knocked up two minutes after I walk in the front door."

Hecht chuckled despite the familiarity. Which was unusual, though

Hecht was godfather to one of Consent's children and had helped sponsor his conversion to the Chaldarean faith.

Sedlakova retailed the punch line to a crude joke. "Me so horny."

"And that's the truth," Consent said. He did things with his arms, overhead and beside himself, that caused movement down where the shadows were creeping out of sight of the rising sun.

Hecht saw others of his senior people on the far ridge, up and ready for action.

Sedlakova said, "Time to tighten the circle." He gestured with his one arm. Consent continued his own signals, using both arms. Movement began, hard to see because of the brush and trees.

A LITTLE WATERFALL DROPPED A MODEST STREAM INTO A COLD, DEEP blue pool. The foliage nearby was especially verdant. The air was cool. The Patriarchal soldiers surrounded the area, high and low, almost shoulder to shoulder. Every falcon the force owned was there, inside the circle. Some of the soldiers carried the smaller man-portable falcons with the one-inch bore, double charged and loaded with iron shot. They were to employ their slow matches only if the Instrumentality survived the falcons.

Sedlakova was now on the side of the stream opposite Hecht. Like Hecht, he was twenty-five feet above the stream leaving the pool. The Brotherhood man waved and pointed at dense growth beside the pool, against the cliff, in a sort of armpit formed by the turn and meeting of the high ground. It would be dark in there all day long.

Kait Rhuk accompanied Hecht. Drago Prosek, senior falconeer, was at the head of the waterfall with Colonel Smolens, tasked to lay the falcons so as to get the most from their fire.

Rhuk grumbled at his crew captains. Never satisfied. But, in an aside, he told Titus Consent, "Lieutenant, when the smoke clears off, I'm jumping into that damned pool. That sure looks good."

Hecht thought so himself. And the thinking was universal. In fact, why wait? The monster wasn't going anywhere. Let the men have a dip, take the tension off.

He found himself rubbing his left wrist. Startled, he looked down. Then looked around. Several men were in the initial stages of undress.

"Rhuk! Consent! With me!" He stepped to the nearest falcon, seized the slow match from the chief gunner. "Lift the back end. I want it pointed right at the middle of the water."

Consent and Rhuk did as instructed. Which both would regret.

As he touched match to primer Hecht saw a face on the surface of the water. It did not last. The falcon bellowed. Consent and Rhuk howled when the recoil threw them back. Silver and iron darts whipped the surface of the pond.

Thunder began a continuous roll as every falcon crew assumed the first blast was the signal to fire.

Godshot shredded the shadows in the natural armpit.

No one could hear. Hecht moved Consent and Rhuk back, examined their wrists while the falcon crew swabbed and reloaded. "Put the shot into the water!" he shouted in the crew captain's ear. "That's where it is!"

The center of the pool rose, a pillar of dark water that took human form. That morphed into a naked woman. An incredibly sensuous woman. Twice life-size.

The Patriarchals were practiced at deicide. Most kept their heads. Lighter weapons began popping. A few falcons shifted aim. Their shot tore the water woman apart.

She did not rise again.

The firing faded. The weapons reloaded. The troops awaited their commander's will.

The Captain-General wished the Ninth Unknown were handy. He did not know how to identify success.

His officers seemed as uncertain as he. "Titus. Can you hear me now?"

"Yes, sir. It's only really bad if you get in front of the falcons."

"You went through this with all the others. How did you know when they were done?"

"You just felt it. You knew. The earth itself seemed overwhelmed by sorrow."

"Meaning we haven't gotten our guy."

"Not fatally. What came up out of the water wasn't Rook. That was some local Instrumentality. Too big for a dryad. Maybe a water horse . . ."

A falcon spoke, someone having seen what he took for movement. In a moment every weapon discharged, mostly into the pit that had been the main target before. With the brush destroyed and the rock laid bare, now, the darts ricocheted, buzzed, and whined off in every direction. A man died and a dozen were wounded before the firing stopped.

Hecht asked, "Do you suppose he's laughing at us? For being so panicky?"

"No," Titus said. "I think he's been hit so many times that he's more scared than we are. He was right down there where we guessed he'd be. Because there was nowhere else for him to be."

"And he didn't fight back. An Instrumentality, a revenant deity, and he didn't fight." Shade had put up a fierce fight. Men had died. And the revenant had left a husk of a corpse that the Patriarchals ground in a mortar and scattered a pinch at a time.

"He was never that strong. And he's been getting cornered and escaping now for more than half a year. Each time we get close we hurt him. This is the end. Stirring the undine, or whatever that was, was his last hope. If we thought it was him we'd killed . . ."

Consent was rattling. Stream of consciousness pouring out his mouth. Hecht had seen it before in men under stress. Had been guilty himself when he was younger.

A soldier yelled. Another did the same. A third called, "Hey, General, there's some guy down there."

Hecht squinted. Sure enough, he saw a bony, pale character in rags who looked like one of the Grolsacher fugitives Count Raymone and his bloodthirsty wife were hunting out of this quarter of the Connec. The man had both hands in the air. He kept bowing.

Hecht asked, "What do you think?"

Consent replied, "I think Rook is still with us."

"Bring him up that gully. Rhuk, I want a whole battery positioned to rip him apart. Have him stop on that piece of white stone. . . ."

Rhuk was frowning and shaking his head. Hecht saw the problem. If the falcons fired while the man was right there shot would ricochet into the troops on the far slope.

"All right. He stops a yard short. The ricochets will mostly hit him."

The man seemed to be waiting for someone to come get him. "It isn't going to happen, fellow," Buhle Smolens called down from the head of the fall. He had a pair of falcons discharged in the man's direction.

Hecht said, "Bonus for Smolens."

A shadow flickered over the ground. "Raven," Kait Rhuk said. "Landed in that big oak behind Sedlakova. Just to the left."

No one knew how much power the revenant had over ravens today. The legendary Prince of Ravens had had a great deal. But the troops were ready.

A skilled crossbowman dropped the bird the moment it stopped moving.

That was the only raven seen, though they flew in mated pairs.

Vultures had begun to circle high above, though.

Moved by gestured orders, the man below waded the stream and started climbing toward Hecht. He was emaciated. Starved. Weak.

There was not one ounce of sympathy amongst the watchers. Grolsacher or Instrumentality in refugee guise, this was no one capable of generating compassion in men who had been in the field for more than half a year. Most wondered why the old man didn't just kill him and be done.

"Stop him. Move a couple falcons to make the point."

Rhuk did as directed.

Across the way, Clej Sedlakova repositioned his falcons to get a better angle of fire into the little shadow left down below. Buhle Smolens had his men drop firebombs, including some from the precious nephron supply.

Rhuk returned from moving the weapons. "He stinks, boss."

"Probably has a religious problem with bathing."

"A bath won't help this smell. Never has since God created the world."

The Instrumentality could not mask the stink of corruption.

"Before you do that," the disguised revenant called, in a strong bass voice, as Hecht started to give the fire command, "a word."

"Quickly."

"A crisis is coming. You'll need all the allies you can muster. Especially across the boundaries of the Night."

Hecht rehearsed what he knew about the Old Gods and crises pending.

He made a hand gesture out of sight of the revenant.

Rook had some power in reserve. It prevented the match men from firing their falcons. All but one.

One was enough. Rook's concentration broke.

The falcons began to bark. Raggedly.

Belatedly.

Rook collapsed into a seething mound of maggots.

Kait Rhuk did not need to be told. Injured wrists and all, he helped tilt a falcon so it could fling its godshot into that mess before many maggots could wriggle away.

Hecht felt the sensation Titus Consent had talked about earlier. An abiding, deep sorrow that an age had come to an end.

Ravens began to gather. Hecht said, "Take iron tools and mash those maggots. Throw coals on them. Do whatever it takes." An Instrumentality as old as Rook must have had several ways of evading ultimate death. The evil always did in old stories.

This one would get no help from Piper Hecht.

Titus Consent said, "You didn't consider his offer."

"It would not have stuck to the bargain. It couldn't have. That was not its nature. It would've turned on us."

Everyone got busy destroying maggots and cleaning up. Hecht sat on a boulder and contemplated the pool. It had changed color. Maybe because of the changing angle of the light. Maybe because of something else.

That water was cold and uninviting now.

Something did not want to be disturbed.

Let it be. It would harm nothing now.

Hecht sensed that it grasped the "Or else" implicit in his clemency.

The men all talked about what they would do now. Everyone assumed there would be downtime. Maybe a lot. They might all be unemployed soon.

Not one man decided to go swimming.

THE PATRIARCHAL ARMY LEFT THE WILDERNESS, HEADED INTO GARRISON in Viscesment. From Viscesment Hecht intended to return to Firaldia, where he expected his force to wither. The Patriarch would start letting soldiers go, now. He had no need for them anymore.

Riders on exhausted horses came hurrying up the old Imperial road beside the Dechear. They caught the army two leagues east of Viscesment. Pickets brought them to the Captain-General. Who picked one out and snapped, "Pella! I told you to stay . . ."

"Dad, the Patriarch sent me! Bellicose himself! He thought I could find you easier than anyone else."

Hecht saved his thoughts, including those about a boy so young being abroad with only four lifeguards in these anxious times. "What is it?"

Pella swelled with pride as he handed off a courier case bearing the Patriarchal seal. Hecht felt some pride himself. So much trust for one so young. Pella had come far since the streets of Sonsa.

The boy said, "It's about Arnhand invading the Connec. In defiance of Krois and the Collegium."

Hecht sent orders for the companies to tighten up, then had the trumpets sound Officers' Call. And kept moving. The soldiers came alert. Something was up. They feared that something was unlikely to be good.

A message from Count Raymone arrived during the officers' meeting. It reported rumors of an Arnhander army headed for Viscesment, to capture the bridges there before invading the Connec. The Count had friends and agents in Salpeno. And Anne of Menand had enemies willing to betray Arnhand if that would burn the whore.

"Gentlemen, it's clear. Anne of Menand has defied the Patriarch. She's sending troops into the Connec to cleanse it of the Maysalean Heresy. Her real motive is probably the same old grab for property and power. There seem to be three armies. One is coming our way. It numbers between two thousand and twenty-eight hundred, the leadership mostly people Anne of Menand would like to be shut of. It should accumulate Grolsachers along the way. The Patriarch wants us to stop these people. We have the numbers and the skills. And these won't be men eager to die for Anne of Menand. So we have to delay our holidays. In the meantime, we need to secure Viscesment and its bridges."

He expected grumbling.

There was a lot of grumbling. The officers reminded the men that while commanded by the Captain-General they had never missed their pay. How many soldiers could say that?

In many armies the leaders considered the opportunity to steal money meant for the men to be one of the perquisites of command.

Titus Consent, possibly the most disgruntled Patriarchal of all, said, "There may be irony at work, here."

"Yes?" Hecht asked.

"It's well known that since Regard took the throne Anne and her Church cronies have taxed Arnhand blind. She must have sent some of that with her crusaders."

Consent launched a long-winded explanation of his reasoning. Hecht listened with half an ear, already worrying how best to carry out his orders while minimizing the suffering of his troops. "What was that?"

"I said if they bring as big a war chest as they'll need to finance a long campaign, we could take enough to keep the troops together."

What next? was on the minds of thousands.

"Maybe, Titus. Maybe. One thing at a time."

The Patriarchal army reached Viscesment with days to spare. The Arnhander crusaders did not want to be in the field. They moved just fast enough to soften the screeches of the Society monks. The force had been raised according to the laws of the feudal levy. Their forty days were rolling away. They might never have to fight if they dithered long enough.

Consent was right about the war chest. The bishops who considered themselves to be in charge intended to keep the army together by taking its men into pay. Once they had completed their feudal obligations, they could not imagine the nobles and knights not being willing, even eager to continue. They would be, after all, doing God's work.

Titus Consent sent agents to meet them. Those assessed the on-

coming troops, took names, estimated individual wealth. Disgruntle-
ment vanished in the face of confidence and the expectation of ran-
soms.

The grumbling changed character. Now the men groused about not
getting a chance at the bigger Arnhander columns out west, where
richer prizes could be taken. Even King Regard, in the field again because that was the only way to escape his terrible mother.

The Captain-General was less sanguine. What was he missing? Why
would Anne send a force so small—even counting on it being reinforced
by essentially useless Grolsachers—against his own veteran force?

Count Raymone Garete and Socia offered an answer that fifth evening, two before the crusaders were expected to slouch into view.
Hecht was entertaining them at a small, private supper.

"You're ignoring faith, Captain-General. You're overlooking the fact
that Anne is so sure her cause is righteous, she can't imagine that the
Church would do anything to stop her. Corrupt as her life may be otherwise, she truly believes she's doing the work of God in this. She *knows,*
beyond *any* doubt, that you'll step aside after a token gesture to maintain
the pretense of honor. I have friends inside Arnhand's councils. The
people most devoted to this crusade absolutely believe that your soldiers
will defect before they risk their souls fighting God's Will. They're also
convinced that you won't resist a chance to finish what you started last
year."

Hecht asked, "Titus. Do you know any of our men who actually
think like that?"

"A few may. Possibly. I haven't run into them. I know some who
say they've let Society spies think they feel that way. Hoping they'll
keep coming to the harvest."

Always there were complications. Problems guessing the true loyalties of various men. Hecht believed he could count on most of his
people. But adding religion to any equation altered its balance unpre-
dictably.

Men would do bizarre things when they thought their immortal
souls were at stake.

"Let's not disabuse them of their illusions. Once Count Raymone
leaves us, and has gotten a good head start, start a rumor that I plan to
arrest him. Count, I've come up with a fairly complicated scheme that
could help us succeed at slight cost."

"I'm all ears."

"As may be these walls. The Anti-Patriarchs had several fine quiet
rooms. I suggest we use the nearest after supper."

*     *     *

ARNHANDER SCOUTS INFORMED THEIR COMMANDERS THAT THE
Captain-General's troops were headed back to Firaldia. A few remained
in Viscesment, getting ready to go chase Count Raymone Garete as soon
as an accommodation with the crusaders had been reached. If they could
not capture the wicked Count they would, at least, cut him off from
Antieux.

"We'll find out how much those people are slaves to their own
wishful thinking," Hecht said. "Titus. Has it been going smoothly?"

Consent was one of few staffers who hadn't been sent to set up
what was coming.

"Like clockwork."

"I worry when things go too well."

"And you worry when they don't. You just plain worry."

"Oh. Yes. I guess I do. And something that's worrying me now is,
I don't see any Deves around anymore. Have we lost them?"

"Yes. I get very little out of the Devedian community anymore.
When I do I'm not sure it's any good."

"Why?"

"They feel badly used in the matter of Krulik and Sneigon."

"*They* feel badly used? *They* do?"

"No point yelling at me. They think they have the right to do whatever they want with their product as long as they fill your needs first.
The constraints imposed after the explosions, and after they were found
out, they consider unreasonable. Outright oppressive, even."

Though inclined, Hecht did not say that he was fully capable of
showing those people some real oppression.

"Where are they building their secret foundries?"

"Sir? Piper?"

"I'm not stupid, Titus. Nor are you naive enough to think they've
accepted the rules we set down. They see a chance to get rich fixing
the rest of us up to kill each other more effectively. It'll take more than
one rebuke for them to get my message."

Consent's eyes narrowed. His face hardened. "Was Krulik and
Sneigon destroyed on purpose?"

"No. But I might've if I'd known what we found out after we got
into their records. I wouldn't lose any sleep, either. The way they were
operating, they would've sold the powder Rudenes Schneidel's thugs
used to attack Anna's house. They don't care how their product is used
as long as it's paid for."

"I do understand. . . . What, Berdak?"

"A gentleman wants to see the Captain-General. He says it's life-

and-death critical. He has plenipotentiary credentials from the Imperial court."

Ferris Renfrow. Or, if not Renfrow, Algres Drear. Which could have dramatically different implications.

"Send him in. Stay, Titus. Unless he asks you to go."

A moment later, "Ah. Renfrow. Not a gentleman after all. How long did it take you to get past all the people who don't want me to find out what's going on in the world?"

"Not so long. I have a golden tongue. People listen when I tell them it's important."

"So, then, tell me."

Renfrow glanced at Consent.

"He'll know in a minute, anyway."

"A quiet room, at least? So the whole world doesn't know in a minute? *Some* people need to be kept in the dark."

"Titus? We have a small room right back there." To Renfrow, "They're all over the Palace. The Anti-Patriarchs were justifiably paranoid."

Titus Consent did not know Ferris Renfrow, other than by reputation. Clearly, he wondered how Hecht knew the man.

Hecht shut the door of a tight little room that had been used to hide female visitors more than to protect conversations.

"Crowded," Renfrow observed.

"The sooner you tell it the sooner we're back out where we can breathe."

"Bellicose is dead. Your old friend Bronte Doneto has arranged to succeed him. That will be decided on the second ballot. A bull forged in the name of the Collegium is on its way. It will direct you to forget Bellicose's orders. You're to place your forces at the disposal of the Arnhander crusaders. This isn't a legal order now. It will become legal once the Interregnum is complete and Doneto takes full control. Tomlin Ergoten will take over from you the day the Interregnum officially ends."

"Who is Tomlin Ergoten? A Brotherhood import? I thought I knew everyone of standing in Firaldia."

"Tomlin Ergoten is a false name meant to protect Pinkus Ghort. Some people are afraid you won't cooperate if you know Ghort is going to replace you."

"Some people being Bronte Doneto?"

"Exactly. The man has a hard-on for you."

"Hang on," Titus Consent said. "An Interregnum. It lasts twenty-six days. When did Bellicose die?"

"About four hours ago." Renfrow's expression dared Consent to pursue that.

Titus knew a waste of time and energy when he met it head-on. Renfrow would not explain. He nodded, left it to his commander to ask questions.

Hecht remained impassive. With an effort.

Where was Cloven Februaren when he could be particularly useful?

There had been no sign of that old man for ages.

"Tomlin Ergoten. Strange name."

"Sounds like a disease," Renfrow said.

"Wonder where they came up with that?" But curiosity was pointless. "How long till the orders get here?"

"You have something in mind?"

"Just a gesture. To leave Bellicose's stamp on the world." The latest Patriarch could not have taken a more controversial reign name. He had wanted the world to know he was one militant bastard about the true mission of the Church.

Renfrow said, "Give me an idea. Maybe I can contribute."

"I can crush the Arnhanders headed this way. Capture most of them. Ransom them. So my men go into unemployment with some prospects."

"It could be made difficult for couriers to get through. But your men don't have to be unemployed. Take them with you."

"With me? Where?"

"Don't be coy, Captain-General. The Empress wants you to lead a crusade to liberate the Holy Lands. A most ironic turn of the wheel. Take the job. The barons will scream but there's a lot of Ferocious Little Hans in Katrin. She'll get what she wants. Once you take the job, you can bring your own people in to help."

Piper Hecht had no desire to lead another crusade.

"I'd say you don't have much choice. You'll get no work in the Patriarchal States. Bronte Doneto must be nursing a huge grudge."

"He knows he can't count on me to be his tool instead of the Church's."

"Sure. That sounds good."

Titus made a growling noise. He was not best pleased by the Imperial.

Hecht asked, "You speaking for the Empress?"

"She hasn't heard the news."

"Let's see where she stands once she has." Hecht signed Consent to silence.

Renfrow bowed slightly, with just a hint of mockery. "Fine, then.

As general information, you could probably get on with Anne of Menand. If her captains show their usual overpowering incompetence."

After another slight bow, Renfrow departed.

"What was that, Piper?" Consent asked.

"Huhm?"

"The man said a lot that he wasn't saying. If you see what I mean."

"He was. My problem is, I'm too literal to understand most of it."

Consent was not convinced. He did not pursue the matter. He knew his way around his boss. He did ask, "Are we on the brink of becoming Imperials?"

"Possibly. We have an army to care for."

"The army is in no grave danger. Only those of us that Bronte Doneto knows he can't tuck in his pocket."

Consent had a point. Several key staffers were Brotherhood of War. If Bronte Doneto had an arrangement with the Brotherhood—which seemed likely—Pinkus would inherit a ready-made staff.

Consent continued, "We ought to consider the implications."

"Meaning?"

"Doneto was all set to jump when Bellicose went down."

"It does seem like. But he can't take full power till the mandated mourning time is over."

"Sure. But I'm thinking, if he had his election rigged, maybe he rigged some other stuff, too. How about a deal with Anne of Menand? As much as any Patriarch, he'll need money. The greedy ones all want to plunder the Connec."

"And Doneto does have an old grudge. I'll send a warning to Count Raymone."

"Good. Meantime, let's get ready for the crusaders. Maybe they've been dawdling because they're waiting for this news."

Hecht did doubt that. The Arnhanders were slow because they did not want to come at all. They were giving forty days a chance to pass without them having to bleed for the Whore of Menand.

"NOTHING ELSE WE CAN DO TO GET READY," COLONEL SMOLENS TOLD his Captain-General. "I don't know if it'll work. There are bound to be locals who sympathize with the Arnhanders."

"If Titus did his job—and hasn't he always?—they'll hear so much conflicting stuff from so many sources that they won't believe anything. Especially not that we might fight with the few people we have left here."

Those responsible for baiting the trap rode out to meet the captains of the crusader force.

"Titus, if you don't have anything pressing? I want to talk falcon manufacture."

That earned looks from several staffers as they returned to their duties. But they shrugged. It was typical of the Captain-General. He would turn to unrelated matters at the most difficult moments.

"YOU WANT TIME OFF?" HECHT ASKED TITUS CONSENT. TITUS looked exhausted. Threads of gray had begun to appear at his temples. He was losing the hair at his crown.

"I do. Of course. But to business. I've got what you wanted to know about iron production."

"Let's be quick. We'll be at war in an hour." He did not recall asking Titus anything about iron.

"Iron is now the metal of choice in falcon production. It stands up better to heavier charges. But it's hard to work. Only Krulik and Sneigon have figured out how to cast and cool it reliably."

"Meaning anyone they want to share the wealth with will find out."

Titus frowned. Though a convert, he still resented stereotyped observations about the Devedian people. "Possibly. But listen. It will take a major operation to manufacture iron falcons in any number."

Hecht seated himself, cleared his mind. "Go ahead."

"The first thing is, wherever they locate, it will have to be forested. With old hardwoods. It's astounding how much oak it takes to make smelting quality charcoal. Then it takes almost two hundred cubic yards of charcoal to smelt out twenty-five pounds of what they call malleable iron. The light iron falcons weigh almost a hundred pounds. Immense amounts of charcoal are consumed all through the process. Which is also labor-intensive. I couldn't get exact figures but the Krulik and Sneigon records suggest hundreds, maybe even thousands, of man hours are needed to make one iron weapon.

"As a labor example, making a simple iron sword, of basic utility and ordinary hardness, using malleable iron already smelted, takes about two thousand pounds of charcoal and up to two hundred hours of smithing."

It never occurred to Hecht to be curious about what it took to create the tools of his profession. "Krulik and Sneigon make swords, too, don't they?"

"They produce a complete range of weaponry. Most of us carry something of theirs. I'm fearing the explosion in Brothe may have been a blessing for them. Their productivity has always been constrained because of their location. They had to bring the iron and charcoal to the manufactory. There are no decent forests anywhere near the Mother City."

"I see. They'll be able to offer better prices, now." He and Titus shared a chuckle. "Or to improve their profit margin."

"Yes." And, as though thinking out loud, Consent said, "Charcoal is also an ingredient in firepowder."

"Yes?"

"Just occurred to me. I've been thinking in terms of regions that have a lot of hardwood near iron deposits. There are a lot of those. But if you add a need to be near sources of chemicals to make firepowder, the possibilities shrink."

"Artecipea. It's the main source of natural saltpeter. There are iron deposits, copper deposits, some low-grade sulfur pits. We saw forests."

"We saw softwood evergreens. But there are hardwoods at lower altitudes, in the east part of the island. And it isn't that far over to the south coast of the Mother Sea. And right there, in what used to be the Imperial province of Pharegonia, are mines that have been producing first-quality sulfur for two thousand years."

"So you think they'll relocate to Artecipea."

"I would. Because Artecipea has one more resource, maybe more important than all the rest."

"Which is?"

"It's outside the Patriarchal States. In territory now beholden to King Peter of Navaya. No Patriarch or Patriarch's Captain-General can tell anyone how to run his business there."

"I see. We'll see. Keep after that. In your copious free time."

"Yeah. I told the quartermasters to round me up a set of brooms so I can sweep up when I don't have anything else to do."

"Believe it or not, Titus, I know how you feel. I'm thinking I might enjoy being unemployed."

"For the first few minutes, maybe."

"Yes."

THE CONSULS OF VISCESMENT HAD TOLD THE APPROACHING CRU-saders that the city would not resist their passage. Pass through, cross the bridges, head off into the Connec, no bad behavior along the way. The crusaders had agreed despite knowing they could not control their Grolsacher hangers-on. Nor even the more fanatic members of the Society for the Suppression of Sacrilege and Heresy, who damned Viscesment for tolerating the Maysalean Heresy.

The consuls did insist that the common soldiers, Grolsachers, and camp followers surrender their weapons to the armorers and quarter-masters during the passage through the city.

The pliable Arnhander nobles acquiesced. The Society churchmen gave the consuls promissory scowls.

The Captain-General lost patience. He sent a message telling the consuls to get on with it.

In the end, the crusaders were granted use of one broad, paved street leading to the Purelice Bridge. The Grave Street. The Purelice Bridge was the broadest and longest of the three Viscesment boasted.

The crusaders found the cross streets all blocked with carts, wagons, and furniture, the barricades backed by local militia. The distrust shown by the locals accentuated an ages-old southern attitude toward the cousin in the north.

The Purelice Bridge, named for the Emperor who ordered it built, humpbacked over the middle of the Dechear to make it easier for traffic to pass under without having to unstep masts. Today, few riverboats or ships depended on sail power.

The bridge was straight. The west end could not be seen from the east end because of the hump. The bridge's west end had been barricaded. Eighteen falcons loaded with pebbles backed those barricades. Buhle Smolens and Kait Rhuk were in charge. They had several companies of archers and spearmen in support.

The rest of the Patriarchal firepowder weaponry was scattered along the Arnhander route of march, hidden, sited by Drago Prosek. The point was to stun the crusaders into surrendering. If they failed to be convinced by the cruel logic of their situation.

Should the falcons be discharged they would generate noise and smoke enough to summon the rest of the Patriarchal force to cut off retreat to the east.

From the bell tower of Sant Wakin's Church—the Anti-Patriarchs' own—the Captain-General could observe both ends of the Purelice Bridge and most of Grave Street. Nowadays, nobody knew why the street was called that. Some locals would not use the name for superstitious reasons. The street filled. First came determined Society types who suffered catcalls and occasional thrown stones as they excoriated the locals for being sinful. Then came the gaily caparisoned nobles who commanded the army, followed by their lances, foot, and train.

"What a lot of clutter," Hecht said. "We aren't that bad on the march, are we, Titus?"

"Not so much. But if you let the men bring their families . . ."

That touched a nerve. That was one way Piper Hecht differed from other captains. He did not allow a lot of noncombatants to form a tail that impaired his mobility.

Despite his efforts, though, the force inevitably developed a drag whenever it remained in place more than a few days.

The leading priests reached the height of the hump in the bridge. And came face-to-face with dread reality.

Hecht said, "I wish I was out there. I should've gone out there."

"Better you're here where you can control everything but Smolens and Rhuk."

"Looks like the priests are yelling for their bishops and archbishops." His breath came faster. He trusted Colonel Smolens. Yet . . . Bishops were clever. One might convince Smolens that . . .

"Smolens will stay the course," Consent said, reading his unease. "Kait Rhuk wouldn't have it any other way."

"I worry about Kait, too. He enjoys his work too much."

"You're never happy about anything, are you?"

"Not so much. Not at moments like this. Oh, damn!"

The falcons had discharged into the churchmen and Society brothers. Smoke rolled up and drifted eastward, concealing the western end of the bridge. By the time the rumble reached him Hecht knew part of the plan had gone south. Flashes shone inside the smoke. Kait Rhuk's falconeers continued to fire.

Below, a wave of consternation ran back along Grave Street. That turned to fright. Fright turned to panic at the speed of rumor.

"Hold off, Prosek," Hecht muttered. "Hold off. Let's don't kill anybody we don't have to."

Consent gave him an odd look, then whispered to a messenger. The messenger dashed off to give that word to Drago Prosek.

The rattle in the distance slackened, then stopped. Smoke continued to conceal the far end of the bridge. Hecht could see only mass confusion as mounted nobles and knights tried to push back east into a street already filled. While below the bell tower calmer crusaders continued to push west.

The panic faded after the falcons fell silent. Attempts to break through the street barricades declined. The militia showed remarkable restraint.

Hecht began to breathe easier. "All right. We killed a bunch of Society priests. That isn't so bad. They weren't going to survive anyway." If Count Raymone had a say.

Firing resumed at the bridge. One salvo. "Fourteen weapons," Hecht said. "That means several are out of service. Unless . . ."

Titus Consent observed, "You do need to take time off."

"Where's Pella?" Continuing to worry. Realizing that he had not seen the boy for two days. Feeling sudden guilt because he had not been giving Pella much of his time.

He did not know how. He had not had a father of his own.

"Tagging around after Kait Rhuk. He's infatuated with the stinks and bangs."

"And Rhuk doesn't mind having him underfoot? With all his life-guards?"

"Knowing Rhuk, Pella is getting his tail worked off. His lifeguards, too."

"Speak of the Adversary."

Madouc had invited himself into the belfry. He had not been seen much lately. "A messenger from the consuls, sir. They want to know if they can begin accepting surrenders."

"Remind them that the Arnhanders are ours. Otherwise, yes. Let's move on. I want to get home as much as any of you." After Madouc ducked out, Hecht asked, "Does it seem like he's changed?"

"Absolutely."

"How? Why?"

"He's not doing his job for you, now. He's doing it because the Brotherhood wants him to."

Hecht grunted. Kait Rhuk was raising hell on the west bank again. Why? He wasn't being attacked. Why waste valuable firepowder when a handful of fanatic churchmen could be brought down by archers and crossbowmen?

"I messed up with Madouc, didn't I?"

"Yes. But that was bound to happen, you two being who you are. And it isn't a dead loss. He still respects you. Make sure to show your respect for him."

"What the hell is Rhuk up to?"

"A demonstration, I'm sure. That's just one falcon, now. Talking slow."

"Ah. Right. I got it. He's probably letting Pella play. Using Society brothers for targets." He saw dust from far beyond the bridgehead. That should be Count Raymone.

THE MAIN HALL OF THE PALACE OF KINGS WAS FILLED. THE MAGNATES of Viscesment, the Captain-General's own champions, Bernardin Am-berchelle and Count Raymone's lady, Socia, and the greats who rode with them, and the leaders of the defeated crusaders, all were gathered. Some in despair, most in high spirits. No invader churchmen were present. The few survivors had been claimed by Bernardin Amberchelle. The Captain-General had given them over, bishops and all. The Connectens could ransom them. Or not.

Titus Consent brought Madouc to the high table. Seating him to the Captain-General's left. "His report is ready."

"Ah. Good," in a soft voice. "Madouc?"

"Seventeen dead priests, sir. And more than a hundred wounded. Including two bishops, one of whom won't survive. A stone opened his gut."

"It could have been worse, all the firing Rhuk did."

"Showing off." Disapproving. "Just two Arnhander knights were wounded. Back up the column, there were minor injuries among the foot, taken trying to escape. And one man dead. From a fall. He landed on his head."

"That's good. The consuls will get a lot of labor out of the prisoners. So. The treasure? And the Grolsachers?"

"The treasure is secure. It's not as big as you hoped. The bishops expected plunder would cover their expenses starting around fifty days into the taken into pay period. And the news isn't good for the people of Grolsach. Again."

"Is there anyone left up there?"

"There'll be less competition for resources now."

Hard but true. Count Raymone and his band had gone north to cross the Dechear and get into position to intercept the fleeing Grolsachers. Raymone meant to stop those people coming to the Connec—if he had to exterminate their entire nation.

His attitude toward Arnhand was no less fierce.

"Madouc, have you made any plans?"

"Sir?" Sounding honestly puzzled.

"We're near the end of our run. Bellicose's health is fragile . . ."

"Bellicose is dead. Sir. That may not be common knowledge but it isn't a secret anymore."

Hecht reflected briefly, scanning the crowd. Typically, knights from both sides were catching up with relatives on the other. The Arnhanders were relieved about not having to feed Anne of Menand's ambitions.

"All right. My question stands. And becomes more pertinent."

"I'm a Brother of a holy order. I'll do what my superiors tell me."

"As will we all, of course. I hope they reward you well. Though I always felt fenced in, you did an amazing job."

"Thank you, sir." With no great warmth.

He had lost Madouc for sure. He had wasted the honor of seating the man so close.

Madouc yielded just the slightest. "I'm hoping for a command in the Holy Lands. Addam Hauf sounded positive when I spoke to him. When we were in Brothe."

"Perhaps we'll meet again overseas."

"Sir?"

"Not really. I'm done crusading. I'm thinking about buying a rural tract somewhere and retiring. Spend my last days with Anna, making wine for Colonel Ghort."

Madouc did not react to the mention of Pinkus Ghort. He had no feelings on the matter. Or lacked knowledge.

Hecht said, "When we're done here I want a private word with the Viscount Dumaine."

"Yes sir."

For the remainder of the evening Hecht mostly observed. Keeping an eye on Pella, in particular.

Anna had gotten a few social skills to stick.

MADOUC REMAINED IN THE QUIET ROOM WHILE THE CAPTAIN-General saw the Viscount. It was the largest quiet room in the Palace of Kings but not so big that the chief bodyguard had to strain to eavesdrop. Madouc was less inclined to avoid the Captain-General lately.

"How can I help you?" the Viscount asked. Politely, conscious of being a prisoner but unwilling to stifle his pride of class completely.

"Sit. Share coffee with me. And tell me about Vali Dumaine."

The Viscount did the first two, not concealing his delight at being offered the rare and precious drink. But he thought some before doing the third. "Vali Dumaine is my sister. She's Countess of Bleus. Why do you ask?"

"To find out. What you just said is a variation on what I've already heard. I thought she was your wife. I didn't understand why your wife would be Countess of Bleus while you were Viscount of . . . what is it?"

"Klose. You can throw a rock across it. Once I've been ransomed it'll belong to someone else. I'll have to go live with my sister. Or join the Brotherhood. You haven't told me why you're asking."

"I haven't." The Captain-General let that lie there. "Do you have any connection with Sonsa?"

"I? None. My father traveled on a Sonsan ship when he went on crusade. Him and his three brothers. He was the one who came home. The one who inherited even though he was the third son."

"The Holy Lands are a harsh mistress. They devour all who come there. Are you involved with the Special Office? The Witchfinders in particular?"

"No. We don't see that kind back home. There used to be a Brotherhood chapter house outside Salpeno. You'd see a few of them in the city. But they pulled out before Charlve the Dim died. Cherault, one of Anne's clever villains, had a scheme for confiscating their assets. They found out. They left with all their wealth. Cherault contracted a wasting disease. It causes him a lot of pain. He'll be a long time dying."

"Are the two connected?"

Madouc was very attentive. And contemplative.

"Unfortunately, the world doesn't work that mechanically. Bad people don't get what they've got coming. And good people die young."

"And all we can do is trust that it's part of God's plan. Yes. You have children? On either side of the blanket?"

The Viscount glowered. "I insist on knowing what this is about."

"Sit. Viscount. You don't insist on anything. I'm a lowlife hiresword with no noble blood and no honor, even if I do command the Patriarch's armies and embarrass his enemies regularly. How can you count on a man like that not to drop you off a bridge, or have you strangled and burned to deny your hope of resurrection? Or any of the other wicked things a man like me might do?"

"You'd lose your ransom."

"Hardly a problem. The Count of Antieux will buy all the Arnhander prisoners I'm willing to wholesale. He wants to send their pickled heads to your sweet King Anne. Or he could sell them into slavery across the Mother Sea. He talks about that when he's feeling particularly vengeful."

Viscount Dumaine had turned pale. But he did not disgrace himself.

"He's a mad dog, Count Raymone. If you Arnhanders insist on plundering the Connec, Raymone will make you pay in barrels of blood. But I don't want to talk about that. I'm interested in a girl child named Vali Dumaine. About thirteen. Possibly younger. Found as a captive in a Sonsan brothel. She claimed she was being used as leverage to force her father to do something. Everyone who can answer to the truth or falsehood of the claim is dead. I look into it when I get the chance. This was a chance. You and your sister are the only Dumaines I've ever identified."

"I can't solve your mystery. Sorry."

Hecht wished the Ninth Unknown was making a nuisance of himself, still. He could help with this. The Viscount was being truthful, in the main, but something not quite right was happening, too.

Might be interesting to have him stripped, to see if he didn't have some little hidden tattoo.

Hecht asked, "You haven't gone on crusade? Never been to the Holy Lands yourself?"

Dumaine eyed him several seconds before making a decision. "I went with my father." That would be a matter of record, hard to hide. "I was a child. Eight when we left. Twelve when we came home. I pray God never again requires my presence in the east. Hell can't be worse than the Holy Lands in summer. Or winter. Or any season in between."

Hecht nodded. Some westerners felt that way. Others liked the Holy Lands well enough to stay. There were generations of crusaders, now, who had been born in the east and who offended their western cousins by having adopted local clothing and customs.

"I felt the same about Firaldia when I first came down. The summers were too hot and they never seemed to end. And snow was a rare treat instead of the natural state of the world."

"I hear that's changing."

"It is. Definitely. People in the Chiaro Palace have been tracking the changes. They're dramatic. With worse to come."

Once Dumaine left, Hecht brought in Titus Consent. "There's something not right about that man. Keep an eye on him. Have him be the last we let go home. Have you seen Bechter?"

Sergeant Bechter had been scarce of late.

"He's still sick. They say he tries to get up and come in every day. Most mornings his body won't cooperate. He's old."

"I miss having him underfoot."

"If he could, he'd be there."

"Is he getting good care?"

"He should be shipped back to the Castella. Let him live out his last years with his brothers."

"He asked? You haven't sent him?"

"I've asked him. He wants to stay here. Says this is where he belongs, now."

"The old coot is too stubborn for his own good."

"Lot of that going on around the heart of this army."

Hecht refused the bait. "You checked up on Pella?"

"He's having the time of his life. He's decided that firepowder artillery will be his career. Rhuk says he has interesting ideas."

"That'll change. I just want to know that he's all right. Don't want to fuss in his life like I'm his mother."

"He's fine, Piper. But, really, he could use a little more interference in his life. He's too raw for the independence you give him."

Anna would agree. "All right. Create a training program for falconeers. Put him in. Keep him close and busy." That should sound good to the boy. And needed only last till Bronte Doneto fully assumed the Patriarchal throne.

Hecht asked, "What future do you see for your boys, Titus?"

"These days, maybe the priesthood."

"Security."

"Yeah. Only, I'm afraid the opportunity won't be there when they're old enough. The monasteries are full of freeloaders now."

Titus might be pulling his leg. It was hard to tell. "There're always careers in military staff work."

"But how many? Assuming I'd let my sons get into this insanity?"

Hecht frowned.

"You still don't realize what you've done, do you?"

Hecht felt, too frequently, that he had no idea. He raised an eyebrow in invitation.

"There hasn't been anything like the Patriarchal force since the Old Empire. Not in the west. In the Eastern Empire they have professional soldiers, enlisted and officers alike. Here, since the fall, there's been no need. We mainly fight our neighbors, on the smallest scale. And a fear of standing forces, plus contempt for mercenaries, is the standard. The warrior class is especially hard on men who fight for pay. Except when they go into pay after their forty days themselves. But they'd argue that that's a different animal."

Why did Titus want to remind him of the obvious? Oh. Because he really was changing the shape of thought about professional soldiery.

Titus went on, "All of which is about to be undone."

"Indeed?"

"Pinkus Ghort isn't Piper Hecht."

"Piper Hecht won't be out of work."

"So you'll sign on with the Grail Empress."

"I don't see any alternative." Whenever he considered retirement, as he threatened so often, a disappointed Helspeth Ege wormed into his thoughts and, like a song getting stuck, would not go away. "For a while. But don't count on me actually invading the Holy Lands."

"How would Noë and the boys fit in Alten Weinberg?"

"I don't know. It's cosmopolitan. People from all over the Empire live there. I didn't see much prejudice. But it's bound to exist." And in some minds Titus would always be a Deve, whatever religion he pursued. "I hear so much about the Holy Lands from pilgrims and returned crusaders, I *know* I don't want to go there."

Titus gave him an odd look but kept his thoughts to himself. He was fully invested in Piper Hecht's imaginary past. If Piper Hecht fell, Titus Consent would follow.

Madouc stuck his head into the room. "Can I interrupt, Captain-General?"

"Of course. What is it?"

"It's Bechter, sir. The healing brothers say he's slipping. They don't understand why. He should be recovering. I thought you'd want to know."

"Yes. Is it . . . ? Do they think it could go fatal?"

"Very likely. And it might not be long."

"Titus, I have to go." He felt the sorrow rising. Another way the west had infected his soul. He had become a servant to his emotions.

Consent asked, "Can I tag along? Bechter has been a force in my life, too. Almost a father since I converted."

Hecht was surprised. He had not noticed. But it could be. He did not pay close enough attention to the lives of those around him.

Madouc waited outside. He explained, "Now would be when a villain might think we were relaxing."

Hecht took the point. "Of course. Lead on."

The Patriarchals had complete control of the Palace of Kings. A hospital had been established there. It served the troops principally, but aided poor locals where it could, in the name of Bellicose. That paid dividends. Titus Consent kept in touch with the nuns and healing brothers, who were not shy about passing on useful information.

Redfearn Bechter was the sole tenant of a room featuring pallets for four. A healing priest sat with the old soldier, no longer trying to battle Bechter's illness.

The room stank.

The Captain-General met the priest's eye. Who shook his head sadly.

Bechter heard them enter. He cracked one eyelid, recognized the visitors. He struggled to lift himself.

The healing priest pushed him back.

Hecht knelt beside the old man. Took his hot, dry, fragile hand. Could think of nothing to say. He could remember only a sutra from The Written about finding love for one's enemies. Redfearn Bechter was that most cruel of foes, a soldier of the Brotherhood of War. And the Sha-lug Else Tage, having transmogrified into the Patriarchal champion Piper Hecht, had grown to care for the man.

Bechter said nothing, either.

Hecht considered some banter about shirking, about hurrying up and getting back to work, but Bechter knew. The end was at hand. So the Captain-General said, "I have one last task for you, Sergeant. I want you to deliver a message when you stand before the Divine. Ask Him to show me His Design. Ask Him to still the turmoil in my heart by granting me a clear vision of His Will."

Bechter did not speak. He could not. But he managed a slight inclination of his head. He had heard and would comply.

Hecht ignored his other duties till the end came. And that was not long delayed. The healing priest reported, "He was running on sheer willpower. He was determined not to pass over without making his farewells to those he loved."

That idea startled Hecht. Redfearn Bechter had been the consummate Brotherhood warrior. He should have loved nothing but his own secret creed.

NEWS OF BECHTER'S PASSING, AND THE CIRCUMSTANCES THEREOF, swept through the army.

One uncalculated gesture won the Captain-General an even fiercer loyalty. None of the soldiers had ever heard of a high officer entrusting a trooper to carry a message to God Himself.

Hecht said little when he heard, other than to express bewilderment to Titus Consent.

Bechter's latest assistant, Vladech Gerzina, onetime bodyguard, turned up asking for a minute of the Captain-General's time. Hecht had no cause to refuse.

Gerzina carried a teakwood chest two feet long, fourteen inches wide, and nine inches deep, with an arching, hinged top. The old wood was almost black. The corners and edges of the chest were protected by fittings of brass. "Sergeant Bechter asked me to bring you his personal things, sir."

Hecht could think of nothing appropriate to say. "Personal things?" Members of the Brotherhood were not supposed to accumulate personal things.

"Memorabilia, perhaps? Bechter was in his seventies. We think." Gerzina was Brotherhood. He was not dismayed by Bechter's bit of worldliness. "We all pick up souvenirs to remind us of key moments. Don't we, sir?"

"Yes. I suppose." Hecht still carried one small white pebble, twice the size of a chickpea, that had been in the load of the falcon he had discharged in Esther's Wood. It connected him to the most critical moment of his life. No one else would know what that pebble meant.

Gerzina set the chest on a bench the lifeguards used when they kept watch on some dubious visitor. "I have to get back to work, sir. I'm behind because of the emotional distraction."

"What's in the box?"

"I don't know, sir."

"It doesn't appear to be locked."

"It isn't my place to look."

Hecht considered the man closely for the first time.

Physically, Vladech Gerzina was nondescript. Average height, neither good-looking nor ugly, his colorings unremarkable. He was a few pounds overweight, which was unusual in a soldier.

A walking illusion. A man with a big don't-notice-me spell on.

Maybe.

Gerzina's body language shifted suddenly.

He didn't like being noticed.

"Can you do Bechter's job?"

"Sir?"

"I don't believe I mumbled."

"Yes, sir. I've been doing it. All of it. I don't know how he managed, at his age."

"He had an assistant. You're the man, now. Officially. At least till the new commander comes in."

"No, sir. Begging your mercy, sir. I have to decline. And, no sir, it's not because it's too much work. It's a cush job." He patted his belly. "Enough to eat and warm in the winter. And not one heathen Praman in sight. But a time of change is on us. Sir. Those sworn to the Brotherhood have to leave you. Or the man who replaces you."

"Oh?"

"There's been word from Addam Hauf. The Master of the Commandery will send reinforcements to the Holy Lands. Men, material, and money. Which he's having some success gathering since the Patriarch doesn't have to use all his resources to stave off predatory Emperors."

"I see." And, though Hecht had not considered it before, he did.

Katrin's peace had eased life dramatically for the Patriarchs. Bronte Doneto would see no need to consult Imperial ambitions at all.

"I'd better get everybody together and see who needs to be replaced. Help with that. Before you go."

"Yes, sir. It won't be right away. Sir."

Alone again, Hecht sat down with Bechter's chest.

He had worked up an expectation of something dramatic. Reality proved disappointing. Memorabilia, indeed. Bits of cord. Several stones. A small dagger rendered useless by means of having had an inch of its business end broken off. Several iron arrowheads of Lucidian design. Assuming Bechter followed Brotherhood custom, those had been removed from his own flesh. Then several scraps of paper, one crumbling, one in an unreadable hand, another a pass to be shown while traveling on Brotherhood business. A locket with a bit of brittle hair inside,

uncharacteristic for a warrior-priest. Several small wooden boxes, beautifully made, all but one unlocked. One contained a perfectly preserved
moth with a wingspan over four inches. Hecht had never seen its like.
But he understood that it must have been beautiful when it was alive.
And, in death, had been treasured by a man Hecht could not help but
honor.

He opened two boxes that contained nothing, then one wherein lay
a shredding little cotton sack containing several dozen copper coins
from almost as many polities, forming a metal log of Redfearn Bechter's
journeys.

This was a life. Seventy years, plus.

Why had the man wanted him to have this?

As a message? A warning?

"Vanity of vanities. All is . . ."

There was still the box that was locked. The key was there in the
mix with the copper coins, itself brass and as green as any of the money.
Hidden in plain sight, perhaps without much concern.

The box contained a thin, bound book, its leather cover at once
stained, worn, and grown brittle. Hecht opened it carefully.

The first page was done in artful calligraphy, in a language Hecht
could not immediately identify. Till he suffered an epiphany: He was
looking at Melhaic written down using the Brothen alphabet. Melhaic
was the ancient language of the Holy Lands. He could read that clumsily.
In its native characters Melhaic was inscribed across the page in a direction opposite that customary for most of the languages of the region.

He had just discovered that the book was a history recorded by
Grade Drocker when Pella burst in, so startling him that he jumped.

"Dad? Pinkus Ghort is downstairs."

"Pella. What're you doing here?"

"I thought you'd be kind of down. Because of Sergeant Bechter. So
I thought I'd see if I could do anything. I ran into Colonel Ghort in the
street."

How the devil had Ghort gotten here so fast? What was Bronte
Doneto up to? The news about Bellicose was not yet general knowledge. The Interregnum had weeks to run.

"You're right. I am in a bleak mood. Here's how you can cheer me
up. Get your butt on back home and get into school. Make something
of yourself. So you don't end up like Sergeant Bechter. Like I might end
up any day."

"Whew! It does have its claws in you."

"It does. Bring Ghort. Tell Cederig I want some of the red wine I've
been saving. Might as well get Pinkus started on it. Save the trouble of

hauling it to Brothe and back." And a few cups might loosen Ghort's tongue.

"DAMN, MAN!" GHORT SAID AS SOON AS HE WALKED IN. "YOU LOOK like shit on a stick. You need to get more sleep."

"Put the wine on the desk, Cederig. And stand by. Pinkus, I'll be getting all the rest I can stand starting real soon."

"You know what's up."

"Of course I do."

"Consent's still got eyes in Brothe."

"That, too. More importantly, several Principatés aren't happy about Doneto taking over. Some hoped I would overrule the election."

"Care to name names?"

"I don't think so."

"What do you think?"

"I'm not some old-time legionary commander who wants to control who gets to be the next Emperor."

"Yeah. The boss figured you'd see it that way. I meant, what's your opinion? About Doneto."

"He's the best man available. But I wish he wasn't nuts about the Connec."

"Yeah. I don't know for sure but I got a notion your Count Raymone won't get no joy out of him."

"Raymone will have plans in place. Doneto should let the old grievances go. He's supposed to be everybody's Patriarch."

"Told him that myself. I don't think he was listening. Hey. Pipe. No hard feelings?" Ghort was well into his first bottle. He had begun to slur.

"No reason. You didn't fire me. Actually, I might've quit if I hadn't been fired. I've had about all of this that I can stand. I couldn't work for a busybody like him. I want a boss who tells me what he wants, then gets out of the way and lets me do it."

"That scares the busybodies. Makes them afraid they might get run over themselves."

Hecht understood that. He had dealt with it most of his adult life. It was the reason he had been sent west. Gordimer was afraid of getting trampled. "The problem is, those men see the world in the mirror of themselves."

"Huh?"

"They're scared because they know what they'd do in my place. Which means that they start from a different notion of honor."

"Gotcha. But, hey, Pipe, you can't never claim you don't pull a slick once in a while your own self. Damn, this grape juice is fine."

"Me? A fast one?"

"I ain't as dumb as I look. You knew the change was coming. You jumped in on them crusaders anyways."

"I did. Yes." Hecht grinned.

"Doneto ain't gonna like that."

"What's he going to do? Fire me?"

"That's rich. I don't know. He can be a vindictive prick. Like what he figures on doing to Count Raymone and Antieux."

"Which would be?"

"I don't know, Pipe. Not yet. But I ain't gonna be nowhere near that berg when it happens. I don't want to be remembered for what I'm scared is gonna happen."

"In that case, I regret being so effective against the revenants."

"Thanks, buddy. That's all I need. Them goddamned spook demons traipsin' round behind me, kicking my ass every time I bend over."

"It would keep you humble."

"This stuff right here keeps me from gettin' bigger than myself." Ghort took a long draw of wine, stared at his feet for a dozen seconds. "An' I keep wonderin' how long it'll be before he fires me."

"Look at it this way. Who could possibly replace Pinkus Ghort?"

"A good question, Pipe. A fine question. But you gotta remember, Doneto has got some huge blind spots. That might be one of them."

"When do you plan to take charge?"

"Officially? When the Interregnum is up. If you want to work it that way. Otherwise, anytime after my core staff gets here."

"You going to fire my guys, too?"

"Have to. Most of them. What I was told. I figure they wouldn't stay on, no how. The Brotherhood ones is all gonna report back to the Castella. That Addam Hauf is a ball of fire. The rest are loyal to you. According to Doneto. My first job will be to vet all the officers, to see which ones need to go and which ones are loyal to the Church or their pay."

"Too bad. This was an effective force. It won't be anymore."

Ghort shrugged. "Way of the world, Pipe. Sad way of the world. I need a place to lie down. This shit was just too damned good." He put the wine bottle aside. Empty.

THE CAPTAIN-GENERAL DID WHAT HE COULD TO HAMSTRING A NEW crusade against the Connec. Falcons disappeared. Firepowder, likewise.

Titus Consent's records, and those of the quartermasters, turned sloppy, incomplete, and confused. Hecht suffered considerable guilt. Which he handled by telling himself Pinkus Ghort would still get paid. He would just have to work harder to start making the Connec miserable.

Most of the soldiers did seem inclined to stick. Few were pleased but an income was an income. There were a dozen refugees willing to replace any veteran afflicted with excessive scruples. The staff, though, did have theirs. Hecht had trouble keeping them in place till the day of the changeover.

Hecht overheard one staffer tell Ghort that his departure was not personal. Another insisted he had no problem with the new Captain-General, just with the villain behind him. Hecht passed the word that they might want to feel a little less free to speak their minds.

Bronte Doneto was less popular with the soldiers than Hecht had expected. They recalled Doneto's behavior during the Connecten Crusade.

Hecht's last official act was the release of the Viscount Dumaine and other remaining Arnhander captives. Those who had not yet been ransomed would send the money themselves. Their honor demanded that they not renege.

The change of command was no drama. Hecht shook Ghort's hand and went away, leaving the new commander frazzled and dismayed.

"What do we do now, Dad?" Pella wanted to know. He had begun to stick close. He was not welcome among Pinkus Ghort's artillerists.

"Go home. Settle in with your mother. Loaf." Those who would make the journey to Brothe were gathering. The company seemed curiously small. Hecht needed a moment to work out why.

There was no Madouc. Nor any of Pella's constant companions. There were no bodyguards at all.

For all that he had resented Madouc every moment that he was underfoot, Hecht found himself feeling naked now. And constantly uneasy.


## 13. In the Frozen Steppe with the Talking Dead

The Chosen of the central steppe and northern waste assembled. They would crush the enemy of their god. Defiant Tsistimed had come far enough into the cold that the Windwalker himself could join in.

The Chosen, whipped on by a dozen fierce copies of Krepnight, the Elect, probed and retreated, probed and retreated, drawing Tsistimed and his sons deeper into the realm of winter. The Chosen neither knew nor cared what was happening among their enemies. They did as they were told.

The warlords of the Hu'n-tai At recognized the enemy strategy. They used it themselves. It was as old as men riding horses. They did not care. The Chosen would not retreat forever. When they turned they would be obliterated.

No army survived the Hu'n-tai At.

The ground chosen by the Windwalker was wild and stony, a vast sprawl of sharp-edged, tumbled basalt. Harsh mountains rose within a mile, to either hand. Ice rimed most of the stone. Ice and snow masked the brownish gray rock of the mountains. This was not a place where horsemen would enjoy an advantage. The Krepnights, the Elect, should prosper there.

Tsistimed dismounted his warriors and sent them to hunt. He accepted the disadvantages of the ground. This enemy did not know what he had chosen to fight. The Hu'n-tai At were not just the fiercest warriors alive, they boasted the most skilled and ruthless warrior-sorcerers as well.

The warlord of the Hu'n-tai At, in turn, did not understand that one of the oldest, cruelest, darkest Instrumentalities would stalk the battleground himself. These days the gods did not meddle personally.

Tsistimed learned too late.

The collective power of the Hu'n-tai At sorcerers bothered the Windwalker no more than a circling bat annoyed a traveler hurrying home at dusk.

The slaughter was epic. For the Hu'n-tai At it was like nothing they had ever known. They faced an enemy more stubborn and fearless than themselves, though of little skill and limited endurance. Most were on the edge of starvation.

Tsistimed gathered his sons and generals. The Windwalker was a pillar of darkness drifting about, squirting lightning. The warlord admitted, "We cannot destroy that thing."

A leading sorcerer observed, "We can destroy those who serve it. Even those tiger-skinned monsters do fall. Eight have been overcome already."

The warlord nodded but did not agree. In the fog of war those at the tip of the spear always imagined successes greater than what had been achieved. Sure enough, soon enough, reports had the tide of fighting turning ever less joyful. The monsters were hunting down the power users among the Hu'n-tai At. And the Instrumentality was developing a taste for destroying life himself.

One of Tsistimed's sons suggested, "Perhaps we should go collect another army. There'll be few enemies left when this is done."

Tsistimed considered the indeterminate darkness that seemed about to hand him his first defeat ever. Even in early life, when wrestling other boys, he had never been less than completely victorious. His very soul shrieked, go forward! Compel that thing to his will! But he had not become Emperor of all Men by letting his ego lead him into choices unsuitable to a longer view.

A general observed, "If we choose to go raise another army we ought to do so soon. The god has noticed us."

The tower of darkness was miles away but had stopped. The warlords sensed it feeling the world around it, trying to locate them. They were hidden by the most potent sorceries available, but this thing . . .

Something happened.

Something changed.

The Instrumentality coalesced. It hardened. It took shape. That shape seemed indecisive, though. One moment it resembled a man two hundred feet tall but far too squat and wide, the next it was a toad on its hind legs. Then it became something very wide, with vast wings of shadow. Color could not be discerned.

A great tongue darted down, pulled back with a struggling man whose allegiance could not be determined at that distance. The Instrumentality's eyes fixed on the mound where the lords of the Hu'n-tai At had gathered. But maybe they did not see. For the god seemed distracted. Its tongue acted again, without apparent conscious direction, as the Instrumentality fed absentmindedly.

It rose from its toad slouch into its tallest manshape, turned, leaned westward. Tsistimed sensed an immediate change in the flow of battle. The Chosen were no longer getting help from their grim patron.

The Instrumentality leaned a little farther, took a tentative step. It sniffed the air. Then it loosed a great groaning excited rumble, shook all over, and began walking, the battle forgotten. It headed west.

Cries of despair rose from the jungle of shattered stone, the Chosen bewailing their abandonment.

They fought. The many-fingered monsters fought. Mourning would blanket the continent. Never had so many Hu'n-tai At fallen in one battle. Never had so many fallen in one generation.

Kharoulke the Windwalker strode steadily westward.

# 14. The Lucidian Frontier: Skirmishes

Nassim Alizarin's raiders never neared Gherig closer than two miles. They engaged the crusaders only when there was no alternative. They intercepted couriers. They forced caravans to choose more difficult routes. And they made mock of Black Rogert. The strategy was transparent. And warmed the heart of Indala al-Sul Halaladin in far Shamramdi.

Young Az had brought several hundred warriors to support the Mountain's efforts. The boy had firm instructions about bowing to the wisdom of the veteran. Indala remembered Nassim Alizarin as an enemy. He considered the Mountain his equal. Nassim's Sha-lug had routed a larger force of Lucidians, long ago, during one of the periodic collisions between Lucidia and Dreanger. Only one other could claim to have bested Indala on the battlefield: Gordimer the Lion.

The boy showed his character. He accepted his relative's directives. He did tell Nassim, "It grates. If I were any of my brothers or cousins, I'd ignore Indala. They do, too often, despite his having shown no reluctance to discipline his own blood."

Nassim thought about his murdered son. Hagid would be about this age. Without as much promise. "You remind me too much of my son. I'll probably be too soft to teach you what you need to learn."

Old general and youth were astride horses, in the shadow of a rock spire in the dun badlands, observing Gherig. Smoke signals were rising there. No knowing what that meant. But they suggested a season to be wary.

Rogert du Tancret might be angry enough to move against Tel Moussa.

Young Az asked, "Were you too soft with your son?"

"Possibly the opposite. He was desperate to prove himself. That got him killed." Nassim did not share the details. He would not, other than to reiterate his indictments of Gordimer and the sorcerer er-Rashal. He did not want to explain why the boy had gone to Brothe.

Captain Tage could not possibly maintain his charade indefinitely. But he would not be betrayed by the Mountain. Nassim Alizarin owed that man a debt of honor. He could repay it no other way.

He grumbled, "It's a complicated world."

"Certainly one where few men see past the sunset."

"Eh?"

"Nobody thinks beyond the moment. Especially those who serve God. They just don't get the concept of consequences."

Nassim grunted. That was true, though more characteristic of Lucidia than Dreanger. The kaifate of Qasr al-Zed was, before all else, tribal. The kaifate of al-Minphet was more unified, with the Sha-lug there to enforce the will of the Marshal and Kaif.

He supposed the western kaifate was more like the Lucidian than the Dreangerean. A continuous dance of changing tribal alliances, a game that had begun millennia before the Praman Conquest.

Nassim asked, "Are the eastern tribes still being difficult?"

"Absolutely. You'd think they're convinced that Tsistimed has gone for good."

"If Indala can't hold the kaifate together, then it can't be done. His passing will bring on a long, dark age of chaos."

The boy seemed slightly miffed.

Nassim amended his observation. "Somewhere among the young there could be one with the character and will of an Indala. But there isn't among his contemporaries. His brother and uncle and cousins are talented but they aren't Indala. They're the kind of men who make an Indala great. They execute the Will but they aren't the Will itself."

The youth considered that. He responded with a nod. "I'm here to learn."

The general had the boy working with old Az, Bone, and that band. He would be in the middle of everything. He would find out what it meant to be the hand on the spear.

The boy said, "There's a big group coming out of Gherig."

Right. Light cavalry first, with infantry behind. Then heavy horsemen. Crusader knights. Nassim wondered what they planned.

Young Az suggested, "Maybe you've stung Rogert so much he has to make a demonstration in order to feel better."

That was in keeping with the man's reputation. "A pity we can't lead him on, into waterless wastes, the way Indala did."

"Is even Rogert stupid enough to let that happen again?"

"He is. But those around him would rein him in." Nassim chuckled. "For which God be thanked. I can't imagine how awful he'd be on his own."

Wagons and camels emerged from Gherig. The column turned eastward. Gisela Frakier rode ahead, scouting and screening.

Young Az guessed, "They're going to besiege Tel Moussa."

"I expect. Not even Rogert du Tancret would dare go farther than that. We should get back." Nassim was sure that other, younger observers were ahead of him with the news. "A pity there's no army to cut them off once they settle in." Nassim chuckled again. Rogert du Tancret would try to starve Tel Moussa into yielding. Even fools would not storm the tower without the assistance of some severe Instrumentality of the Night. Every topographical advantage lay with the defenders. Only the lack of a natural source of water served the besieger.

"That smoke concerns me," Alizarin said. "It must be meant to let somebody know that this has started."

"Other Gisela Frakier. Tribal allies. No one else. . . ."

"They aren't enough in awe of Indala to refrain from dealing with Rogert?"

"Some don't think that big. The al-Yamehni, for example, might consider an alliance with a strong crusader more attractive than their present role protecting the flanks of their ancient enemies, the al-Cedrah and the al-Hasseinni."

The crusaders had been manipulating tribal hatreds since their advent in the Holy Lands. Never numerous, they had to make politics a strength. Fractious tribes with timeless squabbles made manipulation easy.

Neither the old fox nor the young lion could make out which tribe had chosen to aid Black Rogert. But they were quick and efficient. They streaked toward Tel Moussa, quickly threw a loose screen around it. Nassim and the boy did not get back ahead of them.

Others would be in the same straits.

Black Rogert's move was an obvious one. So were the likely results. There was a plan in place.

There was a spring in the hills north of the Shamramdi road. Those caught outside the tower would assemble there. Or nearby, if the enemy knew about the spring and chose to deny it.

Late afternoon saw Nassim and young Az watering their mounts. The Mountain took the reports of those already gathered, then others as they arrived. Alizarin said, "There must have been a hundred Gisela Frakier." Exaggerating slightly, perhaps. "How did they assemble without us noticing?"

The youngster said, "Our encirclement was porous. One man and one horse, on a path unknown to us, by moonlight? Easily done. We do the same. In any case, we were denying food and supplies. More mouths only worsened their position."

All true. The boy was paying attention. But Nassim Alizarin did not like to admit that a general of the Sha-lug had been outwitted by Rogert du Tancret.

"So. What will they do now?"

"Simple enough. Keep Tel Moussa locked up. . . . Uh."

"Good. You're thinking. Anyone else want to guess why they'd do this now? Why not last month? Or next winter? There are no campaigns being readied on either side. Rogert isn't strong enough to launch one of his own." Though Nassim was not sure about that. Rogert du Tancret might be arrogant enough to think he could defeat Lucidia on his own.

Certainly, he was arrogant enough to start a wider war over the harassment of Gherig.

Still . . . "Time will unmask him."

TIME WITHHELD ITS JUDGMENT. NASSIM BEGAN TO SUSPECT THAT Black Rogert had acted impulsively because he had found himself in possession of several momentary advantages. He had the Gisela Frakier for only a few weeks. And he had recruited a sorcerer, about whom Nassim's spies could learn nothing. Not his name, whence he came, how he managed to work beside Rogert's Brotherhood allies, notorious for loathing sorcery.

Three times the sorcerer acted against Tel Moussa. Thrice his efforts did no obvious harm. Three times Bone and old Az hunkered down inside the tower, remained calm, and endured.

Black Rogert stayed in the field himself only a few days, then returned to the wicked pleasures of Gherig. He left the siege work to others.

The crusaders did not patrol far from their line of investiture. Nassim gathered fighters in the hills nearby. Reinforcements came from Shamramdi. Indala was concerned.

Nassim ambushed the Gisela Frakier when they started back to their tribal territories, up on the frontier with the Rhûn. They fought bravely and appealed to Gherig for help. Help did not come. Black Rogert was done with them. They were on the discard heap. No matter to him that he might want to hire Gisela Frakier again tomorrow.

Nassim did not have the strength to exterminate the traitor Pramans. He did hammer home the point about the folly of becoming an ally of Rogert du Tancret.

A week later the truth made itself known.

The crusaders attacked a vast, rich caravan from Dreanger headed for Lucidia and the silk road beyond. The caravaneers had refused to take the harsher but safer path through the eastern desert. They believed a bribe to Rogert would guarantee safe passage.

Rogert seized all the goods and made captive the few people not slain outright. Those were all people who could be ransomed. The dead and captured both included important Chaldareans from the Eastern Empire. Among the dead were Dreangerean diplomats headed to Shamramdi and Lucidian ambassadors coming home.

Young Az observed, "At least this time there were no women from my granduncle's family."

But there had been Praman pilgrims by the hundred, going to visit shrines in the east or returning from shrines in the west. They had been robbed and butchered without concern for their religion or status. To Rogert they were all Unbelievers and vermin. There was no market for them as slaves. Murder was the obvious way to be shut of their hungry mouths.

"He'll get a war for this," young Az predicted. "It's a prince's duty to protect pilgrims. Even Unbeliever pilgrims."

"Or, failing that, to avenge them so nothing wicked happens to the next band."

Nassim bemoaned the disaster. But it had happened miles away and without warning. It was over before the news reached him. He could have done nothing, anyway. His forces were not concentrated. In retrospect, though, he thought he should have anticipated something of the sort, based on du Tancret's past behavior.

Before the attack the crusaders bled most of the strength from the lines around Tel Moussa. Nassim took advantage of that to launch frequent counterattacks against what, in the end, proved to have been a calculated distraction.

A brace of new falcons arrived from Haeti, having evaded interception along the way.


## 15. Wrong Place, Wrong Time

The Perfect Master approached Khaurene late in the day. The setting sun liberally splashed the golden light for which the Connec was famous. He meant to bypass the city and would have done, but circumstance adjusted his thinking.

A year earlier Brother Candle would have gotten behind Khaurene's walls to escape Patriarchal invaders and revenant things of the Night. Now the great dangers were bandits and itinerant heretic hunters from the Society for the Suppression of Sacrilege and Heresy. The Writ of several recent Patriarchs banning the Society had not taken hold in Arnhand, where those grim monks had been multiplying like mice, with Anne of Menand's blessing. There was a new Patriarch, Serenity, now. Society vermin were coming out, getting into everything, everywhere, excepting those counties in the eastern Connec where the locals were not in the least reluctant to invite them to become participants, as targets, at archery practice.

Bandits were no threat to a wandering Maysalean Perfect. Bandits were a homegrown peril. Those desperadoes knew the holy men carried nothing worth stealing. Even their ragged clothing had no resale value. Society brethren, though, would happily rob the Perfect of their lives. And, though those villains were not yet numerous in the Connec, they were so absolutely convinced of their righteousness that most people had not the courage to stand up to them. They were fanatic about keeping lists. Including lists of what people were worth.

And they had the threat of Arnhander crusaders behind them.

King Regard himself was headed for Khaurene with an army, rooting out heretics as he came.

The Khaurenesaine had recovered substantially from its recent travails. Crops were in. Vineyards seemed restored. That which had been damaged or destroyed had been repaired or replaced. But the folk the old man met did not smile. They were worn down, exhausted, but had not lost hope. Not even in the face of this latest invasion.

The Connec had the greatest soldier of the age behind it.

Peter of Navaya's Queen was Duke Tormond's sister. And Peter had guaranteed the safety and independence of Khaurene. Peter of Navaya, hero of Los Naves de los Fantas, was the most beloved, honored, and respected monarch of the Chaldarean west. Not even Serenity dared try to call him to heel. If Serenity assayed the usual holy bluster and bullying he might find himself master of nothing but what he could see from Krois. He might even lose allies his predecessors had gathered so painstakingly.

Among Peter's devoted battlefield allies was Jaime of Castauriga. There was no love between those Direcian monarchs but Jaime was unshakably hitched to the Navayan star. And was worshipped by the Grail Empress Katrin. Who had a vast capacity for making any Patriarch's life more miserable than ever Peter might.

All this Brother Candle heard on the road from Sant Peyre de Mileage. It piled emotion atop emotion, luring him ever farther from Perfection.

He might yet have avoided Khaurene had he not needed to dodge Arnhander scouts that afternoon. They roamed unchallenged. Regard himself was tied up harassing the gentle folk of the Maysalean-tolerant communities of the Altai but did have strong recon patrols surveying the countryside around the Connec's greatest city. He was, at least, making a grand show.

A show was the best Anne of Menand had yet gotten from most of the men she bullied into going after the Connec's heretics. Only the fanatics of the Society were enthusiastic. And their captains were notoriously incompetent as warriors.

Brother Candle entered Khaurene just before the gates shut. When he was young the gates never closed. Often they went unguarded because the old men charged with the task failed to show up for work. Now everyone who entered Khaurene enjoyed a personal chat with a young, fit, and suspicious soldier, usually Direcian. The soldiers were practiced and efficient and familiar with the local dialect. They asked quick questions while their comrades watched. Society infiltrators usually betrayed themselves by the lies they told.

One soldier murmured, "Take care in the streets, Master. We still haven't controlled all the gangs." Religious violence had become part of city life.

"I've been here before. I know which streets to avoid. But thank you for reminding me."

"Fair weather and good fortune, then." Since he could not wish a Seeker "Godspeed."

"And you as well, young man. And you as well."

King Peter had chosen his soldiers well. Or, more likely, Queen Isabeth had done.

Sometimes the Perfect thought Isabeth loved Khaurene more than did her brother. Duke Tormond seemed to find his role an oppressive burden.

So Brother Candle entered the capital city of the End of Connec, that had stood since before men began keeping records. He had no specific plan but knew he would have to reveal himself to the local Seeker community. He could not survive here, otherwise. He had no money. He had no family here. He had left those things behind to become Perfect.

No choice seen, he made his way toward where the weavers, dyers, tanners, and leatherworkers dwelt. Those trades found the Maysalean philosophy congenial. That area was where he stayed regularly. If those people had recovered from the siege and defeat Khaurene had suffered he should find hospitality there again.

He arrived shortly before nightfall.

Grim news. Brother Candle was too well known. He had been recognized. News of his coming had raced ahead. Raulet Archimbault, the tanner, intercepted him as he turned into a street where all the tanners, spinners, and weavers were Seekers After Light. A plump Madam Archimbault hurried after her husband. Both brought the reek of the tannery with them. The entire neighborhood shared that stench. Weather could only make that worse, never weaken it.

Archimbault definitely showed the consequences of life in a time of stress, having regained few of the pounds he had lost during a grim winter spent hiding in the Altai. His wife had been eating well, though, and actually seemed younger than the Perfect remembered.

Archimbault swept Brother Candle into a great embrace. "We feared you had gone on, Master. No one knew what had become of you."

"I went into isolation. To find my way back to Perfection. But the world wouldn't let me be."

"Come. Come. You'll stay with us, of course."

The wife said, "And you're just in time to eat."

By the time they reached the Archimbault home the whole neighborhood knew that Brother Candle had returned. Scores came out to see. It would be hard to slip away again.

He observed, "The house seems bigger and quieter." Madam Archimbault scurried about, winkling out bread, cheese, wine, olives, and pickles of a dozen sorts.

Archimbault said, "It's awfully quiet with the children gone. Empty, too."

Brother Candle held his tongue, afraid he might open a wound. Every family in Khaurene had lost someone the past couple years, either to crusaders, or to disease and hunger after the fighting stopped.

Madam Archimbault expanded: "Archimbault doesn't like to talk about it. He doesn't like to admit error."

Her husband muttered but did not argue. Equality of the sexes was one of the great heresies of the Seekers After Light.

"Soames turned up. After we started looking for a new husband for Kedle." Kedle being their daughter. "The story he told is a barrel of dung. He wouldn't say where he'd been or what he'd done. The men from his company say he ran away before the fighting started. Some think he surrendered without a fight and might be a spy for the Society, now. He has no explanation for why he didn't join us in the mountains. He knew Kedle was near her time." Madam Archimbault had a huge anger against her son-in-law, rigidly controlled. "He's already got her with child again."

Archimbault made a noise like a hissing pot. His anger was larger than his wife's. He would say nothing because he did not want to look bad to the Perfect. These were the sorts of cares a Seeker was supposed to put aside.

Madam Archimbault confessed, "I blame myself. It's all my fault. I urged the boy on Kedle. She wasn't really interested. I bullied Archimbault into approaching his family."

Brother Candle had been surprised by the match, back when.

Though then it had been a coup for the Archimbaults because Soames's family was so prominent.

The woman said, "Soames has all the family property, now. Which must be the real reason he came back. Only his grandfather was still living when he did. Soames had become the only heir."

Archimbault grumbled, "That family suffered so much misfortune in so short a time. People said it was because of Soames's bad behavior. And Soames is the one who benefited."

Madam said, "He insisted that Kedle and baby Raulet go live with him." Angrily. As an afterthought, she admitted, "Kedle doesn't mind."

"It lets her put on airs. Master, the child has strayed from the Path. She may never find her way back. We need your help. Desperately."

"The times try the faith of the best of us." The Perfect tried recalling Kedle's age. Still under eighteen, he thought. Of an age to sway in every philosophical breeze.

Visitors began to arrive. Domestic talk ended. Brother Candle was always a favorite with the local Seekers.

Khaurenese stayed up late, seldom sitting down to the last meal till the tenth or eleventh hour. They rose with the sun but took an extended nap during the heat of the afternoon. Spirited talk continued till well after the Perfect fell victim to exhaustion.

A different breed of visitor appeared next morning. Early, but not wickedly so. His appearance demonstrated the speed with which news spread in the tight environs of the city.

A groggy Brother Candle found himself face-to-face with Bicot Hodier, Duke Tormond's chief herald. The old man was too sleepy to manage his manners perfectly. "Hodier? That's you? I thought you died in the fight with the Captain-General. You were with Sir Eardale Dunn."

"No doubt there were people who hoped that was true. As ever, I continue to disappoint. The Duke wants you to come up to Metrelieux. Please don't frustrate him."

"No." Though Tormond was another reason he had wanted to pass Khaurene by. "I can't."

"It would be disrespectful of you to visit these friends but not him."

"I know. I know." And Tormond was a friend. Or had been, when they were boys. After a fashion. Now they were just two tired old men.

Brother Candle had not visited the fortress Metrelieux for some time. "Improvements have been made, I see."

"Isabeth's Direcians are pushy. Though it's only the gate." Hodier shrugged. "The rest is cosmetic. Militarily, the Direcians are more interested in upgrading the city gates and walls."

Brother Candle had noted the physical improvements where he had entered the city. He had seen patrols in the street, mixed Direcian and native. "Do you think a siege is a sure thing?"

"That decision will be made by King Regard. Meaning, by his mother. King Peter will make sure the city resists."

"His soldiers seem to be everywhere. How many are they?"

"Fewer than some like, more than make the Patriarch's friends happy."

"Meaning you don't know."

"Clever, Master. But the question can't be answered. By me. Perhaps by Principaté de Herve or Count Alplicova. The garrison turns over constantly. Nor do they want spies being able to establish anything certain. The soldiers are here to teach our people to defend themselves. Most seem willing to learn."

A member of the Collegium was in Khaurene representing interests opposed to the Father of the Church? "So the debacle when they met the Captain-General convinced the survivors that they have some shortcomings."

"Indeedy do, Brother. Indeedy do. Wait in here. I'll find out how soon the Duke can receive you."

Brother Candle settled in one of Metrelieux's quiet rooms. He had waited there on other occasions. Usually someone turned up wanting a private word before he saw Tormond. Which seemed to be the point of the delay.

This time was different. Hodier was gone a half hour but no whisperer materialized during the wait.

"He's ready, Brother. You'll understand the delay once you see him. Be prepared for changes. For the worse."

The worse? And Tormond was still alive?

"Sorry, Brother. I don't mean to sound dramatic. But, as I said, you'll understand."

He would. Almost. But, more, the Perfect was tempted to decline into despair.

The Great Vacillator, Tormond IV, last of his line because he had no surviving issue, had become a drooling ruin. He was confined to a wheeled chair. He stank. He could not lift his chin off his chest, so weak had he become. He was little more than a stick figurine.

Hodier said, "This time there's no sorcery and no poison. This time it's just age and poor health."

This, Brother Candle suspected, would be the last time he saw his friend among the living. His resentment over having been dragged up to Metrelieux faded. "Has he made a religious commitment? Will he take Church rites or the consolamentum?" The latter being the final ritual for the dying Seeker After Light.

"He's the Great Vacillator. Unto the extremity itself. Bishop Clayto, Bishop LeCroes, and the Perfect Brother Purify have been standing by. His Lordship won't choose among them."

Brother Candle thought that must be Brother Purify's fault. One of Brother Candle's most persistent failings was his inability to think a single charitable thought about Brother Purify. They were flint and steel. But he also started at the mention of Bishop LeCroes. His onetime friend had been caught giving Tormond slow poison at the behest of Sublime V. His reward was to be exalted status once the Church gained control in Khaurene.

Publicly, Bries LeCroes had been the senior local supporter of the Anti-Patriarchs, not a Brothe man.

Bicot Hodier noted his response. "One thing the Duke does do is forgive. Sublime is dead. The threat of Patriarchal troops is gone. So he pardoned everybody. Including every noble who worked with the Captain-General during the time of the crusade. And for that we're paying already. Now they're conspiring with Arnhand."

Knees grinding in protest, Brother Candle sank down in front of Tormond. He considered the healing brother behind the wheeled chair, saw nothing to indicate that the man was anything but what he pretended.

The Perfect thought he would see the serpent of darkness lurking behind the priest's eyes if he was a Society tool.

Tormond's eyes glittered. He was as aware and alert as could be, trapped inside that deteriorating flesh. But he could not communicate easily.

The meeting took place in an audience where Brother Candle had conferred with Tormond and his councilors before. Tormond had asked his opinions about everything, always, but never took them to heart. This morning the room was damp, chill, gloomy, barren, and almost unpopulated. Hodier was there. The healing brother was there. The Duke and the Perfect were there. Where twenty to thirty usually gathered, raucously, with fires roaring in the fireplaces.

Brother Candle observed, "Between us we have over two centuries of experience. And the priest is just a boy."

The healing brother said, "I can give him an infusion that will restore his control of his body briefly. We seldom use it. It sucks up what resources he has left. Is now a good time?"

The priest had bent to ask that question beside Tormond's ear.

Brother Candle caught a flash of mischief in Tormond's rheumy eye as he managed a tiny nod.

The priest hustled away.

Hodier said, "This infusion does work wonders. But the cost is cruel. Hours like this, or worse, after barely a quarter hour of creeping over just this side of the far frontiers of normal. Don't waste what time you get."

Brother Candle could think of no appropriate response. He shifted the Duke's chair so they could face one another once he parked himself on a bench so he did not have to grind his knees into the hard oak floor.

"We've all enjoyed several seasons since last we met."

Tormond offered a gurgled grunt.

The healing brother rematerialized. "This won't look good. But it's how the job has to be done." He seized Tormond's wispy hair and forced his head back. Tormond's mouth opened as his head tilted. The priest gave him five heartbeats to clear his windpipe, then dumped a small clay cup into his mouth. The contents looked like dark tea. Brother Candle smelled nothing. That meant little. His own senses were not what they used to be.

The priest pinched the Duke's nose, forced a swallow response.

Tormond downed his medicine without choking or aspirating.

His response was not long coming. And was dramatic.

"Almost magical," Hodier opined, perhaps tongue in cheek.

Color came to Tormond. His slight palsy stopped. His drooling ceased. Then, laboriously, his chin came up off his chest. "Charde ande Clairs. My most faithful friend."

There was a pathetic indictment of relations between Tormond IV and his world. And the Duke's own fault. He never took charge. He let himself be managed and manipulated and got stubborn over the wrong things at the wrong times. Everyone tried to take advantage, excepting Sir Eardale Dunn, who had died defending Khaurene. And Brother Candle, who had been Charde ande Clairs in an earlier life, when he and the Duke-to-be had shared childhood adventures in contravention of the rules of station.

"I'm here."

"But, almost certainly, had to be dragged." Tormond could not overcome a slur and a lisp, nor did he rattle on as was once his wont. He could, however, be understood. And it was clear that he wanted to speak directly to Brother Candle. "Bicot, find Isabeth. Bring her. No excuses. Fornier, go get coffee. That was supposed to be here by now."

The priest inclined his head. "As you wish, Your Lordship."

"He took that gracefully," Brother Candle said. While searching the room for shadows that did not fit.

"He's a good man, Charde. Unlike most of his tribe. We have little time. I need you to listen." Tormond beckoned the Perfect closer. "Among my many ills, lately I'm cursed with glimpses of what the Instrumentalities of the Night see when they look into the face of to-morrow. Usually while this drug infusion is fading."

"Uhm?" Carefully neutral.

"Charde, the future is not a friendly place."

Not exactly an epiphany.

Tormond took Brother Candle's hands into his own. He eased something out of his sleeve into that of his guest. The Perfect concealed his surprise.

"Not friendly at all. Great sorrow is coming. Fire will scourge the Connec. There is no way to avoid it. Tell Count Raymone that I regret everything. Though I don't see what I could have done to make things come out better. Give him my blessing. Tell him to salvage what he can."

A wisp of darkness stirred behind the Duke's eyes. The effect of the infusion was approaching its peak already.

Fornier returned with coffee service so fast Brother Candle had to believe coffee preparation had been in progress after all.

Queen Isabeth and several Direcians blew in moments later, all frowns. As Tormond failed his demesne became, ever more, an extension of Navaya. King Peter's men would not be pleased with random old contacts who wandered in and caused distress.

Brother Candle recognized none of the Queen's men.

He eased the packet in his sleeve to an inside pocket.

Brother Candle had known Isabeth since birth, though never familiarly. For reasons he never understood there was more warmth on her part than his. Bright with concern, she demanded, "What's going on?"

The Perfect gestured. "Your brother sent for you. Not I."

"Sit, Isabeth," Tormond told his sister. "Listen. This may be the last chance I get to speak."

The Duke rattled along as though there was more in need of saying than he possibly had time to say. He had been having apocalyptic visions. Disaster could not be avoided but its harsher details were not yet fixed.

Twice Isabeth started to interrupt. Twice Brother Candle stopped her with a gesture. This would be a grim race. Tormond had no time for interruptions.

He did not get as specific as anyone wanted. Always the trouble with sibyls, though Brother Candle did concede that all futures were fluid as long as they still lay ahead. The Night saw possibilities and probabilities but could fix nothing to its place or temporal point before it happened.

Still, some things verged upon certainties. None of Tormond's futures boded well for Khaurene.

Tormond's flirtation with lucidity degenerated into a gurgling mumble. The Duke vainly trying to communicate, still.

Isabeth eyed the Perfect. He stared back. She said, "It will start before we're ready."

"The future always arrives before we're ready. Whatever you do, the ambush comes when you don't expect it. But he did tell you a lot that you can use." In a way. The personalities set to dance in the coming storm thought too much of themselves to deliberate what might be best in the long term.

Isabeth said, "I'll have to inform Peter. He'll have decisions to make. And you. You can't waste time. Go preach to your people."

He had other obligations, too. And might succeed in fulfilling none.

The dying man's most dire visions had presented as the most determined futures.

And Tormond *was* dying. No doubt about it. He had given them a choice of three dates, all inconvenient. Two could be beaten by taking action to prevent them. Action entirely within the domain of Father Fornier.

Brother Candle suggested, "Whatever you do, be clear and don't sugarcoat. Your husband's choices will be hard. He deserves the best information possible."

Isabeth considered him for several long seconds. She was no child. And she was not her brother. If anything, she could be hasty making decisions. "You accept what he told us, Master?"

Brother Candle did not correct her usage. She had done that deliberately, for the benefit of her companions. Most Direcian nobles were solid Brothen Episcopals, if openly contemptuous and defiant of the Patriarch himself. They were willing to exterminate the inquestors of the Society—mainly because those fanatics presented a threat to the nobility's temporal power.

Isabeth was suspect religiously. She sprang from this nest of heresy. She had to tread carefully.

Brother Candle said, "I accept his visions. My creed tells me I must accept what is. The Night is. The Instrumentalities are. None of us can deny those facts because they're inconvenient."

Nothing he said contravened Chaldarean doctrine. So long as no one accorded the Instrumentalities any status but that of devils or demons.

Truths like that did not please the kind of soul that found completion only in a Society for the Suppression of Sacrilege and Heresy. A soul determined to coerce God Himself to conform.

Brother Candle said, "I've played the part your brother created for me. Which was to make sure he got his say and you people listened."

Isabeth was skeptical.

She was a tired, graying woman who had spent her adult years enmeshed in the politics of her brother and husband. She had seen little of the stylish court life enjoyed by most women of standing. From the moment the Connec went into continuous crisis she had scant opportunity to enjoy the company of her husband or son. Who would be walking and talking and making life an adventure for his nurses, now. And whose name, Brother Candle realized, he did not know.

Embarrassed, he asked.

Isabeth rattled off a string of names. Direcians liked to get their favorite ancestors and saints involved. "But just Peter, or Little Peter, for everyday." Wistfully.

Brother Candle got away soon afterward. Bicot Hodier accompanied him to the citadel gate. "I can't walk you all the way, Brother. Tormond will need close watching now. He sometimes suffers after using Fornier's infusion."

"I understand. I know the way. I'm not senile yet. I just walk slower."

THE PERFECT DID NOT WALK ALONE. HE SOON REALIZED THAT HE HAD a tail, a brace of rogues who did not appear to be moved by benign intent. But they suffered a change of heart soon enough. A half-dozen Direcian troopers came jogging down from Metrelieux and by coincidence seemed headed whatever direction the Perfect was.

"I DON'T KNOW WHAT THAT WAS ALL ABOUT," BROTHER CANDLE TOLD the Archimbaults when they got home from the tannery.

Archimbault hazarded, "Must have been Society thugs. The capture of the notorious heretic Brother Candle would be quite a coup."

The Perfect did not argue. Archimbault might be right. There was no fathoming the reasoning of some people. "Possibly. I need to get back on the road. Before I become a distraction."

He could become one in a huge way.

After reaching the Archimbault home and making sure he was safe from stalkers and prying eyes, he retrieved the packet Duke Tormond had slipped him.

The contents could rock the Connec.

Within it were the ducal seal, the ducal ring of office, and a relic of Domino that had been in the Duke's family since Imperial times. Each was an item only the true Duke of Khaurene could possess. They were the talismans of the office. Also included were documents inscribed in a tiny hand, copies of the legal instruments that confirmed Duke Tormond's family as lords of the End of Connec. The originals went all the way back to Imperial times. Each copy was signed with incontestable sworn attests that it was an exact and true copy in every respect. Multiple signatories had witnessed every page of every document. The names ranged across the spectrum of Khaurene's religious leadership.

The key document, the prize that could shake the world, was one in which Tormond IV legally adopted Count Raymone Garete of Antieux and made the Count his heir in all respects.

That would upset everyone. People had been jostling for position for years. Peter of Navaya led the pack. Isabeth had been Tormond's only heir for a decade.

Adoption had not been much employed since Imperial times, when the more thoughtful emperors used it to assure the Empire of a competent successor. But adoption remained a viable legal maneuver. So long as it could be established beyond challenge.

Brother Candle considered the list of witnesses. Every man was highly respected, excepting Bishop LeCroes. And LeCroes had been rehabilitated.

There were too many of them. Honest men all, yes, moved by loyalty and the best of intentions, surely. Yet someone would say something to someone. That was human nature. The news would leak, if it had not done so already. Someone with ambition and a streak of villainy would start trying to undo Tormond's scheme.

Thus, Brother Candle saying he had to get on the road. He needed a good head start before anyone began to suspect that a lapsed, superannuated Maysalean Perfect had smuggled the emblems of state out of Metrelieux for Tormond IV.

Brother Candle considered taking Archimbault into his confidence. Archimbault was as good a soul as they came. And the man thought better of Tormond than did most of his subjects. Archimbault could be valuable in the effort to execute Tormond's plan. But Archimbault had a life, a wife, a family, a career, and an important role in the community. He did not deserve such cruel peril.

Archimbault and his wife both tried to talk the Perfect out of going. The Maysalean community did not want to share him. They did not like Brother Purify, who was the only other Perfect available.

Identical arguments were offered later, once the evening meeting started. The Seekers enjoyed themselves. Debate became spirited. And, to a soul, they insisted that their gatherings were never so enjoyable when the Perfect was not there to teach. Meaning, by implication, to referee.

Brother Candle put more into the evening than usual. The Seekers had to be warned that dark times would return. "The trial that's coming will be harsher than ever the Captain-General was. The Captain-General was a gentler, more honorable man than the commanders we'll see now. And that time of tribulation, terrible as it was, lasted only a few seasons. The next trial might last for generations. Till the last Seeker has been burned." The Society had shown a fondness for burning heretics.

Tormond had not mentioned prolonged persecutions. His focus had been on the near future. But the crushing darkness of the deep future had been implicit in his every word.

Brother Candle finished the evening by saying, "Please awaken me early. I want to be on the road to the Altai with all the day ahead."

He felt badly about the misdirection. Which, no doubt, would be of little efficacy, anyway. Anyone chasing him for what he might be carrying would know that he had to take it to Count Raymone. In which case, he ought to head into the Altai after all, then travel eastward through the wilderness.

BROTHER CANDLE REACHED THE NORTHERNMOST OF KHAURENE'S several gates only to find it shut. A lot of military activity was under way. There had been a bloody fight in the assembly area just inside the gate.

The soldiers and militia were not looking for an old man smuggling the emblems of state. Brother Candle approached a Direcian who did not appear to be overwhelmed, asked what had happened and when the gate would open.

"King Regard's men are outside, Father. They tried to capture the gate during the night. They had inside help. They failed. The survivors are licking their wounds but they haven't gone away. If you want out you'll have to use another gate. They won't be watching them all. They're too busy here."

Brother Candle thanked the soldier and backed away. The man had not said so but it looked like the troops were getting ready to sortie.

He was amused by having been called "Father." Though for a

Direcian that could be a term of respect for the aged, not necessarily a title for a cleric.

Brother Candle headed for the eastern quarters. One of the gates there should let him get to one of the roads to Castreresone.

## 16. Other Worlds

There was no night in the Realm of the Gods. The Ninth Unknown assumed that there must have been, once. The Aelen Kofer must have taken the diurnal and seasonal cycles with them, leaving only a changeless silvery gray sameness.

How long had he been there? There were no temporal milestones. Not even the sonic rhythm of the world changed. Hunger only worked till the food ran out. Bowel movements became erratic before that. His digestion did not tolerate traveler's iron rations well.

For a time he had concentrated on reaching the Great Sky Fortress without having to walk the broken rainbow bridge. A young warrior, a hardened commando type, might have climbed that sheer gray stone. If there were no traps and no hazards less obvious than those Februaren saw from points he could reach riding his own weary flesh.

He had to admit he was a bit past his prime.

Maybe the ascendant could make the climb without using the bridge. He could change into something built for that. But the ascendant was not here to help.

Februaren had not yet gotten a ghost of a hint of a means of opening the way between the worlds. Nor of escaping himself. No good trying to call on the Construct, either. From inside the Realm of the Gods there was no sign that great growing engine existed.

He had dropped himself into a room without doors.

He was not powerless. If anything, his sorcerer's abilities were enhanced. But they were no help, except insofar as he could charm his stomach into believing that it had not gone out of business.

Despair did not defeat him. There was that of the "northern thing" in his character. No surrender. Battle on till the Choosers of the Slain arrived. Or whichever deathlord followed on after the Gray One's beautiful daughters.

He prowled the dwarf town till he knew it like he had been born there. He found nothing of value or interest. The Aelen Kofer would have taken the wood and mortar and stone had they not been loaded down with night and the seasons.

They had that reputation in myth and legend.

Must be a lot of truth in the old tales. Februaren had yet to uncover a contradiction to the little he knew of the Old Ones.

But in the Night everything was true.

In time spells no longer silenced his hunger. Soon he would stop thinking logically and linearly. Something dramatic needed doing.

In desperation he fashioned crude fishing apparatus. Something lived out there in the oily gray water of the harbor. The surface often stirred to movements underneath. He had no bait. He would have devoured that long since had he been able to find anything. He made a shiny lure and stained it with his blood, then went down to quayside. He boarded the derelict tied up there, began fishing off its bow. He hoped he was a better fisherman than hunter.

He had enjoyed no luck trying to catch the few rats, squirrels, other vermin, and birds still inhabiting the Realm of the Gods. As desperately hungry as he, they were the fiercest survivors of their species, too fast for an old man not used to hard work. He thought they might be hunting him.

Not even sorcery availed him. These creatures were indifferent. Maybe they were immune, simply by always having lived inside the supernatural.

He expected no better luck with the denizens of the harbor. But in just minutes he felt a tug on his line so determined it was clear something down there was fishing for dinner, too. Februaren pulled. The thing pulled. The old man had more success. He glimpsed something like a miniature kraken. A squid. He had eaten squid all his life. Squid was popular throughout Firaldia. Too bad he had no olive oil or garlic.

This squid was miniature only by comparison to the krakens of nautical legend. It outweighed the Ninth Unknown. And had the reach on him, too. Its long tentacles were a dozen feet in length. It failed to take Februaren only because the old man had the better leverage.

The monster would not give up.

The Ninth Unknown was just as stubborn.

Tentacles slithered up over the edge of the quay. The monster began to lift itself out of the water. It turned, tried to reach over the rail of the hulk. Its eyes . . .

Startled, Februaren stared down at a face almost human, contorted in desperate effort. Those eyes were intelligent but mad with hunger.

It let go the quayside, hoping to topple Februaren with its weight. He did stumble but not enough to go over the rail. Just enough to see the tentacles reaching. Enough to see the water suddenly churn and give up three heads that looked almost human. Shoulders and torsos and weapons followed. Short harpoons in manlike hands plunged into the monster's unguarded back.

Februaren surrendered his fishing gear. It was time. Time to get off the hulk, too. He watched the struggle as he went. The people of the sea were gaunt with starvation. They were weak. Though they were three and the monster one he knew they would get the worst of this. The kraken would feed.

He employed his last resources once he reached the quay, hitting the monster with a spell meant to paralyze. The spell would immobilize a human for hours. This kraken was not human. But its struggles did turn sluggish.

Februaren collapsed.

He went down with enough reason left to make sure he kept stumbling away from the water as he did.

SOMEONE WAS SINGING. THE VOICE WAS REMOTE AND EERIE AND THE words were alien but the melody was familiar. It went with a love song sung first in the dialect of the western Connec a hundred years ago. Cloven Februaren recalled making love to the refrain out of the Khaurenesaine.

He smelled a powerfully fishy stench.

He lay where he had fallen, right cheek hard against cold, damp stone, palms burning from abrasions. He cracked the eyelid nearest the pavements. What he saw so startled him that he gave himself away.

Five feet away, seated cross-legged, facing him, was a young woman, singing while she worked. She wore nothing that had not been on her at the moment of her birth.

Had he the strength he would have turned away. She might be without modesty but he had his, even after all these years. But he was too weak to do more than flop and make noises even he did not understand.

The song faded into gurgling laughter.

The mer got onto her knees. Putting those together. She extended a hand with something in it. The fishy stench grew more powerful. "Eat!"

After struggling into a seated position, Februaren could see what the mer had been doing. Carving flesh from a tentacle.

He was much too hungry to worry about what that flesh used to be. Or how badly it smelled now.

His stomach would soon rebel. But sufficient to that moment the evil. He seized the food.

The girl said, "I have . . . been sent out . . . to watch. Our debt. Your spell saved . . . many lives." Clearly, she was not accustomed to speaking a human language. But she did warm up quickly.

The little Cloven Februaren knew about the people of the sea he had learned from books. They could change shape and walk among men but only for a short while. Only in extraordinary circumstances would they put themselves through the pain necessary to gain legs. The change, in this case, had been perfectly mimetic. And the mer had deliberately revealed that.

She cautioned, "You don't eat too much. Small bites. Chew, long times. Or get sick. When you get stronger, make fire. Cook."

She spoke a dialect of the northern Grail Empire. One he had known well as a youth but had not heard in a century. He gestured at her to keep it slow. He took her advice and ate slowly, too.

She stopped needing thought pauses between words and phrases but never spoke at a conversational pace. "You are not the only sorcerer. But you are the one who had the right spell."

The raw kraken lost its savor. Februaren supposed that was his own body telling him to stop eating. So he tried to concentrate on the girl. Without having his gaze drift downward.

She was admirably equipped, there, just a hand below her chin.

He supposed her capacity to distract was why she had been chosen to speak for the mer.

"You may think we fed you in gratitude for your help. In less desperate times that would be true. We are a peaceful, hospitable people. But that luxury has been taken from the mer who are trapped here. We feed you, instead, by way of investing in our own survival. You have legs. You can make the journey even the greatest hero of the mer could not endure." To his frown she replied, "I cannot go far from the water. I have to return to the wet frequently. Please. Tell your story."

Little splashes behind Februaren told him he had an audience broader than a single shape-changed girl.

He told ninety percent of the truth. And no deliberate lies.

The girl said, "We are after the same thing. The opening of the way. Otherwise, we all die. And the world of men will follow. Unless . . ."

"Yes? Unless?"

"We are at the mercy of the Aelen Kofer. Only the Aelen Kofer can open the way. Only the Aelen Kofer have the skills to rebuild the rainbow bridge. Only the Aelen Kofer can save the Tba Mer. And . . ."

The girl wanted him to ask. "And?"

"Only you can go where the Aelen Kofer have gone. Only you have legs to survive the dry journey. Only your human lips can shape the magical word that will compel the Aelen Kofer to hear your appeal."

"Magic word? What magic word?" A swift riffle through his recollections of north myth exhumed nothing. "Rumplestiltskin?"

"No! Invoke the name of the one whose name we dare not speak. The one you named in your tale."

"All right." He would have to think about that. It must be Ordnan, whose name was not to be spoken though everyone knew it somehow. But the Gray Walker was gone. Named or unnamed, he had no power anymore. How could an extinct god compel the Aelen Kofer? "But I can't make any journey if I'm sealed up inside here."

"Only the middle world, your world and mine, is denied us. The Aelen Kofer went down into their own realm."

"Down? I thought they sailed away aboard the golden barge of the gods."

"No. The barge is right behind you. You were on it. It is involved, but the dwarves went down. Back to the world whence the Old Ones summoned them in the great dawn of their power. Back when they were the New Gods and the Golden Ones."

The girl stopped talking. The old man was pleased. He had time to do more than labor after what she was trying to say.

She was patient. As were the mer in the water behind Februaren.

"I don't know the stories of this world as good as I should. How does one move from this world to that of the dwarves?"

The answer was absurd on its face. And explained why someone might think the Aelen Kofer had gone away on a barge.

His acquaintance with religion suggested that most were founded on logical absurdities easily discerned from outside. And yet, each was true, courtesy of the Night. Somewhere. At some time. At least part of the time.

A dozen Instrumentalities of the grand, bizarre old sort had shown their resurrected selves of late. He had come here seeking help dealing with the worst of the breed.

He could almost feel the bitter cold breath of the Windwalker.

ABSURD. BUT REAL. FEBRUAREN BOARDED THE ROTTING SHIP AGAIN. Gingerly, afraid the decay might be so advanced that ladders would collapse under his negligible weight. But time had not advanced to meet his dread.

The ship was not large. It was low in the waist, rising only a few feet higher than the quay. Februaren doubted that it drew a dozen feet heavily loaded. The main weather deck was six feet above the waterline. The tub was short and wide and indifferent, like one of his earliest wives. It did not resent his presence enough to react. Magic ship or not.

This ship was not the same size inside as out. Which was no stunner to the Ninth Unknown. Space needed only to conform to the Will of the Night.

The only deck below the main weather deck was the bottom of the cargo hold, loose planking on cross frame members, concealing the ballast voids, bilges, and keel. Half the ship was nothing but a big, empty box that stank because it had not been pumped clean in far too long.

The hold could be examined from above simply by moving a hatch cover. It appeared to be accessible—safely—only through the bows or stern castle. Februaren had instructions to go down. The mer had told him to use the stern route, past the master's cabin.

The master's quarters were on the main deck level, behind a pathetic galley. Februaren ransacked that, found nothing more useful than several rusty knives and an ebony marlinspike that had to be a memento. It was too heavy to be a practical tool.

Done there, Februaren descended a steep stairs. Seamen would call it a ladder. The deck below constituted quarters for two or three officers, so low even a short man had to bend to get around. How much worse for the seamen up forward? Had they even had room to sling hammocks?

Had there, in fact, ever been an actual crew? Did the gods need one?

Light leaked in from above and through skinny gaps in the hull. It revealed little of interest. A fine deposit of dust. Webs whose spiders had been hunted out long ago by rats and mice who had since abandoned ship.

He had been told to keep going down. He descended to another cramped deck where food and ship's stores might have been kept. Then down again, and again. Counting steps, he was fifteen feet below the ship's bottom when he ran out of ladders. There was no less light here than there had been up above. The tired old light leaked in, around, and through cracks in a crude plank door. Which, in theory, ought to open on the cargo bay but could not possibly because it had to be beneath the bottom of the harbor.

The rotten latchstring broke when he pulled it. Why had it been left out? Had someone been left behind? Or did it just not matter?

He slipped the blade of the thinnest knife through a crack and lifted the latch. Which proved to be a wooden strip so slight it would have broken if he had just pushed the door hard.

"Hatch," he reminded himself as he eased through, cautiously. Sailors called their doors hatches.

What lay beyond the hatchway was no ship's hold. It was a mountain meadow in summer, without the direct sunshine. Lightly wooded hills rose to either hand. Mountains more fierce than the Jagos loomed beyond, all around. Mountains all dark indigo gray, most with white on the tips of their teeth.

Cloven Februaren stopped halfway through the hatchway, saw what was to be seen, withdrew. He swung the rickety door open as far as it would go, used one of the plundered knives to jam it so it could not swing shut. He collected a loose plank from those covering the bilges, laid it down so a quarter of its length protruded into the world of the dwarves. Only then did he step on through.

He removed his pack, extracted his spare shirt, fixed it to the plank end by hammering in another liberated knife. The shirt hung there like what it was, a rumpled, dirty yellow rag. Attached to a board protruding from a blot of darkness the eye could not fix and could not have found again without knowing the correct magic—had he allowed the hatch to close.

He found nothing better than a few stones so tossed those through to strengthen the connection between worlds. Then he walked slowly uphill toward a standing stone on sentry duty a hundred yards away.

With each step a little of the gray around him went away. A wash of pale color entered the world. It waxed but never became homeworld strong. It was a pastel world when the old man stopped in front of the standing stone.

The menhir was covered with dwarfish runes. The gods had borrowed them, then gave them to the children of men so they could record their prayers. Cloven Februaren stared at three runes inked onto his left palm, then found a matching sequence on the face of the stone. He traced each of the three with his right forefinger as he spoke the names of the runes. He was careful with his pronunciations.

The air shimmered. It shuddered and pushed against the Ninth Unknown. It twisted. Then the space between him and the stone filled with an old, hairy, bewildered Aelen Kofer who rubbed his eyes and squinted, rubbed his eyes and squinted. He did not want to believe what he saw.

Februaren said, "The Aelen Kofer are required." He used the tongue he shared with the mer. He had been assured that the dwarves would understand.

If his recollections of the mythology were correct, the Aelen Kofer would understand him whatever tongue he used.

The dwarf gulped air behind his beard. Doubtless, that had sprouted before the first men turned sticks into tools. He rasped, "Son of Man!" and made it sound like the worst swearing he could imagine.

"Kharoulke the Windwalker is awake and free. The middle world is going under the ice. The Aelen Kofer are required."

The ancient looked like somebody was beating him with an invisible shovel.

"Others like the Windwalker are wakening, too. There is no power to keep them bound."

"Stop!"

One word, so heavily accented Februaren almost failed to grasp it.

"Do not . . . speak . . . again."

The Ninth Unknown waited, feeling the world around him.

The realm of the dwarves was thick with magic, the way the middle world had been in antiquity. Its wells of power must be boiling, flooding it with magical steam. Yet the power of the dwarf world was slightly different. Februaren clawed at it but it slipped through his sorcerer's grasp like quicksilver between cold, stiff fingers.

"Son of Man. You stand before Korban Iron Eyes."

Februaren heard the "Iron Eyes." It took him a moment to connect that with Khor-ben Jarneyn Gjoresson, the son of the dwarf king in the commoner northern myth cycles. He was supposed to have made several magical rings and swords and hammers for various gods and heroes.

Februaren stifled an urge to tell Iron Eyes that while he was older than expected, he did not look his age. His sense of humor was moribund lately.

"Cloven Februaren, Ninth Unknown of the Collegium, in Brothe. The Aelen Kofer are required."

The dwarf grunted. He wanted time to think.

Februaren felt a rising dread. This would not go quickly. Dwarves were not immortal but their lives did stretch back to the dawn of memory. They knew no urgency. He glanced back. The doorway remained visible. The world continued to gain color, maybe as his eyes adapted.

Korban Iron Eyes turned to the standing stone. He talked to it as, slowly, he rested his palms on a dozen runes in succession, naming them in turn.

Reality quake. Silent thunder. A moment when the lightning of all darkness met. And a moment beyond when the old men of the Aelen Kofer joined their Crown Prince. Including the ancient Gjore himself. Nobody spoke. Everybody stared at the outsider.

These were the pride and glory of the Aelen Kofer?

The tribe was in bad shape. Maybe as bad as the Realm of the Gods.

The Old Ones must have taken steps to make sure they would not go down alone.

The dwarves talked among themselves. Februaren heard the Windwalker mentioned several times.

Iron Eyes faced him. "Son of Man. You say the Aelen Kofer are required. Divulge the full truth if you hope to see your arrogance overlooked. What do you want? What do you mean to do? How did you find your way into our world?"

Februaren told it. Without lying. Without overlooking much. Without admitting how powerful he was in the middle world. The Aelen Kofer of myth had a mystical horn that trumpeted whenever it heard a lie. No horn was on display. But it would be around somewhere.

The Aelen Kofer began to debate.

Language was no mask for the dispute. There were two points of view. Which seemed to verge on turning deadly.

One side wanted to go right on doing nothing. The Realm of the Gods meant nothing to the Aelen Kofer. Let the Windwalker have his way with the middle world. Let both worlds die if that was their destiny. The fates of men—and of trapped mer—did not concern the Aelen Kofer.

The opposition held that the dwarf world had begun to grow pale. It was dying, in its own way. And, the fate of the world aside, Kharoulke the Windwalker was the most vile, hideous, ancient, and implacable enemy of the Aelen Kofer. Whose cleverness had been enough to imprison him in the long ago. In time, come for the Aelen Kofer he would. In time, make himself Lord of the Nine Worlds he would. Unless someone stopped him.

Februaren's ears pricked up. Nine Worlds? That exceeded the census of myth by several. And, how the devil *was* he following all the argument? Till minutes ago he had never heard a word of dwarfish spoken.

Magic.

One man in ten thousand would not just say, "Magic," shrug, and walk away. The one guy, a Ninth Unknown, would begin fussing about it immediately, driven to find out how it worked and why.

The debate raged. The dwarf elders remained balanced precariously on the cusp of violence. Cloven Februaren thought about what could go wrong. He recalled what he knew from the Aelen Kofer myth cycle.

"Oh-oh."

He was in a typical story. And a story of this kind—not just in the northern tradition—tended to launch its hero onto a whole ladder of quests. If that pattern held the dwarves would agree to help but only if he went to the land of the giants to steal something only a Son of Man could carry away. But before he could do that he would have to pilfer something from the world of the elves so he could unlock the way. And whatever that was could be handled only by someone who had been thrown down into the icy wastes of Hell. . . . And once he got home they would wed him to the King's daughter and the old monarch would abdicate in his favor.

Something to look forward to. If he lived that long.

The inaction party had a good argument. Saving the world was too much work.

Iron Eyes announced, "It's been decided. A compromise has been reached. Those who think the Aelen Kofer ought to respond to your petition are free to do so. Word is spreading. Those who aren't interested will stay behind and forget you ever crept into our world. The rest will join you in the Realm of the Gods."

Iron Eyes did not bring up a need for a talisman from the Land Beyond the Dawn. Februaren chose not to raise the question. Iron Eyes said, "Organization of the expedition has begun."

"Excellent. Meanwhile, any chance I could get something to eat?" It had been a while. The kraken was no longer coming back. And he had harped on the hunger all through the telling of his tale.

"Of course."

Iron Eyes touched the standing stone in a pattern of pats and whistles. He vanished, leaving a *pop!* and a tuft of beard drifting toward badly trampled grass. Cloven Februaren moved nearer the menhir. It must have something in common with the Construct.

Dwarves began to reappear, attired and equipped for war. Fighters were not what Februaren had come to get. He needed magical engineers. Masters of their trade. Not breakers of bone and stone.

Well, maybe they did come equipped with mystic tools. Hard to tell. Each had loaded himself down with a pack bigger than he was.

Should he despair? These dwarves were the oldest of the old. The grayest and hairiest of the extremely hairy and gray.

Iron Eyes came back armed with two packs. The puny one he handed to Februaren. "For you."

The mass bent the old man to the ground. "You did hear me when I said I've been around over two hundred years?"

"Barely out of nappies."

"That's extremely old, for a man. Since age has come up, why are only the grandfathers volunteering?"

"They're the Aelen Kofer who believe there's a problem. They remember the Windwalker and his brothers. The youngsters think the old folks exaggerate. They do about everything else. Times always used to be harder. In any case, some think that the Windwalker was cruelly done. We didn't try hard enough to talk out our differences before we resorted to violence."

Cloven Februaren touched his chin to make sure his jaw had not gone slack. The Aelen Kofer were nearly immortal. How could a rational being who had survived more than two decades possibly think that way? Kharoulke's idea of a peace conference would be to eat the delegates the other side sent. By offering to negotiate you announced that you had already accepted the probability of defeat. You wanted to weasel out of the worst consequences.

With Instrumentalities like the Windwalker there was nothing to discuss. He offered victory or extinction. The Night saw no in-between.

"Don't be shocked, Son of Man. Your tribe doesn't have an exclusive claim to the production of fools." Iron Eyes changed subject. "This adventure will be hard. We have to make the walk between worlds by actually walking. No eight-legged horses. No changing into hawks or eagles. There isn't power enough left for any of that. Tell you truly, Son of Man, I'm surprised that the Realm of the Gods has survived as well and long as you say. It ought to be farther down the path to extinction." At the end, there, the dwarf seemed bitten by a sudden, dark suspicion.

"Time is wasting," Februaren said. He started downhill toward the shadowy uncertainty of a doorway.

THE CLIMB OUT OF THE SHIP WAS NOT THAT LONG, INTELLECTUALLY. Physically, it was a harsh challenge for Cloven Februaren, weak and unaccustomed to labor. He felt every one of his years when he collapsed on the main deck of the barge.

Some Aelen Kofer were equally drained by carrying all that weight. The more spry went to the rails and called to the mer. Much of what they had dragged up the long climb was food.

Iron Eyes said the mer would have to find the seams outlining the gateway to the middle world. The Aelen Kofer could not.

The people of the sea showed little interest. Having eaten, they began to display a certain animus. Understandably.

Februaren reminded them that the Aelen Kofer were not obligated to feed them again. And recruiting the dwarves had been their idea. They had to help save themselves.

The mer then declared their unwillingness to stray from areas they considered safe. The slain kraken was not the last of its kind. There was a white shark out there, too. It had produced pups not long ago. Those, most likely, had been eaten by something.

All smaller forms of life, barring things able to burrow deep into the bottom mud, had been hunted out. Nothing remained but the top predators, eyeballing one another, desperate for an opportunity.

There were six people of the sea. Four males, in their prime before becoming trapped, the female who had shape-changed, and a fiercely protected female child. Had she been human Februaren would have guessed her to be four.

Korban Jarneyn said, "There is little magic left. We need to be niggardly with it. Opening the gateway will bankrupt us."

"How large a hole do you need? My associate on the outside can get through a rat hole if he has to."

"The bigger the opening the more outside magic we can pull in."

The Aelen Kofer hoped to catch the tail end of the burst of power in the Andorayan Sea. None, Februaren noted, suggested drawing on the more accessible magic of their own world.

"Will a small hole let you draw power to make a big hole?"

"If we find the seams so we can force any hole at all." Iron Eyes glared at the timid mer. He looked up the mountain. Its peak lay hidden in clouds. Most of the Aelen Kofer had gone to study the rainbow bridge.

Februaren said, "Make the way safe for the mer. Even if that leaves only power enough to force a finger-size hole."

Iron Eyes scowled. He muttered. He bobbed his head once, fiercely. "The alternative is defeat without having fought."

And that, of course, was not to be endured. The fight was the thing. To battle without hope, yet battle on and battle well. Thither loomed immortality.

Korban collected a half-dozen dwarves. They formed a circle facing inward—excepting Gjoresson himself. He faced the harbor.

The mer made frightened noises. They crowded into the tight space between the barge and the quayside. They wept, sure something would winkle them out.

A shark's fin broke water a hundred yards out. It headed straight at the dwarves.

Something brought mud boiling to the surface beside the quay. Tentacles followed. Cloven Februaren slashed one reaching for the Aelen Kofer. That fixed the kraken's attention on him.

The Aelen Kofer were teasing the desperate hunger of the monsters of the harbor.

The kraken got no chance to taste the Ninth Unknown.

The shark arrived. The quay shook to its strike. Then another kraken materialized, rising into the death struggle.

Satisfied, the Aelen Kofer broke their circle.

"Better than any dogfight," Gjoresson observed. "Son of Man, ask the mer if there are any more monsters out there."

The answer was, there were no more known dangers.

The shark tore the first kraken apart. But the second got hold of the shark and hung on, out of the reach of lethal jaws. Its beak was sharp enough to slice through shark skin. Shark blood and kraken ichors filled the water.

Februaren remarked, "If there's anything else out there that will bring it."

Iron Eyes lamented, "Those krakens are as intelligent as us. But their minds are more alien than you can imagine. They were created by the Trickster. Accidentally. It's a long nightmare of a story about giants and incest and revenge gone awry. The krakens hate the Old Ones, the more fervently because they could never do anything about it."

"Uh . . ."

"They hate the Sons of Men almost as much. The mother of them all was a mortal fathered by the Trickster. These are the last of them. Unless some escaped to the middle world when the way was still open."

The krakens out there were far bigger than these. These could not pull down anything larger than a coracle.

"The closing ought to put the Aelen Kofer on their list, too."

"Oh, right at the top. Yes."

Februaren muttered, "With the Night all evils are possible and most are probably true."

The shark rolled, thrashed, then sounded. And that was that for several minutes. Then the killer fish broached so violently that for a moment it was entirely free of the water. It rolled, came down with the kraken between it and the water. Stunned, the kraken lost its grip.

"There's the end, then," Iron Eyes said. "The shark will finish the kraken, then bleed to death." He gestured to his companions.

The dwarves boarded the ship, took in the rotten mooring lines. The mer protested vigorously. The combat continued out in the harbor. The kraken had to get back on and hang on if it hoped to live. It could not run to safety.

The dwarves found oars somewhere. Gjoresson explained, "The Aelen Kofer built this barge. Employing our finest arts. There's more to it than what you see. Though you should have seen it when it was new and the magic was everywhere. It needed only to be told what sort of vessel to be and where to go. It didn't have to be rowed."

In its final throes the shark smashed into the side of the ship, breaking oars and leaving a hole at the waterline. The oars could be replaced. Februaren and Korban went below to get a patch on the breach.

The shark stopped thrashing. Two of the mer found the courage to look for the portal to the middle world. Which took only a few minutes to find. The problem became locating a good place to break through.

By then Februaren and Iron Eyes had been replaced at the breach by dwarves no longer needed at the oars. Gjoresson was in continuous conversation with the mer. Once, as an aside, he told the Ninth Unknown, "I see the outlines, now. But no weak spots. We did good work in the old days."

Old days? That was just a few years ago.

"We'll go for the best opening we can force and hope there's magic enough to do." Iron Eyes grinned behind his beard. "And if we fail, you can settle down with us back in our world. I have a grandniece who would find a human wizard endlessly fascinating."

"If need be." But he didn't want to entertain that bleak a future. Instead, he began contemplating a possible alternate method of attack.

The world of the dwarves, in story, had its own connections with the middle world. Maybe the ascendant could be brought to the Realm of the Gods the long way round.

How would Korban Jarneyn respond to that suggestion? Maybe his grandniece would like to play with a newly minted Instrumentality.

Februaren glanced across the harbor. The dwarves from the mountain had returned to the quay. They did not appear to be filled with good cheer.

Gjoresson stayed focused on the gateway. He gathered his companions, muttered with them, then the lot put together something indistinct. They pointed it at the portal, right where it met the dead water.

A spot of ruby fire came to life.

Februaren stared. The bounds of the world could not be discerned by his eye. Harbor and sky seemed to roll right on. Yet ripples caused by the barge made little splashes against something right where the dot shone. Seabirds wheeled in the distance, fishing, but never came close. Clearly, they could not see the barge or harbor.

The dwarves broke up. Most went to the oars. The barge wobbled back to the quay. Iron Eyes said, "I need more help. Particularly from those who closed the way, back when."

Curious. Gjoresson kept talking like those events had taken place in the remote past.

The barge hugged quayside just long enough for the other Aelen Kofer to board. Dwarves were a dour tribe but this klatch were unusually taciturn and grim. A few muttered with Iron Eyes while the barge crossed the harbor. Finally, Korban told Februaren, "The bridge can be restored. We haven't lost the secrets of building with rainbows. But it will take time and require a lot of magic. Which we don't have. We'll have to bring it from the middle world. But, granting that we get the bridge restored, freeing the Old Ones may still be impossible."

"Why is that?"

"Because the entangled sorceries sealing them in were written so that only one of the Old Ones, or one of their blood, will be able to thread a passage through the magical closure. Your soultaken must be a genius. How could he know? Did he know? He did better imprisoning them than they did imprisoning the wicked gods they overthrew. No one has to stay here to keep these spells working. I'm in awe."

And more than a little dishonest, Februaren reflected.

Iron Eyes said, "Unless the soultaken himself gives us a tool, there may be no hope. Those who could open the way are all inside. Even the Trickster, which amazes me. He was always too clever to get caught."

Februaren considered. The ascendant had elements of the All-Father and the Chooser of the Slain Arlensul inside him. He would have drawn on those to imprison the rest of their divine gang. Could their knowledge also bring the walls down?

Had to.

The ascendant would know. The Aelen Kofer were peerless magical architects and engineers. They just needed his direction.

The Aelen Kofer gobbled steadily, gesturing, showing unusual animation. Februaren could not follow.

That little floating ruby dot grew. It burned more brightly. Ruby droplets dribbled down an invisible surface into the dead, colorless water.

There was a *crack!* of an explosion. Water sprayed the barge. A small wind heavy with alien odors knifed in behind it. And kept on coming, whistling.

"Success! Of a sort," Gjoresson declared.

A vertical sword stroke of light three feet long, dropping into the water of the harbor, now hung in the air. It was an inch wide at its broadest, at the water level. Sunshine rushed in with the wind and odors. It was so bright!

Februaren said, "I didn't realize how bleak it is over here." His eyes adjusted. Blue water sparkled beyond the crack.

Where the breach met the harbor surface dull water began to show streams and eddies of color. Februaren felt gusts of power coming in with the wind and smells.

The Aelen Kofer started singing. Iron Eyes said, "The magic will return."

From a world where the wells of power were drying up. Februaren wondered, was the power dying out of all the worlds?

He reminded himself that these worlds existed only to a few Instrumentalities and believers anymore. They were dying for sure.

The white shark broached feebly, halfway to the quay. It lived, just barely. Its eye fixed on the barge for one baleful moment.

Color continued to spread from the crack. Here, there, sparks of gold flashed for an instant on the rotten wood of the ship.

The power from that sea burst, over there, must still be strong.

A great whale eye appeared at the gap.

The Ninth Unknown raised a hand in greeting.

A worm of flesh started wriggling through.

Color spread. It climbed the side of the barge. Cloven Februaren opened himself to what power there was.

THE NINTH UNKNOWN KNEW EXACTLY WHEN THE WINDWALKER SENSED that the Realm of the Gods had been opened.

Iron Eyes shrieked.

Kharoulke had not known about the burst of power in the west. He did now. His attention had been attracted by a sudden, ferocious threat.


## 17. Brothe: Brief Idyll

Piper Hecht's return to the Mother City was uncomfortable for everyone. A thousand men accompanied him, men who did not want to work for Pinkus Ghort. Some Brothens wanted to celebrate their coming. Most did not want to attract the attention of the new Patriarch. Serenity's cronies wanted to shut the gates but did not have the popular support. Hecht had strong backers in the Collegium. Serenity did not, to his abiding mystification.

The moment the Interregnum ended Serenity started swinging Mother Church back to the course long steered by Sublime V. No surprise to Hecht, but a shock to most Brothens, including several Principatés who had taken bribes to vote for him.

Bronte Doneto had done well pretending religious indifference when he lacked the power to enforce his convictions. Now he owned that power. Now he could feed the rage that had festered since the Connec humiliated and nearly killed him.

"I'm not comfortable," Titus Consent said. While coming off the Blendine Bridge, watching Brotherhood members turn upstream toward their Castella dollas Pontellas. Leaving the former Captain-General without his lifeguard.

"As they tell us, be careful what we wish for."

"Yes?"

"I resented every minute that Madouc was underfoot. Now he's not."

More than a hundred men did remain with them, headed the same direction. "We'll be good for now. Later, maybe not so much."

"Uhm. Pella. Stick close."

A mile on, nearing their own neighborhood, with only a handful of friends close by now, Titus asked, "Made a firm decision yet?"

"What?" Hecht had been daydreaming about Anna. And the girls. Then, bemused, reflected that his true home and family were somewhere in the slums of al-Qarn. Possibly. What horrors might time, poverty, disease, Gordimer, and er-Rashal have worked there?

"About what's next. You going to buy that vineyard? Or become Empress Katrin's war tiger?"

"Oh. No you don't. I'm not deciding anything now. It's time for some plain old lazy drifting."

Titus just smiled. He knew. The decision had been made, though Hecht's motivations might not be clear. Even to Hecht himself.

The former Captain-General meant to head north, out of the Patriarchal States, possibly forever.

News of their coming had run ahead. Anna and the girls were out, waiting with Noë Consent and her brood. And with Heris. The Consents left immediately. Hecht went into Anna's house. He had one answer for all of the first dozen questions. "I'm tired. I'm exhausted. Later."

Pella took up the slack. He had plenty to say. And was disappointed when Anna and the girls did not share his enthusiasm for falcon warfare.

Again, "I'm so tired. I just want to vegetate. I don't want to go anywhere. I don't want to do anything." That directed to Heris, who had hinted already that Principaté Delari wanted to see him. "Brothe and everybody got along fine without me. And can keep right on doing without me. Anna. Stop scurrying around. Come over here. Sit by me. Let me drink you in."

Anna did so, managing to blush.

Leaning against her, sleepily, Hecht considered Lila and Vali.

"What's happened with the girls? Other than Vali filling out and both of them wearing better clothes?"

"School. The nuns on the girls' side of Gray Friars."

"Uhm?" A questioning grunt that Anna interpreted correctly. How had she managed to get two girls of questionable antecedents into so exclusive an academy?

"Your name and Principaté Delari's. Plus a surprise legacy from Hugo Mongoz."

"Hugo Mongoz? But . . ."

"Not money. Influence. Bellicose found a letter among his papers. Instruction to an illegitimate grandson that didn't get sent before he died. In it he claimed he owed you a big debt. Not saying why. He wanted the grandson to repay you. The grandson is a monk at Gray Friars. So there you go."

"Oh. I guess that's good. Heris. Heris?"

Vali looked past Pella, said, "She did that turn sideways trick, Dad."

Lila said, "I wish I could learn how to do that. I'd get rich."

Anna told her, "You are rich. Your father has gathered up more prize money than the rest of us can spend in three lifetimes."

Hecht laughed. "I sincerely doubt that."

"What are you going to spend it on? And none of your nonsense about vineyards and latifundia. What you know about agricultural management I could tuck into a thimble with room left over."

"You think? I'd surprise you, heart of my heart. I spent a long time in prison in Plemenza. The only way to pass the time was read old texts about farming."

That gave Anna pause for scarcely an instant. "Which means nothing, practically. You'll never be a farmer."

"You could be right. We need to talk about that. But not now. I just want to wallow in the luxury of having no demands on me."

"Oh, there are going to be demands. But first you're going to have a long wallow in hot, soapy water."

The girls had Anna's big copper bathing tub set up already, with water heating. Anna would not use the public baths. Nor would she let the children. A safety measure, that. She said. But Hecht suspected there was more to the story. She would not discuss it. It was not worth a squabble.

Settled in the tub, with females dumping warm water and Pella contemplating making a break for it, to avoid being next, Hecht observed, "The one thing I'll miss, being on the outside, is the baths at the Chiaro Palace."

"Really?" Anna asked.

"And there you go, letting your imagination get loose. The rumors aren't true. Nothing ever happens there."

"Really?" Again.

Hecht shrugged. "Don't let me confuse you with facts."

HERIS TURNED UP EVERY DAY. SHE HAD LITTLE TO SAY AND DID NOT press. "You'll let me know when you're ready. I just come down to see if you are. There isn't anything crucial. Yet."

But Heris and Principaté Delari were not the only people who wanted a slice of the former Captain-General. Representatives from members of the Collegium, from most of the Five Families, from the Castella, and from the Imperial embassy at the Penital, all turned up during Hecht's first four days at home.

Only Titus Consent and his tribe were allowed in. And Heris, who could not be turned away at the door.

"YOU'VE STARTED GETTING RESTLESS," ANNA OBSERVED. VOICE CAREfully neutral. At a time when she thought the children would be occupied.

"Titus tells me I never learned how to relax."

"Titus is outrageously smart, for his age. So. Is it time to talk?"

"I suppose." He had been puzzling how to put it all together for her. "The Empress wants me to come work for her."

"To help her fulfill a holy obligation. By leading an Imperial crusade into the Holy Lands. I know. That may be the worst kept secret of the age. It was all over Brothe within hours of the announcement that Bronte Doneto would become the next Patriarch. The Penital put it out. Doneto was upset. Pinkus sent some of his trusted men to look out for us. Not that he would brag about looking out for a friend. He was afraid Doneto might do something stupid."

Hecht grunted. Ghort had not said a word. But that was Pinkus Ghort. Never say anything when he did something someone might construe as good or thoughtful. He did not want to tarnish his black reputation. "He'd know if the danger was real." Hecht eyed Anna curiously. Why had she kept this to herself till now? Was she hoping the question of taking service with the Empress would go away?

Probably.

"It turned out to be a tempest in a teapot. Pinkus pulled his men out after Principaté Delari dropped a few one-ton hints on the right people."

That sounded like something Heris would say. After rehearsing before she said anything.

"Muniero Delari and Bronte Doneto have a bitter history. Which I'm not free to discuss. I suspect Doneto will avoid reviving old quarrels now that he has his dream job. Delari is older than stone. Doneto can let time put an end to their squabble."

"Piper, I won't follow you if you go to Alten Weinberg."

And there it was. Not unexpected but not understood. Despite having given the possibility plenty of brooding.

"You know we've only actually spent a few weeks together over the years we've been a couple."

Was that question or statement? Whichever, she was exaggerating. Sort of. He did not say. Because there was a deep truth, down under.

"You're always in the field. If I move I still won't see you. And I won't know anyone but the girls. Nor even speak the language. So I'll just stay here and not see you because you're in the field."

"I'm not really going to lead a crusade into the Holy Lands. I'll get the Empress to change her mind."

"No doubt. You can do anything. You have a knack for getting people to do what you want. But, once all is said and done, you'll be in the field. That's who you are. So, as I said, I'll stay here, where I'm comfortable, and only see you once in a while. I won't have to upset the way I live."

Hecht clamped down on his emotions. Stilled his inclination to pull male rank. He did not own that in this relationship, in this country. Irritably, he batted thoughts of Helspeth aside. This was not an opportunity. "I see." He sensed the children lurking, out of sight but not out of hearing.

"I freely admit that I have more than most wives and many mistresses. Which leaves me too spoiled, besides being too long in the tooth, to take up the life of a camp follower."

"I won't argue. I can't. You've put it perfectly. I am what I am and you, more than anyone, know the truth of that. But I did think Alten Weinberg might be more domestic."

Anna definitely had an answer for that. She did not get the opportunity to deliver it. Heris turned around out of nowhere on the far side of the room. "You have to come this time, Piper. Things have happened. Supper. Anna. Grandfather would really be pleased to see the children, too." She turned and was gone.

Anna caught her breath. "That was a polite invite to a command performance."

"Yes?"

"You might say Heris and I have become friends. The way she carried herself . . . Our discussion might be moot."

Again Hecht offered only an interrogative monosyllable.

"We have to see Principaté Delari before we make any other plans."

A premonitory chill crawled Hecht's back. His own desires could become so much chaff in the breeze should the Night be driving down some rigorous line of its own.

THE DELARI TOWN HOUSE WAS IN THE THROES OF A DRAMATIC MAKE-over. Not just repairs to damage but a total renovation. The staff had expanded by a dozen, all hard-eyed rogues who were as alert as ever Madouc's gang had been. Each hailed from the Principaté's own clan. Which made them kin of Muniero Delari's grandchildren.

Supper was served at the usual table by the usual servants, Turking and Felske. As the first course arrived, Delari explained, "Everything changed when Bronte Donte achieved his ambition. I expect him to res-urrect the conflict that brought us head-to-head not so long ago."

He said this in front of Anna and the children. Who looked to Hecht for an explanation. Hecht did not deliver.

He did say, "Two of us got you out of that. Whatever became of the other one?"

"Armand? I don't know. The little weasel vanished seconds after Hugo Mongoz expired. I suppose it's too much to hope that Doneto's partisans did away with him."

"What's the construction all about?" Hecht asked. "What's going on?"

"Forting up."

"I get that. But what about us, here? This isn't just me and the family stopping in for a friendly supper. You look almost guilty. Which tells me there's something going on. Heris implied as much, the way she acted. Where is she, anyway?"

"She'll be here any minute."

Turking and Felske brought the courses with a noteworthy absence of enthusiasm. As though they were stalling.

Heris came in, roughly dressed. Turking and Felske hustled in the small courses she had missed. Even Mrs. Creedon took a moment to bring her a single marinated cheese and onion–stuffed mushroom. Heris grunted pleasure and dug in. Evidently her story would be shared only if necessary.

Principaté Delari became taciturn, his contribution to table talk vague questions for the girls about their progress at school. To which Lila was the unexpectedly enthusiastic respondent. She found intellec-tual pursuits more interesting than did Vali. Hecht was surprised.

People never stopped not being what you expected.

Turking and Felske came to life. In a trice they produced the clutter of another place setting as Cloven Februaren dragged in.

Hecht observed, "Borrowing from my friend Pinkus, you look like death on a stick."

"No doubt." Cloven Februaren did look like he had suffered extreme starvation.

Delari said, "He's the picture of health, now. You should've seen him this morning. I thought his story was over."

The Ninth Unknown settled. He picked at his food, ferociously. He made Vali and Lila uncomfortable. Anna needed to release those girls into the wild. They needed re-exposure to reality. They had developed amnesia about their own early romances with the harsh side. Februaren said, "I spent a night in Elf Hill. It was worse than any of the stories."

Hecht said, "I don't get it."

Delari said, "You should. It's part of the northern thing. Up there people believe that we share the world with lots of other races. The Hidden Folk, collectively. Pixies. Brownies. The Fair Folk. Light elves and dark elves. Goblins, dwarves, the People of the Sea. And dozens more."

"Not to mention the evil dead," Februaren grumped.

Delari ignored him. "The Hidden Folk get up to all sorts of mischief. Some good, some bad, according to their nature. More bad than good, of course. A favorite trick is to lure a mortal into their realm, where time passes differently."

"Usually a lot slower over there," Februaren said. "In the Realm of the Gods it was the other way around. I used up all my food and was starving. It's true about the food, too. It helped me forget I was hungry but it didn't provide enough nourishment."

Delari said, "The point is, while he was there for months only a few days passed here."

"So you did what you went off to do. You released the . . ."

"I did not. Not even close. The Old Ones are locked up like olives inside a cask closed inside a sealed barrel. My success amounted to opening the way between the middle world and the Realm of the Gods. This being what those involved with the northern thing call the middle world. Because of where it stands in relation to the other worlds involved in their concept of the universe. Oh. Success number two. I talked the Aelen Kofer into helping break the Old Ones out."

Hecht resisted a conditioned response, reminding himself, yet again, that all beliefs were true inside the Night.

The children had grown bored. The Ninth Unknown had not described his adventure in epic terms. Which was a little out of character.

Februaren said, "After all that positive news you just know there's got to be a catch."

Principaté Delari seemed to be hearing all this for the first time, too. "Grandfather. Please."

Februaren's grin was a ghost of itself. "All right. Time is important. The way is open. The magic is flowing in. The Aelen Kofer can rebuild the rainbow bridge to the Great Sky Fortress. We can get that far."

"But?" Delari, with a scowl.

"But the Windwalker is on his way. And we can't get inside. Only someone with the blood of the Old Ones can crack the last barrier."

Delari said, "And those of the blood are all inside."

"Basically. I thought the ascendant could manage. He has chunks of the knowledge of Ordnan and Arlensul. And he shut them in. It seemed logical that he could undo what he did."

"But not so," Delari guessed.

"No. He did the job too damned good. And there is some mythological imperative at work. One even a freethinker like me, because I spent my life immersed in Brothen Episcopal Chaldarean culture, can't get to make sense. What it comes down to is, if we're going to spring the Old Ones so they can stop the Windwalker, we need someone of their blood to kick down the door."

Anna startled everyone by chiming in. "From what I've heard, the male Old Ones doinked every farmer's and woodcutter's daughter they ran into when they visited our world."

"It would be hard to find those descendants," Delari said. "They haven't done that sort of thing for four hundred years. The blood would be pretty thin."

Februaren said, "There's another option. According to the ascendant."

"Gedanke," Hecht guessed, wondering why he even recalled that name. Was he damned eternally because he had acquired that kind of wicked knowledge?

"Right road." Februaren was startled. "How did you know?"

"Lucky guess. That and the fact that most of what happened below the walls of al-Khazen had to do with the feud between the Banished and her father, over Gedanke."

"Most of what happened had to do with the hunger of the Old Ones for the blood of the Godslayer. Arlensul took the opportunity to get revenge. Also, Gedanke was Arlensul's lover. Not the child they created. The ascendant says Gedanke himself was there for the showdown. As one of the undead heroes. Which gave Arlensul added incentive in the fight."

No one said anything. Hecht wondered why Februaren chose to discuss this over dinner. In the normal course, it would await withdrawal to the quiet room. He began peering into shadows and watching Turking and Felske closely.

The Ninth Unknown recognized the moment realization struck. He grinned, nodded, said, "The part of Arlensul the ascendant incorporated offered very useful information about her half-mortal bastard. She did her best to watch over him. He was still alive at the moment of her own demise."

"That should narrow the search. There can't be many men who have been around longer than you and who show the occasional burst of divine power. He would have some of that, wouldn't he?"

"Excellent, Piper. He would, yes. But, chances are, he doesn't know what he is. His mother never told him. He never saw her. He should think he's just a very strange orphan."

Principaté Delari interjected, "He'd have to suspect. If he had any familiarity with the mythology. If you grew up in that part of the world, were an orphan, had unusual abilities, and seemed to be immortal, wouldn't you suspect something?"

"Of course, Muno. As far as I know—the Arlensul part of the ascendant isn't completely forthcoming—the bastard should be a long-lived peasant or woodcutter somewhere in the northeastern part of the Grail Empire. The infant was abandoned in the sacristy of a forest church in the Harlz Mountains of Marhorva, a hundred miles from Grumbrag."

Anna asked, "Could he be the one pretending to be Piper's brother?"

Cloven Februaren chuckled, made a sign indicating that subject ought not to be pursued. Hecht asked, "And you know all this because?"

"Because the ascendant knows most of what the mother knew. Though she couldn't provide any help locating him today. Or wouldn't."

"Meaning?"

"Even in severely reduced circumstances the Banished's personality is still alive and independent. A tiny fraction, but the essence of who and what she was."

Delari said, "Easy work now, Grandfather. Just pop up to that rustic church and work your way out in a spiral search, asking each man you meet if he's four hundred years old. When you get an affirmative, you've found your half-blood god."

"An ingenious strategy, Muno. Piper, the boy always did have a knack for slashing through the fog around the core. Though I have in mind a simpler, faster methodology."

Anna offered, "A man who's been around that long did things to

hide his age. If he didn't he'd have every aging petty lord after his secret."

"Or people would want to drive stakes through his heart," Heris
suggested.

Hecht asked, "Could he be the source of vampire legends?"

The Ninth Unknown replied, "Vampires are the source of vampire
legends. Things of the Night with a taste for blood." Februaren pointed
at Anna. "The young lady is as smart as she is beautiful. No. I daren't
say that. That would declare her a goddess. Let's just stipulate that she's
smart. Concealing his longevity would be a serious problem."

"Flattery will get you everywhere, sir."

"I wish. Piper? You look like you just bit into an unexpected pit. If
my wordplay offends you, tell me to go to hell. I'll take it back."

"So, go to hell, old man." He chuckled. "No. You just stated the
facts. She is all that. But I had a thought. A place to start looking. That
doesn't force you to go all the way back to a church that probably
doesn't exist anymore." He laid his finger across his lips. He did not
want to carry on here. The old men were hamming it up for eavesdroppers, be they shadow or human. Every household had a servant or
relation who did not mind picking up the occasional extra ducat by
contributing to the informational black market.

Principaté Delari, "We'll talk about it over coffee, then. Now, children, you've been quiet as snakes. Why don't you girls tell me about
the Gray Friars? And Pella can tell me about his adventures with Piper.
They tell me you've fallen in love with the falcons, lad."

Encouraged, coaxed, the children came forward with a few details
of their own lives. Bits innocuous enough to be shared with the old
folks.

Heris stood. She had eaten rapidly and heartily. "I'm full. I'll go
help Cook get the coffee service ready."

The youngsters soon talked themselves out. Hecht told Februaren,
"Regale them with tales of your adventures in the lands of the gods."
Pella, at least, should be interested in a fairy-tale realm that was mostly
real.

The Ninth Unknown did regale, employing outrageous exaggera-
tions, sounds, and distinct voices for his characters. He made Korban
Jarneyn sound like a dimwit old gorilla. Even Hecht enjoyed the show.

"I HOPE YOU WERE JUST TRYING TO MAKE YOUR ORDEAL MORE ENTER-
taining," Hecht told Februaren as he accepted coffee from Heris.

"I took some of the grim out, so they wouldn't be too upset, but
that was the way it was. They ate the shark, too."

Principaté Delari wondered aloud, "Why do I find myself doubting you, Grandfather?"

"Because you're such a tightass, Muno. You always were. You don't have an ounce of wonder in your soul."

"Likely not. I've always been too busy picking up after you and trying to hold it all together."

Heris snapped, "Will you old people stop? Piper had a reason for wanting to talk in here. Since you were so blatant about that burlesque downstairs. Get on with it. Before us being hidden has your spies wondering what's really going on."

"She's right." Februaren sighed. "And I was just getting warmed up. Definitely a chunk off the Grade Drocker block. Looks like he did at the same age, too."

"Stop!" Hecht growled. "That's enough. Cloven Februaren. You said you had a plan for rooting out the missing bastard, fast. What is it? Tell us, then I'll explain why I wanted us all in here."

"Another chunk off the Drocker rock. No patience. All right, Piper. The scheme is simplicity itself. The new Patriarch, our beloved Bronte Doneto who happens to be the most powerful sorcerer to assume the ermine in two centuries, has his Instrumentality minions all over you and Muno. I let them hear all sorts of intriguing stuff downstairs. As a result, a very nervous Serenity ought to unleash the whole power of the Church on the problem of Arlensul's bastard."

"Why? He shouldn't really care."

"Wrong. Well, maybe if he knew the whole story. What he's been allowed to know will compel him to care."

"Do take the trouble to explain."

"Key point. He's just found out that I'm still alive. That will rattle him badly. At the same time he'll learn that there's absolute, concrete proof that his religious vision remains incompletely triumphant. That the Old Ones, while no longer seen, are still alive. They survive in the imaginations of hundreds of thousands of rural people who attend church on all the appropriate days, then hedge their bets by following the ancient rituals when those are due. More, the Old Ones will need to be awakened and strengthened if the world isn't to be crushed beneath the hooves of even older and darker Instrumentalities."

Hecht said, "You may have lost me. I understand every sentence. Individually. But how do they all connect up in a way that helps us find our missing half-god?"

"Blood simple, Piper. Blood simple. *Listen* to what I say. I scare the crap out of Serenity by being alive. I terrify him by being eager to find Arlensul's pup. He's already scared Muno will make his life difficult.

So he panics. And deploys all the resources of the Church to find our man for me."

"Clever. But you might have outsmarted yourself. Look. The reason I wanted to talk in here is so I could tell you to look at Ferris Renfrow. We tried to investigate him when we were in Alten Weinberg. We didn't find much but some odd facts did surface."

"Such as?"

"He wasn't well known before Johannes but somebody with the same name has been connected with most of the Emperors since the Grail Empire was founded. Today's Ferris Renfrow claims all those other Renfrows are his ancestors. But we couldn't find anybody who ever heard of any of the Renfrows being married. Or otherwise involved with any human being, male or female."

"That would be unusual."

"He does odd things, too." Hecht repeated what he had heard about Renfrow presenting an apparent eyewitness account of the Battle of Los Naves de los Fantas to Empress Katrin the evening of the battle.

That got some attention. First in the form of denial, mostly by the Principaté. "He must have used Night things to observe the action and report back. Nobody walks the Construct but Grandfather. And Heris, now. We don't teach anyone. We don't *tell* anyone. Even the monks and nuns down there don't know what it really does."

Cloven Februaren was not so certain. "Someone else could have come up with a Construct of their own." The ancient fell into a brooding silence, clearly trying to remember something.

Heris said, "If he's a half-god and near-immortal he might not need a Construct. When was the bastard born? How long ago?"

No one knew. The child was mythical. Februaren grumbled, "At least four hundred years. Probably more."

Hecht said, "You have an eyewitness. A participant. Inside the ascendant."

"Who couldn't say. Arlensul never developed any skill at grasping a place in time in the middle world. A common failing of the Night. Which has kept you alive. So far."

Hecht said, "Whatever else, Renfrow is a place to start. Even if he isn't our man he might know where to look."

The Ninth Unknown blurted, "I've got it! When I was a boy! Younger than Pella. The Sixth Unknown was in charge. The Construct was primitive back then. But we did get more support from the Collegium. . . . You wouldn't have recognized it. . . ."

"Grandfather! Did you have a point?"

"Oh. Sure. There was a brother who worked on the project. Something was wrong about him. Beyond being just plain creepy. A lot of brothers, especially ascetics and monks, are natural-born creepy. It has to do with the kind of personality that's attracted to the life. . . ."

"Grandfather."

"Yes. Creepy. I told my father and grandfather and his father. None of them wanted to hear it. He worked hard and didn't do anything heinous in public. And he definitely had a talent for the work."

Hecht said, "And his name was Brother Ferris."

"No. It was Brother Lester. Lester . . . Temagat! That's it. Temagat. He was way more interested in the Construct than anyone I've ever seen. Including Muno. But maybe excepting Heris. Heris is in there like a fish trying out water."

"I have plans, ancestor."

"Temagat disappeared under what I considered mysterious circumstances. No one else gave a rat's ass. People came and went. The old folks only whined because they couldn't come up with as dedicated a replacement."

"Temagat? Lester Temagat?" Hecht asked. "You're sure?"

"Of course I'm sure, pup. I'm old, not senile. The melon works as good as ever. Why?"

"I know that name."

"Ah! Then talk to me, young Piper."

"When we were in captivity in Plemenza, being interrogated by Ferris Renfrow, Pinkus Ghort told a story about one of his early jobs as a mercenary. He was working for the old Duke of Clearenza. Which was under siege by the Emperor. An Imperial agent named Lester Temagat supposedly murdered Ghort's father and opened the gate during the night. This all came up because Ghort insisted that the man interrogating us was the man who called himself Lester Temagat back then."

"Very interesting."

"The problem is, Pinkus Ghort is notoriously unreliable about details of his own past. He'll tell conflicting stories about the same incident on the same day. I didn't try hard to find the truth about that. But Clearenzans don't recall events the way Ghort did. Till now I'd have bet that the story was mostly true but with Pinkus Ghort in the Temagat role."

"Rather a bleak indictment of your friend."

"He is a friend. That doesn't make him any less a villain to some. It doesn't guarantee that he won't be a villain to me, someday. Especially if he's had too much wine. He can't resist a good vintage."

"Vintage this," Anna said, ending that chatter. "Find out more about Pinkus. If only so we know how he came up with that name."

"Anna?" All three men spoke her name at once.

"Pinkus Ghort is definitely a bastard. So far, he's been our bastard. What are the chances he's the half-god bastard you want to find?"

Futilely trying to be funny, Hecht suggested, "He would have to be several hundred years old to have done all the things he claims." Which failed to stir a smile.

Cloven Februaren said, "You people will have to deal with that. My focus will be the Great Sky Fortress."

"Wouldn't this be part of that?" Hecht asked.

"The hunt for Pinkus Ghort's past? Doubtful. Though my mind isn't working with its usual cool precision. I'm a bit distracted these days."

That piqued Principaté Delari's curiosity. "Explain that."

"The Windwalker is coming. Uh. No. Not here. Toward the entrance to the Realm of the Gods, through Andoray. He knows the way is open. And, before we got started, there was an explosive event under the Andorayan Sea. An immense surge of power. It's fading now but it's still leaking. Every Night thing able to get there is coming to feed."

"You think he might overwhelm the others."

"I'm scared that he'll get strong enough to freeze the water between Andoray and the gateway. If he does, we're doomed."

Hecht pictured a map of the north. "Wouldn't that approach be going the long way round? Coming along the south shore of the Shallow Sea would be shorter. He'd end up in Friesland, which would put him closer to the entrance."

"He can't leave the frozen country. The ice isn't permanent south of the Shallow Sea. Yet."

"I don't recall my mythology that well, Grandfather," Delari said. "Wasn't Kharoulke afflicted with a curse that kept him from crossing open water?"

"Some. He can step over puddles and streams with little discomfort, unless the water touches him. He can wade through liquid water for a short time if he concentrates on managing the pain. If he takes the time, he can make water freeze for a hundred yards around him. One way of handling him, back when, was to make sure he stayed distracted around sizable water barriers."

Hecht said, "This is a winter god who can't abide water? Winter is all about ice and snow."

"He isn't bothered by ice or snow. They just get harder when he's around."

Anna observed, "There's water naturally in the air. It evaporates. Would that explain why this devil is in a bad mood all the time?"

"Could be. Or, like some people, he could just be a natural-born asshole."

"Well, gentlemen, I appreciate you letting me into your club tonight." Anna downed a last sip of coffee, pushed her chair back. "But I'd better go check on the children."

The Ninth Unknown told her, "When you get to the door, stop and count slowly to ten before you lift the latch."

That puzzled everyone. For eight of the requested seconds.

Hecht grew irritated because the old man kept staring at Anna's lower half.

Februaren pointed a finger, spoke a word. The word hung in the air, glowing like hot, violet metal.

Hecht loosed a violent belch, first in a gassy chorus that embarrassed everyone.

High-pitch shrieks erupted from the folds of Anna's skirt. Shadows fell out, writhing, looking like foot-tall humanoids with scorpion tails and an extra set of arms. Nothing cast them. For an instant each shone the same dark glow as Februaren's floating word. Then they collapsed into little piles of black sand. That sand quickly decayed to black dust.

The Ninth Unknown said, "A few seconds more, if you please, Anna. Heris, scatter that dust. Gently. You should find two tiny amber beads. Patience, Anna."

Heris did as instructed. "I don't see any beads. Just two flakes of gold." She placed those in front of Februaren.

"Well, well."

Anna asked, "Can I go, now?"

"Certainly. Catch hold of that word and drag it along. That'll keep any others from sliding in while the door is open. Once you close that, give the word a shove to put it in motion. It'll drift around and rout out any more lurking things. Lurking! I love that word. It should last twenty minutes. The floating word should, that is."

Anna followed instructions, refusing to be impressed or intimidated by the unexpected.

The door chunked shut.

"So what do we have?" Hecht asked.

Everyone stared at the flakes. Hecht downed some more coffee. Finally, Delari said, "Bronte Doneto has gone clever on us."

Heris asked, "Why do you think it was him?"

"Because of the flakes. Any true Night thing would've left an egg. In this size, a bead. These were specially created from Night things, then trained by a sorcerer who had the inclination to spend a lot of time shaping them."

"All that from a couple flakes?"

"All that. I'd guess they represent years of work."

Heris asked, "How did you know?"

Februaren tapped the side of his nose. "Talent, sweetling. Talent. Take my word. Since you don't have it yourself you'll never really understand."

"I understand when somebody is blowing smoke, though." Heris was irked but only mildly so. Februaren had not been condescending. "Won't their disappearance tell him you're on to him?"

"He has half a brain. He should assume that anyway."

"When he doesn't know you're still alive?"

"He'll know that as soon as he gets the news from the show downstairs."

Principaté Delari said, "I have no love for Bronte Doneto. But I have an almost boundless respect. He's done an amazing job of crafting himself, almost entirely in secrecy. I still have no real idea what he was up to in the catacombs with the Witchfinders that time. You be careful of him, Piper. He must have figured out that you and Armand helped me escape."

Februaren added, "Keep an eye out for rogue Witchfinders, too."

"*Rogue* Witchfinders?"

"You've been around the Brotherhood of War most of the time since you arrived in Firaldia. Have you figured out what the Witchfinders were up to in the catacombs? Or in Sonsa, at the Ten Galleons?"

"No." And he had tried to find out. Cautiously.

"Chances are, nobody knows anymore. Except maybe Bronte Doneto, the only survivor. Barring Lila or Vali knowing something they've never reported."

"There's nothing there."

Heris said, "You could always ask the Patriarch himself."

The others chuckled charitably.

The Ninth Unknown asked, "How soon till you go haring off after your impossible fantasy, Piper?"

"Excuse me?"

"I'm sure you won't resist the blandishments of Alten Weinberg. I'm hoping you hold out awhile. So Muno can get you connected to the Construct."

Hecht's response was instant aversion.

Februaren revealed a lot of teeth. Those could have used more attention. "You aren't in the Realm of Peace anymore, Piper. And it's important."

Delari observed, "The Realm of Peace turned its back on you."

"You don't have to do that. I get it. But I don't like it. I don't like being an exile, either. I'll spend as much time with the Construct as I can."

Heris remarked, "Note that he denied nothing about Alten Wein-berg, nor the Empire, nor the two pullets running the farmyard there."

Februaren said, "Oh, we noted."

Hecht's cheeks grew heated.

BREAKFAST AT ANNA MOZILLA'S HOUSE. THE CONSENT FAMILY VISIT-ing. Noë in the kitchen with Anna. Little Consents infesting the place like they were twice their actual number, playing some game where they fled from Pella and the girls, shrieking and running.

Hecht slumped in a comfortable chair, sipped a mint tea, and en-joyed the domestic chaos. Titus occupied a chair facing him. He had said nothing since they finished eating. He sipped from a showy Clearenzan glass filled with grape juice. He, too, was savoring the moment. Finally, reluctantly, he asked about Alten Weinberg. "Are we going?"

Hecht nodded. "I don't know when. I visited the Penital. Told them we'll take the job if the Empress still wants us."

"Us?"

"She takes everybody. Or nobody. Has Prosek decided?"

"He waffles. He loves the stinks and bangs and won't get to play with them if he follows the Brotherhood to the Holy Lands."

"I don't want to lose him. Or Kait Rhuk. By the way. There's a new ambassador. Bayard va Still-Patter. Graf fon Wistrcz got called home. His wife did something to offend the Empress."

"Bayard. Not so good. He didn't like us taking over his place."

"All is forgiven. If he hadn't been made to suffer through that, Ka-trin wouldn't have given him this plum assignment."

"What's holding you here?"

Hecht made a gesture to include their surroundings. "And Princi-paté Delari. That old man is a slave driver."

"Having you do what?"

"He claims it's education. I'm not allowed to talk about it." And did not want to. Encounters with the Construct left him feeling inade-quate, even retarded. Heris said she had felt the same in the beginning. He could accept that intellectually but never before had he had diffi-culty mastering any skill.

"All right. We'll go when we go. I won't need to look for work right away. But I do worry about Noë getting sick of having me underfoot."

"I can empathize with that." Hecht was uncomfortable. Titus no longer seemed able to conceive of life without his being part of Piper Hecht's staff.

Consent said, "By the way, I've found where Krulik and Sneigon are relocating. Which isn't anywhere near where I expected." He took a folded sheet of paper from his sleeve, handed it over. Hecht opened it, smoothed it. On it was a painstakingly produced map of the upper Vieran Sea. A red circle lay in the wild mountains over on the Eastern Empire side. "Somewhere in there. I found it because Krulik and Sneigon are recruiting veterans to defend something. Some of my agents were approached. I had them sign up."

"I presume you know more than this."

"Of course. Hidden in rough country that's mostly empty. Plague wiped out the population several hundred years ago."

An odd and terrible time that had been. The plague hit hardest in the Eastern Empire just as the Praman Conquest reached its ferocious peak. Some believed that the vast movements of peoples at the time spread the disease. Within the Eastern Empire urban populations became so depleted that rural folk flooded in hoping to prosper. Many of them died as well. Vast tracts of country had gone back to nature. And remained wilderness even now, centuries later.

"Why just there?"

"Splendid isolation, yet a river wide and gentle enough for small barge traffic. Vast old forests to turn into charcoal. And nearby ore deposits. Not the best but still good. Especially if they use forced labor. There's no government to interfere. Tribal leaders can be bribed or intimidated. Those wild people are why they hired soldiers. The ownership plans a huge, bloody demonstration first excuse they get. Construction has already begun. They want a huge operation that'll make them filthy rich selling to everybody."

"There are, indeed, fortunes to be made creating the tools for efficient organized murder. What about sulfur? For making firepowder. There aren't any sulfur mines over there, are there?"

"That they have to import. Unless they make the firepowder somewhere else."

"Which would make some sense."

"I'll keep on it. Yes. But you need to remember that we no longer have any legal standing."

"I understand. But we'll pretend. We'll be our own law."

"Also, some new intelligence sources have opened up. Because of that."

"Oh?" Immediately curious.

"A lot of Brothen Devedians aren't happy about what Krulik and Sneigon are doing. Ones who have seen what happens when Deves get blamed. People like refugees from Sonsa. They're sure Krulik and Sneigon will bring down the wrath of the Chaldarean world on the Deve communities."

"You never know." Full of one of Anna's finest breakfasts ever, Hecht wanted nothing more than to go back to bed.

"I know. The hammer will fall because Chaldareans will be terrified the Deves might arm themselves with fearsome weapons."

"And they'd be right."

"Probably. But I remind you, Deves never start the ruckus."

"Titus! Of course they do. Just by refusing to acknowledge a few self-evident religious truths."

"I'm now a devout convert, boss, but bullshit!"

Hecht laughed.

"I haven't found anything useful about Ferris Renfrow or Pinkus Ghort. I don't want to push, especially with Renfrow. I don't want to alert him. His network is bigger, more sophisticated, and more deadly."

"I get you, Titus. He worries me, too."

"Thank you. With Ghort the problem is a lack of resources. I can't send somebody to Grolsach. Assuming Ghort really is from there. The investigator wouldn't survive."

"Naturally. What about the catamite?"

"Not much there, either. He disappeared the day Boniface died. He may have fled to the Empire, in disguise. He might be living on the street. Somebody might have killed him. All three hypotheses have their advocates. Why are you concerned?"

"He lived with Principaté Delari. He heard things. The Principaté is worried that he might repeat them."

For an instant Hecht wondered if Cloven Februaren might have dealt with Osa Stile. He would have to ask.

"I see." Said in a tone suggesting that Titus knew he was not hearing the whole truth.

Heris rotated into being behind Titus's chair. Her mouth burst open. This was a huge blunder on her part. She turned again, hastily.

Consent felt the air stir both times but Heris was gone before he looked back. "What the hell was that?"

"A ghost? Something. It was only there for half a second."

"But . . ."

"If this was my place I'd make Anna move," Hecht said. "Too many weird things happen in this neighborhood. Not to mention too much dangerous stuff, like people blowing up carts loaded with kegs of firepowder. Now what?"

Someone had begun pounding on the door.

Hecht headed that way.

Pella streaked past. And was totally disappointed when he found

Heris at the door. Who told him, "My feelings are hurt just by being here with you, too, Pella. I need to see your father."

By now everyone had come to see what was going on. Pella told Heris, "I thought it might be Kait Rhuk. He said he might come. . . . Uh-oh."

Numerous pairs of eyes bored in. Hecht asked the question. "When did you see Kait Rhuk?" When no answer was forthcoming, "I distinctly recall telling you, more than once, not to leave the house."

Heris reminded them of her presence. "I can provide a convincing demonstration, Piper. It's one reason Grandfather sent me." She produced a shiny brown mahogany dowel an inch in diameter and eighteen long. She found the center of the room, lifted the piece of wood overhead, closed her eyes, and began turning. And singing in a bad voice, words in something like Church Brothen. The mahogany dowel wiggled, wobbled, and writhed.

It vanished in an eye-searing scarlet flash. Two more flashes followed quickly, then one sharp little crack of thunder.

Hecht's eyes adjusted. Three black silhouettes now decorated three different walls, each near a corner of the room. The shapes were knee-high, nearly as wide, vaguely humanoid but without necks, demonic by the standards of every present or formerly held religion of those in the room.

Something more tangible lay a step behind Hecht. Twenty pounds of already rotting, greenish meat, shedding ribbons of lime steam. Severed extremities, shiny and lizard-belly yellow, lay scattered around the odiferous mass.

Heris said, "Pella, this is what we're dealing with. The least dangerous of it. When you go out unprotected, things like these go with you. Some could make you look like that green mess if their master ordered it. Like this." She snapped her fingers. "Piper, you just witnessed a triumph of technical education over an absence of talent. The old people can make a monkey over into a deadly weapon."

Hecht gave Pella a hard, promising look, but asked Heris, "Why are you here? And how did those things get into the house? I thought the Principaté charmed the entrances against the Night."

"There are ways to ride somebody through the wards. If that somebody is in a hurry and doesn't take precautions. Pella."

Hecht said, "Pella, out there it just might be something a whole lot nastier. Something that could kill you before you knew it was there."

Noë Consent said, "Titus, we have to talk. When we get home."

That did not sound promising. Hecht said, "You haven't told me why you're here, Heris."

"That was part of it. Clearing the vermin."

"Please."

"The same reason I always come here when you're in town. I'm Grandfather's messenger. This time, besides getting the bugs out of Anna's house, he wants me to warn you that you're about to hear from Serenity. He wants you to be careful. The other old man has gone away again. Though he did sow some confusion before he left."

As she talked Heris turned slowly, pointing her stick at every corner and shadow. And at Titus, his wife, and all the children. She did not care who might be offended.

Following the path blazed by her surviving male ancestors.

"Nothing got away when I came in. Anna, let's take a quick look around. There may be more. Pella. Stay away from that."

Dazed, Anna left the room with Heris. The children and Consents had sense enough to stay put. Titus asked, "What was all that?"

"You saw everything I did."

Timid Noë wrung her hands, gathered her brood, and looked to the men for a cue.

Hecht said, "Pella. Do I have to strap you to get you to leave things alone?"

"I just wanted to see."

"And what would there be to see if you'd done as you were told? You let those things in when you came back. Boy, there can be real consequences . . ."

Fierce red light. A *crack!* that rattled the house. A roar of rage and agony. Anna squealed in terror in the kitchen.

Hecht and Consent headed that way. As though there might be something they could do that Heris could not.

The blonde appeared. "That will be all of them. That was the big one." She stepped aside, glared at Pella. It was plain there were things she wanted to say but could not in front of the Consents. "Grandfather will send someone to clean up. He'll probably come himself, to fix it so this can't happen again." Pella had begun to wilt. "I'd clean up myself but . . . He'll want better information than I can give. Being just a messenger."

"You did have a reason for coming?"

"I told you. He suspected the kind of problem I just corrected. And he wanted you to know things are happening inside Krois. That you'll be seeing Serenity and should be careful when you do."

Hecht was sure there was more but Heris would not broach it in front of Titus.

She said, "Go comfort Anna. Don't whip Pella. Just make him sit watch on the thing in the kitchen. Sense might penetrate." She went out the front door into a bright morning. Carefully.

ANNA WAS BADLY RATTLED. SHE STOOD IN A CORNER OF THE KITCHEN, hands clasped between her breasts, staring at a mess like that in the other room but five times its size. It was evaporating. It stank. Hecht wondered if it would be all right to open a window.

Best not. Not till an expert said it was safe.

Anna sounded like a frightened little girl when she asked, "How could that thing be invisible? And not make any noise or smells?" Then, more focused and more determined, "I can't live like this, Piper." After a pause, "These things happen because you're you. And they only happen when you're here."

Probably not strictly true but he did not argue. "I won't be long. I can move to the Castella. If that will make you more comfortable."

He watched Anna struggle to behave like an adult. She wanted to scream at him for being willing to desert her. Even though she had told him that having him around was intolerable. Only a short time after telling him that she refused to leave this place for any other. Even if moving put her beyond reach of those inclined to deploy the Instrumentalities of the Night against her.

Anna took deep breath after deep breath. Her color improved. The ugliness of anger faded. He knew she wanted him to utter some magic words that would close the situation neatly. He remained silent. This was outside his expertise. He had a Sha-lug's sense of being a fragment of a larger instrument. He took what was given and did not look beyond. Otherwise, God might find him guilty of hubris.

Anna said, "We're all counters in a game. We don't get many choices, however much we whine about the injustice. I've never regretted following you here. But sometimes I do miss the quiet old life."

Hecht took her into his arms. It felt good, having her there. Felt good having put together this makeshift family from human spindrift, all flotsam like himself. Though he had found a blood family of his own, as well.

"We still have company, Piper."

But not for long. Noë Consent had had all the excitement one timid woman dared enjoy in one morning. Titus was apologetic as he followed his wife to the street.

Hecht told him, "I understand, Titus. If I was Noë and had three knee-highs to worry about, I wouldn't want to be around me, either. Well. Look at this."

Principaté Delari's coach was approaching, surrounded by outriders armed with firepowder weapons. They wore smoldering slow matches on their hats.

Consent grumbled, "How the hell did he get here so fast?"

"Has to have been on his way."

Titus eyed him suspiciously. He did not buy that. Not whole, though it had to be true. Something was going on. He was not trusted enough to be taken inside.

"There's that thing called need to know, Titus."

"I understand." But he was not happy. He considered coach and outriders. "They do say he's a wizard. And he knew there were eavesdropper entities on the premises."

"He *is* a wizard. And a damned sight more scary one than people realize. I'll keep you posted on my plans."

"Be careful. I really don't want to look for another job."

"A vote of confidence. Excellent." Hecht surveyed the street, checking for gawkers interested in Anna Mozilla's house. What he saw startled him. Two of his old bodyguards were hanging around up the way, trying to be inconspicuous.

They were not doing a clever job of it.

Was he still under the protection of the Brotherhood? If so, why? The castellans, the masters of the commanderies, and the overlords over in Runch, they all liked their Patriarchs driven. They had that kind of a man in charge, now. Except that Serenity's obsession was not the Holy Lands.

"Piper? Are you lost in the next world?"

He blinked. Heris's face was just a foot away. And there was Titus looking back, clearly wondering how the blonde could be riding with Principaté Delari. "No. I'm lost in this one."

The Eleventh Unknown, with help from his coachman, had descended and started for the house. Bent and taking small steps.

Hecht asked, "What happened to him?"

"Nothing. Protective coloration. The world doesn't need to know how spry he is. Especially the part that lives inside Krois."

"I understand. They'll be more patient if they think he's on the brink."

Delari straightened up as soon as the door closed. He considered the members of the household. He did not appear to be in a good mood. The look he gave Pella made the boy cringe. Nor was there the customary gentle indulgence when he considered Vali and Lila. "You girls go do whatever you'd be doing if I wasn't here. Pella. You'll clean up the mess you caused." He indicated the green meat. "Starting now!" when Pella opened his mouth to protest.

The boy did not know what he should do or where he should start. Heris took him by the ear and headed for the kitchen.

Delari stared at Anna so long she finally demanded, "What?"

"Are you ready to move to the safety of the town house?"

"What? No! This is my home."

"I can't protect you here. You're too far away."

"I don't need protecting if Piper isn't here. And he's about to run off to Alten Weinberg."

"If those are the facts you perceive, then I bow to your superior feminine wisdom. It's Piper who concerns me, anyway. I offer friendship and protection because you're important to him. It's not something I do lightly. Neither will I argue. You want to be on your own, so be it."

Anna considered Delari with always big, dark eyes gone huge.

Pella stumbled through, headed for the front door. He lugged a chamber pot filled with reeking demon flesh. Heris opened the door.

Delari said, "I won't argue with you, either, Piper. You stay at the town house for the rest of your visit. Stop! That wasn't a request. That was a statement of fact. That's the way it's going to be. Don't waste your breath."

Piper Hecht chose to avoid a squabble. For the moment. This would be one he could not win without losing the Principaté, too. And it made sense. Assuming he still had enemies. Say, someone so powerful he sent Night things to spy in Anna's house.

Hecht caught Anna's eye, glanced at the meat pile not far from where he stood. That thing had come in with Pella, not with Piper Hecht.

She would come around. He hoped.

Though feeling fierce, Anna also saw a fight she could not win. She left the room to see what the girls had found to do.

Pella trudged back in with an empty chamber pot. He started on the mess in the front room.

Principaté Delari heard Hecht's report on events, remarked, "The balance has tilted slightly in our favor. For the moment."

"I don't understand."

Delari shrugged. "It doesn't matter. So long as you exercise due caution. Now. You're going to be summoned by Serenity. Expect him to be unpleasant and verbally abusive without burning his bridges. I want to use your visit to get around his security precautions."

"You know he won't let me in with anything dangerous."

"It won't be anything dangerous. Just the kind of things Heris rooted out here. Pella! That boy is dogging it, Piper. He needs a little more direct encouragement."

"He's a kid. It's what they do at that age."

Delari grunted. "May be. I don't remember ever being that young."

Heris and Pella returned from another trip to the gutter. Pella lugged the chamber pot. Heris carried a covered stoneware dish. She handled it like it was hot. "Are you ready for this, Grandfather?"

"Yes. Set it on that stand."

She did that. Delari removed the lid. Fragrant steam rolled up.

"Damn! That smells good!" Hecht said. He leaned into the steam.

The dish looked to be something featuring lamb and rice, with red beans, fragments of vegetable, seasoned heavily with garlic and fennel and something less familiar.

Delari said, "This would be some of Mrs. Creedon's best work." He took a packet from a pocket, added what looked like a dozen dried button mushrooms. He stirred those in with a wooden spoon presented by Heris. "We'll let this set a minute." Heris replaced the lid. Delari continued, "I'm sure Anna has fed you up just fine. You've filled out some already. But when I tell you, you should gobble this down. The mushrooms are particularly important."

"Why?"

"I'll explain when you get back. Also, we need to get Grandfather's amulet off you before you head out. That's the sort of thing they'll be looking for. Bronte Doneto is already suspicious because you've survived so much. We'll reinstall it when you get back. Be especially careful while you're doing without."

Hecht had a library of questions but got no chance to ask them.

"Time to eat." Delari lifted the stoneware lid. Heris proffered a tin spoon. Pella slumped past, grumbling because he had to do all the work.

A clatter rose outside, the Principaté's coach leaving hurriedly. Heris spun sideways and disappeared. She rotated back into being seconds later. Anna and the children gawked like that was something new. Heris said, "The Patriarchal messenger is just a few blocks off, Grandfather. Let's get busy. The watchers out there need to forget seeing anything after Lieutenant Consent left."

"Right. Do what you can while I deal here. Piper. Be honest with the Patriarch. But don't volunteer anything. Make him work to find out anything. Eat, damnit! Those mushrooms. And stick your left hand out here so I can get that amulet off. Anna. You and the girls need to come in here for a second."

THE POUNDING ON ANNA'S DOOR BESPOKE ARROGANCE. BEWILDERED, Anna answered it. She suffered that confusion one has after hastening into a room to do something, then not being able to remember what. The children had the same confused air.

Piper Hecht occupied his customary chair. He shared the confusion. Something had happened but he was not sure what. He rubbed his left wrist. It felt odd. Moist, too. And it itched.

A mild stomach cramp startled him. He belched.

The man at the door was being unpleasant to Anna. Hecht went over, pushed children aside, moved Anna, smacked the man squarely in the nose. "Pella, bring my sword. And a rag for the blood." He wore a short sword when he was out and about. Though the blade had seen action, it was more symbol than substance.

Anna begged, "Don't start anything, Piper."

"I won't, sweet. Much. Except for this asshole. Who seems to have lost the manners his mother taught him." The deliberate use of "asshole" was more likely to get the man's attention than the pop in the snot locker. All Brothe knew that the Captain-General—emeritus, now—used bad language only when extremely provoked. "Or can we expect those manners to improve, Mr. Silo?"

Hecht knew the man, barely. Deepened Silo. Related to the new Patriarch. An ambitious thug with none of the skills necessary to get where he thought he deserved to go. He had been rejected by the Brotherhood, had enjoyed a three-week career with the Patriarchal forces of Captain-General Piper Hecht, then had been asked to leave the constabularii of the City Regiment after failing to shine there. Family connections were all he had.

None of his problems, of course, were his own fault.

Hecht wondered what Silo was doing working for Serenity, family or no. Bronte Doneto seldom let sentiment ignore incompetence.

Silo was, undoubtedly, scheduled to become a throwaway in some underhanded scheme.

"Do I have your attention, Mr. Silo? Or shall I break something else?"

Venom sloshed behind Deepened Silo's eyes. There would be paybacks for this humiliation. But, right now, he just wanted the pain not to get any bigger.

"Yes, sir. No, sir. I was just . . ."

Hecht drew back, ready to indulge himself again.

"Sir, the Patriarch sent me to bring you to see him. He wants to consult you. In person."

Curiously put. A summons, but just slightly soft.

"Is that so? Then I'd better get going." He strapped on the sword

that Pella handed him. He tested the ease of its draw. As encouragement to Mr. Silo. "Thank you, son."

AN INTERESTING JOURNEY, THAT TO KROIS. THE PATRIARCH'S MEN
had not come with a coach or horses. They walked, soaking up the
morning sun. The Patriarch wanted to deliver a message to the rabble.
Hecht did not think they were getting the one Serenity intended. He
saw anger over what appeared to be the arrest of a hero.

So. Maybe Bronte Doneto felt threatened by Piper Hecht the way
Gordimer the Lion had felt threatened by Else Tage.

Everywhere he looked, along the way, Hecht saw a tall, hard-eyed
blonde watching from the shadows. Silo and his henchmen failed to
notice.

Heris must have made herself familiar with every inch of Brothe.

Absent his amulet, Hecht felt countless focal points of malice, low-
grade concentrations of the Night he would not have noticed normally.
His companions, though, sensed nothing at all, or just ignored what
was there.

Must be something to do with Cloven Februaren's amulet.

What was that old man up to these days?

HECHT WAS SEARCHED AND CHECKED AND FOUND FREE OF BOTH
offensive and defensive weapons and sorceries. During the process he
belched twice, massively. That problem had grown steadily during the
walk to Krois. He belched again, violently, as he entered the Patriarchal presence.

During his obsequies he tendered an apology. "My stomach refuses
to adjust to Brothen cuisine."

"Is that painful?" as another, smaller burst gained its freedom.

"It is, Your Holiness. It is."

Serenity seemed pleased. He got to the point. "I'll be straightforward, Hecht. I'm not pleased with you."

Without saying so, and without demonstrating defiance, Hecht made
it plain that he did not care. He could argue but would not. There was
no point. Bronte Doneto's universe revolved around Bronte Doneto. The
rest of the world existed to advance Bronte Doneto's ambitions.

"You have nothing to say?"

"No, Your Holiness."

"The Penital is putting it about that you're transferring your allegiance to the Empire."

"I find myself unemployed. The Empress has offered me work."

"I understand she offered you work before. You turned her down."

"I had a commitment."

"Suppose I forbid you?"

Hecht shrugged. "I don't work for you."

"I'm the Patriarch."

Hecht shrugged. "The Empress might consider that an inappropriate incursion of the Church into Imperial prerogatives. At a time when she's under tremendous pressure to return to the policies of her father."

"Are you trying to bully me?"

Hecht belched thunderously, accompanying that with a toot from the nether orifice. "Your Holiness? No! I'm trying to make you aware of how other people might perceive your actions. And how some might respond. I wouldn't want to bring up painful memories. . . ."

"But?"

Hecht waved a hand to hasten the dispersal of gas he had jut passed. "Please recall what happened in the Connec, with other people who didn't admire you so much as you do yourself."

Ouch! Not the best way to say that.

Anger floated across Serenity's face, went away. The Patriarch suspected that he was being baited, probably not intentionally. "There is one other matter. Well, two other matters. One is the disappearance of weapons and equipment belonging to our forces."

"Your Holiness? Everything was accounted for when I turned over command. My staff kept meticulous records. The kind of corruption you see in most forces wasn't allowed to take root under my command."

Serenity did not sound pleased when he admitted, "So I've heard. I heard complaints during the Interregnum."

"People actually complained because I wouldn't let them steal from the Church?"

"They did. Though they made it sound like something else."

Hecht released more gas, less quietly. "You Holiness, if you're having problems with things going missing, you should talk to the people you sent to take over." Now he passed a long, silent stream of gas, moved to evade the worst of it.

"I was hoping it would be simpler than that."

"Pinkus has the records." He hoped Ghort was not stealing. "We had inventory numbers marked on everything. Who had what will be in the records."

"I'll take another look, then."

"The other thing?"

"The relationship you've developed with Muniero Delari. I'm curious about that. And I'm even more curious about what goes on inside that town house."

"You expect me to tell you anything? I owe Principaté Delari a great deal."

"I gather. He took over sponsoring you when Grade Drocker died. Though Drocker's interest in you never made sense. Now I hear there's another villain lurking in that town house. One Cloven Februaren, who styles himself the Ninth Unknown. But Cloven Februaren is supposed to have died before I was born."

"I assume you're talking about the old man they found living in a room in a part of the house that hadn't been used for decades. He claims he's the Principaté's grandfather. I don't know much about him. He's not around much. When he is, he's mostly pulling practical jokes. The Principaté doesn't like him. Talks like he wishes the old man would just go away. I think he's scared of him."

Hecht recalled Delari cautioning him not to volunteer anything. Was there something in the air? Something designed to loosen his tongue? "Oh, God!"

"What?"

"My stomach. Oh, Sweet Aaron!" He grasped his gut. This time the fart energy exceeded everything that had gone before. The odor pursuant was the worst ever to grace Piper Hecht's nostrils. It took only a moment to reach Serenity. It distracted the Patriarch from his rising anger. When Hecht repeated himself, almost immediately, Serenity demanded, "Has this been going on long?"

"Not this bad. Your Holiness." A cramp shook him. If there was something in the air this gas should overwhelm it.

The Patriarch began barking at his hangers-on: Get a draft moving through the chamber. Bring in candles and torches. Do *something*!

Nothing helped. It got worse. Serenity wanted to bully and badger his former Captain-General but the disruption was too great. Too much for Hecht, too, who finally begged, "Excuse me, Your Holiness. Please. There's something bad wrong. I need to find a healing brother." He failed to stifle the most ferocious rumbler yet. He managed to create an expression of deep suspicion. "What did you do to me?"

The grand toot was the precursor of a parade of lesser expressions. Candles and torches did not help. The Patriarch angrily ordered Piper Hecht expelled from Krois, grumbling something about interviewing him later. He denied any connection with Hecht's affliction, in the face of Hecht's growing pain and passion.

The Patriarchal Guards did not seem inclined to believe their master. Hecht's digestion was almost normal by the time he reached the south bank of the Teragi. Shaking, he settled on one of the stone benches at the edge of the Memorium, considered the thousand monuments to victories and personalities of antiquity. He tried to stay alert, but the tail end of his suffering sucked his attention inward.

He was unaware of Heris till she sat down beside him. "That was way more harsh than Grandfather intended, Piper."

"Humh?"

"I watched. I got as close as I could without getting caught in the tangle spells. You were just supposed to have a giant case of the silent farts."

"You were in there?"

"Sure."

"They'll know. Doneto is the most powerful sorcerer in the Collegium."

"He's supposed to know that something was there. That it came in when you did and it left when you left. You have a guardian Instrumentality. They won't look for some other outside agency. We're just reinforcing what they're already thinking."

Gas escaped Hecht. It whipped away on the breeze. "So what have I done?"

"You took a pack of shadow spies into Krois. Inside you. So no one knew that you were smuggling. Very clever of Grandfather."

"Yeah. Right. Should we be talking here?"

"With the sun so high and bright? Well . . . Maybe not. Somebody might wonder about us being together."

"Really?" Heris was not well known. Still, she might arouse some curiosity, juxtaposed with Piper Hecht. "Serenity really wanted to interrogate me about the Principaté, our relationship, and about Cloven Februaren. The gas saved me having to deal with that."

"For now." She laughed. That startled Hecht. She had no discernible sense of humor. "He may have you watched so he can catch you in a gas-free mood." Another snicker. "I was behind a tapestry fifty feet from that room when you all came out. You had me gagging. I'll let Grandfather know he's developed a potent new weapon."

"He wants to use it that way, he'd better feed those mushrooms to people he doesn't mind losing." He released a small rumble. "The pain wasn't worth it. And it feels like it's coming back."

"Oh! Let's travel on. You need to get to the town house, anyway. You need to get your amulet back on. You don't want to be exposed any longer than you have to be."

Hecht farted again, gently. He surveyed the Memorium and river's edge and spied several observers. There was nowhere someone could hide and still be close enough to keep watch. "If us getting together will set off alarms, then the bell is already clanging." One more look at the Memorium. "I'd rather go around. Bad things can happen in there." As they walked he told her about having been ambushed by a hidden archer there, and about fighting Calziran pirates among the monuments.

"If the Ninth Unknown is halfway honest, which is questionable, you ought to feel the same way almost anywhere. He had a full-time job keeping you alive, back when."

"Things should be different now that I'm unemployed."

AFTER QUESTIONING HECHT ABOUT HIS PATRIARCHAL AUDIENCE FOR twice the time that visit had lasted, Principaté Delari observed, "You might consider leaving town before Serenity pulls you in again." The old man was very self-congratulatory about having inserted shadow agents into Krois. "If he can't question you he can't get answers."

"You're probably right. Though I'll miss my sessions with the Construct."

"Sarcasm duly noted."

"Sorry. I *am* starting to get the hang of using it to communicate."

"I have a work-around. Is there more coffee in that pot, Heris?"

"There is, Grandfather. But we need to find a smuggler. We're almost out of beans."

"Tell Turking. He knows the man who knows the man who knows where to get the beans. Here's what we'll do."

HECHT'S PEOPLE STARTED REPORTING WITHIN HOURS OF HIS HAVING sent out word of his intentions and his hope of getting through the Jagos before bad weather arrived. The Imperial ambassador provided a headquarters suite at the Penital. Unattached staff were invited to move in. Where they got to work eighteen hours a day in return for room and board.

Titus Consent knocked on the frame of the doorway to the little room Hecht had commandeered for his own use. Beckoned, Consent stepped inside. "I think we've heard from about everyone who is going to respond. More of them than I expected. Kait Rhuk can't wait to get going. I let him, Vircondelet, and a dozen others get started this morning. Hagan Brokke is with them. The others are spies or quartermasters. Oh. Drago Prosek says he's in. Claims the Brotherhood will survive without him."

"Efficient, as always."

"It's a curse. Couple of things came up today. Surprises, sort of. First was a letter from Smolens. He says he made a mistake when he decided to stay and work for Ghort. He wants to know if you'd have a job for him if he quits the Patriarchals."

"What do you think?"

"I like Smolens. He did good work. But I'd always wonder if he'd come to us just to spy for Ghort or Serenity."

"And we were sure of him before? He was forced on us the first time. And, like you say, did good work. I hated to lose him. I'll leave it to you. If you can think of a way to use him that leaves him no chance to cause harm, bring him back."

"I'll find a way. Meantime, second surprise. I just got finished talking to Clej Sedlakova. He says he convinced Addam Hauf that the Brotherhood needs to keep somebody close to you. Somebody besides Prosek, who cares about nothing but his falcons."

Hecht laughed. "I'm not surprised. I know Clej. His real motive is, he wants to skate out of the Brotherhood buildup in the Holy Lands. He's been there. He lost the arm there. He's welcome. But I'm really thrilled about Prosek. He is *the* master of artillery. Both kinds."

"Don't let Kait Rhuk hear you say that. He thinks he has that title wrapped up."

"One is as valuable as the other. Rhuk is more the theoretical guy. Though that was Prosek when we started. How soon can you be ready to travel?"

"Half an hour? No. Make it an hour. I need to go get Noë knocked up before I grab my stuff. Don't give me that disgusted look. Tell me you won't give Anna a special goodbye."

Hecht shuddered, uncomfortable with that kind of talk. "I can't say for sure exactly when we'll go. Not before I have a solid idea what I'll have to get started and what I'll need to pull together. Mid-level officers, for sure. And I'll want everybody to travel in small groups. The country can't stand a big mob moving through all at once."

With the best of will an army could not prevent disruptions and damage.

"So your plan is, you'll avoid angering the Patriarchal States till Katrin tells you to jump on them."

Hecht nodded. He hoped to redirect the Empress into pursuing her father's old squabbles with the Patriarchy.

Consent said, "I wish I knew more about how her head works. We could build an interesting future if we knew how to manage her."

Hecht laughed aloud. "Titus, you've got to know that every noble in the Grail Empire is thinking that exact same thing. And, so far, she's been Hansel's daughter and has manipulated them."

"Now you mention it. But the idea is still valid."

"Let's get things moving."

PIPER HECHT'S LAST HOURS IN BROTHE INCLUDED AN INTENSE, POSSI-bly ultimate night with Anna Mozilla, and some vigorous discussion with Principaté Delari in the quiet room at his town house. He did avoid further congress with Serenity by contriving to be elsewhere whenever the Patriarch's messengers came looking for him. Which he managed because Heris seemed to be reading Serenity's mind.

She said, "They say Krois is haunted. They're right. I'm the haunt. Along with your fart children."

Principaté Delari grumbled, "Language, woman. You're getting as bad as my grandfather."

Heris did not argue. Neither did she appear chastened. Delari said, "I wish we'd had more time with the Construct, Piper. But what time we did have will pay dividends. Heris. Break out the medallion."

She brought a pendant, gold and amber with inlays of jade and lapis lazuli, presented it to Hecht. "Heavy," he observed.

The metal portion took the form known as an Ihrian knot, very complex. It had a turban shape at its center and four equal arms surrounding it. The Ihrian knot was one of the earliest symbols of the Chaldarean faith.

"Show him," Delari said.

"You're connected to the Construct now. No matter where you are. Use that to touch it back. Tap the inlays in the right order, you can send a message one character at a time. Here. These are the code sheets. I tried to write them down so it isn't obvious that the code is connected with the pendant. Someone who gets hold of the sheets will look for letters written in the same substitution cipher."

Hecht examined the pages, considered the inlays on the medallion. "I see it. I can memorize this."

"Good."

"Just for fun, why don't I send my messages in Church Brothen?"

Ignoring that, Delari said, "Be careful, Piper. You've never been as vulnerable as you'll be the next few weeks." Mainly because of the need to travel in small bands. "Heris has caught whiffs of several potentially unpleasant schemes."

Heris said, "People you've never even met want to get you just because you're you, Piper."

"I'll become caution itself. We'll disguise ourselves and take a route that stays mostly in the Imperial territories. We'll be all right once we get to the Remayne Pass."

"Be wary of false friends. Serenity is wooing weather vanes like Germa fon Dreasser."

"I know who I can't let get behind me, Grandfather. And I'll go armed with all the legal instruments the Penital can provide."

"So va Still-Patter has developed an affection for you."

Heris sneered. "He hopes Piper will help him achieve his own ambitions."

"An understandable basis for an alliance."

It was not yet light out. Hecht said, "Titus is outside. He'll be getting impatient. I'd better get gone before Serenity finds me and has me dragged in. What's his problem, anyway?"

Heris said, "He's really worried about his falcons and firepowder. Ghort says he can only find a few falcons. Most of those are damaged. Serenity counted on having scores to use against Antieux."

"He won't let that go, will he?"

"Not as long as he lives."

"I couldn't help him with the falcons. I told him to take a closer look at his own people. There are always crooks around our homegrown Patriarchs. Plenty would sell military stores and equipment to line their own purses."

Delari said, "I'll start a rumor, give it a few days, then raise the question in the Collegium. We have the right to insist on an accounting of where the Church's money is going. That will put him on the defensive."

"Add a little pressure by insisting on being told where it's coming from, too."

"Anne of Menand?"

"She's always in the mists somewhere, isn't she?"

FOURTEEN RIDERS LEFT BROTHE WITH HECHT AND CONSENT, A LARGER party than Hecht wanted. His men would not let him travel with less protection.

Heris quickly developed a habit of turning up when nobody was looking, like her remote ancestor before her. She kept Hecht posted on wickednesses hatching inside Krois. As had been the case with Sublime V, Serenity had almost no idea what those around him were doing in his name. He might not want to know. He refused to hear what the Collegium had to say. He was almost completely fixated on next spring in the Connec.

"And what would be the plan for today?" Titus Consent asked, the fifth morning. He became more surly and suspicious daily. Hecht was too obviously shutting him out of the secrets.

"Your choice today, Titus. Either road will bring us to the Remayne Pass day after tomorrow." They were crossing the rich farmlands of the Aco River floodplain, well east of the direct road from Brothe to the pass. Heeding Heris's warnings, Hecht was directing his company out of harm's way. He had not explained. Not in detail. "By now the villains will have decided to catch us at the mouth of the pass."

"I won't ask how you know. You wouldn't give me a straight answer. But I am interested in why you're determined to avoid these villains. There are sixteen of us. None of us virgins."

"All right. I have a friend. A sorcerer. He watches them and keeps me informed. That's all you need. I've avoided the fight because I don't want it to reflect back on the Empress." Which was true. Though mainly for show. He had no objection to renewed conflict between the Patriarch and Empire.

"Things are changing. And I'm not comfortable with some of that."

Hecht shrugged. "We'll get back to normal once we get to Alten Weinberg." He hoped.

Consent remained sullen for hours, upset because he was not trusted. Which could lead to trouble someday. Though, intellectually, Titus had to see that trust was not the issue. What a man does not know he can never reveal, no matter what.

Consent came to Hecht later. "I know how we can deal with these people who worry you so much."

"Tell me."

"We have a thousand men on the move. Maybe more. Mostly behind us. Why don't we just sit down and let them catch up? Your villains won't take on a whole army, will they?" Consent had a hard time believing that Serenity, or his henchmen, would risk angering Empress Katrin by attacking Piper Hecht. But the former Captain-General was adamantly attached to the opposing view.

There was a faction inside Krois that was as stubbornly anti-Imperial as the Anti-Patriarchal faction in Alten Weinberg was stubborn. It had not gotten much voice under the last three Patriarchs. But the new one was not paying attention. The new one had obsessions in another direction.

"You're right, Titus. Why not just show them so many spears that they'll just run away?"

*    *    *

HECHT ENTERED THE REMAYNE PASS ACCOMPANIED BY KEY STAFF, three hundred veterans, and armed with an up-to-the-moment scouting report from Heris.

There were people up ahead. Their intentions were not friendly.

Drago Prosek had found a dozen falcons somewhere. Hecht had not checked their inventory numbers. Prosek put them out front. Random blasts of creek pebbles thrown up the brushy slope flushed the ambushers. Who would have tried nothing against such numbers, anyway. There were scarcely two dozen of them.

Prosek brought prisoners. "Shall I have them put to the question, Commander?" As Hecht had no official title those who dealt with him direct called him whatever came to mind.

"To what end?"

"It might be instructive to find out who hired them."

"I already know. You'll be happier being ignorant."

"You think?"

Titus Consent shook his head slowly. "Silly-ass discussion."

Hecht said, "You prisoners. Two of you were with us during the Connecten Crusade. So you know where you stand. Remind your friends. And keep it in mind when Mr. Consent talks to you."

Consent wasted no time. He asked questions. The prisoners answered. They had nothing illuminating to say. They had been recruited by a Race Buchels. Buchels had paid well, half up front.

There was no trace of Buchels. He had gone missing as soon as the smoke from Drago Prosek's falcons rolled over his position.

Most of the prisoners thought Buchels had worked for somebody in the Collegium. A few picked Anne of Menand. And one liked those nobles in the Grail Empire who did not want the Empress getting any stronger.

Hecht told his inner circle, "Buchels works for one of Serenity's associates. An idiot who decided to do his boss a favor and eliminate the nuisance Serenity is always grumbling about. An idiot who can't look past the moment far enough to see that he could start a war with the Empire."

Heris said the fool's name was Fearoé Durgandini. She thought that was funny. Durgandini meant "woman of bad smells" in one of the languages she spoke. This Durgandini was the illegitimate son of a Doneto cousin. He was determined to make his mark handling Serenity's unpleasant chores. Heris suspected that Durgandini operated under deniable orders.

Titus Consent observed, "It doesn't matter in the end. We'll go where we have to go. Whoever gets in the way will get trampled."

There were no more human intercessions. The road was busy now that no monster lurked in the high Jagos. And the season was late. Travelers were trying to get through before weather got in the way. The Night took no more than a normally malicious interest. After a few small punishments it pretended indifference.

"BAYARD VA STILL-PATTER OFFERED THE USE OF HIS HOUSE, GAVE ME letters to prove it, and I don't intend to be shy about taking advantage," Hecht declared as he neared Alten Weinberg. To va Still-Patter retainers sent by the Ambassador's father to discourage the hiresword interloper from taking advantage of the son's generosity. "I won't let my men steal whatever they overlooked last time."

He faked a light, playful mood. He did not look forward to the incessant politics plaguing every center of power. He was exhausted. Though the threats had been minimal the mountains left him wanting nothing more than to disappear and recuperate.

The pass had been colder than ever for the time of year. And, though the Night itself had shown little interest, someone had sent numerous noxious minor Instrumentalities to make him miserable, presumably in hopes he would turn back.

Heris had been no help.

He had not yet had time to pull off his boots, once inside Bayard va Still-Patter's, when the invitations and petitions started. He told Rivademar Vircondelet, "You've been here a week. You're rested up and familiar with the local situation. This crap is on you. Anybody wants an audience, tell them to go through the Empress. I work for her. If it's the Empress, though, say I'm too sick." Hecht did not strictly lie about being sick.

"Won't be the Empress, boss. She's out in the sticks doing what they call a progress. Which sounds like just showing herself off so people know she really exists. At their expense, of course. I hear Johannes started it so he could save on what it cost to run the court. Anyway, we'll actually have a few weeks where the load stays kind of light."

"That's good. That's real good. It'll give me a chance to recover."

He did not like being sick. He could not recall the last time he was really sick.

Titus told him exactly, when he arose, recovered but weak, three days later. Titus had consulted his personal journals. But it did not matter, other than to illuminate the fact that people pushed old seasons of pain out of mind.

"What's on the schedule?" Hecht asked.

"It's really piled up while you were loafing, boss. Everyone wants a piece, now that you're here. Both of them."

"What?"

"Almost everybody who is anybody is out making progress with the Empress. The elder va Still-Patter is not here to aggravate us only because his gout is so bad he can't get out of bed."

"Again, then. That's real good. I want you all to learn everything about this city while you have the chance. Now. Let's put me to bed."

## 18. Cape Tondur: Andoray

A supernatural wind blew south southwest along the coast of Andoray. Little of the power from beneath the sea made it inshore, where scores of ravenous Instrumentalities prowled the brink of the forever ice, eager for any taste of power, dodging or preying on one another.

For all but the greatest a moment of inattention meant certain destruction.

The most terrible doom was the vast white toad squatting atop a promontory of ice that thrust miles out into the sea. That ice creaked forward a yard or two every day. And lifted vertically several feet. Or more, if the Windwalker caught a lucky gust of power. Or if some desperately hungry lesser Instrumentality strayed within range of the Windwalker's lightning tongue.

There were human worshippers attendant upon the Windwalker, initially. Cold and starvation took most. Their frozen remains lay scattered around the great toad. Most resembled the Seatt peoples of the northernmost north of ancient times.

Not all the Windwalker's Chosen elected to perish beside their god. One family took advantage of a distraction on the god's part to flee into the Ormo Strait aboard a boat found caught in a crust of newly formed surface ice. These fugitives were the first Chosen to shake the mad god's control. His strength was limited and his attention rigidly fixed elsewhere.

Kharoulke the Windwalker had no room in his divine consciousness for anything but hunger: for the power out there, and for revenge on those filthy come-lately divines who had driven his generation into a terrible captivity.

Middle-world time rolled past swiftly. Those who had known the Windwalker elsewhere did not mourn his absence.

Kharoulke sat at the end of the ice, five hundred feet above the frigid indigo waters of the Andorayan Sea. Only a few miles now separated him from the gateway to the Realm of the Gods. He could see through that. The waters beyond were subtly different. He saw but could not reach. A mighty and dark god he was but he had almost no power left. He could not collect enough more. He might not get there in time to sabotage the restoration of his most hated enemies.

Can a god know despair? Particularly a god who knew what it meant to be imprisoned for millennia?

Maybe not. But certainly something very like despair, which had built in the understanding that Instrumentalities of the Night were not armed with a sense of time like the one so critical to those ephemeral mortals who shaped the gods.

There was no longer any guard on Kharoulke's back but the dread of him. Among the scattered, frozen Chosen, now miles behind, there were, as well, several Krepnights, the Elect. They had not had the strength to survive the frozen dreams of the god who had imagined them, either.

Something flickered into existence behind the great white toad, was gone in an instant. The same shimmering disturbance came and went a dozen times before the cold and hungry god realized that something not of the Night was very active back where he was not watching.

Kharoulke the Windwalker began to turn. He began to change his form.

Thunder spoke, sharp and businesslike.

A thousand invisibly fast iron and silver needles pierced the god, driving deep into his being. The agony was like nothing he had ever known. It raped away all reason.

Kharoulke continued to change, growing taller and more man-like. The pain worsened. Those needles were barbed. Movement made them cut their ways forward, deeper into the divine flesh. Till they were expelled or absorbed they would continue the hurt and would sap Kharoulke's little remaining power.

In ragged-ass volley a dozen kegs of firepowder spent their chemical energy, not against the Windwalker but against the ice on which he had begun to shift his bulk.

The Instrumentality made one move too many. A crack zigged and zagged from one explosion site to the next, dashing east to west across the promontory. The ice groaned, grumbled, roared.

The Windwalker boomed in rage, so loud his fury could be heard a thousand miles away. He saw. He knew. He began to shift to another shape, angelic, sprouting a vast spread of white wings. But he was a thing of the most intense cold. He could not change quickly. He did not make this change in time.

The tip of the ice headland descended into the sea. The Windwalker followed, plunging deep into the painful, poisonous indigo water. The agony inside the dark god gained accompaniment over all his surface.

The Windwalker's thrashing only caused the needles within to do more damage. The storm surge waves he generated were powerful enough to wreck small boats when they reached Santerin's shores.


## 19. Lucidia: Border War

Rogert du Tancret could be everything ever accused, twice as dark and twice as ugly. But the man was cunning, and Delphic at anticipating personal danger. He would not be lured into any deadly strait, however tasty the bait. When he could not resist he sent someone else to spring any trap.

Azir asked, "Would the same be true if we took the danger to him?"

The Mountain shrugged. It had been a hard several months. He was exhausted. "I've lived too long. This kind of war is a young man's game."

"You don't have to be out here. You could be in Shamramdi right now."

Nassim grunted. Disagreement. This was the point of the spear. This was where Nassim Alizarin had to be. The Mountain would not die in bed.

The Mountain did hope to die having had his revenge on Gordimer and er-Rashal. Sadly, he saw that goal receding. His mission, now, was to open the way to Tel Moussa. "I wouldn't fit. I wouldn't be welcome. The emirs already know everything worth knowing."

"You're fishing for excuses to avoid any chance of being given more responsibility."

That was so near the truth that Nassim had no answer. This boy was sharp. He would be a worthy successor to Indala.

Azir laughed outright. Nassim's face had given him away. "Sometimes you're obvious, General. I know your heart pulls you another direction. You have my word, if none other, that you'll get all the support you need."

Nassim scowled. The promises of princes . . . But this prince, if such he could be called, was chosen of Indala al-Sul Halaladin, whose word was as good as that of God. Whose word, being executed slowly now, promised the destruction of Rogert du Tancret.

Azir continued, "Sir Mountain, you are a mighty warrior and a great captain. Your dearest enemies confess it. But your personal skills are questionable. I suspect because one purpose of a Sha-lug upbringing is to freeze the Sha-lug warrior at the age of fifteen."

"Ah. Now you're repeating something you've heard, not something you worked out for yourself."

Azir used both hands to gesture like he was a balance scale. Meaning, "Some of this, some of that." Or, "Six of one and half a dozen of the other."

Nassim scowled again. This pup was just too damned bright.

The scene was a mountain spring back on the edge of the Idiam. The fighters had fled into the haunted country several times while running from the enemy. Brotherhood warriors were tenacious. Tonight a strong breeze stirred the campfire and tossed sparks up like short-lived stars. It was unseasonably cold. The moon was halfway up the sky and nearly full. Nassim thought it looked like a big wheel of ice with some chips knocked off one edge.

The pup said, "My uncle will send more troops. Militias from the hundred towns and cities he's enlisted in his hope of liberating the Holy Lands."

Towns and cities that Indala had conquered, by the spear or the tongue, in the Mountain's eye. They had enlisted in Indala's vision as an alternative to fire and sword.

Indala al-Sul Halaladin, as he aged, became ever less tolerant of the narrow tribalism of the Believers.

Nassim did not remind the boy that the westerners believed they were liberating the Holy Lands, too. And that the Devedians had been there before Pramans or Chaldareans. And the Devedians were children of the Dainshaukin, who had come into the Holy Lands two thousand years ago, having been guaranteed possession by a violent, psychopathic deity who occasionally insisted that his followers murder their own children for his glorification.

"General?"

"What?"

"We lost you there. For a moment."

"The curse of growing past one's Sha-lug training."

"Meaning?"

"I was reflecting on the endless torment inflicted on the Holy Lands. And wondering if maybe the wells aren't closing down deliberately so the land can shake off its human lice."

"An interesting notion. One so heretical that if you expressed it anywhere but out here, it would get you flogged or stoned."

Nassim shrugged. That was not going to happen. He was too valuable. For the moment. And he had his own accommodation with

God. God did not seem to mind Alizarin's occasional unorthodox speculation. "Why the manpower largesse?"

"He wants to expand the pool of veterans. And to identify the best
warriors. He wants an army of the best when he does move to cleanse
the Holy Lands of the western Unbeliever."

There was more. A lot more, Nassim was sure. He was one small
stone in the structure of Indala's strategy.

The Mountain would remain pliable. He would trust Indala. He
would do his part. He would abide, preparing himself for the moment
when it all came together and he could bask in the warmth brought on
by the restoration of the balance undone by Hagid's murder.

Young Az said, "Whatever else happens, our mission will be to in-
convenience Black Rogert. Every day. We have to become more aggressive. My granduncle won't want du Tancret in any position to influence
the other Arnhanders. None of them are as fierce."

Nassim nodded, though at this stage of life he found himself short
on lethal ambition. Again, outgrowing that Sha-lug arrested develop-
ment.

The boy continued, "First order of business, the siege lines round
Tel Moussa."

WITH MORE MEN AND NO SPECIAL NEED TO HUSBAND THEM, THE
Mountain harassed Rogert du Tancret constantly. He sent blooded
warriors back to Indala. And corpses to Black Rogert. Who got little
support from his co-religionists. They had been appalled by his foul
behavior.

Du Tancret's strength declined. Each day a man or two slipped off
to take service with some more honorable captain. One who was less
likely to get his people butchered.

Falcons often featured in Nassim's quick strikes, at some point when
the enemy was in close pursuit. Crusader horses refused to charge the
thunder and smoke.

Nassim found a fanatic young Believer in one of the militia contingents. A boy who wanted to be a hero. A boy determined to win fame.
Rogert du Tancret had offered a huge reward for a falcon or a supply of
firepowder. Nassim offered the youth an opportunity to become immortal. The youth jumped at the challenge. Though he did not believe he
would be martyred.

He was so sure God walked at his elbow he insisted that Nassim
promise to take him to the finest taverns and brothels in Shamramdi
when he returned from his mission.

Nassim promised.

Nassim Alizarim pursued the forms of religion because that was the politic thing to do. His secret but sincere conviction was that most of his contemporaries were also hypocrites. But the night before the martyr's big day he lay awake late, begging God to guide him.

The Nassim Alizarin of Tel Moussa was not the Nassim Alizarin who had commanded a thousand Sha-lug. That Nassim had perished when his beloved, only son had been murdered to further er-Rashal's ambition. The new Nassim was only too aware that a martyr was someone's son.

As in the past, God did not trouble Himself over the agony of a lone supplicant.

The pain ran deep because only two living beings knew this martyr remained true to his God and his people. Not even Azir had been inducted into the scheme.

Nassim would not think of the martyr by name. There was less guilt when he was just the boy or the martyr.

The scheme went well to start. The boy collected camels, loaded them with kegs of firepowder, slipped away unnoticed. He managed with ease because he was the warrior entrusted with the watch on that side of the camp.

It took longer than Nassim expected for someone to notice the boy missing. It took longer, still, for someone to figure out that six camel loads of firepowder had disappeared at the same time.

The Mountain's ego was bruised. He had believed these men to be better trained and more alert. He had taught them himself.

A soldier appeared. "Lord! Bad news! Ambel appears to have deserted. And six camels are missing. Along with most of the firepowder. It looks like he means to collect Black Rogert's reward."

Nassim raged around the way he would if every bit were true. And raged even more in frustration over the desultory response in camp. No one seemed inclined to do anything. They all wanted to talk. Those who knew the boy from back home were adamant. He would never do what he seemed to have done.

Cursed by their commander, most of the company finally howled off after a traitor. As Nassim had hoped.

The pursuit had to be loud and it had to be real. Otherwise, Black Rogert's sixth sense would save him again.

Nassim joined the chase, though he only followed, at a pace suitable for an older man.

The martyr's lead was, of course, insurmountable, though a couple of bucks from the boy's own town almost caught him by killing their horses.

Nassim Alizarin was himself in sight of Gherig—and of Tel Moussa and the weakened siege lines around it—when the act played out.

The martyr talked his way into Gherig, steps ahead of men obviously determined to murder him. One of those shrieked when hit by an arrow from the barbican wall.

The Mountain did not know when the plan went wrong. He just knew that six camel loads of firepowder, nearly half a ton, cooked off before the martyr could possibly have penetrated the fortress proper.

The massive barbican, larger than the tower at Tel Moussa, came down majestically, the collapse mostly hidden inside a dust cloud of mythic proportion.

"Damn," Nassim swore under his breath. "Too soon. Too damned soon. No way Black Rogert was close enough."

He spoke without thinking, focused on Gherig, totally.

"Excuse me?" Azir asked. His tone demanded further explanation.

Nassim obliged. The secret needed no keeping, now.

Riders charged the spreading dust cloud, rushed into it. The spontaneous assault carried the ruins and captured the still lowered bridge over the perilous dry moat splitting the rock between the barbican and Gherig proper.

The Mountain never had any intention of storming the unassailable, even had the martyr performed his task ideally. Gherig without Black Rogert would be immune to storm, anyway. But Nassim had not anticipated the scope of the destruction, despite having seen firepowder used against Arn Bedu. His interest was the murder of one man. The rest was beyond his ability to imagine. And he had lost control of his fighters.

The inexperienced militia, especially, surrendered to the excitement and noise.

Gherig had stood immune to storm or siege for all time. That did not change. But later it would be argued that the fortress survived only because the troops besieging Tel Moussa broke away to save it. Their counterattacks forced the Lucidians to leave. But the final tally was: advantage Lucidia. The siege of Tel Moussa had been broken. It would not resume. Gherig had been forced onto the defensive. Several Brotherhood knights died in the explosions. More perished in the fighting afterward.

Rogert du Tancret had been rushing in to celebrate his coup when the firepowder went up. The wicked knight lost his hearing, his sense of balance, and his ability to give sensible commands.

He would recover. But he had enemies among the crusaders as well as the Believers. The Brotherhood ordered him out of Gherig, his disabilities being the excuse. Rogert tried to refuse. He was too damaged to resist the men who took him away.

The Mountain returned to Tel Moussa. The besieged received him with cheers and dramatic gestures of gratitude. Basking in the adulation, he told young Az, "Rogert will really be angry, now. He'll find some way to do us evil. We need more."

"Evil is what men do. That one more than most. But you've enjoyed successes beyond my granduncle's dearest hopes."

"Successes? I don't see many, boy."

"The great roc of evil has been flushed from his nest, General. Black Rogert is out of Gherig, where no power of this earth could bring a blade close enough to strike. His own people forced him out of his shell. He can be reached, now. Half the Arnhanders probably hope that he is." Then young Az asked, "What did you mean, 'We need more'?"

"More fighters. More weapons. More animals. And, more than anything else, more money. Parsimonious as I am, according to some, I've exhausted my war chest." Nassim Alizarin did have a reputation for being frugal. But he had not been reluctant to invest in falcons and firepowder. Especially firepowder. And now that was gone.

He had learned the lesson of Arn Bedu better than most. He wished someone among the Believers knew the secret of the stuff. Believers who were not er-Rashal al-Dhulquarnen. He had only one source for firepowder and that was way out in the Realm of War. Every keg cost dearly.

It was good powder, though.

Azir said, "Having seen what the stuff can do, I'll back you up."

"Thank you."

"Don't thank me yet. I said I'd back you up. You'll have to go to Shamramdi to press your case."

Nassim did not want to do that. After all his time in the wilderness, some spent inside the terror of the Idiam, he had little drive left. The hatred stirred by Hagid's murder had not deserted him, but it had become less compelling. Other interests found room in his heart. He had located the concept of relaxation, though not the skills to manage it.

Nassim said, "I'm a cripple. Too long obsessed. I couldn't function in a normal court."

"That may be," Azir admitted. "We'll find out this winter." In a confidential whisper, "My granduncle will begin the liberation of the Holy Lands come spring grasses."

Nassim sighed. He was exhausted. He did not have much left. And still his allies insisted he use what remained against everyone but those who had made of him their deadliest enemy.


## 20. Realm of the Gods: Time and Tide

The Ninth Unknown felt the weight of each of his years, though he had forgotten all but the most interesting. Nor was he sure his recollections of those were trustworthy. Could anyone be so old? And he was in little better shape than he had been on escaping the Realm of the Gods.

This time he had worn himself out trying to find the son of Arlensul.

THE ASCENDANT, IN HUMAN FORM, JOINED CLOVEN FEBRUAREN IN A place Aelen Kofer magic had made over into a tavern. Into the idea, or dream, or soul, of a tavern. Never did a more taverny tavern enter Februaren's life. There were people and dwarves and, for a few brief minutes, one of the daring mer. Loud talk, ribaldry. A potent, all-pervasive impression that this must be a place far away from anywhere that an honest man would want to be. A place to leave other worlds behind.

Could it be another pocket world?

No. Like so much the Aelen Kofer wrought the tavern was almost entirely illusion.

"Irrelevant," the ascendant said. "How have you fared?"

"I've made my mark in the middle world. As a failure. I've successfully identified ten thousand places where our man is not. That, by the way, is a fact? Arlensul birthed a son?" It would be embarrassing if he had overlooked a daughter through assumption.

"Yes. A son. As the legends say." The ascendant had learned to waste no time responding to, or even acknowledging, what he perceived as the Ninth Unknown's provocations.

"Why did you want to meet here? So I can validate the quality of the brew? I can't do that, brother. These dwarves like it too thick and bitter."

He lied. The beer was astonishingly good, especially for somewhere so far out in the wilds that it was in another world. But, no doubt, the brew would be perfection to any taste.

The ascendant shrugged, indifferent. "The Aelen Kofer are supple artificers. The beer is perfect. Any failing will be found in the drinker. I want you to meet some people."

Cloven Februaren downed a pint, quickly. "Tasty." He considered asking for another. Probably not wise. He was feeling that last already. "All right. Lead on."

The ascendant, in Svavar-form, did so. Out of the tavern, toward the great barge.

"Some dramatic changes there," Februaren observed.

The entire Realm of the Gods had grown less gloomy. The water-front town had returned to life. Color had wakened everywhere, like a spring that renewed every aspect of the world. The ship of the gods had gone from dangerous derelict to opulent barge.

A boat was tied up in front of that, its mast the only evidence of its presence from where Februaren stood. He paid it no mind.

"More changes will come. If the power continues leaking through. This world is still a long way from what it was. But." He stopped the old man, turned him, pointed.

Februaren looked up the mountain. Clouds obscured the Great Sky Fortress, incompletely. They came into being off to the right, whipped past the home of the gods as though riding a mighty wind, then dematerialized again to the left. They waxed and waned quickly.

"The bridge!" Februaren blurted. "The Aelen Kofer have restored the rainbow bridge!" The rainbow bridge, bright and beautiful, arced right up to the fortress gate.

"Pretty much. You can walk across now. If you want to go try."

"I want. Very much." The Great Sky Fortress itself showed signs of rejuvenation. "If this ancient flesh can survive the climb." His turn sideways trick did not work inside the Realm of the Gods, even with the gateway open. He could jump in from outside. Once inside he had to walk. Even to the gateway to get back out. Though taking the barge left his clothing a little less damp.

"The Aelen Kofer have a goat cart that can take you up, when you decide you have to go."

"But we're headed somewhere else, now. Aren't we?"

"We are. To the barge."

THEIR DESTINATION PROVED TO BE A FAMILY, FIVE MEMBERS, ALL pallid, bony, and blond where they had any hair. A grandfather. His daughter. Her husband. Their children, boy, girl, eleven and eight. A lone Aelen Kofer watched them. Februaren did not recognize the dwarf. The ascendant dispensed with introductions. "These people escaped across the Ormo Strait. Former followers of the Windwalker. They found a boat, fled, and turned up here." He exchanged glances with Februaren, so the old man knew he was not without reservations.

"I see. Unusual, that."

"Yes. But the Windwalker has shown no knack for inspiring fanaticism. His worshippers execute his will because what lies ahead is less terrible than what pushes from behind. Kharoulke is a Punisher kind of god."

"Not so many of any other kind," Februaren said. "Can we talk to them?"

"Bluntnose has the dialect. It was spoken in Andoray before the Old Ones arrived, dragging us along."

"Seatt?"

"One of those tongues."

"I thought the Seatts were squat and brown."

"Some were. The name includes all of the ancient tribes of the farthest north. These people . . . It doesn't matter. Their ancestors were entirely surrendered to the Will of the Night. Their sorcery served the Windwalker and his kin. They lost their lands and gods when the Andorayans came. This crew amounts to little. They have no sorcery."

"Let's see what they can tell us."

Bluntnose left her seat on the cargo hatch, joined Februaren and the ascendant. Februaren wondered how he knew the Aelen Kofer was female. What cue had he caught? He could not find it consciously. She said, "These people are desperate to cooperate. They understand their situation. We've fed them. They know we could stop. Also, they lost many friends and relations because of the Windwalker."

Februaren asked, "Do you know who I am, Bluntnose?"

"Yes." With a certain reserved disdain for even the most lethal of middle-worlders.

The Ninth Unknown winked. "Then tell them who I am, sweetheart." While she did, he told the ascendant, "They don't look much recovered."

"They were in bad shape to begin. I didn't think they'd make it. The Aelen Kofer worked some deep magic but you can tell from the missing bits that frostbite was too far along for even dwarf magic."

The ascendant related what the Seatts had reported so far. Which was that the Windwalker was angry and hungry. "Pretty much his normal state, though maybe more so now because he knows what we're doing."

Bluntnose said, "I told them, wizard. Your name failed to strike terror."

"That's a pity." Using Bluntnose to translate, he interrogated the Seatts.

From the barge Februaren could see the cliffs of ice away toward Andoray. He saw shapes and shadows atop them. The ascendant followed his gaze, captured his thought. "He's getting close. We have to try a new tack. Soon."

"Something is being done. To buy some time."

Bluntnose said, "They want to know how long we intend to hold them. They don't want to be here when the Windwalker comes."

"They won't be. One way or another."

"What?" Bluntnose turned to see what had the others' jaws dropping.

A fishing smack had appeared outside the gateway. It headed in.

The ascendant said, "Get Iron Eyes. Tell him to bring everybody he can. It'll take some serious artificing to handle this."

Februaren saw nothing worth excitement. Other than that the smack's approach was deliberate.

Typically, in myth, visitors to the Realm of the Gods did not arrive of their own accord. Not until recently. But lately a rush had developed.

Korban Jarneyn and a dozen weighty henchdwarves turned up implausibly fast. Iron Eyes explained, "We felt them cross over."

The Ninth Unknown could now distinguish the "them." "I've heard of these things. Though never of more than one in one place at a time."

The boat was filled with Krepnights, the Elect. Februaren got a different count each time he tried a census. The average was a dozen. So many that the boat had almost no freeboard. Februaren could not imagine how it had made the crossing without swamping.

Aelen Kofer kept turning up, each as heavily armed as an individual dwarf could be. They brought along all the magic they could manage, too.

There were a surprising number of dwarves. Many more than had made the climb with Februaren and Iron Eyes.

They were getting ready for something.

Likewise, the ascendant. He had backed off to have more room as he experimented with several ferocious shapes.

An unpleasant animal musk preceded the smack. It reminded Februaren of the den of something large and filthy. A bear, perhaps.

"No fooling around here," Iron Eyes said, apparently to himself. He rattled orders in a language Februaren did not understand.

The boat lurched up out of the water. It continued landward at the same steady pace but climbed higher and higher.

Iron Eyes barked a command that had to be, "Now!"

The boat fell. From eighty feet, it plunged to the quay. Pieces and things were still scattering when the Aelen Kofer swarmed the impact site.

Februaren said, "Try to save a couple for questioning."

"Go teach your grandmother to suck eggs, mortal."

The butchery did not last long. Nine hairless, tiger striped things ended up dismembered and, before long, consigned to a bonfire built special to accommodate them. Three captives suffered hamstringing. They could neither flee nor fight.

They would not talk. It was unclear whether they could if they wanted.

"This is a puzzle beyond me," Iron Eyes said. "These things are constructs. Not unlike a number of mythical creatures the gods made to amuse themselves. Only, these are deadly tools. They have no feelings, no fears, no insides, nothing but an obsessed determination to execute the will of the Windwalker. Who breathed just enough of himself into each to give it the strength to do what he wants done."

Februaren went to the ascendant, who seemed determined to turn into a giant jumping crab. He had not participated in the reduction of the striped creatures. "Any way you could look inside those things?"

The ascendant seemed surprised by the question, then irked. "Why would you ask that?"

"Because you're what you are. With bits of god packed up inside. Your god stuff might be able to burglarize their god stuff."

"I don't get anything but cold. And a fair certainty that they'd tear me apart if they could just get at me."

Februaren said, "I may have another tool. But I'll have to take one of them somewhere else."

"More time," Iron Eyes grumped.

"More time, Mr. Gjoresson. You're going to get it. I have something going. It will buy us a lot of time." But he was uneasy. In fact, he was damned worried and getting more so by the hour.

It should have happened already.

Cloven Februaren was in a state approaching panic, more frayed than he had been in centuries. His schemes were coming unraveled. Heris should have done her part three days ago. He had to get out of the Realm of the Gods. He had to find out what had gone wrong. What had happened to Heris.

He should not have listened when she volunteered.

He had to check in on Piper. Piper ought to be in Alten Weinberg by now.

Maybe that was why Heris was running late. Piper might have gotten into deep trouble and she was digging him out.

The old man was on the quay, staring over the Seatt boat, out the gateway into the middle world. Korban Jarneyn joined him. "Not much to see out there."

Exactly. Just haze and a bleak dark sea where waves had begun to run high in anticipation of an approaching storm. As true winter closed in it became ever more difficult to see all the way to the land of always winter, with its monster denizens, now drawn so close.

When the old man did not respond, Iron Eyes asked, "Why so dour and distant of late, friend?"

"The Night may have chosen to instruct me in the matter of hubris."

"Interesting. I don't know what you mean, but that's interesting nonetheless. I'm here to report that the Aelen Kofer have come to a wall. There's nothing more we can do."

"What?"

"We've taken our part to the point where we can't do anything more till you do your part."

Cloven Februaren said, "I thought too much of my own skills as a teacher." Which did not fit.

"Find Arlensul's whelp, sorcerer. Or the course is run. That thing out there, that horrible toad in the mist, will drive the ice this far before spring. If ever it does return. Unless you . . ."

Red-gold light flared in the mist, far away. A second flash followed, shorter, brighter, and more yellow. Then a dozen more flashes, in varying shades, followed quickly, creeping from right to left.

"What would that be?" Gjoresson mused.

The Ninth Unknown had a sudden, sobering thought. "Can you close the gateway? Quickly?"

"After all this time prizing it open an inch at a time?"

"We're going to get deadly wet if you can't at least make the hole a lot smaller."

The dwarf heard his urgency. "All right. I trust you to worry about your own skin."

Februaren explained while Iron Eyes worked at whatever Aelen Kofer did when they tinkered with magic. It was not dramatic. Nor ever was, till it was over and there stood something like the rainbow bridge. Iron Eyes did not understand the Ninth Unknown's explanation.

The gateway's diameter had shrunk ten feet before the first dull, protracted, barely audible *crump* arrived, forerunner of a series of thumps, cracks, and crunches that whispered about very big noises having been birthed a long way away, across cruelly cold water.

The bellow of an outraged god soon followed. It had so much anger behind it, it might be heard for a thousand miles.

The Ninth Unknown's mood improved dramatically. "She did it! She did pull it off! I was right. He had no one guarding his back." But fear returned as he recalled the certain consequences of success.

"We've got to close the gateway."

"Who just did what, sorcerer?" Iron Eyes demanded.

"Get the gateway shrunk down as small as you can without leaving us locked up here."

The ascendant arrived at a trot, moving fast for the first time in months. "Best do as he says, Gjoresson."

The dwarf wanted to bicker but sensed that wasting time might prove uncomfortable shortly. This was not a moment for reasoned, deliberate, parliamentary discussion.

Februaren was not unreasonable. He tried to explain again while Iron Eyes worked. The dwarf just did not understand.

Another divine racket arose, a staccato salvo of screams that got Februaren to imagine a hundred elephants being slowly roasted alive.

The ascendant asked, "What was all that?"

"The Windwalker taking an involuntary, full emersion dip in the Andorayan Sea. Keep shrinking the gateway, Iron Eyes. The wave is coming. I promise. In fact, the rest of us ought to be headed for higher ground." He told the crowd of dwarves, "Shoo! All of you! Find someplace high. Run! Argue after I turn out to be an idiot."

Iron Eyes reduced the gateway to ten feet wide and five high before the wave arrived. That was taller and wider than the opening. Water exploded through the gap. It shattered the Seatt escape boat, pounded the barge, and sank the smack belonging to the striped killers. But it did not have energy enough to drive on inland.

"LET US CELEBRATE OUR WET FEET," CLOVEN FEBRUAREN DECLARED. "And then let's get to work."

The water had subsided. The gateway had started growing again. The harbor was a plain of jade glass. The sea outside was calm, clad in its bleak winter colors.

The screams of the Windwalker continued. Februaren pictured the god clawing his way along the foot of the ice cliffs, looking for somewhere to drag himself out of the torturing water. "Sounds like he's having serious problems."

Gjoresson said, "The sea is eating at him like a weak acid. It will devour him completely. If he can't get out. Though that could take years. There's a lot of him. And the water is freezing. If it was hot it would eat him up a lot faster. Still, he's in so much pain he can't concentrate enough to use his divine power. So, for now, he's just a big, stupid brute wracked by agony."

The Ninth Unknown and the ascendant were pleased. The longer Kharoulke remained immersed the weaker he would be once he escaped the water.

Februaren said, "I bought time. Now give me one of Kharoulke's bully beasts and take me outside the gateway."

Hours passed. The barge needed repairs. Eventually, the Aelen Kofer took it out into the Andorayan Sea. They went only a hundred yards beyond the opening. They crowded the decks, soaking up the rich magic of the middle world.

Februaren had two of Kharoulke's artifacts. He would not need to return for a replacement if one died. He worried that he might be doing the wrong thing.

The ascendant and a dozen Aelen Kofer were watching. Everyone would pay devoted attention to whatever he did now.

No help for it.

He pulled his prisoners in close, thought of a particular place, made his sideways turn.

He stepped into a grove in Friesland. Heris was waiting. She had a fire burning. No need to fear discovery. The people had gone away. The Instrumentalities, great and small, had run off toward the waning power in the Andorayan Sea. She said, "Let's go home. I need to get warmed up. Then I need to check on Piper."

He made sure of the constraints on his cargo. "What took so long with those explosions?"

"I had to make sure Piper settled in safely. What the hell are those things? If they were any uglier we'd have to kill them to put them out of their misery. Why are they tied up like that?" And, "You need a rest. You look awful."

Februaren knew of no reason why he should appear unusual. He snapped, "Tell me!"

"Your plan called for me to set off firepowder in a dozen different places. I did fourteen. But you gave me no help coming up with the firepowder. I had to deal with that on top of wet-nursing Piper."

"You should've taken it all from him."

"He watches his. So. I had to raid eight different armories, five of which I had to find for myself. So don't get snippy. I do know where I

can swipe a couple more that I could set off under your cranky ass."
She glared, daring him to say something.

"All right. All right. The job got done. Big Ugly God got dumped
in the drink. And he's in too much pain to do big ugly god stuff. We've
bought time."

"Thank you, Heris."

"Thank you, Heris."

"All right. Now. What the hell are these things, all bundled up in
ropes and blankets and stuff?"

Februaren explained. Then, "If you take one and I take the other,
we can get home in a couple of skips."

"They really stink, don't they?"

"They do. They're dying. Kharoulke is too busy saving his own
scary butt to keep them topped up."

"Then we shouldn't waste time swapping tall tales."

Februaren indulged in a small smile as he seized an artifact and
turned sideways. The woman had shown dramatic growth over the past
two years. Maybe, just possibly, she could be primed to assume the calling that Piper could not.

Muno was no pup anymore.


THE NINTH UNKNOWN TOOK ONE OF HIS CAPTIVES INTO THE HEART
of the Construct and tested it to destruction. When he took the health-
ier one in he knew enough to mine the communal memories of the
Krepnights, the Elect, who were all the same beast.


JARNEYN GJORESSON JUMPED INTO THE AIR, LITERALLY. FEBRUAREN
said, "Sorry. I've never seen a startle response that dramatic."

The dwarf scowled more fiercely than usual. He growled, "You have
something to report?"

"I've found a place to look for the Bastard. It was in the group memory of the monster. One of the first accompanied a band of Chosen
raiders into the wilds of the Empire. They were supposed to kill a particular man who could be found at a particular rustic fortress. The Windwalker gave no reason. But there was a sense that Kharoulke foresaw a
dire threat. The mission failed. The god has been too busy since to send
another expedition against a target now aware of the interest of the
Night."

Iron Eyes immediately confounded Februaren. "What is the Empire?"

So the Ninth Unknown spent several hours updating the dwarf on
the middle world.

"Things happen fast there," the dwarf said. "Last time I was over for any length was during the hunt for Grinling."

"Oh?" Februaren had heard Piper mention that magical ring. "And?"

"It evaded us. Even me, and I did most of the work making it. A lesser Instrumentality from the south threw it overboard in the deepest part of what you call the Mother Sea."

Februaren grunted. Not good. Legendary magical artifacts could not be banished that way. They always found a way back.

Februaren said, "I need you, and the other Aelen Kofer, to come to my world for a while."

The dwarf grunted.

"It will take strength and cleverness to capture the Bastard's stronghold. Thirty picked Chosen and a Krepnight, the Elect, had no luck."

"That's encouraging."

"They were slaves of a god. Not Aelen Kofer."

"Transparent, mortal. But still in need of response. Tell me where you want us to go and what you want us to do."

Cloven Februaren said, "I found the place. I walked around it before I came back here." He described what he had seen and told Iron Eyes what he thought needed doing. After consideration, the Crown Prince of the Aelen Kofer agreed that Februaren's strategy was appropriate. For the moment. Given the intelligence available.

Preparations began. Hurriedly.

This would be a long mission. There was no way to reach the target other than by walking. In winter. Across a realm no longer in awe of the Aelen Kofer. Across a world where, for the most part, the Aelen Kofer had been forgotten.


## 21. Empire City: The New Life

Alten Weinberg was extremely quiet. The Empress and Princess were away, on a progress, though Katrin was supposed to be far advanced in her pregnancy. Most of the Imperial hangers-on were out there with her, creeping from castle to town like a swarm of locusts. Personages of note remaining in the capital city were careful to avoid being seen anywhere near Katrin's new general. They were sure everyone still in town would be a spy for the Empress, her sister, or Ferris Renfrow. Nobody wanted to get onto a list of suspects.

Hecht was pleased. Mildly. Both at being left alone and at seeing how far the sisters had managed to wriggle out from under the thumbs of the Council Advisory.

The daughters of Johannes Blackboots made everyone around them nervous. If they continued strong, they would rival their father in a few years.

Titus Consent had a stream of spies in to visit and report. Some had been at work since the Captain-General's wedding visit. Few had learned anything of interest. The absence of the Imperial court had left Alten Weinberg in a state approaching hibernation.

Rivademar Vircondelet said, "There are other spies everywhere, boss. Anybody who isn't an apprentice or employee is watching everybody else for somebody who can't be here personally."

Vircondelet began to ramble.

"Stop!" Hecht said. "I understand. They're all watching each other. I knew that already. How about something less obvious or more interesting?"

"There's this. Something is wrong with the Empress's pregnancy."

"Explain."

"She insists she's pregnant. That she's carrying Jaime of Castauriga's son, who will unify the Direcian and Imperial lines into one grand dynasty."

"But?"

"People are starting to wonder if it isn't all in her imagination."

Hecht had his staff spend time on the biological math—with and without Jaime as a factor. He had them mine every rumor, hundreds of those, for anything that might be factual. Katrin faking would be huge. Her relationship with Jaime had become so strained that it was unlikely she would ever see the man again. It could be that the strain was not exclusively due to Jaime's distaste for his wife's bony charms. There might have been an incident, vigorously covered up, involving the Princess Apparent. Jaime might have made inappropriate advances that, to his amazement and wrath, were soundly rejected. Continued importunities resulted in Helspeth arranging for Katrin to witness what she would not have believed otherwise.

Ferris Renfrow might have put a warning bug in King Jaime's ear. Jaime was too arrogant to listen but people around him did enjoy a more intimate relationship with reality.

Hecht said, "So our new Crown Prince should arrive anywhere from next week to ten weeks from now—if Katrin takes about a full year to deliver."

Sedlakova said, "She's still doing a progress, boss. Maybe she isn't as pregnant as she thought. Noblewomen usually go into confinement about the time they start to show."

Kait Rhuk opined, "If I was King Jaime about now I'd be starting to have my doubts about me being the daddy."

"Indeed." Disdain for the behavior of women of estate was owned by lower-class culture everywhere in the Chaldarean world.

Titus suggested, "She may not be following routine because she's afraid to withdraw. She's surrounded by jackals."

Hecht said, "We're all enjoying this, but in the end it's something that will take care of itself. I need to know more about the people around the Empress. The ones who think they have some influence, or want to have some influence. The ones convinced that the future of the Empire has to be reflected in their own special mirrors."

Hecht cringed. This time he would have to play the political game. "Titus. Find Algres Drear."

"Drear?"

"The Braunsknecht captain."

"I remember. I was just surprised."

KATRIN'S CONDITION COMPELLED HER PROGRESS TO PROCEED MORE slowly than usual. The date of her return kept getting pushed back. Unseasonable weather did not help. Communication through the Jagos ended six days earlier than ever it had before. Hecht's quartermasters made sure of a fuel supply early, before prices started to rise. Hecht's status as favored of the Empress made his credit good.

Consent observed, "This might be a bad winter. By the time it's over maybe nobody will be interested in gallivanting off to the Holy Lands."

"More likely they'll all want to go because it's warmer there."

Titus shrugged. "Just thinking out loud."

"A man can't help that, can he?"

Unsure if he ought to be miffed, Titus went off to do something useful. Hecht muttered under his breath, something about Consent turning into a gossipy old woman. About having to bring Noë and the children north next spring. Titus was more tractable with his family close by.

Once he chose his quarters Hecht gave orders that no one should enter without invitation. He wanted to create a space where Heris or Cloven Februaren could appear unnoticed. He did not want to be accused of having secret congress with the Night.

Heris turned up soon after Titus left. Hecht said, "You don't look so good."

"Grandfather's grandfather is testing us all to destruction. And it's hard to argue with somebody who has two hundred years on you and does more than he wants you to do. That old bastard don't believe in sleep, Piper."

"He's just showing off."

"I'd say it's more like he's trying to prove something to himself."

"So. What news?"

"Anna is well. Sends her love. The girls are well. Not thrilled about school. Pella has the whooping cough. The rest expect to have their turns. Grandfather has, in my way of thinking, been getting too bold in the Collegium. He's deliberately provoking Serenity."

"Of course. There's a history. And he's counting on Serenity to be worried sick by the continued existence of Cloven Februaren. The Ninth Unknown had a nasty reputation in his time. Several old-time Patriarchs regretted attracting his ire."

"Piper, Serenity doesn't know any of that. He's almost completely ignorant about the Unknowns. And about anything before his own grandfather's time. He doesn't care about old times. And he was never invited in on the Construct project. Hardly anyone knows about it anymore, other than the orders involved and those who do the funding. Meaning just a few members of the Collegium. Grandfather's cronies, who are all sure that the fall of the old world is right around the corner. The last Patriarch who expressed an interest in the Construct was Pacificus Sublime. When he was still the Fiducian. He wanted to know where the money was going but never looked at the project up close. Something blindered his thinking."

"Something like the Ninth Unknown?"

"Probably. Grandfather says Hugo Mongoz knew a little but that was only because he'd been around so long he couldn't help it. Bellicose knew nothing. Serenity won't, either. Neither will whoever comes after him. That's the way the old people want it. They're thinking about sealing off access from the Chiaro Palace."

Hecht wondered: How would that impact all those monks and nuns who worked on the project? Some had done nothing else for fifty years.

There were other ways to get to the Construct. For the dedicated worker. Of course. Since nuns were not supposed to be inside the Chiaro Palace in the first place.

"Did you have anything exciting to report?"

"Sure. We gave the Windwalker a bath. And the really old man thinks he's found the place where the Bastard lives. Getting there and doing something with the information might be problematical, though."

So. Someone had put a label on the man they sought. "Expand, please." He had no idea what Heris, the Ninth Unknown, and Muniero Delari were up to. Only Heris was ever forthcoming. And seldom did she have much to say.

She told a long story now.

"You have been busy."

"We're going to get busier. I won't be able to pop in here half a dozen times a day to spoon-feed you information. You need to use the pendant. That's what it's for." She sounded like the mother of a stubborn child, patience exhausted.

"I was hoping I could get you to haunt Alten Weinberg the way you haunt Krois and the Chiaro Palace."

"I'd like that, Piper. I really would. You think you could get them to do me the courtesy of speaking Firaldian or Church Brothen? Or maybe Melhaic?"

"All right. Sarcastic exposition of obstacle noted. I'll do my own haunting."

"I mean it about the pendant, Piper. I'm really busy."

"I understand. It's good for me, too. There won't be so many questions about who I'm talking to in here."

There had been questions. Concerned questions. Partial truths had sufficed, so far. He had a spy whose identity only he knew. The spy wanted it to stay that way. The staff worried about how she came and went.

An informal bodyguard had begun to form.

EMPRESS KATRIN WAS COMING IN FROM HER PROGRESS. AT LAST. Forerunners had been arriving for days, for their own purposes or hers. When word came that Katrin had reached the Eastern Gate Hecht ordered work stopped and the men turned out to line the way, to do the Empress honor. They were snappy, which pleased the Empress and her sister both.

The Imperials passed by.

Titus whispered, "They're carrying her in that sedan so people can see her. But she doesn't look like a woman about to give birth."

Hecht agreed, though he had been distracted by the Princess Apparent. He could not help imagining having seen both hunger and promise there. He turned to say something to Consent.

Something slammed him violently from behind. He felt metal drive through the padded scale mail shirt he wore. Felt it enter his back, turn on his shoulder blade, and so miss his heart. There was no pain.

He had been wounded before. He knew it would be a while before his body began to protest the damage.

He staggered a few steps, aware of shouting. His first reaction was incredulity. There had been no warning from his amulet. But there would be none when the attack was worldly. He offered a silent apology to Madouc, wherever he might be.

The bad guys had gotten him at last.

He began to worry about his men, about Anna and the children, even about the woman in al-Qarn and her daughters. He had not been able to provide for them.

His right hand stole inside his shirt almost without conscious thought.

Hands caught hold of him. Bodies surrounded him. Shields built a turtle over him.

The shouting went on. He was not the only one hit. And the men were responding.

Confusion. His mind would not work right. His heart was not doing its job, either. Still, he tapped on his pendant till consciousness fled.

PIPER HECHT WAKENED TO FIND HIMSELF SURROUNDED BY GRIM-faced men, some with light wounds, all angry and every one frozen still as a statue. Time had not stopped, though. Several had fallen, stricken in midstep.

Heris said, "It's working. He's awake."

Hecht could not see her. The Ninth and Eleventh Unknowns, though, entered his field of vision. The elder said, "The arrow was poisoned. Fortunately not with anything fast. There was no damage to your organs."

Februaren was thoroughly unhappy. He could not express himself fully. There was no telling what the frozen men would recall when they recovered.

Heris said, "He's starting to show some color."

"The poison actually helped once his heart stopped."

"It's racing, now."

"Yours would be, too. We got lucky. We were quick enough. He'll make it."

Delari mused, "I wonder how this will change him."

Februaren grumped, "It might finally get the idea through that there really are people who want to kill him."

"I meant changes because he's been one with the Night."

Hecht wanted to tell the Principaté that he was wrong. He had not had congress with the Night. He had been unconscious.

"Scrub those minds, Muno. Quickly. So we can get your ass out of here. We've been here too long already. It's a miracle no one's walked in on us."

"No miracle. I spelled the door. Anyone who gets close forgets why he came. He'll wander off trying to remember. There. That should do till they get a healer in. I'm ready."

Heris appeared. She touched Hecht's cheek. "Be more careful, Piper." She and Februaren placed themselves to either side of Muniero Delari, locked arms with him. Somehow, despite the clumsy configuration, they managed the sideways turn.

There was a soft *poof!* as they vanished.

Sound and confusion. A dozen men all asking one another what had happened, helping one another get up, asking each other if they were all right.

"Holy shit! Lookit here! The boss is breathing. Hell, he's awake!"

They crowded round, some helping others stay upright. Hecht noted several bandaged wounds, none as dire as his own.

"Ain't this some shit?" Kait Rhuk demanded. "Ain't this some I ain't never seen the like of it before shit? The man was stone-cold dead. I was sure."

Someone out of sight snarled, "About goddamn time your ass got here, padre!"

A healing brother entered Hecht's field of view. He was old, certainly past sixty. He owned a round, ruddy face with a white furze of beard. A natural tonsure occupied the top of his head. He looked like a man who always had a smile in store. Though just one man, he gathered over Piper Hecht. He laid healing hands on while auditing the history of the incident. He became disturbed. He jumped away as though burned when told that his patient had died and returned to life.

Several men said they thought they remembered spirits moving among them while they were . . . Well, they could not explain what they were, other than able to do nothing. Most had no recollection of having been in that state.

The priest said, "My talents would be better applied somewhere else. Anywhere else. The dead who get up can only be creatures of the Night. Of that side of the Night ruled by demons, the undead, and the Adversary."

Clej Sedlakova took station in the doorway. He had only one arm but lacked no skill with a blade. "Not this way, Brother. Turn around. Treat the man."

Remarks from the others made it clear there was no other option.

And once he finished with Hecht they would generously let him deal with the lesser injuries they had sustained themselves.

Hecht had fallen asleep. He wakened again when he felt the healing brother's hands. The priest's touch was almost sensual. It left good feelings, new energy, a sense of well-being. In minutes Hecht felt strong enough to sit up. And to speak. He rasped, "Talk to me, gentlemen. What happened? What did you do about it?"

He got frightened looks and silence in response.

He was strong enough to think. "Damn! You superstitious dolts! Look at me! I'm not dead. Obviously. I was never dead. What the hell is the matter with you? You'll get people who don't know any better thinking that I rose from the grave. You'll get us all thrown into a pit of burning oil. Think! Don't be superstitious morons. You! Priest! What happens when we die?"

The healing brother mumbled some confused Brothen Chaldarean dogma.

"None of which happened. No bright lights. No darkness. No angels, no demons, no voices. No black ferryman with his hand out. No nothing but a huge headache. I was unconscious. And in shock." Sucking energy off the priest, he was becoming manic.

He saw flickers of a will to believe.

Hecht definitely preferred his current situation to the one that had obtained a short while earlier. But his resurrection was sure to complicate life.

Titus Consent, shivering, said, "We did get the assassins."

"What? Plural?"

"A pair. Lovers, I think. We haven't done anything with them. Except lock them up."

"Separately, I hope. I'll want to see them when I'm stronger. Priest. Do your sorcery on this wound. Who took the arrow out?"

"That would be me, boss," Hagan Brokke said. Brokke was one of the men with lesser wounds.

"Thank you. You kept the arrow?"

"It's in pieces. But yes."

"Good. I want the arrowhead. For a memento. For God's sake, priest! I won't break. I just survived an arrow that went right . . . Oh! That hurt. The prisoners have anything to say?"

"Not yet," Titus replied. "They will."

"No torture. Just keep them alone, in the dark. Let their imaginations wear them down. Ah! Back off, Clej. He's doing his job."

A subaltern came to the door. Sedlakova let him in. He made his report. And saw his commander being treated.

"Good on you, Clej," when the boy left. "That should kill the craziest rumors. What did he say?"

"They want to know, downstairs, what to tell the people who keep turning up wanting news. He says the Empress and the Princess Apparent have been especially insistent."

"Keep a log if you're not already. Knowing who is concerned might be useful. How much longer, Brother?"

"Only a few minutes, sir. Then I'll need to get you bandaged and to get your left arm immobilized."

"Anything for pain? I'm starting to feel it."

"I recommend inactivity. If you sit still and don't put any strain on it the discomfort should be tolerable. If you don't, enjoy the result."

Hecht drew breath for an angry answer. Pain shot along the path the arrow had taken.

"Let nature do its work. Yours will get done without you. If you don't take my advice you'll suffer. And keep tearing it in there so it never heals right. And you end up losing use of the arm."

"It will heal, though?"

"If you let it. I've given it the chance." The healing brother bandaged Hecht slowly, letting everyone else see what needed doing and how it should be done. The dressing would have to be changed.

As he started to immobilize the arm, though, Hecht told him, "I need to get dressed first."

"Excuse me?"

"I have to go out and show myself. To hearten some and dismay others."

"Meaning you intend to ignore my advice already."

"Just this once. It's important."

"Very well. And it will be important every time, won't it? Fortunately, it isn't Brother Rolf Hasty who has to pay the price. Though I'm sure he'll hear a lot of whining about the arm not working right." The healing brother refused to help Hecht dress.

Titus stepped in. "We'll make sure it's just this once, Brother."

Hecht could not restrain a groan as Consent moved his arm to get a shirt on him. A fresh shirt. "You can cut it off when I get back out of it."

Hagan Brokke presented the bloody scale shirt Hecht had worn when hit. He said, "You want this on, I'll get it cleaned up."

"I'll do without. I couldn't handle the weight. I'm beginning to get really sleepy, gentlemen." He considered the mail shirt. "Didn't slow the arrow down, did it?"

"Punched right through. The head was an armor piercer. For use at short range. Don't see those used much by longbow archers."

Minutes later Hecht was dressed and the healing brother had strapped his arm into place. Titus asked, "What now? Assemble the troops? It's important. You told the healing brother."

"Titus . . ." He found himself considering Piper Hecht with disdain. "No. I need a nap first. I have to face it. I won't be able to stay awake. Have somebody trustworthy babysit me. All of you, get back to work. We've only got six months . . ."

He slept fourteen hours. Fitfully, if Titus was to be believed.

"Do I talk in my sleep?"

"No. You're good about not doing that." In a tone that set Hecht to wondering if Consent might not have tried to interrogate him.

"Where do we stand? The world didn't end while I was snoring, did it?"

"It seems to have gotten on without you."

"It would, wouldn't it?"

"And it's turned back normal since word that you survived got out." Titus remained uneasy about that. "The Empress and Princess Apparent want in-the-flesh proof. They're afraid the rest of us are covering up so we won't lose our jobs. The Imperial treasury, by the way, handed over our start-up money."

"I'll see Katrin as soon as I'm able. A short visit. Unless she wants to come see me here. Where I still won't last. I've been awake how long? And I'm ready to sleep again."

Might his people be drugging him for his own good?

Titus said, "There was a letter from Buhle Smolens. He's on his way. The weather will slow him. One of my agents says he had a real knock-down, drag-out with Captain-General Ghort when he resigned."

"That's not good." Could it have been staged?

"Ghort took it personally. He wouldn't listen to excuses about not being able to work for Serenity."

"Again, not good."

"Considering the loss rate among veterans he's suffering, no. Those men have been to the Connec before. They don't want to go back. The Connec doesn't deserve what Serenity wants to deliver."

Hecht managed a nod and grunt.

"Your friend might be in over his head."

"And that wouldn't be good for him, Serenity, the Church, or the Connec." Hecht could imagine a frustrated Ghort and Serenity deliberately unleashing a massacre like the inadvertent bloodbath at Antieux during the earliest Patriarchal incursion into the Connec.

"Nothing good will happen in the Connec, Piper. King Regard has left an investing force outside Khaurene. They don't have the numbers

for a siege but they're tearing up the countryside and making Khaurenese life difficult. And that has the Direcian kings and princes pissed
off. King Peter has told King Regard and the Patriarch both to back off
or face grim consequences. He's already negotiated truces with the surviving Praman princes. Who are only too happy to buy time to recover
from the disaster at Los Naves de los Fantas. The Direcian Principatés
are getting loud in the Collegium, too. Where Serenity has lost most of
his support. The Principatés have decided that they made a huge mistake, electing Bronte Doneto."

"Interesting times. All right. I'm going back to bed. Much as it
gripes me to admit it, I need somebody to take care of me till I recover."

"The progress has been back long enough for the prostitutes to
have gotten caught up."

"Titus."

"Sorry. It's the company I keep."

"You told me Pinkus Ghort was still in Viscesment. That's his kind
of joke."

"You should've let Pella come along. It would be perfect work for
him."

Hecht growled softly. He did not want to think about family.
"Have you located Algres Drear?"

"Yes. He's willing to talk whenever you're recovered."

"Do you remember why I wanted to see him?"

"You didn't say. Is there a problem?"

"I've lost some memories. Nothing much. Little details from the
last few days before it happened."

"You do remember who Drear is?"

He did. "That's still in there."

"Then your answer should be involved with who he is."

"Politics, maybe. He knows the players and the secret rules. He
could be an informal adviser."

"If he was willing."

"There is that." But that was not it, he was sure.

THE EMPRESS INSISTED ON SEEING HER HIRED GENERAL BEFORE SHE
went into seclusion. Hecht had himself carried to the audience in a
sedan chair, then entered the presence in a wheeled chair pushed by
Terens Ernest, one of Titus Consent's clerks. Ernest had become Piper
Hecht's keeper. Who would, undoubtedly, monitor and report the boss's
every breath.

Many staffers were not yet comfortable about his return to life.

Hecht had used his pendant, one-handed, to warn Heris that he would no longer be alone nights. When Ernest was not hovering another of Consent's minions was.

Isolated, bored, he spent a lot of time toying with the pendant. Too much. Heris's responses became curt, irritated.

His left arm and shoulder were bound in bandages and splints which made him look worse off than he was. Though that was bad enough. He was tired of the pain.

The show might not have much impact. Brother Rolf Hasty, lately, had become the most popular healer in Alten Weinberg. Everybody wanted to quiz him about the new general's health.

Arrangements had been made to let Ernest help Hecht with his ceremonial obligations. The Empress was in a flexible mood. She had chosen to interview him in the same venue, Winterhall, where first she had asked him to come over to the Empire. As then, there were few witnesses, though more than before.

The Princess Apparent sat to her sister's right and below, slouched but quietly attentive. Her truce with Katrin continued. An heir was on his way. Katrin did not feel threatened.

Helspeth met Hecht's gaze boldly.

First thing the Empress asked, after the formalities, was, "Have you found the men who attacked you?" She wore a thin smile. She knew the answer, of course.

"We have. I spoke to them myself, just this afternoon. An odd pair. My slum-divers tell me they're local criminals with a reputation for daring murders. They had a factor, one Willem Schimel, who found work for them. Master Schimel was last seen just before the arrow hit me. Living or dead, he's no longer to be found. That's all we know."

Not true. Piper Hecht had been sixth on the assassins' list, bearing one of the smaller bounties. The killers had been late getting into position. The more lucrative targets, the Imperial sisters and members of the Council Advisory, had passed the ambush site before they settled in.

The killers had no idea why any of the targets was wanted dead. They had not cared. Great wealth would have been theirs had they been able to clear the list. Schimel had been confident in the trustworthiness of his contact. The assassins had been confident of their ability to vanish in the chaos following such dramatically important murders. But they had not moved fast enough.

Hecht kept all that to himself.

The Empress did not look like a woman already past due to deliver. Though extra attendees hovered, midwives lurked in a room nearby and healers waited in another, on a moment's call. About to say something, Katrin started violently. "Oh! He kicked! I really felt that one. It won't be long now."

Hecht considered the faces nearest Katrin. Each was a study in absence of expression. Those women were determined to do nothing to trigger Katrin's displeasure.

The donning of masks was so careful and so universal that Hecht knew the growing suspicion of the capital was, in fact, the truth.

The Empress was not pregnant.

She thought she was pregnant. She believed she was pregnant. She wanted to be pregnant so badly that she showed most of the signs. She was convinced she was about to produce a son. After which, no doubt, she expected Jaime to return and be her one true love.

"Excuse me, Captain-General."

"Of course, Your Grace." She liked that. It suggested high religious standing in addition to Imperial status.

"You and I, each in our way, are denied our potential by our bodies. You have a prognosis for your situation?" She was intently watchful. Looking for evidence of tainting by the Night.

He was used to that. Everyone held that secret reservation. *Everyone.* He might never be free of that, nor ever become comfortable with it.

Honesty was his only recourse. She knew whatever Brother Rolf knew. "Guardedly optimistic. I'm told I'll be good as new, someday. If I don't try to do too much before I'm ready. I don't think I will. My staff are masters at nagging me."

"Will you be ready in time for spring campaigning?"

Ensued an extended discussion of what had to be done before the Empress could launch her expedition to purge the Holy Lands of the Praman infestation. Katrin let formality slide while military business was on the table. She and her sister both impressed Hecht with their knowledge—Helspeth even more than Katrin.

The Princess Apparent flashed a grin. "We had to be the sons the Ferocious Little Hans always wanted."

Katrin agreed. "We grew up looking over his shoulders. Living this stuff. Being mascots around the headquarters. The warlords all thought it was cute when we were five or six."

"Then she started to fill out and it suddenly became scandalous."

Katrin bobbed her head. "It's get-even time." She waved a hand. "Enough of that. General, I'm impressed by what you've accomplished, given the limited time and cooperation you've had. And your wound, of course."

"Your Grace, I did the hardest part when I built my staff. They're talented men. Though sometimes a little rough dealing with what they call friction."

"That would be?"

"The lack of cooperation. Politics, I guess. People trying to pull them this way or that, trying to get them to do this or that. They're used to being left alone to make the clockwork run."

Not strictly true. But here in the Empire "friction" could become more of a problem than when they had been Patriarchals.

"We can't stop that completely. It bleeds off surplus energies. When it becomes a serious impediment, tell me. As Empress I have ways to make it stop. I can ask what they think my father would have done with them. If they can't take that hint I can refer them to Ferris Renfrow."

Hecht wanted to ask about Renfrow, who had not been seen for quite a while. But the Empress started, groaned, rubbed her belly. "I need to come up with a fancy title for you. Captain-General was good but it's thoroughly attached to the Patriarchy. Your fault." She did not ask for suggestions. "Back to friction. I considered easing that by handing off one of my duchies. If you were a duke you wouldn't have to put up with as much. But what we find out about your family doesn't stand you in good stead. Even my allies among the Electors wouldn't tolerate that dramatic an elevation."

Hecht was startled. Even shocked. And, from Helspeth's smug look he concluded that the Princess Apparent might have come up with the ennoblement suggestion.

"I'm flattered beyond my capacity to express, Your Grace, that such an honor should even occur to you. I wish my father could have heard you say it." Grade Drocker or the imaginary Rother Hecht.

"I can knight you. That would help. But I've decided that I'll build my crusade outside the Church and nobility. If we can make that work. I know several priests who can preach a cause in the mode of Aaron."

The woman was smarter than he had thought. Much smarter.

He had to forget her sex. Helspeth's, too. He feared the younger sister was brighter than the elder. And more deviously clever.

Definitely the Daughters of the Ferocious Little Hans.

"As you will, so shall it be."

The Empress started, then seemed pleased by the unusual formula. "If you're right—and I see no flaw in what you presented—we have a year and a half to get my Electors and nobility tamed."

"There are a lot of smart, talented nobles who will make outstanding warlords. They're bred to it. They grow up being trained to it." That ought to play well with the husbands of the Empress's attendants.

"Had they the capacity of seeing themselves for what they're sup-posed to be." Katrin offered no definition herself. Her attitude was un-mistakable: deep, abiding contempt for a class of men determinedly seditionist and obstructionist. "The whining arrogance . . ."

"Your Grace. I'm none too strong yet. My wound still pains me a great deal, and . . ."

"Yes. Of course. As you told the Grand Admiral and the Grand Duke when you decided you had nothing more to say to them."

Hecht began to feel truly uncomfortable. Katrin, for sure, had be-come the hard-ass son of Johannes. When she was not being crazy.

The Empress barked instructions at her women. Their languor ended. They scurried. Piper Hecht found himself being chivvied into the quiet room he had shared with the Imperial sisters before.

The Empress said, "I don't really have anything to say here. But I want those women to think I do. There'll be coffee in a minute." She grunted, settled into the biggest chair, rested both hands on her belly. Helspeth got behind her, began kneading her neck and shoulders. While making daring eye contact with the former Captain-General.

Katrin said, "I find myself mortally frightened, General. First, that this pregnancy won't turn out any better than my last one did, and that if it does go well for the baby, giving birth will be the death of me."

Hecht had nothing to say. Helspeth's mugging warned him not to say it.

This would be sensitive ground.

One of Katrin's women brought the coffee service. She did not stay. The door closed. The Empress gestured. Helspeth took what looked like a funerary urn off a marble side table. She removed the lid, turned the urn over. Drops of darkness fell like a rain of heavy honey. Neither sister explained. The Princess Apparent placed the urn on its side on the floor. Katrin poured coffee.

The drops of darkness did what they were supposed to do, then crawled into the urn like fat black slugs.

The Empress said, "They didn't sneak anything in this time. Enjoy, General."

Helspeth managed a lingering touch when she brought Hecht's cof-fee. She looked like a woman under sentence of death, with her big day not far off.

Minutes passed in silence. The Empress had something on her mind. She got to it at last. "I'm going into seclusion till the child comes. For a month, at least. Possibly several."

Hecht tensed up. The Empress had a reason to use the quiet room after all. And he feared that he was not going to like what he would hear.

Katrin said, "Instead of saddling you with some overblown title, why don't we go for understated but to the point? Something like plain Commander? Or, for a little more punch, Empress's Commander?"

The Princess Apparent suggested, "How about Lord High Commander of All Commanders?"

"You're being a smart aleck, Ellie."

"Sorry. Commander of the Crusaders, then. Or Commander of the Righteous."

"You don't sound sorry. I don't believe you're sorry. For your penance I'm putting you in charge till my confinement is over. Hush! You need a taste of how awful this role is. Commander of the Righteous. Helspeth's job will be formidable. Give her the backing she needs to succeed. Keep your men in the city instead of sending them to Hochwasser. I'll write formal orders. The nobles will whine. It isn't customary. Ignore them. You understand?"

"Of course, Your Grace." While reflecting that, sanity aside, the Empress was very clever. She had been working toward this the first time she tried to hire him. She now had a potent counterweight to the Electors, the Council Advisory, and anyone else who wanted to take advantage of a weak girl.

Helspeth protested. "I don't want . . ."

"So you've insisted since Mushin died, Ellie. Again and again. I never believed you. I'm not sure I do now. But I insist on you. Commander of the Righteous. Become the shadow of the Princess Apparent. Make sure she doesn't get carried away."

Hecht did his best to bow. Somewhat impractical for a man in a wheeled chair. Nevertheless, he held it. Keeping his face hidden lest it betray his wild thoughts. "As you will, Your Grace, so shall it be."

"Excellent. That's what I'd like to hear from all my officers. Ellie! Stop shaking. The doom that you dread is upon you. I've executed the legal instruments already. Orchard Vale should be rehearsing the Grand Duke in the facts of life as we speak."

Orchard Vale would be one of Katrin's more obscure secretaries, a priest from the local bishop's retinue. That Bishop, Brion of Urenge, new to the job, was dedicated to the Brothen Patriarchy. He had spent time in exile while Johannes was Emperor. "When you leave this room, Ellie, you're going to be the It."

Hecht watched Helspeth wrestle with herself. Saw that she thought she was being cruelly used. Was being forced into a place where nothing she did would be right. And saw that Katrin was wickedly pleased by having put her there.

The other daughter of the Ferocious Little Hans, the one so often accused of being too much like her father, saw no way out. "As you will it, sister, so shall it be, till you're able to resume your duties."

Hecht's mind raced through lists of things that needed doing. Of opportunities a smart man would take care to avoid. And sniffing round Katrin's undeclared assumption that the Commander of the Righteous should let no conspiracy against her take root while she was away.

Katrin kept growing ever more pleased with herself.

"EVERYTHING HAS CHANGED," HECHT TOLD HIS STAFF, WHO HAD BEEN gathered and waiting. He explained.

Titus said, "The military part shouldn't be hard. We have enough people here. Add the fact that, more than anything, the Grail Empire runs on inertia. The Empress being offstage for a while shouldn't give anybody time enough to get up to much mischief."

"Our job is to make sure. To that end, I want to see Algres Drear. And Ferris Renfrow, if anybody can find him."

"He's been scarce for months, boss. Which isn't unusual, I take it. They have a saying here: 'Comes the day, comes the man.' Meaning somebody will rise to the occasion, whatever it might be. It's a sort of nickname for Ferris Renfrow. If there's a need, he turns up."

Hecht grunted. That was not what he wanted to hear. He preferred to see Ferris Renfrow when he wanted to see Ferris Renfrow.

Titus asked, "Commander of the Righteous? Really?"

"I didn't pick it."

THE PRINCESS APPARENT'S REGENCY WAS NOT THE HARSH TRIAL SHE expected, nor the debilitating strain Commander Hecht anticipated. The old men of the Empire showed an uncharacteristic restraint. Titus Consent reported an abiding anxiety, an undirected dread, abroad in the Empire. No one could identify a specific cause. Everyone seemed willing to wait and see and stand united if the unknown birthed some bleak certainty.

Winter neutralized all external threats, except possibly from the north. North centered every sense of foreboding.

One change obvious to the dullest mind and dimmest eye was a sharp increase in incidents involving the malice of minor Instrumental-ities.

"WE'RE LIKE A COUPLE OF MASTIFFS SIZING EACH OTHER UP," TITUS told Hecht. Speaking of the nobility round Alten Weinberg. He and the Commander of the Righteous, Hagan Brokke, Drago Prosek, and Clej Sedlakova were enjoying a dinner honoring Buhle Smolens, who had

arrived that afternoon with thirty-two disgruntled fellow former Patriarchals. Hecht was still weak but could walk around for short periods.

Consent continued, "Their noses are all bent out of shape but our
legend is so big they mean to be very careful making things right."

"Right?" That was Smolens, hands resting on his full belly. Hecht's
former number two was laconic by nature, seldom having much to say.
Tonight, though, he wanted to get caught up. To manage that he had to
talk and ask.

Hecht observed and wondered.

And wondered about himself as well. He had developed a strong
strain of paranoia, lately.

Smolens had turned into a mass of contradictions. He had gained
weight, yet still gave the impression of being gaunt. His face had become more round. He had lost hair. He had stopped wearing the thin,
well-trimmed beard he had affected for years.

And he had the shakes.

Not obviously. Not all the time. And in no obvious connection to
what was going on around him. But the tremors were there. They came
and went, seldom lasting more than a few seconds.

Everyone noticed. No one mentioned it. But Smolens understood
that the tremors were no secret.

"All right," Smolens said. He took a deep breath, tried to relax.
"You're all suspicious because I quit the Patriarchals when I've been on
Krois's payroll since I was a sprout. Most of you probably think I'm
here to spy."

Consent admitted, "The thought had occurred to me."

Hecht said, "Pinkus Ghort is rough around the edges but he isn't
hard to work for."

"It isn't the Captain-General," Smolens replied. "Are we secure
here? Or do you care what might be listening?"

"I'll stop you if you hit something I don't want the world to know."

"All right. You're correct. The Captain-General isn't hard to work
for. Easier than you, mostly. His expectations aren't as high. He's not
the problem. That would be the people collecting around him. Against
his will. Witchfinders and really spooky Society thugs. Going underground didn't improve those people. And, lately, several sorcerer types
have shown up. Not Special Office people. They don't even pretend to
be agents of God. They go around greeting each other, 'Surrender to the
Will of the Night.' Yet they came with patents from Serenity. He'll tame
the Connec if he has to have the Adversary do it for him. I couldn't
take the strain."

"And Pinkus?"

"The Captain-General chooses to quell his conscience with fortified spirits. Which makes the villains unhappy but they can't do anything. The troops stay loyal to Ghort because the Society brothers make themselves so obnoxious."

Hecht wished the Ninth Unknown were around to eavesdrop. Or, better, Principaté Delari. Muniero Delari was the natural foil to Bronte Doneto.

Maybe the roots of their encounter in the catacombs had begun to show.

Consent muttered something like, "Give a man the power to excuse himself and his true heart will always shine through."

Smolens said, "I decided to leave after I overheard some Society brothers making plans for next spring. I tried to tell the Captain-General. He didn't want to hear it. I couldn't stay after that."

"We'll discuss the details in private," Hecht said. "Welcome back."

"You do have a job for me?"

"I told you I did. Just not the job you had. That's been split between Hagan, Clej, and Titus. Hagan got the hard part. You'll be my provost of the city. We have too many soldiers and not enough to keep them out of trouble. We haven't had any serious problems yet. It can't stay that way. I want to head off trouble before it starts. Pick five big bruiser noncoms to help. I expect firmness, fairness, finesse, and no favoritism to our men over the locals. Nor the other way around. Take no crap. You answer only to me. I answer only to the Empress." For the benefit of eavesdroppers. "If you do find yourself downwind of somebody wearing some really big pants, let me know. The Empress is hungry for excuses to throw a leash on some of these people."

THE COMMANDER OF THE RIGHTEOUS WAS AS UNCOMFORTABLE AS HE could recall ever being, though the Princess Apparent was trying to make it easy. She had women with her. Impropriety would be impossible. They faced one another across a table crafted of some rare, dark wood polished smooth. He took comfort from its protection.

He had come prepared for an extended, serious exchange concerning the business of Katrin's crusade. Cost estimates. A proposal for sending quartermaster scouts, come summer, to explore possible routes. A suggestion that diplomatic missions get busy negotiating rights of passage. The Eastern Empire would be crucial. Katrin's army would have to travel overland. It would be too large for the available shipping. Though shipping would have to be contracted in order to supply the army with what it could not carry or buy along the way. Acquisition of materials to fill those supporting holds had to start soon because it would take a long time to collect it all and move it to the handiest sea-ports.

And so forth.

This kind of warfare was not a pickup game.

Throat tight, Hecht said, "We need to hammer out some way to en-force good behavior. We can't have dukes and barons and their contin-gents dropping out to plunder along the way. Monestacheus Deleanu isn't the weakling that Anastarchios was."

Monestacheus was the current Eastern Emperor. Anastarchios had been Emperor eighty years ago, when last a Crusader army had gone to the Holy Lands overland.

That crusade had become an exercise in chaos. Too many proud kings. Too many desperate poor. No firmly established command, no detailed preparation, and no overall plan.

Born in shining idealism, the crusade lapsed into ugly adolescence before its tail departed the Grail Empire. The wealthy lords out front bought up local surpluses as they moved. The poor coming along be-hind had to forage. Which led to plundering. The slow progress, just a few miles a day, left a swath of devastation thirty miles wide. Once into the Eastern Empire it left whole cities destitute or destroyed. Cities home to good Chaldareans who also wanted the Holy Lands torn from the grasp of the cruel Unbeliever.

The Princess Apparent said, "We expect you to make things work better than they did back then." Her voice was strained. Her hands would not stay still, except when she realized what she was doing and forced them. But that never lasted. "I hear you've found Algres Drear."

Drear had not been hidden.

"Yes. I brought him along. I want you to take him back as chief bodyguard. I'd feel more comfortable with Drear between you and harm." Having the Braunsknecht close to Helspeth would place in-debted eyes near the seat of power, too. Drear owed Hecht.

"I don't know about chief bodyguard. But I do owe Captain Drear. I ruined his career."

"You did, didn't you?"

Flash of anger, quickly shoved aside. "I'm not that girl anymore. Still willful, though. But not ready to drag others down with me."

"Glad to hear it. The welfare of millions depends . . ."

"Yes." Sharp look. Estimation. Calculation. Leaning forward. In a voice meant for no other ears, "Things aren't going well for my sister."

Hecht sensed fear. Sparked by his remark about the millions. "How so?"

"I'm not sure. It's being hushed up. Most of her attendants aren't allowed out of the Quill Tower. Those who are won't say anything. And they look grimmer every day. One thing's certain. The baby hasn't come. That wouldn't be kept secret."

"I see."

"My sister can get ugly when she's upset. Which explains the moods of her people. They'll feel the sharp edge of her rage first." Helspeth told the story of her winter exile. "If it hadn't been for Ferris Renfrow I'd have died of hunger or exposure. And not because of Katrin's malice. Not entirely. Malice put me out there. But when she wasn't angry anymore she just forgot me." In an even softer voice, "My sister isn't sane, Commander. And she'll get worse every time she's disappointed."

Hecht glanced around, turning too quickly. His wound presented him with shooting pain.

"Are you all right?" Frightened concern.

"I moved too much, too fast. They tell me pain is a good teacher. I'm not sure. If I'm not hurting I'm not paying attention. How much do you trust these women?" She had, after all, been keeping her voice down.

"They'd overlook an indiscretion." Said with timorous challenge. "But nothing political. They all have husbands and lovers."

As he forced pain-born tension out of his muscles Hecht felt Helspeth's real meaning. Her women would not retail gossip but matters political were fair game? Strange, these people.

Helspeth said, "I can't find Ferris Renfrow."

"Nor can I. Makes you wonder, doesn't it?"

"Wonder? Not so much. If you grow up here you're used to Ferris Renfrow, the unpredictable apparition. It frustrated Father no end. But Renfrow was never missing when it really counted."

Hecht saw Heris seldom and the Ninth Unknown never, these days. He did communicate, via pendant, often. They had nothing to report about Ferris Renfrow, either. They said they were working on it.

Hecht felt starved for information.

He had access to more and better intelligence than anyone, possibly saving Renfrow, but remained painfully aware that there was much that he did not know.

Intelligence was like opium. The more you tasted, the more you wanted. The craving could not be satisfied.

The session never slipped the bonds of propriety. But it did go on. Helspeth always had another question. Hecht began doling out bits of thinking he had not yet shared with Titus, also to prolong their encounter. Before they did part, Helspeth suggested that they make an evening briefing part of their schedules. So that, when Katrin returned, she would find her crusade developing perfectly.

Hecht's men worked long days. They drilled. They performed weapons exercises. They performed fatigue duties. They helped clear snow from thoroughfares. They were involved in restoration of the city fortifications and a study of its arsenals and emergency stores. The latter, as in so many cities not recently threatened, existed mainly in wishful thinking. Shortages had sparked several scandals already. No names of consequence surfaced, naturally, so punishments were draconian.

Mostly, the Commander wanted his men seen. Wanted everyone aware of them constantly. He wanted potential villains conscious that a new factor had to be reckoned with and that factor was beholden to the Ege sisters.

He did not want to be lord of a praetorian guard. The politics of the Grail Empire, however, pressed him into the role of Imperial shield and hound.

He accepted that because he wanted to lead the next crusade. Which, if the Empress had her way, would be the biggest ever.

Katrin meant to buy her way into Heaven.

Loyalties blanketed Hecht in layers. He was several people, the created become most real. He forgot Else Tage completely for long stretches, as Else Tage had forgotten Gisors. Duarnenia and a childhood with Rother and Tindeman Hecht usually seemed more real. He rehearsed that past every day. And each time he talked about his boyhood new details accreted.

Alten Weinberg enjoyed a quiet winter. Weather in the Jagos was terrible. Not so in the capital. People remained content to mark time. Men of standing told Hecht that Alten Weinberg had not been so quiet since the heyday of Johannes's power. A popular effect. But that could change when Katrin came out of seclusion.

Helspeth's ladies were not as tight-lipped as she predicted. The heightening tension between the Princess Apparent and the Commander of the Righteous was the object of considerable delicious speculation. Nothing had happened yet, but, oh, what about tomorrow?

Privately, several Electors petitioned their God to make it happen—publicly enough to compel official notice.

The instruments establishing the Ege line as the Imperial succession just might be overturned if the Princess Apparent got caught in something sordid with a base-born, foreign-born soldier of fortune.

Crueler realities, filthy of tooth and claw, prowled the shadows of tomorrow. The first would come shambling out long before the first thaw.

# 22. The Chosen: The Wounded God

From the nethermost orient to the eastern shore of the Shallow Sea a grand migration was under way, though the families, clans, and decimated tribes braved the heart of winter. The Windwalker was hurt and distracted, somewhere far away. There might never be another chance to escape.

Few were welcomed. Resources were strained everywhere. Often there was fighting more bitter than when the Chosen were war slaves of the winter lord.

The empire of Tsistimed the Golden was an exception. Refugees were welcomed where willing to become subjects, so great had been the Empire's losses fighting the Windwalker.

Tsistimed seethed continuously. Those near him feared he would suffer some final outrage and succumb to fatal apoplexy. The Ghargarliceans were pushing back. They had recaptured several cities where the nomads had demolished the walls. The kaifate of Qasr al-Zed remained defiant, scorning all ambassadors and executing merchants and traders caught scouting.

Never had Tsistimed known such difficulties. He railed against his commanders like a spoiled child, till the more thoughtful began to wonder if it was not time to decide which son ought to succeed.

Winter, though, was time to rest and recover. Tsistimed himself had to wait out the season. He came to terms with reality.

He *had* been through this before, early on, on a smaller scale. Time and patience were the remedies. He could await a new generation of warriors. Meantime, former enemies could fill the holes in the ranks. Most of his warriors had ancestors who had been his enemies.

The refugees were willing. They were too hungry to scruple.

A MOUNTAIN OF ICE CALVED OFF THE SOUTH SHORE OF EASTERN Andoray, knocked loose by savage tidal bores roaring back and forth through the Ormo Strait. Sliding away, the berg exposed acres of stony beach. The monster toad crawled onto that, now more a two-legged transition between tadpole and adult. The withered god lay motionless, most all strength gone. And did so more than a month.

Kharoulke had escaped the sea. Continued existence remained problematic. He drew power out of the ether at about the rate he consumed it to remain viable.

Darts of silver-tainted iron remained at work throughout the Windwalker, blessing him with their poison.

Kharoulke's great advantage was his bulk. It would take him an age to perish, even in his current dire circumstance.

Smaller Instrumentalities—those quick and clever enough—streaked in and carved off bits of foul god flesh. The small eating the great, rather than the reverse. Familiar in the middle world but unseen before in the Night.

Vigorously engaged in resisting the embrace of the ultimate, the Windwalker became ever more intimate with the time-point where he was engaged in the awful struggle. Being thus tied and preoccupied, a fragment of his consciousness opened to happenings in that one present and one particular world.

He sensed the movements of his enemies. He could follow those. But he did not have the power to act. His emotions were like those of a man who had been buried alive.

He made no headway recovering. And, because time participated in an inevitable progress, summer would come.

Warmth, even just to the point of surface thawing, was no friend of a winter god.

## 23. Lucidia: Shamramdi

The Mountain honored the martyr Ambel by standing in for him in the wicked dives of Shamramdi. He drank in taverns belonging to Antast Chaldareans, for whom wine consumption was no sin, and whose customers were mostly Believer sinners in disguise. He whored in brothels high and low, a vice he had indulged at no time before, even when young. He had a wife . . .

In truth, he had no idea what had become of the woman. He had not seen her since his last approved visit to al-Qarn, years ago. His agents in al-Minphet reported nothing. He suspected they were making no effort. They would not care. Women were of no consequence. Plus, getting close risked bringing them to the attention of er-Rashal al-Dhulquarnen.

TONIGHT, HIS FIFTH IN SHAMRAMDI, NASSIM WAS DRINKING IN A place with an unpronounceable name. Its signboard showed faded keys, dice, and a strange fish. The managing family spoke numerous languages, few of them well. Nassim communicated good enough to keep the wine coming. Coins did most of his talking.

He did not like the wine. It lay sour in his mouth.

The great question tonight was why he went on when he loathed the wine and was ashamed of what it did.

He persevered. Alone. In Ambel's memory. Though there was a young man in shadow across the way who seemed inclined to flirt.

An alternative accepted by many Faithful. Nassim Alizarin was not among them. The idea repelled him. Nor was he capable of wrapping his mind around the sophistry involved in justifying the act.

The Written proclaimed homosexuals an abomination in the eyes of God. They were to be slain wherever discovered, preferably by stoning. Yet across the Realm of Peace it was acceptable for an older man to relieve his needs by using the body of a boy. Shamramdi had its male brothels. Even holy men indulged. No stones got thrown.

Nassim drank wine and was glad his comrades from Tel Moussa were not witnesses. Though they, more than most, would understand.

Ambel, really, was nothing to him. A boy he had known only by name before he went off to assassinate Black Rogert. A boy who, in the normal course, might have fallen anyway, before his time in the field ended. Whose loss, in that event, would have touched the Mountain no more than that of any other warrior.

The flirt did not become discouraged. The Mountain first thought the lad had no idea who he was trying to attract, then decided that the opposite must be true. There was villainy afoot. More appealing and much more likely targets were available.

The wine, however, encouraged Nassim to play along, to find out what was up. Which might have suited yon blackguard just fine, Nassim having failed to consider the full range of possibilities.

As soon as Nassim began to feign taking the bait, he found a drunk settling at the low table, crossing his legs. He came armed with a bottle of wine, mugs, and an aggressive personal aroma. He mumbled an unintelligible self-introduction as he flung a hand into the air and beckoned someone the Mountain could not see. Nassim was in no mood to squabble about sharing space. Sharing was expected in a crowded public house.

He watched the newcomer pour wine, studiously creating identical portions. His desert clothing was filthy. It boasted fresh dust over the filth. His headwear suggested generations of insects had nested and feasted there. The man had lost his right eye and, apparently, could not afford a patch to conceal the resulting scar. He grinned at Nassim.

Fate had not been kind to his teeth, either.

A brace of rogues as tasty as the first sat down. The one-eyed man offered Nassim a cup, grunting as though unfamiliar with the local dialect.

The flirt, who had started toward Nassim, decided to turn his attention elsewhere. He changed course.

The one-eyed villain tossed his hand up, as though to another acquaintance. And, in a cultured whisper absent any influence of wine, said, "You should be more cautious, Nassim Alizarin. We can't always watch over you."

The flirt headed for the exit. The one-eyed man muttered, "Tears will be shed in al-Qarn." He poured more wine. After a while, he said, "The lord Indala will see you tonight."

THE MOUNTAIN WAS SURPRISED. THE FAMOUS INDALA AL-SUL HALAL-adin was as short as rumor claimed. And as old, though he bore his years with grace.

He looked every inch the lord and champion he was said to be.

He was, reputedly, fiercely insistent on his dignity, yet would set status aside entirely once convinced you accepted that dignity. In the Mountain's instance he dispensed with formalities immediately.

"Sit, General. Make me understand the circumstances in which Rashid and his brothers found you."

Indala's dignity must be honored absolutely, here. Nothing but honest, straightforward truth would do. So Nassim told it, without embellishment, analyzing himself, sparing himself nothing.

"So, after the fact, you see yourself the same as the man by whose order your son was murdered."

Nassim bowed his head.

"Despite all the obvious differences between the situations."

"Acknowledging those seems like self-justification."

"I understand." Indala contemplated his folded hands. "Often the choices that affect the least number of people are the ones that trouble us most."

"Exactly. Which makes acceptance all the more difficult. How many men have fallen since I took charge of Tel Moussa on your behalf? It must be more than three dozen."

"Fifty-three dead or missing," Indala told him. Revealing another facet of the character that made him the most honored chieftain of Qasr al-Zed. He would know most of their names, tribes, cities, and how they had died, too. If the stories were not greatly inflated.

"It was his idea," Indala said. "He volunteered."

"Yes. But I knew what he was giving up. And I let him do it anyway."

Indala again contemplated his hands. When his gaze rose it was piercing. "Tell me, have you been damaged permanently? Can you go on? Can you send other mothers' sons into the fire between Heaven and Hell? Will you hesitate in the critical instant when hesitation could be fatal?"

Nassim understood. His future depended on his answer. And Indala would be unerring in tasting his sincerity, or lack thereof.

"I am Sha-lug." And, though he suspected Indala understood perfectly, he clarified. "I'll come through this. It won't fog my mind nor stay my hand when the arrows are in the air."

"Well said." Then, "Just a moment." A man had appeared. He looked like young Az with three decades added. Indala gestured, giving him permission to approach. He came, whispered into the sheikh's ear. Indala nodded. Nassim thought he was unhappy behind his aplomb.

Indala said, "I'll send instructions before I retire."

The message bearer bowed his way out. Nassim thought he lacked enthusiasm.

Indala said, "That was interesting. Gherig has a new castellan, Anselin of Menand, younger brother of Regard, King of Arnhand. He arrived at the head of a great troop of westerners, most of them Brotherhood of War."

Nassim had nothing to say, other than an unhappy grunt.

"It would seem you worry them, General."

"I doubt they think that much of me."

Indala said, "Perhaps. So. Tell me about the boy, Azir."

Surprised, Nassim did so.

"He has potential, then?"

"A great deal. So long as he receives proper guidance now. He's brilliant. He's quick. Men like him, most of the time."

Indala nodded. "Good. I'd hoped. That was his father's brother who just left. The son of my second youngest brother. They're competent soldiers, too. But their men don't like them."

"Do they take on airs of privilege?"

Indala's forehead crinkled into a deep frown. Then, "Exactly. They think too much of themselves. Because they're related to Indala, Nirhem, and Sufik." Nirhem and Sufik were uncles of Indala, deceased, who had been champions almost as great as Indala himself.

"Family connections. Being an outsider, I can tell you that family connections are the burden that keeps this entire kaifate from moving forward."

"Most men won't trust anyone but family."

"So you marry your cousins and can't imagine any allegiance beyond a tenuous loyalty to tribe. And that's why a handful of Arnhanders were able to carve a kingdom and a half-dozen lesser principalities out of the Holy Lands."

"That and most common folk don't care who runs things as long as they deliver peace. Which isn't common in the Holy Lands, historically."

"One more reason the Crusader states persist. They've provided decades of peace where they're in control. They've prospered because of that and the pilgrim trade. At Tel Moussa we fought Gisela Frakier."

Indala chuckled. "Of course. We Believers of Qasr al-Zed would rather squabble amongst ourselves. Though I'm changing that. I wonder, then, why al-Minphet and the monolithic Sha-lug haven't reclaimed the Holy Lands. Gordimer the Lion can't be beaten in battle. And has hordes of warriors trained up from birth, probably the best in the world."

Nassim started to respond. Indala raised a hand. "The question was rhetorical. The answer is: er-Rashal al-Dhulquarnen and Gordimer the Lion. Neither can escape the conviction that an army operating so far from their immediate control represents a personal threat. And they'd rather not take the field themselves."

"The paranoia of princes."

"Always justified. The higher you rise the more men want to bring you down. And those two create enemies indiscriminately, casually, willfully, almost deliberately. As though daring Fate to do its worst."

"Add stupidly. They had no need to turn me against them. As they have no need to tempt the spite of the Night."

"Let us consider those two. In particular, let us consider Gordimer. How much under the sorcerer's thumb is he?"

"At the risk of sounding like a fakir, Gordimer is more under the Rascal's control than he could ever believe. At the same time, he's far less so than er-Rashal thinks. The relationship hasn't been tested. It's been ages since they faced anything where their ambitions diverge. Nowadays, Gordimer wants nothing but to hole up in the safety of the Palace of the Kings, where he indulges all the vices he found so despicable in his predecessor. Er-Rashal makes sure that he can indulge. So he gets a free hand."

"Didn't er-Rashal have the same understanding with Abad?"

"You know he did. Abad was farther gone than Gordimer is ever likely to be. If the honor of the Sha-lug faces a large enough challenge the Lion will find his roar. He'll come out and fight. If that challenge crosses the sorcerer's ambitions in a way that they need different outcomes to satisfy them, things might get interesting."

"That's worth some thought. Especially how to goad Gordimer."

"An army from the north," Nassim said.

"Yes?"

"There was a prophecy, when Gordimer removed Abad. It was vague. Those things always are. Gordimer interpreted it to mean that an army will come to al-Qarn to overthrow him. That it might consist of his own people is the nightmare that torments him."

"In other words, you."

"Could be. I wish. But, think. He does have enemies who aren't Sha-lug. We all do. The New Brothen Empire wants to launch another crusade."

"The Chaldareans talk about it all the time, General. But when the armies come together they fight their own kind." Indala held up a hand to forestall a response.

Indala had not been aware of the prophecy overhanging Gordimer. Might that have been a true vision passed along by the Night? Might Gordimer fall to Qasr al-Zed? Unified, Qasr al-Zed and al-Minphet would have the power to drive the Unbeliever from the Holy Lands.

"This is marvelously interesting, General. Food for a feast of thought. But I'm feeling my years. I need rest. Before we part, though, I must tell you that your would-be paramour tonight claims to have come out of the Idiam. Says he's a resident of the dead city."

"That can't be true."

"I've never visited the haunted desert. I have no idea what's true there and what isn't. But I'm inclined to agree. The young man is one of er-Rashal's agents. He may be Sha-lug. He may not. Er-Rashal's men are good at not attracting attention. Remember that they're out there. Stay out of places like the one where you were found tonight. Pull yourself together. Azir speaks highly of you. He thinks you're invaluable. I want you to demonstrate that to the full war council tomorrow."

When Nassim merely bowed his head in acceptance, Indala said, "I had a taste for vice myself when I was Azir's age. If you stay here long you'll hear of my adventures from my relatives. But a man of attainment has responsibilities. You have responsibilities. I want you here tomorrow afternoon, alive, sober, and not hungover."

"It shall be as you say."

"My personal guards will see you to your house."

Nassim had been given use of a small establishment not far away. He shared it with Bone, old Az, and several young bucks from Tel Moussa.

Indala's guards would make sure the Mountain did not wander during his journey. The message was plain.

Nassim did not look forward to the disapproval he would face from Bone and Az once they heard from Indala's men. Those old campaigners had little give or understanding left.

Decades had escaped since a young Nassim had faced a disappointed professional sergeant. That Nassim had learned from those instructors then. He prayed that his lessons would take this time, as well.

There was a near full moon up. He enjoyed the silvery light. It went well with the chill of a winter night.

Later, it would cloud over. Snow would come with the dawn. It would stick for days, something alien to Shamramdi.

The children would enjoy it immensely.

## 24. Brother Candle: Full Circle

The Perfect Master spent more than a month hiding amongst Khaurene's Seekers, none people with whom he usually associated. The Maysaleans smuggled him out, finally, during the excitement after King Regard abandoned his siege. Most of Regard's soldiers returned to Arnhand. They would not come back. But a minority, with no prospects elsewhere, stayed. They captured several small castles, murdered heretics—anyone the Society indicted—and built a rambling, inadequately fortified camp only miles from Khaurene.

Thoughtful Arnhanders feared the coming summer. The lack of bluster out of Khaurene and, more so, out of Direcia guaranteed a fiery reckoning.

The most stubborn Connectens, rural lords who shared an attitude with the iconic Count Raymone Garete, harassed the Arnhanders constantly, determined to wear them down before Anne of Menand gathered new swarms of bandits. They responded rudely when Serenity threatened them with excommunication.

Count Raymone and Antieux continued to give heart to those who refused to accept foreign dominion and religious bullying. Though now, with the Viscesment Patriarchs gone, legal pretenses for defying Brothe were more strained.

It had become harder to make a case for the Brothen Patriarch being a tool of the Adversary. God did, after all, have the option of overruling any Patriarchal election.

HUNDREDS FLED KHAURENE WITH BROTHER CANDLE, FOR AS MANY reasons as there were people fleeing. The siege, though never fully effective, had discouraged many would-be travelers. Brother Candle went out in disguise, as part of a family rejoining relatives in Castreresone. The gate guards were not looking for a party of twelve, nor for one old man. The guards were looking for the things Duke Tormond had given Brother Candle, in the possession of one old man.

Those left Khaurene through a different gate. The youth carrying them had no idea. He met Brother Candle near Camden ande Gledes, of grim recollection. The Perfect took the treasures and headed east with his adoptive family, who suspected the identity of their companion but were vague on why the authorities wanted him. They assumed religious crimes.

Castreresone was controlled by Navayans, to whom the White City had passed when Isabeth inherited. The people, including local Seekers, were content. The only grumbling came from those close to the Brothen Church. They did not grumble loudly. Count Raymone had friends in Castreresone. They outnumbered Serenity's.

Brother Candle spent several weeks seeking those friends, who might be men he knew and trusted, but enjoyed no success. In time he left the White City, hurriedly, because members of the Maysalean community bragged that a famous Perfect was among them. And that word reached Count Diagres Alplicova, Queen Isabeth's proconsul.

Out of sight of the city's white walls, Brother Candle changed into his Seeker travel wear. That would mark him for his enemies, yes, but in the Connecten countryside it would mark him more clearly for his friends. And, sure enough, he fell in with bandits that same afternoon. Bandits who, recognizing him as Perfect, never asked to see what was in his pack.

Those fourteen men played only a brief role in the Perfect's tale. They fed him and protected him on the road to Sheavenalle. He learned only a few names, Gaitor, Geis, and Gartner, who were brothers. The band presented a social history of the past half decade. These men came from several countries, had deserted several armies, had been driven from their homes by fighting, or were criminal fugitives from the cities. A half-dozen ragged families followed them, mostly women in circumstances more dissociated from the main than those of their men. In gratitude for their assistance, and despair over what the women and children were suffering, Brother Candle found the means to write a short message. He gave it to Geis. "Take that to Antieux. Give it to a man named Bernardin Amberchelle. Your fortunes should improve."

Geis thanked him, though he was suspicious. No one did them favors. Geis could not read, nor could any of his companions, so there was no way to be sure the note would not betray them to the authorities. But, on the other hand, the author was a genuine Perfect Master. Those people did not play cruel games.

Geis promised.

THE MAYSALEAN COMMUNITY IN SHEAVENALLE HAD ABANDONED that city during the Connecten Crusade, shortly before it fell to the Captain-General. The rest of that city's religious minorities had gone, too. Only a few returned when Pacificus Sublime called the crusade off and sent the Captain-General to fight pagans on Artecipea. Brother Candle had trouble finding the modern community, then was uncomfortable among them. Though they called themselves Seekers After Light, their doctrine differed from that practiced farther west. Brother Candle found them too worldly, while strangely otherworldly.

They disbelieved in the marriage sacrament, but not in physical abstinence, so held one another in common. Likewise, property, such as survived. And they believed in a different form of reincarnation.

Errors, Brother Candle thought. They had come into being because these Seekers had no Perfect to guide them. Then he learned that their erroneous thinking came from Firaldia. Seeker doctrine there had come under the influence of thinkers in remote reaches of the Eastern Empire. Brother Candle met several Firaldian Seekers there, and was dismayed. They were as militant as the brethren of the Society for the Suppression of Sacrilege and Heresy.

He left Sheavenalle as soon as he found passage aboard a coastal trader that meant to sail up the river Job. Agents of the Society, of Navaya, of anyone else interested in what Brother Candle carried, might be watching the approaches to Count Raymone but he doubted that anyone would anticipate him arriving by ship.

The vessel was small. Its cargo seemed to be salted fish. Its crew were all related and fit perfectly Brother Candle's idea of coastal pirates. They would indulge, too, no doubt, if they thought they could get away with it. They might have robbed a passenger, too, were they sure they could be rid of the body effectively. But they gave that no thought in Brother Candle's case. Being what he was, he would have nothing of value. And preying on a Perfect would be begging to bring a curse down on the family.

Brother Candle was ever amazed that supposed holy men, good or bad, enjoyed so much deference. Especially these past few years, when so many had been so blatantly predatory.

He did not fail to take advantage of that deference.

At his urging the sailors waited till dusk to tie up at Antieux's waterfront. Time of arrival made no difference because tidal effects were minimal on the Mother Sea.

The waterfront, such as it was, lay outside Antieux proper, downstream, and consisted entirely of slapped-together facilities. Several sieges in a few short years left people unwilling to invest in structures that could not be defended. It was an article of faith that the new Patriarch would seek revenge on the city that had injured and humiliated him.

THE PERFECT FIRST SEARCHED FOR FELLOW MAYSALEANS. AND FOUND them in numbers. Count Raymone had made Antieux a haven for Seekers After Light. He knew they would fight when the Patriarch's men came. But the Perfect could find no one he knew, personally or by repute. Carrying what he carried, he dared not reveal himself to strangers.

It was not a good time to have no place to stay. Winter had its teeth out.

The warmth of the coast had vanished after just a few miles of river travel. There had been ice floes the rest of the way. Brother Candle tried life on the streets but gave up after one night.

He was too far past his prime.

He went to a Maysalean church that helped Seekers in need. A church! That was a wonder in itself. Seekers did not have churches. But this one had been taken from the Brothen Episcopal Church because of the bad behavior of its priests. To make his point loudly, Count Raymone had handed it over to local Seekers, who made of it a charity shelter and hospital for refugees.

The Perfect received a thin mattress filled with wheat husks. He was allowed to fill his begging bowl with soup from a communal pot. The man dispensing the soup, a tanner by his odor, apologized. "Usually it isn't so thin and we don't limit how much you can take, Brother. But business is too good. Weather like this. Most of these people aren't really Seekers. But if they know the words we don't turn them away."

"As should be. Charity stands at the heart of our faith." But, his worldly side reminded, it also posed a danger.

There would be agents of the Society among the ragged and forlorn evading winter and the dank of Night, making lists.

Three days of scouting left Brother Candle confident that there was no hue and cry for one Charde ande Clairs, alias Brother Candle, in this end of the Connec. Those who wanted him kept away from Count Raymone must be lying low, waiting for him to come to them.

Each morning Brother Candle pursued a careful routine, following his begging bowl, affecting a cane and bad limp, wearing an eye patch, with hair and beard gone fallow. He could not disguise his age or poverty so he exaggerated them. Though tempted, he did not add feigned madness. He adopted the name Brother Purify. Nothing he did could abuse that man's reputation.

One morning he settled on the steps of the burned cathedral. He meant to rest just a moment. Sleep ambushed him.

Prodding wakened him. He looked up, groggy. Three men faced him. By his dress one must be the new Brothen Episcopal bishop. One of the Bishop's companions had been poking him with a truncheon. Vaguely, he wondered why anyone would accept the see of Antieux. Bad bishops had a brief life expectancy in Count Raymone's demesne. And only worse and worse examples seemed willing to assume the risk, especially since Bellicose ended Antieux's brief turn as an archbishopric. He supposed most of them hoped to get rich when the Church came triumphant.

"Yuck!" said the man with the stick. "There's stuff running out from under his eye patch."

"Then we won't talk to him. Just beat him and send him along."

"An excellent idea," said a horseman who had materialized behind the threesome. "Only let's make it the black crow who takes the cane."

Brother Candle met Bernardin Amberchelle's merry eyes. He did not want this but dared not speak up.

The Bishop's men knew Amberchelle. Still, they were inclined to be uncooperative. Till more horsemen arrived.

Amberchelle said, "Lay into it, men. I want him to remember his place. I'll stick him with my sword when you're done. If he squawks I'll have you beaten, too."

This Bishop was new. He thought he could bully the boldest priest-baiter in this end of the Connec.

Amberchelle kicked him in the mouth. "That's the way you feel, I'll kill you now so I don't have to keep looking over my shoulder." He drew his sword.

Brother Candle bit down on his tongue.

Amberchelle held back. "I find myself feeling merciful. Carrion bird. Bishop. If you offend me again I'll take your head. No courtesy warning. Just a quick chop. And stay away from the cathedral. It's Antieux's memorial to all the evil done in Brothe's name."

The Brothen Episcopals staggered away, the Bishop unbeaten but bleeding. Amberchelle peered down at the old man. "I thought so. Come along, then. Want to ride?"

"I'd rather go looking like a prisoner."

"You want the boys should hit you once in a while?"

"You don't have to make it that authentic."

Amberchelle laughed. "A pity." Then, "I sense disapproval, even though I didn't beat that vulture. But you know *nothing* we do will appease the Church. So I might as well enjoy sticking knives in while I can."

The old man did not respond. He should, he knew. Something about multiple wrongs not adding up to a right. But what Amberchelle said was true. Nothing short of the will of the Chaldarean God Himself would keep His Church from designing and conspiring in one of the great evils of history. The more people talked about a Connecten Crusade, the more carrion eaters would begin to circle.

Brother Candle dragged it up from his deepest heart but did say, "You could be right, Bernardin. Maybe we should make sure the rape of the Connec is something so bad that it's never forgotten."

"Come on, Master. People are starting to wonder if you're our prisoner or our pal."

"So it's true," Amberchelle said. "You did make off with Duke Tormond's baubles."

Brother Candle was infatuated with his first decent meal in weeks, but did respond. "I made off with nothing. Tormond forced them on me. He gave me no chance to refuse."

"That's such a crock, I think I'll believe you. I never knew Old Indecisive. I figure that's exactly the kind of thing he'd pull if he ever did make up his mind. I wish I could read his letters."

"I wish you could, too. I'd give it all to you and let you worry about getting it to Count Raymone."

Amberchelle indulged in what he called his evil laughter. "No way, old-timer. He's up near Viscesment, working out how to bloody the new Captain-General's nose when Serenity turns him loose."

The Perfect shook his head. Nothing would be gained by beating his head against that particular wall. He had argued for peace a hundred times. Peace had been rejected just as often.

Amberchelle asked, "You think they know what you have? The people back in Khaurene?"

"Of course they do. Why else have they been hunting me?"

"There's your winning personality. And your message."

Brother Candle started to reply, stopped short.

Bernardin Amberchelle, the seriously violent thug, sounded much too thoughtful and subtle.

The mindless thug grinned. "Messengers are on their way to Ray-mone. Three, just to make sure word gets through. Sometimes odd things happen. Especially at night."

Brother Candle had experienced little of that during his travels but had heard fearful stories from the country people. Though the last Captain-General had rid the Connec of major revenants he had done little to quell the malice of lesser Instrumentalities. Those crowding in from the north excited those already resident in the shadowy out-of-the-ways. All of the Instrumentalities seemed inclined to take it out on the nearest unwary mortal.

It should not be so. Simple precautions, of the sort undertaken by anyone with half a brain, were enough to leave a wise user nearly un-aware of what haunted the darkness around him. That had been worked out two thousand years ago.

Brother Candle said, "Let me pass the tokens and instruments on, now. Their weight is crushing."

"Oh, no. Bear up, Brother. I'm a wicked man. You don't want to put that much temptation in my way." Wearing a wistful sort of look.

"I see." Bernardin might win Count Raymone's title, rescission of excommunication, and pardon of his sins and crimes in exchange for the treasures in Brother Candle's keeping. "A man should recognize his limits."

"I'll send you on to Raymone."

"No. No. I'm almost as old as the limestone under the Connec. I've been on the road forever. This old dog needs to curl up on the hearth and nap. For months."

"As you will."

"Where is Socia?"

"Out there. With Raymone most of the time. Off on her own when she thinks he isn't aggressive enough."

"Frightening."

"More than you can imagine, Master. More than you can imagine."

"Explain."

"She's started hearing voices. Telling her how to defend the Con-nec. Telling her how to deal with our enemies. Raymone tried to stifle her. He failed. She's started recruiting her own Companions. Each time she massacres some invaders more young men rush to join her. It doesn't hurt that she's such a handsome woman."

"Raymone can't control her." An observation. He was not sur-prised. He had had charge of Socia Rault before their marriage. The child was willful and ferocious. A Seeker whose sole adherence to doc-trine was to equality of the sexes.

"He never could. The challenge was what attracted him in the first place."

Brother Candle agreed.

Count Raymone saw himself mirrored in his wife. . . . O wicked dread!

"You don't think they might get into a competition? Trying to show each other who's more bloodthirsty?"

Amberchelle's face darkened. "Brother, there's some of that already. There was news last week about her taking the castle at Suralert Ford. Among the captives were a distant cousin of Anne of Menand and a viscount who was popular in Salpeno. There was a bishop, several priests, and a dozen members of the Society. She beheaded the knights and nobles, no exceptions. She burned the churchmen. She applied the torches personally. But the common soldiers she disarmed and paroled."

Brother Candle closed his eyes and shook his head. "Socia, Socia. Bernardin, I knew she had the taint, but not that bad."

"Brother, she promised them safe-conduct to win their surrender. Then went back on it. She said God doesn't expect us to keep faith with agents of the Adversary."

True enough. Church people claimed that all the time. "Didn't the Society execute 'heretics' when they captured that same castle?"

"They did. Two Seeker students. Two. Who were confused about what to do if they were captured. The garrison surrendered without a fight."

Brother Candle learned that Socia had, improbably, taken the Suralert stronghold with thirty-six men. Only three suffered injuries. The defenders had numbered eighty-four. They had had supplies enough for two months. Socia executed twenty-two prisoners. A twenty-third, Bishop Morcant Farfog, decided to change sides. . . .

"Farfog? *Morcant Farfog?* The Farfog who was with Haiden Backe when he attacked Caron ande Lette? Who took command of the mercenaries after Backe was killed? The Morcant Farfog who had several wicked titles under several wicked Patriarchs and the Arnhander Crown?"

"Uh . . . Yes. Interesting turn, eh? He turned coat and made speeches denouncing the wickedness of the Society. His other option was the stake."

"Ah. Yes. St. Morcant the Martyr. I knew him well. And good for him. But, just one problem, Bernardin. Morcant Farfog was an Archbishop. And he was murdered in Castreresone way back when the Captain-General occupied the city."

"Uh-oh, then. I must've got it wrong. Or Socia did. Hey! Maybe it was that other famous Arnhander asshole Bishop, Austen Rin-poché."

"The hunchback? Didn't he get killed somewhere along the way, too?"

"No. He was the one, I'm pretty sure. My mistake. I can't tell one Arnhander Church dick from another. It had to be Rinpoché, the special idiot. Anne's favorite idiot. She kept trusting him with missions. He kept screwing them up. I heard she's started nagging Serenity about making new seats in the Collegium so she can pay off her clerical lap-dogs."

"The Patriarch can't expand the Collegium. Only the Principatés can do that. And that won't happen. The Firaldians have too thin a majority. One that won't hold up if Serenity comes at cross-purposes with the Empire."

"Then let's hope our new shepherd of souls offends the Empress."

"Let us hope." A chill had shaken Brother Candle. He was no student of Church history but did recall that more than one Patriarch had tried to reshape the communal attitude of the Collegium by eliminating Principatés of insufficiently sympathetic attitude in order to replace them with men whose views were more compatible.

BECAUSE BERNARDIN AMBERCHELLE WANTED THE WORLD TO THINK the Perfect was a prisoner Brother Candle became, in practice, a loosely confined prisoner. He had freedom of movement inside Antieux's citadel but was not allowed out.

Three times Bernardin reported taking prisoners who admitted having been sent to recover the treasures the Perfect had carried away from Khaurene. That hunt had grown vigorous, now.

Socia Rault turned up one morning as Brother Candle was breaking his fast. Nine days had passed since Bernardin found him. She had cleaned up but it remained obvious that she was not long off the road. She held a finger to her lips, tapped her ear, swept her hand round to indicate the plentiful shadows.

Brother Candle was not sensitive to the Night but had felt the chills and creepiness supposedly associated with the presence of lurking Instrumentalities. Did he care what they overheard? Those interested in him ought to know everything worthwhile already.

Socia produced a doeskin sack a good foot deep. She shoved a hand inside, winced, then flung a scatter of something all round. It rattled like pea gravel against the walls of the cell. Socia licked bloody spots on her fingers.

Whatevers from the handful rolled back toward Brother Candle.

They did look like bits of dark gravel. Then they opened like sow bugs uncurling, took a moment to get oriented, considering him and Socia first. Then they headed for the shadows, fast.

"Not rolly-polies," he said. Sow bugs had no speed at all.

"No. I'm not sure what they are. I bought them from a pagan witch out in the hills. Don't mention them to Raymone. They work better than any charm." She counted on her fingers as she talked, dropped the doeskin sack at a hundred beats. The creatures began to crawl back inside it. "We can talk, now. They ate everything spying on you."

Brother Candle did not understand, had no idea. "You'll have to explain someday. Though I'm not sure I want to know."

"It isn't just the Old Gods wanting to come back. Little things are stirring, too. They didn't interest the Captain-General. He was after big revenants." Then, "Is it true? Duke Tormond adopted Raymone? He sent Raymone everything he needs to become the next Duke?"

"It's true. All wrapped up in a legal package so neat that the only way to break it is to voluntarily, publicly, choose eternal damnation."

"Meaning a lot of people are going to be unhappy."

"A lot of people are thoroughly unhappy already, child. Ask Bernardin. He's already run into squads of agents sent to get me before I turned the baubles over. Expect a flood of immigrants now that my whereabouts are known."

"Bernardin and I will enjoy the hunt."

The old man shuddered. Socia was almost a daughter. He loved her like his own. But the more he heard about Socia today the more troubled he became.

She was possessed of a soul both dark and cruel. Her husband's enemies had cause for dread.

WINTER WAS CRUEL IN THE CONNEC. EVEN THE OLD FOLKS ADMITTED that its like had not been seen before. There were ices floes in the Dechear. At Viscesment citizen crews worked for weeks to keep the ice from damaging that city's precious bridges.

The cold forced an end to all campaigning. Even Count Raymone Garete's hardiest fighters abandoned the field once they started losing fingers and toes.

The Arnhanders harassing the Khaurenesaine suffered the worst, though winter was less harsh in the west. They had failed to show the season adequate respect when they wasted the countryside. Depriving the enemy meant depriving oneself. Food, fuel, and fodder had to be dragged in from far away. Other than in the few overcrowded castles shelter was hard to come by. Huddling for warmth elsewhere could turn fatal. Well-fed and well-clothed Navayans or Khaurenese almost always attacked when smoke gave a gathering away. They tried to recapture the castles whenever it looked like they could manage cheaply.

Despite all, King Regard kept a force in the field. He stayed in the End of Connec himself. Which occasioned humor on both sides.

There would be an invader army on hand when spring came. The Arnhanders believed the campaign would go their way once the weather turned. Then Khaurene would pay the butcher's bill.

COUNT RAYMONE CAME HOME AT LAST, COMPELLED BY THE COLD outside and the heat within. He and Socia were shameless in demonstrating their affection.

BROTHER CANDLE WAS ONE OF A DOZEN GUESTS AT A SMALL FEAST. Something private was being celebrated. No one said what. Brother Candle suspected that Socia was pregnant. He was not sure why he was present. The other guests were all intimates of Count Raymone.

The merry mood was unjustified, in the old man's view.

This was no world to bequeath a child.

Something he said inspired Socia to poke him in the ribs and declare, "You're the perfect pessimist. The world is going to hell in a chamber pot. You ought to be dancing a jig. Every gloomy day we get more evidence that Seekers have it right. The world is the Adversary's playground. You get validated anew before every sundown."

"That may be, child. But I don't exult in the torment of my fellows."

Bernardin Amberchelle laughed like that was the joke of the decade.

"These are apocalyptic times," Count Raymone said. "And the most learned Perfect is here to witness and to guide us through."

Sarcasm? Hard to tell. Brother Candle could not help saying, "I don't like the sound of that."

Socia responded, "That's because you're a sour old badger who only expects the worst."

"And the worst is about to rain down like a ton of gull droppings, isn't it?"

Count Raymone said, "This once your pessimism may be justified."

"Just this once, though, of course. Right?"

"Of course." The entire gathering showed amusement, though the Perfect could tell that only Bernardin, Socia, and the Count knew the secret.

"Maybe you ought to give me the really bad news."

Amberchelle shifted his bulk. "You look a lot better than when I saved you from the Bishop."

"That doesn't seem likely."

Count Raymone combed his fingers through his thinning hair. "This is the plan, Brother. I want you to get yourself arrested by the people who want to take you back to Khaurene."

The old man was speechless. What?

"That's less risky than you think. Those people know you're important to the Duke. And they know you have my protection, which means a lot more. They know it'll go hard if they aren't gentlemen."

Brother Candle frowned. That would not be the whole tale. Raymone Garete's enmity was not a dread as potent as the Count might wish. Enemies did not worry about exciting his wrath every day. "And what have I done to earn this further trial? At my time? The victims of God's insecurities in the scriptures of the Devedians and Chaldareans weren't forced to face such tribulations."

"I know. It's terrible of me putting this on a man your age. But no other messenger, no other witness, can relay what needs relaying as effectively. Nor can anyone else disappear into the sea of the people like you. Once you reach Khaurene you'll vanish. Then do the talking I want you to do."

Brother Candle did feel much better than he had when Bernardin found him. He had gained several pounds. He no longer dragged. He was, occasionally, bearing witness to the locals and auditing their evening meetings.

The local strain of the Heresy resembled that prevalent in Sheavenalle. There was more pressure to conform and less acceptance of debate. It was, like Antieux's Count, militant. Still, unlike the Church, the Seekers of Antieux did not feel compelled to crush dissent completely.

Count Raymone's scheme revolved around a challenge to the arguments of a Firaldian Perfect known for his intolerance and inability to step out from behind his ego. Bernardin Amberchelle thought that this Brother Ermelio would deal with intellectual competition by whispering to those who wanted to carry Brother Candle away.

"That involves a lot of ifs," Count Raymone admitted. "But Brother Ermelio is an idiot. We've used him before."

Bernardin added, "The surest way to provoke him is to question his Perfect status. His behavior makes me think his Perfection was self-endowed."

Count Raymone said, "I think he's an agent of the Society. But he's so useful I can't bring myself to have his throat cut."

Bernardin contrived to have Brother Candle cross paths with Brother Ermelio. One evening's meeting, though Brother Candle held his tongue, left the Perfect despairing of the collective wisdom and intelligence of Antieux's Seeker community. Which was large and militant and dumb as a bundle of broom handles. And left him further despairing of the Seekers of Firaldia.

He did have to grant that those there were scarcer than their Connecten cousins and were constrained to be less open. They faced a more determined persecution.

Following the meeting, as he headed back to the citadel, shadowed by Bernardin's guardian angels, it occurred to him that Brother Ermelio might be a confidence artist. He seemed more a carnival barker than a religious witness. Then it occurred to him that Count Raymone was a confidence artist, too.

And then, so suddenly it startled him, he felt stupider than all the local Seekers put together.

Socia was the only one he could find. She had waited up. She asked, "What's wrong?"

"Brother Ermelio isn't Brother Ermelio. He isn't Society, either. He works for the Captain-General. Probably the new one. We saw him when we were in captivity at Castreresone. He's disguised himself but he hasn't changed his voice. It wasn't till I was almost back here that I remembered where I'd heard it. His name is something like Bogna, or Bologna. I'm sure he knew me right away."

"You're sure?"

"Completely."

"If he's gotten that far inside the Seekers that means we really don't have any secrets."

"I'd guess not. I'll bet he's been using Raymone and Bernardin by letting them think they're manipulating the petty personality he showed them."

"We have to do something. No telling how much hurt he's arranged already. Does he know you recognized him?"

"I didn't recognize him when we were together. I debated him on reincarnation and the Wheel. Briefly. He got huffy, then angry."

"I'd better waken Raymone. This might be important."

"Perhaps. I have a question for you, child." He was sure Socia could not consider him a throwaway. "Is my journey something that really does need doing?"

Socia's response would not have pleased her husband. "The fate of the Connec won't be riding on you. It's a calculated propaganda move meant to give the Duke and his supporters heart."

*      *      *

BROTHER ERMELIO HAD AN OUTSTANDING NOSE FOR DANGER. COUNT
Raymone's men could not find him. They got nothing sensible from the
old Seeker couple who had given him a place to sleep. He was just gone.

Bernardin Amberchelle could not believe that Brother Ermelio had
gotten out of Antieux. He kept the search going.

Agents of Direcia did find Brother Candle one night, being insufficiently alert while returning from a Seeker convocation.

A JOURNEY THAT HAD TAKEN MONTHS, HEADING EAST, LASTED A LAZY
sixteen days going the other direction. With a strong escort and a seat
aboard a cart Brother Candle was safe and was obligated to exercise only
as much as he liked. The cart, though, threatened to beat him to death on
the crude roads. He walked most of the time. And complained like an
old woman whenever his escort took a shortcut.

There were hints of impending spring as the party approached the
queen city of the Connec. Brother Candle did not notice. He was shaky
following a skirmish with lean, ragged Arnhander soldiers.

The camps and engines Regard had spent fortunes to build had all
been destroyed or captured. Some of the engines now served in Khaurene's defense. Patrols protected citizens outside, as they undid the damage the invaders had wrought. The laborers included the occasional
Arnhander who had surrendered rather than go on suffering the fury of
winter.

News of the old man's coming outpaced his party's progress. Deliberately so.

He and his companions entered Khaurene through the Castreresone
Gate. The soldiers on guard were militia. They asked few questions.
They were nervous about a situation developing behind them, up the
hill.

Moments later a riot engulfed the Perfect and his party.

It seemed Khaurenese devoted to Duke Tormond, to Connecten independence, to the departed Viscesment Patriarchy, or who just plain
loathed the Brothen Church had joined forces to hunt down fellow citizens suspected of being in cahoots with King Regard, the Society, or
Serenity. An old sport finding new life, near as any sense could be wrung
out of the confusion.

At the height of that confusion Brother Candle became separated
from his escort.

# 25. Alten Weinberg: Bleak Spring

Helspeth appeared grimmer than ever. The Commander of the Righteous asked, "What is it?" He had been summoned to confer in the morning rather than awaiting the usual time in the evening.

"My sister."

Helspeth was so pale Hecht leapt to a conclusion. "What happened?" There had been a lot of activity at Winterhall lately. Imperial Electors had visited. Members of the Council Advisory had visited. Only Ferris Renfrow had not been seen. And the Commander of the Righteous had not been consulted.

Hecht had put his men on alert quietly. His falcons were charged, manned, and sighted in. Key points were under observation. There would be no deadly surprise.

Helspeth replied, "Nothing's happened. But this week everyone who's anyone . . ."

"Yes?"

"They all agree. It's time. Something's got to be done."

Hecht began to get it.

She stated it. "The Empire is paralyzed. I can't make commitment decisions even though things happening in Arnhand might affect us."

King Regard, under fierce pressure from his mother, intended a massive new invasion of the Connec. The Maysalean Heresy would be the excuse. Annexation of the Connec and the taking of titles in reward to the Arnhander nobility would be the real goal.

The Captain-General of Patriarchal forces would invade at the same time, supported by levies from the Patriarchal States. And the jackals of the Society would follow along.

All predictable without spies or the random report from Heris, via pendant.

Hecht was tired of that. He would prefer an occasional visit. But something ate up all her time.

"Are you going to take over?"

"No!" Horrified by the suggestion. "*Katrin* is Empress till God calls her home. Sainted Eis! Not even the Grand Admiral suggested anything like that. Don't ever say that again."

"It was an inquiry, Princess, not a policy suggestion." He did not check the audience to which Helspeth played. "I had to make sure that I needn't call my men out to protect my employer's rights."

"Nobody is thinking that way, Commander. *Nobody!*"

"All right. I'm listening."

"Nobody! Even Brothe's steadfast enemies are more interested in keeping the peace than pushing their own agendas. Probably because of you. But everyone agrees that things aren't moving forward."

He admitted, "I'm nose against a wall myself."

"So. Katrin has to be pushed."

Hecht raised an inquiring eyebrow.

"We'll make her have her baby." Stated in a tremulous voice. "Or not." Because only the Empress herself believed in the Imperial pregnancy anymore.

"I see."

"We've collected the most skilled midwives . . ."

"Don't give me details. Give me instructions."

"There aren't any. Except to stand by to keep order."

Hecht nodded, not pleased.

Each day Hecht's force became more of an Imperial bodyguard, in every mind but his own. Most people seemed comfortable with the notion. It promised an alternative to chaos.

HECHT WAS WITH HIS STAFF WHEN WORD CAME TWO AFTERNOONS later. The Empress had been delivered of a male child. The news stunned Hecht, his staff, and, he was sure, all Alten Weinberg.

"How did they manage?" Titus demanded, cynicism kicking in. "Did they ring in an orphan?"

Clej Sedlakova said, "No way. Even the suspicion would poison the succession. There would've been a platoon of unimpeachable witnesses."

A vigorous discussion began, driven by worry about future employment. It lasted only minutes. A second message arrived.

Katrin's son had been born dead. She had carried a dead baby all this time. It had developed only to about the sixth month.

"Is that possible?" Hecht asked. "Can a woman carry a dead fetus for half a year?" He had no idea how all that worked.

Nor did any of his staff, though Buhle Smolens opined, "She could if there was sorcery involved."

Sorcery, or the suspicion thereof, soon animated rumor. Some wicked power had stilled the future Emperor in the womb. He would have been greater than his grandfather had he lived. Further wickedness had been worked by spelling the Empress so the death would go undiscovered for months. The finger-pointing began.

The potential villain had a hundred identities. Hecht was on the list, but well down it. At its head, despite Brothe's romance with the Empress, was the Patriarch. The logic indicting Serenity was convoluted.

If it was not the Patriarch, then surely it must be the Collegium.

Hecht wondered if Katrin had, indeed, been touched by the Night. He seemed alone in his curiosity, though.

THE PRINCESS APPARENT MANAGED A MEETING WITH JUST ONE witness present. The woman was not formally presented but Hecht knew she was the notorious Lady Delta va Kelgerberg. Such a profligate was unlikely to broadcast the indiscretions of her friend.

That birthed an excitement so intense it distracted him almost completely.

Helspeth was painfully aware, too, but fought through. "How is your health? Is your wound still a problem?"

"I'm better. Some. I can't go riding. I can't indulge in work that requires physical effort."

Helspeth glared. The va Kelgerberg woman flashed a knowing smirk. "Why do you ask?" An out for the Princess.

"I want an honor guard. Yourself leading. For the funeral."

"Funeral?"

"For Katrin's baby."

"There's a baby?" He blurted it, surprised.

"Of course. Haven't you been paying attention?"

"I thought . . ."

Helspeth leaned in to whisper, "There is an infant. Katrin has been holding it and crying for two days. We'll take it away soon. Even in this weather it will putrefy. It will lie in state tonight. Tomorrow we'll inter it with my father and brother. The lighting will be bad. Katrin won't look so awful with the shadows around her. I hope she'll have her hysteria controlled. Come dawn we'll close the casket. You and your men will guard it and Katrin during the night, then take the casket down to the crypt. Katrin's favorite churchmen will handle the rites and prayers. Then Katrin can get back to ruling the Empire."

"I see. Of course. I'll play my part." Never being sure what was real and what was playacting.

All the appurtenances of a state funeral—for a stillborn child. But without them the Empress might be lost.

Hecht had a hundred questions. He dared ask none. The va Kelgerberg woman might have no part in the plot. If there was a plot.

Helspeth saw his confusion. "Someday. As pillow talk." Boldness on which she almost strangled.

THE COMMANDER OF THE RIGHTEOUS STATIONED HIMSELF AT THE end of the tiny gold casket. He wondered where it had come from on short notice. Titus, beautifully turned out, stood at the other end and gently urged people to keep moving.

It would not do to have the little corpse examined too closely.

So Hecht felt.

He thought it looked nothing like the Empress. It was as dusky as King Jaime. He thought it looked nearer full term than six months, too. Though in the available light it was hard to tell, and he was no expert.

Katrin occupied a light throne behind and overlooking the casket. No reason had been given. It was not customary. But she was Empress. She could do what she wanted. She had cried a lot. Then she had fallen asleep.

She slept well, except for one brief crying jag and a short absence to relieve herself. She did not reclaim her place among the living till after the viewing ended. Hecht's picked men were about to close the casket.

"Wait, Commander. I want one last look."

Hecht signed his men to step back. Katrin rose with difficulty. Hecht asked, "Do you require assistance, Your Grace?"

"No. But I've decided not to look. I just slept for the first time. I should let go now, not torment myself any further. Close it. Take it away. Priests! Do your duty."

Hecht performed the stiff, shallow bow expected of a senior officer. "As you command, Your Grace." And wondered how Katrin would have reacted to seeing her infant in the light of day.

THE FUNERAL WAS APPROPRIATELY SOMBER. HECHT SAW NOTHING TO suggest that anyone considered this playacting for the benefit of the Empress. These people really believed.

"Maybe I've gotten too cynical," he murmured to Titus Consent. "I was sure this was all set up so the Empress could save face. Yet, near as I can tell, everybody believes it but me."

"Sometimes the unlikely can be true, too. And villains don't have to be black-hearted all the time."

"Yet I hear no conviction."

"What I think doesn't matter."

"It does to me." Hecht brooded. In time, he decided that only Katrin's conviction mattered, but she was not alone in her conviction.

If Helspeth and others had worked a scheme, its outcome was good for Empress and Empire.

THE EMPRESS WHO HAD LOST A SON WAS A NEW EMPRESS: HARDER, more focused, and less tolerant than the Empress who had gone into confinement. This Empress meant to slay her pain by working herself to exhaustion. And she meant to carry Alten Weinberg along with her.

The Unbeliever had better beware. A furious storm was gathering.

Hecht's weary staff cornered him one evening. Clej Sedlakova said, "I've been elected to speak for everyone."

"Can you hurry? I have a meeting with the Empress."

"The woman is eating you alive." Someone snickered. These were soldiers. "She's devouring all of us. We need a leader here. We need a decision maker. If you want to spend all your time dancing attendance, leaving us to work ourselves numb best-guessing what we're supposed to do . . . Well, you need to delegate somebody to be in charge if you aren't going to be yourself."

Surprised, Hecht had to admit that the one-armed man was right. For nineteen days he had spent most of his waking time with the Empress. And not just preparing for her crusade. She insisted. He had become her emotional crutch. He tolerated it because it gave him a chance to see Princess Helspeth, often in circumstances less chaperoned than when he had conferred with her every evening.

They had moments to talk and—more or less—flirt.

Two days ago Katrin had asked, clumsily, "Did you two manage to dampen your ardor for one another while I was confined?"

Helspeth had reddened and sputtered. Hecht had done nothing. He was in no position to contradict the Empress, nor to argue with her outside the realm of war planning.

"Ah. You didn't. Ellie is still valuable on the marriage market. But she is getting past her bloom. How droll. How sad for you both." There was a cruel edge to her laughter.

Katrin was going through changes. Hecht feared she would turn into one of those tyrants who practiced their worst cruelties on those nearest them.

Katrin said, "You two don't hide what you're thinking. You look at each other like ferrets in season. But, never mind. As you will. So long as it doesn't sabotage Imperial policy."

A small cruelty, there. After suggesting that Helspeth might be on the marriage block again.

Hecht did not speak into the silence. Nor did Helspeth.

Katrin tired of waiting. "I'm pleased with what you've done, Commander. Especially during my confinement. I'm also pleased with your efforts, Ellie."

Hecht smelled a "but." "Thank you, Your Grace. It was a strain. I'm sure it will be less so now that we have you back to guide us."

"You have requests and reservations?"

"Nothing new, Your Grace. It's all in the reports. Excepting recent difficulties having to do with me overworking my staff. If you like, I'll have my recommendations separated out of the body of the reports so you can review them without the distraction of drayage censuses, blanket and tent inventories, and the like. A messenger could have that here in the morning."

"Yes. Do that." Said in a way implying that she had not had that in mind.

The Empress had moments where her mind slipped its moorings. When she went away somewhere. She never explained, never acknowledged that anything had happened. Perforce, those in her presence shared the pretense.

"As you command, so shall it be."

"In all things?"

Uncertain of his ground, Hecht went for cautious honesty. "Almost all things. There is my higher obligation to God. I won't sell my soul. I won't surrender to the Will of the Night, though I love you as a man must love his greatest earthly lord."

"An answer Mother Church and all her swarming little priests would applaud. Good enough. Suppose I were to order you to carry my sister into one of these private chambers and spend the rest of the night making her fantasies come true?"

That edge of cruelty was back in Katrin's voice, stronger than before. Time to be very careful.

"Much as I might, as a man, wish for such a night, I think that the situation, as you present it, would come near asking me to sell my soul."

The devil left its place behind Katrin's eyes. The urge to be cruel evaporated. "Very well. If I can't help, I can't. You two will just have to manage it by bumbling and sneaking. Go, now, Commander of the Righteous." A hint of mockery there? "I want that report right away."

THE EMPRESS SEEMED TO LOSE INTEREST. HECHT'S MEETINGS WITH her came further and further apart as winter headed toward spring. He was not alone in enjoying less of her time. She was withdrawing. Her periods of distraction grew longer and more frequent. There were rumors of physical complications left over from her delivery.

There was talk of erratic behavior, though Hecht never faced it during his visits. He did see the harsh consequences suffered by some who managed to displease their Empress.

The same period saw the Princess Apparent growing ever more frightened. She told Hecht, "She's worse than she was when she sent me off to die in exile. It's only a matter of time before she turns on me. On all of us, eventually. Nothing we do will change that."

Hecht wished he could reassure her. But the Empress he saw in meetings was not the Empress others saw when he was not around. There was plenty of smoke to give that fire away.

"Piper, she's clever at covering it, but my sister is quite mad."

"Maybe. You should be less melodramatic, though. The walls have ears." Katrin kept setting up situations where they might think they were alone. But someone was watching. Possibly Katrin herself.

There were ugly whispers about the Empress ordering persons from the court to couple while she watched.

That, Hecht suspected, was enemy talk. Somebody wanted to paint Katrin in a repulsive array of colors. But caution would not hurt.

Helspeth whispered, "We need an exorcist. Something dark got into Katrin that night. It's taking over."

"Which night?"

"When she had the baby. Don't be an idiot."

"The night she . . . But . . . I thought . . ."

"What?"

"That you took a dead baby and made the whole business up. To stop her self-delusion."

"You really did?"

"Of course I did. That's what a lot of people think. While admiring how well all of you in the conspiracy have held your tongues."

"Understand this, Lord Commander of the Righteous. One last time. It was real. Katrin's pregnancy, Katrin's delivery, Katrin's baby. All real. I was there. I saw that thing come out. It was awful. The midwives made it look a lot better before they put it in the coffin. They were terrified. They kept babbling about sorcery and the Night."

"Hold on." Even now Hecht had trouble believing in Katrin's pregnancy. "Any chance somebody besides Jaime could have been the father?"

"Piper! None! How dare you . . ."

"It's a process. Seduction of the truth. Save your indignation. So. Before, your sister was rude, self-centered, uncaring, and bullheaded. Everything we admire in a monarch once they're safely dead. But now she's more of all that, and crazy religious besides."

"Yes. She lives according to her faith. As she sees it. But what she sees keeps changing and getting uglier."

"If she's devout, then she didn't have knowing congress with the Night. That she birthed a monster wouldn't be her doing."

"Wrong! Of course it's her fault. She let that animal Jaime spill his seed inside her. She wanted him to. She begged him to."

"It wasn't a match ordained in Heaven." Hecht looked around hard. Where would an eavesdropper be lurking? Along with what else?

He tried to caution Helspeth with a hand sign.

She forged on. "For Katrin it was. It still is. She's blind about Jaime. Say something against him and you're on her bad side for sure. I loathe myself for it, but I feed her fantasy."

Hecht had trouble staying with the discussion. Just sitting there, frightened, Helspeth distracted him. She stumbled over her words. "It's different when something really could happen. Consequences start rattling around inside my head."

"It's not naughty letters to somebody hundreds of miles away anymore."

"The consequences . . ."

"Could be awful. Could be deadly."

"Katrin talks about it every time I see her."

Hecht frowned. And stared. And could think of no response.

"It's her new way to torture me. She couldn't enjoy my misery when she sent me to Runjan. This she can. She asks embarrassing questions in front of people."

Hecht sighed. An enduring fantasy seemed doomed to a humiliating demise.

"She's looking for a husband for me again, too."

"You'd expect that. Now that she isn't carrying the next Emperor. She'll feel more insecure."

"I did expect it. It took her longer than I thought. I did good looking out for her and her interests. She needed time to find some arcane way to think that was all a plot."

Still concerned about eavesdroppers, Hecht said nothing.

Helspeth understood. "I just wish there was some way to make Katrin understand that I'm not her enemy."

Her good intentions could be irrelevant. The Princess Apparent was not just a person, she was a symbol. She represented a ready alternative to an unpopular monarch.

Helspeth changed the subject. "How's your wound? Can you go to the field?"

"Do you know something?" Spring was not far off. Hecht had men training to help with the floods. If they came. They did, three years out of five. "I still have some pain when I'm not careful."

"Katrin might be thinking about using you against her critics."

"Not a good idea."

"Oh?"

"It'd create more problems than it could possibly solve." Stated for the possible audience.

Using foreign hirelings against her own nobility would enrage the whole class, who resented the central authority already.

"And if she orders you?"

"I'll carry out my orders. After I do my best to explain why there must be a better way."

Helspeth winked. "We haven't gotten much done. But you'd better go. I can't restrain myself much longer. I don't want to reduce my market value yet."

"Nor do I." Inasmuch as that would be a lapse of trust on a par with outright treason.

EVEN TITUS CONSENT SEEMED TO BE HOPING FOR SALACIOUS NEWS. "It was just another meeting, troops. Nothing for any of you. Though I did gather that our employer's reason is slipping. You all go on to bed. Except you, Titus." Alone with Consent, he said, "Katrin is thinking about giving us crazy orders once the weather turns."

"Not good, considering the foreign situation."

"You've had news?" Having no regular contact with Heris or Cloven Februaren left him feeling blind.

"I had two reports today. Just coincidence, that. One came from Arnhand, the other out of the Eastern Empire."

"Bad news?"

"It could be. In Arnhand they're preparing a massive invasion of the Connec. Anne of Menand bought a truce with Santerin by giving King Brill most of what he claims is his."

"Guaranteeing bigger trouble there, someday. And it doesn't bode well for our friends down south, now."

"I'm sure Anne had her fingers crossed. She'll turn on Santerin as soon as Arnhand controls the wealth of the Connec."

"Probably. And King Brill deserves it if he lets her get away with it."

"Anne hasn't bought the Empress off, though."

"Uhn." Hecht thought he might suggest that Katrin just overlook whatever her frontier barons did to take advantage of Anne's Connecten preoccupation.

"But the other report is the real bad news. Krulik and Sneigon have begun offering their weapons and firepowder. The Eastern Emperor and Indala al-Sul Halaladin have shown a lot of interest."

"Not good from our point of view."

"No. They've heard from Serenity and the Patriarchal States, too."

"That would be Pinkus's fault. Bet you. He'd want to stock up. He loves falcons almost as much as Prosek and Rhuk do. But with all the demand, how will Krulik and Sneigon manufacture enough weapons?"

"They might not. They've only made sample deliveries so far. They're taking orders against future delivery, no credit offered."

"That's smart, considering the people they're dealing with. Pinkus might never see a new weapon. Unless Bronte Doneto is a better money manager than his predecessors."

"Yes. Here's a problem. They've figured out how to make big lots of firepowder. They're experimenting all the time, trying to improve it. One formula includes nephron from Dreanger. I don't know what that means but someone thought we should know."

"Nephron is used by mummy makers. I know that. I'll have to tell the Empress about this, first chance."

"What good will that do?"

"Who knows? Maybe none. But she has those moments when she's as fierce and brilliant as her father." Hecht knew what Johannes would do, Monestacheus Deleanu be damned. "Have your agents dug out Krulik and Sneigon's future plans?"

"No. But they're obvious. Get filthy rich producing the instruments of murder."

"The very best instruments. Of which, you'll agree, they can produce only so many."

"Of course. Maybe they'll go to auctioning their weapons." That was basic economic sense, every man's daydream—and a good way to get butchered by an exasperated prince.

"Or?"

"Or what?"

"Or they could pick and choose who gets what. They could steal the power to decide winners and losers."

Titus grunted unhappily.

"Does that noise have meaning?"

"Krulik and Sneigon moved out to that wilderness in part because they're so greedy their own people would have turned on them if they had stayed in Brothe."

"A point you made last year."

"Keep it in mind."

"I'll consider it. I need to rest. The wound is really barking tonight."

"Want something?"

"No. I don't want to get addicted."

That night Hecht spent an hour tapping on his pendant. He received only a curt acknowledgment from Heris.

He had not seen Heris in months, nor Cloven Februaren in twice as long. He had not weaned himself from emotional reliance on the Lord of the Silent Kingdom. The protection of the Ninth Unknown had been there as certain as the dawn.

The pain in his left shoulder was a solid reminder of the change.

What were those two doing? Why such focus? How grim had it become?

A WARM WIND CAME UP AROUND THE END OF THE JAGOS, PUTTING smiles on every face. Though pessimists like Titus Consent still talked doom and gloom through their exposed teeth.

The snows might melt in a rush. The Bleune and its tributaries could flood. That was the case, three years out of five.

The Commander of the Righteous felt no compassion for those who would suffer. "The waters *do* rise three years out of five. Anybody who keeps living where they're sure to get wet deserves whatever they get." But he would help with the relief effort.

PIPER HECHT WAS OUT REVIEWING HIS TROOPS. THEY, WITH THEIR animals and equipment, had assembled in the Franz-Benneroust Plaza, in front of the main citadel. Franz-Benneroust had been a weak, early Grail Emperor, forgotten except for his public works, though he had ruled longer than any Grail Emperor since. He had spent most of his income improving Alten Weinberg and Hochwasser, and building bridges. His own descendants did not recall him well enough to connect him with the name attached to so many buildings and bridges.

Hecht knew because he accumulated such knowledge. It was a compulsion and a defense mechanism. The more he knew the safer he felt. He was better able to fit in.

For the first time in an age he wondered where he would be if er-Rashal had not made Gordimer fear him.

For the first time in an age he examined the question of why the Rascal needed him dead or out of al-Minphet permanently. As ever, he found no answers.

For the first time in an age he wondered if Gordimer and er-Rashal knew he still lived. Or if they cared, since he was out of their way.

Him leading an Imperial crusade ought to remind them. He could go south from the Holy Lands. It should not be hard to convince

Katrin that Dreanger needed liberating, too. Dreanger had been critical to the early history of the Chaldarean faith. Definitely more important than Firaldia had been till the Praman Conquest inundated that end of the world.

He reminded himself that Katrin Ege was the daughter of the Emperor Johannes III and far more clever than she pretended. She would not be led easily.

The parade went off with minimal difficulties. His soldiers were paid up, well fed, not overworked, had several sorts of sharp new uniforms, and could not be in better morale. There were fourteen hundred of them now. Almost to a man they were living the dream that had drawn them into service. Only absent was the part where they got to smash enemy cities and get rich on the plunder.

They were sure that part would come soon.

Drago Prosek and Kait Rhuk concluded the event with a thunderous concert from their falcons. Sulfurous clouds of firepowder smoke drifted through the city in sulfurous clouds, potent reminder of where the power lay.


## 26. The Chosen: Transitions

The Windwalker's thrall had fallen off half a frozen world. Wherever they could, wherever they were bright enough, whole peoples took flight.

The edge of the ice became the realm of fury, of war and chaos. Few princes or peoples were as welcoming as Tsistimed the Golden and the Hu'n-tai At.

But Tsistimed did rule the steppes and mountains for six thousand miles.

In the west geography and history made the situation a little different. The refugee problem was not as troublesome. The lands above the Jago Mountains had not been heavily populated, initially, and many natives of the northern principalities had migrated south already. Only around the cities was there a significant impact. Thousands could live off the land in the wilds. And only thousands had escaped the Windwalker's reign.

The god had spent the rest.

Few escaped the lands above the Shallow Sea, most of those by crossing the Ormo Strait on a bridge of ice that formed briefly during the winter.

The handful who failed to make that crossing would not see summer's return.

A DOZEN FIGURES PROWLED THE SHINGLE WHERE THE FALLEN GOD lay, all encompassed by the feeble *thrum-hum* of the life still animating the Windwalker. Seven were men. One was a wild-haired woman. Those eight were all mad, dedicated priests, the last of Kharoulke's local adherents. They protected him from lesser Instrumentalities. They prayed and performed rites in an effort to waken him. They grew weaker by the day. They had little to eat but dead things found on the ice, or washed ashore during those brief times when the tides were not roaring back and forth.

In the main, they scavenged the gaunt corpses of fallen Chosen.

Of the other four, two were Krepnights, the Elect. Feeble imitations of the original. The big one stood four feet tall. The other barely topped two. Both had the look of work hastily done by an exhausted artisan.

Like the mad priests, they tried to protect their creator.

Two more madmen roamed the shingle. They were not the Windwalker's friends. They wanted to murder the god. They did not know how to manage it but they had perfect faith that it could be done.

They were more cunning than the Windwalker's protectors, whom they had been picking off and eating almost from the moment Kharoulke dragged himself out of the water.

Once a woman came who tried to show them how to realize their ambitions. They attacked her. She did not speak their language so, clearly, could not be trusted.

She hurt them both and went away.

They saw her again, occasionally, never up close. She must be some powerful Instrumentality. She appeared when so inclined and vanished the same. Her visits always marked the start of a setback for the Windwalker. Most visits produced explosions and clouds of noxious brimstone smoke.

Yet Kharoulke kept recovering.

Divine healing went slowly with the wells of power going silent. Kharoulke's progress suffered frequent setbacks. But the trend was definite.

And Kharoulke was timeless. The pesky mortals could try as hard as they liked. They would fade. They would die. One day, one century, Kharoulke the Windwalker would rise from the shingle as he had risen from the prison where his supplanters had bound him. He would reclaim his frozen realm.

His pain was exquisitely terrible, and without respite.

Kharoulke managed it by fantasizing about himself in the future middle world, exacting his revenge. The dream was much like the real thing would be. Sometimes he lost his way in time and thought he was there already. But his condition did join him to the moment more tightly than usual for an Instrumentality of his magnitude.

Vaguely, he sensed the surface of the nearby ice start to slicken and run.

Now a season of warmth would add to his miseries.

## 27. The Holy Lands: Fierce New Blood

The Mountain and Azim al-Adil had their first serious encounter with the new castellan of Gherig, at Indala's suggestion, as spring began to threaten the Holy Lands. Indala wanted to test the Arnhander prince, who was little older than Azim.

Reports said Black Rogert's successor was businesslike. He was better liked than du Tancret but considered cold and aloof. How he would handle combat remained a mystery. He had gone to Los Naves de los Fantas with his brother but had not been allowed to join the fighting, being thought too young.

In the event, Anselin of Menand proved as valiant and fierce an opponent as any warrior could want. Azim al-Adil and Nassim Alizarin avoided death in addition to humiliation only by being equipped with the faster horses.

The Praman infantry suffered. Those who survived did so by fleeing into terrain where their less numerous enemy dared not follow.

Having learned what he wanted to know, Indala sent reinforcements and orders to harass Gherig relentlessly. No traffic was to move westward out of Lucidia till he led the way himself, at the head of all the armies of Qasr al-Zed.

Azim admitted that there was a scheme afoot but he could not share details. He knew nothing. He had not been invited into Indala's confidence.

ROGERT DU TANCRET GATHERED HIS CRONIES IN VANTRAD. THEY LAID wicked plans. Black Rogert made no effort to hide his ambition, which was to usurp the Holy Diadem, the supposed Crown of Aaron, which went to the kings of Vantrad. The Diadem, nominally, elevated Vantrad's kings to lordship over the princes and counts of all the Crusader states.

King Berismond was fourteen, plagued by congenital infirmities, chronic diseases, and a marriage made out of political convenience. He always wore gloves and a veil. Clothilde, his queen, was twice his age. Her family had connections with the du Tancrets going back to the home countries. Clothilde had no objection to replacing her mostly useless, heirless, third husband with a fourth who had proven himself a real man.

The lords and knights of the Crusader states had strong feelings about Rogert du Tancret, and about honor. Individual interpretations led men to choose, to stand with Black Rogert or against him. Armed dispute seemed likely.

Both parties began wooing Gisela Frakier, du Tancret's with less success. Some people did remember from one day to the next.

In Shamramdi Indala al-Sul Halaladin put in long hours rehearsing provocateurs who would try to get a deadly squabble started.

NASSIM ALIZARIN UNDERESTIMATED ANSELIN OF MENAND JUST ONCE. Thereafter he made the Prince's life a hell on earth. Indala gave him the tools. He kept them sharp and used them often.

## 28. The Ninth Unknown: Castle in the Wilderness

Pure misery. Misery rendered down, concentrated, coagulated, then force-fed to those experiencing it. Thus did Cloven Februaren think of his recent life. In a namby-pamby sort of way.

The decision to bring the Aelen Kofer to the fortress of the Bastard started the misery. That misery had not yet ended. That fortress had not yet been attained.

The Aelen Kofer could not be touched by the Construct. They could make no contact whatsoever with its powers. Neither Heris nor the Ninth Unknown had the strength to move the smallest, lightest dwarf using the Construct. They had to be sailed from the Realm of the Gods to the mainland. Then they had to walk. The sailing part took many trips over two weeks. The weather was that foul.

Iron Eyes insisted that his entire following make the winter trek. He feared the new middle world.

Cloven Februaren was expected to provide supplies.

He had no problem with the essential concept. It was winter. There was little to be had out there, by theft, hunting, foraging, or purchase.

Most of which options would bring the Aelen Kofer to the attention of middle-worlders. Iron Eyes did not want to be noticed.

Cloven Februaren had a problem with the execution. The work involved was overwhelming. Supplies in quantity could be obtained unnoticed only in Brothe. Then they had to be transferred out to where the dwarf company labored across the icy landscape. Which going proved murderous early on.

Cloven Februaren and Heris put in eighteen-hour days just to keep the Aelen Kofer from starving.

It was a long journey and dwarves were hearty eaters. Weather never stopped being an evil challenge.

On the other hand, the Night was no trouble at all. The minor Instrumentalities seemed thoroughly dedicated to shunning the Aelen Kofer.

Dwarves were slow travelers. And reluctant, quarrelsome travelers. Some days the band did not move at all. Which left the Ninth Unknown thoroughly frustrated as well as exhausted.

Further complications arose once they reached lands where middle-worlders still lived.

Iron Eyes wanted to remain mythological. Forever, if possible.

Though the dwarves formed a sizable company, remaining unnoticed was not difficult at first. But that did take increasingly careful scouting. Which, of course, further slowed progress.

Februaren held off exhaustion long enough to get a meal inside himself. Iron Eyes intruded. "This would be easier if the Old Ones were still in charge. We could ramble around wherever we wanted and the folks would be eager to help."

"Too bad they're all sealed up, then. We could bust them out, easy, if they just weren't all locked up."

"You've got a sour attitude on you lately, you know that?"

"I expect it's because of the company I keep."

For sure. The Aelen Kofer were making him crazy. He was worried about his health. At his age he ought not to face prolonged stress and physical labor. Though he had the Construct to support him—he was, practically, part of that machine—there were limits to what he could overcome.

Most of today's Grail Empire was wilderness. That had not always been the case. But the fall of the Old Empire and several passages of plague had reduced the population by two-thirds. The Aelen Kofer mostly went unnoticed when they stuck to the wilds.

There were incidents. Even deep wildernesses got visited by hunters, woodcutters, and just plain wild men who could not stand the stress of civilization. The more self-confident of those reported having seen dwarves.

The news caused no excitement. Country people knew strange beings lived in the woods. No local prince or count called up the levies.

THE FORTRESS HAD NO NAME. THE NEAREST VILLAGE WAS EIGHT MILES away. No one there talked about the castle. The villagers seemed unaware that it existed. Few ever went into the forest more than half a mile. Yet a ghost of a road led to the fortress, a recollection of a way that might have been important in some century now forgotten.

Cloven Februaren used the Construct to be waiting at a gateway through what looked like an innocent boundary defined by a split rail fence. On his side, that frozen memory of a road, a biting wind, and scattered precipitation that felt like a shower of frozen needles. Beyond the fence, possibly a little less enthusiasm for winter. But only a little. Patches of ice and piles of snow were plentiful. There was a glistening glaze on otherwise barren branches. Some wore little icicles, like rows of teeth, on their undersides.

On the top sides there were crows.

The Ninth Unknown stared, only vaguely aware of the racket being made by the Aelen Kofer approaching. He tried to guess how many crows. How many hundreds of crows. Or maybe ravens. He could not tell the difference with them just sitting there. Nor did he much care when faced with the question of why they were silent and still.

Crows were never silent, and seldom still for long.

Sorcery.

"Of course it's sorcery, you ass!" he muttered at himself. "The question is, what kind of sorcery? And to what point?"

"Double Great?"

Februaren jumped. Heris had turned into being beside him, unnoticed. "Just thinking out loud, child. You want to take a turn? Why are all those damned crows over there? And why are they so quiet? They ain't sparrows but they still bicker in their damned sleep."

"Somebody spelled them so you'd work yourself into an apoplectic lather worrying about why they're quiet." Then, in her best spooky voice, "Or maybe they're not crows. Maybe they're demons spelled to look like crows."

"Muno is still laughing about inflicting you on me, isn't he?"

"I was drafted. But I bet he is sitting in front of a nice fire, maybe with a cute little boy on his lap, drinking coffee and chuckling. What's this over here?" Heris headed for the gateway.

"Stay back! We can't just go prancing in! No telling what that might trigger."

"I'm not going in, Double Great. I'm looking to see what this is." She indicated a chunk of weathered board tangled in the remains of last summer's weeds.

"It does look out of place," Februaren admitted. Grudgingly. Because he should have noticed himself. Long ago. Maybe even the first time he came exploring.

Heris pried the board loose, cracking it lengthwise in the process. The old man took it, again failing to note an important point. He rotated the board so he could see the wet side. "Something written here. It must have been a sign. Hard to make out. Ah. In Firaldian, roughly, it says, 'Beware of the wolves.' And something else that I can't make out."

"Never damned mind that! Look!" Heris pointed. Vigorously.

A skull and some long bones lay where the sign had hidden them, sunken into the frozen mud under the dead weeds.

"Well," the old man observed. "That's something to keep in mind." He eyed the crows again. They seemed mildly amused. He had stumbled across an old acquaintance of theirs.

Heris asked, "You think they're hoping we'll join this guy?" She shuddered. The cold had nothing to do with that.

A heavy tread approached from behind. The old man recognized that step. Khor-ben Jarneyn. Tired and hungry. "That the place?"

"It is," Februaren admitted. "I'm pretty sure. I've never dared go look."

Iron Eyes pushed between man and woman. Other dwarves rattled and clanked and came to a halt behind them. "How come?"

"It might be dangerous. Why take chances before you need to?"

"To have some fun? Huh! Might be dangerous?" Iron Eyes stepped up to the opening in the rail fence. The crows began to stir, but settled again when he stopped a foot short. Iron Eyes spent two silent minutes glaring straight ahead, at what looked like some kind of structure looming behind a dense growth of leafless trees. Then he came back. "Lots of magic in there. We'll camp. We'll rest up. We'll eat and get our strength back. See if you can bring in some goats. When we're full of piss and vinegar again we'll go grab the Bastard. I'll pick bits off till he says he'll help us."

Februaren considered insisting on wasting no time. Anytime now the Windwalker might . . .

Iron Eyes would remind him that the Windwalker was beached on a stony Andorayan shore, barely able to keep himself together. If

Kharoulke regained strength enough to start something he would send his Chosen out long before he regained enough power to do anything directly. The Aelen Kofer would love that. They were spoiling for a fight.

A dustup with the Ninth Unknown would suit them if he started questioning their tactics.

Februaren said, "You all just get comfortable, then. Enjoy your time off. Heris and I don't have the luxury. Come, Heris." He touched her so they would stay together while the Construct moved them.

They materialized inside a little-used room in an out-of-the-way wing of the Delari town house in Brothe. Februaren said, "If we're going to waste time resting we might as well be comfortable."

Heris grunted and nodded and said, "I can buy into that. Though I don't expect to do a lot of loafing. Those dwarves need to eat. But not before I get a hot bath and a couple decent meals inside me. Food. Glorious food. If Piper could just not bug me for a few days I'd be in Heaven."

So, naturally, valuable loafing time got wasted on talk about what was happening in Alten Weinberg.

KHOR-BEN JARNEYN NEEDED THREE DAYS TO STEEL HIMSELF FOR THE next phase. During that time temperatures rose enough for the ice and snow to start melting.

"Spring is in the air," Februaren declared. No one got the joke. He sulked, muttering about a congenital Aelen Kofer immunity to humor.

That third morning Iron Eyes said, "We've determined the bounds of the place and the three general classes of sorceries protecting it. Since you two aren't the usual hero type that charges straight in just to see what happens, we'll experiment before we do the time-honored Aelen Kofer slithering attack."

"Slithering attack?" Februaren asked.

Iron Eyes ignored him. He barked orders in dwarfish. A couple dozen crossbows materialized, the dwarfish variety so powerful their bolts could punch through granite. So the Aelen Kofer claimed. The weapons began a moaning chorus of strings slicing air, slapping stops, and bolts humming downrange.

The crows over yonder shrieked, outraged. A score had become explosions of blood and feathers. Cursing, they took wing, their cries and pounding wings overwhelming the aria of the Aelen Kofer crossbows. The dwarves impressed the Ninth Unknown by downing the birds on the fly. Maybe fifty, total, died in Jarneyn's experiment.

The dwarf said, "That didn't bring anybody out. Maybe the Bastard doesn't worry about his far-seers."

"He can afford to lose a few more than Ordnan since he started with a thousand." The All-Father of the Old Gods, the Gray Walker, had had only two ravens to keep him informed: Thought and Memory.

"You could be right, sorcerer." Iron Eyes chuckled.

"You laughing means what?"

"The magic here is familiar. Old Gods magic, crudely done. The kind the Aelen Kofer have worked for thousands of years. The Bastard would appear to be self-taught and hasn't had to operate around people who know what he's doing."

"Meaning?"

"Meaning he's never dealt with anybody who knows what he's doing. Was I that opaque?"

The Aelen Kofer began to jabber all at once, in their own language. Heris remarked, "Sounds more like a gang of crows than a gang of crows."

Aelen Kofer, and Iron Eyes in particular, were conservative where their dignity was concerned. Jarneyn heard Heris. He bellowed. The bickering stopped. Jarneyn barked something else, the essence of which must have been that it was time to get to work.

There was a plan. Despite all the noise. The dwarves jumped to it.

They ignored the gateway. Parties broke through the rail fence fifty yards to either hand, behind potent protective spells. Two parties of ten dwarves each advanced parallel to the remainder of a road. Four dwarves from each breach came along the fence, toward the gateway. Other fours followed the fence going away.

The rest of the company, fifteen Aelen Kofer including Iron Eyes, waited with Heris and Februaren. Jarneyn said, "You two keep your heads down. Pretend you're not even here. You can be a big, ugly surprise if we need one."

"That makes sense."

Heris said, "Sure. Let him think it's the past catching up when he's really getting mugged by the future."

Iron Eyes scowled. He did not understand Heris.

The crows became distressed. They tried swarming the dwarves. The Aelen Kofer did not mind. The birds could not hurt them. Helmets, beards, and armor protected them perfectly. Still, they were covered with gore and feathers when the birds left off.

The parties of four reached the gateway. They talked to Iron Eyes. One dwarf was kind enough to choose a language Cloven Februaren could follow. He delivered an entirely technical report about the architecture of the sorcery protecting the forest island.

In the Aelen Kofer view it was crude peasant fieldstone construction compared to an Aelen Kofer finely crafted formulation.

The craftsmen went to work on the gateway.

Minutes later Iron Eyes said, "The way is open, now." He trundled through the gateway. "Definitely instinctual work. All self-discovery. But still damned powerful."

"Must be nice to have a god for your mom," Heris said. "All that kick-ass power. He must've been hell on wheels when he was a baby."

Iron Eyes launched a tedious exposition about demigods not coming into their powers till puberty.

Cloven Februaren interrupted, "Another benefit: He's been around and healthy for about a half-dozen centuries."

Heris gave him a look but did not comment.

Iron Eyes, irked at being cut off, got in no hurry going forward. But, then, haste was a killer when dealing with sorcerous defenses. "Ah. And here come the wolves. We definitely caught this mob napping."

These wolves were of a breed unknown to Februaren. Those now becoming scarce in Firaldia were gray and mastiff size. These had dark tan and almost black coats on their backs. They were larger. Some might go two hundred pounds. There were a lot of them and they were ferociously upset.

The Aelen Kofer did not mind the wolves, either. Foursomes crouched in a little shielded square and hacked at anything in reach. When one square broke under a torrent of wolves the dwarves just rolled up in balls and let their armor protect them while crossbows elsewhere worked on their attackers.

Februaren asked, "Why would the Bastard think wolves would be effective against people in armor?"

Heris snapped, "He doesn't get many visitors wearing armor?"

Iron Eyes told her, "He doesn't get any wearing Aelen Kofer armor. These beasts would shred regular mail like rotted cloth. You two get into the center, here. You aren't wearing Aelen Kofer armor."

Iron Eyes's party formed concentric circles round Heris and Februaren.

The wolves came. All of them. Once. They tried leaping the outer ring. Many suffered from upward thrusts of spear, sword, or ax. But they were amazing jumpers. Several smashed into dwarves of the inner circle, on the fly, and bowled the Aelen Kofer over.

Februaren took Heris's hand. They turned sideways. They then stood inside the tree line of the woods beyond the fence and observed.

The dwarves of the outer circle did not break discipline. They did not turn to help those behind them. They let Iron Eyes and his companions dispatch the wounded wolves.

The two parties paralleling the road stopped to lend supporting fires.

The wolves recognized failure quickly. The biggest and darkest howled. The survivors raced away, too fast to be targeted. Their tails were down but not so far as to concede defeat.

Heris and Februaren rejoined Iron Eyes. Who said, "That's a damned useful trick, old-timer. You sure you can't teach me?"

"Not if you insist on remaining Aelen Kofer." He did not mention having noted that Aelen Kofer had more pathways to their own world than they admitted. How else to explain their company being more numerous now than when it had left the Realm of the Gods? It expanded only when there were no humans around to see it happen.

Februaren had a feeling the journey would have gone faster and more comfortably had the Aelen Kofer understood middle-world geography. They could have done the overland part in their own world, in a more gracious climate.

Februaren did not raise the subject. Iron Eyes would admit nothing. Allies need not share every secret.

Iron Eyes said, "It's too late for me to pick something else to be. This is your world. Have you ever seen so many wolves in one place?"

"No. I can't imagine a pack numbering sixty or seventy."

"Definitely not natural."

There were seventeen dead wolves. Injured animals disappeared into the wood. The rest remained out of range but watchful. Respectfully opportunistic.

Heris said, "That's not natural, either. And they aren't interested in us because they're hungry."

The wolves all radiated health. They were well fed and well groomed. Februaren asked, "What next?"

Iron Eyes said, "We go kick the door in and yell, 'Surprise!' "

"That does sound like fun. Heris and I will be right behind you."

Iron Eyes awarded the old man a narrow-eyed, sour, almost suspicious scowl. But he got his people moving. The crows raged in protest but kept their distance. Death came suddenly when a bird ranged too near the Aelen Kofer.

Likewise, the wolves. Awaiting their chance.

The bolt from an Aelen Kofer crossbow moved so fast you might only note a flicker before it hit you.

A grim, gray little castle lay at the heart of the wood. It looked deserted. Its drawbridge was down and had been for so long that weeds had crept in over its edges. The moat was turgid but the water did move. Barely. It was not frozen, nor was it more than two feet deep, but it was thick. The bottom was foul, loose mud that went down at least that much farther.

The surface of the drawbridge boasted dried leaves, a few dried weeds that had grown between the timbers, and several dangerous patches of ice. Around it, for thirty feet, lay a scatter of human bones.

Iron Eyes grumbled. "Those bones. I remember. Did you plan to remind me before . . . What?" The crows had gotten excited.

Two elderly men had appeared on the drawbridge. One carried a rusty old bill, the other a lance that had seen its best days centuries ago. They lacked no confidence. They prepared to hold the bridge.

Iron Eyes muttered something about mercy for the mad. But he did not get carried away. "Shift them without hurting them. If they won't be shifted, make them a feast for wolves and crows."

The latter were in the air, excited.

Iron Eyes had used the dwarf language. The old men heard. They seemed amazed. Then decided they were overmatched after all. They went back inside, pursued by the derision of crows.

The entrance loomed dark as a fathomless cave.

Iron Eyes again asked, "You were going to keep me from marching straight in, weren't you?"

"I don't know. Maybe. On the other hand, it might be instructive to see how Aelen Kofer mail stands up to a falcon's bite."

The old man was guessing, based on Piper's speculations. Layers of hearsay and imagination could be hiding something but it seemed most reasonable to suspect the presence of firepowder weapons. Which he had explained to Iron Eyes when the expedition was forming. "You see any unusual bones around here?"

"I see a lot that are busted up strange. You mean the striped creature? Like the ones that tried to invade the Realm of the Gods?"

"Yes."

"They don't look so different with the meat off."

"Extra fingers and toes."

"There's that. But the small bones are scattered, probably for miles. But sometimes theirs are black. Don't ask why. We found out getting rid of the ones we dealt with before. How should we do this? Can you just pop inside?"

"No. I don't know what I'd be jumping into. There might be spells to make me unhappy. But I could get up on the wall . . . Girl!"

HERIS TURNED, PERCHED AMONGST PANICKY CROWS, LOOKED DOWN, turned again to rejoin Februaren and Jarneyn. "Not one falcon, Double

Great. Two. One the kind Piper calls a hound. The big kind he got rid of because they worked so bad at Clearenza. The old men are beside them with torches. I didn't see anybody else. If it wasn't for them I'd say the place was deserted."

Februaren told Iron Eyes, "Move your people out of the way, now." He indicated an arc, narrow end at the gate, that he thought should be dwarf-free. "And tell them there's going to be a lot of noise. These machines talk loud."

Heris asked, "What's the plan?"

"We get those people to think the whole mob is charging in. They fire. Then the whole mob charges in."

Februaren and Iron Eyes made the arrangements. Crows and wolves observed, remaining at a safe distance. The crows kibitzed. An occasional wolf crawled forward, got hold of a fallen pack mate, dragged it away until one of the Aelen Kofer decided to object. Iron Eyes told Februaren, "That's clever. The perfect trick."

It tricked no one.

Iron Eyes, not counting chickens, already had another plan running. Some of his people brought rails from the fence. Wolves paced them but took no risks.

Heris wanted a look at the countryside roundabout. She went up top, came back down. "The wolves are waiting for something." The beasts were gathering out where they could not be seen, with numerous comings and goings. At least two dozen more had come from somewhere.

"Probably expecting the Bastard."

Aelen Kofer work parties used fencing to bridge the moat off to the right of the gate. They started building a ladder. Heris told them, "Wait." She took a coil of rope from a dwarf, turned sideways, then dropped one end from the top of the wall. A half-dozen dwarves swarmed up. They climbed like monkeys despite the clutter they carried.

Those six readied their crossbows, stepped forward, sighted on the two old men. Then dove back so violently that one knocked Heris right off the wall. She did miss the makeshift bridge. Which meant an intimate encounter with icy, nasty, shallow water. She came up cursing, turned sideways, got back up top in time to watch a fog of burned firepowder clear from the little courtyard. Dripping, starting to shudder in the breeze, she demanded, "Anybody hurt?"

The dwarves could not hear her. The bellow of the hound had stolen their hearing briefly. Heris had trouble hearing herself, but because of water in her ears. She had been falling when the hound roared. The wall had sheltered her from the noise.

A dwarf pulled her back as the lighter falcon barked. The glimpse she had gotten was of two old men reloading the hound, now aimed for a blast through the gateway.

All six dwarves popped up and loosed quarrels. Shrieking crows whipped around them. There were no cries from below.

Heris turned sideways. She materialized four feet behind the hound. One old man had his left hand pinned to its wooden mounting frame by an Aelen Kofer bolt. Heris smacked the other one with her fist. "Ow! Goddamn! Why didn't I bring something with me?" She grabbed both torches, turned sideways, chucked them into the moat from the top of the wall. "That's your cue, Double Great!" She swatted a diving crow. And watched just long enough to make sure the Ninth Unknown understood.

She turned yet again.

One groggy old man was trying to cut the bolt nailing the other to the hound's frame. Which, at a glance, told Heris why Piper had rid himself of the big bore weapons. The machine could not be moved easily. And recoil had cracked its supporting frame after one firing.

A mob of dwarves trundled into the courtyard. Overhead, angry crows registered their disapproval by defecating on the fly.

Cloven Februaren and Korban Iron Eyes were not among the arrivals. "What now?" She decided to go see. Nearing exhaustion, she walked out this time. And reached the drawbridge in time to see Iron Eyes and the Ninth Unknown become involved in another engagement with more wolves than ever before. Wolves who seemed desperate but unenthusiastic. This time they encountered Aelen Kofer and human sorcery before they got close enough to be ripped up by Aelen Kofer steel. This time the survivors left with their tails all the way under and their bodies riding low.

Februaren and the dwarves grabbed lupine corpses and headed inside the castle. Crows followed. Several died as dwarves lost their senses of humor.

Heris needed not ask why all the excitement. She had her answer once she got a look at the dead wolves.

Some of the fallen from the first attack had begun to shift shape. The largest wolves, the ones with the heaviest, darkest fur. The leaders of the vast pack.

"I don't know," Februaren said, answering a question she had not yet asked. "Changed by the Night. By the one who lives here, maybe, using whoever was unlucky enough to be passing by. Making himself a fierce pack of protectors who dared not run away. Because everywhere else would mean an agonizing death at the first hint of a change. Damn those things!"

A skilled sniper of a crow had gotten him in the forehead with a nasty load.

The old man dug into one of the pouches hanging from his belt while muttering in Archaic Brothen. He found something, flung it into the air, shouted. To Heris it looked like a fistful of peppercorns.

Each peppercorn shot off toward a crow. The air filled with little pops as those hit feathers at high velocity. A hundred birds gave up flying, fell, lay twitching. The rest fled, making more noise than ever.

"Not a very nice man, the Bastard."

"Blood will tell, child. What about in there?"

"The falcons have been captured. And the two old men. I don't understand what's happening. The dwarves were standing around waiting for orders when I left."

The dwarves had gone into the fortress while Heris was outside. They had found nothing remarkable. The dizzy old men were the only inhabitants. Though there was a suite on the second level that showed signs of regular use.

Its user appeared to have been absent for some time.

The inside of the castle consisted mostly of storerooms generously stocked with supplies suitable for use by men, dwarves, or wolves.

Howling from the woods roundabout made clear what those beasts thought of the change of management. The crows were out there, still, but had grown contemplative.

The Aelen Kofer indulged in a huge feast, underwritten by the Bastard. They ate their fill, drank their fill, burned firewood profligately. Februaren and Heris joined in, some, though she spent time communicating with Piper while Februaren tried to crack the glamour imprisoning the minds of the two old men. He had no luck.

They were automatons shaped by the man who was not there. They did not speak. Left alone, they went back to managing the castle. They ignored the intruders now that they were inside.

Februaren told the Aelen Kofer, "Leave them be. Let them work. But keep them away from any weapons."

It was late. Heris said, "I need some sleep. I'm seeing things that aren't there. Our guy hasn't come around. So what's next, Double Great?"

"We wait. The Bastard will come home, eventually. And the things you're seeing *are* there. The Night is strong and active here. Much more so than anywhere you've ever been before."

"There's a confidence booster. That'll help me nod off. Just wait?"

"Yes."

"Won't he notice that something is wrong as soon as he gets near the place?"

"He may. I doubt it. He won't be looking for it. He's never had this kind of trouble."

The Aelen Kofer had found no stable inside or associated with the castle. There was no sign that horses had visited in modern times. The Bastard came and went by extraordinary means.

That was troubling.

But maybe he just walked.

THE WOLVES MADE A LAST TRY AT MIDNIGHT. A DOZEN WORE THE shapes of men. They came in the company of swarms of minor Instrumentalities, but otherwise unarmed.

Though they had been warned not to relax most of the Aelen Kofer had shed the misery of their mail. Several would pay the price in blood.

The Ninth Unknown had created booby traps using the hound and the falcon. They made the difference.

Nevertheless, the struggle was grim.

Come sunrise Februaren counted corpses and concluded that the Were had been exterminated. They had not appeared interested in surviving. Lacking leadership the ordinary wolves should now move on.

Not so. These wolves had been attached to the castle for generations. Despite events, they showed up at a postern to be fed by the two old men.

Februaren allowed it.

The crows watched. Quietly, mostly. They were everywhere. The Aelen Kofer tried to make them more miserable. The birds gave back no joy.

THE NINTH UNKNOWN, IRON EYES, AND SEVERAL PROMINENT AELEN Kofer were drinking and basking in the warmth of the little castle's master suite. A spirited discussion had begun, fueled by boredom and beer. Spring was a definite threat. Its tentacles might reach Andoray in a month. Many Aelen Kofer were tired of waiting. They had convinced themselves that the Bastard would never show while they squatted in his home. If he even existed.

Some thought the Bastard was a product of the human sorcerer's imagination. The human sorcerer responded with the observation that the Aelen Kofer appeared to exist despite being considered imaginary by some.

Heris had gone back to Brothe, to recuperate at her grandfather's town house. She was under orders from the Ninth Unknown to visit and reassure Piper's family, on pain of . . . Something. Which she would have done without the encouragement. Anna Mozilla was her friend.

Februaren was not thinking clearly. A lot of ale needed drinking. He did his part. The two old men, from whom the disdainful Aelen Kofer were removing stubborn glamours with the delicacy of craftsmen harvesting fur from a dozing leopard, were master brewers. Their names were Harbin and Ernst. They could not recall a time when they had not been part of the castle. They thought one of the Fredericks, or maybe German the Fat, might be Emperor. Celestine of Electon would be Patriarch. No one had taken the reign name Celestine in Februaren's lifetime. He did not recall an Emperor named German. The history of the Grail Empire was sprinkled liberally with Fredericks and Freidrichs.

Iron Eyes observed, "These characters make you look like a callow boy."

"And they make good beer."

They did. And had been brewing for the Were for ages. It was not hard for them to adapt production to the needs of a horde of dwarves— assisted by Aelen Kofer brewing magic.

Iron Eyes had told his grumblers they would stay as long as it took to collect the Bastard. Or till the ingredients for making beer ran out.

The grousing did not end. One of the great joys of dwarfish life was the creative complaint. That died down some. The Aelen Kofer had something to look forward to, for a while.

Jarneyn prowled the castle night and day, muttering, like some symbolic ghost in a passion play. The unheard conscience listened to only the ever-present but now stubbornly silent crows. The rest of the Aelen Kofer enjoyed themselves, knowing circumstance would, in time, drive them back to their world or the Realm of the Gods.

Iron Eyes grumbled, "Right here in this place, sorcerer, you see why the Aelen Kofer don't rule the Nine Worlds. The instant adversity steps aside we lose our focus. We suffer from a cultural absence of ambition. We can weave a bridge out of rainbows if somebody orders one up but we won't raise a silver hammer to do ourselves any good. We'll throw up a Great Sky Fortress with fanatic attention to the tiniest details but we won't build decent homes for ourselves."

"A little down tonight, eh?" Februaren asked.

Jarneyn sat down facing him. "Enjoying an all-night loving session with despair. Thinking my folk are too much like our new friends, Harbin and Ernst. Automatons. Totally limited . . ."

The iron eyes shut. Korban began to snore.

The Ninth Unknown's adventures had revealed a truth unmentioned in myth and legend. Dwarves snored. Always. Regardless. Relentlessly.

Februaren thought the dwarf had demonstrated initiative and inspiration. He ambled off to the chamber he had claimed, dove into a featherbed he suspected must belong to the Bastard himself. He drifted off wondering if they would ever get their man. Or if there was a point to continued pursuit, since the Windwalker still lay on the Andorayan shingle and showed no sign of recovering.

"GET YOUR DEAD ASS OUT OF BED, DOUBLE GREAT. SOMETHING IS about to happen."

Heris had returned moments earlier, armed with routine news and luxury comestibles. The crows had begun going crazy. Now the wolves started up.

The castle filled with imminence—and the rattle of Aelen Kofer hastily unlimbering their mystic tools.

Noise and panic had nothing to do with her arrival. She came and went regularly without causing a stir.

"It's time," said the Ninth Unknown. He got out of bed and forced himself upright. He smoothed his hair and clothing while observing, "He doesn't get in a hurry, does he?"

"His way isn't ours, obviously." Heris turned sideways, moved only far enough to place herself in a shadowed corner behind a glob of shimmer that was the source of waxing imminence.

A shape formed, as a dark, flat ghost that became humanoid, then gathered color and three-dimensionality. It took nearly a minute for the man to arrive, staggering. The shimmer vanished. The newcomer bent over, hands on knees, gasping. He panted for several seconds before he realized that he had an audience.

Both later wondered if what they heard as soft curses might not have been the muted screams of crows and howls of wolves from outside.

Still gasping, the Bastard forced himself upright. "You? You! But . . . How did . . . ?"

"Ah, Brother Lester. Welcome. There have been changes. And your assistance is required. Allow me to explain."

At which point Heris smacked the Bastard in the back of the head because of what he was doing with a hand hidden behind him.

Khor-ben Jarneyn arrived.

The Ninth Unknown announced, "We have him."

"That fellow?"

"That's him."

"He doesn't look like his mother at all."

"Maybe he takes after his dad."

"I never met Gedanke. I don't know. Tuck him under your arm and take him back."

"Uh . . ."

"The stranger his surroundings when he wakes up the more likely he is to listen when you explain. He'll want information so he can figure out what's really happening."

Februaren eyed his captive. He hoped Iron Eyes was right. "Heris? Shall we?"


## 29. Alten Weinberg: Spring

Titus Consent tapped on the frame of the open doorway.

Hecht said, "Come ahead." He set Redfearn Bechter's memory chest aside. "What?"

"Algres Drear is here. He wants to see you. He seems distracted."

"He say why?"

"Not straight up. Not to me."

"Bring him in. And feel free to eavesdrop."

Hecht expected that to happen with or without his approval. His people got more protective every day. There were times when he missed Madouc's easygoing ways.

He resented the increasing isolation. He went back to contemplating Bechter's bequest.

He did that when he was feeling low. Wondering if there was a deeper message. Was it part of a pattern? Was it proof that the world was essentially random? Was his own passage through life part of a divine plan or just a stream of events with no real meaning?

He could argue both ways. Were he in an epic it would, for sure, lack a traditional plot, everything connecting to everything else and coming together in the end. His epic consisted of a lot of little plots entangled.

Titus Consent coughed, held the door for Algres Drear, then disappeared. Drear peered around. "No armed guards in the inner sanctum?"

"Don't give them ideas." Drear was back in Braunsknecht livery, with an extra band of black silk around his wrists.

"It might already be easier to get to Serenity than it is to reach you."

"I find it tedious, too. Then I have a shooting pain in my shoulder that reminds me why. I try to tolerate the overreaction of the people who want to keep me among the living."

"Not to be critical. But if you let them isolate you, pretty soon you won't have any idea what's going on."

Which echoed Hecht's fears.

"You aren't here to warn me about that."

"No. I have a different warning in hand."

"If it's time-sensitive you'd better spit it up."

Drear decided not to take offense. "There's a new plot afoot against you. It appears to include some serious players."

Hecht considered. "You did go back to work for the Princess Apparent, didn't you?" He knew the answer, of course.

"I did. In part thanks to you. I owe you for that. Plus, I want to shelter the Princess from the ambitions of her supposed friends."

"Ah. Do go on."

Drear told his story. He named no names because he had most of his information second- and third-hand. But there was a cabal, embracing some of the Electors, the Council Advisory, and senior court functionaries. They planned a palace revolution. The Commander of the Righteous would be arrested before all else. And killed, if he resisted. Katrin would be replaced with the more tractable Helspeth.

Hecht observed, "Those kinds of rumors have been around since Lothar went belly-up."

"And the plotters never have the balls to take the plunge. I know. But Katrin's recent behavior has given them fresh courage. And I don't want my benefactor hurt by power squabbles amongst the Empire's most spoiled nobles."

"And you especially don't want your principal to become a pawn in a game not of her own devising." Hecht suspected that Drear harbored deep, well-hidden feelings for the Princess Apparent. Possibly more realistically founded than those of an itinerant war fighter who was not at all sure of who he was or where his true loyalties lay. He suspected, as well, that Algres Drear was perfectly aware of the weakness of the Commander of the Righteous where the Princess Apparent was concerned.

Captain Drear, married man, was offering to found a conspiracy of would-be lovers who dared not touch.

"I especially don't," Drear agreed. "With the Empress getting more erratic, more unpredictable, and more harsh, I don't. She could have Helspeth executed this time. She'd be sorry and penitent afterward but it would be done."

"If somebody does something really stupid and says he acted on her behalf."

"That's what I'm trying to stop. If we can make it to summer, and the diplomats find a court interested in a marital alliance, Katrin wouldn't feel so threatened. Although Helspeth getting married won't change the succession. Katrin has to produce an heir to do that."

Hecht feared Katrin's enemies would feel pressed to act before Helspeth could be dealt on the marriage market. "A lot of old men would be thrilled if they could just get Helspeth out of the country. If Katrin died they might have years to run the Empire if they could keep Helspeth away. If they could get her to abdicate. I understand that Anies is senile but healthy as a horse."

Anies, Johannes's sister, followed Helspeth in the succession. She was old but likely had a decade left. Hecht had not met her, though she shared Winterhall with the Empress and Princess Apparent. Indeed, she was the grande dame of that establishment.

Drear grunted unhappily.

"Dynastic troubles. There must be a better way," Hecht mused. "How could we get Jaime of Castauriga back here for a while? He could solve all our problems with a five-minute effort."

"That would be ideal. But we'd have to kidnap him. Witnesses agree, Jaime developed an abiding, irrational loathing for Katrin while he was here. As potent as her obsession with him. Who knows why? Nobody knows what happened in private. But it's there, and Jaime's feelings are so strong he's even lost interest in gaining the Empire through his descendants."

Titus Consent held the same opinion. But would that continue to be the case? The opportunity had to be gnawing at Jaime. When he fell asleep at night. In that twilight state when he was wakening. And every time one of his family reminded him what he was putting aside.

He could be the father of an Imperial dynasty.

Hecht said, "Maybe Helspeth should marry. She'd be safer. Her husband would have a vested interest in protecting her."

Sourly, Drear agreed. "It would make her safer. But because Katrin has no issue there'll always be knives with Helspeth's name on. The temptation to meddle might even increase if it looked like a foreign line might come in. Especially if a match with Regard of Arnhand turned up."

There had been resistance to that from all factions before. But that had begun to change when Katrin created her own lifeguard legion while steadfastly refusing to wilt like a woman.

Hecht said, "It could happen. The flaw, though, is that Arnhand is so supportive of the Brothen Patriarchs. That's where Anne of Menand doesn't restructure her values when a change might be convenient. And she's definitely not somebody anyone here wants playing the wicked mother-in-law. Katrin would be the best match for Regard."

The moment he said that he started to worry. He saw the identical fear take root in Algres Drear.

Katrin Ege was close to Serenity. Jaime of Castauriga was not. Jaime remained an adamant supporter of Peter of Navaya, who made no secret of what Serenity could do with his Connecten ambitions. There would be armed confrontation this summer. Anne of Menand had to scramble to hang on to allies who were not inclined to face the victor of Los Naves de los Fantas and the hardened troops of the Direcian Reconquest.

The Empress could not divorce Jaime. But no especially clever Church lawyer would be needed to develop an annulment action. Katrin's pregnancy problems could be laid off on Jaime's whoring and consorting with the Night.

Drear nearly moaned. "If Katrin's crowd think of that, they'll be at her day and night. Her loving Jaime will become irrelevant. They'll argue the good of the Empire. No Ege can resist that."

"You're right. The religious angle could make her spite her emotional attachment, too. She really does believe the souls of her subjects are her responsibility."

"Just keep her fixated on the Holy Lands. Feed that obsession and starve the rest."

"Of course. Don't mention any of this to anybody. Those people have proven that they can get up to plenty of mischief on their own."

Drear nodded.

Hecht continued, "I know you don't want to accuse anybody. But how about suggesting a few people that I should keep an eye on?"

Captain Drear's conscience proved more flexible than he pretended. He produced a generously annotated list. "Some of these won't be deeply involved. Others you'd expect. And some might surprise us if it came time to take a stand."

Hecht read. Drear's penmanship was obsessively precise. And his rating of suspects definitely did include surprises.

Drear said, "I should get back. I don't like leaving her unguarded."

The Princess Apparent was not, of course, unguarded. She just was not guarded by Algres Drear.

"All right. Thank you. Real food for thought, this. One thing. Don't take it all on yourself. The weight could break you. Then what good will you be? If you can't trust anybody else, holler at me."

The men locked gazes. Drear nodded. "I will." He left.

Titus knocked.

"Come. You heard?"

"Not all, but enough."

"Here's his list. You'll find some surprises. Maybe with personal meaning to our Braunsknecht friend. Watch as many as you can. Carefully. If Drear isn't making it up, go ahead and make it obvious that we're watching. That'll start them complaining. But it should make the weaker ones run scared. I want to see Sedlakova, Rhuk, and Prosek as soon as they can come in together."

AFTER THREE TRIES THE COMMANDER OF THE RIGHTEOUS CAUGHT the Empress feeling well enough to attend a demonstration in support of an idea he had presented and she had given a supportive nod but not final approval. "The actual show will take only a few minutes, Your Grace. But it does have to be seen to be understood."

So the Empress, her sister, and a handful of functionaries joined him on a cavalry training field two miles north of the city wall. Katrin was not in a good mood. Captain Ephrian, commanding her guards, insisted her disposition was its sunniest since the funeral.

She left her sedan demanding, "Why couldn't you show me this in Franz-Benneroust Plaza?"

"The danger, Your Grace. You'll understand in a minute."

"I hired you. I suppose I have to trust you. So do it! While I'm still well enough to care." She began to needle Helspeth.

Hecht left the review stand. Rhuk and Prosek awaited him. Titus Consent joined them. Consent murmured, "I keep reminding myself that I didn't believe her when she told us she was pregnant."

"Meaning?"

"That now she might really be badly sick."

"I thought that was obvious. She's been going downhill since the baby came."

"Not quite true, boss."

Hecht had been about to give the order to fire. He lowered his right hand. "Explain."

"Near as my guys can tell, she made a turn for the better when we started dogging the folks on Drear's list. I consider that suggestive."

"She's had help getting sick?"

"That would be my guess."

Hecht pretended to study the field. He had detailed twelve falcons and four heavier pieces for the demonstration. They stood in line abreast. The falcons pointed toward a hundred rude scarecrows made up to look like advancing infantrymen, at ranges up to a hundred yards.

Clej Sedlakova and Buhle Smolens had found enough junk armor to partially equip each scarecrow.

Amongst the scarecrows there were bales of straw.

Two larger targets had been prepared, too. Both were derelict stone buildings proved up for the occasion.

Hecht gave the signal. The falcons popped off in succession, left to right.

Most of the scarecrows went down. Several nearer straw bales scattered downrange.

Rhuk and Prosek let the smoke clear, then fired the four squat, almost bowl-shaped weapons they called mortars. Each spoke with a deep rumble. Sixty-pound stones arced through the air, easy for the eye to follow. Three of four landed on the lesser stone structure, demolishing it.

The smoke cleared off again. Kait Rhuk lighted a powder train laid to be obvious to the observer. Sparkle and smoke raced toward the larger stone structure.

A corner and one side came apart. The sound arrived a second later, like a kick in the stomach. Smaller debris fell within yards of the reviewing stand.

Hecht went over. "Your Grace, if you will, I'd like you to examine the weapons and what they did to their targets, close-up."

The Empress's entire party seemed dumbfounded. That would be because of the noise and smoke. An effect that did not remain intimidating long, he knew.

Katrin nodded. "I'm impressed, so far." She rose, refusing help, and made her way slowly to the firing line. Drago Prosek, flustered, explained the two types of falcon, muzzle-charged and fast fire, and the mortars. "Which we called that because they kind of look like an apothecary's mortar."

Hecht guided Katrin to the target area. "We used stones in the falcon loads today. Pebbles are free. In battle we'd want to use metal shot because it's more effective."

The old armor had not stood up to the stone shot, out to about eighty yards.

Katrin said, "Archers could do as much damage, couldn't they? And they'd be cheaper."

"Cheaper, perhaps. But trained soldiers aren't at great risk from archers. Falcon shot, though, will rip right through shields and hauberks. And you need to take into account that these weapons are already obsolete where we're headed. Krulik and Sneigon are making them bigger and more reliable and are manufacturing better firepowder. And they're letting Indala order as many as he can afford."

Katrin made her way slowly back to the fast fire falcons, cast to Kait Rhuk's design. "I don't believe your Krulik and Sneigon have anything like this. Do they?"

"No, Your Grace. Kait?"

Rhuk showed the Empress how the preloaded pots went into a breech in the rear of the tube. Turned a few inches, a protruding knob moved into a slot and held the pot in place. A touchhole in the pot needed charging with a dram of firepowder. A falcon supported by a dozen pots and an experienced crew could fire four or five times as fast as the crew of a front-loading weapon.

The Empress was appropriately impressed. But Rhuk held Hecht back when Katrin decided to move on. "Don't try to sell her on the fast firers. I'm not going to have any more made."

"What? Why not? They were a stroke of genius."

"The pot needs to seat into the breech perfectly. The founders can't cast them with enough precision. We can't get them to line up right. Which isn't a huge problem if we're shooting gravel but metal warshot can hang up and damage the weapon. Solid shot can hang up enough for the pot to explode. The weapons would have a very short life under field conditions."

Hecht sighed. This was an old story. The human mind could invent things that human hands could not make work. "I understand. But don't give up on the idea completely." He hurried to overtake the Empress.

Katrin went straight to her sedan. She had had all the activity she could take. She told her Commander of the Righteous, "I'm inclined to turn you loose. Next planning session bring your best assessment of the weapons makers. We may have to alter our strategy. Meanwhile, I'll be flooding the Eastern Empire with embassies this summer. Maybe they can do some good."

"As you will, so shall it be, Your Grace."

"HOW DO YOU THINK IT WENT, BOSS?" PROSEK ASKED. HE HAD NOT yet recovered from having to speak to the Empress directly.

"Relax, Drago. She's as human as you are. Just more dangerous. And a little crazier. I think we did well. She got what we wanted her to get."

Prosek muttered something.

"What?"

"I just said them two women are too damned smart."

"You could be right."

*    *    *

HELSPETH SAID, "YOU'RE GOING TO GET WHAT YOU WANT." SHE SIPPED coffee, looked at Hecht over the rim of her cup. "From my sister."

"Really?" In a teasing tone that surprised him more than it did the Princess Apparent.

"I could tell what you were thinking. Wicked man."

"Ouch! Then I'd better kill you before you tell somebody."

"Smart aleck."

"Can't help it. I get distracted."

Helspeth smiled a small smile.

Hecht said, "And I'm as happy as I've ever been. Life is good. I have a job I like, working for somebody who is interested and supportive. If a little scary sometimes. What more could I ask?"

"Ask? Maybe nothing. Want? I could make a suggestion but these old cows might hear."

There did appear to be an extra ration of chaperones.

"Well, yes. There's something that would be nice."

Helspeth said, "She isn't a little scary, she's very scary. Almost enough to make me hope they find some fool prince who wants to carry me off. To safety. For as long as Katrin hangs on."

Was that a hint of something hidden but important?

Helspeth leaned in to whisper, "The Council Advisory has sent a delegation to Castauriga. Very secret. To get Jaime to come back. Katrin doesn't know. Yet. She'll figure it out."

Hecht had not known. Titus had missed that.

Numerous delegations had departed Alten Weinberg in recent weeks. Several of Algres Drear's suspects had been posted to one or another. Almost, Hecht thought, as if the person handing out the appointments had a good idea which of her subjects might be most useful farthest from town.

Helspeth said, "It's risky. No telling what Katrin will do if Jaime flat refuses to see her again."

"I hear rumors that she's not well."

"Rumors? You saw her the other day. Did she look healthy?"

"No."

"No is right. Her physicians keep looking grim. At the same time, a lot of people who are never nice to me have been stricken kind."

"Good. Have the physicians told you anything?"

"Not really. They thought she was being poisoned. Caches of arsenic and belladonna were found in the Winterhall kitchen. The cooks disavowed any knowledge. They didn't seem to be lying. There's no sorcerer available who can backtrack and identify the culprit." And that villain would have been busy covering trail.

"I wondered. Because of how she looked. But she started improving."

"Because of you."

"What?"

"People notice things, Piper. Like you having your men tag along behind half the nobles in the city. Things like thugs who try to discourage your men ending up thoroughly discouraged themselves."

"Really?" He had not known about that. But he did not need to know. "The people being followed are supposed to notice. The idea is to encourage them to behave."

"They're encouraged. Katrin's health started improving right away. So much that she noticed and worked it out for herself. So she started handing out ambassadorships to people you seemed not to trust."

"It's all working out, then."

"Except that she's still sick in her head and heart. In her soul and her body. A lot of people think she'll die even if she isn't being poisoned."

"Which they thought about your brother."

"And Lothar died."

"But years later than even the optimists were betting. Your sister does still have something to live for. Her crusade."

"Her mad expedition that she hopes will make her more famous than Hansel Blackboots."

"Is that how you see it?"

"Don't you?"

"No. I believe her. She's so sincere it's terrifying. When you consider where her determination might take us. What it might cost the world."

"You puzzle me, Piper. Truly. I'd expect you to be a butcher. The nature of your profession. But you do care about the harm you do. Maybe that's what . . . No. That's animal. It started the first time I saw you. Anyway, my father cared, too. A great deal."

"Cared but didn't let caring keep him from doing what needed doing."

"Nor will you."

"No. I won't."

"You showed that in the Connec."

"I hope the world understands the points I was trying to make. But I doubt it. Most people can't get anything more subtle than a hammer between the eyes."

Helspeth poured fresh coffee. She contrived to touch him several times as she did.

Several women noticed. None seemed to care.

Hecht wondered if there might not be a faction hoping a liaison developed. That could take Helspeth off the marriage market for a decade at least. Once a woman reached a certain age she was no longer expected to be an innocent maiden. Especially if she came equipped with a handsome dowry.

What could be more handsome than an entire empire?

To the pleasure of some and the despair of others the Empress regained her color and strength and energy, if not her full grasp on reality. She became bold. She braved the streets with a handful of lifeguards. She looked fortune in the teeth and sneered. She passed many of her more tedious duties to her sister and spent her time watching the troops train, both those assembling at Hochwasser and her own Righteous, as she now styled Piper Hecht's force. Which she authorized to increase their numbers twice over the course of just two weeks.

She bestowed the incomes of several of her grander holdings upon the Righteous, having seen little waste and less corruption there.

There being no stemming the flood of money, Hecht armed Buhle Smolens with an additional mission and the power to enforce it.

Temptation toward corruption would be growing. Hecht made it absolutely clear that graft and corruption would not be tolerated. Not even where local custom made it acceptable.

He did not find these sins morally abhorrent, just detrimental to the image and reputation he wanted to create for himself and the Righteous.

The Remayne Pass to Firaldia was not yet open when the Righteous moved out, intent on circling the Jagos to the east. The mission was to begin preparing the country in that direction for next year's passage of armies.

Those looked likely to be bigger than hitherto hoped. The Empress would send priests to preach the crusade in Arnhand, Santerin, Direcia, and all the lesser principalities of the west.

With permission from the Eastern Emperor quartermaster companies would move into foreign territories to scout out the best routes overland.

Dozens of Imperial knights and nobles invited themselves along. Hecht thought they wanted to keep an eye on him more than they meant to contribute anything to the cause.

The Empress invited herself, as well.

The woman was in pursuit of her childhood. She brought out the armor she wore when she and her sister followed Johannes south for the Calziran Crusade. That armor was much looser on the older Katrin.

The Empress seemed happy. Her health continued to improve. Reports from the people who had gone to Castauriga were encouraging.

Hecht found them suspect. Those people could not have traveled that far, worked their way into the presence of a disinterested King Jaime, then have had time to get a messenger back to Katrin, all the way to Glimpsz.

The lands through which the Commander and his troops passed were strange and mostly wilderness. The farther the Righteous marched the more palpable the presence of the Night became. In the nebulous region between empires the Instrumentalities had a presence sensible even at high noon.

It was a presence aware of and intimidated by the passage of the Godslayer.

The Godslayer had his firepowder weapons travel charged with godshot. Men with slow matches paced them, always ready should the Night do something unfriendly.

Heris would not explain but during widely separated, brief visits did promise that big things were happening elsewhere. Eventually, the Night would notice. He needed to stay alert. The Night's ire might turn his way.

After each whispering visit Hecht wondered again what she and Februaren and the revenant were doing. He had only the vaguest notion. His cynical side suggested that they were up to no good and were hiding the details because he would take it in the neck if their scheme went sour.

THERE WAS NO DEFINED, FORMAL FRONTIER BETWEEN THE GRAIL Empire and the Eastern Empire. That remained in dispute, always. East and west were, instead, separated by a myriad of minuscule principalities informally attached to one empire or the other, usually by the claims of the respective Emperors. Though they paid tribute these states were independent in the minds of their princes, who never proclaimed that independence lest they spark a response by bruising an imperial ego.

Hovacol was an exception. Cleverly, though, Hovacol chose not to lie directly between empires. Instead, it lay to the east of the geographic pinch. King Stain declared he was no one's running dog. Of late he had begun making noises about extending his own sway over his neighbors. The empires were busy elsewhere. Emperor and Empress seemed content to ignore him.

Those folk of Hovacol who were not still pagan preferred the Eastern Rite. A tenth of the population shared a heresy close cousin to the Maysalean of the Connec.

All that tripped Katrin's intolerance trigger.

The Commander of the Righteous established his forward headquarters near Glimpsz, yards from a line which, if crossed, would make the Rhûn observers yonder nervous. His quartermaster scouts had gone on, to make maps and blaze routes, supervised by the Eastern Emperor's men. He passed his days being intimate with mixed feelings. He was excited about what he was doing. It was historically unique. But he was unhappy about being far from developments in the west. And about being away from Anna and the kids. And away from Helspeth. And he was growing frightened of the changes taking place in his employer.

The Empress grew stranger by the day, in ways difficult to define. The changes were taking place inside. She wanted to hide them.

Katrin summoned the Commander of the Righteous. Hecht entered the Imperial Presence reluctantly, though he had rehearsed himself for the moment. Katrin wanted to deploy his idle forces against Hovacol. That kingdom's people refused to give up their romance with the Eastern Rite. They tolerated heresy. They accepted the presence of pagans. They even ignored a few wicked Pramans.

She had hinted for days. He had, so far, managed to appear too thick to come to the idea on his own.

Rehearsed, Hecht spoke first. "My staff tell me enough reports are in, Your Grace." He feigned an excitement too great to conceal. "We have all the work done. A way to do it, fast, without attracting attention, suffering minimal casualties, without offering direct insult to the Emperor. The infiltration routes are set. The men have been chosen. We can go when you give the word."

Katrin *had* to be distracted from side issues like Hovacol and its preening bantam rooster king.

Hecht's ploy worked. This time. What could have become an unpleasant evening devolved instead into celebration. Which developed its own dark side soon enough.

The Empress imbibed too much strangely flavored local water of life. Her speech became difficult to follow. None of the witnesses, including the Princess Apparent, failed to understand when Katrin invited the Commander of the Righteous to share her bed.

Those witnesses were appalled. Hecht was as frightened as ever he had been. How to get out of this?

Katrin soon proved too far gone to pursue the notion, but suppose she added that to her obsessions? Too often she did drag her frustrations to the center of her life.

The Empress remained isolated for two days, recovering from a massive hangover. There was no indication she recalled her bad behavior. No one reminded her.

Even so, when the raiders slipped into the Eastern Empire Piper Hecht went along. And Helspeth headed for the safety of Alten Weinberg.

Only after trudging southward for two days, reviewing those events all the while, did Hecht realize that a huge milestone had slipped past without his having noticed. And it was one he could in no way blame on the bad behavior of his employer.

He had moved swiftly to keep Katrin from distracting herself from her determination to rescue the Holy Lands. A committed agent of Gordimer the Lion, al-Minphet, and al-Prama would have welcomed the opportunity to wander off into Hovacol, to fritter wealth and strength butchering other Chaldareans. He would have sprung at the chance to ruin the Grail Empress's reputation when she made that offer.

So. His loyalties had worked themselves out to the satisfaction of his soul. And he had noticed only now, well after the fact.

The job at hand, and the dread potential inherent in the interest of the Empress, left him little time for self-examination concerning that silent decision.

## 30. Khaurene: Death Dancing

The pavane in the Khaurenesaine progressed inexorably farther into the realm of dark fortune. King Regard turned aggressive as soon as his countrymen began to join him. Always outnumbered, he succeeded, nevertheless, more often than he failed, through vigor and ferocity. He was willing to act, often without forethought.

The Khaurenese habit was to dither. To try to gather enough information to be on firm ground before making a move. The Direcian garrison had picked up the disease.

Towns and castles fell. The Arnhander forces grew stronger daily.

The King's mother was at her most persuasive.

Regard's successes stirred a swift response from Navaya and Castauriga. King Peter brought four thousand veterans of the Reconquest. Jaime of Castauriga brought twelve hundred, every man a blooded veteran of Los Naves de los Fantas. Coming along behind were fourteen hundred more contributed by other kings and princes.

The lords of Direcia were determined to keep Serenity and the Church from becoming too powerful in the Connec.

Thousands of Connectens headed for Khaurene, too. The Arnhander bandits would face overwhelming odds once all those fighters came together, with the armed men of Khaurene behind them.

This time Regard meant to concentrate his force instead of acting in driblets, striking in every direction. He wanted a quick conquest of Khaurene itself.

The prospect of Serenity and Anne of Menand enforcing their will in the End of Connec was so unpopular that several counts who had abandoned Tormond during the times of chaos now offered knights and soldiers for his defense.

Even Terliaga offered troops. Queen Isabeth, at Peter's request, asked the Terliagans to concentrate on defending the Littoral. They ought not to offer Serenity further excuses for inciting religious conflict.

The Terliagans were clever enough to understand.

Brother Candle thought they were clever enough to make themselves look good with an offer they expected to be refused. Fielding Praman troops against Chaldareans in a purported Chaldarean religious squabble could irk even Peter's best friends.

The Perfect was staying with Kedle Richeut, daughter of Raulet and Madam Archimbault. With Kedle and her husband, Soames. Who did not like the arrangement but who kept his mouth shut. Soames had no friends. He wanted no more enemies. Brother Candle found him creepy. Absolutely creepy.

More than one Seeker reminded the Perfect that Soames had returned from captivity a changed man. That he was an agent of Arnhand, or even the Society. Brother Candle acknowledged those warnings with a smile and a nod. They might be true. Likely were true. He considered that a good thing. For him. In the fork of a cleft stick, Soames dared not betray him. Further, Soames likely hoped to deliver him to his secret masters once Khaurene fell.

The Perfect might be the coin wherewith Soames purchased safety for himself and his family.

In brief, for the moment, Brother Candle felt safer and freer in the house of the enemy. Too, he was sheltered by Kedle's upbringing. The girl had problems but she was no running dog of the Adversary.

Brother Candle felt comfortable going out amongst the Seekers of Khaurene. Because Regard was terrorizing everything north of Khaurene, and getting stronger by the day, Tormond's Direcian allies, and those Khaurenese who wanted the Duke's succession scheme to fail, had little time to hunt a missing Perfect.

When he did preach Brother Candle always worked in a few words about Tormond's adoption of Count Raymone. Though embarrassed, he sang Raymone's praises, too. Strictly as a patriot.

Time fled at a blistering pace, headed for an apocalypse. Khaurene desperately wanted more in which to prepare. But, long before anyone high or low wanted, Arnhander crusaders appeared north of the city.

Brother Candle joined the crowds on the wall, weakly disguised, usually with Kedle and her children. Sometimes he went out with other elderly Maysaleans taking a break from getting ready to spit in the eye of doom. He saw smoke in the distance several times, never explained. Nearer to hand the enemy did not repeat past mistakes by destroying resources he might need later.

Regard was confident that he would be able to deny the countryside to Khaurene's defenders.

They did say the young King lacked no confidence in himself—so long as he was outside the reach of his mother's voice.

Skirmishes happened. King Peter's proconsul, Count Diagres Alplicova, believed in harassing an enemy mercilessly, to bleed his strength, steal his sleep and comfort, keep him off balance, and force him onto the defensive. No Arnhander foraging party, patrol, or smaller action force could expect to get through an assignment without running into Direcians accustomed to using similar tactics against their Praman foes.

Word spread: Regard meant to force a battle. Then he would take Khaurene. He was completely certain of the superiority of the Arnhander knight over all other fighting men.

Brother Candle observed, "The Night never lets such hubris go unpunished. Or is it arrogance? We have a chance. It could be that soon every bell in Arnhand will ring in mourning."

"Let's hope," Kedle replied. Grown withdrawn under Soames's regime, the girl was, nevertheless, as ferocious as Socia Rault. On the wall she left the babies to the old man while she helped work on the nearest missile engine. Khaurene's women faced a worse fate than any of its men.

The old man saw legends in the making. Should it come to a siege.

THOUGH SPRING HAD MADE ITSELF KNOWN, BELATEDLY, WINTER REfused to retire. It made repeated comeback bids while the armies collected, skirmished, maneuvered. Random late snowstorms came and went, inconvenient and annoying. Then came a final heavy fall and hard freeze, more cruel to the invader than to the invaded.

The Arnhanders scattered into whatever shelter they could find. Meaning they split into three concentrations plus numerous smaller forces. King Regard and his force, three thousand strong, settled into and around a the castle at Repor ande Busch. The King, surrounded by priests set on him by his mother, spent his time fasting and praying. Outside Repor ande Busch, which could house only two hundred eighty in crowded discomfort, Regard's force camped in misery on the banks of a creek known sometimes as the Envil and otherwise as the Auxvasse. It was narrow and shallow and muddy, carrying away excess moisture from the vineyard slopes behind the castle and from marshy ground between Repor ande Busch and Khaurene. The creek provided just enough water for the needs of the camp. Thick, unpleasantly flavored water.

Three miles northwest of Repor ande Busch the Captal du Days and four thousand men hunkered in the relative shelter of a narrow, deep valley known locally as the Raffle. The biting cold wind did not get down to its bottom. The men huddled there had no inclination to leave but there was no food, little fodder, and not much water. Firewood consisted of scrub brush.

The third concentration, commanded by Anne of Menand's cousin Haband, including the strongest religious campaigners, coalesced round Peque ande Sales, six miles north of the Raffle. Their right flank and back lay against the mountainous wilderness whither Connectens fled in the worst of times. Partisans of one sort or another were always close by. Haband's force numbered fifteen hundred at the onset of the late foul weather.

Several thousand more men were scattered in smaller clusters, within a day's brisk march. All prayed for better weather.

THE SITUATION SEEMED IDEAL TO THE NAVAYAN CAPTAINS. THE ENEMY was scattered, hungry, and dispirited. Many of them were unblooded. Count Alplicova hoped to silence Arnhander ambitions in the Connec for at least a generation. If the Direcians attacked with the vigor they had shown at Los Naves de los Fantas, Arnhand might never come back.

One sharp, quick, thoroughly bloody engagement. With King Regard taken prisoner. His ransom would be his sworn word to leave the Connec and never again torment that land. Nor ever again presume upon the rights of Peter of Navaya and his allies.

Overly optimistic planners thought native Connectens could silence the Society once that wicked brotherhood had no national power behind it.

*    *    *

BROTHER CANDLE WAS ON THE WALL WITH HUNDREDS OF SPECTATORS, mostly old folks, women, and children. He held the youngest of Kedle's babies. Raulet Archimbault had the older, wrapped in a heavy, ragged cloak. Some of the crowd eyed Raulet harshly. He was not too old to be out there defending his city.

Kedle stayed close to the Perfect. Her husband was nearby but made no effort to keep her warm.

Soames drew more potent stares than did Raulet. He ignored them, disdainfully, yet did seem tense, nervous, worried, even frightened. This could be a bad day in the life of Soames Richeut.

The Navayans looked ragged, advancing toward Repor ande Busch. King Peter's standard was not out there with them. Rumor said the King had spent the night drinking and sporting with a woman who was not Isabeth of Khaurene. Count Diagres Alplicova, whispered to bear an un-requited passion for Queen Isabeth, had taken command.

Brother Candle thought the Navayans seemed unsure they wanted to follow today's commander.

Soldiers moving left of the Navayans were the Castaurigans and their King. Jaime's mission was to interpose himself between Repor ande Busch and the Raffle so the Captal du Days could not reinforce King Regard.

Khaurene's militia formed behind the Navayans. Brother Candle was surprised to see so many. And was further surprised to see Duke Tormond's own standard out there with them. He told Archimbault, "I'm amazed that he could get that armor on. He hasn't had it out in twenty years."

Other Connecten forces, though, were not yet present. Scattered, hiding from the weather, they were reluctant to assemble. There was too much confusion for anything to happen.

THOUGH DETERMINED TO FORCE A DECISIVE ENCOUNTER NEITHER PE-ter nor Regard was prepared for the opportunity. Both were still abed when the first arrows flew. Peter was the worse for a terrible hangover. His people did their best to get him up, get him dressed, get him armed, armored, and mounted. He departed Metrelieux under the stern eyes of his Queen, her gaze so flush with anger that, hangover and all, he pre-ferred a battle to explaining himself.

Peter joined his knights after the fighting became chaotic, neither side pursuing any strategy deeper than hacking at the man who was nearest. Contingents of Navayans sat their mounts outside the fray and

326GLEN COOK

did nothing because they had received no instructions and had no initiative. Many Arnhanders did the same. And the Khaurenese stayed well back from danger.

On the wall, beside Brother Candle, Raulet Archimbault grumbled, "I feel like I'm hearing this story for the second time."

Kedle responded, "You are, Dad. But last time it was the Captain-General. And he was ready."

Archimbault grunted. "Handed us our heads and hearts and sent us scurrying into the Altai like terrified rats." He eyed Soames but said nothing.

Kedle, the Perfect noted, did not so much as glance at her husband.

Archimbault said, "Things were different, then."

Indeed. The Patriarchal forces had been disciplined and well led. For them it had been another day's work at organized murder.

The Navayans approached to within bowshot before the Arnhanders wakened their sovereign. Regard had spent the night with an equerry named Thierry, sure there would be no fighting for days. The weather made campaigning impractical.

The enemy did not agree. He began making probing attacks. Frightened courtiers brought word that several of Anne's favorites had fallen already.

The situation looked desperate.

Regard would not be hurried. He refused to hear talk of flight. He performed his morning religious obligation, demanding added blessings for a warrior headed into harm's way on God's behalf.

Panic found a home in the hearts of some awaiting the King's appearance, particularly those in the Connec out of greed rather than conviction. Several dozen knights chose to leave Regard in God's keeping before he completed his obligation. Among them were three of his cousins, his mother's brother, and Anne's latest pet priest, Bishop Mortimar du Blanc. Du Blanc was a senior member of the Arnhander branch of the Society for the Suppression of Sacrilege and Heresy.

The omens were bad from the beginning. Regard's squires broke the laces on his mail shirt as they tightened them. While they hunted replacements news came that the last hint of organization had fled the battlefield.

More faint hearts discovered a conviction that they would be of more value at home than at Khaurene. Anne might spit and swear but she would not leave them facedown, dead, in freezing Connecten mud.

Several contingents from counties that had shifted allegiance from

Tormond IV to Charlve the Dim moved off, refusing to participate, having no desire to make a permanent enemy of Peter of Navaya.

The Navayans had similar problems. Many Direcian allies would not engage unless Peter himself took command.

Elsewhere, King Jaime of Castauriga exceeded his instructions. Rather than block the road to Khaurene he stormed into the Raffle, a valley poorly suited to fighting on horseback.

At Repor ande Busch King Regard's back cinch broke when he put weight on his stirrup. He fell. His left shoulder and the back of his head hit hard. He did not break his skull, only knocked himself dizzy. But he hurt his shoulder so he could not raise his shield more than a few inches.

His right leg also turned back under him when he fell. Some who were present later claimed they heard bone break. Regard himself only ever admitted to injuring his ankle and knee.

Several dozen more reluctant warriors saw the last evil portent they could stand. They joined the dribble headed north.

Once Regard did settle astride his great gray warhorse the animal at first refused to accept commands. Another ill omen.

Barely two hundred lances followed the Arnhander King when, finally, he rode out to face the victors of Los Naves de los Fantas.

SEVERELY HUNGOVER, YET STILL DRUNK, PETER OF NAVAYA ARRIVED on the battlefield at the same time. He cursed Count Alplicova for not having been more forceful and aggressive while, at the same time, damning as an idiot any petty-minded count or prince who had failed to carry out Alplicova's directives. He ordered them to assemble.

Some nobles arrived looking sheepish. Some arrived defiant. More than one, obliquely, indicated that Peter's disrespect for his Queen had cost him much of his own respect.

It was not so much that he had bedded a woman not his wife but that he had done it in his wife's home castle, making no effort to be discreet.

Peter, King of Navaya, honored by most Chaldareans and respected by his enemies, nevertheless stood second in the hearts of millions. Good Queen Isabeth's admirers believed her destined for sainthood.

Peter's state did not leave him best capable of temperate thinking and reasoned decisions. His allies saw that.

They had no faith at a moment when faith was all they needed.

KING REGARD LED A CHARGE AS SOON AS HE GOT HIS MEN ALIGNED. When that line surged forward a dozen horsemen did not move.

The Navayans were not prepared despite Regard's slow, lackluster preparation for the attack. However, there were a lot of Navayans. And most of the Arnhanders who followed Regard did so out of obligation, not enthusiasm.

The Navayans were no more enthusiastic once it became man-to-man.

Regard set his eye on Peter's standard and kept pushing that direction.

He kept having dizzy spells. He had trouble staying on his horse. His friends had to protect his left and keep him in the saddle.

No one knew who did what to whom. The chaos only worsened. It became ever more every man for himself. Navayan numbers and experience should have told quickly but did not gel. Count Alplicova never gained tactical control. King Peter had arrived too late. Many of his knights never knew that he had come to the fray. Quite a few got bogged down in the marshy ground while trying to circle the disorganized and confused Arnhanders.

At one point someone knocked Regard off his horse. His men surrounded him. He managed to remount as his foes mistakenly began shouting that he was dead.

The entire engagement was one of the most ill-starred and incompetently managed of the age despite the presence of the veterans, the trained fighters, and the famous commanders. At the root, no one had any idea what they were supposed to be doing.

AFTER WHAT SEEMED AGES OF INCONCLUSIVE, HALFHEARTED, CHAOTIC fighting, King Peter lost control of his mount. The animal had had enough. It bolted. He fell off.

While fighting the Pramans Peter had taken to wearing plain armor so he could not be singled out. Praman Direcian princes considered him a demon incarnate. In every engagement their whole strategy would hinge on their destroying him first. He had followed habit here, though his standard-bearer did stay close.

Stunned by the fall, Peter failed to make his identity known. A foot soldier who could have grown rich ransoming Peter of Navaya instead killed an unknown knight. He used a mason's pick-hammer to punch holes through Peter's helmet.

No one noticed. No one knew. The chaos continued. Count Alplicova strove to bring order but had no luck. He began moving his own followers out of the fight, meaning to disengage long enough to re-form.

The Khaurenese militia watched from a slope a few hundred yards distant. They did nothing because no one gave the order.

The Connecten counts did not show, though messengers had gone to their several camps.

Tormond IV, given a powerful draught of medicine, had been led out to inspire his people. But all he could do was remain upright in his saddle.

People on the city wall cried out in anguish, anger, outrage. Who dared send Tormond into battle? They wept. The most devout pacifists among the witnesses agreed: Someone, anyone, had but to give the order and the Arnhanders would be overwhelmed. They were scattered, disorganized, outnumbered. Their King kept falling off his horse. It was a raging, diabolic miracle that the Navayans had not crushed them already.

Arnhander reinforcements were sure to come soon, from the Raffle and Peque ande Sales, then from the numerous scattered small contingents.

KING JAIME AND HIS CASTAURIGANS SURPRISED THE CAPTAL DU DAYS. The Arnhanders hunkered down in Raffle were confident that the weather precluded enemy action. Their only warning came moments before the Castaurigan storm, brought by fleeing foragers.

King Jaime was as vicious and aggressive a warrior as he was a lover. And today he was inattentive to doctrine developed through centuries of battlefield experience. He did not take time to assemble and array so his charge would have maximum impact. He just rushed in and started killing.

The slaughter was terrible amongst those who were not knights, the majority in any camp. The knights themselves, once they donned their armor and mounted up, managed well enough.

Just as in the struggle nearer Khaurene, the fighting went on and on. The living on both sides neared that point where they might collapse from exhaustion. King Jaime still drove his followers. So great was the slaughter, and so numerous were those who fled, that the Castaurigans developed an advantage, including one in leadership. The Captal had been killed. So had most of his captains and champions—unless they had run away.

Jaime's advisers wanted him to leave while his men and animals had strength enough to return to Khaurene. Fresh Arnhanders could arrive anytime.

Thirsts for blood and glory ruled the young King. He refused to go. He meant to spend the night in the camp of the defeated. He thought Haband would be too frightened to come out of Peque ande Sales.

But Haband came. Though hardly fresh after a six-mile forced march, his men were less exhausted than the Castaurigans. Fugitives from the Raffle added weight to Haband's force, professing eagerness to redeem their earlier cowardice.

Haband's men were inexperienced. Most were the useless sort of night crawler who concealed natural-born cowardice by hiding inside the Church and Society. They could be terribly fierce with an enemy already caught and disarmed, but with an armed and angry knight, not so much.

For a while it seemed there would be an afternoon of epic slaughter in sequel to the morning's butchery, with the same result. The faint of heart from earlier had found no additional courage. Most ran away again.

Then a fighting bishop, quite by accident, knocked King Jaime off his exhausted mount. The youngster ended up in the midst of a wild tangle of men on foot.

Responsibility, later, would be claimed by every bishop who survived. Haband himself would lay claim, though scores of witnesses put him miles away already, with companions who believed they were too valuable to die in that cruel valley.

Credit mattered not. It might even have been a stray Castaurigan blade that delivered the first wound, unintentionally.

The Castaurigans lost their stomach. They backed out of the fight. Jaime's brother Palo, just sixteen, tried to rally them. He wanted to recover Jaime's body. No one would join the effort. His advisers insisted that he ransom it later. So bullied, he led the survivors south.

In fact, no one had seen the King actually die. But no one expressed any doubt that he was dead.

They did remain professional in retreat. They ambushed those who pursued them, and killed all the Arnhanders they encountered along the way.

BROTHER CANDLE HAD BEEN SHAKING HIS HEAD FOR HOURS. IT HAD become a tic. He could not control it. Like every Khaurenese and Direcian still breathing he could not believe that the militia had remained paralyzed all day. Any idiot could see what needed doing. The old man began talking to himself. He had been mad to leave Sant Peyre de Mileage. He should go back to Navaya Medien before the insanity here twisted round to where the crusaders were on the inside, with the Seekers and true Khaurenese driven out.

The world now imposed itself. His muttering faded as he realized that all those who had shared the ramparts with him had disappeared.

He conjured vague recollections of Raulet and Kedle trying to get him to go. Fear must have forced them to abandon him.

Still he stared. This disaster, likely to echo through the centuries, had happened only because his oldest friend could never make a decision. Though, to be fair, today's Tormond had all he could do to stay upright and breathe.

"Master!" The voice was impatient. It had been trying to get his attention for some time.

Brother Candle turned. "Hodier! Why aren't you out there with the Duke?"

"Because Isabeth made me stay here to deal with you."

"There's no dealing to do. The thing is done. Count Raymone has the tokens and instruments."

"I know." Tormond's herald stepped forward, separating himself from his escort, Direcians all. "Yet there might be cause to delay the transition." Hodier pointed. "Out there. King Peter didn't apply his genius because he has so little to gain. Tormond still breathes but can't do anything. The magnates won't do anything because they dread losing Tormond in battle. The consuls are hiding under their beds."

Hodier rambled on, a soliloquy for his mother city. The old man listened in silence. Succession complications. They plagued all lands, all the time, and caused endless dislocation, confusion, and misery. There had to be a better way.

He did not expect to see it in his lifetime.

Every plan, every scheme, every social experiment broke down as soon as people became involved.

"Arrest me, Hodier. Take me away if you must. You're wasting your time. And mine. What little I have left. These days I'm nothing but a spectator." He moved half a step so he could lean on a merlon. Nearer the gate carpenters had started putting up hoardings.

Hodier appropriated a nearby merlon. "Tormond was aware. He hardly slept last night. He wishes he had done things differently. Once his mind and body started going he decided he wanted to ride out on a day like this so he could leave Khaurene remembering the Great Vacillator defending his city. He could go out a hero. Then a more confident, savage hero, Count Raymone, could come avenge him. He built that whole legend in his mind."

"But?"

"But Peter of Navaya. Peter wants to be the great champion of the Chaldarean world. Bigger than the Grail Emperors. As big as the emperors of the Old Empire. Despite his successes he hasn't become that to anyone outside Direcia. And he's convinced that if he doesn't add the Connec to his diadem he'll never get to be what he wants to be."

"He needs to work that out with Count Raymone." It could be done. Count Raymone Garete had a big ego. He was the product of his class. But he was a fierce patriot, too, capable of swearing fealty to the kings of Navaya if that would save his motherland.

Hodier said, "I believe that to be in line with what the Queen hopes to accomplish."

"The Queen?"

"Isabeth. She sent me. I told you. She sees a way past the dilemma. I imagine she wants you to take her message to Count Raymone."

"Oh, for Aaron's sake! Look at me! In another week I'll turn sixty-seven. Everybody older than me is already dead. I'm not likely to survive another journey across the Connec."

"That may be. It's not for me to decide. My job is to bring you to Isabeth. You can quibble with her."

Brother Candle stared out at that fraction of the fighting visible from his vantage. What he saw was still mostly chaos. And looked like it could come out favorably if only the Khaurenese militia would do something.

THOSE WITH DUKE TORMOND, PRETENDING HE WAS IN CHARGE, FI-nally made a decision. The militia would return to the city. At the moment when a few Connecten knights finally began to appear.

When battered driblets from the Raffle and Peque and Sales began to arrive Count Alplicova ordered his Navayans to follow the Khaurenese. He remained unaware how few the Arnhander reinforcements would be. He had had no news from the Castaurigans, who were retreating past the city to the west.

It would be determined later that four thousand Arnhanders and allies perished in the day's fighting. More died later from wounds. Navayan, Castaurigan, and allied losses amounted to fourteen hundred, more than a hundred of those being men taken prisoner.

Tormond IV's Khaurenese militia suffered twenty-three casualties, six due to enemy action.

BROTHER CANDLE JOINED A GRIM, ANGRY ISABETH. SHE HAD JUST DIS-missed men covered with filth and sweat and blood. The Perfect guessed their news had not been good. Finally, she said, "They think Peter is dead."

The sun was low in the west. Its light poured in through high, arched windows, splashing the audience with gold. Not appropriate, Brother Candle thought.

Isabeth added, "Jaime is dead, too. The Castaurigans are withdrawing. They say they left the Arnhanders badly weakened. They killed a lot of fugitives from the fighting here."

Brother Candle sighed, focused on the afternoon light. An omen of darkness to come. Turnabout on the old saw about darkest before the dawn.

A runner announced that the Khaurenese magnates had made up Tormond's mind. They were on the move, back into the city, with never a blow struck.

Isabeth suddenly looked old. She told the Perfect, "Remember what Tormond was like last time you saw him."

"It wasn't that long ago, if you'll recall."

"Oh. Of course. But the Tormond who went out this morning was in worse shape than back then, despite all that wizards and physicians did. He shouldn't have gone. But without Eardale Dunn we had no one else. Mas Crebet and Casteren Grout are bad jokes." She meant the consuls, Khaurene's equivalent of a mayor.

"There is Your Majesty," Hodier observed.

"Crap. They won't follow a woman."

Brother Candle observed, "It might have been worth a try. But that opportunity has fled."

"Who knows? Jaime is gone. Peter is gone. Tormond is next to extinct. Count Raymone is at the other end of the Connec and Regard is at the gate. So it comes down to me, anyway. We will find out who'll follow a woman."

The Perfect was at sea. He had been brought to Metrelieux to discuss a matter that had been pushed aside by subsequent news. The world had changed, for everyone, wherever they stood.

Isabeth said, "The lords of Navaya will be back, soon. That could get exciting. I need to steel myself."

Brother Candle could see that. Without Peter to curb them the Direcians were likely to treat Khaurene as an occupied city instead of an ally and dependent. They would feel justified. The Khaurenese could have overwhelmed the Arnhanders but had chosen not to act.

That would not be forgiven.

"We need to be quick," Hodier said.

Isabeth waved that off. "I became a queen mother today. But my son is practically still a baby. In the normal course Count Alplicova would become regent until Little Peter comes of age. I'll push for that.

But Fate was wearing her big stomping boots today. Dead or alive, I lost my brother, too. Dead or alive, he'll no longer be a factor in the considerations of princes. Nor of the Patriarchs, whom Tormond did, at least, always make nervous."

A minor chamberlain burst in. "A band of Brothen Episcopals led by Society brothers are trying to take control of the north gate."

"They're wearing colors?" Isabeth asked.

"They are, Your Majesty."

"Then kill them. If they surrender, throw them off the wall."

"Your Majesty?" Appalled.

"No exceptions. If they have families, kill them, too."

Though appalled himself, Brother Candle did the cold equations. A show of ferocity now would save lives later. Nor could he summon much empathy for people who meant to burn him at the stake.

The chamberlain went away.

Isabeth said, "I'll do everything I can till they come take it away." She went silent for a moment. Brother Candle said nothing. Eloquently. Isabeth finally mused, "They killed King Jaime, too."

Hodier murmured, "God willing, then, Death will claim King Regard, as well."

"God willing. He's been reported down several times. But he keeps getting back up."

Brother Candle finally worked himself up to ask, "Why am I here?"

The Queen replied, "Because you're an agent of and apologist for Count Raymone Garete."

"I wouldn't say that."

"I would. You were Tormond's friend. He thought. Mine, too, but not so much. My conscience wouldn't trouble me if I had to drop you down a well. Count Raymone."

"What about him?"

"Exactly. Tormond made Raymone his heir. The men best equipped to keep Raymone from inheriting all died today. I want to know what we can expect from Antieux. Does Count Raymone want to become Duke? What kind of man is he?"

"Yes to the first and stubborn to the latter. Count Raymone Garete is everything people always wanted Tormond to be, only twice as much. He'll become Duke because that will give him the power to punish any foreigner who refuses to leave him, Antieux, and the Connec alone."

"I might like this man better than the Count Raymone I remember."

"A caution. If Raymone assumes the Dukedom, there'll be war."

"We've got war now."

"I mean a war involving man, woman, and child, all out, until

Raymone Garete draws his last breath. Or until Arnhand and Brothe
fold their hands and direct their ambitions elsewhere. Even Raymone's
death might not be the end of it. The Countess, Socia, is more bloodthirsty than he is."

Another underchamberlain rushed in. He reported that the captains of the militia, who had chosen to do nothing all day, were now in
a demanding mood.

"Where is Alplicova? I want him here. Tell those people I'll be with
them shortly."

It took more than a few minutes to locate Count Alplicova and
chivvy him into the Queen's presence. He was in no fit condition to be
there. His wounds had not yet been treated. He had been busy readying
Khaurene's defenses rather than getting cleaned up and patched up.

Isabeth demanded, "Are you well enough to endure the demands of
command, Count?"

"As ever, I will do what must be done. There is no one else."

"You could be right. Collect some reliable men and bring them here.
Quickly. The magnates are in a mood to make demands. After all they
did for us today, on the battlefield, I'm not inclined to be indulgent."

"I understand completely, Your Majesty."

"Master."

Isabeth's sudden attention startled Brother Candle, who had slipped
into a dark reverie. He failed to remind her that "Master" was inappropriate. "Your Grace?"

The Navayan Queen failed to remind him that she did not like being
"Your Grace." "I don't have time for you, now. Keep yourself available."

"As you wish."

"At the moment I wish you to find my brother. Someone brought
him back, I expect still breathing. Find him. Attach yourself. Take care
of him. Hodier. You just became the Master's shadow. Where he goes,
you go. Do what he says needs doing."

"As you command." Said without pleasure.

The Perfect and the herald left the Queen's presence, two old men
glad to get away.

To the distress of few outside their own families Isabeth arrested the leaders of the Khaurenese militia. Rumor soon claimed that
several had taken bribes from the Society—or from Anne of Menand,
or from the Patriarch—to shun the fight. Treason being a more attractive explanation than indecision or incompetence.

There was a lot of anger in Khaurene. Brothen Episcopal Faithful suffered the brunt. Anyone even vaguely suspect dared not show himself lest he be thrown down to the befuddled Arnhanders trying to initiate a siege.

The scattered smaller Arnhander companies had begun arriving.

KING REGARD WAS SO STIFF AND BRUISED HE COULD BARELY MOVE. His concussion caused occasional brief blackouts. But he saw an opportunity. He was determined to strike while the Khaurenese remained stunned.

Regard, however, lacked followers who shared his vision.

Those who had fought and survived, those who had not deserted, were too exhausted to do anything but go through the motions while the bands coming in were cold and tired and hungry. And they all faced heretics determined to fight. They would not flee to the Altai this time. Not this early in the season.

Once the sun set, siege work proceeded desultorily by artificial light. It was difficult to see arrows in flight. Meaning it became difficult to dodge.

BICOT HODIER DRAFTED A COUPLE OF GUARDS HE TRUSTED AND HAD them accompany him and the Perfect. "Just in case. Some people may consider today an opportunity."

Brother Candle grunted, saved his breath for keeping up. But he understood. Khaurene teetered on the brink of chaos. Adventurers would see opportunities that, likely as not, existed only in their own imaginations. But they would act anyway.

Count Alplicova began arresting city magnates and militia captains before the herald and Perfect located Tormond. The Duke had been whisked into the home of the consul Sieur Casteren Grout. Grout and his fellow consul, Sieur Mas Crebet, had not turned out for morning muster and, thus, had not been with the militia in the field. A gross dereliction by Crebet, whose principal responsibility was to lead the city levies when they were called out.

Brother Candle wondered if there might not be some substance to the bribery rumors.

The consuls were not pleased to receive fresh guests. But Sieur Casteren Grout grasped the precarious nature of his position. He put on a grand show of concern for his Duke's well-being.

Tormond was, indeed, in terrible shape. Brother Candle insisted that he not be moved. He sent for Father Fornier. And more trustworthy soldiers lest Grout and Crebet suffer a further bout of stupidity.

*        *        *

Isabeth told Brother Candle, "We've exploited you mercilessly lately. And you've given your best. But I have one more request before you go back into the wilderness. The Arnhanders intend to storm the north gate tomorrow. The defenders there are mostly Seekers. It would hearten them if you were there with my brother."

Khaurenese morale was poor. Those who thought they might not suffer if King Regard triumphed were vocal about negotiating a surrender. Those threatened by the Society and the Church took the opposing view, as did Queen Isabeth on behalf of Navaya, her husband, and her son.

Navayan strength had dwindled as Isabeth sent out streams of messengers, across Peter's empire, to warn every garrison and proconsul that unrest could be expected.

It would be hard to cling to all of Peter's gains, however faithful Count Alplicova and his peers remained. Alplicova himself she sent back to Oranja to gather the reins of state on her son's behalf. And to make sure Little Peter would be safe from anyone with secret ambitions.

Brother Candle understood what Isabeth wanted. He and Tormond would be companion symbols of Khaurenese defiance. Harmless old men, cornerstones for the reconstruction of Khaurene's self-confidence.

The woman was clever.


Father Fornier reanimated the Duke enough for the man to stand. With assistance. He and Brother Candle took places on the wall two dozen yards west of the northern gate, well protected by hoardings. The Perfect wore an uncharacteristic white robe. He drew cheers from the defenders, many of them familiar. Just ten feet away Madam Archimbault, her daughter, and her neighbors made up the all-female crew of a light ballista.

Where were Raulet and the men? The only men to be seen were nearly as old as Brother Candle.

Somewhere, every man who could move was being assembled for a counterattack. Given past performance, that might prove disastrous.

The Arnhanders began moving engines toward the city. That was not easy work. They had to advance up a slope, under fire. Literal fire, frequently. The Khaurenese engines flung burning missiles. The slope of the ground and height of the wall gave the defenders a range advantage.

The flaming missiles did little serious damage. The two siege towers had been covered with fresh hides. Some genius had faced the mantlets with water-soaked thatch, which made them heavy but, essentially, fireproof. Likewise, the tortoise bringing a ram up to pound the gate. Other little houses on wheels would shelter sappers who would try to burrow directly through the wall. Elsewhere, other sappers were, likely, starting tunnels.

King Regard had assembled a formidable array of artillery, all standard stuff, similar to the captured engine. He readied his weapons, protected them appropriately, then began dueling with the amateurs behind the hoardings atop the wall.

Regard made no effort to disguise himself. He wore gaudy armor and livery and traveled with heralds and standard-bearers. His party became a favored target.

Everyone who paid attention saw that there was something wrong with Regard. He was slow, suffered bouts of clumsiness, and dizzy spells. But he refused to be anywhere but up front, heartening his crusaders and directing artillery fires. He took savage pleasure in sniping at Khaurenese personally. He snatched crossbows from infantrymen and dashed forward to discharge the bolt. He was an excellent shot. The hoardings saved numerous lives.

Brother Candle could not help being amazed by the spirit of the ferocious Seeker women operating the nearer missile engines. Kedle told him, "We have the most to lose if they get inside."

The woman had a talent for murder. Once she usurped command of her particular ballista every shaft it sped struck where it would have an effect. Her marksmanship silenced several enemy engines. She also slaughtered several men trying to advance to the nearer siege tower.

Her unexpected talent caused a stir along the wall. People came to see what she was doing right. She could not explain. Ammunition bearers made sure her crew never ran short. An old mechanic stood by in case her engine needed a repair.

The girl showed the Perfect a fierce grin, reminding him of Socia Rault. He forced an answering smile, then went to watch the deployment of a weapon similar to one used by warships in classical times.

The tortoise protecting the Arnhander ram snugged up to the gate. The men inside started a work chant.

An argument broke out behind the Perfect. He turned.

Soames Richeut had materialized. He was determined to remove Kedle from her post despite venomous abuse from every woman within range. Soames glared at them like he wanted to remember their faces.

Kedle would not leave. Her companions made it clear they would not let her be coerced.

Brother Candle wondered who was taking care of the children.

Soames yelped in pain when his mother-in-law barked him one with the butt of the shaft she was about to load into the ballista.

Brother Candle turned back to the crane swinging its long arm out above the Arnhander tortoise. A one-ton stone "dolphin" on a chain hung from the arm. The Perfect had no idea where that had come from. It looked more like a penis than a denizen of the deep. Whatever its name or provenance, it was effective when it struck.

The first drop cracked and shifted the massive timbers of the tortoise. It took the crane crew twenty minutes, under fire, to hoist the dolphin again. The second drop smashed through the timbers and injured several men. The third time the dolphin fell two yards farther out, made sure the tortoise could not be dragged away for repairs.

Direcian veterans issued through a sally port, butchered the ram crew, and set the tortoise afire.

The Arnhanders would have to clear the wreckage before they could bring another ram to the gate.

The crane operators began to shift it to attack the sappers chipping at the wall—though those men had to deal with hot sand, quicklime, and firebombs already.

Brother Candle kept up a conversation with the Duke, as though Tormond understood and was in charge. Tormond had been positioned in such wise that he could be seen by nearby defenders, all of whom conspired in the pretense.

In fact, there was no real command, insofar as Brother Candle could see. People just did what they thought needed doing, feeling around for what they could do best.

Soames Richeut went away for an hour, then returned to berate Kedle again. He was not kind. Nor were Kedle's friends kind to him.

The Perfect lost patience with the bad husband. He went to admonish the man. Kedle's crew shifted a hoarding so she could loose another deadly shaft.

Someone outside awaited that opportunity.

Richeut stepped in front of Kedle's ballista to block her aim. The Arnhander bolt hit him in the right temple and passed on through his head. The marksman shouted, "Thirteen!" in an accent from the Pail.

In the calmest murder Brother Candle ever witnessed Kedle Richeut avenged her husband before his body stopped twitching. Almost before the celebrant outside finished congratulating himself.

A slowly building tumult developed amongst the Arnhanders. When Brother Candle dared look he saw gaudy King Regard being held erect by his heralds. Kedle's shaft had transfixed him. He was alive but that would not last. The gut wound would kill him slowly. Only the absolute best sorcerer's care would help now, unlikely in an army ruled by the Society.

Kedle did not wait on peritonitis. She sent a second shaft. It passed through Regard's equerry, Thierry, then the King, then lodged in the haunch of the King's confessor, Simon du Montrier.

Brother Candle started, turned, found that Tormond had been led up to see the enemy. Tormond gurgled something the Perfect thought sounded like, "There'll be no getting over that."

Brother Candle mused, "This is history. This is a tipping point. Three kings in one week. Possibly the three most important in the western world. Everything is going to change."

The future could be bleak indeed. The successes of the Calziran Crusade, the Artecipean campaign, and the triumph at Los Naves de los Fantas might all have been rendered naught these past several days.

Only the Perfect thought that way. There was dancing and singing on the wall and a shower of abuse on the enemy. There would be city-wide drunken celebrations later, after the militia finally fought. And succeeded to the point where only the fastest scuttlers among the Arnhanders and Society scum managed to escape.

The Khaurenesaine had been saved, at incredible cost. But the storm still loomed over the rest of the Connec.

# 31. Lucidia: End Around

Per instructions from Shamramdi Nassim Alizarin shut down traffic past Tel Moussa. He drove his soldiers to exhaustion harassing the Unbeliever. The enemy, he was sure, would realize that something was up. Lone travelers could not all be intercepted. Those who did get through would carry rumors. Throughout the Crusader states the Arnhanders would gird themselves for the worst, though even Indala's captains remained ignorant of what their ruler planned.

Indala's grandnephew participated in every action. He distinguished himself each time. He worked harder than the Mountain himself till a courier arrived with a summons from Indala. The boy left immediately, accompanied by a few warriors his own age.

The Mountain stood in a high parapet. He watched till the only trace of Azim was a distant hint of dust. He had become emotionally invested. Azim was everything he could have hoped Hagid would become.

Someone said, "And a new age is about to dawn."

Nassim came back to his everyday world. He shared the parapet with Bone and old Az, the core of Tel Moussa's renegade Sha-lug.

Azer er-Selim had spoken. Nassim responded, "Meaning what?"

"Look out there. Farther than you were. Do you see a fuzziness that makes the horizon indistinct?"

Nassim looked but did not see. "Must be your bad eyes. I see what I always see out there. Don't play games, Master of Ghosts."

Bone remarked, "He can't help it, General. When they teach these camel-fuckers their trade they whip them if they say anything in plain language. The point is to keep it murky so later nobody can claim they got it wrong."

Nassim eyed Bone for several seconds. Bone seldom had much to say. This was a week's worth of chatter in one lump.

Er-Selim was surprised, too. And irked. He said, "All right, but only so it's all done before the old-timer embraces the Angel of Death. Our employer, never trusting us completely, has been hiding the fact that he's going to invade al-Minphet."

"What?"

"Indala has spent a year pretending he's getting ready to charge into the Holy Lands. He's convinced everyone. We've been key in convincing both sides."

"But you know something different?"

"Yes. Because I took advantage of our visit to Shamramdi. I poked my nose in. I listened. I exercised my reason." Old Az paused briefly, then added, "It's obvious if you watch Indala's family and trusted companions. And you ignore the chattering fools of al-Fartebi's court."

The Mountain said, "Dispense with self-congratulation. Tell me."

"I did. Indala means to invade Dreanger, capture al-Qarn, and unify the two kaifates."

Nassim let that simmer, then observed, "That poses a moral dilemma, doesn't it?"

"Only if you insist. Though being in revolt against Gordimer the Lion isn't the same as joining in a foreign enterprise meant to put an end to Gordimer and al-Minphet. The moral quandary is what Indala has spared us by keeping us ignorant."

"We'll suffer for this."

"Whether Indala succeeds or fails the Sha-lug will blame us."

"Should we send warning while we still have friends there?"

"Could we manage? Unnoticed? Won't Indala know who to blame if he finds the Lion prepared?"

"He can lay that blame no matter what we do."

"We do make convenient scapegoats."

Nassim mused, "The Lion may have gone rotten, and the Rascal even worse, but they aren't the Sha-lug, nor even Dreanger. There were Dreangeran agents in Shamramdi. Nothing this big is ever completely secret. Rumors have been reported back to al-Qarn. They'll be given credence because geography compels Indala to approach from the north."

"The prophecy. Certain to excite the Lion."

Nassin reflected, then said, "It will be interesting if this *is* the prophecy fulfilled." Then, "We'll just do our job. Nothing more. Nothing less. That was our commitment."

Nassim wondered if Indala meant to use him as a puppet Marshal. He said, "We'd best see to our defenses. If I were a Crusader prince I'd charge Shamramdi if Indala and Gordimer were locking horns behind me."

Bone seemed to be somewhere else. Not unusual with him. But now he asked, "Do we have any idea what's become of the Rascal?"

That sorcerer, only briefly rehabilitated, had had another falling-out with Gordimer, religious rather than based on bad behavior. The Lion did not mind er-Rashal being a murderous villain so long as he remained a devout Praman murderous villain. But he crossed a line when he kept trying to resurrect ancient devils.

It had taken the Marshal an age to understand that his henchman had no more love or respect for him than he had had for the apprentice Sha-lug Hagid, whom he had ordered murdered for a reason that, even today, only he understood.

Gordimer had not gotten the message meant to be conveyed by the presentation of the head of Rudenes Schneidel. He had been blinded by er-Rashal's immense and ferocious utility. But he came to the truth eventually.

Er-Rashal el-Dhulquarnen was a declared, dedicated enemy of God.

"He's hiding out again," Azer er-Selim said. "Most likely among his ancestors in the Hills of the Dead. That's where he went before."

The Mountain said, "None of that concerns us now. Once the decision has been handed down by God . . . We'll know how to face our tomorrows." He stared due north, toward the distant Idiam. And worried that the dead city there, though a hundred miles away, had infected his soul. He had not gone near it, yet, during his flights over the border of the dead realm. He had seen nothing to suggest that the nearer reaches of the Idiam differed from regions around it. There was even evidence that someone lived in the haunted territories.

No good Praman ventured there by choice.

Nassim feared Andesqueluz like he feared for his soul. Yet he seemed drawn to the haunted city. If only to slake his curiosity.

"Bone. Az. Tell me about Andesqueluz again."

Bone said, "There's nothing new to tell."

"Try."

Azer said, "Its reputation might make you think it was a major city, long ago. Yet I doubt that a thousand people ever lived there at one time. It's on top of a mountain. Not that great a mountain, but *the* mountain, Asher. The buildings are all either carved from Asher or built from stone the mountain provided."

Nassim grunted. "Their holy place."

"The holiest of holies. For those pagans. Which they kept a closed kingdom. They raised their food on tiny mountainside plots. Pilgrims were required to bring a basket of soil to gain entry."

"So few, yet we remember so much." Vaguely suspicious of al-Azir's knowledge.

"Every wall has its pictographs. They're easily read. Andesqueluz exported fear. Its sorcerers extracted tribute from all the kings in this part of the world."

"At a time when kings were little more than village chiefs."

"Andesqueluz was powerful but it did something to offend the whole world. The world united and destroyed Andesqueluz, to the last babe in arms, then went away, shunning the city and the Idiam forever. The fear was that the evil hadn't been destroyed, only the people had been. The evil just lay dormant. It couldn't be destroyed because the soul of the mountain, Asher, is the Adversary Himself."

Nassim heard nothing new. Again he asked the question that had been asked so many times. "What did er-Rashal want with those mummified sorcerers?"

It had to do with Asher, surely. El-Dhulquarnen had tried to resurrect Seska, the Endless, another wicked elder deity, already.

Az said, "I have had a new thought about that. After all these years. It doesn't have to do with Asher. But it'll still be unacceptable to the Faithful."

"Do tell."

"I think er-Rashal is after ascendance. He wants to become one of the Instrumentalities of the Night."

"You're right. True Believers wouldn't want to hear that. You could get in trouble just for saying somebody could think that way."

"Which is why the quest for ascendance went out of fashion."

"I'm sure. Az, anything to that notion? I heard something similar on Artecipea. Would the Rascal have gotten involved in such a dangerous scheme on speculation? Wouldn't he make sure he *could* become a god before he took chances?"

"I don't know. He never thought like normal Faithful. But trying to become a god was common in pagan times. The pictographs in Andesqueluz say ascendance was the city's reason for existing. The pagans must have succeeded once in a while. Which might explain why the Idiam is said to be haunted. If wicked ancients are still prowling the night."

"You saw direct evidence?"

"No. But we all felt like we were being watched. All the time. Captain Tage's bogon was our only direct contact with the Night."

Nassim sighed. "Always nothing. Oh, well. We should enjoy an interesting summer here. What do you think? Will the Arnhanders help Gordimer? Or will they sit back and enjoy the spectacle?"

Er-Selim said, "That might depend on who barks loudest. Vantrad would center any action. It's the biggest Crusader state and the one nearest probable points of contact. And Vantrad is positioned to interfere with Indala's line of communication. But King Berismond is a diseased boy under the thumb of an older wife with a diseased mind. Whom Indala bought off somehow. There'll be other Arnhanders, though, who'll see the danger of a united kaifate."

Nassim looked to the northwest. "This could be a situation made for Rogert du Tancret."

"If Berismond is seen as indecisive or weak. And how can he not be with Clothilde manipulating him?"

"Al-Adil hinted that something might happen to Black Rogert."

"That's always a possibility. For any of us. An assassin could get in here, too. But du Tancret has a phenomenal sense for personal danger. The love of the Night, perhaps. Don't base any strategy on the assumption that assassins will push him aside."

"Just thinking out loud. It's not my problem. We have enough to keep us busy here."

Nassim went downstairs, thinking about Azim al-Adil. Young Az had found a way into his heart. He would be devastated if the boy followed Hagid and Ambel into the dark.

Indala had asked if Ambel's end had left him a broken tool. Broken, not. But there were cracks.

The Sha-lug Mohkam approached Nassim as he approached his own quarters. He whispered, "There's a letter came from Akir. He's succeeded in buying twelve hundred pounds of firepowder. It will come by ship to Shartelle. We need to have people there to meet it. The Deves also offered a battery of six four-pounder falcons at six hundred eighty Aparionese ducats apiece if we take the set."

"That's cheap. What's wrong with them?"

"They're obsolete out there. Akir says they've survived repeated test firings, though."

"If that's what we can get. We can adapt. Why so generous with the firepowder?"

"Akir says they've found a way to produce it in quantity, less expensively."

"Then the face of war will change."

Mohkam shrugged. He was not one to care.

"Thank you," Nassim said. "I need to rest, now."

## 32. Tsistimed and the Chosen

There was no forgiveness in Tsistimed the Golden. And he was methodical about eliminating enemies. His biggest challenge in generations were the Chosen and their weird companions. No other enemy had come after him in more than a century. Others were content to wait for their doom to find them.

Ghargarlicea would enjoy a respite while he exterminated the threat from always-winter.

The Hu'n-tai At moved with the spring melt. They pursued the retreating freeze, guided by Chosen who had deserted their foul winter god.

It was not a war with much conflict. There was little left to find, other than starved bodies frozen alongside roads leading toward friendlier climes. Before summer's peak the great lord of the steppe knew the Chosen would be no further threat.

No living humans remained north of lands Tsistimed ruled. He could shift ambition to the Ghargarlicean Empire, though that conquest would not now go as quickly as he would like.

The Hu'n-tai At needed time to regain strength. That could take decades.

Tsistimed was not pleased.

The wells of power continued to wane. He would not survive them by long.

Their power, and that of the Night, sustained him. While they went on, Tsistimed the Golden went on. When they failed, Tsistimed the Golden would die.

# 33. Realm of the Gods: Great Sky Fortress

Korban Iron Eyes and his troop followed their own path back to the Realm of the Gods. When Heris and Cloven Februaren arrived with the Bastard, Heris blurted, "Shee-it, Double Great! They beat us! I'm going to crack some heads! They screwed us, taking all damned winter to get down there to that damned castle."

"Not really. Be calm. They can't walk across to our world wherever they want. They have to go there on foot first, from an entry point they already know."

"Like me with the Construct when I first started."

"Like that. But, remember, time passes differently here."

That might be. Iron Eyes had not taken advantage of the differential to clean himself up.

Heris recognized the ascendant instantly—though, in retrospect, that was no prodigy. He was the only unfamiliar non-dwarf. And, even in Asgrimmur Grimmsson form, he radiated a powerful presence. More so while he studied the Bastard, son and grandson of the fragmentary Instrumentalities inside him.

The Bastard did not react to the ascendant. The Bastard was unhappy. Bizarre myth had caught him up, had kidnapped him, and he could do nothing about it.

When the ascendant drew near, though, the Bastard jumped as though pricked.

"He believes it now," Februaren said.

The Bastard's gaze rose to the Great Sky Fortress and restored rainbow bridge. "It's real."

Februaren responded, "It's all real. Whatever your beliefs."

"I believe in Ferris Renfrow. Nothing more."

Heris asked, "Not even the New Brothen Empire?"

While Februaren said, "Then Ferris Renfrow is true inside the Night, too. Let's adjourn to the tavern. We'll get comfortable. Jarneyn and Svavar can fill you in on your family history."

The ascendant growled. He insisted on leaving Svavar behind.

Februaren had provoked him deliberately, to keep the shattered souls inside from exerting too much influence.

GALLONS OF EXCELLENT AELEN KOFER BEER PASSED THROUGH THE principals while the Bastard learned. He had heard various stories about Arlensul and Gedanke but insisted that never had he suspected a personal connection. He had bought into the Chaldarean worldview. That old stuff was rustic folklore and discredited mythology.

"Never?" Heris asked, incredulous.

"Not once. It's too outrageous. And heretical. And when I was young, every charlatan with any magical talent claimed he was the spawn of Arlensul. The most convincing ended up being murdered by the Church."

"You didn't suspect even after you knew you had all your power?" Heris had made herself lead interrogator. She had not downed as much beer as the males. And she was intrigued by Renfrow.

"Why would I? Did Februaren think he was the Bastard?"

"Well, he is. For sure. You should try working for him."

Februaren wasted no time being amused. "Heris!"

The Bastard said, "I suspected a lot of things. That I might be the get of discredited gods wasn't one of them. Understand?"

The Ninth Unknown swatted Heris on the behind. "Be quiet. We're trying to save a world, here."

"You'd better get ready to do it on crutches."

"Runs in the family," Februaren told the others. "Her brother . . ."

Heris interrupted, "I can save the world by myself, no Bastard necessary. Give me a falcon, a ton of firepowder, and two hundred pounds of silver-plated beads. The damned thing just lies there." She gave Februaren a glare meant to remind him that her brother had no part in this. Especially considering the other hat the Bastard wore.

Februaren nodded, asked, "When did you last visit?"

"Ah. You could be right. It's been a while. But that option is there and doesn't require all this stuff with other worlds, lost gods, and cranky mythical people."

"Watch your tongue, cutie," Iron Eyes gurgled.

"There is something to be said for solving a problem by hitting it with a really big hammer. Still, let's focus on what we're doing here."

The Bastard drained a flagon. Heris said, "Right there is proof that he's a supernatural. I'd be destroyed by what he's put away already. But he isn't showing a sign."

Not quite true, but close.

The Bastard said, "I might be what you claim. I can't figure out how to make it not true. That being the case, let's get down to the mystical business and get it done. I have obligations back in the real world. People get into mischief when I'm not there."

Februaren conceded, "An excellent point. I haven't checked my own folks in much too long. Svavar . . ."

"Last chance to get it right, old man. Not Svavar. Asgrimmur, if you have to, but not Svavar."

The Bastard said, "And I prefer Ferris Renfrow. Bastard has unfortunate connotations."

Februaren glanced at Korban Iron Eyes. The Aelen Kofer shrugged, shoved another tankard into his beard. "I'm just the labor, Son of Man. One of the fetch and carry folk, the Aelen Kofer."

Februaren did not argue. That was what Iron Eyes wanted. A squabble for entertainment. He and his tribe had not yet surpassed that constituent of the northern thing. The Ninth Unknown said, "Asgrimmur, you have to take charge, now. We got the . . . the man you needed. He's here. You know what you did to seal the Instrumentalities up. You know what needs doing to break them out. So now I'm like Iron Eyes. I'm labor, sitting here waiting for instructions."

The ascendant produced a rumbling from deep within, like something from a much bigger monster. Which could have been. In the Realm of the Gods forms and attributes often existed beyond the visible.

Ferris Renfrow and the ascendant put their heads together. Renfrow mostly listened. Februaren and Jarneyn bickered about something that made no sense to Heris. She had been brought up in the Eastern Rite of the Chaldarean faith and had become Brothen Episcopal by directive after her rescue by Grade Drocker. The dormant mythos of the east did not much resemble that of the north. Which, she suspected, must have confused its own pantheon often enough.

She asked, "Is there any reason for me to stick around here, Double Great? We've done our part. We rooted the Bastard out and brought him to the job site."

"We did. And there probably isn't much more you can contribute. But you're walking through living myth. Aren't you even a little curious about the Great Sky Fortress and what's inside?"

"Marginally," she admitted. "But it isn't going anywhere, is it? I can come back when you've gotten it under control."

"Which might be in just a few outside hours."

The ascendant and the Bastard concluded that they needed to go up for a firsthand look at the Great Sky Fortress. They had to see what was possible before they decided what to do. The ascendant admitted, "I haven't been up farther than the foot of the rainbow bridge. I didn't want to disturb anything without experts handy to fix whatever I break."

Iron Eyes said, "Aelen Kofer have crossed the bridge to test it but they haven't gone inside the fortress."

Februaren suggested, "Let's all get some rest. We'll head up there first thing in the morning."

That was a joke. Only Jarneyn got it. He awarded the effort a scowl. It was always high noon in the Realm of the Gods.

HERIS DID NOT LEAVE. SHE CLIMBED THE MOUNTAIN.

That was a great fang rearing up all by itself. The view was spectacular. There was more to the Realm of the Gods than a harbor and an Aelen Kofer town. Or had been, once upon a time.

Spring had come to the nearest forests, sprawling out inland. But color faded with distance, green dwindling quickly to the hue of grass long covered by a rock. Farther still, gray ruled, occasionally tainted by shades of pale brown. The ascendant explained, "There wasn't enough outside power to quicken the whole world."

Cloven Februaren wanted to add something but was breathing too hard. The climb was killing him but he would not let the Aelen Kofer put him into one of their goat carts.

Aelen Kofer goats were the size of middle-world elk.

Heris said, "Maybe it's because the magic is thin but everything that isn't up close looks artificial. Like it's all a clever painting. Like if you headed out that way, you'd run into a wall with the rest of the world painted on it."

Iron Eyes nodded. "You'd be right. In a manner of speaking, though not literally. This world does get less real the farther you get from the Great Sky Fortress. That was always true. It's just more obvious now. If we shut out the middle world entirely, a few thousand years from now nothing would survive but Aelen Kofer artifacts."

Another dwarf interjected, "We build for the ages!"

They reached the rainbow bridge.

Jarneyn grinned broadly enough for it to show through his thicket of beard. "Here's where we sort you out."

The rainbow bridge was just that. Not a huge arc as after a storm, just a curved piece of the arc's top spanning a chasm a hundred feet wide and a thousand deep, its bottom hidden by mist. The bridge was a bright tangle of brilliant hues. And transparent.

The mist below stirred, visible through the rainbow. The faces of the chasm were basalt knife edges all the way down. Some boasted the bones of giants fallen during one or another of that race's periodic assaults on the Old Gods, ages gone.

"That's a reassuring view," Heris said.

"A fine moat," Renfrow observed.

Jarneyn said, "Stick to the middle of the bridge. Have faith in what your feet tell you. Your eyes will lie. And don't think inimical thoughts." He grabbed the lead of the foremost goat cart and headed out onto the tangle of color.

Cloven Februaren gasped, "My pride is going on the shelf for now."

"You going to crawl, Double Great?"

"I'm going to get into a cart."

The Aelen Kofer crossed in single file, enjoying the discomfiture of the humans. Renfrow boarded a goat cart, too, and sealed his eyes.

The ascendant asked, "Heris? Will you take a cart, too?" The implication being that she had best hurry. Opportunities were dwindling fast.

Something in his tone, like a spark of condescension for the weakness of women, irritated Heris. "No. I'll walk." She strode forward, following Jarneyn's advice. Trust feet, not eyes nor instinct. Don't think inimical thoughts, which she could not have done, anyway. Her entire being focused on her feet.

The ascendant crossed behind her, close enough to catch her if she missed a step. She did not know.

Februaren, after dismounting, waited at the end of the bridge. He caught Heris's hand as she stepped onto solid footing. "There you go. Now, take a look at Renfrow." Still in a goat cart and shaking. "Most powerful man in the Grail Empire, maybe. Child of a god. Notice anything?"

"Not really. Unless the point of the lesson is that he's in a cart."

"There's that. And the fact that his eyes are still closed. And his hands are still shaking."

"So. The lesson is?"

"Don't let your pride get you killed. You didn't need to show anybody anything, girl. You needed to get across the gap alive."

"Uhm?"

"Really. You don't need to impress Jarneyn and his cohorts."

Iron Eyes remarked, "She doesn't, but it was still worth seeing, her walking the rainbow bridge. The list of middle-worlders who have managed is quite short."

Heris snapped, "Let's just get on with it!"

Renfrow descended from his cart. "All right. You people have me ninety-eight percent convinced." He glared at the rainbow bridge.

Februaren said, "Let's go inside and arm you with total conviction." He eyed the bridge himself. His voice quavered.

Heris understood, suddenly. He was afraid. The Ninth Unknown was frightened!

Hell! After a studied look around she realized they were all frightened. Even the Aelen Kofer and the ascendant.

"Double Great, you haven't planned this out, have you?"

"Child?"

"The plan, stated so far, is: You go in there and open the way. And
hope these Instrumentalities are going to behave. That they'll be grateful and cooperative."

"That's a little simplistic. . . ."

"But essentially true. Is there anything in the mythology to make
you think they'll respond the way you want? Aren't they all vilely self-
centered?"

"You're being too harsh."

Renfrow interrupted, "She's right. Dwarf. Iron Eyes. Did you have
any plan deeper than what the girl just described? Did you, Asgrimmur?"

The ascendant said, "I intend to make them swear oaths to behave
and help in return for their release. Beforehand."

Uncertain if she ought to resent or appreciate being referred to
as a girl, Heris said, "I grew up in a different part of the world. I
don't know the fine details of northern myth. But isn't one of the prisoners the Trickster? Won't his very nature compel him to mess with
us?"

Iron Eyes grunted unhappily. "You have a point. A definite point."

Heris said, "Then we ought to have the means to compel him. Or
any of the others who don't want to cooperate."

"They're gods, woman. They won't take to having their arms
twisted."

"I don't care what they like."

Iron Eyes shrugged, turned away. "Ascendant. This goes to you,
now. Look inside yourself and find an estimate of . . ."

"Already done. She's right. Though he might risk eternal imprison-
ment, the Trickster will try something. But we'll have the time it takes
for the Old Ones to get a read on the present. The others should accept
terms for freedom."

Heris asked, "Do we need the Trickster to handle Kharoulke? Can
we just leave him in there?"

The ascendant said, "We'll need them all. And, given a chance to
understand the situation, even the Trickster will behave till the grander
threat is gone."

The Ninth Unknown's eyes narrowed to slits. "Heris. Girl. You're
scheming something. I beg you. Not against the gods. Not even pagan
gods."

"I won't do anything stupid. But I want all this to stop. Now. Let's build a point-by-point operation, absent the influence of beer."

They were just steps from the tower gate of the Great Sky Fortress.

Iron Eyes announced, "This used to be a hundred times more glorious. Now it's about as beautiful as a castle in the middle world. Only bigger."

"Focus, dwarf!" Heris snapped. "That's irrelevant. We're here to deal with Instrumentalities."

Renfrow muttered something to Cloven Februaren, who replied, "Would you believe that three years ago she was scared of her own shadow? I blame my grandson. And her brother, a little."

"Double Great, you talk too much. Family matters should stay family matters." Then Heris swore. If Renfrow had not gotten the point from hearing the old man, she had made it plain that he ought to take note.

Renfrow, however, did not seem interested. He was overawed by his ancestral home.

The gates of the Great Sky Fortress were open, as the ascendant had left them. One leaned on a damaged hinge. Korban Iron Eyes said, "We came no farther forward than the end of the bridge. Repairs to the Great Sky Fortress aren't necessary."

The ascendant said, "The place gives me the creeps," as he headed through the gateway.

Inside, the place was dull, gray, lifeless. The power from the middle world had not reached the top of the mountain.

Behind the gate lay a level, open field. To either hand were what had been gardens and orchards. The magic was gone.

The ascendant said, "I don't remember much. First time round I was a prisoner. What I saw was less colorful than this. Last time, I was too crazy to notice much. The Aelen Kofer will have to guide us."

Heris stared off to their left, at the bones of an orchard, recalling that it had been sacred to one of the Old Goddesses. The remains of the apple trees were covered with scale and fungi.

Did that bode ill for the larger mission? The gods had depended on that fruit for their immortality. But it looked like the orchard depended on the gods in turn. "Did all that die since you were here?"

The ascendant responded, "I don't know. Maybe."

"Double Great, this might not be as dangerous as I feared. But let's take every precaution anyway."

The old man looked puzzled.

The bulk of the Great Sky Fortress reared ahead, climbing far higher. There was no color in it. Sunlight fell upon it and died.

Heris continued to quiz the ascendant. Who continued to insist, "I was just a prisoner here. I don't know anything."

She glanced at Iron Eyes. The dwarf lord shrugged, said, "It's been a long time. We weren't invited in much once the place was finished."

So she snapped at the ascendant, "Parts of you lived here. All of you knew enough to turn the place inside out."

The ascendant went rigid. Then he began to swell.

And Heris could not hold her tongue.

"Yeah. Go ahead. Get all huffy and pissed off. Turn into something uglier than you already are. That'll be real productive." She turned her back. "Double Great, this whole expedition is about to turn sour. We're just plain not ready, except maybe for Asgrimmur. He's all set to tremble and shake if the Old Ones won't cooperate."

Though she was not behaving well the old man seemed more pleased than troubled. "You keep making the point. I heard it. Now say something useful."

"We need to make sure there's no way they can get out without them doing what we want. Meaning all the damned doors better be locked before we open the way. Meaning we have to use up all of whatever magic still exists here. Meaning we have to send the Aelen Kofer home so the Old Ones can't bully them into engineering their escape into the middle world. I might even borrow some of Gisors's toys in case we have to enforce an attitude adjustment."

Februaren grinned. "Darling girl! I think we've found our Twelfth Unknown. Clever, that. And I do see your point. Gentlemen. My student has, again, made a powerful argument. We dare leave nothing to chance. We won't be conjuring everynight demons."

Eyeing Heris, Ferris Renfrow observed, "The overconfident sorcerer has become a cliché. There's a reason things become clichés."

Heris showed him a thin smile. Remarkable. She said, "Iron Eyes. We can adjust to this. With Aelen Kofer help. Come talk to me." She headed back toward the rainbow bridge.

Cloven Februaren watched. He glowed with pride. He muttered, "She's coming along just fine." Then, "Boys, how about we explore this dump while we're waiting?"

## 34. Commander of the Righteous: Raiders and Invaders

The move into the Eastern Empire by the Commander of the Righteous was a complete surprise. The immediate reaction to the news, everywhere, was that people up there on the frontier were in error and unduly alarmist.

Hagan Brokke and Clej Sedlakova led mounted infantry in swift dashes to isolate the Krulik and Sneigon works. Carava de Bos and Rivademar Vircondelet got the opportunity to demonstrate that Titus Consent's faith in them was not misplaced. They roamed the wilderness around the establishment, romancing the locals, then the mercenaries protecting the manufactory.

The Commander of the Righteous reached the sprawl of smelters, foundries, timber ricks, and charcoal kilns five days after launching the incursion. There was no resistance.

Carava de Bos brought out the managers. Hecht had spoken to some of the same men after the destruction of their Brothen enterprise. They had pledged to restrict sales of their product to the Patriarchal forces.

Hecht ignored their pleas. "De Bos. Do you have an inventory?"

"I don't have enough fingers, sir."

"What?"

"Sorry, sir. A poor joke. It's incomplete. There's so much firepowder we may not be able to haul it all away. That could be true for the weapons, too. I've found nearly sixty finished pieces already. They'd just started to make deliveries."

"Then we got here in time."

"We did, sir. Shall we start pulling things down?"

"Yes. And don't waste time. Sooner or later someone from the Eastern Empire will decide that something has to be done."

Hecht spent hours touring, inspecting, and being amazed. Krulik and Sneigon had performed prodigies here.

LOCALS HELPED WITH THE DEMOLITION. HECHT LET THEM TAKE WHATever they wanted, excepting only weapons, firepowder, and the belongings of guards who had stood with the raiders. Everyone else would be bare naked but alive when the Righteous left.

Titus Consent chose not to show himself. He needed fashion no more enmities amongst the Devedians. Instead, he headed downriver to Liume to hire coasters. Hecht wanted to get his plunder into Imperial territory as fast as possible. The nearest friendly country lay across the Vieran Sea.

Clej Sedlakova approached Hecht the second afternoon. "What'll we do with all these Deves, boss?"

"You don't think we should just leave them naked in the rain?"

Head shake.

"Why not?"

"They'll just start over. Maybe here, maybe somewhere else. But right now they figure you're gonna kill them so they can't."

"And you think they've got the right idea?"

"Just don't ask me to do it. I'm not that hard."

"Be a serious waste of talent and knowledge. Let's take them with us. We can lock them up in Hochwasser. They can pursue their trade in service to the Empire."

"Make slaves of them?"

"Forced labor. My father would find that delicious."

Sedlakova showed confusion. "Sir?"

"Nothing. Identify the most valuable people. Have Vircondelet take them away as soon as he can."

"Yes, sir." Sedlakova's relief was obvious.

Why had the man not believed that they would be left naked and starving?

Hecht reflected briefly on the legacy left him by Redfearn Bechter. Had there been more to that than just Grade Drocker's journal? If so, he could not figure it out. And Drocker had not been the sort to indulge himself with deep puzzles and riddles.

THE EMPRESS, ACCOMPANIED BY FEWER THAN A HUNDRED COMPANIONS and guards, arrived as Sedlakova went to deal with the prisoners. She did not look comfortable. Hecht thought she was sick and putting on a bold face. He ran to greet her, stifling the protests she was sure to have heard a hundred times, already. She was here. He would have to pretend to be pleased.

Katrin made no effort not to be noticed. "I want Monestacheus Deleanu to know that this was my adventure, not a rogue action by my Commander of the Righteous. God's enemies cannot be allowed to arm themselves with these horrible weapons."

Then greed flashed. Her thinking included the savings this meant for the Imperial treasury.

The presence of the Empress only added to the chaos.

*          *          *

THE COMMANDER OF THE RIGHTEOUS RECEIVED A SUMMONS TO THE
Imperial Presence the evening of the day following her arrival. The lifeguard who brought the message told him the Empress expected him to
dine with her. He should dress accordingly.

That meant a hurried bath and a change to his other clothes. He
traveled light in the field, seldom dressing better than his soldiers.

He grumbled because this might cause a delay in leaving.

He was ready to go, having accomplished his mission.

The Empress had taken the quarters of the directors. Living rough.
She did not mind, though she had only two distraught young women to
manage her needs, leaving much to her lifeguards. Who, Hecht noted,
went about their business grimly.

Protecting this impulsive Empress might be more difficult than had
been protecting the Captain-General. Katrin had no real need to go
dangerous places. She did not have to be difficult. But she did feel compelled to be her father's daughter.

Katrin was not in a good mood. "Is that the best you have to wear?
You look like one of your foot soldiers."

"It is, I fear, Your Grace. I did not anticipate a need for anything
better."

Katrin dropped it. "This went well. What next?"

"Back to Hochwasser and Alten Weinberg. Then steady training
and planning for next year. For now, we should send an advance party
to the Holy Lands. What we know now isn't much more than rumor."

Katrin had established herself behind the bulwark of a large, rude
table. She remained there, unmoving, occasional flickers of discomfort
darkening her features. She was, for sure, not well.

One of her lifeguards brought a chair, placed it opposite her. She
indicated that Hecht should sit.

She began to talk the business of crusade and empire but seemed
vaguely distracted.

The first course arrived, something local that Hecht neither recognized nor appreciated. It was a dough ball filled with shredded meat, unfamiliar spices, and strange chopped vegetables. The Empress observed,
"Their people weren't big on luxuries. Especially food."

Hecht caught a whiff of coffee. It made him sit up straight and
look toward the doorway whence the server lifeguard had entered and
departed.

Katrin managed a smile. "Some things are too marvelous to give
up, however much I don't mind living rough."

The coffee arrived with what turned out to be both the main and final course, a roast slab of unidentifiable beast the attending lifeguard divided according to status rather than capacity.

Hecht tied in, ate slowly, talked planning, and hoped the disappearance of the lifeguards and the absence of courtiers did not foreshadow another difficult situation.

Katrin did get personal. And became personable. A little food, a little wine, doing wonders for her mood.

She quizzed him about his past and plans, about Anna Mozilla, the children, what he thought of Helspeth as a person and his feelings toward her. She knew an uncomfortable lot about Piper Hecht. As always, she came to the question that seemed to consume her: Had he and Helspeth yet been intimate?

"This is difficult, Your Grace. The answer is, no. We haven't. Nor will ever be. Though I might find it difficult to keep my place if she insisted." He might want to sell a dangerous lie later.

"Helspeth wouldn't insist. Helspeth is dutiful to the needs of the Empire. But a well-timed nudge could tip her over with her heels in the air."

Katrin was tormenting him. Trying to provoke him. Being jealous of Helspeth. Again. "I'm not comfortable discussing these things, Your Grace. My role is to help you liberate the Holy Lands."

"As your Empress we're free to interpret your duties as it please us, Commander of the Righteous." Using an Imperial "we" for the first time in his experience. With a tremor in her voice.

Hecht was frightened now. He had a notion where Katrin was headed. He did not want to be there when she arrived. But he saw no way to escape.

Katrin said, "Have you heard rumors about my private court, Commander?" Voice more tremulous.

He could not deny that. "I have, Your Grace. Canards put about by your enemies, surely. All rulers suffer such things."

"But you're afraid there might be some truth there, aren't you?"

"It isn't my place to be concerned. My mission . . ."

"Those rumors might be true, Commander. I've become infatuated with human coupling. I've made some of my ladies mate with their lovers while I watch. Some find that exciting."

Most, he suspected, had been humiliated. Their humiliation would be what Katrin fed the darkness within her.

"You don't think well of me. For that. I don't think well of myself. I did stop watching those who objected. I just wanted to satisfy my curiosity, anyway."

Which left Hecht puzzled. And disinclined to believe her.

"Of course. I'm no virgin. Why should I be curious? Because Jaime is my only experience. Jaime was never the kind of lover my ladies whispered and giggled about when they thought I wasn't listening. Jaime was a brute. He did nothing to make me want to be there while he spilled his seed. My agents found other women he used during his stay in Alten Weinberg. His ill usage wasn't reserved for a disdained spouse."

"Your Grace, I beg you. This isn't something I need to hear."

"But you do. Jaime of Castauriga is, was, *the* watershed event of your Empress's life. Jaime of Castauriga created what you see: A woman sick in body and soul. A woman who can't fulfill her foremost duty to the Empire. I can't produce an heir."

Hecht tried to be reassuring. He failed.

"Commander, I know there are diplomats out west trying to lure Jaime back. For my sake. For the sake of the succession. For the sake of their own ambitions. It doesn't matter. He won't come. The conflict between the Jaime I imagined and the Jaime of reality will shape me for as long as I go on. My problem at the moment is my terror, knowing I may not go on long."

Hecht grew uncomfortable in a different way.

Had he misjudged? Was she just venting secret torments? Ridding her soul of things she could not share with anyone else because anyone else would use her revelations as political tools?

"Commander, I'm dying. Slowly, but definitely getting there."

"Uh . . ."

"It isn't just the poison. Though I'll never fully recover from that."

"But . . ."

"The second pregnancy. It did something to me. Sometimes I'm deathly sick. The physicians and healing brothers can't figure it out. Can't make it go away. I piss purple and turn blue. It brings on episodes of madness. I don't know that while they're happening. People tell me, afterward. When it's sometimes too late to undo the damage."

Hecht was becoming more comfortable in his discomfort. This was, indeed, just a guided tour of Katrin's inner hell. "Not to insult you in any way. Have the healers considered exorcism?"

"I'm sure they've discussed it. They haven't had the nerve to suggest it. Should I raise the matter myself?"

"That might ease their fears."

"When we get back to Alten Weinberg, then. Meantime, I have a new assignment for you." Katrin left her seat, moved to a shadowy corner where she fiddled briefly with a wall hanging. Her hands were shaking. "Help me with this, please."

"All right." He shoved his chair back, rose, went.

Katrin's gown collapsed around her. There was nothing but pallid, lean woman underneath. She stepped out, spread the gown around, dropped to hands and knees atop it, lowered her forehead onto her folded hands.

"Your Grace!"

"You know what you have to do."

"I can't! It's not . . ."

"Then I'll have a new Commander of the Righteous in the morning."

Her tone left no doubt she meant what she said.

Even so, he had to debate himself before he began, reluctantly, to unbuckle.

This could not be good. In no way. It might cost him big, and forever. But he could not give up being Commander of the Righteous to avoid it.

His choices might have nothing to do with his intellect if his flesh refused to perform.

"Your Grace, this isn't the best way."

"This is the way I know. This is the way Jaime taught me. He wasn't interested in any other way. Sometimes he missed the proper channel. He didn't care."

And still the man obsessed her.

Hecht could think of no escape save resignation.

His body was more easily swayed than his mind. He had been away from Anna for a long time.

Hecht executed his Empress's demands, amazed to find her ready and further amazed that she responded once she understood that he would not be brutal.

Katrin was made different than Anna, in there. He did not have enough experience of women to understand what that might mean. If anything.

Self-loathing, dread of potential repercussions, even concern that he might disappoint the Empress, made him last longer than ever he had with Anna.

Katrin became deeply embarrassed after it was over, Hecht suspected more because of her behavior during than because of what she had done to make it happen. He had no idea what to say except to express an unromantic concern. "What happens if that quickens?"

"Another of my husband's blessings, Commander. I told you. My last pregnancy left me barren."

"I didn't know." That was explosive news.

"No one should. I shouldn't have told you. That information could be dangerous to the Empire, internally and externally. Don't mention it to anyone. Especially not those idiots who are always scheming in my sister's name."

"Of course not." She had just pulled him in further. He was deeply invested in her. He needed her reign to go on. Those idiots who schemed in Helspeth's name did not love him. Verbally, he admitted what he had confessed with his flesh. "My post is too important to me to risk on gossip."

Possibly not the best thing to say despite the absence of romance in the situation. But Katrin was no more experienced than he.

"Thank you, Commander." She finished shrugging into her gown. "For everything. Are you all right? You look pale."

"My wound. I didn't feel it while . . . It's reminding me that I'm not supposed to indulge in strenuous activity. Even now."

Flicker of a smile. Self-congratulation? "You'd best get back to less arduous labors, then. Before someone imagines a reason for a new wicked rumor."

"As you command, so shall it be, Your Grace."

"Of course." To herself more than him, she said, "A pity I couldn't be Helspeth." Louder, "Commander, this didn't happen. I had an idea about attacking Hovacol on the way home. I sent the others away because I'm convinced that one of my lifeguards is spying for King Stain. I'm quite mad on that point. In fact, I'm starting to see spies everywhere. It took you all this time to talk me out of the invasion." She paused, then added, "I really have been thinking about Hovacol. I talked it over with my people."

"Smart thinking, Your Grace. But, don't. It's a side issue."

Just how smart? Was she manipulating everyone? Had the past half hour been the product of a longtime scheme? If so, how often were her sicknesses and mad spells tactical?

On reflection, he concluded that was not the Ege style. Both daughters wanted people thinking they were more fierce, straightforward, and stubborn than their father had been.

VIRCONDELET WAS WAITING WHEN HECHT RETURNED TO THEIR makeshift headquarters in the former employee barracks. "Wow! You don't look so good, boss. What happened?"

"The wound is barking back. I got excited and tore something. What're you still doing here?"

"They'll move out at dawn. With de Bos doing the moving, if that's all right. He's got something going back in the berg. I don't. How did you tear it?"

"I lost my temper. I'm starting to think I outsmarted myself, signing on with this madwoman."

"Sir! That kind of talk . . ."

"I'll be more circumspect. I promise." He settled into a rickety chair, gingerly. There would be no sudden moves for a while.

Others from the duty section began to gather.

Again, Vircondelet asked, "What happened?"

"She was all about Hovacol and King Stain again. She wanted to attack them on the way home. And wouldn't listen when I told her we don't have the numbers and we'll be too busy hauling falcons and firepowder and trying to avoid Eastern troops to go haring off on an adventure she dreamed up because some pipsqueak local tyrant doesn't share her religious prejudices."

Several men groaned. Vircondelet asked, "Do we have to? We'll need to start planning right now."

"No. I talked her out of it. For now. But she won't forget it. I just need to keep her eyes on the Holy Lands. By the way. Don't mention this to her people. She's sure some of them are spies for King Stain."

Hecht saw nothing to suggest suspicion of bad behavior on his part.

A clerk asked, "What is it with her? All this holy war stuff."

"She isn't well. And she thinks she's sicker than she really is. She doesn't want to be another Lothar."

"She wants to make a splash that will buy her passage into Paradise?"

"So it would seem, Mr. Tharep. With luck, stubbornness, and a lot of yelling, I weaseled us out. Now, if we have to travel tomorrow I'd better go lay me down and let this wound recover some."

Nervous discomfort. Some of these men could not get past their commander having been slain, then returned to life. No argument could quiet their conviction that the Night had intervened. Not that it was, ipso facto, always bad to be hallowed by the Night.

They were unaware that the Night already knew him as the Godslayer.

HECHT LAY BACK ON HIS COMMANDEERED COT AND FAILED TO FALL asleep. Katrin would not get out of his thoughts. Inevitably, when he replayed specifics, she morphed into the Princess Apparent.

Try and try again, he could not get events as they had occurred to fit his prior expectations—least of all that Katrin Ege would take such pleasure from the encounter. Maybe the exercise of absolute power had moved her.

His flesh began to respond to his recollections.

"WELL. LIVING PROOF THAT IT'S A GOOD IDEA TO KNOCK BEFORE EN-tering."

Hecht started up, in a panic of embarrassment. He dragged his blanket across his lap. "Heris? What the hell are you doing here?"

"Sweet welcome. I didn't come to see that. I'll tell Anna you miss her."

"Heris, I . . . I . . ."

"Forget it. I'm embarrassed, too. I had to remind myself that you're my brother."

Which left him just that much more unsettled. "What do you want? Why are you here? What's happened? You seem different."

"I am different. Keep your voice down. Your mother hens will be all over us. Let me talk." She plunged into everything she had seen since last they had visited. Hecht did not interrupt. Heris had a knack for re-porting essentials.

"So you're all set to release those devils."

"All set to try. But not real sure we can pull it off. Which is why I dropped by. I need some weapons," she explained.

"Damn! I ought to give you to Rhuk and Prosek. They could use somebody who understands firepowder as well as you do."

"Even a girl?"

"That could be a problem. Drago is a total cocksman. Anyway, your timing is good. There's about every type firepowder weapon ever imag-ined here. Tell me what you need. I'll leave it behind."

"A lot of firepowder. Several light falcons. And some of those hand weapons you don't let your men use anymore. Why is that, anyway?"

"I do let them. Some of them. But giving them to everybody— besides being expensive—is counterproductive. Originally, the idea was for every man to have a weapon he could use if he came up against some Night thing. But they won't hold back. If it's dark and they're scared they go straight to the smoke and bang. They end up hurting each other."

"God, Piper. You sound like Grandfather giving a lesson on the Construct."

"Sorry. Any news from home? Have you been?"

"Not for a while. Last time I was there, Anna was all upset because the girls were spending so much time with Grandfather. He has them learning the Construct. And Pella was being a handful. Anna has to remind him about the incident with the rotting demons all the time. He should be out here with you."

"He should find something better to do with his life."

"Anna would agree. But, what? Think about his background. The best he can do is have your light shine on him. I'll let you get back to what you were doing. I'll pop over to the town house and steal a night in a real bed. Don't forget to leave me my toys."

"I won't. How will you shift them?"

"Dwarf power. I've got troops of dwarves I can call in. All mythical and imaginary, of course. Me being a true-believing Episcopal Chaldarean."

Heris turned sideways, leaving Hecht unable to ask further questions.

As with everything in life, departure took longer and was more aggravating than had seemed likely beforehand. Everyone wanted to know why Hecht was leaving a cache of firepowder and falcons in the barracks. He refused to explain.

While questions were asked and going unanswered a courier arrived. He bestrode a badly blown bay gelding. He was as bad off as his mount. He belonged to the party that had gone down to Liume. Hecht and Vircondelet helped him dismount. He had just enough will left to hand over a folded note. Vircondelet helped him lie down, which was all he wanted now.

"Vircondelet. I have something to do. You're in charge till I get back. Keep things moving. And be ready for trouble."

"The locals say there're no . . ."

"Ready for trouble, Mr. Vircondelet. It's stalking us now. Don't let it surprise us."

"Yes, sir. As you command." Clearly puzzled.

Hecht strode through the ruins of the manufactory, bent by his burden. He found Katrin's lifeguards in a frenzy of activity. They had no specific invitation, and seemed determined not to coordinate, but were not eager to be left when the Righteous departed.

Hecht cornered Captain Ephrian. "I need to see her. Now. *Bad* news." Rather than argue, he presented the note.

"Oh, shit. Holy fucking shit. You think it's true?" In a flat, stunned monotone.

"I can't imagine my men sending the news the way they did if it was just a rumor."

"I'll take you to her, she likes it or not, because I don't want to be the one who tells her."

"Coward."

"Damned straight."

"She'll take it hard."

Ephrian growled, "She'll go way beyond the bug-fuck she already is. I'm willing to bet."

Hecht would not have stated it that colorfully but he agreed. Katrin would do something dramatic.

She was not pleased to see him. She tried to avoid talking to him.

"Your Grace. I've just received terrible news from my intelligence chief. You need to know. Right now."

"Speak. And it had better be interesting, Commander."

"There was a battle near Khaurene, in the Connec. Connectens and Direcians fighting King Regard of Arnhand, who invaded the Connec at the bidding of the Patriarch." Underscoring the obvious.

Katrin went from imperious and impatient to pale, bowed, and bleak. "Tell me."

"King Peter of Navaya and King Jaime of Castauriga were slain in the fighting." He did not try to soften the reality. He wanted to get in quick, deliver the blow, get out, and let Katrin bring her Ege iron to bear.

Katrin barked, "Don't toy with me, Commander! I made you. I can unmake you in an instant."

"You can, Your Grace. I merely report. How you respond is up to you. But the fact remains, there's been a disaster in the Connec."

The Empress fixed him with a searing gaze. She did not speak. Her attendants began to shuffle and mutter, worried. Hecht met her eye steadily. He did not like what he saw, a huge internal collision between personalities, each demanding control of the mind's interface with the exterior world. A momentarily dominant personality asked, "You hired ships to move the material you captured?"

"I did. With what success isn't certain. The courier who brought this news knows. But he collapsed before he could report."

"There'll be ships, then. We'll cross the Vieran Sea."

"What? Your Grace? What?"

"Serenity's mad greed has made a widow of me. Now I'll make him long for the quiet, gentle affections of my father before I kill him."

Hecht gulped air. He gurgled. He trembled. This was . . . He could not find an adequate metaphor. He looked to the heavens. For a sign? In an appeal for divine intervention? The heavens did not speak. He saw nothing but a low overcast. Rain was coming.

Katrin said, "Forget the Holy Lands, Commander. We won't be

going till my barons have had their fill of what they've wanted since I took the ermine." In a fainter voice, to herself, she said, "I can't believe he betrayed me."

Hecht concealed mild elation. He would not have to make war on his religious kin. For now.

Then he thought about Pinkus Ghort and other friends still active in the Patriarchal forces.

"That's your decision, Your Grace?"

"Yes. Irrevocable. Serenity must be punished."

"Then I'll leave you. I have fresh work to do."

THE COMMANDER OF THE RIGHTEOUS WATCHED UNHAPPY SOLDIERS board ships, none of those large. The horses were less pleased than the men.

Titus Consent arrived, gasping. "It's really real, what I hear?"

"Yes. And completely off the cuff. Great job pulling the transport together."

"Not really. I had only to say the Empress wanted to hire ships. There isn't much work for these sailors, these days. That's every boat and coaster capable of being bailed fast enough to not sink."

"We'll use them all. I'm taking four hundred men and the captured falcons. Messengers are headed for Glimpsz with orders for men there to get down to the coast so they can be brought along next."

"You intend to invade Firaldia with four hundred men?"

"They won't be expecting me. And Katrin will call out the garrisons of the Imperial cities."

Consent grumbled, "I don't believe it."

"It's a challenge."

"Sounds like a suicide run."

"The first Praman army to invade Direcia numbered seven hundred."

"It isn't so much the numbers. What gets me is, we're getting distracted from our proclaimed task again."

Hecht frowned. "Explain."

"Once upon a time we were hired to help tame the Connec. You were, actually. I didn't know you then. You ended up conquering Calzir instead. Then, a while later, you were back in the business of taming the Connec and doing a damned good job, thanks to my help. You had the eastern half in the bag. Then we get a new Patriarch and we're off to pound on some pagans in Artecipea instead. So. Now we're supposed to be getting ready for the biggest damned crusade ever to head into the

Holy Lands. And we're getting on with it really good. But. So. All of a sudden, here we go again, getting aimed in a different direction."

"You could be on to something. Makes you wonder about divine intervention, doesn't it?"

"Divine distraction, maybe." Titus counted ships. "If I was inclined to worry, I'd wonder why God is suddenly pissed off at Serenity."

"Maybe the Maysaleans are right. Maybe their Good God is stepping in."

Titus was appalled. Titus took his faith seriously though he was no fanatic concerning points of dogma.

No one told the ship owners and sailors where they were headed till after the troops and cargo were loaded. The soldiers themselves were not informed till it was too late for news of their coming to beat them across the Vieran Sea. Thirty-two vessels put out with the feeble evening tide.

The Mother Sea was landlocked. Tides there were minimal. Only in very narrow places were they of much import.

There was vast confusion. The sailors had no experience sailing in convoy. Despite that, collisions were few and did no harm. Only one small vessel was lost. It went hard aground on an unexpected rock near the Firaldian coast. Crew and passengers survived. The weather turned no worse. The wind blew just hard enough to carry the fleet across quickly enough to let the landing start at sunrise, after forty-two hours at sea.

The landing took place on a beach of Vis Corcula, one of the least of the Patriarchal States, though a principality. It was not strong. Prince Onofrio was not fanatically devoted to the Patriarchal cause. He should do little more than go through the motions.

Ashore, Hecht polled his troops, looking for someone who knew the territory.

He settled for a peasant couple whose curiosity brought them too near and whose cupidity overruled their patriotism.

By midmorning a comfortable villa with a sea view had become Imperial headquarters. By noon the Empress herself had taken up residence, her presence undesired but her behavior beyond reproach. She did not interfere. Having declared the strategic objective she was content to let her Commander deal with operational details. For the moment.

Piper Hecht pushed on with two hundred men and fourteen falcons, toward Fuerza. His lieutenants took smaller bands to show the colors in the principality's villages.

The Imperial advent was completely sudden and unexpected. There was little resistance. One firepowder barrage discharged outside Fuerza convinced the would-be diehards.

PRINCE ONOFRIO TAGLIO DI FUERZA BENT THE KNEE TO THE GRAIL Empress at the Fertelli villa thirty-two hours after her arrival.

Katrin was not harsh. Hecht had convinced her to be gentle with those who cooperated. His reputation, from the Connec, would give thought to those inclined to resist. Terms were: Onofrio had to provide some foodstuffs, some drayage, and fifty armed men who would not be required to fight the Patriarch. Onofrio had no trouble agreeing. In return there would be no plunder, no rapine, no murder—so long as the Prince and people of Vis Corcula did not hinder or harm the Imperials.

Heris popped in as Hecht was about to lie down his second night in Firaldia, in a villa near Vis Corcula's western frontier, beside a road that crossed the Monte Sismonda to the Old Empire's central military road, which, in time, reached Brothe.

He could reach the Mother City in three days if he wanted to push it hard. If nobody got in his way.

He had numbers enough to cause panic but not nearly enough to attack a sizable city, even taking it by surprise. Nor would Bronte Doneto allow himself to be captured. And that would be the only way to end this quickly.

Heris observed, "You should be too tired to be that jumpy, Piper."

"I'm tired, all right. Of . . ."

"Don't waste time. I've got to go lead my dwarves to the promised land pretty soon. Here's what you need to know. The news about Katrin being pissed off and after Serenity's guts hit Brothe a couple hours ago. About one hour before word that you're here in Vis Corcula, in a bad mood, and headed that way."

"Word gets around fast when the news is bad."

"You don't know the half. The city is in a panic. The Collegium worst of all. You really got the hoodoo on some of those old men. I don't get that."

"Blame Principaté Delari."

"Grandfather?"

"He's no adventurer. But he knows how to lay down a lie and make it smell like gospel. I'd bet he started some rumors."

"Could be."

"He doesn't like Bronte Doneto."

"Serenity has been screwing with him since you signed on with the Empire."

Hecht sighed. "Life is strange. And keeps getting stranger."

"Preaching to the choir, little brother. Ten years ago I was a slave, hauling water and lying down for an asshole . . . No! That's all gone. Though I did birth a couple of children I wonder about sometimes."

Hecht grunted. This was news. "Do the old men know?"

"I never mentioned it. I'm not sure why I'm telling you."

"Did Drocker know?"

"If he did, grandchildren didn't interest him."

"Same with me. Though I didn't know who or what he was till you and Delari told me."

"You have children, too?"

"Two daughters, last seen in al-Qarn. By now they may have starved, died of a pox, or been murdered by the regime. I was promised that they'd be cared for. I have no way to know what actually became of them. Now I've made Anna, Pella, Lila, and Vali into a new family. Serenity better let them be!"

"Calm down, Piper. Grandfather will look out for them. And Serenity knows they're protected."

"I'm calm. How pressed are you?"

"Depends on what you want."

"It would be useful to know what the rest of the Righteous are doing and how soon I can expect them. It would be nice to know how the Patriarch hopes to keep me from making the Empress happy. And I'd love to know how this is playing in Alten Weinberg and Hochwasser."

"You don't want much, do you?"

"If I'm going to wish I might as well wish for the stars. Information is addictive."

"Sure. I'll do what I can. But, like I said, I've got a herd of dwarves to keep in line and a clutch of gods to bully."

"All . . ."

Someone pounded on the door to the room, tried to get in. Hecht had barred it.

Heris stepped into a dark corner, turned but did not leave. She could vanish without notice if necessary. Hecht opened the door. It had begun to creak as people shoved against it. He found Rivademar Vircondelet and several self-appointed lifeguards about to use a bench for a battering ram. "What in God's Name are you doing?"

"Kinzer heard voices. We thought you might be in trouble."

"Did I call for help?"

"No, sir. But . . ."

"Go away. And don't do this again."

The men behind Vircondelet were trying to see inside. They looked less sheepish than they ought.

Hecht shut the door.

"They're worried about you."

"They're more worried about themselves. They watch me close because they think that I died and came back to life."

"You did. But you weren't possessed by the Night. We kept all that at bay."

"I did? I died?"

"I thought you understood that."

"I . . . No. I thought . . ."

"Don't you go getting silly, too. There's nothing different about you. A lot of people have been gone much longer than you were. They came back untouched. Will you still be here tomorrow night?"

"Probably. I don't have the manpower to take this much farther. An unexpected diplomatic success could change things, though."

"See you tomorrow night, then."

AN UNEXPECTED DIPLOMATIC SUCCESS OCCURRED. THE HIGH ROADS of Firaldia swarmed with messengers, Imperial and Patriarchal. On the Imperial side the news they carried was good. The nearest Imperial cities quickly affirmed their support for the Empress. Several nearby Patriarchal dependents volunteered to stay out of the squabble. "Promises written on air," Titus Consent observed. "They'll turn on us if Serenity has any success."

"Of course. That's Firaldian politics. They'll never change."

"Unless a strongman comes along and ends it."

"Someone strong and long-lived. Johannes might have managed if he'd survived al-Khazen."

Consent shrugged. "He did, we'd be on the other side, here."

"No doubt."

"I'm thinking Johannes's offspring might have what it takes, too. If it interests them. If they have the drive."

"Meaning?"

"Katrin and Helspeth are both capable of making the tough decisions. And their people seem accustomed to the idea of a female monarch, now. But the Empress doesn't seem to have the commitment."

"Uhm?"

"She's changeable, boss. We could be knocking on the gates of Brothe and she'd get distracted by some ephemeral ambition somewhere else."

"She'll be constant till she's shoved Serenity against a wall and made him explain why her special guy is no longer among the living."

"You're enjoying the hell out of this, aren't you?"

"Titus?"

"You've changed since the Empress changed her mind about Serenity and the Church. You're happy about it. Even though we're likely to end up having to face friends we campaigned with before."

"I hope it doesn't come to that, Titus. I hope we can give Katrin what she wants before Pinkus can disengage in the Connec." Word from that direction had the Captain-General facing serious difficulties. Serenity had few friends in the eastern Connec. Count Raymone Garete and his Countess had harvested the crop.

Hecht did think that Serenity would scream like a scared little girl when he understood what was headed his way. He was very much the product of his past.

His Plemenzan captivity had not been harsh. It was just time taken out of his life. But torments he had suffered earlier in the Connec remained tattooed on his soul. Never again would he allow himself to be at the mercy of another.

Failure, defeat, surrender, captivity, none were acceptable options. Unless God deserted him completely.

Hecht desperately hoped to see Heris again. The more he eyed the chances of success the more worried he became for Anna and the children.

There was an ancient saying: "Children are hostages to Fortune." And, unhappily, any other asshole who could lay hands on.

A GRIMLY WEARY HERIS TURNED SIDEWAYS, INTO BEING, SECONDS after Kait Rhuk and Drago Prosek left Hecht. She grumbled, "I know. I can sleep after I'm dead."

"You can't tell if there's somebody here before you do that, can you?"

"Sometimes. Mostly not. I can halfway arrive and keep from being seen if I'm rested enough."

"You missed popping in between Rhuk and Prosek by five seconds."

"That would've been embarrassing."

"You think?"

"Worried about them finding out?"

"Absolutely. About anyone finding out. We have a huge advantage as long as nobody knows. We lose that fast as soon as they do."

"Get one of those folding screen things to drag around with you. Wherever you set up shop, put it in a corner so I can pop in behind it. That way I can get away again without anyone seeing if you've got somebody with you."

"That might work. What do you have for me?"

"You don't have a social life, do you?"

"What?"

"I know. All business, all the time. Saves having to deal with stuff. Story of my life, too."

Hecht was confused. This was not the Heris of his experience. "You're hanging around with the Ninth Unknown too much. You're turning into another him."

"I am a bad girl, little brother."

Heris proceeded with a long report, some of it not very interesting. Since her last visit she had been a fly on the wall in a dozen venues, including Krois in Brothe, Pinkus Ghort's camp a dozen miles above Antieux, Alten Weinberg's Winterhall, Hochwasser, and even briefly in Salpeno, where Anna of Menand was ecstatic about the deaths of kings at Khaurene. There was panic in Krois and elation in Alten Weinberg because Katrin had come back to her father's path. There was crippling indecision in Ghort's camp. Pinkus himself was willing to carry out orders but he was up to his ears in legates, envoys, Society angels, and other pests, all of whom insisted on telling him what to do.

Though the news about the Empress was fresh, levies had been assembling at Hochwasser for weeks, according to annual custom. Those forces were in motion already, according to a marching plan laid down in the reign of Johannes II. That plan was no secret. Once through the Jagos the Imperial main force would advance down the West Way toward Brothe. Resistance would arise mainly at river crossings.

Thus it had been with invasions and defenses for two thousand years. Thus it would go. Geography dictated it.

"Nothing remarkable there," Hecht said. "And though they'll make a lot of racket, they won't move with any vigor. How close to Serenity did you get? What's his plan?"

"Close enough to sit on his lap. If I wanted. Close enough to blow hot air down the back of his neck. Close enough to convince him that his favorite wing of Krois is haunted by Ostarega the Malicious and Ostarega doesn't love him."

"Ostarega the Malicious?"

"One of the early Bad Patriarchs. His reign name was Clement. The Second. He was awful. God had the Collegium bend him over a wine cask and hurry him on to Paradise by impaling him with a white-hot iron rod. So there would be no blood spilled."

"Strangling or drowning would've worked."

"That wouldn't have made a strong enough point. It was personal."

"I guess so. Serenity's plans?"

"The reason I keep him jumping. The haunted wing of Krois is where the good quiet rooms are."

Hecht controlled his impatience. If he barked too loud Heris might just go away. So he said, "Good thinking."

Heris did a little jig, absurd for a woman of middle years. "I'm so smart!" Like a child. Grinning. "All right. I'm done messing with you. He means to pull together every man he can and come straight at you, through the Shades." The Shades being the nearest stretch of the Monte Sismonda, the mountain range forming the spine of the Central Firaldian peninsula. Why the local stretch was called the Shades had been forgotten. It had been the Shades when the Old Empire arrived.

It would have something to do with the Night.

"That wouldn't be smart. If I don't go meet him."

"He means to swarm you before you pull together enough Righteous and Imperials to turn into a real nuisance."

Which did not make Hecht nervous enough to suit her. "He isn't playing around, Piper. He'll order the prisons turned out. He's already summoned the militias. He's posted a call for mercenaries. He could have twenty thousand men here by the end of the week."

"Twenty? *Thousand?*"

"That's what he thinks. There're a lot of hungry people in Brothe. And he's offering good money."

"Twenty thousand." That was a kick in the gut. Even if Serenity's plan was fifty percent wishful thinking. "A rabble, though."

"Sure."

But there would be men he had trained among them, giving them backbone.

"Are you all right, Piper?"

"Just in shock. I didn't count on Bronte Doneto being another Tormond IV but I did think he would dither awhile."

"He's thought about this, Piper. Knowing he might have to butt heads with you someday. He knows you won't let him have time to waste. So he's done what he has to do."

Hecht began to pace, muttering, "Twenty thousand."

"Think about the others instead of Serenity."

"The other what?"

"The other men involved. The ones Serenity has to rely on. Who aren't him. Are they eager for a fight? Will they drag their feet, hoping you'll go away? Because they're afraid of you? Because they'd have to leave Brothe filled with uncontrolled enemies if they came out to meet you?"

Hecht muttered, "Twenty thousand men."

"Will you get over that?"

His mind did slide past it. He began to think like a general. A general faced with a hopeless task.

First, he had to protect the Empress.

Then he had to protect and salvage the Righteous. And the firepowder weapons. Having provoked the Eastern Emperor so thoroughly he could not let that prize get away.

And he had to ensure the safety of such Firaldian allies as had begun to accumulate. That was only right.

"I wish I could talk this over with the old men."

"No help for you with Double Great Grandpa. He's inside the Realm of the Gods. But Grandfather is a possibility."

"I don't see how . . ."

"I can skip there. And take you with me."

"You can what?"

"Come here."

Hecht did as she said, still distracted by the possibility of having to face an overwhelming Patriarchal force within a few days.

Heris seized him in a fierce grip, twisted, wrenched him violently.

Darkness followed.

DARKNESS SWARMED WITH DREAMS THAT WERE MOSTLY NIGHTMARES. Terror pounded Hecht. He was sure he would be trapped there forever.

"DAMNED GOOD THING YOU HAD SOME GET-ACQUAINTED TIME WITH the Construct," Principaté Delari said. "That gave Heris the leverage she needed to drag you all the way through."

Pale, exhausted, Heris still shook, minutes after arriving. There had been unexpected problems.

Also shaking, Hecht grumbled, "Wonderful. Marvelous. What the hell happened?"

"Calm yourself. I don't know. I don't use the Construct that way. Heris hasn't had this problem before."

Heris said, "Tell me what you saw, Piper. That might give me a handle."

"Crawling chaos. Ghosts. Nothing that made sense. Nightmares and monster games. What should I have seen?"

"Double Great and I see the world without much color, other than reds and darkness. With everything moving a thousandth the speed of normal when we're traveling." She explained that her journeys took her through a thousand shades of red, few of them dark. She went where she wanted by thinking about it hard. Now that she was experienced, she could go places she had not visited before.

Hecht was frightened but also amazed because here he was in the quiet room of Muniero Delari's town house, only minutes after Heris had taken hold of him a hundred miles away.

ANNA AND THE CHILDREN SOON LEARNED OF HECHT'S PRESENCE. Principaté Delari had insisted that they move to the town house to shelter from Bronte Doneto's malice.

Hecht thanked Delari for that, enthusiastically. Then he thanked Anna for swallowing her pride and letting the Principaté put the family where they would be harder to reach. "Lover, Doneto is a bad man." He eyed Delari, wondering where the feud between the Principaté and the Patriarch stood.

Anna said, "Don't pat my back before you hear the whole story."

"So you did try to be stubborn, eh?"

"Absolutely. Nobody was going to bully me and my kids. Not even the Infallible Voice of God."

"But?" Hecht was having trouble keeping his hands off her—though he did keep it clean enough for the presence of family.

"That new man at the Castella, Addam Hauf? He came to the house. He said Serenity wants to take us hostage. That was before the news about you landing in Vis Corcula."

Delari said, "The Brotherhood of War has no affection for Serenity. Their obsession is the liberation of the Holy Lands. Serenity is interested only in his vendetta with the Connec."

Hecht made a snorting noise.

Delari continued, "Serenity's personal crusade has not gone well."

Hecht then first heard about the death of King Regard. "Does that mean Pinkus Ghort is out there on his own?"

"No. There are several smaller Arnhander forces roving around, commanded by Society priests. Complete incompetents. However fierce she is, Anne of Menand can't manage the intervention herself. With Regard gone she'll probably abandon Ghort and Serenity.

"She'll be scrambling to hang on to power till Anselin hears the news and comes home. Which he might not do. He has no love for Anne and might make her regret it if he does come home. He has an independent streak. He might not suffer the abuses that Regard did."

Anna and the children grew more sour while Delari talked. They cared nothing about any of that. Hecht was their interest.

As they were his, for the moment.

He was startled by how much emotion seeing them brought up-welling. And how much guilt he felt on recalling his involuntary inter-lude with the Empress.

In truth, he doubted that Anna believed he would remain celibate while away. He was a man. Indulgence was expected.

Delari gestured at Heris, who said, "We'll let you enjoy one an-other for a while, now. Piper. Remember. I need to get you back in time for your morning staff meeting."

That did not improve Hecht's temper. "Early enough for me to have time to get myself together?"

"Good idea."

Heris and Delari began arguing softly. Hecht paid no attention. He gathered his family round, suddenly fearful that this might be his last chance to enjoy them all together.

Anna wanted them to be alone.

But the children were determined to get a share of him, too. Hecht was touched that the bonds of family included Lila, now.

He led everyone to a lounging room where the furnishings were low divans and large pillows. Delari called it his orgy room, though nothing of the sort had happened there in recent centuries. It was a comfortable place to relax with loved ones.

Hecht took the opportunity to catch up on all their lives, devouring the trivia. What seemed so dull when it was there every minute, all around, was a treasure from afar.

Pella claimed he was going crazy. That he had to get out. And not to any stupid studies at Gray Friars or down under the Chiaro Palace. And, damnit! Yes! He did know that actually doing what he wanted might well land him in the clutches of somebody who would use him to gain leverage on the Commander of the Righteous. It was not fair! He never asked for this!

"That's life, boy. If you're lucky, you'll have problems for another hundred years."

Lila was still too shy to chatter about herself. Vali, however, had lost all her reticence. Hard to believe that she was the quiet little girl who had attached herself to him and Pinkus in Sonsa.

She said, "Pella is right. Gray Friars is really, really boring. Espe-cially if you're a girl. But afterward we get to go to school with Grandpa Delari. That's fun."

"Doing what?"

"Learning the Construct. I'm not so good with it and Pella doesn't pay attention but Lila is like a genius. She already knows how to . . ."

Hecht finally cut her off. Despite having no private time with Anna he was pleased to have these rare hours with his unexpected family.

"TIME TO HEAD OUT, LITTLE BROTHER." HERIS SHOOK HECHT'S SHOULder again.

He had fallen asleep with Anna and the children piled around him. Only Anna and Vali stirred as he extricated himself.

Heris whispered, "It'll be dawn in an hour. We need to go."

He whispered, "I'm not sure I can take that again."

"No option, Piper."

"I know." He scratched his left wrist.

Anna wakened. She got her feet under her, got up, leaned against Hecht groggily. "I wish you didn't have to go."

"I wish I didn't, too."

"There's so much to talk about."

"I know. If everything goes right I could be back in a few days." He scratched again. Then started, raised his hand, and stared.

Anna clung. Vali joined her. Lila and Pella went on snoring. Anna said, "I'll pray that it goes that well. But I don't have much hope."

Nor did he.

"Piper! Come on. We're running out of time."

"HERIS, I NEED TO SEE GRANDFATHER FIRST."

"He isn't awake. There isn't time. Come on."

"Then you need to tell him when you get back. There's something coming. Something dark. My amulet started nagging me a few minutes ago. It hasn't done that for so long that I thought it had stopped working."

"Let's hope nobody knows you're here. I like Turking and Felske." The implication being that those two could be the only sources of leaks should news of his presence get out. And that the price they would pay would be dear.

There was a harsh soul inside a harsh woman, Heris. Very harsh.

Hecht did not remind her that their enemies had darker and sneakier espionage resources. Though he imagined that it did take human eyes to look inside Muniero Delari's house.

The harsh soul promised, "I'll see him as soon as I deliver you. If something is headed our way he'll deal with it."

"I'm holding you to that."

"Piper, enough! Let's go."

HECHT FOUND THIS TRANSITION NO EASIER THAN THE LAST. AND IT could have been worse had he not been distracted by concerns about Anna, the children, and Principaté Delari.

Their situation was sure to grow riskier by the day.

TITUS CONSENT ROUSTED HECHT OUT. HECHT CONGRATULATED HIM-self on having unbarred his door before he collapsed, too exhausted to dwell on nightmares seen during the transition. Consent said, "Time to get up, boss. Work to do. Man, you look like shit warmed over. What's the deal?"

"Nightmares. Bad news nightmares, Titus. I think they mean that there are some Night things around here and they're looking for me."

"Sent by someone? Or just local spooks?"

Hecht shrugged. "One, the other, or both. Doesn't matter."

"I'll look into it." Consent's tone suggested deep skepticism. "There have been no reports. And the villa is warded at double and triple depth."

"Was it exorcised before we moved in?" He was taking the pre-tense too far but could not stop.

Consent said, "That might be it. We'll move you to a room far away from this one."

"That's all right. I like this one."

"Despite the nightmares? You're getting scary, boss. I wish you'd stop."

Hecht understood perfectly. He had done a lot, lately, that Titus considered troubling.

"Titus, I don't do it on purpose."

Consent seemed to understand what he meant.

HECHT TOLD HIS STAFF, "YOU'VE ALL BEEN WORRIED ABOUT ME LATELY. I point out that I'm still doing my job. And the Empress and I expect you to go on doing yours. Which will be whatever she tells us it is. I don't expect you to be happy about that. I'm not. But the discretion I enjoy will be limited because she's right here with us. I *can* argue with her. She tolerates that. And lets me change her mind occasionally. But that's only when there aren't any witnesses. If someone is watching she won't budge to save her own life."

Clej Sedlakova asked, "What's your point?"

"That, going forward, we won't have the freedom of action we're used to. We'll operate according to the Empress's mood because she plans to stay right here with us."

Rumble rumble. Somebody growled, "That'll draw unfriendlies like shit draws flies."

Hecht nodded. Having trouble staying awake.

Sedlakova quickly established himself as the loudest voice. "Boss, we need to get a lot stronger before we go racing around in open country. I'd bet they could have a force ten times the size of ours up here by tomorrow. If they're really in a mood to be nasty."

Consent observed, "That all depends on one man. Serenity."

Hecht asked, "You suggesting we go on the defensive, Clej?" Disinclined to mention Heris's suggestion that Serenity might field a mob twenty thousand strong.

"We aren't known for that, I admit."

"But that's your recommendation. And I agree. Much as I'd like to go whooping through the hills and vales toward Brothe, setting fires and ruining Patriarchal vineyards. That's why I have all those scouts out. They're looking for a place to make a showing if we're forced to. That's why you're all supposed to be thinking about ways we can protect ourselves while we wait for our friends to show up." Twenty thousand. He could not get that number out of his head.

"Will she be patient?"

"She's impulsive but she isn't stupid. She'll listen."

Drago Prosek asked, "You think we can count on the Grand Duke to answer her summons?"

The key question, perhaps.

"I do. For reasons to do with his character rather than his notion of an obligation to the Grail Throne."

Consent inquired, "So now we buy time?"

"Aggressively. As aggressively as we dare. Making Serenity focus on our trivial force while the real storm gathers behind him." Twenty thousand.

Prosek said, "That'll be easy. All we need to do is what they did with Sublime, back when. Destroy his family stuff. Whatever he sucks money out of."

Sedlakova did not like that. Neither did he like Serenity. But he could never be comfortable while hearing a Patriarch accused of corruption, even obliquely.

"Come on, Clej. Even you got to admit . . ."

"Never mind," Hecht snapped.

Kait Rhuk, who had just arrived, settled next to Hecht. "I found the place. It's perfect. I've got people moving up there already. Hey! You all right, boss? You don't look so good."

Hecht muttered something about the pain from his wound. Then he fell asleep right there, in the middle of the meeting.

He dreamed unpleasant dreams.

## 35. Realm of the Gods: Triangulation

Heris guessed right, first try. The entire brain trust of the divine lib-eration expedition had assembled in the Aelen Kofer tavern on the waterfront to refine nebulous plans by lubricating them liberally. Cloven Februaren started barking the second she stepped inside. "Where the hell have you been, girl?"

The Ninth Unknown was not a happy man. There had been no mischief whatsoever for him to get up to for however long he had been confined to the Realm of the Gods.

With no clear proof Heris could not be sure, but after her several passages to and fro, she suspected the time differential between the middle world and the Realm of the Gods was inconstant. There might be a predictable cycle, though time would never pass slower here than it did at home.

She told Februaren, "There were things going on in the real world, Double Great. None of them happy." She offered a synopsis. The old man plucked additional meaning from between her words.

He and Ferris Renfrow immediately insisted, "I have to get back there."

Heris said, "I'm only an amateur observer but I thought the great horse of chaos was galloping along just fine without either one of you yanking on the reins."

Neither was in a mood to be chided. Each wanted to drag her off for a private interview.

The ascendant, who never spoke, had a glint in his eye, too.

Heris ignored them all. "Iron Eyes. I came up with an arsenal of the kind of weaponry we ran into at the Bas . . . At Ferris Renfrow's palace. Plenty enough to give us the edge with these Instrumentalities. I need Aelen Kofer help getting them here, though."

"Indeed?" Sourly. Then, "Really?" with more enthusiasm, as some stray thought wandered through his head.

Which Heris identified in one.

The Aelen Kofer were the artisans of the gods. How hard could it be for them to improve the new weapons? Dramatically?

Might not be the best plan, letting them get intimate with such deadly but essentially simple tools, the efficiency of which was limited only by the difficulties inherent in casting them.

Clever artificers like the Aelen Kofer would be quick to find alloys, casting and cooling processes, and spells that would help them create bigger, lighter, more accurate, and more deadly falcons. Especially when they had the temporal advantage of working under the hill.

Februaren and Renfrow went on fussing about their obligations in the middle world.

"So go!" Heris growled. "Asgrimmur and I can manage things here."

It turned out that there would be serious problems. The Aelen Kofer could not reach the Krulik and Sneigon works directly. There would be a lot of walking the middle world needed. Though, Heris discovered belatedly, that would not require the whole dwarf race to go traipsing across the Grail Empire in a loud, gaudy mob. One skilled magic-using dwarf could do the walking and opening of the way. Which, evidently, was an escape skill many Aelen Kofer learned early.

Of course, a gang would be needed to haul the weapons away. But they, and their goats, could make the journey in lazy stages on the other side. The dwarves never mentioned their rune-laden standing stones.

"Double Great! Before you bail out on me. You heard what we've been talking about."

"No. I wasn't listening."

"Listen now. I have a cache of weapons over there with nobody guarding them. I didn't think about that when I asked . . . for them. You understand me?"

The old man sighed and nodded. "Give me the gruesome details. I'll take care of it." Like Pella, she reflected, when he was asked to do a chore. Totally put-upon.

Cloven Februaren was an eternal adolescent. Incredibly powerful, a genius—with all the acquired personal skills of a spoiled fourteen-year-old.

With all that talent and genius he had no need to be mature.

CLOVEN FEBRUAREN AND FERRIS RENFROW WENT AWAY. THE AELEN Kofer followed, leaving only a skeleton crew. In time, Heris had only the ascendant and three sour, elderly dwarf women for company. And, occasionally, a young mer who called herself Philleas Pescadore. The mer thought that was funny but never explained. She shifted shape and

left the water, stark naked and achingly beautiful, only when Asgrimmur was around.

Heris knew she was imagining actions and motives because the fact
was, Philleas needed Asgrimmur to translate in order to communicate.

Philleas was both intensely curious and deeply naive about the
world above the waterline. For her that world was more mythical than
was hers to humanity. Only a few mer in any generation, most female
and young, could change and pass for human, briefly. Naked young
women who dared not venture far from the sea would not see the best
of land dwellers.

Philleas was doubly ignorant. Her entire world had been the harbor. The dangers she knew were shark and kraken.

Heris found the girl more irritating than interesting. She never
stopped asking questions.

Out of the blue, a few days after the old men left, Asgrimmur announced, "I'm not interested in Philleas the way you think. She isn't interested in me that way, either."

"What?" Taken completely off guard.

They were on the quay. The ascendant wore his most manly man
form. He stared through the portal at the brilliance of the middle world.

The gateway was open so Heris could go if she must.

"Her people have found the survivors of another pod out in the Andorayan Sea. They mean to merge pods by uniting Philleas and Kurlas,
a mer her age in the other pod. That should be interesting. Philleas has
picked up a lot of romantic notions from us. Especially from the old
man. Meanwhile, the sea pod has spent a century hugging the warm
water round a slow power leak. They'll have turned quite strange."

Heris grunted, not much interested. She just did not want to see the
mer in human form and have to compare herself.

It was not fair. Not even a little. The girl was not even human.

The ascendant said, "I believe Februaren thought he was playing a
clever practical joke."

"He would. Sometimes he's an idiot. I'm surprised he didn't exploit
her naiveté."

"Who knows? He may have. It wouldn't matter. What Philleas
does in human form is separate from what she does as a mer. I couldn't
guess the old man's proclivities—if he has any at his age—but his sense
of humor would be intrigued by the fact that Philleas starts out a virgin
every time she takes human form."

"Oh, now that's just! . . . All right. I don't know how he'd think
about that. You don't go sneaking around, trying to find out if your

oldest living ancestor is some kind of pervert. Asgrimmur, let's stop. This stuff makes me uncomfortable."

"So let's go climb the mountain instead."

"Excuse me?"

"Let's pack some food and go explore the Great Sky Fortress. You are curious about it, aren't you?"

"Of course I am. The same way I'm curious about seeing what happens when a ship founders and everybody drowns."

"An odd way to think of it."

Heris shrugged. "I'm an odd woman. I've survived an odd life. I see the world through skewed eyes."

"I thought it might be useful to walk the field before the battle. Save us time once the others get back. Winter will come. When it does it will serve Kharoulke far better than it will us."

"I can't say you're not right about that."

THE RAINBOW BRIDGE REMAINED BRILLIANT AND THRUMMINGLY PO-tent. Heris had no difficulty crossing. The Construct had no direct potency inside the Realm of the Gods but using it outside had built up her self-confidence.

The ascendant followed, fearless himself. And had no reason to fear. Should he fall he need but change. . . . A random gust did push him off his footing. In an instant he developed tentacles that snagged hold of the rainbow. He dragged himself back onto the bridge, where he turned into a huge bird that hopped the last few yards on one foot. He had his trousers clutched in the other.

"That was impressive," Heris said, noting that one wing seemed stunted. "Those stories about people changing into animals always made me wonder what they did about their clothes."

"You lose them if you get in a hurry. Otherwise, you make arrangements." He remained generically bipedal till he finished wriggling into the trousers. He became fully human, then, but only momentarily. His exposed feet and upper body changed again. He developed lionlike feet and a heavy pelt above the waist.

It was cold up there.

Heris observed, "You're going to be an adventure for some demigoddess."

"I dropped the sack. There's water up here but nothing to eat."

"It'll be a short adventure, then. I have a question."

"I may have an answer."

For reasons uncertain Heris turned toward the dead apple orchard once they passed through the gateway. "Your missing . . . whatever.

That comes and goes. You always have the right number of hands and feet when you're human. When you're something else you always have a crippled limb. Which is why you lost your shirt and the food."

"And other valuables as well."

"And? So?"

"The hand is also missing when I'm human. But when I'm a man I don't need to invest much effort holding the form. I can create the illusion of a hand."

"Illusion? I've seen you use it."

"Have you? For sure?"

"Uh . . . No, actually. What happened?"

"I attacked somebody when I was the mad monster of the high Jagos. He didn't panic like the others. He chopped it off. That was not pleasant. But it was useful. The pain eventually wakened what little sanity I had left. That and a savage ambush later that almost killed me."

Asgrimmur extended his right hand. It began to shrivel. "Kind of creepy, isn't it?"

"You might say." Heris stepped through a gap in the dry stone fence surrounding the orchard.

For an instant the gray went away. The garden offered a vision of itself in olden times. A gorgeous blond goddess plucked a golden apple. She placed it under a small flagstone, made a sign Heris assumed was a blessing. She looked in Heris's direction as though thinking she had heard something coming. She saw nothing, evidently. Distress warped her beauty. Then the vision ended.

"What just happened?" the ascendant asked. "I felt something when you stepped through the fence."

"I'm not sure. A flash from the past? I might have seen what the orchard looked like, back when." The tree from which the goddess had picked the apple lay at Heris's feet, rotted. Without a termite.

Like the power, insects were not returning to the Realm of the Gods, if only because the gateway was in the middle of a freezing sea. Though all the recent comings and goings probably meant that fleas and lice had become reestablished.

Heris said, "It's sad, all this having to go. It was magnificent."

"Have you forgotten what lived here?"

"No. But I bet they weren't worse than any other Instrumentalities from their era. Were they big on human sacrifices?"

"They demanded it. But not often. The victims were usually condemned men, cripples, or people about to die from disease anyway. Or, after the Chaldarean cult reached the northern world, missionaries.

But when times were extreme the gods sometimes demanded a real sacrifice."

"Did you enjoy your time with Cloven Februaren?" Heris stepped back out of the orchard, strolled toward the entrance to the "keep" of the Great Sky Fortress. Keep was appropriate based on design but a deep understatement by the standards of middle-world fortifications. The structure sprawled to left and right and rose up and up and up.

"I did. The man has a unique mind. Most of what you're looking at is an illusion. The real fortress goes more back into the flesh of the mountain than it goes up."

"Not the answer I was looking for."

The ascendant frowned. He took a moment, as though trying to craft a response that would be approved. "I'm sorry you were disappointed. I'm never sure how things are done. Nor why I do what I do. The Walker and the Banished were powerful personalities. Even as ghosts they sometimes work some wicked magic."

Heris started to say that that was not what she was looking for, either, but stopped herself.

Asgrimmur continued, "I do enjoy time spent with the old man. My stay at Fea was a pleasant interlude. I enjoyed him even more, here, while you were away. He has an insatiable curiosity. But he likes to start arguments. He squabbled with the Bastard constantly."

"I'd say he has an infinite capacity for making mischief. What did he get up to when I wasn't watching?"

Asgrimmur gave her a blank look. Again, she had trouble connecting him with the brute raiders who had come out of Andoray centuries ago. Then she recalled the Ninth Unknown suggesting that he might have absorbed knowledge from the people he had killed during his mad seasons.

She asked, "So what do we do now?" Trying to distract herself.

That old man with the insatiable curiosity would have been up here countless times while she was away. Maybe she could get Asgrimmur to let her in on what they had learned. Maybe she could get him to explain how he had become such a changed man.

"Come."

She followed.

He showed her a place she refused to visit again.

"This is where my brother and I and our boyhood friends were kept while the Instrumentalities waited to turn us loose. This is where the heroes of the north, scavenged from battlefields by the Choosers of the Slain, awaited their destiny. This is where those who served the Old

Ones well in life hoped to spend eternity. The Hall of Heroes. A paradise that has a lot in common with your Chaldarean Hell."

Despite countless years gone on the smell of death remained.

There was little light back there, inside the mountain. For which Heris was thankful. In the area she could see there were scattered limbs and bodies so terribly mutilated that they had not been able to answer the call to battle when the Walker summoned them to save the Night.

Before the Old Gods went, there had been no corruption in the Hall of Heroes. Just a stink of fresh death. But, now, corruption had found its way into the Great Sky Fortress. Slow, slow corruption, constrained by cold and alien physical law.

"How did you trap them?" Heris asked.

"Clever. Trying to catch me by surprise. But no help. I must have been inspired. But I was too mad to remember. I ripped the necessary knowledge out of the All-Father and the Banished like tearing out their lungs, I expect."

Heris suppressed a gag reflex. "The smell is too much. How did you stand that for a couple hundred years?"

"It wasn't that short. Time differences, remember? But we were lucky. We were unconscious. Though that was bad enough. There were dreams. My brother . . . No point tormenting myself with that."

"I understand." Recalling what the ascendant and his brother had done once the Old Ones turned them loose.

"I make no excuse more powerful than that I was trying to take care of my brother. As you would if you had one."

"All right. Yeah. Whatever. Show me something else."

There was little to see. Certainly nothing dramatic. Just more and more rooms, large and small, where nothing remained but dust. And that mostly dust created by the slow decay of stone, one mote at a time.

"There aren't any furnishings," Heris noted. "No matter where we go. Not one shred of old cloth or one bit of corroded metal. It can't have been that long, even if time does run different here."

"The glory that was existed because the Old Ones were here to see it. The Aelen Kofer of antiquity were ingenious artificers. Even the form and dimensions of some parts of the Great Sky Fortress would change in accord with the whim of the beholder."

"Those would be the same Aelen Kofer we're working with today?"

"No doubt a point worth keeping in mind."

"You speaking from memory?"

"Memories not my own. But, yes. There's still a thrill of pride in the ghost of the All-Father, though he did no more than compel the dwarves to build what he wanted. The genius was that of the Aelen Kofer."

"If they were geniuses, how did they end up the next thing to slaves?"

The ascendant stopped, faced her, stared for several seconds, then said, "Though the dimmest Aelen Kofer are a dozen times more clever than us that doesn't make them a dozen times stronger. Nor more willful. They aren't . . . They're . . . They're artificers, Heris. Merchants and tradesmen. Folk who take orders and execute them."

Heris noted the first time use of her name but gave it no weight. She knew what he meant about the dwarves. She had been there. She shifted the subject. "You don't sound anything like an Andorayan pirate should."

The ascendant frowned, worked out what she meant. "You have some practical experience? You think you know how a pirate sounds?"

"An Andorayan pirate, no. But I do have direct experience. Though I'll stipulate that I'm female and I was young at the time." Younger than he should be thinking now.

The ascendant just looked puzzled.

Heris said, "Show me where the Old Ones are locked up."

"There isn't anything to see."

"Then show me all the nothing."

There was a hall. An empty hall, empty like every other hall, of any size, that Heris had seen anywhere in the Great Sky Fortress. This one was thirty feet by forty-two, with no distinguishing features. She prowled its bounds. Unglazed windows in an exterior wall admitted ample light, though this was the time of day when passing clouds were thickest. Nothing marked the room as unique.

"Where are they? Is there a direction? A point? Something?"

Asgrimmur spread his hands. "This is where I ended it. That's all I remember. Any more questions would be a waste of time. I don't know. I went through it with the old man twenty times. That's all I can tell you. I don't know. Though I am sure I can undo it with help from the Bastard, Iron Eyes, and the old man."

"It would be so handy to know what direction I ought to be looking when you guys open the way."

Asgrimmur shrugged. And managed to look apologetic.

"All right, big dummy. I'm standing here. The way opens. I watch that, wherever it develops. What am I going to see? What will be behind the opening?"

"I can be a little more useful, there. There'll be . . ." His words slowed, stopped. He looked baffled. Like his mind had become a blank.

"Don't tell me. You just fogged." Heris thought she might know why Asgrimmur had memory problems.

"I did. I'm blank."

"One of the soul chips in you is more powerful, more rational, and more independent than you thought. It's sabotaging you."

Asgrimmur stared at her dolefully. Then started violently. "I believe you're right."

"So. Which one? Arlensul, wanting to keep her family locked up? Or the One Who Harkens, working on a jailbreak?"

"Heris, I don't know. I'm no good at this Instrumentality business. I don't have much contact. Not like us standing here talking. Most of the time they're just ghost voices, way far away. I only catch a few words. Sometimes their voices get lost in all the others."

Did he mean the voices of those he had killed and eaten when he was the mad monster of the Jagos?

He said, "The Old Ones are the strongest voices. But all the voices come and go."

"What do they tell you?"

"Mostly they scream. Including the All-Father and the Banished. At the most intense moment of their existence, they were all in extreme agony."

Heris shuddered. This was grim stuff.

Asgrimmur said, "We should go. There isn't anything we can accomplish here."

He was listening to something else. The screams inside? Or the Old Ones imprisoned nearby?

Heris suspected the latter.

Asgrimmur continued, "Let's go back down to the tavern and see what the Norgens say."

"The Norgens?"

"That's how I think of those crone dwarves Iron Eyes left to babysit us. Norgens figuratively, not literally."

"What would Norgens be?"

He frowned. How could she not know? "Southerner! Norgens are something like the Fates. Three crones who spin the threads of destiny. More or less."

"If they were still in business would they be in the bottle with the Old Ones?"

"They're long gone. A different kind of Instrumentality. They've faded into whatever afterlife claims used-up Instrumentalities."

A subject on which she and the Ninth Unknown had wasted hours speculating, as an intellectual game. She thought the old man had it right. Instrumentalities did not die in the normal course, they faded into obscurity and quiescence, becoming one with the mud in the swamps of the Night. Unless somebody actively tried to kill, consume, contain, or shatter the Instrumentality. Then it could cease to be. Except, possibly, as a constituent fragment in another Instrumentality.

Eyeing Asgrimmur as she thought that.

His Norgens might be out of business but they would be out there, somewhere. Sleeping. A clever someone might find a way to waken them. As clever someones had been wakening grander and more terrible Instrumentalities.

"All right. Let's go talk to the old women. But tomorrow we come back with paint and chalk and measuring lines. We'll lay out fields of fire."

The ascendant looked baffled. And was.

The soul at the heart of him was a man two hundred years out of his native time. He had not lived through the changes of all those years.

Thus his gods had taken even more.

HOURS WITH THE RELUCTANT DWARF WOMEN EQUIPPED HERIS WITH the key details about the Old Ones. She wrote everything down on parchment provided by the dwarves, using quills and inks manufactured by the Aelen Kofer.

Thus, when she rose in the morning what she had written the evening before was still there, despite what might have become of her memories. What she left herself included notes and messages about the rest of the information and thoughts about how it all could be used.

Heris visited the Great Sky Fortress every "morning." She explored new areas each time but always visited the hall that Asgrimmur insisted was the one where he had imprisoned the Old Ones. She used a lot of chalk and paint, both in there and for marking routes through the confusion.

"ASGRIMMUR. IT'S EIGHT DAYS SINCE EVERYBODY LEFT."

"Which could be only hours in the middle world. A day at most."

"Not so much my worry."

"Then?"

"I need you to take a trip with me. I want to show you something. Out there." She waved a hand at the gateway.

The old dwarf women started complaining before Heris finished explaining what she wanted.

"Enough," the ascendant said. "Do as you have been told." He began to change.

Heris was behind him. She did not see what he showed the dwarves. It made an impression. The complaints stopped. None of the three spoke again till they brought their small boat to a stop just outside the gateway to the Realm of the Gods.

"Good fortune attend you," said the eldest.

"Fair weather attend you," said another.

And the last, "Take no needless risks, girl."

All three used a language Heris understood, albeit with brutal accents.

"Thank you, grandmothers." She meant it. "Come here, Asgrimmur."

"DID YOU HAVE VISIONS OR STRONG EMOTIONS WHEN WE WERE TRANS-lating?" Heris asked.

"I visited Hell. A darkness infested with nightmares." He was shaking, not because of the cold.

"Then it must be me. Something I'm doing."

"What are you talking about? And what is that foul smell?"

They stood on a cold gray hillside amid lifeless broken rocks, most of which boasted sharp edges. Ice filled any crevice the sun did not reach. A steady wind brought both a bone-biting chill and the reek of corruption. But the sky above was a cheerful expanse of pale blue occasionally marred by the hurried passage of a twisting cotton puff.

The wind also sang with a thousand voices as it played amongst the massive shards of stone. The chorus was a dirge.

Heris said, "Follow me. And stay low. We don't want to silhouette ourselves against the sky."

Asgrimmur finally understood that he was far from the old dwarf women. "What did you do?"

"Quiet would be a big help, too."

Heris crept to the ridgeline, thinking she had changed a lot in very little time. Relatively speaking. Not just since Grade Drocker rescued her but since Grandfather Delari brought Gisors—Piper—back into her life. Not so long ago she had been a slave, a Chaldarean used and abused in what the idiots there were pleased to call the Realm of Peace. Now she was a wild adventuress clambering across an arctic hillside with a demigod, thousands of miles from the cities of her shame.

She reached the vantage she wanted, slowly lifted her head. She beckoned Asgrimmur. "Come up here. Slowly."

The ascendant did so.

"That's it, Asgrimmur. The monster god. And his worshippers."

Two starved forms huddled for warmth beside the Instrumentality's putrescent flank, probably so mad and weak they could do nothing if they did spot the watchers.

The stench was overpowering. Heris breathed through her mouth but that helped only a little.

"That's the dread Windwalker? That's why we need to free the Old Ones?"

"That's him. But others of his kind are loose, now, too."

Kharoulke the Windwalker, in summer, sprawled across the shingle, just above the agonizing touch of the sea, resembling nothing so much as a decaying jellyfish more massive than a beached pod of blue whales. Unhealed wounds leaked treacle-darkness that dribbled down the god's side to the shingle, then crept away into the brine.

The ascendant asked, "Why are we worried about that?"

"Because the Instrumentality, diminished, survives inside that of-fal. Waiting. Because winter always comes. And winter here is long and bitter. The Windwalker will thrive in that. If we don't conquer it first."

Heris had to admit it was hard to consider that stinking mass a threat. It was hard to believe that she could not destroy it herself, given logistical and technical support.

She would not get that. However much the Ninth Unknown said he believed in her, he would never support her the way he would her brother.

There was just no way to improve the thinking of men.

The ascendant asked, "Are you going to do more than look?"

"No."

"It knows we're here."

"What?"

"I feel it calling someone to deal with us."

"The rot. Is it just camouflage . . . ? Asgrimmur?"

"I'm all right. I was . . . It senses me, not us. It smells the part of me that conquered it two thousand years ago. It wouldn't have noticed you by yourself. It's sending someone to deal with me."

Heris could get her mind around that. The ascendant belonged to the Night. She, on the other hand, could come and go, ephemeral, un-noticed until she attacked that stinking earthly aspect down there.

"We should probably leave, then." Heris began backing away.

"Too late."

A spotted thing, brown on a snake's belly color background, popped over the ridge, fast. Distilled ferocity, it charged the ascendant.

It was no bigger than a squirrel.

Asgrimmur snatched it out of the air. It tried to bite. He smashed its head against a rock, then examined its fingers. "Somebody exagger-ated, didn't they?"

Heris caught her breath. "No. The god's power to create, and to influence the world around him, has gotten real weak. Can you sense anything on the supernatural level?"

Asgrimmur turned the miniature creature, poked it. "The Instrumentality is disappointed. This thing was Krepnight, the Elect. It was created by the god. It was supposed to be my size but faster, deadlier, and more single-minded."

The slope shuddered. Rocks shifted but the tremor was not violent enough to initiate a slide. The beached god wobbled and jiggled.

"It's crazy with rage but doesn't have strength for anything but trying to stay alive. For a long time, naturally."

"Handy skill, reading a god's mind without getting your own baked."

"I'm not reading its mind, Heris. It would love to have me try. It would make me over into an ascendant Krepnight, the Elect, in three heartbeats. Then it would turn me loose on you and the others."

"You know that without being able to read its mind?"

"It's simple. I feel its emotions. I think about what the god side of me would do in its place, if I had its power." Asgrimmur moved up for a better view of the shingle.

Heris joined him. "Is this safe?"

"It is now. For a while. If you want, you can go throw salt water on just to be nasty."

"I didn't remember to bring a bucket."

"You'd be destroying only what it's written off already, anyway."

"And there are the priests." She pointed.

"They're no problem. He used them up to make Krepnight, the Elect."

Hungry seabirds surrounded the dead already.

It seemed instructive that carrion eaters would not touch the Windwalker.

Heris asked, "Are you learning anything now?"

"I'm always . . ." He realized that the question was not general. "From the Instrumentality? Yes."

"Is it anything we might find useful to the fight? Because if it is, I'll stay here till my eyeballs freeze. But, otherwise, not. Otherwise, I'd just as soon get the hell out of here, now."

"Give me a few minutes. Unless you have a pressing need."

"I do have a need. But, go ahead. Knock yourself out. I've got nowhere to go but home."

# 36. The Connec: Journey

Brother Candle had no trouble getting away from Khaurene in the confusion after the fall of King Regard. He did not go alone. More than thirty Maysaleans joined him, bringing carts, wagons, livestock, and wealth, as though begging for the attention of bandits.

They could help him, yes. He was sure he could not survive the journey alone. But, on the other hand, they could get him killed.

They wanted to leave Khaurene in a clement season, before Anne of Menand extracted her vengeance. Which they knew would come, as surely as nightfall.

What they would not hear was advice. What they would not hear was the Perfect's warnings about the dangers of travel.

He told them to head south and cross the Verses Mountains into Navaya Medien, where the Church and Society had little reach and Arnhand had none. Where heretics were welcome so long as they brought useful skills and a willingness to work. Navaya Medien was a land depleted of people, first by a long-ago plague, then by two centuries of vicious, no-quarter warfare between Chaldarean kings and Praman kaifs.

Peace had returned. Peter of Navaya had pushed the war zone away to the south. The Chaldarean triumph at Los Naves de los Fantas guaranteed that the Pramans could not become seriously obnoxious for a generation.

But these emigrants were all intimates from the Khaurenese Maysalean community: the Archimbaults and their neighbors. Most were folk with whom Brother Candle had shared exile in the Altai. Ferocious Kedle Richeut, née Archimbault, was now a leader, possibly the most respected. But these days she wore a new name: Alazais Record, after a female Perfect murdered by the Society.

She used the false name because it was no secret that a young Maysalean mother named Kedle Richeut had loosed the shaft that made an end of Regard of Menand.

The band followed the southern road to Castreresone. That passed through friendlier country. At Kedle's insistence each member of the group old enough to heft a weapon had brought arms out of Khaurene. Those had been easy to acquire in the confusion. Brother Candle added a codicil to every prayer imploring the Good God to shelter his people.

Nevertheless, trouble came near Homodel, which still showed evidence of the fighting during the Captain-General's scourging of the Connec. Castreresone was not half a day's journey away. But bandits were out and bold.

The travelers found the road blocked by four armed men. The leader wore knight's armor but showed neither pennon nor device. He was the only mounted man. He held his helmet in his lap. His contempt for Maysaleans was manifest.

Brother Candle did not follow what the man said when first he spoke. His accent was thick. The gist, though, was that they should clear away from his wagons and livestock.

In a strong, calm voice, while handing her baby to her cousin Guillemette, Kedle said, "Clear the road. You get no further warning."

At which the mounted man laughed.

His companions were less confident.

He bent to tell them something . . .

Kedle swung a ready crossbow out of a donkey cart and put a bolt into the knight's right eye. She traded the crossbow for a spear and rushed the men on foot.

Every witness *knew* the girl was going to kill all three and there was nothing they could do. The bandits themselves knew.

The youngest, clearly unwell and only about fourteen, bolted.

Kedle hit the others like Death's angel, wasting not an instant of their stunned inaction. She wounded the heavier by stabbing him in the inner thigh. He staggered back, making a whimpering noise. The other was twice Kedle's size. His weapon was a rusty long sword. He wielded that with both hands, in wild strokes. Kedle backed away, circled, got the fallen knight's horse on her shield arm side.

Strange things happen on battlefields. On this one the knight's horse did not move after its rider got hit. The knight himself fell off and lay on his face in the road, his left foot still tangled in a stirrup.

The girl pricked the horse. It surged forward, dragging its erstwhile rider, shouldering the bandit with the sword. His guard was open for an instant. She slipped the head of her spear up under his chin and shoved. Then she went after the wounded man, who was making a limping effort to escape. He was losing blood. She ignored his pleas. She stuck him till he stopped moving. She seemed possessed.

She returned in a rage. "What is the matter with you people? Not one of you lifted a finger to protect yourselves. What if there had been more of them out there in the woods?"

Raulet Archimbault said, "Poppet, that's why . . ."

"That isn't why. You froze. Every last one of you. Like rabbits who hope the fox won't notice. What happened to all those loudmouthed wolves who were howling before we left Khaurene? And you. Old man. Master. You're the experienced traveler. Why did you just stand there with your thumb in your mouth?"

"I'm used to talking my way through confrontations."

"You're used to being too damned poor to rob and to not having women along. There wasn't going to be any talking your way around those four." She dropped to her knees beside the fallen knight, tried to recover her bolt. It would not come loose. She kicked the corpse viciously. Then she took his foot out of his stirrup so the horse would not have to drag a dead man everywhere. "Go on, horse." She faced the party. "There would've been rapes and murders. You know it."

She was right.

Kedle returned to her cart. She took the crossbow out and spanned it again, the while glaring around. "You people better not get my children killed." Then, "Othon! Let the dead be. They don't have anything we want."

"But . . ."

"Othon."

The man, twice Kedle's age and twice her size, left the dead knight. Kedle said, "Let somebody else plunder them and get caught with the evidence." She returned the ready crossbow to the cart, took her youngest back from Guillemette, said, "Let's go. And nobody says a word about this when we get to Castreresone. Or ever."

The rattle, clank, and squeak started up.

No one spoke for a long time.

The earth had shifted under all their feet.

"Not a word, Master," Kedle said when he fell in beside her. "I won't hear your nonsense."

"As you wish."

The silence got to her eventually. "I was moved by a grand example, Master. Duke Tormond IV."

"But Tormond would not have . . ."

"Exactly. He would have procrastinated. He would have temporized. He would have talked. He would have done everything to avoid making a decision that might upset somebody. Or, worse, would compel him to act. As a consequence, we would find ourselves with a homeland where half the people were persecuted, foreign armies would roam around as they pleased, and it would be lethally dangerous to use the roads."

The old man could not answer that.

There was a counterargument. Pacifists always had one. But he had become embedded too deeply in the everyday world to bring a good one to mind.

He did mutter, "But three men are dead," understanding that it was an absurd remark as he made it.

"Leaving the rest of us, the people we care about, alive and unharmed. Eh?"

How did you argue with true believers in mathematics and human nature?

THERE WERE PROBLEMS AT CASTRERESONE. THE CONSULS HAD DEcided not to let any more refugees into the city, whether or not they had relatives inside. But those relatives could come out and talk. They could provide food and drink, blankets and clothing and such.

Castreresone had not yet fully recovered from its romance with the old Captain-General. The suburb called Inconje, where the big bridge crossed the Laur, had been abandoned by its original inhabitants. Now it housed a thousand refugees. Brother Candle saw many familiar faces. All were tired of travel and its constant fear. Many had lost everything to bandits.

Brother Candle's group did not want to face those risks anymore, despite his assurances that they would be welcomed by Count Raymone Garete. Pettish, the Perfect told Raulet Archimbault, "I'm probably wrong about that welcome, anyway. He's looking for people with some spine. People willing to help turn the tide of evil drowning the Connec." He stopped. Kedle sneered at him from the shadows beyond the communal fire. Little Raulet snuggled under her left arm. The baby nursed at her right breast.

The old man left the fire, rolled himself into his blanket. He was well and truly lost. He was further from Perfection than most raw students. They were blessed with an eagerness to learn, to achieve salvation. Too much exposure to life had made him over into a cynical old man. He would have to go round the Wheel of Life several times to get back to where he had been, arriving at St. Jeules for the synod of the Perfects, not that long ago.

Come morning Brother Candle rose determined to go on alone. He had obligations to Queen Isabeth and Count Raymone. He was slow to get started, though. He dithered round the communal fire, snuggled Kedle's baby and played with the toddler, found an excuse to exchange words with everyone before he finally hoisted his pack. By then it was nearly noon and it looked like he would spend his afternoon walking in the rain.

As he stepped off the east end of the Laur Bridge he spotted another familiar face. Or faces. The bandit Gaitor and his brothers, Gartner and Geis. Who were not thrilled to be recognized. They tried to slink away, hoping he would not follow. The Perfect shouted, "I'll yell out everything."

"Clever, that, Master."

"What?" Heart hammering, he turned. Kedle was there with her donkey cart, children aboard. She had a spear in hand. "What are you doing?"

"Going with you. Stop arguing. Your friends are about to ditch you."

"They aren't friends. They're men like the ones outside Homodel."

"Then you'll definitely need me to watch your back." She yanked her donkey's lead.

Brother Candle sighed. He would deal with this after talking to the bandit boys. "All right."

He met Gaitor and his brothers on the riverbank thirty yards down from the remains of the tower that had protected the eastern approach to the bridge. They stared at Kedle. Her presence disinclined them to be rude or crude. Geis asked, "Who's your friend?"

"Alazais Record. You don't want to make her unhappy."

"What do you want, Master?" Gaitor asked. Of the three he most obviously did not want to be seen talking with a Maysalean.

"I just wondered how you were doing. I wondered if you followed my advice and took your case to Count Raymone. You do look more prosperous these days." He told Kedle, "Alazais, these people helped me during my last journey to Antieux."

"They look like bandits."

That struck a nerve with Gartner. "Not no more! We work for Count Raymone, finding real bandits and spies. And Society creeps."

Gaitor and Geis gaped. Gartner seldom talked. Gaitor exploded, "Gart, what the hell is wrong with you?"

"I don't want him thinking we're the kind of guys we used to be before we run into him, that's all."

Kedle's infant began to fuss. A hunger fuss, Brother Candle realized. That baby was the unfussiest he had ever seen. Nor was Raulet ever inclined to be trouble. He was standing up now, looking over the side of the cart, taking everything in. It was easy to forget that Raulet was there.

Four men stood in numb silence while Kedle gave the baby the breast. With a spear still ready in her right hand.

Gaitor muttered, "You must be right, Master. Some kind of shield maiden. But not so maiden anymore."

"You've gone honest, then."

"Ninety percent. Definitely not doing anything to make the Count or his woman angry."

Brother Candle said, "I need to get to Antieux. I have messages for the Count. I was traveling with a group of refugees from Khaurene. They've decided to stay here."

"Her, too?"

Kedle had leaned her spear against her cart in order to deal with dirty nappies. The reformed bandits were no less intimidated.

"She says she's coming. I hope she changes her mind."

Meantime, Gartner took a couple careful steps toward Kedle. "You need some help with them bitties, missus?"

Startled, Kedle looked to Brother Candle for his opinion. He shrugged. "Up to you. He was good with his own children."

"Miss them, too," Gartner said, taking a couple more steps, careful not to alarm Kedle.

"He does," Gaitor said. "We didn't think we'd be out here so long."

"You managed to settle your families?" Such as that desperate mob had been.

"There's room for them as accepts the Count. That's another thing we do. Spread rumors that Count Raymone will take on anybody that's willing to give him as much loyalty as he gives. Lookit there."

Gartner had taken a leather bucket from Kedle's cart. He headed down the muddy riverbank. Then he and Kedle used the water to clean Raulet and the infant. Kedle accepted the help but never let Gartner get in snatching distance of her spear.

Gaitor asked, "How old is she? She don't look near old enough to be so hard."

Brother Candle tried to add it up. "Eighteen, nineteen."

"No husband?"

"Not anymore. Took a crossbow bolt through the brain during the siege of Khaurene." Soames was gone. No need to speak ill of him now.

Geis wanted to hear all about that.

Brother Candle offered a few sad details.

Gaitor said, "So when you hailed us you was really hoping you could con us into looking out for you on the road to Antieux."

"I did have thoughts along those lines. Yes."

"I don't want to do it. We was just starting to fit in here. But after so many people seen us talking to you, with you being known for working for Count Raymone, I guess we ought to go away for a while. Let suspicions die down."

"Your generosity . . ."

"Master, we owe you. Much as I wish we never ran into you. We couldn't have got through last winter. It won't take long, anyway. The roads are safe between here and Antieux. Them bandits who wouldn't learn have been hunted out."

Something came up between Gartner and Kedle. Sharp words. But the woman did not grab her spear.

Brother Candle warned, "Take care with Alazais. She's volatile."

"I noticed. Master, if we're gonna travel together I need time to get ready. Can you wait till tomorrow?"

"If I must, I must."

"At the end of the bridge at sunrise, then."

Brother Candle inclined his head in acknowledgment. He went to speak soothing words to Kedle's donkey. The poor, put-upon beast.

THERE WERE A FEW CHANGES OF HEART. KEDLE'S PARENTS AND HER cousins Guillemette and Escamerole, plus Scarre the baker and his wife. Seven companions, obviously prosperous, of whom three were nubile women. Two probably virgins. How could Gaitor and Geis resist? The Perfect needed to forge an alliance with slow but essentially honorable Gartner.

Or, maybe not. Kedle equipped her cousins with several edged weapons apiece.

The bandits turned spies were waiting as promised. They were mounted. Not on the best of steeds, but mounted nonetheless. Gaitor asked, "How come there's a bunch more?"

Brother Candle said, "They changed their minds."

"They don't look like much. All heretics, right?"

"True. But I'm the only one who isn't a fighter."

"Lot of women and old folks."

"You can just say the hell with us."

"I could. But then I wouldn't have no excuse to go see my family, would I? What's that?"

Some sort of disturbance had broken out across the Laur. It involved a lot of shouting and a few cheers. It did not sound like a riot.

Brother Candle said, "We're ready to go but we might find out what that's about. In case it affects us."

Gaitor scowled. "You do something? Got the garrison after you?" There were people coming down from the White City. A Navayan garrison still quartered there.

"Not us. Unless the Society took over since we got up this morning."

"Then it must be news. Big news." He gestured at his brother Geis, indicating that he should investigate.

The rest started walking.

"How dangerous is this likely to get?" Raulet Archimbault asked. He was terrified on behalf of his grandchildren.

Gaitor said, "Shouldn't be no trouble till we get close to Antieux. Count Raymone hunts down brigands who won't join him. He's quite stern. He's more interested in stamping out banditry than in scrapping with the Captain-General. But Patriarchal patrols might be a problem near to Antieux."

Archimbault said, "This new Captain-General doesn't seem as vigorous as the old one."

"There's some of that," Gaitor conceded. "Mostly he's ineffective because of the Patriarch, though. Serenity has buried him in incompetents and people pushing their own agendas. He can't get anything done on account of, no matter what he tries, somebody gets pissed off and wants him to do something else."

"Good for us, then."

"Exactly. The hard truth is, Pinkus Ghort would be worse than Piper Hecht if everybody backed off and let him."

GEIS DID NOT CATCH UP FOR TWO HOURS. GAITOR KEPT A GOOD PACE. When he did arrive Geis went to whisper with his brothers.

Kedle took station beside the cart where her weapons were stashed.

Gaitor announced, "Folks, there's been a big shift in the world order. The Grail Empress has gone to war against the Patriarch. She blames him for the death of her husband, Jaime of Castauriga. She's in Firaldia already, with the former Captain-General. I wouldn't want to be in the Patriarch's shoes right now."

Brother Candle received that news with less joy than did the others. He knew such things became exaggerated. Likely the news would go through several serious transmutations before curdling into its historical form, which was sure to be its least dramatic shape.

Even in a tepid form, though, this was good news for the Connec. The Patriarchal forces harassing Count Raymone would have to be recalled. Faced with the wrath of the Grail Empire Serenity would have neither a man nor a ducat to spare for anything but self-defense.

THE TRAVELERS REACHED COUNTRY WHERE PATRIARCHAL TROOPS HAD expressed their displeasure with Count Raymone.

Word was, the Captain-General's initial instructions had been for Ghort to remain in place and waste the countryside. Then he had been directed to launch an all-out attack on Antieux. He refused. That would waste his soldiers' lives. Given no other option, though, he had attacked, achieving the predicted results. His force had been decimated. It never came close to succeeding.

Then Serenity ordered the Captain-General back to Brothe, fast, collecting the full feudal levy of every Patriarchal State along the way. He was to accept no excuses and make no exceptions.

"Desperation," Brother Candle said.

Gaitor agreed. "Sounds like Serenity's fortunes went into the shitter, fast."

Brother Candle saw what Count Raymone would surely see. An opportunity granted by God Himself. A respite while Serenity fought for his life. A chance to throw light into the nooks and crannies where Society vermin hid and bred.

Briefly, Brother Candle wondered what kind of noble Raymone would have made had he lived in a peaceful age.

News from farther east became the subject of so much speculation that time just flew. There were no adventures other than a brush with a band of Society brothers fleeing retribution. They lacked the courage of their convictions that morning.

Brother Candle saved their lives. He talked Gaitor into letting them go. "Ye reap what ye sow."

Kedle responded, "What we'll reap is rats bred up a hundredfold. Remember those faces, old man. See if they aren't in the mob that ties you to the stake someday."

"Blood drinker, that one," Geis whispered.

Brother Candle nodded. And could not shake the truth underlying what Kedle said. Someone would pay for his kindness.

A PATROL FROM ANTIEUX FOUND THEM TEN MILES WEST OF THE CITY. The soldiers had heard of Brother Candle. They formed an escort and sent a rider ahead to report the coming of an important messenger.

Count Raymone was away harassing stragglers from the Patriarchal force, Society fugitives, and brigands. His prey often fit multiple categories. Socia, though, was in the city, busy being pregnant. She came out to meet Brother Candle. She was as effusive and excited as if he were her own father. Her pregnancy had begun to show. She was sensitive about that. She had dressed to make it less obvious.

She asked, "You're carrying communications from the Queen?"

"I am," Brother Candle replied.

"We've been hearing a lot from her. I expect your message won't be anything new. But she says you speak for her. She thinks we'll trust you to do what's best for the End of Connec."

"Oh, no. Socia . . . Countess . . . no! I was born on the third day after Creation. I'm *old*. I need to rest. It's a miracle the Good God hasn't called me during this journey."

"He left you in place because He knows you have work to do."

Kedle chuckled.

Brother Candle said, "These people saw me through. They're good people, mostly. Though that girl with the baby needs some rough corners knocked off."

Socia grinned at Kedle. Kedle grinned back. Socia's chief lifeguard whispered to her. She said, "I know who she is. We spent a winter in the Altai together. Kedle. Two babies now. So either Soames turned up or you found out that he didn't have the only one."

Storm clouds crossed Kedle's face. But she nodded. "He turned up. Got me another baby, then got himself killed. By the very King of Arnhand. Six kinds of poetic and ironic justice there."

"Ha! They're calling you the Kingslayer. You know that? So I like you even better. But I'm jealous. I wish it'd been me. Well, maybe someday. The Arnhanders won't stop coming till we're shut of Anne of Menand."

Brother Candle eyed Socia narrowly. Was there a sinister inflexion there?

He said only, "Some of these people are almost as old as I am, Countess. And we're all exhausted. *And* it's going to rain. Again." Wet weather had been common the past ten days. It was not coming up off the Mother Sea, which was the norm, but was sweeping down from the northwest, often accompanied by thunder and occasionally by hail and savage winds. More signs that the world was changing.

Socia gave orders. "You. You. You. Stay with me." She indicated Gaitor, Kedle, and Brother Candle. "We need to talk. Martin, Jocelyn, take the rest to the quarters I had prepared."

Brother Candle said, "Kedle has children to . . ."

"Bring them along." Socia eyed the band. "Every one a heretic." Most she would remember from the Altai. "I know you from our time in the mountains. You, though. I don't remember you."

"Escamerole, and it please Your Grace. I didn't go into the Altai. My parents wouldn't leave Khaurene."

"Relative? Cousin? Yes? I see. Come. Help Kedle manage the children." She considered little Raulet. "He's come on fine, considering the rough start."

Brother Candle thought Escamerole might melt. She was Kedle's mirror image. He told her, "Be brave. The Countess only eats Arnhanders and churchmen." A remark that did not leave Socia best pleased.

Socia took it out on her lifeguards. They jumped to.

It was obvious they worshipped their Countess.

In hours it was clear that Socia had, in Brother Candle's absence, become the object of a cult of personality amongst Antieux's young soldiers. It was equally clear that Antieux itself now existed for one purpose: war. Continuous war against the enemies of Count Raymone and the Connec had become the city industry. Man, woman, and child, Antieux subscribed to an apocalyptic vision. It would be obliterated by evil but the fight it fought would render it immortal. For a thousand years wherever righteous men and women strove against the darkness Antieux's memory would be invoked.

Near as Brother Candle ever determined, no one preached that doctrine. It came into being as a shared civic nightmare.

He muttered, "The Night created humanity and humanity creates the Night." He feared he was present at the birth of a self-fulfilling prophecy. As the populace imagined it, so it should be.

Socia's destination was the same comfortable room where he had conferred with her during previous visits. Food and drink were brought. Kedle and Escamerole focused on the littles while Brother Candle and Socia caught up. Then Socia surprised the old man. "Being pregnant has given me a new perspective. A deeper appreciation of what you tried to teach me, all those years. I still don't agree but now I understand what you were saying."

"Glory in the highest."

"I smell rampant sarcasm."

"Possibly. I may have lost my faith. I may have lost any ability I ever had to enjoy a faith."

"You're just feeling sorry for yourself because the real world won't leave you alone. Every time you start to crawl back into the comfort of your faith somebody like me smacks you with a cold, dead, rotten fish of reality."

"What?"

"I've been rehearsing that for months. It didn't work when I said it out loud."

"It worked, child. I think, no matter our root faith—and you're welcome to name any one you want—this is one of those times when despair is the only sane philosophy."

"Bah. Crap. My family were Seekers After Light. My brothers— may the Good God bless and illuminate them—never lost faith. But they never laid down their arms, either. I don't know what the hell I'm talking about, Master. Maybe I should've been born a thousand years ago, when defeat was inevitable and your greatness was measured by how fierce a fight you put up before the inevitable got you."

"Surrender to the Will of the Night."

"Master?"

"What you're saying is an iteration of the attitude of most people before Aaron of Chaldar. It doesn't matter what the individual thinks, feels, or does. The gods do as they please. So yield and be less damaged."

She disagreed. "Defiance, Master. Not acquiescence. Struggle till the end, then fight on."

Kedle said, "I'm sure this is all fun for you two. But there'd better be a reason for dragging the rest of us around."

Brother Candle considered Kedle and Escamerole, each with a child in her lap. "It's a good point, Socia."

"Yeah. Yes. All right, old man. Tell me about your journey. Tell me what the Queen wants. And what you think about that. You girls feel free to interrupt because, much as I love him, the Master wears a big pair of blinders."

Brother Candle spent an hour telling his story. Kedle interrupted twice. Escamerole never said a word. She kept Raulet entertained till exhaustion overcame him.

Socia said, "I don't know when Raymone will be back. Maybe when all the invaders are dead. More likely, in time to see his first son born. Meantime, he trusts me to handle things. So be frank, Master. Why did Isabeth send you? What does she want?"

Brother Candle presented his documents. He said what he had been told to say. Socia did not respond. Finished talking, in danger of an exhausted collapse, he begged to be released. The Countess said, "Thank you, Master. You'll be in your usual cell. Go." She began to talk to Kedle about mundanities like nursing and labor.

COUNT RAYMONE RETURNED THREE WEEKS AFTER BROTHER CANDLE'S arrival, not in a happy state. The Captain-General had departed the Connec in good order. The Society had slipped away with him. There were no more enemies to torment and butcher, except as necessary to maintain civil order.

Raymone Garete was not quite sure what to do with himself in a world where he lacked enemies.

# 37. Lucidia: The Great Campaign

Indala's effort to unify the kaifates of al-Minphet and Qasr al-Zed won the title "The Great Campaign" while it developed. Indala al-Sul Halaladin could not have wished a better champion to shield the flank of his line of communications than Nassim Alizarin. No caravans passed Tel Moussa, westbound or east. No reconnaissance companies got by to go spy on Shamramdi. The Arnhanders of Gherig enjoyed their customary daily pressure—though it was necessary to be wary of the young castellan. Anselin of Menand was vigorous, clever, and determined. He gave as good as he got.

Nassim Alizarin developed an admiration for the boy.

They fell into a routine of patrol and counterpatrol, each trying to lure the other into making a mistake. The Mountain held a slight edge in number of successes. Anselin's youth did work against him occasionally. He suffered moments of impatience.

The news from the south, that summer, was less than golden. Despite the disadvantages Gordimer had created through bad living and an increasingly bad character, despite his having alienated the friendships of those he dealt with daily, the Marshal of the Sha-lug had not lost the genius that had made him a dread opponent.

Gordimer's mystique was founded on the fact that he never lost a battle when he was in charge. As a boy, in school, he never lost a skirmish with a fellow student. As a young officer he carried out every assignment successfully and brought his companions home.

He had known defeat as a minor participant in two lost battles. Neither time had he been in charge, nor near those making decisions, but he had been close enough to see defeat develop and understand why.

Nassim Alizarin had been there near Gordimer throughout the early years, a clever captain himself. He had risen as the Lion rose.

None of the news from the south surprised the Mountain.

The forces of al-Minphet—only a minority Sha-lug, especially early on—crumbled before the Lucidian host. Till Gordimer himself left al-Qarn and met the invaders at Nestor, where the desert gave way to the green fecundity of the Shirne delta. There the superior numbers and quickness of Lucidian horsemen did little good. The Sha-lug fixed them in place on boggy ground while engines aboard Dreangerean galleys in channels nearby punished them with continuous missile fires.

The again rehabilitated sorcerer er-Rashal al-Dhulquarnen aided the Dreangerean cause dramatically.

The engagement at Nestor was unusual. It occurred in brief, sudden bloodlettings over several days once the initial massive exchange subsided. Indala tried to draw Gordimer out. Gordimer worked Indala's flanks, keeping him fixed within range of the ships. The Lucidians had no means of silencing those.

Each side suffered a level of casualties considered unacceptable in an engagement that would not prove decisive. Indala finally chose a genuine withdrawal into the desert. Once there, out of sight, he sent a substantial force south, through the wilderness. Meanwhile, Indala demonstrated in front of Nestor. That kept the Dreangerean main force in place while the southern group presented itself at the gates of al-Qarn. The city was defended by local militias and retired Sha-lug.

Azim al-Adil ed-Din was one of the commanders in that adventure.

Admitted to the city by traitors, the Lucidians ran wild. They were fierce and merciless, murdering anyone who resisted. A day after getting past the wall they reached the Palace of the Kings and forcibly assumed protection of Kaseem al-Bakr, Kaif of al-Minphet.

The invaders continued vigorous in suppressing resistance, for which they paid. The elderly and retired Sha-lug of the staffs of the various palaces of state refused to yield. Those old men were slower than the Lucidian youngsters but they were crafty and they knew their ground.

The cost of taking the civil center grew too heavy. The invaders took Kaseem al-Bakr and settled in at one of the city's great temples.

All this news reached Tel Moussa eventually, as it wended its way back to Shamramdi. Nassim strutted around as proud of young Az as if he were his own son.

Other news arrived as well, with Akir's firepowder and two of the promised falcons. Bad things were happening in the Eastern Empire, specifics uncertain till Akir himself arrived. He had made a side trip to Haeti, to the Dainshaukin founders there. The rest of the four-pounder battery would not be coming.

Raiders from the Grail Empire had overrun the Devedian manufactory before those could be moved out. Akir himself had gotten away, "By the thickness of one of God's whiskers. Had I wasted another half hour they would've caught me."

There was more. The raiders had taken all the firepowder and weapons, and all the craftsmen as well. They had destroyed the works. Then they had crossed the Vieran Sea to invade Firaldia.

"Why would they do that?" Nassim was confused. Akir seemed unable to tell his story linearly. Too, he wandered off into speculations about what God must be thinking, causing these things to happen.

Nassim listened with the rest of the garrison, during supper. After the meal he told Akir, "Join me for prayers. I have a few questions."

The Mountain fulfilled his obligation in the highest parapet, with the sun already set and a sliver of moon pursuing the evening star. It was getting chilly.

Akir prompted, "Your questions, General?"

"Your report was confusing. You had so much to say that you didn't get it out in any sensible order."

"And that would be the truth."

The general did not push. Akir could not recall every critical fact if he became excited.

Nassim interspersed questions with comments about a remarkable meteor shower. "The angels are flinging death stones by the score tonight." He wondered who and where the targets might be. The streaks of fire all headed west.

The Mountain's efforts brought out news that would not reach his crusader neighbors for days, nor Indala for more than a week.

Three western kings were dead. The three who had crushed the flower of the manhood of al-Halambra. God is Great! The death of one had turned the Grail Empire against the Brothen Church. It now looked like the greatest of all invasions of the Holy Lands might be stillborn. God is Great!

The death of another king placed the heir to one throne right over there in Gherig. God is Great!

Nassim tried to winkle out what Else Tage might be doing along with the real prospects for the Grail Empress's greatest of all crusades.

Surely she would set that aside, now. And once she fed her hunger for emotional equity, she ought to have no crusader spirit left. Right?

The history of the wars between the Patriarchs and the Grail Emperors was, largely, one of futility. The lords of the scores of little Firaldian polities played them one against the other. They had an interest in chaos. It inflated their importance.

Still . . . Much would depend on Captain Tage. He might be the man to shatter the deadlock so he could head east, to address his own grievances. Gordimer might survive Indala only to find himself chin to chin with the Grail Empire.

"Akir, tell me more about what happened at the place where they manufactured the firepowder weapons."

Akir had nothing else to tell. He had had to flee before he could learn anything useful. "The critical point, General, is that the Grail Empire controls all those weapons and the craftsmen who make them."

"My heart bleeds, Akir. No good will come of this."

*       *       *

THE MOUNTAIN KNEW ALMOST TO THE INSTANT WHEN NEWS OF RE-gard's death reached Gherig. Bells started ringing. Their clangor was annoying even at Tel Moussa's remove.

Nassim had been awaiting the distraction. He began raiding imme-diately. He enjoyed some success, but only briefly. The Arnhanders of the region dashed inside their fortress. Gherig was like a tortoise pulling in head and legs. The foreigners regained their balance, then counterat-tacked.

Nassim hoped he could harass Anselin of Menand enough to keep him from leaving. The longer it took him to get home the more chance for chaos to breed there. Arnhand, more than any other infidel king-dom, fed and financed the crusader movement.

Anselin refused to be managed. He came out in force, scattered Nas-sim's raiders, drove them back into Tel Moussa and the desert, then headed for the coast. Untroubled.

NEWS CAME UP FROM DREANGER. IT WAS NOT GOOD. GORDIMER AND er-Rashal had faked a withdrawal from Nestor. Indala and his generals had believed what they saw. Indala took half the remaining troops and scurried off to see al-Qarn. He was forty miles south of Nestor when the Sha-lug attacked the troops he had left behind. The surprise was complete. The slaughter afterward was very nearly so.

The Dreangerean success put Indala in a position where he *had* to win his war to survive politically.

His dead all had families to mourn them. Many had relatives of standing who could raise difficulties if they believed lives had been wasted. Further, the unity existing inside Qasr al-Zed did so because of the respect and admiration Indala's family had inspired by their many successes. Indala must continue to succeed to retain that respect.

Following his triumph the Lion did leave Nestor. He used the great fleet ported at Iskendemea to leapfrog the mouths of the Shirne to that second greatest of Dreangerean cities. There he reorganized and refit-ted. His intent was to march up the west bank of the Shirne, hoping that Indala would come over and fight. The numbers lay with the Sha-lug and Dreangerean forces.

Indala had achieved most of his goals. He held al-Qarn. He had possession of Kaseem al-Bakr. In the Lucidian mode of thought that should have ended it. But Gordimer and er-Rashal gave those facts no special weight. They were annoyances. Inconveniences. They could be rectified.

The world awaited an outcome.

In the Holy Lands the lords of the Crusader states got ready to jump on the back of the winner.

THE MOUNTAIN WAS DRAFTING HIS MONTHLY ACTIVITIES REPORT FOR the clerks in Shamramdi when old Az appeared. "Big news, General. And it isn't good."

"Indala got his head handed to him?"

"No. Not that. That's still in the hands of God. I'm talking about Queen Clothilde bullying Berismond into giving Gherig back to Black Rogert."

"Oh." Nassim sat in glum silence for more than a minute. Then, "What do we know? Where will he be coming from? And when?"

## 38. Vis Corcula, the Shades

It was a beautiful summer dawn in the Shades. It started chilly. That would change dramatically once the sun climbed high. It had rained off and on all night. A mist now concealed the wildflower-strewn ground out in front of Piper Hecht. Somewhere beyond that, a few miles downslope, lay the encampment of the army sent to clear Vis Corcula of this tumor called the Righteous.

Hecht, Titus Consent, and Rivademar Vircondelet had slipped down there in the darkness and rain. They had not gotten a good look because of the weather but what Hecht had seen assured him that he faced big numbers, entirely disorganized. Heris had been right about Serenity being able to roll out a large mob.

The rain had made hearing unreliable. They avoided getting too close, fearing they might stumble into a sentry post because they could not hear the sentries complaining about having guard duty in foul weather.

There had been a lot of fires, both inside of and outside a low stockade meant to manage sheep and cattle. The camp centered on a longtime livestock operation belonging to the Benedocto family.

Wherever Hecht wandered next morning, willfully alone, the soldiers watched nervously. They wanted to believe he could work a miracle. They wanted to believe they were the best of the best and invincible. But they were daunted by the numbers. A disparity still growing as more troops arrived down below. A plan was in place but was so weird the men did not believe it could be the real plan. It had to be a plan the Commander wanted the Patriarch's spies to discover.

And that was true. With Hecht hoping the enemy gave it less credence than did his own men, who understood the concept despite its
departure from doctrine.

Clej Sedlakova joined Hecht between hummocks that might have
been faded recollections of prehistoric burial mounds. "They're getting
nervous, boss. You still haven't told anybody the real plan."

"Smoke and mirrors, Clej. That's the way it stays. What our men
don't know those people down the hill can't find out. Tell them to do
what I say when I say it. What about the meadow?"

"It gets soggier by the minute." Drainage was not good. Hecht saw
several sheets of water, none deep enough to overtop the grasses and
wildflowers but definitely deep enough to have gotten into his boots on
his way back from scouting.

"Good. That'll make the footing worse." He licked a finger and
stuck it in the air. "I don't know about that, though. I can't decide which
way I'd rather have it blow."

"Either way, somebody ain't gonna be able to see shit."

"Yeah. Send me Rhuk and Prosek."

"Again? Haven't you pestered them enough? They know what
they're doing. And they have plenty to do. Let them do it."

"All right." That used to be his strength. Giving a man a job, then
letting him do it. "You're right. They can handle the details. You'd better
get going if you want to get there in time."

"And if they don't come today? Or if they just want to talk you
into giving up?"

"If not today, tomorrow. They can't have brought a lot of supplies.
They didn't have time to organize it. If they want to talk, I'll talk. And
be obviously stalling till my situation gets better."

"You *want* them to come at us?"

"No. I want them to think that's what I want. So they'll be confused.
And, maybe, not give me what I want. Oh, damnit! Go gently tell the
Empress that it's not good for her to be wandering around where a mas-
sacre could break out any minute."

Katrin, in armor, roamed the slopes making a studied effort to connect with the soldiers. A cynical effort, to Hecht's thinking.

"Will do," Sedlakova said, not bothering to remind him that she
would have heard it all from Captain Ephrian already. "She's probably
scaring the men more than giving them heart." He left, humming a tune
that had been a favorite of Madouc's. If he spoke to Katrin Hecht
missed it.

Hecht felt the ghost of a whisper of moving air. A soft voice asked,
"You do intend to make a stand here, don't you?"

Hecht tried and failed to hide his surprise. "Well. Hello. I thought you'd gone off to another world."

Grinning, the man in brown said, "I did. I'm on holiday while your picky sister makes some arrangements. A detail-oriented girl, our Heris. She'll do well as the Twelfth Unknown. If we survive all this."

"We? You're joining in here?"

"I was speaking generally. But, here? Yes. Good timing, eh?"

"Suspiciously."

"Not so much. When Heris brought the latest news the Bastard and I decided we had to come back and add to the confusion. I've been around for a few days."

"Really?" Hecht looked round to see who might have noticed the Ninth Unknown. The old man appeared to have generated no special interest.

"Two days. First I had to go over and make sure Heris's falcons don't end up in the wrong hands before the Aelen Kofer show up. Then I had to see Muno and poke around in the dark corners in Brothe. Not a pretty city, right now. Serenity is out to make it uniquely his own. Muno and his cohorts are undermining him."

"What were you thinking of getting into here?"

"Mischief, dear boy. Malicious mischief. And lots of it."

"Like?"

"Well, an invisible man can cause a lot of confusion. Orders could go astray. A general could say one thing and a captain could hear something else. There could be ghosts. Or Night things. Who knows? The options are infinite." Februaren turned sideways, vanished. Then turned right back into being. "Forgot to tell you. They're going to attack today. The first wave is on its way. They won't parley. Their orders are to find you and overwhelm you, at whatever cost."

"Not very sporting."

"Serenity thinks like you, Piper. This is serious business. Time to go. People are starting to wonder."

Terens Ernest and the self-anointed lifeguards arrived momentarily. Ernest demanded, "Who was that? Where did he go?"

Terens Ernest was a dangerous man. He was always around, somewhere. And Hecht seldom noticed. No telling what he heard and saw.

Ernest wilted under the glare of the Commander of the Righteous. He could not match Madouc's immunity to his principal's attitudes.

"A man who spies for me. Forget you saw him. Did I call for you? Any of you? You have assigned posts. You haven't abandoned them, have you?"

The response consisted of nervous yak about being concerned. He was in the presence of a stranger, with no help close by. And it was not that long since he had proven that he was not arrow-proof.

Hecht stifled rising anger. It was unreasonable anger. These men should not be crushed for listening to their consciences. However much he found their concern inconvenient. "That will be all, then. Back to your posts. The enemy is coming. Terens, tell Mr. Rhuk and Mr. Prosek to attend me as quickly as possible." This time he did have something new to say to those two.

"Quiet. I need to talk fast." Prosek and Rhuk had fewer problems with his ways than did most of the others. Rhuk grunted. Hecht continued, "They're coming. They're not sure where we are. They expect us to be farther back than this but they don't really care. Let's make it a nasty surprise. Everyone wait till I light the candle. Everyone. Understood?"

Rhuk told Prosek, "I do believe the boss wants us to note an important point."

"Yeah."

"Can the smart-ass stuff. There won't be any parley. Their orders are to swamp us and finish us. All. No exceptions. We'll get through this only if nobody panics and everybody does his job. Pass that word and keep reminding them."

"Yes sir."

"Thank you. Go. I hear company coming now."

There were no drums, no horns, no pipes, only the clang, clatter, and chatter of a mob of rowdy drunks.

Could that be?

Commanders in some armies did get their soldiers drunk before an attack. In the days of war elephants they got the beasts drunk, too.

Hecht jogged a couple hundred yards back, uphill, to the eminence whence he meant to observe and hoped to be seen by the attackers and thought to be a picket.

Seconds after he was in place the Ninth Unknown turned into being behind him. "They're coming."

"I hear them. Are they drunk?"

"Some may be. I did work a little mischief with that last night. Any of them who did any drinking will be sluggish and miserable by now."

"How many are coming?"

"You don't have enough fingers and toes to count them. Not all of you put together. But you do have an advantage. You didn't have to hustle uphill for three miles with a hangover to get here."

Most of the mist on the meadow had burned away. From this vantage the standing water was more obvious. There was more of that than Hecht had thought. But it was still seeping down off the surrounding slopes.

Shapes appeared in the mist beyond the meadow. In moments it was clear that Serenity's force lacked all discipline. But they made a big crowd.

The Empress materialized as suddenly as had Cloven Februaren. Hecht started and looked around. The Ninth Unknown just stood there wearing a goofy half-wit look. Katrin brought Captain Ephrian and four lifeguards with her. Hecht could not help barking, "What are you doing here?"

"The same as you, Commander. Being seen by those who serve me."

"That isn't what I'm doing, Your Grace. I'm pretending to be a picket so the men coming up the hill think they have to trudge on a while yet before they make contact."

"Then I apologize for destroying that illusion. Nevertheless, I insist on a more respectful attitude."

He was set to explode. He did not need vultures perched on his shoulders, muttering in his ears. But, out of Katrin's view, Captain Ephrian shook his head desperately, warning him not to make a scene. Hecht took a deep breath, said, "As you will, Your Grace."

"Yes. Always. Do not forget that. Who is this man in brown? I don't recall having seen him before."

"An agent. I've known him for several years. He's reliable."

Februaren chuckled. And would not keep his mouth shut. "An agent of the Night. Piper. Pay attention. It's time."

Correct. The men would be getting nervous. "Hand me that slow match there."

Februaren did so, then took a step backward. Then took another. And a third at the moment when Hecht applied the match to the firework Kait Rhuk had fashioned.

A dozen balls of fire leapt fifty feet into the air over a meadow filled with floundering men cursing water and mud.

One hundred forty-six hidden firepowder weapons—including every last piece taken from Krulik and Sneigon—spoke during the next dozen seconds, each hurling six or more pounds of loam and stones.

Everything out front vanished in the smoke. There was no telling the effect of the salvo. It did have one. The mob did not emerge from the smoke.

That, initially dense enough to harm lungs, drifted westward, off the meadow and down the slope of the Shades.

Now Hecht needed his men to execute their orders without flaw. The men had to form crews at previously designated weapons while the enemy was stunned. They had to reload those and fire at the biggest enemy group they saw. No defense other than the falcons would be deployed.

The auxiliaries from Vis Corcula were supposed to drag any idled weapons to positions farther back.

The smoke thinned, unveiling the nearer meadow.

Hecht was horrified.

No sounds came from down there . . . He heard nothing because of the violence done his ears by all those explosions. There had to be a lot of screaming out there.

The smoke continued to drift and disperse.

Serenity's men had stopped moving.

Hecht heard the dull ghost of a falcon's bark. Somebody thought he saw something worth a shot.

Hecht said, "This is where the smoke could be a huge problem." He got no response. Cloven Februaren had disappeared. He wished that Katrin had done the same.

The enemy resumed his advance.

A falcon bellowed. Another followed. Then another. Then one blew up. Hecht could make out the screams that followed.

The wind picked up and shifted as much as the terrain allowed, a couple points to the north. That pushed the smoke out of the way a little faster.

Soon the people down the hill stopped slogging listlessly into the kill zone.

The smoke cleared entirely, betraying the full horror. Using Katrin's lifeguards as messengers, Hecht nagged his officers to get the falcons repositioned, reloaded, and retrained. As many as time allowed.

The Empress said nothing and did not overrule his use of her companions. Captain Ephrian was not pleased but kept his peace.

Katrin spoke only after full use of her hearing returned. She did not say a lot, though, and Hecht ignored her as much as he dared. He hoped none of the enemy recognized her. But, so long as she insisted on being on the battlefield, he hoped her presence stiffened the resolve of the Righteous.

The work of the falcons was gut-wrenching awful but no victory had been won. The attackers, if not overawed and intimidated early, would realize the weapons took a long time to recharge. And only few could be kept in action after the initial salvo.

On reflection, though, he decided the enemy would have to know as much about firepowder weapons as he did to understand how vulnerable he really was.

Silence again. The only smoke visible was way off down the slope, nearing the plain. Hecht looked for signs of Sedlakova's presence down there, saw nothing.

"How many casualties out there?" Katrin asked. "A thousand?"

"Or more." Most not yet dead. The least badly hurt trying to help other survivors. The standing water now red. And Hecht suspecting that many of the dead might have drowned.

Signals and messengers informed him as each battery came ready for action.

Downhill, out of range, men roamed about helping the injured, peering and pointing, often obviously arguing. Serenity's captains trying to decide what to do next, unaware that each minute granted the Righteous would make their next surge that much more deadly.

Hecht considered the higher hills to either hand. Not terribly difficult ground if the enemy wanted to try going around.

Small groups of recently arrived Imperials were out there. He would be warned if Serenity's captains did try the harder going.

The officers down there were no more eager than their men. Only after a full hour did they launch another mass charge, straight ahead.

This attack involved more men. So many they kept tripping over one another. Not to mention the dead and wounded.

Some nervous fool could not wait. He touched match to touchhole.

One premature discharge led to a score, then to all the rest, raggedly. Men went down like wheat blown over in a high wind.

The smoke closed in. That was worse this time. The air was almost still.

Hecht saw shapes moving through the smoke. Big shapes. Shapes not human. What were they? Illusions? He could not tell if there was sound associated with them. His hearing was gone again.

A lesson that should have been learned long since. Men around falcons needed to protect their ears.

He withdrew upslope a short distance, then crossed to a vantage he hoped would offer a better view beyond the smoke. He noticed that the men did have their ears protected. So it was just him.

The Empress followed. She had been jabbering for some time and he had not heard a word.

She and her lifeguards had protected their ears, too, with pieces of cloth.

The falcons designated to stay in action after the initial salvo did so, blindly—with little likelihood of failing to hit something. They had been laid according to patterns designed by Kait Rhuk and Drago Prosek. Their stone storm should sweep the meadow regularly, invisible or not.

A few men did stagger out of the smoke, glazed and watery of eye, driven by inertia.

Hecht did hear the Empress say, "I thought more of them would get through."

He said, "I did, too. And they may still. There could be thousands in that smoke, still." The big shapes were not there anymore.

There might be thousands in the smoke but only dozens emerged. Dully. Numbly. Ineffective except where they forced a falcon crew to stop work while they defended themselves.

That was what Hecht had feared from the moment he chose to make this stand. Each time a weapon fell out of the firing rotation more of Serenity's men would get through. And that was the way it went, till many of the Righteous could not work their falcons. Though some never ceased firing and others came back quickly after handling a local threat.

The air began to move again. The smoke began to thin. That let falcon crews sight their weapons on the biggest clumps of men moving up.

The carnage was beyond anything Hecht imagined beforehand. It was beyond what Prosek and Rhuk had imagined, and those two always produced grim forecasts. The meadow had vanished under heaped bodies. Attackers had to clamber over and around the dead and dying, whose bodies continued to be torn by stone shot.

The breeze turned brisk enough to clear all but the freshest smoke. The attackers came on in tens, now, instead of hundreds.

Katrin demanded, "Why aren't there more of them? They almost had us."

"I don't know, Your Grace." Hecht was more interested in finding out what those shapes in the smoke had done. He saw nothing. "It might be Sedlakova's fault."

"Sedlakova?"

"The one-armed man. Running my cavalry."

"I know who he is. What is he doing that might affect what happens here?"

"He's supposed to be down there attacking their camp."

"With fifty riders?"

Hecht spread his hands. "If he gets a chance to cause major misery."

The Ninth Unknown might have done something distracting, too.

Hecht would not admit it but he had bet everything that his first salvo would panic the enemy.

That did not happen. They took incredible casualties and kept coming. And more were on their way.

The fighting fell off but continued. Prince Onofrio's men, tasked with moving the idle falcons, did not do so with any alacrity. Some, with the weapons, got overrun.

"There's something wrong, Commander of the Righteous."

"They're dogging it. They want to get caught. With my weapons. This isn't going well, Your Grace. Leave before it starts again."

The Empress snapped, "I don't mean the Prince's men. I mean Serenity's. Look at them. Something's been done to them. They wouldn't keep coming, otherwise."

She was right. They kept coming despite blasts that knocked them down twenty at a time. "Captain Ephrian. Might I borrow some men for messengers?" He had kept no one with him. He had foreseen no need to pull strings once the engagement began.

Ephrian glanced at Katrin. She offered a barely perceptible nod.

Hecht said, "Captain, I fear this won't go as well next rush. Please move Her Highness to safety." Looking Katrin in the eye. "She may not like it but she'll be alive to punish me later."

Ephrian flashed a nervous grin. Katrin flashed anger. Hecht gathered in the two men the captain volunteered. "I need you to run out to where the tripwire forces are hidden. One each way."

"Those Imperials?"

"Correct. You know where they're supposed to be. And what the hell is that?"

A roiling cloud of smoke rose over the distant enemy camp.

"Sir?"

"Right there! Oh. I see. So. Go. One to Consent, one to Vircondelet. Tell them I want them to swing in and hit these people from the sides. Downhill, out of falcon range, and don't try to win the war in one skirmish. Just hit them, confuse them, panic them if possible, then get the hell out. This is just an experiment to test Her Grace's hypothesis about them being englamoured. Plus, I want the distraction. Afterward, catch up with Captain Ephrian and the Empress."

"Sir. Yes, sir."

"Follow her for as long as it takes. All the way back to the coast if you have to. This could turn real bad." He suspected a third and bigger wave was forming up out of sight. The dribble still coming was challenge enough.

"Yes, sir." They split up and left. Katrin had gone with Captain Ephrian but was not happy about it.

Hecht wondered how Helspeth would have behaved in similar circumstances. He thought her sense of duty would have kept her away. She was not as self-indulgent or impulsive as Katrin.

THE ENGLAMOURED OR DRUNKEN SOLDIERS KEPT PUSHING CLOSER despite inspired work by Rhuk and Prosek. Hecht guessed five thousand dead and dying men littered the meadow. More lay scattered right up to and past his own position. The nearby dead included half of Prince Onofrio's treacherous levy.

The attackers treated Onofrio's men as they did the Righteous. They would hear no claims of friendship. Hecht thought they might not hear at all.

Vircondelet and Consent launched the attacks Hecht had ordered, uncoordinated, like mosquitoes assaulting an elephant.

They hit the gathering mass Hecht had anticipated, doing much more damage than their numbers promised. The Patriarchals were slow to respond. Their focus was straight ahead.

Titus Consent hit first, from the north. He was in full flight when Rivademar Vircondelet struck from the south.

The spoiling raid delayed the third wave just when the fighting above the meadow had most of the Righteous engaged hand-to-hand.

Hecht personally fended off two attackers. One he thought he remembered from the fighting against the Calziran pirates. The man did not recognize him. He, his companion, and the rest of the attackers moved slowly, as though part of some army of the dead.

Hecht had seen, smelled, and fought exactly that at al-Khazen. This did bear the stamp of the Night but was not the same.

Deeper analysis would have to wait.

Only a score of falcons still barked regularly. Twice in rapid succession, then a third time, Hecht heard weapons explode. Heard falcon crews scream. Caught whiffs of burnt flesh. And thought Krulik and Sneigon might not be totally clever after all.

The lessened rate of fire was more than matched by a lessened flow of attackers. The assault finally high-watered, then receded.

Titus Consent arrived, so far out of breath that he could do nothing but suck air for half a minute.

Once he had breath enough to dare, he puked. Done with that, he gasped, "They're trying to come around our flanks, now, boss. They're like the undead, or something. I can't stop them all."

A falcon exploded just twenty yards away. Iron shrapnel took the feather off Consent's helmet. "God just busted me back to the ranks."

"No. He just showed you He loves you enough to make that miss. Here we go again."

Another cloud climbed the air over the enemy camp, way down at the bottom of the slope. "Think that's Clej?"

"About time."

Could not be Sedlakova, though. He and his horsemen were barely strong enough to mount a harassment. There was no evidence that they had done any harassing. Nor had they taken explosives with them.

A half minute later something changed.

Hecht watched it come, a wave racing its way through those Patriarchals he could see. He felt it himself but the impact was slight and without personal meaning.

It meant everything to the attackers.

The assault collapsed instantly.

Serenity's troops stood around stupidly gathering their thoughts. But the falcons continued to talk.

Serenity's men ran.

Hecht told Consent, "Get back to your men. See if this helped."

"Right." Titus looked abidingly suspicious, like he thought Hecht had orchestrated everything by sheer wishful thinking.

THE WORLD GREW STILL. THE SMOKE CLEARED AWAY. BETWEEN LONG periods of restful inactivity the surviving Righteous positioned their surviving falcons to greet another assault. Damaged and suspicious weapons left the line.

Time passed. No attack came. The enemy seemed interested in nothing but recovering his casualties. Hecht did not interfere. His officers began to feel comfortable enough to come report. They found their commander overwhelmed by his success.

So far.

He was sure another wave would come. He concealed his confidence that it would be successful.

The reports were good. And they were bad.

The good news was that friendly casualties were implausibly light. Initially, Hecht heard about forty-three killed and wounded, the majority victims of exploding falcons. According to Rhuk and Prosek, those casualties could not be laid at the feet of Krulik and Sneigon. Falcons exploded when panicky crews got into too much of a hurry. They failed to properly clear a weapon's bore of sparks before trying to reload. Or they shoved in multiple loads before remembering to apply the match. Or they measured their firepowder wrong. Or they decided to double charge. All of which happened more often as men grew tired and the acid of fear gnawed at reason.

"Falls into the realm of lessons learned, Kait. Drago. Work on it when we have time. Measure the powder ahead of time. Come up with a work song with a rhythm that reminds them to follow the proper steps in proper order. Something like that. Oh. And find a way to protect their hearing. I like to went deaf and I wasn't on top of a falcon."

Both men eyed him like they were having trouble believing what he had said. "Boss, we've been doing that for two years."

"Oh. So. Maybe I ought to pay closer attention . . ."

Shouts from several directions declaimed, "Here they come again!"

In an instant Hecht was alone. Men scurried in every direction. Then he was not alone. A funny-looking little man in brown was there beside him.

"What do you think of that, Piper?"

"Looks like a false alarm."

"Not that."

"Then what do I think of what?"

"You were having big-ass problems with enemy soldiers who didn't see any reason not to trudge on into the teeth of your marvelous killing machines. Right? Out there? Five deep. They just kept coming, right?"

"Yes. But then they all ran away."

"So say thank you, honored ancestor."

"For?"

"I cribbed an idea from your sister. I took a keg of firepowder and planted it where it was likely to do some good when it went boom."

"Say what?"

"Took me two tries but I got the Collegium asshole responsible for the sorcery. Name was Portanté. Principaté Catio Portanté."

"I don't know the name. Looks like it wasn't a false alarm." Enemy troops were on the move, though not many. "A probe."

"I never paid attention to him before, either. He was lowlife and low-key. From one of the cities up north, related to the Benedocto by marriage. So related to Bronte Doneto, obscurely."

"My guess is, Serenity has a lot of friends we don't know."

"Muno knows them. You should let me take you down to see him."

Hecht shuddered. "Of course." A falcon bellowed greetings to Patriarchals who had come too close. "I'll just pop out during a battle. No one will miss me."

"See, this is why I never let myself get roped into big responsibilities.

They eat you up. They keep you from doing what you want. Like this right here. Here come some of them dicks that need you to think for them. And I can't disappear because they've already seen me."

Rhuk and Prosek had returned. The enemy probe was not developing a threat. Hecht said, "Do keep your opinions to yourself while we talk."

Februaren snorted. Shooting your mouth off was another thing you could not do when you had responsibilities.

Prosek seemed interested only in the man in brown. He stared, let Rhuk do the talking. Rhuk said, "Boss, we might consider pulling out after this stops."

"Why?"

"We're worn out and beat up and the weapons are getting fatigued."

"Kait, I'm going to take a second to make sure I have my temper under control. All right. Go. We've had six weapons explode. I know that. I know why."

"True. But our casualty estimates before were way off."

"All right. Tell me."

Rhuk went pale. "Sorry. Sir. We have twenty-three dead or wounded on my side."

"Forty-two for me," Prosek said. "Those people got into several of my positions before they high-watered."

"To which we have to add casualties suffered by Vircondelet, Consent, and Sedlakova," Hecht grumbled. "Unless you counted them already."

Both men shook their heads.

Prosek, still staring at Cloven Februaren like he suspected the man of being the Adversary incarnate, said, "Manpower isn't the problem. We're running low on munitions. Charges, especially."

A falcon roared. Hecht looked toward the meadow. The probe was fading. The live people out there, now, were looking for wounded to take to the healing brothers. "Are our men more worn out than those people?"

Prosek shrugged. "I doubt it."

"Position your weapons. Load them. Lay them. Vircondelet and Consent will be back soon. Draft their men as replacements. One inexperienced man to a crew. Get me a census on our munitions. We can't possibly have used all that firepowder. It took seven ships to haul it."

"Oh, no sir. There's still tons of firepowder. Just not up here. We didn't have the drayage to bring even a fraction of it. Nor would we have brought it all if we could have. Too much risk of losing it."

Rhuk said, "We're low on firepowder, boss, but even lower on

charges. We started out with twenty to twenty-five for every weapon."
An almost unimaginably immense number, Hecht understood. Tons
upon tons. Wagon after wagon. "But the stuff goes fast. None of the
crews have used up all they started with but some are down to their last
two or three. There isn't anything around here that we can substitute.
We're having what's left redistributed. It won't last long if there's another big attack. Oh. Each team had one charge of godshot. In case. But
we don't want to use that."

Hecht stepped on a flash of anger. This was not their fault. This
was his. They had done what he had told them to do. In truth, they had
done more.

He had not expected this to last. He had counted on massed fire to
panic the enemy. But he should have considered the possibility that
they might be manipulated by a maniac sorcerer willing to spend them
to the last man.

Hecht said, "Things didn't go the way I expected. But there have
been dramatic changes over there. I'm told." Slight gesture toward the
man in brown. "So, for now, we hold on, every weapon loaded. Instead
of spreading your munitions around, though, concentrate them with the
weapons that will keep firing after the first salvo."

Hecht looked to Cloven Februaren, hoping to hear something
about the improbability of another serious attack.

The old man understood but could promise nothing.

"Don't kill people trying to clean up down there."

Prosek said, "We might have a problem with theft. I'm missing several kegs of firepowder."

A ghost of a smirk shadowed the lips of the Ninth Unknown.

Hecht understood. "They didn't go to waste, Drago."

The respite stretched for hours. The enemy removed his dead and
wounded amid gathering carrion birds and insects. The Righteous took
care of their own.

Cloven Februaren contrived to vanish without being noticed.

The Patriarchal force did not move again till late afternoon, when
Hecht had begun thinking about standing down for dinner, then slipping away.

There must be a castle somewhere big enough to hole up in till the
weight of the Empire made itself felt elsewhere.

But he did not want to abandon his falcons.

He would have to if he ran.

So standing his ground was his only real choice.

He worried about Clej Sedlakova. There had been no word.

The day's costs haunted him already.

Some key veterans had fallen, men who had been with him since the City Regiment days.

And Titus had suffered his first serious wound.

"Here they come!" went up across the slope. And this was no false alarm. The enemy entered the meadow and crept forward on the flanking hills. Hecht said, "Titus, I didn't look at it close enough before I decided to do this. If this goes bad . . ."

"Never mind, boss. I put myself here. It's all right." Boldly said but it was not all right.

Hecht knew he needed to have a face-to-face with his soul if he survived. He was not sure if hubris, arrogance, overconfidence, or a combination of those was his trouble, but there was something.

A smile tickled his lips as he recalled feeling like this in every tight situation where his enemies gave him time to brood. He began to have irrelevant thoughts, too. As usual.

He should have studied the Construct more diligently. He would have a way out of here, now. Though he might be at less immediate risk than his men. Serenity might want him taken for special attention later. He seemed the sort.

Fire discipline held. The falcon crews waited.

The advance slowed as it approached a suspected kill line. Most of those men had seen what had happened to those who had gone before them.

Officers safely farther back cursed and threatened.

The advance stopped dead.

A tremendous explosion took place out of sight, down the road. Gray smoke rolled up into the late-afternoon light, accompanied by shouts and screams. Everyone out front jumped, surged, surprised.

Hecht ordered, "Fire the full salvo."

The falcons roared. Reddening sunlight tinted the smoke a fierce orange-red.

That smoke, for a short while, drifted upslope, pushed by marginally warmer air from down the mountain. Soon, though, the air cooled. The smoke drifted downhill again. No one and nothing emerged from it.

The smoke concealed the sources of a lot of noise. Something was going on in there. To Hecht it sounded like every man turning on his neighbor. Partly true. Each man had become desperate to get away. But sorcery that messed with men's minds added to their desperation.

Hecht gave orders that there be no firing unless the attack developed.

Darkness came. The smoke went away. Indifferent stars came out. Rivademar Vircondelet reported that the Patriarchals had withdrawn from the meadow, around a sheltering knee of mountain. The meadow was carpeted in a fresh human harvest. The enemy was removing their wounded. Night scavengers were moving in.

At some point, unnoticed till he spoke, Cloven Februaren had rejoined the Commander of the Righteous. Hecht's people paid him no heed. They stepped around him but did not speak to him or ask about him.

Februaren observed, "It's over, Piper. They've given up. You might still hear from the Night, though. It wouldn't hurt to have a few of your toys charged up with godshot, just in case. Take care of that, then I want you to take a walk with me."

"Why? Where to?"

"Down there. To talk to people from the other side."

"Should I ask you questions?"

"You can if you like. You may not get the answers you want to hear."

"What I figured. Titus!"

"Sir?"

"How are you feeling? How's the arm?"

"They say I'm going to live. Only fourteen stitches but it aches like hell."

"Good to hear. I don't know what I'd do without you."

Februaren grumbled, "I don't want to intrude on a budding romance, but . . ."

"Just making sure Titus is fit to join us. Titus, you can carry a truce flag, can't you?"

"If you insist."

"Good. It's a sure thing that there'll be people we know down there, one way or another." Hecht shook a finger at the Ninth Unknown. "My way, old-timer."

Februaren scowled but did not argue.

Hecht asked, "Is this likely to take long? I haven't eaten all day."

"You should take better care of yourself. Grab a loaf, cheese, and sausage and let's go. You can nibble along the way. It'll be slow going."

"That's all right. I can wait." The scenery would not be appetizing.

The old man snickered.

Hecht thought the Ninth Unknown was on his way to becoming something more than human. Was there such a thing as an apprentice ascendant? Like an accidental ascendant? Unaware of his status?

Asgrimmur Grimmsson could be presented in evidence.

Frowning, Titus went to work rounding up lanterns and lifeguards.

TITUS SAID, "OUR NEW WEAPONS DO TERRIBLE THINGS."

Terens Ernest, swollen proud to be accompanying his commander, said, "Not worse than swords and axes. Praise God, they didn't come at us on horseback. I couldn't stand it if we had to kill a couple thousand horses."

Cloven Februaren snorted but did not otherwise express an opinion.

Hecht said, "The real horror is how fast and impersonally we can kill. Some of those men firing falcons never saw the enemy up close. And guys like Prosek and Rhuk will keep finding ways to reach out farther, faster, and more accurately. They love the challenge. They never think about it in human terms."

This was the bloodiest battlefield of his acquaintance. There were many bloodier encounters on record, a few quite recent: Los Naves de los Fantas and what had taken place outside Khaurene. But there was an industrial feel to what had happened here that he found disquieting.

Titus asked, "What will Serenity do when he hears about this?"

"He'll spew Writs of Anathema. Of Excommunication. Bulls of all sorts, blustering. Blaming everyone but himself. He's turning into his cousin."

The Ninth Unknown would not remain silent. "And no one will take him seriously anymore because he's showing such a great talent for looking as goofy as Sublime. He's not that blind and dishonest but we've had some straight-arrow Patriarchs for contrast. He looks like a throwback. What's happened here could finish him with the Brothen mob."

Hecht did not believe that. Bronte Doneto was much too crafty. "How about we concentrate on the moment?"

He was nervous. The darkness seemed unnaturally deep. The lanterns did not push it back to a comfortable distance. The killing field stank of spilled bowels and coagulated blood and flesh already corrupting. He kept tripping over dead people. The nasty water got inside his boots. He was hungry and his head had begun to hurt. Though the altitude was high and the air was chilling the sounds of insect wings seemed like the hum of primitive death gods at their after-the-fighting chores, like those old devils he had finished off in the Connec.

His amulet declared the night free of all but the most trivial Instrumentalities.

He was nervous about the possibility of imminent treachery. Titus had a bum right arm. The Ninth Unknown was older than the ground underfoot. Terens Ernest was an unknown quantity. Rivademar Vircondelet considered himself a lover, not a scrapper.

Consent, Vircondelet, and Ernest were along because they felt mistrusted and left out. So. This time they had a chance to be there when the hammer came down.

He did not introduce Cloven Februaren.

Other than Titus, who was burdened with the truce flag, everyone carried a lantern. Hecht, Ernest, and Vircondelet also carried spears and a standard array of sharpened iron. The spears proved useful in dealing with the treacherous footing.

The Ninth Unknown had armed himself with a foolish grin.

These five were not likely to give an account of themselves that would echo down the ages.

Once past the end of the meadow they spied torches and small fires behind the knee of the mountain. About twenty men awaited them, two hundred yards off, in that weak light.

More small fires at intervals marked the road to the plain. There was movement on the road.

Hecht muttered, "I should have made them come to me."

Cloven Februaren said, "You're much too paranoid, Piper." And, "Learn to believe in yourself."


HECHT KNEW MANY OF THE MEN AWAITING HIM. MOST WERE NOT friends of Bronte Doneto. They included representatives of four of the Five Families of Brothe, including Paludan Bruglioni of the powerful Bruglioni family. Paludan had been at death's door when Hecht last saw him. Principaté Gervase Saluda, Paludan's lifelong friend, was there, too. Both remained seated in the wooden frames that had been used to carry them up the mountain. The Arniena agent was Rogoz Sayag, with whom Hecht had worked while employed by that family and later, during the Calziran Crusade.

The Cologni and Madesetti were represented by strangers. Only the Benedocto, Bronte Doneto's tribe, had no obvious agent on hand.

Someone would report back. Espionage and treachery were heart and soul of Brothen city politics. And Brothen city politics shaped the larger policies of the Church.

Overall, these people made an unlikely alliance. Some had been backstabbing each other for generations.

Which pointed up the depth and breadth of the developing crisis of confidence in the current Patriarch.

How had Doneto managed so swift a decline?

Hecht wondered more about how Paludan and Gervase, both badly crippled, had managed to be on scene so soon.

A man Hecht did not know stepped forward. "I'm Acton Bucce of Bricea," he said. "Acting captain of what survived your sorcery." Acton Bucce was a sad and angry man controlling his emotions tightly.

Bucce asked, "Would it be acceptable to add fuel to the bonfires? I'd like more light and warmth. So many ghosts will make this a cold, dark night."

Hecht glanced at Februaren. The old man nodded. "Go ahead. I met some of those ghosts coming down here."

The fires grew fast. Everyone on the Patriarchal side seemed cold and haunted. Hecht touched his amulet lightly. Still it offered no warnings other than the usual nascent itch.

The swollen bonfires bruised Hecht's night vision but flung light far enough to reveal corpses laid side by side, touching, their feet at the edge of the road.

"You wanted to talk, Acton Bucce?"

"Twelve hours ago I commanded a regiment called the Free Will Swords. Short-term mercenaries from Brothe's poorest quarters. Twenty-two hundred men, mostly experienced. Thirty-day enlistments, fifteen paid ahead. Now I have thirteen hundred men barely in shape to take care of themselves. We have so many dead we can't take them back with us. We'll bury them in marked graves, where there's enough man left to identify, so their people can come get them if they want."

Bucce paused as though inviting comment. Hecht said nothing.

Bucce continued, "All told, the Patriarch sent about seventeen thousand men. At sunup I was eighth in the chain of succession. Now I'm the senior officer surviving. These civilians are urging me to indulge my inclination to save the men who're still alive. We're working on that but still have bodies to recover. We've collected more than four thousand already. And the wounded outnumber the dead. Sepsis will claim a lot of those because the healers can't get to them all."

He paused. Hecht asked, "How many were conscripts?"

"Sir?"

"Every man in your army chose to be here. Each one was a mercenary bent on murdering me and mine."

"That's true. Though it could be argued that poverty conscripted them."

"It could. But they did choose to try to kill me. By my calculation, trusting your numbers, my men need to put in one more hard day to quash this Patriarchal fantasy forever."

"The Patriarchal fantasy is moribund already. Tomorrow I'll bury my dead. I'll release each regiment once it cares for its own. Unless you force a fight. Then fight I will."

"I had no desire to fight in the first place."

Bucce's lips tightened. His opinion might not agree. "I'm determined that no more lives be wasted till Serenity relieves me. I'll not have them on my conscience."

Lips never moving, whispering so softly that only Hecht heard, Februaren said, "The man is sincere. What he isn't telling you is, most of his men have deserted."

Hecht hid his surprise. "Captain, what was the ultimate purpose for this meeting? And why are all these people here?"

"They came with the army. To observe, I'm told. I think they hoped for a disaster as ugly as what we got. Our Patriarch is no longer loved by his own class."

"I understand the politics, more or less. But you haven't said why you wanted to meet."

"I have. I want the killing to stop. And, then, these people insisted."

Hecht glanced at Titus Consent. Might Consent know something about Bucce?

Bucce said, "The way I understand it, these people want you to be able to drive toward Brothe unhindered, for a showdown with Serenity."

"I presume you've all changed your minds about your votes, last election."

No one responded. They stared at something in the darkness behind him. Had Prosek manhandled a few falcons down to strengthen the Imperial argument?

He glanced at Cloven Februaren. The old man was not concerned. "Tell me more."

"That's it. From me. Talk to them." Bucce was frightened. He stared past Hecht, too. "I won't interfere as long as you let us manage our dead and wounded and go."

He was repeating himself. For whoever was back there.

Voice tired, strained, feeble, Paludan Bruglioni said, "He speaks for Serenity's hirelings. We'll talk once you're done with him."

Hecht eyed Bruglioni, then Gervase Saluda, as though Saluda might explain how Paludan could have survived.

Paludan did not notice. He was fixed on the presence behind Hecht.

A ghost whispered in Hecht's ear, "The Empress is back there."

"I thought so. Your Grace failed to heed the advice of her Commander of the Righteous." Not looking back.

"It was advice, only, Commander. I have more confidence in you than you have in yourself."

This was no time for an argument. "Thank you for your faith, Majesty. Have you heard enough to understand?"

Katrin stepped up beside him, to his left. He glimpsed an abashed Ephrian behind her. "These people have decided they backed the wrong racing team. They hope to save themselves and maybe snatch some of the spoils by changing Colors."

Even after years in Firaldia Hecht did not fully grasp the concept of Colors, which tied together fan support for famous racing teams at the hippodrome, local politics, and, more broadly, made a statement about one's position on the long power struggle between the Brothen Episcopal Patriarchs and the Grail Emperors.

Katrin's statement was bare-boned truth.

But they could still crush the Righteous. And in grand style because they could grab the Grail Empress herself.

The Ninth Unknown whispered, "You rate yourself too small. You changed the world today. Again. But you recognize it no better than you did in Esther's Wood."

Hecht neither understood nor believed. But it was worth some thought.

"Acton Bucce of Bricea, of the Free Will Swords, I am here. Her Most August Imperial Majesty. What do you have to say?"

"I thought I was clear, Your Majesty."

"You said you won't bother me if the Commander of the Righteous lets you go. Which has its appeal. On the other hand, exterminating you all so we don't have to deal with you again later also has its charm. Too, we wouldn't have people like these here if somebody wasn't fishing for special consideration."

Paludan Bruglioni admitted it. "You're right. We came here in anticipation of your success. We hope to negotiate the safety of our houses."

Cloven Februaren muttered, "Bullshit. But he does mean it when he says it."

Saluda took over. "We all pledge to provide no aid or comfort to Serenity. Nor will we impede the Righteous in any way."

The Empress laughed, a peal with a donkey's bray edge on it. "It won't be that easy. It won't be that cheap. There'll be no lurking on the middle road till you can jump in on the winning side. Choose. And let the world know. Your lives, your fortunes, your honor. I want them declared, dedicated, committed."

Februaren murmured, "Somebody is a little overconfident."

"Just a bit," Hecht agreed.

But Katrin had not overplayed her hand. Nobody stomped away.

The spokesmen for the Five Families agreed to negotiate articles of association after the Patriarchals dealt with their dead and wounded and headed home.

Titus said, "I'm not sure about this, boss. Feels like we're letting them off too easy."

"After what we did to them?"

"The Empress said it. We might have to deal with them again."

NEXT DAY RIGHTEOUS SCOUTS PUSHED DOWN TOWARD THE PLAIN, advancing as the Patriarchals buried their dead. Reinforcements arrived, two hundred men come over from Glimpsz. More were en route. An army was assembling in Alamedinne. Imperial garrisons were demonstrating in every north Firaldian city that owed allegiance to the Empire. The same was not happening in the Patriarchal States.

News of the slaughter in the Shades spread fast and grew with the telling. People who should have known better took the wildest stories as gospel.

The whisperers of Krois murmured canards against the Empress and her Commander of the Righteous: They had surrendered to the Will of the Night. There would have been no disaster had not all darkness answered the conjuring of the witch queen and her mercenary familiar.

Journeymen rumor-tinkers of an opposing view charged Serenity with consorting with the Night and with being the man behind the monster that kept returning to the catacombs, however often the good Principatés put it down. Those accusations found the popular mind more welcoming. Almost as far back as the collapse of the hippodrome there had been gossip connecting Bronte Doneto with events in the underground world.

Such was the news Cloven Februaren brought back from his Brothen visits, where his espionage was less subtle and clever than Heris's had been.

He enjoyed sabotage too much.

CLEJ SEDLAKOVA SURFACED AFTER THREE DAYS. ONLY EIGHTEEN MEN accompanied him, most all injured. They had been ambushed by an enemy who had known they were coming. Sedlakova and these men were the last survivors of a long running fight.

\*       \*       \*

THE RIGHTEOUS BURIED THEIR DEAD. THEY EXAMINED THEIR FIRE-powder weapons for defects. They brought up ammunition and supplies, and welcomed further reinforcements.

The Commander of the Righteous twice eluded halfhearted advances by the Empress. Her self-control seemed to be slipping again.

Hecht was not alone in noticing.

Rivademar Vircondelet stuck his head into the tented space Hecht had taken in the Patriarchal camp. Vircondelet had begun to assume some of Titus Consent's duties as Consent became more intimate with field command. "Captain Ephrian is begging to see you, boss. Can you spare a minute?"

"Send him in, then."

Ephrian came bearing bad news.

"Sit, Captain, and tell me the problem."

"The Empress. Of course. I can't take much more. She won't cooperate. She will do what she wants, when she wants."

"Kind of goes with the job."

"I understand that. I remember how Johannes could get. But he was never like her. No matter what happens, it's never her fault. . . . That goes with the territory, too, some. Right?"

"Most of the time."

"Here's the problem. She's into one of her downward spirals. It might be the worst since the Prince was stillborn. We've tried the usual gimmicks. I've worn my butt out taking her riding. That works better than anything. She loves a good gallop. Not this time, though. I'm scared she'll do something to damage or embarrass herself."

"What can I do?"

"I don't know. She won't listen to me when she isn't out of her head. She does listen to you, sometimes."

"Really? I must have missed that."

"I did say sometimes."

"An odd duck, our Empress."

"She's more like a frightened girl. She lets childish emotions drive her. These black moods . . . They keep getting worse. She could cause problems we'll never get over. Something bigger than invading a friendly empire or declaring war on the Church."

Interesting. "We aren't at war with the Church, Captain. We're at war with Serenity. That might sound like a minor distinction but the difference is critical."

"Serenity believes he *is* the Church."

"A common flaw of Patriarchs. What would you have me do with our flawed mistress? I'm a hired sword who's overstepped his bounds already."

"I don't know. I said she listens to you sometimes. I hoped you'd have some inspiration."

"Captain, I'm not that imaginative. The magical way to make everything right got past me. I wish she'd lasted a little longer. Midcampaign is a bad time for your employer to lose her mind."

"Just be warned. She might turn strange."

"I'll think about it. I promise. Now, I do have an order of march to ready."

Ephrian made a face but said nothing. He knew that in no practical sense could the Righteous attack Brothe. The city was too big. And even an unpopular Patriarch had vast resources.

He had found seventeen thousand men willing to go into the Shades.

Hecht really just wanted to become a presence that dared not be ignored while the might of the Empire gathered. He wanted to become a symbol to all Brothens currently disgruntled with their Patriarch. A hope in the mist.

The heavy lifting would be done by armies from beyond the Jagos.

There were skirmishes all across Firaldia. Whatever the feudal obligation of a given city, principality, or kingdom, some citizens or subjects held the opposing view and were determined to regularize their polity's status. Riots were not uncommon, even in the Mother City, where a frightened city senate voted a huge new subsidy for the City Regiment.

Years of parsimony had left that force little more than symbolic.

THE RIGHTEOUS ENGAGED IN SKIRMISHES. SERENITY DID HAVE HIS supporters. But, after the Shades, few could find soldiers willing to face the Righteous.

Superstitious folk convinced themselves that Empress Katrin and her Commander of the Righteous had used sorcery. The Shades had seen the worst day's butchery in Firaldia since the collapse of the Old Empire. Those who knew better, survivors of the battle, told everyone that there had been no sorcery at all. And that, where it was believed, scared thinking people more than did babble about sorcery.

Use of massed machines of destruction was especially frightening. Falcons took the skill and honor out of combat. Which really meant the highborn recognized that they would be at as much risk as, and therefore of no more value than, the lowest, poorest, mallet-armed churl.

Falcons did not care who your father was. Falcons did not take the well-born for ransom. Worse, falcons could be manned by any illiterate peasant's son after just a few hours of training.

Such an engine had to have sprung from the dark mind of the Adversary.

THE RIGHTEOUS WERE ON THE MOVE WHEN WORD CAME THAT THE PA-triarch, supported by his dwindling faction in the Collegium, had issued a bull declaring firepowder weapons the work of the Adversary. No true Chaldarean would employ them. All firepowder weapons were to be destroyed immediately.

Hecht was up with the van as it approached the Bruglioni estate southeast of Brothe. The messenger missed him. When he got back to his staff he found them mocking the Patriarch. "What's going on?"

"Listen to this." Rivademar Vircondelet read the bull.

Titus Consent said, "Right now, throughout the Chaldarean world, men cursed by possession of these organs of evil are rushing out to ignore Serenity completely. Instead, having heard about the Shades, they'll try to find a supplier who isn't Krulik and Sneigon."

"No doubt. That's human nature." Other Patriarchs had tried to ban weapons, too. Those remained in common use.

THE COMMANDER OF THE RIGHTEOUS AND SEVERAL LIEUTENANTS, fiercely uncomfortable about the Empress tagging along, entered the Bruglioni villa. That was a classical collection of limestone pillars and red tile roofs squatting on a ridge in wine country, near enough to Brothe for the filthy air over the city to be seen. Parts of the villa dated to Old Empire times. The Bruglioni claimed it had been built by one of the Imperial families before the time of Aaron of Chaldar. It had figured in several major historical events. Paludan grumbled, "And it looks like the old hovel is going to get to do that again."

Paludan was in a wheeled chair, his destiny for however long he survived. The masters of healing magic could do no more than control his pain. Gervase Saluda also remained confined to a wheelchair but did have hopes of walking again, given an artificial leg. Saluda said, "I hear tell that no good deed goes unpunished. I guess this is our punishment for letting the Arniena talk us into giving you work, back when."

"You're right. But you did get your money's worth. This is just Katrin's way of putting her mark on you."

All the representatives of the Five Families who had sneaked out to the Shades were now visiting the Bruglioni estate. Serenity should soon have reports about them.

"We aren't looking for a fight here," Hecht said. "We just want to

fuel the fire of unrest. We pose a bigger problem sitting here not fighting than we would by getting into something we'd probably lose."

Hecht had realized that a falcon-heavy force could not be an aggressive or agile force. It had its best luck when doing what it had in
the Shades. It was a defensive force.

With all the reinforcements of recent days Hecht's force still numbered fewer than a thousand. A thousand veterans employed in most
Firaldian squabbles would be considered huge, but in this contest,
against this opponent, no.

To the consternation of Paludan and Saluda alike Hecht prepared
defenses for the estate. Rhuk and Prosek sited weapons so raiders would
regret getting too close. Sedlakova and Consent roamed the countryside
in search of creek beds where rounded pebbles of an appropriate size
and hardness could be harvested. They also sought loamy soil that could
be used to fill the empty spaces between stones in a charge.

Rivademar Vircondelet led mounted patrols toward the Mother
City so watchers could see actual Imperial banners close by.

Serenity closed the nearer gates and did not contest their presence.

Cloven Februaren wakened Hecht deep in the night. Lila had accompanied him, shyly proud that she had enough grasp of the Construct to make the twisted journey. She kept quiet. No doubt she had
orders to keep her mouth shut.

The Ninth Unknown whispered, "Serenity has lost it, Piper. He has
squads roaming Brothe, arresting anybody he fancies. The Castella
shut its gates. The Five Families are forting up because he attacked the
Bruglioni citadel yesterday. What's left of it."

"Gervase and Paludan won't be happy." Though their property
was an indefensible ruin, anyway.

"And less so after they hear that a dozen deaths were involved.
Their people resisted."

He watched Lila rove around slowly, almost a wraith. "Anna needs
to get some food into that girl."

"Anna and the girls aren't eating well right now."

"What?"

"Muno let Addam Hauf move them into the Castella. Because of
Serenity."

"You really sure he's lost it? He's good at pretending to be doing
one thing when he's up to something else entirely."

"He could be perfectly sane and trying some sleight of mind. But I
don't see him having time for that kind of foolery. He'll go after Muno
sometime soon. That will trigger a revolt in the Collegium. Fur will fly.
Meantime, Imperial troops are pouring into northern Firaldia. Your

friend may have stayed in the Connec too long. He might have to fight through an Imperial army, now. And while Serenity is praying for Ghort, an Imperial army from Alamedinne and Calzir will be closing in from the south."

"Anna and the kids are definitely safe?"

"Anna and the girls. Note that I didn't mention the boy. The headstrong boy."

"Lila?"

"Yes?" The girl sort of drifted his way, like only her toes could reach the floor and those barely touched.

"What did Pella do?"

"He got bored. He left. That was when we were still at Grandpa Delari's house. Maybe he went back to Sonsa to see about his sister."

Hecht cursed.

Februaren said, "What can you expect? The boy has survived on his own before. And he's been brought up on stories about the brave Duarnenian who left home at an early age."

"I hope he doesn't get himself killed."

"Your imagination didn't get you killed."

"Not yet. Men less lucky than me have gotten killed by the dream."

"Enough. There'll be serious trouble in the city soon. Be prepared to take advantage."

"I could take particular advantage of your special talents."

"My special talents are employed to the limit, now. I'm an old man, Piper. And I don't get to spend my days lounging around a posh villa. You know these people have their own heated bath?"

"I do. I haven't been. My people haven't. I've made life hard enough for the Bruglioni already."

The Ninth Unknown cataloged some of the mischief he hoped to work over the next few days, said he would be gone at least two, then turned sideways. Leaving Lila.

"Hey! You forgot Lila."

"It's all right. I can get back on my own." The girl met his eye momentarily, clearly something she found hard to do. "I'm good at it. And he wants me to do some of the work after he goes back north."

"But you're just a kid."

"I'm almost fifteen. What were you doing when you were almost fifteen?"

Campaigning with the Sha-lug. Not for the first time. But that was different. Yet the only argument he could make was that she was a girl.

Lila said, "You worry too much about us. Except Anna, maybe. She had the sheltered life. She can't believe in really wicked people."

That used up all the courage the girl had. She would not look at him anymore. Again, he was stricken by how pale, how spectral, she seemed.

"I can't help worrying, Lila. I made you my family but I'm never there."

"You make me feel bad when you worry. I don't deserve it. I try. Hard. But I'm always scared that I'll lose it and turn back into what I was."

He understood why Februaren wanted Lila here. She was desperate for reassurance.

"Don't let the past rule you. You did what you had to do. This is now. Be what you want to be." Lila was at a fragile point. She needed to be needed. Desperately. She needed to be needed, she needed to be trusted, she needed to be forgiven. Given all that, she might forgive herself for having walked the roads of hell and returned. She might concede that she had value and deserved to survive. She might start to believe that she was not a soul already damned.

Hecht wanted to hold her while he reassured her but feared there would be an emotional risk. A hug would work with Vali. Vali would not misconstrue because Vali lacked Lila's haunts.

Hecht and Lila talked more than ever they had since he had sent her to live with Anna.

Before Lila left Hecht gave her a note for Anna, suggesting he might see her before long.

His left wrist began to itch. "You'd better go. Something is about to happen."

"Yes. I feel it. Thank you. Father."

He did hug her then, for an instant, careful to use one arm and not press.

Lila turned sideways and disappeared.

Hecht scratched his wrist. It suggested a serious probe by an Instrumentality of some weight.

The usual wards protected the estate, supplemented by those of the Righteous and those of Katrin's lifeguard. The latter were truly brawny. But something fierce and powerful wanted in. It kept looking for a weakness.

It was not alone. Scores of lesser Night things accompanied it.

It failed to break through. But Hecht did not get much sleep.

After breakfast and morning reports Hecht collected Kait Rhuk and went hunting.

The Instrumentality, not quite bogon in magnitude, was dismayed by how easily the Godslayer found the fox's den where it had holed up for the day. It did not have long to enjoy its dismay.

Next night more entities came, all smaller and all frightened. Veterans who had learned their trade in the hunt for Instrumentalities in the Connec trapped and exterminated the lesser entities where they could. They took the opportunity to teach the subtleties of god killing to men with no experience. The knowledge might be critical to their survival sometime later.

Hecht did what he could to create conflicting reports. He knew information would get back to Serenity, despite his trappers. These entities were like mosquitoes. However many you swatted, there were more.

CLOVEN FEBRUAREN FAILED TO RETURN AS PROMISED. HE DID NOT return at all. Lila did, late the third afternoon of the occupation of the Bruglioni estate. She materialized behind the screen that Hecht had acquired at Heris's suggestion. She had been paying attention. But she arrived while Hecht was engaged in conversation with Hagan Brokke, who had just arrived with several hundred Righteous and Imperials from beyond the Vieran Sea. Titus Consent and Rivademar Vircondelet were there making notes.

Lila stepped out from behind the screen before assessing the situation.

Consent gasped. Vircondelet jumped to his feet. He did not know the girl. He leapt to the wicked conclusion. The Commander of the Righteous liked them young and skinny.

Brokke just looked confused.

Lila froze, horrified.

Hecht managed, "This is business, Lila. Stay in the other room till we finish."

She was quick. She had survived on her wits. "Yes, Father."

Clever girl. That and Titus's testimony would ease the speculation. Some.

Hecht said, "What we need to look at is how best to use this new strength. I'm afraid the Empress will insist on a demonstration. She doesn't understand that the Shades was a onetime thing."

Brokke rumbled, "Give them a miracle and they figure you can do it to order."

# 39. Kharoulke: In Pain

Misfortune tightened its grip on the Windwalker. Slowly, inevitably, the Instrumentality became more anchored to the present, though still with enough grasp of potential futures to see that few could turn out favorable.

His sense of this world, as a whole, and of the broad vistas of the Night had grown intensely feeble. His brethren, his hated brethren, were all failing in their returns, too. It would not require the concentrated bile of those who had imprisoned them to abort their rebirth. Human indifference and the failure of the wells of life would be sufficient.

The seeds had sprouted after lying dormant for ages. But their revenant shoots had emerged into ferocious drought.

For the first time in an existence that stretched back to a time before memory, the Instrumentality discovered emotions not intimately entwined with lust, hunger, rage, and hatred. Once he wasted his secret reserve creating a Krepnight, the Elect, that some feeble imitation of an Instrumentality crushed like a roach, he began to know despair. And fear.

For the first time in millennia, if not epochs or even aeons, Kharoulke the Windwalker conceived the possibility of an utter, permanent, inalterable end to the cosmic consciousness known as, and known to itself as, Kharoulke the Windwalker.

If only summer would end.

# 40. Alten Weinberg: Princess Apparent

Circumstance had thrust the mantle of empire onto Helspeth again. Katrin, now quietly being called "the Mad Empress," was far away with her private army, prosecuting her private war.

News of Jaime's death met Helspeth on the road from Glimpsz to Alten Weinberg. She knew Katrin would not respond rationally.

That was the universal expectation.

Helspeth came home and immediately suffered the attentions of lords and knights who wanted permission to rush into Firaldia. Katrin's pro-Brothen cronies had turned invisible. Anti-Patriarchals were everywhere, busy getting ready to do what they had wanted since Johannes was Emperor.

That pressure eased once official word came saying Katrin did intend to turn everyone loose on Serenity for having deprived her of a husband. Told to get rolling, the Imperial war machine sparked up and ran itself.

Everyone told Helspeth she was doing a marvelous job, standing in for Katrin.

She signed a decree, now and then.

She worried about the Commander of the Righteous. She worried about obsessing about the Commander of the Righteous. And she worried because the Commander of the Righteous had not sent a letter since last she had seen him.

She wondered how long it would be before Katrin chose one of the greedy suitors who were sure to start swarming, like maggots in the carcass of a dead dog, now that she was a widow. She prayed Katrin would remarry quickly.

THOSE WERE HALCYON DAYS, WORRIES ASIDE. THE USUAL CRUEL POLItics had gone into abeyance. Energies were oriented toward delivering the licking Serenity and his cronies deserved. Men from the breadth and depth of the Empire headed south eagerly, in no special order, intent on joining the Grand Duke for the capture of Brothe. A few took the eastern routes to join Lord Admiral fon Tyre's campaign on the Aco floodplain, down the east coast of Firaldia, and on the islands of the Vieran Sea.

Those who passed through Alten Weinberg all paused to pay respects to the Princess Apparent.

Helspeth asked Lady Hilda Daedle, "Have you noticed how nice these men are lately? It's like, give them a foreign war and they turn into decent human beings."

"It's not the war, it's your sister."

"Excuse me?"

"You must have heard the rumors. About her behavior? About her health? About her mental state?"

What Helspeth had heard had been edited. No one wanted to make a bad impression. "No. Tell me."

"She . . . She's not behaving responsibly, running up front with the Righteous. Everyone is afraid she'll do something stupid. Or madness will . . ."

"Hilda, this isn't like you."

"It's delicate. It's frightening. But the truth is, everybody thinks you'll be Empress before long. Unless Katrin gets a grip on herself."

"I don't think I want to be Empress."

"You'd defer to your Aunt Anies?"

Long silence. Brief, strained chuckle. Anies Ege was almost a stereotypical elderly, timid maiden lady. A recluse even here inside Winterhall. Anies should have been delivered into a cloistered nunnery thirty years ago. But her brother Johannes doted on her and would not compel her to do anything: marriage or religious vows.

"I think not. The wolves would tear her apart. The Empire would follow."

"So. You see. No choice. Ah. Here's something."

One of the daughters of the ladies of the court advanced diffidently. "Your Highness. Captain Drear asked me to tell you that an important visitor would like to see you. He recommends an audience at your earliest convenience."

"Did he say who this important visitor is?"

"Yes, and it please Your Highness. Ferris Renfrow, Your Highness."

Long pause. Ferris Renfrow! The prodigal. "Very well. Tell the Captain yes, immediately, in the quiet room. Go! Hustle! Hilda. I want wine, coffee, refreshments. And incense. If Renfrow conforms to custom he'll have come directly from somewhere unpleasant and will have the aroma to prove it."

RENFROW DID NOT CONFORM TO HABIT. HE HAD BATHED. HE WORE clothing that was not only clean but new.

"Where have you been?" Helspeth demanded, almost breathless. "Times are desperate. We need you." Hustling him into the quiet room.

"Sadly, Princess, I'm only one man. I have to choose which desperate situations to attend. I'm here to report. In story form. It's an epic. It will take a while. You aren't to interrupt with questions, nor to ask questions when I'm finished. I'll tell you what you need to know and that's all I'll tell you." He faced Lady Hilda. "You. Shut the door tight. Then discover yourself temporarily deaf."

He made a gentle sign. Hilda Daedle stood there with her mouth open, rubbing her ears. Renfrow took a pewter box from an inside pocket. Opened, it shed a half-dozen sleepy things resembling translucent night crawlers armed with dragonfly wings. They zipped around the quiet room, sniffing the walls. They landed and insinuated their bodies into cracks where they exuded something dark brown that smelled of pungent cheese.

· Ferris Renfrow said, "I am amazed. Somebody has to be sabotaging this room. You'd better start tracking who comes and goes."

There were so many little breaches four Night creatures used themselves up making seals. The other two did not have strength enough to flutter back to their box. Renfrow collected them and put them away.

He told his story. He did not let the Princess interrupt. He did not accept a single question when he was done. "I told you what you need to know, not what you want to know. We're headed into a crucial time. Not because of what's happening in Firaldia, the End of Connec, Arnhand, or anywhere else, but because of what's happening in the Night." Most of his story had concerned his part in a scheme to release trapped gods that the Church insisted never existed.

"But . . ."

"Rule well, dear heart. Don't forget the mistakes your sister made. Avoid them. Consider avoiding your passions as well."

"Sir!"

"Your infatuation has been obvious for years. Control it. The man isn't who you think he is. He isn't who I always thought he was, either. He may not even be who *he* thinks he is. I'll be going shortly. They need me in Firaldia. Serenity has some clever and deadly people working for him. They could give the Grand Duke some bad days. I'll be back, though. Probably within the week."

"I will wait with bated breath."

Renfrow was startled. "Sarcasm? Hmph! Just try to make time for me when I get here."

"Always. There's a chance you might let me ask a question."

Renfrow showed an uncertain smile, took a sip of coffee, then made a gesture at Hilda of Averange.

Lady Hilda burst out, "I can hear again!" She gave Ferris Renfrow a dark look but reserved what she was inclined to say.

Renfrow shoved the door open, glared at people who had been trying to eavesdrop. "Here's some names worth collecting, Your Highness."

Soon afterward Renfrow was nowhere to be found in Alten Weinberg, though a dozen people eager to see him searched diligently.

EIGHT DAYS PASSED BEFORE FERRIS RENFROW REAPPEARED. HELSPETH took him into the quiet room immediately, though he seemed less secretive this time. Other than for a desire to conceal the fact that he had toured the length of Firaldia and had taken part in several skirmishes where his presence had made the difference. The Captain-General of Patriarchal forces was a clever rogue and had, twice, lured the Grand Duke into situations where Imperial forces might have been decimated. But for the intercession of the heroic Ferris Renfrow.

"Serenity's half of the Collegium is very involved," he said.

"That hasn't happened much in recent times."

"Not in more than a century. But people are becoming almost as polarized as they were before the schism that caused the Viscesment

Patriarchy. Your sister turning on Serenity released a lot of pent-up passion."

Helspeth sipped tea. She had not had coffee prepared. She waited, hoping Renfrow would understand his decline in favor.

"I visited the army straggling up from the south. It's more talk than power. Sixteen hundred men, knights, sergeants, squires, and foot all counted. With a tail of several thousand hangers-on. The fighters are experienced. Joined with the Commander of the Righteous they'll create a formidable threat south of Brothe. They'll isolate the city from that direction. The Grand Duke will close off the north. And Admiral fon Tyre, probably late but not never, will eventually cross the Monte Sismonda and close down the east. It's too bad the mercantile republics won't get involved. They could blockade the Teragi and cut the Mother City off from the sea, too."

"Uh . . ."

"I did see the Commander of the Righteous. Though not deliberately. I meant to visit your sister. Which I did. But Hecht and some of his people spotted me."

"And?"

"He appears to be doing well. Your sister, on the other hand, is not. Her attendants and lifeguards are doing everything they can, including keeping her a virtual prisoner so she can't harm herself or the Empire. But they're just responding to symptoms. They aren't treating the disease."

"Katrin has had attitude problems since we were little. They never had much to do with what was going on outside her. She was just moody."

"Her problem isn't something that's wrong with her mind."

"What?" Helspeth looked to her left, thinking she had seen motion there. There was nothing to see now.

"There is a problem. But it's her brain, not her soul or spirit."

"Is she possessed?"

"She's considered that herself. But what possesses her is her own body. Something inside her doesn't work right."

"There's a disease that makes you insane?"

"Several, actually. Ergotism is common."

"But that's caused by rotted grain, isn't it?"

"It's a poison from rye that gets infested with mold. In Katrin's case, her own body produces the poison. The disease runs in her family."

"I could go crazy . . . ?"

"It's on her mother's side. One of her grandfathers died of it. That was a spectacular long bout of madness. They kept him in restraints for sixteen years. His sister died of the same disease as a baby. There were others who suffered from it, too. Every other generation or so, going back hundreds of years."

Helspeth made a grand intellectual leap. "Could this disease be why Katrin's babies died before they were born?"

"Maybe. Or two bad pregnancies could have pushed her into a more virulent stage. All politically disappointing, certainly. So much more dramatic to fling about accusations of baneful sorcery."

"But . . ." There was that eye-corner flicker again, with nothing there when she looked. "But Katrin has all those uncles. Her mother's brothers. None of their families have suffered mental problems."

"That we know about. The lords of Machen keep the family burden quiet."

"So. Stipulating all that, what's changed for me?"

"First, believe that Katrin is past her time of sporadic and mild flare-ups and is headed into a phase where the disease will distort her thinking most of the time. If it isn't recognized and dealt with she could do a lot of damage. More damage, and bigger. Her recent choices have been irrational. Though sheer boldness has seen them work out."

"She has the Commander of the Righteous to make that happen. What can I do? I won't conspire against her."

"Discuss it with her uncles when they pass through here, headed for the war. Invoke me as the source of your concern. They'll listen. They'll have to buy in before anything can be done."

"Damnit! What's going on over there?" Helspeth pointed. She had sensed movement in a corner to her left. And something like a worm of black smoke had begun to emerge from a crack near the base of the wall in front of her.

Renfrow swore. "I assumed the room would stay good because I was gone only a little while. Lesson, Princess. Never assume."

Renfrow released his surviving flying worms. They had recovered nicely. They attacked and devoured the worm of smoke. Renfrow repeated himself, shaken. "Never assume." Because, suddenly, there was another man in the room. A man all in brown.

Helspeth thought she had seen him before. In the background, around Piper Hecht. He offered a slight bow, an amused smile, and told Ferris Renfrow, "Time to go to work, Brother Lester. You're out here having fun while everybody else is getting old waiting at the Great Sky Fortress."

Renfrow seemed both at a loss for words and cowed. Which

stunned Helspeth. This man must be something fierce if he intimidated Ferris Renfrow.

The man extended a hand. "Let me do the honors, Brother Temagat. Your method is too slow."

Renfrow allowed him to take hold.

"Count downward from ten," the invader ordered. He looked Helspeth in the eye. "Piper sends hugs and kisses." Then he turned edgewise somehow with Renfrow and they disappeared.

Renfrow had not recovered his flying night crawlers. Helspeth left them to rule the quiet room. She got out. Noting exactly who was nearby and might have been trying to spy.

Hugs and kisses? She shuddered. It felt delicious. And she felt silly as a thirteen-year-old peasant girl being admired for the way she had begun to fill out.


## 41. From Brothe to the Great Sky Fortress

Cloven Februaren's busy life got busier. Leaving Piper Hecht, he turned sideways into a Delari town house in the process of being invaded by a mob. Muniero was not home. Mrs. Creedon was absent as well. Felske was sprawled on the main hall floor, bleeding. Her husband was being beaten nearby.

The invaders had begun to spread out to see what they could steal.

The Ninth Unknown flickered into being only for the instant it took to assess the situation. Then he flickered around the town house with a dagger only slightly wider than a knitting needle. He was fast. He hit from behind. The results were not pretty but cleanup would not be onerous. Nobody did much bleeding.

The man in brown gave those who tried to leave first priority, picking off ringleaders and those tormenting Turking when there were no would-be escapees. Lastly, he worked on isolated looters.

He was determined to make a statement not to be forgotten.

He worked at murder quickly and efficiently, but with less success than he had hoped. So many transitions left him disoriented. Then some raiders did manage to get away.

The Ninth Unknown kept at it the best he could, till he calmed down enough to recall that he had left Lila with Piper. If she translated into the town house . . .

The last invader fled. Februaren turned to the fallen. He discovered that Felske was not dead, just badly mauled and unconscious, her honor uncompromised. Turking had suffered more physical damage.

Februaren's healing skills were slight but he did what he could. And worried about Muniero and Mrs. Creedon.

Snicker. Maybe they eloped.

Principaté Delari returned shortly before sunrise. He did not ask what had happened. The obvious declared itself. He went into a cold rage so fierce that it made the Ninth Unknown uncomfortable. "Take it easy, Muno."

"I'm under control. Angry enough to chew granite, but under control." He glared around. "We need to get going with the cleanup and repairs. How are those two?"

"They'll live. And recover nicely if you get a healer in soon. Any idea what became of Mrs. Creedon?"

"No. Sometimes she goes to help with her mother, who's dying. I'll get the healer in a minute. What about Lila?"

"She didn't come back here. I assume she went straight to Anna."

"Make sure. Did you inspect the quiet room?"

"No. Been keeping these two breathing. And chasing off people who want souvenirs."

BRONTE DONETO'S HABIT WAS TO KEEP HIS PRIVATE LIFE PRIVATE AND well separated from his public life. He had neither wife nor children, but like most high churchmen, he had a mistress, the little-known Carmella Dometia. He kept Donna Carmella in a comfortable house close by his own city home. Carmella's husband's career kept him overseas, in Hypraxium of the Eastern Empire, where, till recently, he had overseen Benedocto commercial interests. Fortune smiled upon Gondolfo Dometia when the Interregnum ended and Serenity assumed office. Gondolfo became Patriarchal ambassador to the Golden Gate. Which he would remain as long as Bronte Doneto sat the Patriarchal throne.

Serenity's fortune did not shine as brightly upon his beloved.

Donna Carmella seldom saw her lover. Not that she minded. She had a limited appetite for men. Doneto was not blind to that but loved her nonetheless. She was, perhaps, the only soul outside himself that he did love.

Donna Carmella maintained a staff of four. Much of the time a small guest suite housed a woman who shared her peculiar tastes, though seldom the same woman for long. Carmella Dometia's infatuations did not last. Her passions were blistering but brief.

Donna Carmella wakened in the heart of a night when she had set extra wards because of unrest in the city. Her connection with the

Patriarch might be unknown to the mob but it was no secret in Collegium circles, where Serenity's enemies were found.

The extra wards did no good. Death came calling.

He wakened her himself.

She was more startled than frightened. Her visitor was old and shabby and frail. He smelled like he had not bathed in weeks.

"Who? . . . What?"

"Your good friend made a lethal mistake, sad, beautiful lady. He tried to have murder done. Failure doesn't absolve him. I shan't be as cruel as his emissaries."

A lightning thrust drove a slim blade in under a generous breast.

THE OLD MAN DRIFTED FROM ROOM TO ROOM. HE LEFT NO ONE ALIVE. The message had to be as loud as the blare of a brass trumpet beside the ear.

He left six human corpses, two dead dogs, two dead parrots, and a dead cat. Then he conjured forth rats and mice to make clear the full extent of his displeasure.

He was in the kitchen, dealing with the last rat, when he sensed life sparks down below.

Had someone hidden in the cellar?

No. Some unanticipated victims of Bronte Doneto were imprisoned down there. People with special significance to the man who had taken the miter. People whose fate he wanted kept hidden from everyone but himself and his wicked woman.

The assassin knew regret. Regret that he had slain the woman who had the answers before he discovered the need to ask her questions.

THE NINTH UNKNOWN TURNED INTO BEING INSIDE THE MAIN DINING room of the Delari town house. "Muno! Come see what I found!" A full day's labor had not cleared all the wreckage.

Delari shuffled out of the kitchen, followed by Mrs. Creedon. The cook moved slower than did the Principaté. She was deathly pale. She was in deep emotional shock. The horror would not let her go.

Delari said, "I was right. She went to help with her mother." The elder woman was known to be engaged in a long, slow, painful process of dying.

"But look what I found, Muno."

Delari moved closer, squinting at Februaren's emaciated, filthy, feeble companion. "Armand? Is that you?"

"It is, Muno. Get that healer back. I've got more to bring." He turned sideways, leaving Delari to deal with the catamite.

"Mrs. Creedon. If you would. Brother Lomas is with Turking and Felske. Bring him here, please."

He studied Armand. He saw no signs of torture but the boy had not been properly fed. He had suffered illnesses as a result. He was sick right now. Doneto must have caught him the day Hugo Mongoz died. Which explained why he had not been seen for so long.

Cloven Februaren turned into being with another liberated guest of Donna Carmella. "I don't know this one, Muno. I'm sure he'll have interesting stories to tell. Unless he's completely mad."

Mrs. Creedon arrived with Brother Lomas. The healing brother was appalled by the condition of the liberated men. "This is unconscionable. Who could have worked this horror?"

Februaren said, "The same man who attacked this house. But you won't say a word. Understand? Heal broken bodies, and hearts if you can, but forget politics. Muno, there's one more. You'll be amazed."

The man in brown left that room before he turned sideways. He reversed the process when he returned. "Last one. Not in as bad shape as the others."

"Pella?"

DAYS PASSED BEFORE THE DEATHS AT THE DOMETIA ESTABLISHMENT were discovered. The comings and goings of carrion birds through glassless upper-story windows, and the buzzing of death flies, finally attracted attention.

The news reached Serenity quickly.

Distraught over damage done his own wonderful city residence, the Patriarch was in a fragile state. This news crushed him. He did nothing for three days. Then he swore an oath: He would take his revenge on an epic scale, though he was not sure who his target ought to be.

The culprit would not have been shy about having his identity revealed. But Heris turned up before the ugliness at Donna Carmella's home was discovered. The old man awaited that discovery as necessary before he took Serenity deeper into a hell on earth.

Ostarega the Malicious was set to demonstrate a good deal more malice.

IT WAS EVENING. FEBRUAREN HAD SPENT A LONG DAY SCOUTING. HE would have Lila relay the information to Piper.

He spent time daily tracking Pinkus Ghort and other players up north. Ghort had suffered savage partisan attacks leaving the Connec, then had fought his way through Viscesment, where the locals tried to hold the bridges. They learned that Pinkus Ghort knew how to get the best out of his few falcons. He left Viscesment burning, its streets littered with corpses.

Ghort passed through Ormienden and Dromedan and the coastal hills, collecting Patriarchal garrisons, then ran into Imperial troops near Alicea. Skirmishing ensued. The Imperials backed off but only until they received reinforcements.

The Grand Duke Hilandle, following plans laid down by Johannes Blackboots, had marched westward across northern Firaldia after leaving the Remayne Pass. He planned to approach Brothe along the West Way. He joined local Imperials harassing the Captain-General and forced him to turn and fight.

The engagement was sporadic. Each side used its few falcons freely. The Imperials deployed some unexpected sorcery when Ferris Renfrow joined them.

On the other side, supposedly plodding Pinkus Ghort demonstrated a flair for cavalry maneuver. His light horse neutralized the Imperial knights by nipping their flanks and threatening the Imperial train.

The engagement remained mainly one of maneuver. Casualties were light. Each commander was amazed by the competence of the other. Preconceptions had to be overcome.

Overall, Captain-General Pinkus Ghort won the honors. He extricated his force. He left the Grand Duke unwilling to launch a pell-mell pursuit.

Such was the situation when the Ninth Unknown returned to the Delari town house in quest of a decent meal and a good night's sleep and found Heris waiting.

"HERIS. GIRL. YOU'RE LOOKING OLDER." HE WANTED TO BITE HIS tongue. To chew the gold right off it. You did not say that even to a woman much less a slave to vanity than the rest of her species. But it was true. Time differences between the middle world and the Realm of the Gods had left Heris visibly more mature.

She needed fresh clothing, too.

"Thank you, Double Great. You're looking well yourself."

"I look like death warmed over. My life is hell on a broomstick. Never a moment's respite. I expect you turning up is a sign that it's all going to get worse."

"The Aelen Kofer brought the falcons. They've completed the other arrangements I wanted. We're waiting on you and the Bastard."

The old man looked to Principaté Delari, who had stood by without comment. Delari shrugged.

Februaren said, "I insist on a decent meal, a good night's sleep, then another decent meal. Muno. How are our guests?"

"Quiet room."

"Yeah. All right." Heris had not heard the story. "After supper. I'm famished. Is Mrs. Creedon still capable?"

"Perfectly. Her kitchen was damaged, not her. The real misery is having to do without Turking and Felske."

That part of the story, Februaren saw, was no mystery to the girl. And nothing there needed hiding from eavesdroppers.

The visit in the quiet room was brief. Delari gave Heris the details of the raid. "They must have watched me for a long time. Sadly, I am a creature of habit. Mrs. Creedon isn't. Her being out at the same time was sheer happenstance but lucky for her."

Heris said, "You mentioned guests. Which is why we're in here, isn't it?"

The Ninth Unknown explained, "I rescued three prisoners from the Dometia woman's cellar. I left two more who died not long enough ago to be skeletons. They hadn't been robbed. They were Brotherhood of War. Muno thinks they were Witchfinders that Bronte Doneto considered dangerous witnesses. Maybe the last two men, besides Doneto, who knew what he was up to in the catacombs, back when. It's an easy guess why he had the catamite, Armand, and Pella locked . . ."

"Pella? *Our* Pella?"

"The very one. He finally got out and had himself an adventure. He should be more pliable, now. If he has the sense God gave a toad. It's pure luck he isn't still down there." Februaren mused, "I wonder . . . You think it might've been a better lesson if I'd left him there for somebody to find after the bodies are discovered? Might've made a huge political splash, too."

Heris said, "They'll find the dead Witchfinders, won't they?"

Principaté Delari said, "I despair of the boy's capacity to learn. He is recovering, though. The others aren't doing as well. They might have been down there too long."

Heris demanded, "The Patriarch meant to get at Piper and Grandfather through Pella and Armand?"

"Mostly your brother, I think," Delari said. "Armand was another agent of Dreanger who came over before Piper did. They knew each other. Armand might have said something he shouldn't and Doneto was saving him for the right time."

Februaren said, "Pella says he wasn't tortured. He can't speak for the others. He was only there a few days, while Serenity was busy looking for ways to save his own ass."

Heris sat quietly, digesting information. Minutes passed. Finally, "Are we going to let Serenity know that we don't approve of his behavior?"

Even Februaren was startled. "Dear girl! You don't think Donna Carmella was enough?"

"Oh. Yeah. I suppose. Was she really that important to him? Hell. Never mind. We'll take a closer look once we're done in the Realm of the Gods. I need time in a good bed and a good breakfast afterward, myself."

BRONTE DONETO, ON BECOMING PATRIARCH, HAD NOT MOVED HIS personal household into Krois. No Patriarch did. The Patriarchal apartment in that great fortress was part of the mystery of the position. As all Patriarchs did, Doneto left his home in the care of trusted relatives, protected by powerful sorceries.

In the wee hours a cloaked figure materialized in the hallway outside the room Principaté Bronte Doneto had used as his personal work space and den, where he kept his most treasured possessions, including an extensive collection of rare wines and spirits. The office was guarded by an equally extensive collection of deadly spells. Anything living entering that room would die instantly. Fallen insects marked the kill line.

The cloaked figure carried a small barrel. Contents and all, that weighed thirty-five pounds. A foot of smoldering slow match protruded from one end. The figure set it down on its side, used a foot to roll it through the deadly doorway. The barrel wobbled and shifted directions but came to rest against the leg of an ornate chair.

The cloaked figure vanished.

THE FAINTEST FORERUNNER OF DAWN'S LIGHT HAD BEGUN TO TAINT the overcast. An explosion ripped a hole through the south wall of the third floor of the Doneto town house. Fragments of gray stone flew a hundred yards. In the stillness following the explosion the structure creaked and groaned. Then the rest of the north face yielded to the seduction of gravity.

Fires burned inside.

The neighborhood panicked. Volunteers poured out. Fire was the bane of all old cities.

This fire failed in its struggle to live and grow.

\*      \*      \*

HERIS AND THE NINTH UNKNOWN TWISTED INTO EXISTENCE QUAYSIDE
in the Realm of the Gods, she seconds after he, though he had left the
Delari town house twenty minutes ahead. He said, "I think I know
why you look haggard this morning, girl."

"I'm not used to a plush bed anymore."

"Oh. Somebody got into the Patriarchal magazine at Krois last night.
A keg of firepowder went missing. One of only six that Krois possessed."

"Intriguing. Why would somebody do that?"

"Got me. But later an explosion took the whole north wall off
Bronte Doneto's town house."

"Amazing. And it couldn't have happened to a more deserving fellow. Here's the welcome crew."

Korban Iron Eyes and Asgrimmur Grimmsson were headed their
way.

A dozen more dwarves were visible, all hard at work.

Cloven Februaren said, "Iron Eyes. I thought we were going to get
your people out of here before we opened the way."

"We will. Meantime, we keep on working to make sure everything
goes right. Heris, everything you wanted is ready to go."

"Even the spear?"

"Twelve spears. Two formulations. Held together by the same
magic that binds the rainbow bridge."

"Korban, I could kiss you."

"Long as my woman doesn't see."

"That's beautiful, Korban. Absolutely wonderful. You're a genius.
Now all I need is a way to get everything over there."

Jarneyn actually winked. "No problem. It's Andoray. Heart of the
realm ruled by the Old Ones. Aelen Kofer can turn up anywhere in
Andoray. And we have. The engines are in place. The spears are ready
to go."

Februaren asked, "What's going on, Heris?"

"I had a lot of time on my hands while we were waiting for my falcons. I cooked up a way to sap the Windwalker's strength."

Iron Eyes chuckled. He approved. Definitely.

Februaren frowned. The girl was up to no good. Again.

Iron Eyes was more amused.

The ascendant seemed equally entertained.

Grimmsson seemed to have taken a vow of silence. He just stood
there looking goofy.

Heris asked, "Where's the Bastard?" Getting no answer, she demanded, "Did anyone bother to let him know we're ready?"

"He's hard to reach," Iron Eyes said. "If you're a short, wide, hairy person who has difficulty with the language. And Asgrimmur is likely to be attacked on sight."

"Asgrimmur, if he put his mind to it, could walk into the throne room of the Grail Empire as anybody he wants to be. I smell a steaming hot pile of laziness. Double Great and I shouldn't be the only ones who do anything."

Iron Eyes just looked back blandly.

"You got a golden tongue on you, girl," Februaren said. "Sorry, Iron Eyes. When she's cranky she has this wicked knack for saying exactly the right thing."

"I've gotten used to it."

"The Bastard hasn't been informed?"

"We don't know. We've tried. My sense is, he's ignoring us."

"We'll see about that." Februaren faced the water. "Take me outside. I'll snag the asshole by his twisty little piggy tail and drag him back."

Heris said, "I never cease to be amazed by your confidence, Double Great."

"You just make sure everything stays set."

CLOVEN FEBRUAREN WAS GONE. HERIS COLLECTED IRON EYES AND Grimmsson and plied them with the best dark ale in the Aelen Kofer tavern. "So what do you think? Should we just hang around drinking? Or should we pass the time trying out my method?"

"I'm up for that," the ascendant said.

Iron Eyes considered Asgrimmur with a veiled expression, then Heris. "My young bucks will be eager. But they'll need to be called in and briefed. Then they'll have to go back to our world to make the transit."

"Or we can just brief them on the way."

"No. We'll keep our world to ourselves. You do your sideways trick."

"More time," Heris grumbled.

"Everything takes time," Jarneyn countered. "That's the curse of being mortal." He headed for the barge. It still concealed the portal to the Aelen Kofer world.

"So what do we do now?" If she had known there would be more waiting around she would have stayed in Brothe. She could cause a lot more mischief there. And could sleep in a comfortable bed when she was not.

"We can check what they did in the Great Sky Fortress."

\*       \*       \*

HERIS HAD LOST ALL FEAR OF THE RAINBOW BRIDGE. SHE WALKED across like it was solid granite.

For no real reason she detoured to the dead orchard. She had not visited since that one time, before. She stepped through the fallen wall. "Asgrimmur."

"What?"

"Look at this. Is this what I think?"

A shoot stood six inches tall where she had envisioned a blond goddess planting a golden apple. The shoot was not healthy. It was a pallid greenish yellow.

The ascendant seemed almost breathless. "I think so. But it hasn't absorbed much magic. It may not survive."

Heris stared. She thought the shoot was aware of her.

The gods would need their golden apples after their release.

"Asgrimmur, we never considered the apples in our calculations and preparations."

The ascendant let that simmer briefly, said, "We didn't, did we?"

"How strong could they be when we release them? How long can they last without the fruit? Because that tree won't produce apples in a human lifetime."

"More likely, never." He turned away, shoulders sagging. He stepped out of the garden, ambled toward the entrance to the keep.

What was his problem?

The ghost of the Walker, disappointed. Beginning to realize that patience was not enough. There would be no restoration. No escape from flesh where he was a passenger without control.

Could he be exorcised? She rather liked today's Asgrimmur Grimmsson.

Heris followed the brooding ascendant to the hall where the return would happen. It was a jungle of color as jarring as biting into an unsuspected hot pepper. Nowhere else in the Great Sky Fortress was there any color.

The Aelen Kofer had created lamps burning oils charged with sorcery to give the color Heris wanted to paint and chalk her cuing lines and signs so participants would know where to stand and how to move. The colors were on floor, ceiling, and walls. Cords ran hither and yon to keep people from moving in wrong or dangerous directions. Six falcons all directed their snouts at an area of interior wall on which had been painted a square in a harsh red. Large black dots marred the red. Two eighteen-inch-wide trestle tables sat endwise to the wall and lengthwise toward the two heaviest falcons, which had their butts to the light from outside. On the tables were hammers, star chisels, copper tubes with silver linings, blow tubes charged with silver dust, oils and unguents, garlic paste, and anything else Heris, Jarneyn, or the ascendant thought had any chance whatsoever of being useful.

Heris discreetly checked to make sure items suggested by the ascendant lay at the ends of the table farthest from the red paint.

Trust leavened by caution. Always.

The ascendant did not appear to mind. Might not, for that matter, have noticed.

There was more. Much more. The Aelen Kofer had invested a middle-world fortune in silver. There was silver everywhere, in everything, in patterns meant to constrain and direct the Old Ones if they evaded immediate control. Silver would channel them into the mouths of the falcons. Silver would subject them to harsh debilitation before they could escape to their hapless world. Any that did win free would have been drained down to the weight of boogies and sprites. There would be nowhere to go but their dead realm after that.

Before the release started Iron Eyes would seal all the exits from outside. Only those inside the Realm of the Gods would suffer.

A dozen heavy glass bottles in the general shape of flat bottom teardrops sat near the painted wall. Their tops bent at right angles and narrowed to a tube just large enough to fit one of the silver-lined copper tubes. The bottles ranged in size from a gallon to more than a hogshead. They were masterworks of Aelen Kofer glassblowing. The thick glass held hints of sparkle, smoke, and gray and purple. Silver dust had gone into the melt.

Heris hoped to move the Old Ones from one captivity to another, where contracts could be forged before the Old Ones were decanted.

The ascendant asked, "Is there anything more you can ask?" Exasperated because she was such a detail-oriented woman.

His main personalities were all smash and grab and deal with the consequences later sorts.

"I'm sure there must be. I'm counting on the Old Ones to be confused and disoriented long enough for us mortals to get control." She watched to see how that played.

Too much of this depended on the ascendant.

He had to have control of the Instrumentalities inside him. Then the Bastard had to do whatever a blood descendant had to do.

Heris never did understand that part. But all the old farts agreed: The thing could not be managed without the presence of the divine blood. They were the ones intimate with the Night. They knew the supernatural rules.

She hoped.

*    *    *

IRON EYES WAS WAITING ON THE QUAY. IMPATIENTLY. "GOOD TO SEE you two. . . ." He did not explain what irritated him. "The youngsters are over there already. Including my only son. The Windwalker is working himself up. He knows the appearance of Aelen Kofer means an attack is coming. It always has. He'll think the Old Ones are free and will turn up after the Aelen Kofer prepare the way. But all he'll get is you. Hurry. I don't want him smashing up the future of my tribe."

Heris scowled. If Jarneyn hadn't been determined to save the dwarf world from outsider pollution she and the ascendant would be there now. "So let's hoist all sail and a-reeving go."

That won no smiles.

They kept saying she had to work on her sense of humor.

Iron Eyes wasted no time moving Heris and Asgrimmur outside the Realm of the Gods.

The ascendant was shaking when Heris took hold for the translation. So. He could be afraid despite all his strength and power.

Out the other side, arriving at the same point as before, with Asgrimmur totally shaken. He needed three minutes to regain control.

"Are the transitions really that rough?" Heris asked. They were like blinking her eyes for her, anymore.

"Yes. And worse each time. That was terrible. I felt trapped. The more time went on the more sure I was that I'd never get out again."

"We need to explore that, then. Come on. Tell me while we're getting set to shoot."

"What do you want me to say?"

"I want you to tell me what you experienced, carefully and clearly. I want to know why it's different from what I experience. And will you look at that?"

There had been a dramatic change in the Windwalker. The great jellyfish blob was gone. The god had traded the protection of two-thirds of its mass for a shape that concentrated strength and required less energy to maintain.

The Windwalker now resembled a gigantic lard toad tadpole about to shed its last remnant of a tail.

Asgrimmur said, "It isn't that hard to explain. When you translate you're a human cutting a chord across the Night. When you carry me you take a part of me back home. The Banished and the Walker were born of the Night. Svavar was imprisoned there for centuries. Svavar is repelled. The Walker and Banished are, too, but they're also drawn. And we can see the entities that dwell there. The hideous souls."

"Souls? It's like Hell? Or Purgatory? Or Limbo?"

"Limbo, maybe. For the souls of gods. Instrumentalities have two souls. They bring one into our world with them. They leave the other one in the Night. It anchors them. I see those when we pass through."

"Well, that sounds good." Distracted. "It's got eyes this time. It's looking at us . . . Down!" She pulled the ascendant off his feet.

The toad-thing's tongue struck where they had been an instant earlier. Heris wasted several seconds wondering how she had anticipated Kharoulke. Maybe repeated exposures during her transitions had left her sensitive. "Why am I wasting time brooding when that thing is about to . . . ? You Aelen Kofer! Why aren't you shooting?"

Asgrimmur tried to say something.

"Yeah. Never mind for now. Come on." She grabbed his hand and yanked, proud that she had remembered which one was real. She headed for the nearest dwarfish ballista.

That, being of Aelen Kofer manufacture, was an amazing engine. Which had been assembled where it could not be brought to bear on the Windwalker. None of the crew admitted sharing a language with Heris.

Asgrimmur interrupted her rant, "They couldn't put it together in a clear line of sight because the Instrumentality would get them with its tongue."

Heris's high excitement wilted. "All this for nothing? Did I outsmart myself again?"

"Again?"

"For the first time. What do I do now?"

"You go to the other machine, which is out of the toad's range, and get it started. Once the Instrumentality is fixed on it these dwarves will move their engine up."

"You follow dwarf gabble good enough to get all that?"

"I filled in based on context. But parts of me did speak the language when they were independent."

"Got you. Hanging around with them probably helped, too. So. Here we go. Off to the other one. Carry on, boys. You're doing a wonderful job."

Jarneyn's son, called Copper, had picked up some middle-world Firaldian from Heris, Asgrimmur, and the Ninth Unknown. Copper was in charge of the second and even bigger Aelen Kofer machine. Heris demanded, "Why haven't you shot the damned thing yet?"

"We were directed not to engage until you were here to see the effect of each shot."

Heris muttered something about beginning to understand the frustrations her brother often felt. "All right. Talk to me. What are you going to do, Copper? And how did you come by that name?"

His companions snickered. Heris did not miss the fact that they understood her question fine. Then recalled that when they cared to the Aelen Kofer commanded the mythic power to understand all languages. When they failed to understand they did so deliberately.

Copper said, "It's a bad joke. I did something stupid a few hundred years ago."

"All right. When I need to know I'll ask Iron Eyes. What are you doing?"

In part, that was obvious. The dwarves were cranking the ballista so tight it shrieked in protest.

Copper said, "Velocity will be critical, first shot. That will be a missile we cobbled together while we were waiting." By gesture he invited her closer to the engine, a bow type with long arms crafted of laminated horn from a beast that did not exist in the middle world.

Done cranking, the dwarves moved to their ammunition, carefully arranged on the flattest ground available. Heris counted eight shafts, each fourteen feet long. They ranged from three to six inches in diameter. The one selected was six inches thick and appeared to be made of ice in imitation of a fluted marble column. The head flared out to a foot wide, beginning three feet from the end. That head was hollowed back in a cone shape a foot and a half deep inside.

"That looks like ice," Heris said.

"It is ice. Carefully frozen, then bound with strings of the sort used on the rainbow bridge. If there wasn't an overcast you'd see the light do marvelous things."

"How can ice hurt the Windwalker? He's a winter god."

"It won't stay ice. Impact will turn the ice to water. Hot water. As one shaft splits into twenty thinner ones. The Instrumentality will have twenty jets of water shooting through him. The pain should break his concentration."

The shaft was in place. The Aelen Kofer moved to where they could begin cranking as soon as the ballista discharged.

Copper said, "This was your idea. All we did was tinker. Which is what Aelen Kofer do. Get up on the king seat and give the old toad a poke in the eye."

Heris allowed herself to be guided to a seat atop the engine, above and to the left of the butt of the ice shaft. Copper said, "You see two oak levers by your right hand. The nearest one is the safety capture. Push forward on that one first. When you want to loose you do the same with the farther lever. Do them in that order, left lever, right lever, or you'll find yourself in big trouble."

"Got it. Forward on the nearest lever, then shoot with the other one." She rested her hand on the safety release. That lever was as long as an ax handle. She focused on the Instrumentality, whose own focus was entirely on her.

The god knew what was coming. It was poised to do something about it. Kharoulke was one hundred percent connected to the moment. Was one hundred percent outside the Realm of Night. This was a fight for existence. No other instant in the entire history of the Nine Worlds or Night mattered. This was *the* moment. Perhaps for Heris and the Instrumentality, both. And she felt the full weight of what will the Instrumentality retained. She should not do this wicked thing. She was Chosen. . . .

Unexpected, sharp pain in her left buttock. She jumped, looked down. Copper winked. "You're going to shoot, shoot, Son of Man. Left side, then right."

Heris shoved levers. That hairy-ass runt would be sorry he had done that. She did not look at the Windwalker till the trigger lever slammed home.

The engine lurched violently as the tension in the great bow released. It slammed down again, jarring the air out of Heris's lungs.

The god's tongue leapt to meet the shaft of ice. For an instant psychic space filled with dark mockery. The god would brush the projectile aside. Then it would accumulate new Chosen.

The Aelen Kofer shaft had to conform to the physical laws of the middle world, in a part of that world where there was little magic left and the deity had squandered its share already.

The monster toad tongue did deflect the shaft. But that was moving too fast, carrying too much momentum, to be redirected much.

It hit just slightly off bull's-eye. Otherwise, it performed as designed. It was, after all, an Aelen Kofer artifact.

Dwarves swarmed around the engine, getting it properly aimed again, spanned again, and loaded again. "This one is mostly salt," Copper told her. "Khor-ben's idea. I know not what muse moved him. Salt shouldn't do much. On the other hand, there are iron knives inside the salt. They'll start spinning when they release."

Heris watched the shaft go into the tray.

Copper told her, "Left lever first, right lever second."

"I remember."

The engine did not buck as violently. The dwarves had seen no need for maximum velocity this time.

As the engine slammed back down Heris saw the other ballista ease into position. It got its first missile off an instant before she launched her third, a long wooden pole filled with thousands of little lead darts, each tipped with a barbed iron or silver head. The lead was expected to separate. The barbed heads were ever so slightly curved. They would not travel in a straight line as they kept creeping through divine flesh.

The wood peeled away while the shaft was in the air. The flechettes hit the Windwalker in a broad spray.

The shaft from the other engine was of the same type.

Thousands of boils and pustules appeared on the skin of the great toad. The god heaved violently, most of its mass clearing the stained and slimy shingle. A scream both physical and psychic froze the assailants. For a half minute Heris was capable of no rational thought at all.

Shaking, she pulled herself together. Downslope, the Windwalker desperately tried to do the same. Its violent heave had caused it to slide. Its leg and tail part were in the water. A sort of gray, foul mist puffed off the god where the darts had gone in.

The scream seemed to have no end.

Working like they were doing so in the face of a high wind and doubled gravity, the Aelen Kofer readied the engine again.

Heris shouted down, "One of you guys want to take a turn?"

Copper bellowed, "We can't do that. We're Aelen Kofer. We aren't allowed. We only make things and explain their use."

Heris thought that claim emanated from the stern quarters of a male bovine. Aelen Kofer could and did act when they thought they could get away with it. Whatever it might be.

Copper was hedging bets. Lawyering. Making sure he could disclaim responsibility somewhat. Despite having brought a full ration of Aelen Kofer ingenuity to the murder at hand.

Thenceforth the fight was an execution. The Windwalker was too weak. It could do nothing but take the punishment and hope to survive. And hope its enemies could not bring anything more to bear before winter came.

Winter would come. Winter would bring salvation. This coming winter would be the most ferocious in an epoch. This world would not emerge from its next winter.

"Let's slow down," Heris said. "Let's let each shaft finish working before we launch another."

The mist puffs coming off the Windwalker had become streamers. They built a cloud around the monster. Heris wanted that to clear.

She got down to stretch her legs. "Isn't that something?" she asked the ascendant. She glanced at the sun. The day was getting on. The light might not last long enough to finish this.

"I don't feel well," Asgrimmur said.

SURRENDER TO THE WILL OF THE NIGHT    459

"What?"

"I'm sick. I haven't been sick like this since I suffered through that minor version of what the Windwalker is going through now."

"But it isn't happening to you."

"No. In theory, it's not. Except to those parts of me connected to the Night. The entire Night is feeling this. It's confused, frightened, angry, and disoriented. And fully aware that something unprecedented is happening."

"Your Old Ones, too?"

"Especially them."

"The other Old Ones?"

"I don't think so. They're in a place outside the Nine Worlds and only the Nine Worlds are connected to the Night."

"Your Old Ones. The rest of the Night. They can't possibly feel sorry for this thing."

"The Banished, not so much. The Walker . . . It isn't sympathy. It's fear and all the things the rest of the Night feels. And . . . No. That doesn't make sense. Does it? A kind of guilt, despair, then another kind of guilt?"

"Who said the man is confused? That's clear as a smack in the teeth. Time for me to take a couple more shots." The steam had cleared off the Windwalker. The mottled, festering remnants of the toad did not retain a third of the mass that had been there before the attack began.

Her first shot set the surface of the Windwalker to bubbling like hot tar. Heris heard the bubbles bursting. Each vented a fat puff of steam. The toad soon disappeared inside another cloud.

Heris leaned back.

The ascendant climbed up and hung on to the side of her seat. "I've made sense of what the Walker is feeling. He sees all this as his fault. He now thinks you'll actually kill the Windwalker. Being selfish, as gods are, he doesn't care what that means for the Night. He does think that it means you won't find it necessary to release the other Old Ones."

"That wouldn't hurt my feelings. Not having to try. Be pretty damned anticlimactic after all the work we've done to make it happen, though."

"Yes. Just so."

"What does that mean?"

"That the Walker is sure you won't let the work go to waste. That, since you don't need them now, you'll bring them out to destroy them."

Heris thought about that. And found it a not unappealing plan. But entirely unnecessary. The Old Ones could be kept forever harmless right where they were.

Asgrimmur said, "The Walker now believes the Old Ones made a huge miscalculation when they conscripted us Andorayans to use against a man who accidentally discovered a way to murder the Instrumentalities of the Night. But didn't know that till the Night itself *made* him understand."

"Yeah. That was a real screwup."

"And now facts hitherto unnoticed have crept into the Walker's awareness. It's possible that the Godslayer himself was misidentified."

"What?" Heris eased a hand toward one of her knives.

"You were a slave when the Esther's Wood thing happened. In the Holy Lands. Less than twenty miles away. An imperceptible separation seen from the Great Sky Fortress, centuries earlier. The Walker thinks distance, time, and coincidence might have resulted in picking the wrong Godslayer."

"Horse hockey." And muttered something about keeping it in the family.

"You're in the process of killing what, once upon a time, was the most terrible Instrumentality of all. A weakened Kharoulke but the real thing, not some ghost of a god raised up by a lunatic sorcerer with a lust for immortality. And you have it in your power to extinguish an entire pantheon and one of the Nine Worlds."

"More horse puckey, Asgrimmur. Get down. Time for another shot."

Shafts from both engines struck the Windwalker. God flesh surged violently but did not come down in the water this time.

The violence continued, as though the god's back had been broken.

Asgrimmur swore. "Oh, shit! Get down from there, Heris."

Copper snarled, "Down, woman! Down!" He and his people started crawling under the nearest chunks of basalt.

Heris felt the imminence. She dropped between skittering rocks, turned an ankle, made cover with an instant to spare.

A blinding flash. A roar that overshadowed all the firepowder roars Heris ever heard. The earth shook, rattled, and bucked. Scree slipped. Boulders went bounding or sliding downslope. Somebody shrieked as his hiding place fell in on him. For an instant the air was too hot to breathe. Then a ferocious wind came rushing downhill.

A massive fireball climbed toward and tore into the low overcast.

"Well," Heris muttered. "This is what Piper saw when the god worm died. Damn! Good thing the old asshole was worn down to where he didn't have anything left."

She could not hear herself. Nor anything else. Just as well. Her companions did not need to follow her ramblings.

She did review what Piper had said about the incident with the god worm.

An egg. There should be some kind of egg. Piper had been collecting those since he started killing Instrumentalities. Better find out if there was one of those here.

Asgrimmur and Copper both yelled and waved as she headed downhill. She did not have to pretend she did not hear them.

The explosion had not consumed the Instrumentality completely. Slime and chunks of rotten "lard" were everywhere, including on the water of the Ormo Strait. The stench was brutal. But there was no more sense of a divine presence. The opposite was true. There was a vacuum, an impression that something important had gone missing. Heris felt an abiding sorrow that was not at all natural.

She spied the egg. It was bigger than any Piper had described. It shed a strong inner light and so much heat that she had to stop fifteen feet away. The light kept fading.

She began to feel other presences, unseen Night things in search of the truth. Not threatening things, just small things come to witness. She began to hear their whispers and rustles.

Copper joined her, as did Asgrimmur. The dwarf squatted. The ascendant stood with feet widespread, his hand behind him. Both stared at the egg. Heris said, "We can go as soon as that cools down."

Asgrimmur asked, "What do you want with it?"

"Two souls. That's the one the Windwalker brought to this world. I want it under control. I want it taken to where it can be destroyed."

"You'd probably be safer just leaving it."

"Maybe. But I'm not going to do that. Copper. Have your guys started breaking down? Though it's a crime to take those beautiful engines apart."

Distracted, Copper shrugged. "They aren't being destroyed, just disassembled. They'll be stored till they're needed again. And they will be. That's the nature of these things."

Heris thought Piper's falcons were more likely to figure in future godly executions.

Asgrimmur took hold of Copper's arm. "I'm not going back the way we came. I wouldn't survive. I'll walk back beside my new best friend. Unless he wants to stay here and set up housekeeping. It'll be fun, come winter. I can teach him to ski."

Heris saw Copper shudder. The dwarf was angry inside. But he did not refuse.

She knew she would get nowhere making the same suggestion.

The dwarf could not refuse. He was Aelen Kofer. Asgrimmur had the ghost of the All-Father inside him. Copper had no option.

Proof that every dwarf had to be out of the Realm of the Gods before any move involving trapped deities.

Heris said, "I understand. Copper. Will you make your journey on foot?"

The dwarf thought before answering, seeing what he might give away. "Yes. It's a one-day journey. Goat carts will move the engine parts."

"Great. You can do me a favor, then. Take this egg to the Realm of the Gods. It occurs to me that it wouldn't be smart to be carrying it when I cut my chord across the Night."

She saw no obvious reaction from Asgrimmur, though he had offered a gentle caution. Copper did respond, but only in the manner of someone who fancied himself serially victimized. He indulged in woe-is-me sighs.

IT WAS ALWAYS HIGH NOON IN THE REALM OF THE GODS so it did not matter that it was after dark when the egg finally cooled enough to be wrapped in leather ammo slings and moved over, whatever secret way the dwarves used, to a goat cart in the Aelen Kofer world. A moment afterward Heris turned sideways and transitioned to the Realm of the Gods.

Cloven Februaren had not yet returned. She was exhausted, physically and emotionally. She vanished into her local hole-up without announcing her return.

THE NINTH UNKNOWN AND THE BASTARD WERE IN THE AELEN KOFER tavern with Iron Eyes when Heris, refreshed, wandered in looking for something to eat. The dwarf and the old man started barking questions.

"Copper is fine. He's on his way. Asgrimmur is with him. He wouldn't have survived another transition. If you've got the Night in you, you can get hung up out there. Forever. Double Great. We're going to need to do some rethinking."

"Rethinking? What do you mean? Rethinking of what?"

"What we're going to do up there." She jerked a thumb in the direction of the Great Sky Fortress.

"Why?" His eyes narrowed. He smelled something.

Heris smelled food. Her usual arrived. Before she tucked in, she said, "Because I killed the Windwalker already. Which I told you I could do, but you wouldn't believe. Yesterday. With help from the Aelen Kofer."

Iron Eyes and her human companions stared. They gaped. And they refused to believe.

"It took almost every weapon I had but I did do it in, Double Great. Copper is bringing its soul egg. Kharoulke the Windwalker is no more. And all the Night is in a panic and disarray."

They still would not believe. They did not want to believe. "Yes. Me. A mere girl. I did it." Her glare dared any of them to claim they had softened the Windwalker up. She had done the heavy lifting from the beginning.

Cloven Februaren said, "She's right about the Night. I've never seen it as agitated as it is now."

The Bastard nodded silent agreement.

Iron Eyes said, "We'll wait on Copper and the ascendant. We'll see what they have to say."

Heris was profoundly irked but knew that was the best she could expect. For now.

## 42. Brothe: Commander of the Righteous

A servant rolled Paludan Bruglioni onto the flagstone patio. The Commander of the Righteous was sharing a morning meal with staff and liaison officers from the Imperial forces of southern Firaldia. Their commander, Prince Manfred Otho of Alamedinne, had refused to dine with a hired sword. The Empress, either drunk or drugged, brooded over the scene from a high seat a short distance away. Her presence dared the southern nobility to try disdaining her desires when it came to naming the Commander of the Righteous master of all Imperial forces south of Brothe.

There would be conflicts if the campaign lasted. The Ege family had little love for Manfred Otho and his father, Manfred Ludovico, both of whom had been conspicuously absent from Imperial ranks during the Calziran Crusade. The southerners could just barely tolerate being ruled by an Ege woman. Having to take orders from a base-born mercenary lay at the frontier of too huge an indignity. Only the prospect of booty kept mutiny from raising its ugly head.

A feeble prospect, plunder.

Agents of the Patriarch were around, whispering. Telling the truth, in fact. Only estates and properties associated with the Benedocto would be given over to sack. The Benedocto were not rich. The Benedocto still owed bribe money from the election of their last Patriarch, Sublime V.

The smarter southerners, though disgruntled, understood that they were in no position to enforce their preferences. The Grand Duke, now with six thousand men, was scarcely forty miles north of Brothe. Admiral fon Tyre was almost as near, though still beyond the Monte Sismonda. He commanded another twenty-two hundred men. Both men would enforce the will of the Empress if the Commander of the Righteous could not do so himself. The Commander's reliable force now numbered thirteen hundred. With all those falcons that had won the battle in the Shades. Plus several lesser engagements since.

Paludan rolled into place beside Hecht. Hecht was not quite startled. He had heard the wheels on stone. "Good morning, sir," he said.

"Good morning. I'll only take a minute. Or two. First, to thank you for the care you took to avoid damaging the vineyards yesterday."

"Thank you for your appreciation. I get some friction but my policy is to minimize damage to friends."

Yesterday had seen a strong cavalry probe come south from Brothe. Titus Consent's friends in the city had sent warnings. Hecht's own horsemen had led that force into an ambush where falcons had torn them apart. Southerners had been there to observe. Their reaction had been to whine about all the horses left unfit for capture once the falcons did their job. Plus, there had been few prisoners to ransom.

Hecht asked, "And your other matter?"

"I don't know what reports you've had. I hear that Brothe is coming apart. The City Regiment can't keep the peace anymore. And Serenity keeps giving stranger and more draconian orders."

"That's what I hear. He's become completely erratic since somebody killed his mistress and wrecked his city house." Hecht had the facts of those events from Lila.

"It could be wishful thinking but my contacts say that neither the City Regiment nor the militia would fight much if you got inside the wall."

Hecht looked Paludan in the eye for several seconds. Then, "Rivademar. This meeting is suspended. I'll let you know when we'll resume. Titus, stay. The rest of you, go enjoy the morning. Or get some work done. Whatever moves you."

Titus moved around the table, settled beside Hecht. The rest of the gathering moved away. Consent asked, "Do we need a quiet room?"

Paludan said, "Unfortunately, the only one here is damaged."

Hecht said, "We managed an ambush yesterday."

Consent nodded. "So we did. By misdirection. Which works as long as Serenity's Collegium friends refuse to be found at the point of the spear."

Hecht asked Bruglioni, "Do you know somebody inside willing to work with us?"

"I expect we all do, in a manner of speaking. In this case, though, I'm talking about somebody involved with the Arniena. Somebody Rogoz Sayag knows."

Hecht nodded, not surprised. Brothen politics being Brothen politics, this was inevitable. But he had not expected it so soon.

Paludan said, "War isn't good for business. Unless it's happening somewhere else and we're selling them the means to butcher one another. If this lasts all summer the cost will become insupportable. Brothe has ten thousand men closing in. Since the Shades Serenity can't find fighters willing to defend him. Only Pinkus Ghort offers much hope. And he hasn't reached Brothe yet. The Grand Duke keeps slowing him down."

Hecht believed Hilandle was either much more clever than anyone credited, or much luckier. He had been doing everything almost exactly right since his advent in Firaldia.

Hecht said, "So if I get there first, get inside, and stun Serenity's friends . . ."

"If you got inside suddenly, and seized several gates, you could probably give your Empress what she wants and, maybe, the rest of us the relief we're looking for."

"We're sitting here talking about it in the wide open. They'll know we're coming."

"Maybe not. Although we don't have a functional quiet room, we aren't unprotected. If we keep our wards in place and up to strength Serenity can't get more than snippets of what we're planning. Go after a gate? Pretty obvious, isn't it? Don't need to be a military genius or have spies riding the Commander's shoulder to anticipate that. But which gate? And can Serenity trust all the men he puts in charge?"

Hecht thought about it. Paludan was right.

The numinous side of life was an incredible pain, even today. How much worse had it been before the Old Empire? Of all the works of the Old Empire—nearly eternal roads and public works, and all the great buildings still used today—the taming of the Night had to be the most valuable. And least appreciated.

Hecht said, "Pull it together, then, sir. You know the people, I'll let you build the plan. See me when you have something workable."

Hecht would work on something of his own, based on information from Titus. Something that could become an alternate course at minimum notice. Or on several such alternates.

The moment Paludan left Hecht said, "Get me a census of healthy falcons, Titus. Anything we do, falcons will be the key."

\*    \*    \*

ONE HUNDRED FOURTEEN FALCONS. ATTRITION HAD CLAIMED THIRTY-
two.

"But Rhuk thinks some can be salvaged."

"What about handhelds?"

"No way to know." Consent shrugged. "Men who have them
don't want us to know. We might take them away."

Hecht felt like cursing and laughing, both. He understood the soldier's point of view. A man's own life was just a whole shitload more important than any cockamamie plan dreamed up by some general or staff
officer. A handheld was number one insurance when a man had to go
into dark places.

Krulik and Sneigon had shown more than two hundred handhelds
on inventory rolls when the Righteous arrived. Twenty-two had been
turned in to Rhuk or Prosek.

Of the heavier pieces, many of which had had to be rooted out of
hiding, only the half dozen put aside for Heris had gone missing. One
hundred fifty-two had been found, many not included on the company
formal inventory. Those off the books had been meant to disappear into
the Devedian quarters of cities all across the Brothen Episcopal world.
One hundred forty-six falcons had seen action in the Shades.

"Have they rigged all the weapons up on carts, or wheels, or some
damned thing?" Getting the weapons moved and emplaced was a pain.
From the beginning Rhuk and Prosek had experimented with ways to
improve mobility. Each idea died once the shooting started. Recoil broke
even the best made carts.

"All set. Pretty rough, though. Prosek wants to build a dual-purpose
cart that can haul stores or tentage but be converted as a replacement
falcon cart."

"That's what he gets paid for. All I'm interested in is being able to
move fast once we're inside the wall."

THE RIGHTEOUS, WITH IMPERIALS FROM THE SOUTH AND A HANDFUL
from east of the Monte Sismonda, moved toward Brothe. Serenity's patrols watched but contested nothing. Hecht halted on grain fields in
plain sight of the wall.

To assuage the bruised honor of the southerners Hecht deferred bat-
tlefield command to Manfred Otho Altomindo, the Prince Apparent of
Alamedinne, for the daylight hours, or till the Empress overruled him.
Prince Manfred was not the senior southerner but his father, Manfred
Ludovico, was senile, bedridden, and a figurehead.

Hecht was giving nothing away, yielding daytime command. Serenity was not going to let God decide his fate on a battlefield.

The Manfreds had no intelligence concerning the true situation, which was that Serenity's advisers had convinced him to go defensive till the southern levies completed their feudal obligations.

Similar limits would obtain for levies raised in the Patriarchal States. But Serenity's cronies were concerned only with themselves and their own immediate security.

The younger Manfred set the order of battle. His southerners made up the center, arrayed for the traditional heavy cavalry charge. The disdained Righteous formed the wings, with a scatter of auxiliary light cavalry out beyond the divisions of the Righteous. Hecht was both appalled and amused because those light horsemen were Pramans recruited from what had been Calzir before the Calziran Crusade.

Nothing happened. Not even a herald came out. Hecht reassumed command come sunset. He ordered camp set, with special attention paid to wards against sorcery and Instrumentalities. Manfred Otho retired cursing the lack of panache shown by the Brothen knightly class.

Reports from the city had the Collegium in a state of civil war. Serenity's partisans had the upper hand in the streets. Their behavior was abominable.

Only the Devedian quarter remained quiet. The Deves had locked up and hunkered down, getting ready for the customary attacks that turned their way whenever there was civil unrest.

Hecht asked Consent, "Do we have any goodwill in the Devedian quarter at all?"

"After what we did to Krulik and Sneigon? No."

"Understandable. They were just trying to make money. That's what Deves do."

Consent gave him a dark look. He loathed the stereotypes and generalizations.

Hecht added, "They'd best get ready to suffer for our success."

"What?"

"Apply the usual logic. Falcons gave us a bloody victory in the Shades. Deves made the falcons."

"And the fact that we robbed the Deves to get the falcons wouldn't enter the argument. You're right. The usual logic."

"It could happen tonight, Titus. I'm going to my tent to pray. I don't want to be disturbed. Please remind Mr. Ernest."

Consent did not reply. He just went off to do his job.

\*       \*       \*

LILA TURNED UP RIGHT ON TIME.

"You look tired, girl."

"I'm working hard. Great Grandpa Delari always has more work for me than I can possibly get done."

"Don't let him take advantage. Say no. You are being careful?"

"Very, very careful. This city is a deadly place right now."

"As long as you understand. Don't take chances. We're coming in tonight."

"And they're expecting you. They already have the gates reinforced." She produced a map, described the welcomes being prepared.

"Dear girl, it's almost like you were sitting in on their meetings."

"Isn't it?"

"They know about the Arniena plan, don't they?"

"There's a Benedocto agent close to Mr. Sayag. The Benedocto have agents inside all of the Five Families."

No surprise, that. Everybody did it. Some of those spies worked for two or three families at once. "Do we know any names?"

Lila produced a scrap of paper. "There are more. These are just names I overheard."

Hecht examined the list, saw nothing familiar. He admired Lila's precise hand. Clearly, she had worked hard to develop it. "I'm loving this, Lila. You're better at this than Heris or the really old man."

"No. I'm not. I'm just doing things the way you want them done. They only do things the way they want to."

"I'll give you that." He studied the map some more. "This isn't good. These sites are all traps."

"I told you that. They'll have crossbowmen on the roofs. And you can't surprise them. They'll be watching with every little brownie and boogie in this end of the world. The Patriarch pulled them in from a hundred miles around."

Hecht stared at the map. And stared. And found no inspiration. "How is Pella?"

"Turning stupid again. He whines constantly. The old old man should've left him where he was. Should've let him ripen. He could've gone back if somebody else didn't find him."

"Rough. And Vali? And Anna?"

"Vali is working hard to make herself good enough to help me. Anna cries a lot."

"What? Why?"

"It's her time of life, I think. It doesn't matter if she's sad or happy or angry. Everything makes her cry. Except when she gets all righteous and wants to go over to Krois and slap Serenity till he starts seeing sense."

"Good for her. I guess. So. Honored daughter. Any ideas about what we should do tonight?"

Lila grinned a huge one. "You attack them where they aren't. I'll smash them where they are."

Commencing sometime after midnight, for slightly more than two hours, about every four minutes, there were explosions in the Mother City. They were scattered and happened according to no discernible pattern—though every one damaged Serenity's friends or the city's defenders.

There were occasional gaps in the timing. Whenever that happened somebody dropped ropes from sections of wall not being closely guarded.

The Righteous failed to achieve complete surprise anywhere. Despite all the confusion some people did keep their minds on their jobs.

Those chosen to climb the ropes took rope ladders up. They were men experienced at dealing with small Instrumentalities and, one and all, were suspected of being in possession of handheld firepowder weapons. They established their footholds, helped more men come up, helped assemble cranes when the parts for those arrived, then helped hoist light falcons and munitions. They expanded their footholds and fended off swarms of minor Instrumentalities.

The falcons crushed counterattacks. Those ceased. The Shades had imprinted an abiding dread of falcons on Serenity's friends.

Pots of explosive tossed into gatehouses encouraged men there to surrender or flee. Two gates changed hands despite the prepared traps, which broke up under falcon fires.

Deeming them likely to be useless except as a cause of further confusion, Hecht let the southerners go howling into the city after he opened the gates.

Hagan Brokke rumbled, "So much for it being impossible to attack the Mother City."

Rivademar Vircondelet observed, "It's not the attack, it's the accomplishing anything once we do. Now they know where we're coming in. They can pull everybody together to deal with us."

Falcons barked not far away, from above, blasting rooftops. Stones rattled off roofing tiles, broke roofing tiles that clattered to the ground, and found spies or ambushers because there were cries of pain.

Meantime, the southerners finished flooding in. Hecht watched them out of sight. "I wonder how many will survive."

"They stick together and do what you told them to do, maybe most of them." Brokke coughed. His lungs were sensitive to firepowder smoke. "But my money is on discipline failing. They'll spread out to start looting and get themselves picked off a few at a time."

They were supposed to roar through the streets cutting down anyone they ran into. Spread enough fear and the streets would clear. The invaders could move north, toward Krois, where an enraged but supposedly more rational than usual Serenity would be straining to get the most out of having his enemies attack as he had hoped.

Vircondelet asked, "We got any real shot at pulling this off, boss?"

"We do. Now that we're inside. Falcons will be handy in the kind of fighting coming up."

"Easy to sweep the streets," Brokke said. "But Serenity is holed up inside Krois. He can just squat there till Ghort comes to save his ass."

"But he won't be safe in there," Vircondelet said. "On account of, the boss knows how to get in going under the river."

"I do," Hecht admitted. "But Serenity knows I know. He's the one who showed me how. He'll have a special welcome waiting down there."

The explosions stopped. Hecht supposed that meant Lila could no longer steal firepowder from Prosek. Or that she had gotten tired enough to quit.

For a while, once the two gates had been taken, it looked like Brothe might be a paper tiger. There was little resistance to start.

That changed when the sun came up.

Did the locals fear the dark more than the invaders? Hecht's amulet had distracted him plenty but nothing big had been on the move.

He did feel something new once the darkness fled, taking the boogies with it. This something had been masked by the rustle of all the smaller entities.

It was down in the catacombs. It was huge. And it was between the Righteous and the river Teragi. It felt like the same old murderous thing that kept returning, however often it was hunted down. This incarnation was stronger than any before.

It would make trouble once darkness returned, guaranteed. It was Bronte Doneto's dark child.

Piper Hecht thought he knew what Bronte Doneto had been up to back when Muniero Delari stumbled into him in the catacombs.

The Righteous made slow headway against stubborn resistance, doing a lot of damage with the falcons. It was not always clear who needed beating down. Serenity's enemies refused to be cautious in getting out to mix it up with the Patriarch's friends.

Southerners began to turn up. As Hecht had anticipated, their gleeful charge into the city's warrens had become a debacle. They had been chastened. Survivors were trying to link up with one another or the Righteous.

Hecht hoped the lesson would not be lost on the men who actually did the face-to-face, bad-breath-to-bad-breath, toe-to-toe fighting.

By midafternoon he was considering falling back to the gates, to wait on the Grand Duke and Admiral. His earlier assessment of his chances appeared to be proving out. He was doing an awesome amount of damage but did not have the manpower to exploit it, even with help from prodigal southerners and local volunteers.

The latter were of little value. They had no interest in submitting to military discipline or in carrying out military missions.

Ever more men had to be tasked to protect the lengthening line of communication from the gates to the point of attack.

Word came that Serenity had ordered Pinkus Ghort to stop dancing with the Grand Duke and get to Brothe, never mind losses.

Come the afternoon Collegium opponents of Serenity began to appear. They sprang from homes in the Empire or Imperial possessions in Firaldia. Serenity's adherents had the upper hand in the Chiaro Palace.

Hecht's heart sank. That was not good. That could portend disaster. If Serenity got to the Construct . . . Pray Heris was right when she said the Patriarch was unaware of the project. Otherwise, his triumph was assured.

Hecht felt the thing in the catacombs ever more intensely. He was getting closer. It was getting stronger. It sensed him, too. He had an ever more powerful impression that it was bigger than anybody thought. And that it was still growing, by the hour and the minute.

And it must be. If the old men were right about it feeding on fear and hatred. Or if the large grew bigger by eating the small. The Patriarch had flooded the city with minor Instrumentalities.

As evening approached more locals came out to work against Serenity. Or, more often, against the Benedocto. Everyone associated with the major families had suffered recently.

Titus insisted the volunteers were more trouble than they were worth. Hecht had him scatter them, making them do something useful like carry things for the fighters.

The advance passed the Bruglioni and Cologni family citadels. The Bruglioni was a ruin haunted by crows, insects, and the smell of death. The Cologni had survived, though that family's less well defended properties elsewhere had suffered.

There was plenty of evidence of fighting but none suggesting any use of sorcery.

As the sun dropped toward the skyline Hecht began calculating how best to deal with the thing down below. It would come tonight. It would get no better opportunity.

It was a thing of the darkest side of the Night, lethally dangerous but not invulnerable. Godshot would tame it. How to fix and target it was the question.

Hecht redirected the advance to pass Principaté Delari's town house. He hoped to find the old man holding out there and willing to give advice. He found only ruin, absent the smell of death. There was no sign of the Principaté or his staff. Refugees from the Chiaro Palace, though, insisted that Delari was alive, making himself obnoxious, and had some special surprise cooked up for the Patriarch.

Where was Lila? Lila would know how to get hold of the old man.

Hecht had begun to worry about that girl. He should have heard from her by now.

The Imperial advance reached the hippodrome, now restored and enjoying a full racing season. Or had been till the death of Jaime of Castauriga changed the world.

There were scores of horses stabled under the stadium. Scores of people who tended the animals or managed the venue also lived in nooks and crannies out of the public eye. Smells of cooking and stables both emanated from the hippodrome.

Hagan Brokke turned up as Hecht contemplated the stadium. "Boss, it's late. And we're too worn down to keep it going after dark. We ought to settle down right here. We can control access . . ."

"You're right. I was just looking at it. Pass the word. Make it happen. And send runners to tell our people to either come here or move back to the gates. I don't want anybody on the streets tonight. It might get ugly out there."

"Night things?" The staff all believed he had some special connection now that he had died and been resurrected.

"Big Night things. Every second falcon should be charged with godshot." His amulet had grown more irritating as the sun sank. It had the same feel as the night that Heris had brought him in to visit.

At first it seemed an evening when the whole city meant to come out and go crazy. There were sounds of rioting, screams in the distance, fires both near at hand and far away. The exterior wall of the hippodrome was high enough to offer a good view in several directions, including toward the Castella, Krois, and the Chiaro Palace. Toward what had been the heart of Brothe for fifteen hundred years. Lights moved around Krois and the Chiaro Palace. The Castella was dark.

Hecht asked his officers to join him up where he could observe the city's torment while they talked. They came, none with any enthusiasm.

And several were unreasonably late. Titus Consent claimed he had been taking intelligence reports from local people. Clej Sedlakova said he was welcoming a company of infantrymen from Alamedinne who had just fought through to the hippodrome. Their addition made it nearly half the southerners recovered.

Hecht gave up on Hagan Brokke. But, then, he did turn up. Not alone.

The Empress tagged along behind.

"What the hell is wrong with that woman?" But he was too tired to get good and angry. He just kept things moving by asking if anyone knew anything about this new version of the hippodrome. He would go through the motions to the end, though Katrin's presence virtually guaranteed death or captivity. How could Serenity resist the invitation to end his war with one quick stroke?

Titus Consent asked what he wanted to know about the hippodrome.

"It fell down because the catacombs caved in. Was anything done to stop that from happening again?" The catacombs offered the monster there a sheltered path of attack, otherwise.

There were several opinions. No one knew for sure. Hecht studied the Empress and Captain Ephrian. Ephrian had gotten himself wounded. He was pale, exhausted, on the verge of collapse. Katrin looked like she had been smoking *kuf*. Smelled like it, too.

Ephrian noted his sniffing. "It actually helps," he said. Then fell asleep.

Hecht envied him.

He began to talk about the likelihood of a serious encounter with the Night, tonight. Tonight could make or break the whole campaign. He made no comment on the presence of royalty. If the Righteous got through tonight they ought to be able to fight through to the Teragi tomorrow, there to isolate Krois and the Chiaro Palace. Then they could relax and wait on the Grand Duke.

Hecht tried to make it sound like he thought this war was as good as won. If they could just make it through tonight.

The night went quiet.

Hecht's amulet itched brutally.

Katrin offered a vague smile to no one in particular.

Something exploded on the other side of the stadium.

A firepowder cart? No. That was huge but down in the ground. Underneath.

There was no big flash or smoke, just a muted bang, and shaking.

Everyone started trading dimwit questions.

The other side of the stadium groaned. Then it rumbled. Then it settled majestically, dustily, into the earth.

"Did they do anything to the catacombs so that wouldn't happen again?" Titus asked. "I'm thinking, probably not."

Hecht said, "We had people and weapons posted over there." Noting that this was not the section that had fallen before. "One more time and we'll have a whole new hippodrome. Get down there and see what needs doing."

Something more than an explosion and collapse had happened. Hecht's staff already believed it had been an attack.

The irritation offered by Hecht's amulet had a whole new feel.

"Wait."

Hecht thought Katrin had spoken. "Your Grace?" But the Empress had drifted into a thousand-yard stare. And Captain Ephrian was sound asleep.

"Father. Here."

"Lila?"

"Here." Inside a shadow hardly big enough to hide a pin.

"You've had me worried half to death, girl. You just plain disappeared last night."

"I had to help Great Grandfather seal off the Construct. Then I had to get some sleep. And then I had to help him set the trap that just got sprung."

"That explosion?"

"That would be the most obvious part."

"He's making a habit of knocking this place down."

"But that's good. For you. It means the monster walked into the trap. It means you won't have to fight it off."

Hecht rubbed his left wrist. "I don't know." It felt like the Night remained plenty active.

Someone called out from below. He yelled back something about looking out for the Empress.

Lila said, "I have to go. I have to help Great Grandfather tonight. Don't worry about the monster. The explosives were silver-charged. They shredded it." She turned sideways.

Hecht turned himself. And found Katrin watching him, not looking the least bit drugged. "Who was that, Commander?"

"My daughter. The sorceress."

THE NEW COLLAPSE AT THE HIPPODROME SERVED TO DECLARE A TRUCE between the working people on both sides. A lot of rescue work needed doing, particularly of horses and the people who lived with them.

It was another long night affording little rest. On the plus side, casualties were amazingly few.

Lila said Muniero Delari was responsible. The Principaté had destroyed the thing in the catacombs again, maybe permanently this time. And the effects were immediate and far-reaching.

Come morning the city was quiet. And flooded with rumors. The squabble in the Collegium had taken a dramatic turn. Serenity's most obdurate supporters had fled into Krois, where they would assist the Patriarch in waiting the several days it would take the Captain-General to come rescue them.

Whether or not Serenity liked it, Pinkus Ghort could not just turn his back on the Grand Duke. That would get him slaughtered. He needed to maintain a force capable of making a rescue.

Loud supporters of the Patriarch were scarce today. Those Hecht did see were in the custody of partisans of families not named Benedocto. There was no resistance.

Could that thing down under have been a revenant old god of strife?

Hecht delivered the Empress and her party to the Penital, where Ambassador va Still-Patter had been under siege for weeks. The besiegers had gone away during the night.

Hecht rubbed his left wrist. The amulet barely tickled this morning.

Principaté Delari had done good. He had done real good.

MILITARY OPERATIONS CONTINUED. KROIS HAD TO BE ISOLATED. THE Chiaro Palace had to be neutralized. The north side gates had to be taken under control to forestall their use by the Captain-General, whose motley Patriarchal levies now outnumbered the Imperials harassing them.

Hecht went to one of the little gates of the Castella dollas Pontellas and asked to see his family. After he had made arrangements for his soldiers with families locally to visit their loved ones, with minimal risk.

Chaos waxed and waned. There were no serious outbreaks. No attack on the Devedian quarter materialized. Hecht was quick to encourage rumors that blamed him for having kept an attack from developing.

HECHT FINALLY SAT DOWN WITH HIS FAMILY. EVEN MUNIERO DELARI was there. Though triumphant, the old man looked like he was on his last legs, and believed that himself. "This time was too much, Piper. Protecting the Construct, harassing Doneto, slaying his monster, trying to turn the tide in the Collegium . . . All too much for one old man. And Doneto is still out there, scheming up something else."

"You stop. He's been thwarted. Leave the rest for someone else."

"There is no one else."

"Pella. I have a mission for you. You can draft Vali to help."

"Dad?"

"Put this old coot into bed and sit on him till I tell you to turn him loose. Brothe will survive without him tinkering."

Vali and Pella closed in on Delari. They did not have to drag him. And he did not protest.

All he needed was for someone to take the decisions away. He could then surrender to exhaustion.

"YOU'VE BEEN UNNATURALLY QUIET SINCE I GOT HERE," HECHT TOLD Anna, lying in bed. She had been powerfully responsive but otherwise uncharacteristically silent.

"I don't know what it is. I can't deal with all this emotionally. It's so frustrating because there's no way to make it change. We are who we are and the world is what it is, and, I firmly suspect, I wouldn't be the least bit happier if everything suddenly changed to be exactly the way I think I want it."

"You always were able to look past emotion. Better than me, really."

"What are you going to do now?"

"This isn't over by a long way. Pinkus is coming and he outnumbers me."

"And you'll fight. Of course."

"Not if I can help it. If I can root Serenity out first . . ."

"No more. Just be here. And save all that for Titus and the others."

"How are Noë and the children?"

"I don't know. I haven't heard from them since all this started. Hauf wouldn't extend the protection of the Brotherhood to a family of Deves."

"Titus went down there. We'll know tomorrow." He felt a deep and selfish dread that the news would not be good.

Bad news might cost him Consent's talents.

He did not want to think about that. He did not want to think. He lost himself in the lovemaking.

RELATIVE PEACE RULED THE MOTHER CITY. THERE WERE SKIRMISHES but no serious bloodlettings. Hecht stayed busy seeing all the people who felt they had a claim on his time. He figured Serenity was just as busy over in Krois.

There was good news. Titus had found his family safe and well and met his newest son for the first time. Further, Noë's family had, at last, forgiven her for having deserted the faith of her ancestors when her husband converted. She had reconciled with them.

Hecht never was convinced that Consent's conversion was genuine so he had no trouble seeing Noë's as illusory.

No matter. He was pleased for Titus.

One of those who made demands was Addam Hauf, Master of the Castella Commandery. Hauf was deeply interested in exploring the Imperial commitment to a new crusade.

"That answer is simple," Hecht told Hauf. "We go next summer, barring disaster. And barring any shortage of funds."

Hauf chuckled. "Catch that rascal Doneto. Hang him up by his ugly big toes. Make him pay. He must have chests full of bribe monies by now."

Not so. One reason some Principatés were deserting Serenity was that he had not yet paid for their votes.

"He might not be so well off, now. Not getting any income out of the Empire since Katrin changed her mind."

"Take it back."

"Excellent idea. Easier said than done with him forted up inside Krois."

Somewhere, remotely, a half-dozen falcons popped off. Probably weapons on the banks of the Teragi harassing Krois. The effort was psychological rather than practical. The projectiles were not massive enough to do serious damage.

Hauf said, "There are passages under the river."

"And Serenity knows."

"Death trap?"

"Absolutely." Maybe. Principaté Delari was working on that. And having little luck.

"The Empire *definitely* is committed to a crusade?"

"Yes."

"Good. Though even next summer may be too late."

"Why is that?"

"While we're fighting amongst ourselves here Indala is involved in a campaign to unite the kaifates so he can undertake a crusade of his own."

"Really?"

"Really. Does that shock you?"

"It's unexpected. And it can't be good for us. But . . . He expects to prevail against Gordimer the Lion and the Sha-lug?"

"He'd have to, wouldn't he? Or he wouldn't have marched on Dreanger in the first place."

"I suppose."

Hecht had paid little attention to Gordimer, Dreanger, and the east these past few years. Could the Lion have sunk so far?

A SUMMONS CAME FROM THE PENITAL, OVER THE AMBASSADOR'S SIGnature. Terens Ernest and ten men in long mail shirts walked Hecht over. He did not see how they could prevent a repeat of what had happened last spring.

His wound still bothered him.

As they walked, Ernest said, "Sir, I'm your height and weight. I've been practicing walking your way, with that kind of shovel handle up the spine and ax handle across the shoulders posture. We should put me in your clothes when we're outside, now. With things slowed down the bad guys will have time to plan all kinds of mischief."

"Terens, I don't know if I should kiss you or tell you you're the stupidest man I ever met. You're right. Extra precautions need to be taken. In fact, we all ought to wear our mail shirts and helmets whenever we go out."

"Yeah." Sarcastically. The Commander of the Righteous was the only man there not wearing a helmet.

Hecht said, "I'll adjust my habits."

THE AMBASSADOR GREETED HECHT WARMLY. "VERY PLEASED TO SEE you again, Commander."

"Tell you the truth, till ten days ago I wouldn't have considered it possible. Your father has been doing amazing things."

"Hasn't he? And not that long ago we thought he was headed for the bone pile."

"You may get to see the new man before long. So. To what do I owe the honor of the summons?"

"She wants to see you. She isn't happy. You don't consult her. You haven't kept her informed since the Battle of the Shades."

Hecht did not protest. That was true. Were Consent, Vircondelet, Sedlakova to operate that way he would knock some heads together. But . . .

That admission did not leave him less resentful of the identical attitude in his employer.

The Ambassador escorted him to a huge quiet room where the Empress waited—after a delay meant to remind him of who was master and who was servant.

He had yet to get it into his head that the Empress was always

there, looking over his shoulder. She was not remote the way the Patriarchs had been when he was Captain-General.

The rich smell of coffee hit him when the door opened. His mouth
watered. The odor seemed a good omen.

On the other hand . . . He saw no servants, no lifeguards, no ladies-
in-waiting as he headed toward the source of the smell. Alone.

Bayard va Still-Patter had not come in with him.

Katrin Ege, at the mercy of *kuf* or alcohol, was also a slave to her
insecurities and appetites. She wore nothing. Her frame was more
gaunt than when last he had seen her unclothed. There were bruises all
over her. Had someone been beating her?

"What the hell?"

"Commander, you know your duty." She slurred her words. She
must have been drinking. And he smelled *kuf* behind the marvelous
stench of the coffee. So maybe she had done both to get into her present state. Meaning she must have been at it for a while.

Katrin got down on hands and knees, rested her right cheek on her
folded hands.

"Your Grace . . ." He wanted to refuse, but after a year he knew
her, knew himself, and knew where he and she wanted to go too well
to try. "You don't look like you've been eating right. And you have
bruises. Has somebody . . ."

"Forget that. I put the bruises there. Punishing my flesh for its
wicked hungers. But my flesh defeated me. Come here. Fuck me."

Hecht was appalled. Repelled. Disgusted. And yet aroused. There
was nothing appetizing about this woman, presenting like a cat in heat.
Yet . . .

No doubt she felt the same things he did, but betrayed by the evil
within, she could not help being receptive.

"Your choices are the same as they were before, Commander."

He told himself he *had* to have this job. He *had* to be Commander
of the Righteous when the next crusade smashed into the Holy Lands.

It was nothing like being with Anna Mozilla, yet, in its crooked
way, it was more exciting. An Empress!

He was master of a king, metaphorically, for those few minutes
when he made the most powerful monarch in the west cry and beg.

SUFFOCATING IN SELF-LOATHING, HECHT DID NOT WANT TO RETURN
to the Castella. He did not want to face his family. He did not want to
see Anna till he found some way to expiate his sin. Or some clever ra-
tionalization.

Katrin's bruises crossed his mind. Her torment must be worse than his. What had she gone through before she surrendered to her lust?

"Sir?" Terens Ernest needed instructions.

"That was not a pleasant interview, Mr. Ernest. Let's take a walk along the river and have a gander at the wonders of the Mother City." This was Ernest's first visit: hardly a pilgrim's journey.

"Might that be risky?"

"Possibly. Stay on my left. Last time somebody tried to kill me here he was down there in the monuments. He used a longbow."

Ernest had heard about it, not from his principal. He knew the story behind each assassination attempt, including some that had not been brought to Hecht's attention.

Ernest asked, "What happened? Can you talk about it? Did you see the Empress? Her bodyguards say she's gone completely nuts."

"I did see her. There was a lot of ranting. She isn't pleased with how I've treated our host city. I'm too gentle for her taste." He stopped, stared back at Krois on its stone-clad island amid the Sacred Flood. Bronte Doneto was out there, scarcely a quarter mile away, completely nuts himself. And completely invulnerable.

Pinkus Ghort should arrive sometime tomorrow, despite the Grand Duke's best efforts.

The worm kept twisting and turning.

Hecht noted signs of substantial explosions over there. Lila's work?

The girl was going to get herself in trouble if she was not careful.

He enjoyed a smirk at his own foolishness.

Shouting broke out back that way, followed by the rattle of horse-shoes on stone.

Brothe, round there, was all stone, including the faces of the chan-nel of the Teragi. A conceit of the Old Brothens. Even the Sacred Flood had been under their control.

Hecht and his lifeguards faced the excitement. Several riders headed their way, pursued by men on foot. The horseman out front went into a gallop. Insanity on this kind of surface.

That lead rider was no man. That was Katrin Ege in her loose-fitting armor, headed for her Commander of the Righteous at the best speed her mount could make.

Hecht's heart sank. This could mean ruin. . . . What the hell? Had she lost it completely?

Ernest grabbed Hecht and dragged him toward potential safety among the monuments.

Too late. Far too late. Shrieking words that never made sense to anyone, Katrin was upon them. Her mount narrowly avoided Hecht and Ernest. Both dove away. Both ended up sprawled on the pavements, with bleeding palms.

Captain Ephrian whipped past, face a mask of despair. He meant to snatch Katrin's reins as she tried to turn to charge in the opposite direction.

The footing was not appropriate for a horse wearing iron shoes.

Ephrian collided with Katrin. The horseman behind Ephrian collided with them both.

Combined momentums pushed Katrin and Ephrian over the brink of the embankment. Screaming, man, woman, and horses all went scrabbling, spinning, and tumbling down the stone facing, into the river.

Hecht was seconds behind. Just the length of time it took to shed a mail shirt and weapons. Terens Ernest was seconds behind him.

Hecht did not think about his actions till later, though the cool water was an encouragement to reflection. He saw Ephrian floundering, a poor swimmer but safely separated from his mount. Hecht went after Katrin, who had gone under while still trying to separate herself from her animal. He got her loose. Her horse drifted on downriver, shrieking at first but soon getting it together and striking out toward the lower northern bank.

Terens Ernest tried helping with Katrin. He was a strong swimmer.

Captain Ephrian made it to the embankment but could find no decent handhold so he tried to stay near the stone while the weak current carried him somewhere more felicitous.

Ephrian would be overlooked despite all the would-be rescuers gathering above.

Hecht was not as strong a swimmer as he believed. Nor was Terens Ernest. They reached the embankment only to face the same problem as Captain Ephrian. There were few congenial handholds.

People up top yelled about hanging on because ropes were on the way.

Ernest lost his weak hold and followed Ephrian downstream. Hecht could not help without abandoning the Empress.

Eyes tearing, he drove bloody fingers into a crack between blocks while keeping Katrin's face above water with his other hand.

He lost consciousness.

PIPER HECHT, COMMANDER OF THE RIGHTEOUS, WAKENED IN AN UN-familiar bed. A headache and upset stomach told him he had been sedated for some time. His left hand ached. The fingers were bandaged. The crust on his eyelids kept him from opening those. He tried to rise.

"He's starting to wake up!" That voice belonged to Vali. It brought several people quickly and others within minutes. Head throbbing, Hecht made noises that were senseless even to him.

A hand went behind his head, lifted. Sweet, cold water filled his mouth. A damp cloth daubed at his eyelids. Anna said, "Relax, Piper. You cheated Him again."

A heavy hand pushed on his chest, forced him back down.

He did will himself to relax. Relaxing had to be good. He would not be in these circumstances if something dire had not happened.

Lamps got lighted. His surroundings became less obscure.

He was surrounded by family. Pella. The girls. Anna. Heris and both old men. What were they doing here?

He remembered. He wanted to ask questions but knew the sensible course was to conserve energy. They would tell him what he needed to know.

The smell of fresh coffee hit hard, like a kick in the shin, wakening memories.

Anna and Pella lifted him and propped him with pillows. Heris put a small cup into his right hand. "You gave us a scare, little brother."

"Yeah?"

"You wouldn't let the woman go."

Anna said, "She drowned. Before you pulled her free. You and her horse were the only survivors."

Hecht teared up. This was insanity. He did not mention Katrin's mother. These people did not know, nor would they understand.

Ernest did not make it? That was just plain wrong.

From somewhere out of sight the Ninth Unknown said, "Piper, you need to quit lying around feeling sorry for yourself. Pinkus Ghort is at the gate."

"Really?"

"Not literally. Not exactly. But he could be knocking by this time tomorrow. We need to take steps to eliminate his motivation."

"Excuse me. Why are you and Heris here?"

Heris said, "We came to drag you off to watch us wrap our job."

Februaren said, "She killed a god, Piper. Just went after him till *boom!* Like that worm on the Dechear. Only this was no pup. This was a true Great Old One."

"Why do you need me?"

Heris said, "Later, Piper. Double Great, quit gushing. And, how about we go give Serenity a double dose of Ostarega the Malicious?"

"Works for me."

With no further discussion the pair turned sideways.

Hecht was on his feet and dressed when they returned, but was woozy. Anna had begun changing his bandages, saying, "This isn't as bad as I thought when they brought you. You'll be good as new in a couple weeks."

Februaren appeared, running. His hair was smoldering. If he had not encountered a wall he would have gone down. Heris arrived bent over. She collapsed into a crouch. Her breath came loud and ragged. Had she been male Hecht would have pegged her for a victim of a skillfully delivered groin kick.

The Ninth Unknown eased over to lean on a table. He gasped, "I think that went well."

"Yeah." Heris tried to laugh. She fell over. "You should see the other guys."

Hecht asked, "What happened?"

"We didn't surprise them. Doneto has some clever friends."

Anna finished wrapping Hecht's fingers. She found a chair for Februaren. He settled gingerly. "We tamed them up some, though. You can get in through the tunnels now, if you want. Unless they flood them. They could always do that."

Hecht kept after them but could not get no more sense out of either. He said, "First chance we get we need to let Princess Helspeth know what happened so she can be ready when the news gets to Alten Weinberg."

Heris and Februaren both groaned and glared.

Lila said, "I can do that."

"No. You can't," Hecht told her. "You've taken enough risks."

The Ninth Unknown said, "I'll do it. In the morning. I'll need tokens from you and the Empress to be convincing, though."

"I'll write you a letter. That should do. She'll recognize my hand."

## 43. Alten Weinberg: Bad News, Bad News

A short man in dirty brown stepped out of the shadows in the Princess Apparent's private bedchamber. She had just risen. Her women shrieked and fled.

"You."

"Me. I have news. Listen closely. It's critical. You'll only get to hear it once before the guards arrive." He told her what had happened to Katrin. He handed her a letter from Piper Hecht, now *her* Commander of the Righteous. He vanished seconds before Algres Drear burst in.

"He's gone, Captain."

"Who?"

"A sorcerer. The same one who took Ferris Renfrow. He brought a message. Get these people out and close the door. With you on this side of it." That done, she said, "Katrin is dead. She fell into the Teragi and drowned. There were twenty witnesses, half of them her own lifeguards. There's more to the story, I'm sure. The sorcerer brought a letter from the Commander of the Righteous. I haven't read it yet. Right now, this very minute, I want you to start getting ready for whatever happens when that news gets back here."

"You believe this sorcerer?"

"I do." She gripped the letter from the Commander tightly, already willing Drear to leave so she could read.

"Then you're right. I'd better get started. And stop talking. It won't be long before someone or something moves in to spy."

"Yes."

Helspeth held on barely long enough to let Drear get out of the room. Then, in her haste to get to read it she fumbled the letter twice. And a moment after that she spit like an angry cat to get her women to leave her alone long enough to find out what the Commander had to say.

## 44. Great Sky Fortress: Heris's Game

Operations in Brothe turned anticlimactic. First came word that Pinkus Ghort, literally outside the gates and getting set to storm them while, at the same time, preparing to tame the Grand Duke, had, suddenly and inexplicably, ordered the levies to go home and his own men to stand down. He did not disarm but said he would not fight unless he was attacked.

Meantime, the Righteous captured Krois. And did not profit after making history. Never in its twelve hundred years had that island fortress been taken.

"They're gone!" Vircondelet complained. "We went over every inch of the place. They're just plain not there."

Some staff remained, people who were, in essence, part of the physical plant. People whose families had been part of Krois for centuries. They reported that Serenity and his associates had slipped away during the night, aboard three boats. They had fled to a ship waiting downriver. The servants did not know where that ship was headed.

Hecht cursed softly. Doneto's boats would have sailed right past the Castella. Brotherhood sentries would have seen them. Would have ignored them. All night traffic on the Teragi was ignored.

HERIS AND THE NINTH UNKNOWN GOT INTO SOME SORT OF SQUABBLE. They did not explain. Hecht thought the old man wanted to go find ships and sink them while Heris wanted to get on with her own project in the realm of legend, myth, and devil gods.

Heris said, "Piper, I need all those eggs you collected after you killed those Instrumentalities."

"Why?"

"Instrumentalities have two souls. One they bring into the world with them and one they leave hidden in the Night. The eggs are their middle-world souls. If an egg and a hidden soul got together your success could be undone."

"How about the thing in the catacombs?" The egg from that had not been collected.

"Double Great is sure it's still down there, under the rubble."

"I don't know how much good I can do, Heris. I never kept those eggs myself. Rhuk and Prosek collected them. They sealed them up in metal boxes but I don't know what they did with them after that."

"Find out. I'll make arrangements to collect and transport them."

"What're you going to do with them?"

"Get rid of them."

But she had to get them to the Great Sky Fortress first. And she could not move them there by translating. The trapped souls might escape while she was cutting the chord.

Hecht was confused. But he did not need to understand so long as Heris and the Ninth Unknown did.

HECHT SPENT A FEW HOURS WITH PINKUS GHORT, WATCHING HIS friend get drunk and listening to him complain. "I'm unemployed, Pipe. I'm glad we didn't have to butt heads, but, shit, man, I'm out of a job."

"That won't last. They'll need an experienced man to run the City Regiment."

The Grand Duke had entered the city to maintain order. The Righteous were already moving out, headed for Alten Weinberg with Katrin's casket at the head of the column. Hecht would catch up later.

HECHT VISITED THE BRUGLIONI ESTATE. HE WINCED AT ALL THE DAMage his troops had done despite their best efforts.

He told Paludan Bruglioni and Gervase Saluda, "The curse of Piper Hecht keeps coming back on the Bruglioni. Gervase, I couldn't talk

Principaté Delari into it so I volunteered you to take over Krois. Somebody has to be in charge there till everything shakes out."

"You're making me Patriarch?"

Paludan laughed out loud. Saluda was not religious. He had gone
into the Collegium only because the Bruglioni had had no better man.

"Pro tem. So there's somebody with a hand on the reins. I'm in a
rush. We need to get hold of the reins in Alten Weinberg, too."

"But . . ."

"You're it, Gervase." Hecht did not stay to argue.

THINGS CAME TOGETHER FAST WHEN THE RICH AND POWERFUL WERE
frightened. Within thirty hours the Commander of the Righteous and the
Grand Duke Hilandle jointly proclaimed Bayard va Still-Patter Imperial
viceroy in Brothe. Pinkus Ghort became master of the City Regiment,
which was to be reinforced by men from his disbanding Patriarchal
force. And Gervase Saluda, numbed, moved into Krois.

After everything that the Princes of the Church had suffered lately,
and with all the grim pressures toward honesty now obtaining, Hecht
thought Saluda might well win an election. If an election were held. If
the temporal Church chose to impeach Serenity, something that never
had been done before. Traditionally, bad or unpopular Patriarchs were
assisted in making an early transition to the afterlife. But this latest unpopular Patriarch could not be found to help along. And, as soon as the
fear began to wear off, his friends would begin to resurface.

"Hopefully in the river," Hecht said.

"Can you leave now?" Heris barked. "Can you goddamned well
leave now, Piper Hecht? You bark at Grandfather because he has to be
there for every goddamned little detail, but you're twice as worse as he
is. Come on! Let's go! Now!"

Hecht's cheeks reddened. Heris was right. And what she implied
probably was, too. As he got older he became less comfortable trusting
details to others. That was not good. That was not what had won him
his reputation. That was not what had lifted him up to the heights he occupied now.

The Ninth Unknown snickered. "Some big-time kettle calling the
pot going on here, Heris."

Heris started pushing people together. There was a plan. Lila and the
Ninth Unknown helped her. Hecht ended up in the middle, with Anna,
Pella, and Vali pressed against him. They were surrounded by the other
three, arms on each other's shoulders, facing inward, squeezing everyone
tighter.

The Eleventh Unknown observed, smiling benignly.

Smashed up inside all that friendly flesh Hecht suffered only a touch of nightmare during the transition to a strange gray place where his amulet became extremely excited.

He saw very little color, except for a gaudy ship tied up not far away. He did not at first look up.

People came out of a genial building not far away. Some were familiar, most were not. All were armed with huge mugs, and they all seemed friendly.

Hecht recognized Ferris Renfrow and the ascendant. The short, wide, extremely hairy people, all helmets, beards, mail, and cutlery, he knew only from stories heard from his sister.

What madness, this? He had been brought up a devout Praman. This was impossible.

He looked up the mountain now, gawked at the rainbow bridge and the impossibly huge and impossibly tall castle.

Heris edged in beside him. She whispered, "How was that transition? Better?"

"Much. But it wouldn't have been if you hadn't put me in the middle. Pella! Freeze. If you even think about wandering off . . ."

Pella took one good look at the dwarves, then sidled over between Lila and Vali.

Vali indicated Renfrow. "I remember that man. He was at the Knight of Wands."

Anna had been stricken dumb. Hecht took her hand, entwined fingers, and held on, afraid she would bolt or faint.

Heris made the introductions. Ferris Renfrow, known in myth as the Bastard. Asgrimmur Grimmsson, soultaken, ascendant, and the once upon a time ferocious Andorayan pirate Svavar. Khor-ben Jarneyn Gjoresson, also mythical and better remembered as Korban Iron Eyes, crown prince of the Aelen Kofer. Behind Iron Eyes: his father and his son, Gjore and Copper. Then this dwarf and that, all of whose names she had harvested and quietly memorized, to their consternation. Then, suddenly, in a dark and dangerous temper, with taut throat, because the mer had both surprised her and had arrived in her most toothsome form yet, leaving a wet trail across the quay, "And Philleas Pescadore, who speaks for the people of the sea."

Anna nearly crushed Hecht's hand. He was so glad she had hold of the uninjured one.

Pella drooled. His sisters hung on and hated the mer for her naked perfection.

All of which went right past Philleas.

Heris said, "We need to get on with this. Most of us have critical obligations back in the middle world. Iron Eyes, Asgrimmur, talk to my brother while I talk to Renfrow."

Hecht wanted to deliver a vigorous kick to his sister's butt. She had said that deliberately.

The Ninth Unknown collected the ascendant and Korban Iron Eyes to one side. It was obvious they were old cronies. Hecht felt left out. And, while he understood that was not deliberate, neither was he accustomed to being an also there, in the margins, not part of what was happening.

Heris just wanted him here to witness. Wanted him to see how clever she was.

Hecht decided he was all right with that. Heris, like Lila, needed validation. Let her be the shining star. She deserved it.

He suspected, though, that several others might consider themselves the star.

He was wrong. Even the ancients deferred to Heris. Heris was the central force. They considered her the real Godslayer, hero nonpareil. Piper Hecht was a passenger.

HERIS INSISTED THAT THEY ALL CLIMB THE MOUNTAIN.

Hecht asked, "But if the Windwalker is already extinct why do anything? Why not just let them rot in Limbo?"

Did she blush? That did look like a bit of color in her cheeks. "I foresee useful results if I take it the rest of the way."

"And those would be?" Unable to keep a taint of suspicion out of his voice.

"Piper . . . If this works out I'll push those soul eggs into Asgrimmur's pocket universe. I'll free him of his haunts. And I *may* be able to enlist some serious Instrumentalities in our cause."

"Uh . . . what?"

"We could end up having some of those Old Ones help us in return for their freedom." She told him about the captive gods, name by name, as she had that information from dwarves who had known the gods personally. The Aelen Kofer bore the Old Gods no love—with two exceptions.

Hecht grunted, scowled, thought this was all just too unlikely to be true. Though it would be marvelous to have an Instrumentality for an enforcer that could gobble a bogon without blinking or burping.

Anna stood around, basically lost. Piper Hecht was a mite less confused only because he had heard so much from Heris. But he still felt like a half-blind spectator. The children took to the Realm of the Gods as though it had been crafted for their entertainment.

One short sleep after a period of planning that Hecht thought went more like a drinking contest and, suddenly, a whole mob headed up the mountain. The Aelen Kofer brought goat carts. Nobody got left behind, though Anna volunteered. Even ancient Gjore trudged along. It had been several millennia since he had poked around inside the Great Sky Fortress.

Anna told Heris, "I wasn't made for adventures. Not of the outdoor kind. All I've ever wanted is a quiet life. And I had that till Piper Hecht turned up at my door one night, calling himself Frain Dorao."

Heris asked, "And what did he do?"

"Nothing. He was a perfect gentleman. A perfect houseguest. Then he went away. Leaving me addicted. The most daring thing I ever did was go to Brothe, find him, and make him my lover."

"You've been tangled up with us long enough, now, to know how messed up we are. So, enjoy the ride. Oh. I promise I'll get you back to the boring same old same old before the sun goes down," she said in a world where it was always high noon.

Hecht listened. And agonized. And kicked himself for letting himself be so affected by the women in his life.

He had not yet shaken the deep impacts Katrin Ege had had, with all her sick needs. Nor could he shed his obsession with Helspeth Ege. Nor could he forgive himself the hurts he had done Anna Mozilla even though Anna had no idea.

Several faces crossed his mind. Recollections from the Vibrant Spring School, Gordimer the Lion at a younger age, Grade Drocker, and Redfearn Bechter. Bottom line, he was becoming a whining, self-involved fool.

Anna seized his good hand. "Piper? Are you all right?"

"No. I'm learning about getting old the hard way." He shut up. Most everyone here was older. King Gjore might be millennia older.

They arrived at the downhill end of the rainbow bridge. The Aelen Kofer loaded people into goat carts. Mostly they offered no option.

Hecht watched Heris practically strut across, well ahead of the cart in which he, Anna, and the Ninth Unknown rode. He had no real idea what was going on or he would have blown up when Lila and Vali headed over behind Heris, with the ascendant close behind them, unnoticed.

Hecht looked down.

He should have kept his eyes shut, like Anna and the old man. He would not have come close to shrieking and losing his breakfast, peering down at giants' bones, sharp basalt knives, and bottomless death.

He would not have seen his daughters walking on air.

He would learn that they had crossed over unaware that the rainbow bridge was imaginary and a thousand-foot fall awaited the least misstep.

Pella crossed in a cart he shared with Ferris Renfrow. Pella had paid attention. Pella had a damned good idea what lay beneath the feet of those who walked the rainbow bridge. He crossed with his eyes closed. As did his companion.

Afterward, with feet on solid stone but soul still drawn by the siren fall, Hecht exploded, "You let Lila and Vali *walk* across that?"

Heris gestured. The girls were already at the gate, talking to a couple of dwarves as curious about human girls as the girls were about dwarves. In a moment they would go look at the only living thing native to the Great Sky Fortress, a sickly, waist-high apple tree.

"Don't you ever, *ever*, put my kids at risk like that again. *Ever!*"

Anna agreed but was so shaken herself she could do nothing but nod.

Heris sneered. "You're just pissed off because I didn't trust you to do something that a couple of girls managed with no trouble."

Not true. But, deftly, she had painted him into a circle where he would look bad if he kept on barking.

"Ever, Heris. *Ever.*"

FOR PIPER HECHT, THEN, IT SEEMED LIKE ONLY MINUTES TILL HE FOL-lowed his sister into a large room filled with colorful clutter. She snapped, "Everybody stays here, inside the green circle, till I tell you what to do."

Aelen Kofer who were there already moved carefully amongst the tables, falcons, giant glass bottles, and things less easily identified. Heris spoke to them quietly, in succession. Those dwarves departed.

"Pella!" Heris's voice was not loud but was compelling. "Stand still. Don't go anywhere. Don't touch anything. There's a stone bench under the windows. Sit on it. Piper, Anna, the rest of you, you, too. Never touch anything unless I tell you to. Otherwise, chances are, you'll get yourself dead. And take the rest of us with you."

Aelen Kofer continued to murmur with Heris, then go. The royal three were among the last. Iron Eyes lighted slow matches at each falcon station before he left. "Best of luck, Heris."

Two teams of two dwarves each brought in a pair of shelved carts that made no sound. They floated. On the shelves were felt-lined trays filled with scores of soul eggs, large, small, and flaked. Most could have passed as bits of amber. There were so many that Hecht could not believe he and his men had created them all.

"Piper. Same thing I told Pella applies to you. Sit down. Anna, hold on to him." Heris turned back to the eggs, showed the dwarves where she wanted the carts hoisted onto the tables. She beckoned Februaren, Renfrow, and the ascendant, muttered with them in the space between tables. The carts came back down off the tables, out of the lines of fire of the falcons. "It'll just be more crowded. I didn't know there'd be so damned many."

Hecht planted himself, let Anna hold his hand and keep him planted. He took in the colorful marvels and listened to Pella complain. He admired Anna.

Anna Mozilla's finest feature was her eyes. They were big and brown and full of warmth. Right now, right here, they were bigger than he had ever seen. She was in complete awe. And trembling. Because she was in complete terror as well.

Heris said, "Lila. Vali. Come." She positioned the girls behind the two falcons farthest out to the flanks. She gave precise instructions about how and when she wanted the falcons fired. "And don't hesitate. When it's time, it's time. You'll have less than two seconds if there's a breach." She approached the bench under the window. "Piper, I want you and Anna to man the two center falcons. Anna? Are you all right?"

"Just a bit overwhelmed." In a voice like a strangled whisper. "I can do it. Just tell me what to do and when to do it."

"And you, Piper?"

"I can handle it." Though he was disgruntled about being one of the foot soldiers.

"Good. That'll free Asgrimmur to help me up front."

"What about me?" Pella demanded, surly.

"I'll let you know what I need you to do. In the meantime, sit. Be quiet. And don't touch anything."

To head off any confrontation Hecht asked, "What happens if somebody fires? Assuming you're loaded with godshot? This is a room where the walls, floor, and ceiling are stone. Might be some ricochets, big sister."

"Taken into consideration, baby brother. Each weapon is aimed at one of those silver glass bottles. The wall behind is coated with ten inches of soft clay and plaster."

She moved on to Vali. Pella fumed, "Why is she treating me this way?"

"Because you're acting that way. No. Listen! What she's doing here could shape the futures of three worlds. Or we could end up dead. And all she sees from you is self-absorbed discontent, apparently because you don't get to do whatever you want. Even though you don't know what that is."

He was not getting through.

"Look, all she has to go on is what she sees and hears. What have you done that would make her think you're trustworthy and reliable? And can be counted on to do the right thing when the crunch comes?"

"Oh, shit!"

Hecht almost snapped. But the boy was reacting to something happening across the room.

Heris had just opened a vein in Ferris Renfrow's left wrist and was taking blood. Cloven Februaren stood by with a bandage. When she had about a scarlet cupful in a silver glass beaker, she nodded to the old man. Februaren slapped the bandage on. Renfrow nodded. "Healing already."

"Pella," Heris said. "Now it's your time. Get up into one of those windows and watch the waterfront. Let me know when the golden barge changes."

Frowning and sneering, Pella climbed into a window opening, leaned out. And said, "Oh, shit! Oh, Holy Aaron!" He eased back inside, shaking. "Dad. Don't . . . I can't do that." He was ashamed and terrified at the same time.

Heris said, "You watch, then, Piper. Pella, take the falcon next to Vali. That's the most important one. You chicken on me there, you kill us all. But don't be firing for no good reason, either. Piper. The window."

He did as instructed. And had no trouble understanding Pella's distress. That was a long, long way down. And it called to him, come, take the plunge!

His gut tried telling him he was falling already.

Heris fiddled. She sent the Ninth Unknown to the falcon beside Lila. She positioned the Bastard and the ascendant precisely. "Nobody moves now, except me. And Piper after he reports. Then he goes to his falcon." She took Renfrow's blood to a point she had calculated to a fraction of an inch. Then she stopped moving, too. Stood looking back at Hecht, waiting.

Hecht lay down on his stomach and gripped the stone of the Great Sky Fortress. He stared all that long way down and tried to conquer terror. No human mind ought to have to endure this.

Dwarves still moved down the switchbacks on the mountain, apparently running. They dwindled, became dots moving toward the golden barge. Dots from the waterfront town joined them. They all streamed onto the ship.

Minutes passed. Then, sharp as a hammer strike—*bam!*—all color went out of the barge and waterfront. The gateway to the Andorayan Sea snapped shut.

Hecht said, "Heris, the color just went away."

"Good. They're gone. The Realm is closed."

Meaning all the Aelen Kofer were gone, with their exits sealed up behind. No matter what happened here, now, none of the Old Ones would be able to follow or escape to the middle world.

Heris asked, "Everybody set? Girls? Piper? Anna? Pella? Double Great? Here we go." She tilted the beaker of divine blood.